THE DEATH OF THE DETECTIVE

ALFRED A. KNOPF

NEW YORK

1974

THE DEATH OF THE DETECTIVE

MARK SMITH

All persons and events in this book are fictitious, and
any similarity to actual persons or events is coincidental.

THIS IS A BORZOI BOOK
PUBLISHED BY ALFRED A. KNOPF, INC.

Library of Congress Cataloging in Publication Data
Smith, Mark, (date)

The death of the detective.

I. Title.
PZ4.S653De [PS3569.M53766]   813'.5'4   73–20769
ISBN 0–394–48766–4

Manufactured in the United States of America
Published June 27, 1974
Reprinted Once
Third Printing, October, 1974

The author wishes to thank
the John Simon Guggenheim Memorial Foundation
for a grant that helped him to write this book.

For Henry Volkening

BOOK ONE

PRELUDE TO MURDER

CHAPTER ONE

BUGHOUSE SQUARE

He has come to Chicago. He has come on foot, in the company of night. He has walked not down roads and sidewalks but first along the railroad tracks, then through back yards and prairies, finally down alleys. When he is hungry he sneaks into a small short-order restaurant run by Greeks, eats a meal of roast lamb and mashed potatoes, with his face in his plate, and steals the steak knife when he leaves. Outside he hangs his head against a wall, and, with the look of a man accustomed to doing things in secret with his hands while his back is turned, inserts the knife like a hatpin through the crown of his hat. He turns north, knows his enemy lives in the north. Emboldened now, he walks upon the streets.

How strange the city seems to him! The beacon on the sky-scraper that revolves like clockwork is from a watchtower inside a prison, while the searchlights that promote the openings of shopping centers in the suburbs crisscross on the horizon in search of planes. The red lights of an airliner that go on and off against the sky are the flashing of a secret code. The neon lights from the nightclubs above the rooftops to the east, the aura of a widespread fire. He can sense the fear and danger in the air. A Gothic city with barbarians outside the walls. Or a modern megalopolis so terrified of an air raid that its citizens can hear the drone of engines in the skies and see the silhouettes of bombers flying through the beams.

Later he rests on a park bench inside a city square. Washington Square, the street guides call it. But anyone along the streets would tell him it is Bughouse Square.

Strange weather tonight in Bughouse Square. Both wind and smog, and a man is wind-blown in one spot and smogbound only feet away. A night for ghosts. The ghosts of old inequities, old violence. Socialists, anarchists, immigrants, hobos, madmen, eccentrics—they are everywhere. They haunt the high windows of the library across the street, looking down upon the haunted square. They grumble in the dust and smoke and shreds of newspapers that blow beneath the street lights. They crowd the park benches until they overlap their arms and legs. They lie upon the grass like corpses worked up from the graves. They become a mob that sweeps along the pavement, splintering their clubs upon the wind, breaking bricks against the smog. "Remember the Pullman Strike," they mean to shout but only whisper. "Remember Haymarket Square. Remember—" a good many things.

The man with the knife in his hat keeps a wary eye on the crowd of people gathering in the street outside the square. A small man in an army overcoat from World War Two stands before it on an orange crate, a newspaper tucked under his arm. His hair is curly, dirty, unruly, his glasses taped with soiled adhesive. The coat hangs to the tongues of his laceless shoes. He looks like a prisoner of war, a fifty-year-old private captured while cleaning latrines, about to be hanged. He holds up the newspaper and begins to speak.

"Shut your mouth, queer!"

"Get off that stand, you commy shithead!"

"Hey, loony, go back to Dunning!"

The shouts of bony teen-age boys who wear their hair in crew cuts and ducktails, or pompadours, and are dressed in silver or powder blue jackets that have luminous stripes running down the sleeves.

On the outskirts of the crowd, men tattooed with snakes and

daggers and the starch-colored women they have their arms around laugh at the heckling as they might at cripples further distorted by funhouse mirrors; are joined by older men who have that fiery satisfaction in their heavy jowls that better suits them on the barstools of their neighborhood taverns or in their back yards when they watch the burning of a pile of leaves. In the face of this the small man on the orange crate seems neither contemptuous nor afraid, and not even patient or resigned so much as disengaged.

A bald-headed man at the foot of the crate is quick to face the crowd, lifting his muscular arms for silence. He wears a clean but faded polo shirt, loose slacks tied with a string, sandals without socks. Already tan, he looks like an impoverished wrestler who has wintered in Miami Beach. He addresses the crowd in an accent that is Italian, possibly Greek. "Gentlemen, I am Mr. George, the moderator of tonight's meeting. I am not ashamed to tell you that I am a dishwasher, that I have washed dishes in all the great cities of America. What I was before I was a dishwasher, I will let you guess." (His arms akimbo, biceps flexed in the pretense of pulling up his pants.) "This is how I choose to live my life, gentlemen. I go from city to city, I wash dishes and go to these meetings in the cities. I have been doing this for over thirty years—long before some of you were even born. On the platform is our old friend, Mr. Evelyn. It is my duty to see that Mr. Evelyn speaks to us tonight. So, gentlemen, you will quiet down and listen, please. If you do not agree with Mr. Evelyn, I promise you, you will be the next to speak. But anybody who will argue with Mr. Evelyn while it is his turn to speak must argue first with me." Legs apart, he grapples like a wrestler searching for a head. His voice, however, has been conciliatory, almost apologetic, and his face is not entirely free of fear. The boys in the crowd grow silent, intimidated not so much by what the man has said as by his size and physique and his audacity to challenge and embarrass them. The dishwasher folds his arms so that his biceps enlarge, and with feigned contempt turns his back upon the crowd.

"I have in my hand a copy of today's Chicago *Tribune,*" says Mr. Evelyn in a voice that in no way contradicts his size and appearance. "I call your attention to what it says not in the headlines but in the small, italicized print below the masthead. It says—" and he traces the print with his finger and suddenly gives out with what he must feel is a ringing and inflammatory shout— "My country right or wrong!" He pauses for a response; there isn't any. The boys talk among themselves or confront him blankly, waiting for him to say more. The dishwasher nods his head in agreement, or at least in acknowledgment that this statement deserves every man's consideration, and peers uneasily over his shoulder at the crowd.

Mr. Evelyn continues: "We overlook those small words below the masthead. We take them for granted. We see them so often we never see them. We want only today's sensational news, the lurid, brutal, flashy, spoon-fed headlines. But there it is, my friends, that most permanent of headlines: 'My country right or wrong!' In the First World War—my country right or wrong! In the Second World War—my country right or wrong! And yes, my friends, in the Korean War—my country right or wrong!"

At the mention of the Korean War, the climax of the oratory, the audience hoots and boos. A man with a union card pinned to his hat shoulders his way through the crowd, shaking his fist at the speaker. "Get off that stand!" he shouts. "Who the hell gives you the right, you red, to talk about America? Get off of there before I break your neck." He hurls his still burning cigar butt at the orange crate.

"Go back to Russia, you four-eyed queer!"

"I'll pay your way to Russia!"

Quickly Mr. George replaces Mr. Evelyn upon the crate. "Perhaps it is our fault you men don't want to hear us talk," he shouts. "We have been content to listen to ourselves make the same old speeches year after year. We want to hear new arguments, new ideas, different news. One of you must have something he can tell us that is important to him, something he wants the rest of us to know, something we cannot know unless he tells us. Come up here —anyone—don't be shy."

The crowd grows silent, restless, pretends to have interests elsewhere, each man afraid he will be isolated from the safety of his fellows.

"You, there—you, sir!" says the dishwasher with the power of a judge having made his choice. He points not at the embarrassed boy in the high-school jacket, as it first appeared, but at the man behind him in the shadows, the man with the knife in his hat who, lurking on the fringes of the crowd, has been busy talking to himself.

"Yes, you!" the dishwasher shouts, waving him up. "Come up here, you! We want to hear what you have been saying. Don't keep it to yourself."

Knife-in-the-hat grins, the way a dog grins, curling up his upper lip to bare his teeth.

He is cheered on by the crowd, is even shoved forward from behind. In response, he shoves back, cuffs someone on the head and, with his cheeks puffed up with rage, fights his way into the clear.

Alone, inside the darkened square, he paces back and forth, muttering. "I'll open up their throats," he says. "I'll hang them by their necks. I'll put my fists through their bodies. I'll open their skulls like eggshells. I'll collapse their lungs like accordions."

Not far from him, the silhouettes of old men on a bench, coaxing the small crowd around them in accents that sound German, Italian, Greek. "Look, we'll sing whatever you young people want to sing."

"Don't be afraid, you kids, go on and sing."

"Maybe they know 'Home on the Range'?"

"Sure they know 'Home on the Range.' Everybody knows 'Home on the Range.'"

"One of you youngsters start up your song. We old duffers will follow."

The palaver of youthful voices that culminates in the languid self-conscious voices of several boys and girls singing "This land is your land, this land is my land." Voices that trail off into hums and coughs as some old men applaud while others complain that they themselves are unfamiliar with the song. Finally one of the old men becomes too lyrical to restrain himself, and his bass voice breaks into song:

O gif me a home
Where de buffalo rrroam
And de deerrr and de antelope play—

His voice fades; no one has joined him. His companions on the bench are still coaxing the young people to sing.

Farther along the bushes a stubby middle-aged woman dances in the street, an oversized flashlight in her hand. Her hair beneath her red beret hangs in a Dutch cut of dirty straw that swings before her painted face. In a loud contralto she celebrates her search for Jesus along with her discovery of the one and only light. Her dance, a hodgepodge of minuet, cakewalk, jig; her song, of church hymns, Tin Pan Alley, jazz. Boys pursue her down the street, cut her off, form a ring around her. Suddenly she grabs a boy, shines the flashlight in his face, and tries to make him dance, revolving with him arm in arm. In response he belly dances, does the dirty boogie, bumps and grinds, only to escape into the crowd. Alone, she lunges for another boy. But the boys retreat, clapping and laughing, combing their hair. She shines the flashlight on and off their faces. She holds up the hem of her red, pleated cheerleader skirt and does her dance, showing brown nylon stockings rolled up to her knees.

"Jesus is waiting in the bushes, Mary!"

"He'll hop you like a German shepherd, Mary!"

"He'll shine that flashlight up your pussy, Mary!"

"Hallelujah," Mary cries. "Praise the Lord!"

The man with the knife in his hat has been listening to noises coming from the bushes he has been pacing up and down beside. Someone in there all right, someone trying to burn him with his eyes, trying to catch a look at him. He gets down on all fours and creeps between the branches. Listen! The intense, erratic beat of someone's breathing. Moves ahead. The acidic urinary smell of cheap wine, the silage smell of cheap Bourbon. Touches a bottle that rolls beneath his hand, touches the sleeping man before he sees him, curled up between the roots of the tree just beyond the bushes.

"Every man," says the voice beneath him, "entitled to his own opinion." The voice of a drunk. Of the drunken pacifier of a drunken brawl saying what he says drunk, what he has said a hundred times earlier tonight, with his head buried in his arms folded on the bar.

"Shut up," says knife-in-the-hat. "You don't know me. Your kind doesn't know a man like me."

The drunken man grunts, struggles to sit up. In the passing headlights of a car the fat, pockmarked, almost Oriental, almost hairless face, the stye in the eye, the filthy clothes, the unbuttoned pants, the bare pot belly. Then darkness. Then that voice again.

"Every man—his own opinion . . ." Curling up, he begins to snore, only to stir when the strange hands reach inside his pockets, saying, "Broke . . . not a dime . . . in the same boat, me and you, Gunner . . ."

"I'm not Gunner."

". . . I'm no hero, Gunner, no big time, no big deal . . . I give my medal away . . . give it away for a beer . . . G.I.'s, Gunner, me and you—the best people in the world . . ."

Knife-in-the-hat lays his hand upon his chest and shoves him down. "Don't call me Gunner," he warns. "You don't know who I am."

"Every man . . . entitled to his own opinion . . ." says the drunk, staying down, snoring.

To knife-in-the-hat how helpless the sleeping drunken fellow seems! And how soft, as though he is all underbelly, no bone. You wouldn't have to worry about a man as vulnerable as this. Such a man he can do with as he likes. It has been a long time coming, too, this freedom to do as he likes. He has not understood its power until this moment. Why, he can do anything, can do anything at all! He puts his hands lightly around the drunk man's throat. To test his power, he tells himself.

Just beyond the tree and bushes the heavy, stop-and-go traffic of Clark Street, the whirr of stopping buses, the compressed air sound of bus doors opening, footsteps on the sidewalk, surprisingly coherent bursts of passing conversations. Then from several blocks away the sudden brassy outburst of a large Salvation Army band that comes marching down the street, drawing down upon the square. Drums and brass, and a march that makes the sentiments of army, church, and tavern seem all as one.

Knife-in-the-hat has yet to hear it though. He is too busy kneeling on the drunken sleeping man as though upon a life-size dummy whose stuffed head he pounds against the roots, its limp, jointless arms and legs flailing out to either side. He shakes the man—throttles —strangles him.

Only when the man is dead does he remember the knife he carries in his hat. He removes it and sticks the dead man several times in the thighs and calves, testing the resistance of the flesh. Once he goes as deep as bone. Then he goes through the dead man's front pockets, rolls him over, and goes through the back.

Mr. George still offers the empty orange crate to someone— anyone—in the dwindling crowd along the street.

The old men on the bench have given up persuading their young friends to join them in a song and are singing "Home on the Range" by themselves in the tremulous bassos and heavy accents of their ancient voices. Since it is one of those songs where the chorus is reminiscent of the verses, and the verses of the chorus, its singers sing on and on, switching back and forth from verse to chorus, ignorant as to where the song should end.

Crazy Mary still dances, still sings of Jesus and the light. The boys still pursue her along the bushes, seeing in her madness a license for that outrage they equate with sex.

Then a high note of Mary's hymn slides up an octave, and after threatening at that pitch to become a croak becomes instead a scream. The flashlight focuses on the gaping, bloodless face of the dead man beneath the tree beside the bushes. Boys jump up and down to peer above the heads in front. What an awesome privilege for some, looking upon a human body that houses the forbidden mystery of death. Others are unnerved, challenged, compelled to grin.

"Maybe Mary screwed him to death."

"Look out, Ralph, he's going to get up and get you."

"Go on, Jimmy, touch him."

"Hey, he looks like an Indian."

"Like a Spic."

Meanwhile the Salvation Army band passes Bughouse Square, turns onto gloomy streets, marches past factories, condemned houses, lots filled with rubble. From now on only the bass drum beats. Only one man in the handful of followers waits in the alley until all the soldiers have marched single file into the back door of a red brick building, his heart beating martially to the rhythm of that drum. His hands go inside his pockets, his shoulders slouch, and he takes long strides with long legs. He wears that funny grin.

He sees eyes everywhere. Not only in the shadowy, featureless faces of the passers-by but between curtains of windows, in the windshields of passing cars, in the keyholes of doors. The eyes are staring at him. The eyes are enemies. All enemies, beware! The old woman in the vestibule of her apartment building fumbling in her handbag for her key had best look out—he goes so far as to poke his head inside the outer door. The girl in the lighted apartment several stories up sitting with her back to the open window—he stops to gauge the climb up the stone facade. The couple in the car parked at the curb, and busy with themselves—he presses his face against the window of the driver's side. He still receives extraordinary pleasure from his killing of the man. Even a fragmentary recollection of his gloating upon the corpse is enough to drive him into waves of ecstasy. He is at a loss to explain why he hasn't killed a man before. What a wonderful ambition, to be the king of heaps of corpses. To rule a world he has himself transformed into an underworld. Why, the people behind those eyes that threaten him, once reduced to corpses, can no longer threaten him. On the contrary, he proves by his ability to kill them that they are his subjects, that in this dangerous world he alone has the power to survive their fate.

He sheds his dupe identity, sees who he really is at last. It explains the magnitude of his powers. It explains why men have imprisoned and restrained him in the past; why he is a king who must have myriad microscopic and inconsequential enemies who despise and fear him and have good reason to attempt to cheat and injure him; why he can extend himself everywhere at once and destroy his enemies; why he is invulnerable to their assaults, further proof of his greatness. It justifies his need to kill. "The death-maker," he calls himself, a name he neither earned nor dared to call himself before.

"Farquarson," he says, naming his enemy who lives up north. "Farquarson," he repeats, as though his voice can cast a deadly spell upon that man he names. No need to walk to Farquarson—he is not a man who has to walk. He will continue his journey in a car, any large car will do. Surely he remembers how to drive a car, even after all these years.

The steak knife he has been holding in his hand he now drops down a sidewalk grate. Beneath a street light he examines the papers in the wallet of the man he murdered. Alvin Raincloud, these papers say.

"Alvin Raincloud," he says aloud, repeating the name with satisfaction, grinning.

CHAPTER TWO

THE DEATHBED CONFESSION

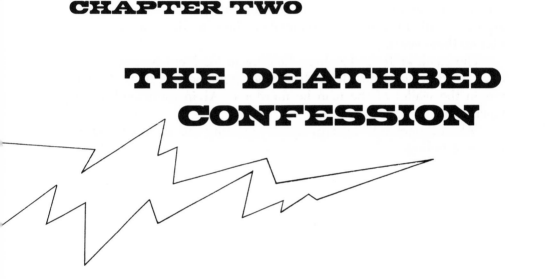

The wealthy lakeshore village of Lake Forest. Wooded, landscaped lakefront estates with lakefront mansions: Mediterranean villas, French chateaus, Scottish castles, English manor houses, Swiss chalets. Casement windows that look out upon the moonlit woods, the moonlit lake, the shadows of the roofs and walls upon the moonlit lawns, the moon. In the great house of Frazer Farquarson the last drape has long been drawn against the moonlight, the last light long turned out, and anyone inside the house knows that all the rooms have long been dark and that the members of the household long in bed, if not asleep. Not so the prowler squatting in the Farquarson woods, his head poking above the bracken. He has long stayed put, confused as to whether moonlight is reflecting on all the windows or some epic but clandestine open house is taking place within the house, candles passing simultaneously through all the rooms.

Finally the moon slides behind the overcast, darkening the windows, and the prowler quits the darkened woods and runs across the darkened lawn, trampling the unseen flower beds beneath his feet. At the front door he turns the doorknob without success and, dropping to his knees, inserts a wire into the lock. While inside the house, as the stairs and corridors go dark, the black woman in the black satin robe begins her journey through the house, the silver flashlight unlit and hidden in the darkness of her hands, her familiarity with the walls and the furniture she has dusted, rearranged, and polished piloting her through the rooms.

From the center of the dark bedroom she enters, the old man's whisper containing no less terror than if he opened up his mouth and screamed: "Hope."

She halts at the threshold, astonished that she should hear his wife's name, and spoken by the very man who by the example of his own silence has forbidden its being uttered in his presence for nearly thirty years. "Hush, for shame," she says.

Then the moon free of clouds, and the man, suddenly moonlit on the flags before the front door, springs up and races back across the moonlit lawn, once more trampling the flower beds beneath his feet. Shaking both fists above his head in the direction of the moon, he bounds into the woods down a twisting, moonlit pathway and disappears in a quiver of moonlit branches and a swirl of moonlit leaves. While the black woman, leery of that moonlit hallway at her back and remembering that the old man's nurse is sleeping in the room next door and imagining nocturnal ambulations and not moonlight at all but flashlights other than her own, shuts herself in that dark, airless, overheated room that encloses sleep, disease, and death, shuts herself among the sour and bitter smells of dry decaying bones poking through dry decaying flesh and alcohol dried upon that flesh and the sweat upon the nightshirts and sheets and the bile that drips into the bottle beneath the bed.

"It's Lena," she says. And after the prolonged silence that greets this revelation, "You know me, Mr. Farquarson."

"Why Lena, why are you here, Lena?"

"You asked me to come."

"What on earth for, Lena?"

"Why, that's for you to know and me to find out, Mr. Farquarson."

The white, withered, waxlike hand cut off by the darkness at the wrist searching for her beside the bed. "No one's there," he says, the hand giving up and falling back into the darkness.

"I'm here all right."

"No one's there," the voice insists. "My eyes are open now." His white, withered face rising as though by levitation from the darkness but not so far as to show the ears, like the face of a drowned man breaking water. "Ghosts," he says. "White teeth. Whites of their eyes." She puts the flashlight against the inside of her robe, turns it on, and the beam seeps faintly through the black weave of the cloth, her flesh coloring like a blue evening turning black. "Ah," he says, the face sinking back into the darkness. "Black on black."

Now she knows the man is drugged or mad or determined even in his pain and infirmity to play some joke upon her. For thirty years she has witnessed and listened to the stories of the practical jokes he has played on his employees, friends, and guests, and she supposes she has suspected all along he would be playing jokes on people up until the day he died. No, she should not have stayed over in the house tonight nor have come to his room at such an hour of the night, and if it were not for the thirty years and that sense of duty and service that the passage of that much time has bound her to she would have been done with this man and in her own house, sleeping in her own bed. "You don't remember, do you, Mr. Farquarson? You just go back to sleep. I'll come back when you remember."

The faint voice: "I remember, Lena."

"You sure you remember?"

"Your voice is frightened, Lena."

"Your voice is frightened too, Mr. Farquarson."

"That's because I am frightened, Lena."

"There's nothing to be frightened of."

"Then what about this epidemic?" And when she doesn't answer him, he adds, "I mean, why are we all sick?"

"You the only one sick, Mr. Farquarson."

"Then why are you here, Lena?"

"Because you asked me to. You don't remember?"

"How can I, Lena? They fill me full of drugs . . . I move and they stick me, I open an eye and they stick me, I moan and they stick me, even when I don't have any pain they stick me. My arms leak . . ."

"What is it that you want, Mr. Farquarson?"

"Can you write, Lena?"

After a pause: "Write what, Mr. Farquarson?"

"Why, words, Lena. Letters, sentences, English—"

"I can write them, Mr. Farquarson." And the sympathy that has been present in her voice turns patronizing, even satirical, mocking herself no less than him.

"Then write a letter for me. Bear with me, Lena. I remember now."

"That's what you want me to do in the middle of the night? Write you a letter?"

"It's a secret, Lena. You're the only person I can trust. All the others have their interest. They're all mixed up in the bag. To them I'm an extra dividend, a check about to be cashed. They wouldn't have your understanding. Oh, I'll pull out of this, Lena. I don't want you to worry. But a sick old man has to take precautions. We can't be afraid to say the word."

"What word is that, Mr. Farquarson?"

"Why, Lena, you know as well as I do, the word is Death."

So the letter has to do with his will, she thinks. And she has been asked to write it not because he can trust her above all the others in this house but because she alone is the disinterested party without expectations of his estate—and the nurse in the house for less than a year and the housekeeper not much longer, whereas she, Lena, has given service here for thirty years, longer even than has Thorsen, the gardener. But the worst injury: he has assumed that she herself not only expects nothing from his will but understands and accepts the reason why she will have nothing, having no human feelings of expectation he can injure. When the dogs cannot trust the other dogs, she thinks, they come to the cats because the cats do not communicate with the dogs, do not eat what the dogs eat and do not want to eat what the dogs eat. The cats are not in the bag with the dogs, or the bones. And she recalls a white chauffeur saying to Max, her husband, once as they idled each before his employer's limousine in the driveway of this house, "You don't see horses mating with cows. You see horses mating with other horses," and Max saying only, "That's right," and she herself overhearing on a Greyhound bus she was taking to the Farquarson summer house in Michigan a white woman telling another white woman sitting next to her, "You put a black pig in a pen with the white pigs and the white ones will gang up on the black one every time and try to bite him and push him out of the pen. They just don't like the black ones. And they wonder why people don't act any different," and she resists butting in and saying that maybe the white woman is content to see herself as analogous to a pig but she, the black woman, is not. So if she feels injured at this moment it must be because she has lived her life not knowing what she knows, not believing what she sees. She is a stranger, a bystander, a passer-by, a traveler down the road whom this man has called into his house to write down some addition or deletion to his will. Until now she has expected nothing from the man. But if some portion of his estate is to be divided among those less deserving than herself, isn't she entitled to her share? Thirty years as a maid. All the furniture. The rugs. The floors. The walls.

She sits in a leather chair and holds the flashlight so that it shines upon the paper and around the black hand that holds the pen.

"Address the letter to Albert Wenzel," he says, spelling it, thrashing in his sheets like a walking stick enmeshed in spider webs.

Clouds before the moon again and the man racing from the darkened woods again and halfway to the house when the moon unexpectedly sails free. Trapped in the middle of the moonlit lawn he turns, and again, shaking his fists with disappointment at the moon and pausing just long enough to stomp malevolently on the flower beds now visible in the moonlight, runs back into the moonlit woods.

She has filled two pages of the letter he dictates in that whisper of dispassion and shamelessness that contradicts the nature of the confession, treating her as though she is a Dictaphone. These are not my words, she has to tell herself, trying to commit them to the paper without understanding or even repeating them inside her head. She guesses at the reason for his fear and secrecy, sees the validity of his precautions, knows why he called her tonight by the name of Hope, why he would have Hope on his mind tonight, his wife from whom he has been separated for thirty years. She shakes her head: he is a bad man, and this is other people's bad business. But he was right to trust her to keep the secret. There is not much that she has seen and heard that she will not tell, she says to herself, but there are some things she will carry to the grave with her lips sealed; some things she will carry even to the throne of Jesus at the Last Judgment, and even if He commands her to tell about this business, even then will she say, Jesus, are you sure?

"Mr. Farquarson," she says, "are you all right now? Do you know what you're telling me to write? You sure you want me to send this letter to the man? I mean, is it . . . true?" This account of insanity, imprisonment, adultery, abortion, rape, venereal disease, illegitimacy, threats of murder, along with less definable actions of inhumanity, sacrilege, perversion.

He waves her to be silent and signs the finished letter she holds before him in the light. Then remembering a second precaution he must take, he asks for a clean sheet of paper around which he cups his hand so that she cannot see and writes in the scratch of his feeble hand:

If I should meet with foul play Mr. Albert Wenzel of Wauconda has in his possession a letter explaining all.

He folds this note and hides it among the stamp albums he keeps beside the bed. Then reflecting on the letter in the envelope Lena is addressing, he smiles and nods his head with satisfaction at the rightness of his present course of action, with the expiation of something evil in his past.

Now she knows why she and no one else was asked to write the letter. She should have known that if his dictation had been concerned with his will he would have had his lawyer to the house and that in case of any emergency, the nurse, housekeeper, and even Thorsen, the gardener, whom she doubts can read or write in English, all would have had precedence before her. But this has been a last testament, not of his properties and monies, but of his soul. He has used her to cleanse the corruption of that soul, as though he thought it common sense to wipe his dirty hands not on any bleached and laundered towel but on one already soiled, as though in herself he thought his own evil would be at last at home.

He calls for the light, fumbles with the combination of the small safe beside the bed, feels among the papers in a strongbox. "Here is fifty dollars," he says, pressing the mint bill against her open palm. "That's for you."

The bill so crisp it doesn't feel like money. Thirty years, she thinks, and fifty dollars. This man is done with her, and she is done with this man.

"And another," he says, laying a second mint bill upon the first, and informing her that this one is for Max, her husband and his former chauffeur, that to earn it he has only to drive over to Wauconda tomorrow and deliver the letter to Wenzel in person.

She holds the bills in her open palm as if offering them to the wind, feels the wet where his moistened finger has peeled and pinched the corners. She seems an actor in an ancient ritual, the participant in an ancient parable, a part of something more significant and timeless than just the two of them at this hour in this room and the hundred dollars she has in hand.

Then a second request is made of her, so extraordinary and unexpected a request that she begins to doubt the sincerity of the confession in his letter and wonders anew if he could be drugged, joking, or insane. Does she belong to a church, he wants to know? She does. Is it a colored church? It is. (He seems pleased.) It isn't a storefront church by any chance? It is. (He is elated.) It wouldn't have a neon sign above the storefront door? It would. (He is ecstatic.) Is the minister a good man? The women like him, the children respect him in Sunday school. (He is thinking.) Can she have the minister visit him tomorrow? She hesitates, wondering if he believes his sins can be comprehended and absolved only by a preacher who is black, and if she dare involve a second party—her own minister no less—in the humiliation and embarrassment that might well be the consequence of meeting with this man. He dismisses her hesitation, insists on his request. She makes excuses. He bullies. She objects. He pleads. She reminds herself that after all his request, if genuine, is Christian, and that in his present mood of consolation and atonement (or madness) he might make a generous donation to her church, and promises to see what she can do.

Then she is in the hallway, returning without benefit of light to the dignity of her downstairs room, frightened of the letter in the pocket of her robe. She pauses along the upstairs balustrade, holds her breath. Noises coming from the dark front door. Someone forcing the wrong key into the lock? She lifts her hem and hurries down the stairs, uncertain as to what, if anything, she will do. A door opens and someone enters the hallway from a dark downstairs room.

"Lena?" a woman whispers.

"Is that you, Mrs. Owens?"

"Yes. What is going on here? I thought I heard someone in the house," the housekeeper, Mrs. Owens, says.

"That's right," Lena says quickly. "That's what woke me up."

"It sounds like someone's at the door."

"That's right. It sounds like someone's at the door."

"Should we call the police?"

"I don't know," Lena says. "Just turn the light on. If anybody's out there he'll go away."

"But then he could see us, Lena. He could look right through the windows and see us." In her voice is the fear that the housebreaker is not after money or jewels but a thick-waisted, sparrow-legged, large-bosomed, middle-aged white woman, remarkably like herself. She grabs Lena by the arm. "What if one of them is already in the house," she says in a breathless and reluctant wonder, "and is coming down to let the other one in? I knew I heard someone prowling about upstairs."

"That must have been me you heard," Lena says. "I woke up when I heard those noises at the door."

"But Lena, your room is downstairs . . . and you were upstairs . . . and Lena, you're not upstairs now."

Indeed she is not. But someone is. Footsteps along the balustrade above, at the top of the stairs and then coming down the stairs, pausing at the first landing. A flashlight switched on and the beam exploring the hall until it finds the two frightened women against the wall.

"Don't scream," the nurse says, shutting off the light and coming down the stairs. "Is someone out there?"

"Yes," the housekeeper says. "Hear it? Hear it? Someone's picking the lock."

Like the generals of a matriarchy the triumvirate of bathrobed women huddle together and take counsel in whispers at the foot of the stairs, the young nurse automatically the leader.

"What do you think, Lena?" the nurse says.

"I don't know," Lena says.

"You'd better get John," the housekeeper says, referring to Mr. Farquarson's nephew.

"He's not here," the nurse says.

"Not here?" whispers the housekeeper, controlling anger or possibly hysteria. "But I saw him go to bed." A feeling of betrayal in her voice.

"I just saw his bed," the nurse says, "and he's not in it."

"Then we should call Thorsen in the carriage house," the housekeeper says. "What is John doing, going off like that? And why is Thorsen sleeping in the carriage house? There should always be a healthy man in the house. We should call the police." Her previous experience has been as a housemother in a fraternity and although she is a divorcee who was married for less than a year she is accustomed to having not one man in the house but nearly a hundred.

"Hush, Mrs. Owens," the nurse says. "Do you hear that, Lena? It sounds like a car."

"I hear it," Lena says. "It could be down in the road, though."

"What will we do?" the housekeeper says. "Why are we three women just standing here? He could break in any minute."

"It's quiet now," Lena says. "Maybe he heard us talking and went away."

"I have a pistol," the nurse says.

"Do you know how to use it?" the housekeeper says.

"I know how," the nurse says.

"Perhaps you should get it," the housekeeper says.

"I already have it," the nurse says, withdrawing it from her military medical corps bathrobe as Lena and the housekeeper back away from her, their hands instinctively across their faces. "Be careful," the housekeeper says, still backpedaling through the dark hall. "It isn't loaded, is it?"

"Yes," the nurse says. "It's loaded."

"There," the housekeeper says. "The noises at the door. They've started up again!"

"Lena," the nurse says, using the barrel of the pistol to point with, "you go to the light switch and turn on the light when I tell you to. Mrs. Owens, you tiptoe to the door and open it when Lena turns on the light. But open it wide and get out of the way. I'll stand in the hall with the gun."

"I can't do that," the housekeeper says, visualizing herself caught in the crossfire between the intruder and the nurse. "I'm too frightened to do that. Let me call the police."

"Then I'll open the door myself," the nurse says, using the barrel of the pistol to wave the housekeeper out of the way. "Lena, you turn on the light."

"I don't know," Lena says, staring at the pistol. "I just don't know. Maybe we should just turn on the light. You know, turn on all the lights."

"Out of the way, both of you," the nurse says, as both women, frightened of the waving pistol barrel flashing in the dark, scurry up the stairs. The nurse switches on the hall light, the porch light, strides to the door, unbolts the door, throws the door open, and stands in the doorway, the pistol in her hand.

Outside on the doormat, John Cavan, the nephew of Mr. Farquarson, stands in creaseless flannel trousers, untied striped tie, and wrinkled corduroy jacket, fumbling with a ring of keys. "Sweet Jesus," he says, falling off the stoop at the suddenness of the door's opening and then, as his eyes adjust to the porch light, slowly raising his hands above his head.

"Put your hands down," the nurse says, replacing the pistol inside her robe. Then to the women behind her: "He's drunk."

And as John Cavan tells the three bathrobed women in the high-ceilinged, oak-paneled hall how he could not find his key, dangling in his defense the key ring with the key missing, a figure sneaks out from behind the garage in which Cavan has parked his car, runs down the driveway between the hedges, and disappears into the street.

Back upstairs Frazer Farquarson, ignorant of the nocturnal stirrings of his household, and made dreamy by the shot of morphine given to him by the nurse who was only waiting for the maid to leave before she entered, confronts the spectre of his wife, Hope. It is the first time he has seen her in any form in the thirty years she has been a patient of those private sanatariums that cater to the mental breakdowns of the very rich. She stands on the threshold, manufactured from the moonlight as it dapples the panels of the door. Her moonlit hair cropped short, the housedress without a belt falling to the thick men's socks rolled down her waxy phosphorescent ankles, her eyes fluttering, looking as though glitter has been pasted to the lids. "Hope," he cries aloud, "can you forgive me?"

She seems to indicate the window. He hallucinates the scraping of a shovel in the garden down below. Imagines he has left his failing body and is at the window, watching Thorsen the gardener with his foot planted on a moonlit spade. He digs among the yews and rhododendrons. Slices the walls, scrapes the bottom with the gleaming point, holds the moon up as a lantern in his hand. Moonlight on a pile of bones. The skeleton of a baby gleaming like tiny eroded odd-sized bars of gold. That in his own mind is not a fetus discarded as so much waste but a child buried in the garden the size of a two-year-old. His son. Or if not his son, a son he should have taken as his own. Who should be here at his bedside instead of down there in the garden, a heap of bones.

He acknowledges his guilt. He has confessed his sins and revealed the secrets of self and family he has no wish to take with him to the grave. The letter he has just sent to Wenzel is the proof of his sincere contrition.

He has gone further still. He has written anonymous letters to Arnold Magnuson, detective, Solomon Chandler, lawyer, and Everett Archer, physician, indicting them as his accomplices of thirty years ago in the locking up of his wife and the abortion of her child. Respectable, honorable men who doubtless are ignorant of their guilt as he has been of his. Who ought to be apprised of their shortcomings and wrongdoings so that, like himself, they can repent and transform themselves before it is too late. If only they could know that sense of rightness and tranquility that he is feeling now, how they would thank and bless him for his accusations! And he can feel it even though his own transformation into the new man is still incomplete! Thank God he no longer has to concern himself with acquiring wealth (he already has it) or social status (he has that too), and is free to ponder moral questions and the matters of justice and guilt. That is what a man has to concern himself with, these days.

He has never doubted that service, charity, and Christian virtues in general are anything less than absolute. But he also knows that throughout his public and private life he has rarely synchronized his actions with this morality, and what is worse, he has unconsciously devised a simple system of hypocrisy to reconcile the two. Too often his intolerance has become his tolerance, his selfishness his charity, his sensuality his love.

But how difficult it is to know for certain that one is genuinely transformed. Until he is gone he will be dying, and the performance of his new self must be within those terms. If only he were poor, how easy it would be. A patient in a veterans hospital shuffling about the wards in a wrinkled seersucker robe and worn slippers, and administering to fellow patients no less in pain and dying than himself. He gives one a glass of water, buys another a magazine from the commissary, helps a third into a wheelchair, engages in small talk to pluck up the courage of a fourth. "Why, the man is a saint," the doctors, nurses, and orderlies would say of him.

But confined to this one bed in this one room in this one house he must somehow prove to his own satisfaction that he has learned the lesson of humility and honesty. All he needs, he is convinced, is the time in which to do it. He has a fear, not of dying, but of dying prematurely. Which, given his condition, means unnaturally. That he deserves to be murdered for his sins he is willing to concede; but above all else he wants to avoid death by violence, and to see, in tranquility and the natural order of things, the man changed instead of ended, his sins absolved rather than avenged.

Ever since this morning when the nurse read him the report in the paper of the escape from a mental hospital of that madman Joseph Helenowski, that former boyfriend and fellow inmate of his wife, he has had good reason to fear he will be murdered in his bed. A dangerous lunatic like that on the loose. Who hates Farquarson. Who blames him for every ill wind that howls around his sorry life. (And not without some cause, he must admit.) Who has sent him letters that threaten him with unmasking, blinding, castration, and death, that accuse him of confining him with madmen so as to drive him mad, of depriving him of wife and child, and transmitting rays that jangle his nerves and jam his impulses and drain his penis and erase his memory and sap the power of his reason until he is duped into believing he is just a corpse. Letters in which he brags that he is richer, more powerful, and a greater captain of industry and native-born patriotic American than Farquarson. Letters full of such terms as The Phantom Realm of the Great Void and The Sphere of Banished Suffering and The Tree of Secret Love Fruits and The Sacred Grove of Transcendent Oaks, and like nonsense. Letters that touched in their fantastic way on Farquarson secrets, that came year in and year out, and that Farquarson burned as quickly as they came.

No doubt about the man's insanity. Only a lunatic would want to murder a man dying nicely in his bed. No doubt either about the real danger he is in. All those threats in all those letters.

Magnuson the detective, one of the three men he has anonymously indicted, comes to mind. Magnuson could protect him until Helenowski was caught. Or until he himself died naturally in his bed. Magnuson could do the job. Didn't he already know all about this Helenowski? Didn't Magnuson investigate Helenowski for him in the past? He must remember something of that investigation and of the evil nature of the man. He resolves to call Magnuson in the morning and secure his services. In the meantime he consoles himself with this thought: men like Magnuson know how to treat the likes of men like Helenowski.

CHAPTER THREE

PINOCHLE

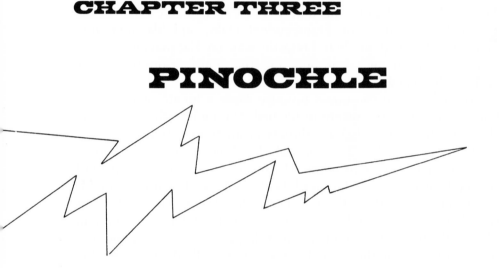

The detective lived on the Gold Coast of Chicago, in a high-rise co-operative of charcoal steel and glass that overlooked Lake Michigan. His name was Magnuson, and tonight he was playing pinochle. So was Scarponi, an old friend, and owner of a string of liquor stores that bore his name and allegedly were connected with the under-world. At the moment, however, because Magnuson was absent and only three hands were left around the table, Scarponi was drinking Scotch, his own brand of Scotch, MacScarp's Highland Scotch, for besides all the standard brands his stores carried their own line of house labels. Not only did they have the Scotch, but Colonel Scarpy's Bonded Kentucky Bourbon, Monsieur Scarpeau's Imported French Bordeaux, Herr Scarpman's Imported German White Wines, Señor Scarpo's Sherry, Scarpovitch's Vodka, and the Royal House of Scarp Distilled Dry Gin. He had brought three bottles of the Scotch to

Magnuson as a gift, proof of his prosperity, and as a joke, for he could appreciate the comedy in the labels. But Magnuson had accepted the bottles without comment or even so much as thanks. Now Scarponi was watching the last of the first of the bottles dribble down the lips of Terence "Tip" O'Neil while the sulking Fritz Schneider, who didn't drink, noisily ruffled a deck of cards. Throughout the evening Magnuson had been disappearing without explanation into the kitchen; he had not played five hands in succession. Each time he had headed for the kitchen Schneider had slammed down his cards, asking of the others, "Where's the guy going now?" Something unhealthy, desperate, and aimless about Magnuson. This was Scarponi's observation.

"Come on," Schneider said. "He ain't in the kitchen now. The guy's gone to bed. Deal them pigs' knuckles three-handed."

But Scarponi ignored the deck and wandered through the room. It was less like a family's living room than a suite in a plush motel furnished by a professional decorator. Lights, like individual spotlights, cut through the dark, above the card table, behind a distant sofa, at the side of a distant easy chair. A feeling of a darkened nightclub with the lone light on the dice table in a remote corner. Scarponi's mind was neither on the card game nor on the mysterious rudeness of Magnuson. While walking down Rush Street on his way to Magnuson's from the nightclub where he had taken supper, he had stopped at a phonograph shop and purchased a recording of an opera by someone named Scarlatti, a work he had never heard before. Scarponi-brand beer sponsored the "Italian Opera Hour" on radio Saturday afternoons and he was always in search of new recordings of old Italian operas. He was weary of Verdi and Puccini. More than anything he wanted to listen to that opera now. He examined Magnuson's expensive German phonograph built in the cabinet on the wall, along with the few records, mostly old sentimental favorites and waltzes, that Magnuson owned. But he could find no earphones, and he was reluctant to play the opera in front of Schneider and O'Neil. He went to a wall-length window, pulled back the drapes and, revealing only the knuckle of his hand to anyone outside, peered down into the street. Suddenly he stepped back; it was raining out, and the wind blew the rain like hailstones against the glass.

"You wouldn't catch me living in all this glass," Tip O'Neil said from the card table. "A little rain sounds like a hurricane. What if you broke a window? You wouldn't break a window, you'd break a wall." O'Neil was a retired Chicago police captain who now lived on his pension in a small cottage on the Florida Gulf coast. He had recently returned to visit his daughter, who was single and worked in City Hall at a cashier's window where she took money in payment of fines for motor vehicle violations and sometimes money for not paying the fines, and lived in an apartment on the North Side in Magnuson's old neighborhood. O'Neil's shirt and suit looked as if he had ridden in them in a bus all the way from Florida, and even when he was on the force his uniform had been shiny, unpressed, baggy, the navy blue covered with chalk, lint, dandruff, anything that was in the air or on the walls. In Florida he rarely bathed, changed his clothes, or had his hair cut. For the most part he did little more than drink salted beer, alone or with the local Crackers, and eat the broiled mullet he was given by the Cracker fishermen who drank his beer. He was small, and although he had been wiry in his youth, his work on the force had almost always been behind a desk; in his old age his legs and arms were thin but soft, and he had a pot belly.

"He'd live in here if he could afford it," Schneider said to Scarponi, indicating O'Neil. Although Schneider wore sunglasses, as did Scarponi, Scarponi assumed Schneider had winked at him.

"You may not believe this, Fritzi," O'Neil said, "but I could be a millionaire and I still wouldn't live in here. If the sun's shining you live in a greenhouse, if you close the drapes you live in a tomb."

"How does he know?" Schneider said. "This is the first time he's been in one of these buildings."

"Now that's true enough, Fritzi," O'Neil said. "But it don't make what I say any less the truth."

"Look at this guy," Schneider said. "He doesn't like sunshine and he lives in Florida. And the dummy talks about telling the truth."

"Sunshine's got nothing to do with it," O'Neil said, pounding his fist on the felt table. "It's living in a goddamned goldfish bowl."

"Horseshit, it's the dough," Schneider said.

"It's not a question of money," O'Neil insisted, shaking his head.

"He's afraid somebody will look in and see him take his pants down," Schneider said.

"I'm not either," O'Neil said. "Although I grant you it's got to be a drawback to these places. But I'd be damned sure to turn off the lights and pull the curtains before I took my clothes off." Schneider laughed and O'Neil, thinking he had said something funny, joined him.

"He's teasing you, Tip," Scarponi said. He remembered O'Neil's tendency to believe, drunk or sober, anything anyone told him. He was a perfect foil, and Scarponi did not wish to serve as Schneider's audience. Schneider rarely spoke to a man directly, and never when he taunted or insulted him; he spoke to third parties instead. This suggested that the man was too insignificant to address and that there were others present who felt the same about the man as he. His victim was simultaneously insulted and isolated from the crowd. He thrived on overfamiliarity and the distance of contempt, whichever served him best, and no one had ever heard him call another man mister, boss, or sir.

At this point Scarponi recalled an anecdote he had heard about their host. Magnuson's wife had been the power behind the purchase of the co-operative, a move Magnuson had resisted to the very end. They had moved into their apartment before the building as a whole had been completed and before there were drapes for the windows. The sunrise and morning sun, of which they had an unobstructed view above the lake, were so intense that the enraged Magnuson in self-defense bought several rolls of tinfoil which, over his wife's protests, he taped to the inside of all the glass. A few days later, van den Burg, the famous Dutch architect who designed the building, was showing it to a group of city planners and politicians when he discovered his clean vertical and horizontal lines disrupted by a row of windows on the sixth floor that formed a blind spot of sunlight, obliterating, by its intensity, a good portion of the building. An argument ensued on the threshold of Magnuson's apartment, Magnuson refusing to remove the tinfoil and restraining the architect by force from entering and doing it himself. But a clause in Magnuson's deed stated that a tenant could in no way interfere with the design of the building and in the end Magnuson had had to take the tinfoil down.

Scarponi told the story mostly for its humor. But Schneider thought Magnuson had been a fool. "Why did the guy buy the place if he didn't want sunlight?" he said. "Anybody else could have just looked at all this glass and predicted what the sun would do."

"Well, Fritzi," O'Neil explained, "he probably didn't see it at the time. But then when he got in the goddamned place . . ." Here he poured himself another Scotch, which so demanded his immediate attention that he forgot what he was about to say.

Schneider worked for the city park district and was the chief of all the youthful lifeguards the city employed in the summer at the neighborhood park swimming pools and on the Lake Michigan beaches. He had been a local high-school baseball star back in an era when schoolboys received as much fame as the college and professional athletes, and back in the thirties he was supposed to have played a game or two in the outfield for the Cubs. He had a short crew cut and he wore short-sleeve shirts even in the winter, when he had little or nothing to do. In the summer he wore only white T-shirts, white ducks, and yachting shoes, and he spent most of his time lying on the sand and in the sun. He would get darker than the Negro lifeguards who worked the South Side beaches, and he liked to place his arm beside theirs, contrasting colors. His job was politically appointed, and he was a strange combination of athletic director (no matter where he was, he always gave the impression of the presence on his person of sunglasses, clipboard, and whistle) and a lazy, politically supported cop.

"Say," O'Neil said, "what's Allegro doing now? I heard he was down in Florida. Lazzaretto's supposed to be down there with him." Allegro was reputed to be the crime czar of Chicago. Lazzaretto, like O'Neil, was a retired Chicago police captain.

"I saw Allegro last time I was down there," Scarponi said. "My girl's going to school at the U. of Miami. Allegro used to be a pretty straight guy. I don't know what he's doing now. I didn't run into Lazzaretto. I don't know him very well. I was thinking I might cross the state to Tampa and see you, Tip, but I didn't want anyone saying you was consorting with known criminals." Since this was a reference to a recent scandalous disclosure in the newspapers that Lazzaretto was seen vacationing in the company of Allegro who, allegedly, was paying his way, Scarponi smirked beneath his sunglasses. His face had the color and structure of an Indian's. His gray gabardine suit looked silver and luminous in the overhead conical light and seemed more appropriate to moonlight and the phosphor of plankton on becalmed seas. More than any man in the apartment he seemed, if only by appearance, to be at home among its walls and furnishings, as though if this were the modern home he was the modern man.

"No, you should have come to see me," O'Neil said seriously. "You're all right. Allegro's all right too. But I told that son-of-a-bitch once, 'Allegro, you punk,' I said—he was a kid then— 'you son-of-a-bitch,' I said, 'I'll break your fucking neck if you get in my way or cross me. I'll have you in a cell before the sun goes down. We'll see who's got the most pull downtown, you or me. Those goddamn judges do anything I tell them and you damn well know it. And don't give me any shit a punk like you's got any judges in his pocket. They know me and say, "How you doing, Tip? How's the daughter?" I'll put you naked in a cell,' I said, 'with fifty filthy drunk dirty tough black naked niggers and then we'll open up the windows' —it was winter then— 'and then we'll turn the fire hoses on you and wash out the cell. The buffaloes hardly ever cry but you dagos always wriggle your way to the bars and start bawling, "*Mamma mia!*" ' After that, him and me were pals. Never had any trouble with the son-of-a-bitch. Never had trouble. He was all right." Exhausted by the monologue, his voice lowered and the Scotch rolled down his chin.

Schneider looked at Scarponi and laughed. "He never said that," he said.

"The hell I didn't," O'Neil said, repeating it again and again in a low voice as he filled his glass.

"That took some guts to say that," Scarponi said, but he felt he was humoring O'Neil.

"He was a punk then," O'Neil said, suddenly, regaining his strength and shouting at the top of his lungs. "Later he got some class and they say he made it to the big time. But he'd always say, 'Hi, there, Tip, you old son-of-a-gun. How's the daughter?' He used to embarrass me. Jesus Christ, I told him not to be so fucking friendly or he'd get me in dutch with the papers. He didn't forget, though. A good egg, Lazzaretto was a real son-of-a-bitch, though. Allegro can't come to no good hanging around with a bum like him. They'll have to screw Lazzaretto in his coffin when they bury him. I never seen such a two-faced crooked cop."

"Him and Allegro went to high school together," Scarponi said. "They're from the same old neighborhood."

"Well, that explains it then," O'Neil said. "There's something to be said for old friends from the old neighborhood. Old pals ought to stick together."

"Where is that guy?" Schneider said, jerking his head toward the kitchen door. "Maybe he's in there learning how to count his meld. Come on, deal the pigs' knuckles. The guy's gone to bed."

Schneider was right. Magnuson was not in the kitchen, where he had gone earlier tonight to lean over the sink of stainless steel or against the copper-enameled refrigerator to try to enjoy the brief interim he had away from the card table and restore his nerves and calm his rage before he returned to play. He was in the bedroom, lying fully clothed upon the bed, his eyes open to the darkness, and the deathlike immobility of his body contradicting the leaps and writhings of his inner rage.

Through the walls he could hear O'Neil relating a story he had heard a hundred times before, of Senator Scott Drummond of Illinois on the floor of the Democratic convention. "The chair was ramming through this motion Scotty didn't like," he was saying, "so Scotty grabs the mike of the Illinois delegation but the chair won't recognize him. That hillbilly keeps gaveling the motion closed and Scotty keeps shouting in the mike, 'Mr. Chairman!' Scotty was for Kefauver and the delegation and the convention was rigged for Stevenson. Why, I met two Minnesota delegates—a shoeclerk and schoolteacher—that went home and found five grand waiting for them in their bank accounts. So I see the mayor snap his fingers like he was calling his Irish setter and he says without even taking his eyes from the platform, 'You guys shut that old son-of-a-bitch up.' And no sooner said than these guys grab the mike away from Scotty, poke him in the guts, get him in a headlock, twist his legs so that he loses a shoe, and begin dragging him out of the hall. One guy's got him by the necktie, another guy's got him by his wavy mop of silver hair and he says, 'Hey, Tip, get these goons off my back,' and I says, 'Scotty, you old son-of-a-bitch, what are they doing to you?' So I steps in and says, 'All right, boys, let go of this guy. This is a United States senator. You'll be downtown in the lockup if you don't let go.' Because I knew the mayor didn't want Scotty roughed up, just pushed away from the mike before he got the chance to start on that golden oratory of his. And later the mayor himself comes down to the station to see me and he says, 'Tip, you old bastard, thanks for stopping those big dummies from roughing up the senator. And how's the daughter?' So these guys knew I meant business and let go of the senator. And Scotty puts his arm around me and pushes back his mop of hair and says to me in that deep voice— you know how he talks—" (and here Tip did his drunken best to imitate the senator's voice, a blend of Russian basso, funeral director soothing the bereaved, and gigolo attempting to persuade a spinster to part with her savings). " 'Tip, my dear and trusted friend, you old bastard. You have my deep and heartfelt thanks from the very bottom of my heart.' "

"Deal them pigs' knuckles," was all that Schneider said.

For Magnuson the voices were alien rather than familiar, emanating more from nightmare than from nostalgia, and they deepened his despair. He had erred in his assumption that a game of pinochle among old friends would, by dispelling loneliness, dispel despair. Pinochle should be played by men in shirtsleeves on Sunday afternoons on a fold-up card table on the wooden back porch of an apartment house, or on the table in the kitchen of a Chicago bungalow, an open quart of beer beside each player; or in the back room at work during the lunchhour or when the job was slack, with someone stationed at the door, watching for the boss. To Magnuson the very game itself was somehow his family, his jobs, his old neighborhood, his old friends, the whole city of Chicago and his lifelong existence in it. For men dressed in suits and drinking Scotch to play pinochle in the evening in such modern, plush, and sterilized surroundings was incongruous, artificial, even patronizing, like stockbrokers and financiers bowling in a blue-collar bowling league.

Wealthy, retired, and widowed, Magnuson lived in the eight new rooms alone. His son was in Europe and at last report was bumming around with an idle company of youths of both sexes and several nationalities, and his daughter was in Africa, in the U.S. Information Service. After several years of cajoling, hints, and even arguments, his wife had persuaded him to leave the old neighborhood where both were born and the small apartment on the second floor of a two-flat brick apartment house in which they had lived since they were married. Within a year of their moving into this co-operative, she was dead. He could not associate these rooms with her, nor with his children, neither of whom had ever been inside them, nor with his jobs and friends, for his friends were either from his old neighborhood or from his jobs, and he had already been retired when they moved in. He had been especially close to his wife, and the feeling of their marriage, in his definition, had almost been that of man to man; he often called her "pal," and in the fashion of Chicagoans, but fondly and with respect, "the old lady." Immediately after her death this disassociation in his home from anything personal had been a boon. Later, when he recovered enough to realize he had no present, nor any future, he was forced back into the past, but the past did not exist within these rooms. The glass and Sheetrock walls, the white Sheetrock ceilings, the unpaneled doors, the floors carpeted from wall to wall in solid and subdued colors, the plastic or veneer cabinets that imitated wood, the wooden furniture that resembled plastic— that stark, square, modern luxury that he sometimes saw as being all satin pads and chrome, a world where nothing was what it appeared to be—all of this was void of an atmosphere of life, as if it were the surface of the moon. He felt in prison in a whitewashed cell beneath a naked bulb, with no pictures, keepsakes, or furnishings. He had invited old friends tonight to fill the rooms with the stuff of the good old days and the old neighborhood, like old photographs, Victrola records, and broken bureaus. But instead they had filled them with the worst of what had been, the baroque quality of their corruption the more magnified in the barrenness of these surroundings, like a bribe made in the middle of the desert, a murder committed on the high seas.

In the early days of the Great Depression he and Scarponi had both served on the Chicago police force, had been rookie patrolmen together in a class instructed by the then Sergeant Tip O'Neil. Within a few years both he and Scarponi had quit the force, the one perhaps because he was too dishonest, the other because he was not dishonest enough, and thereafter each was to go his own way, one into a liquor business that bore his name, the other into a private detective agency that bore his, and O'Neil, who remained on the force, was finally to become a captain. Over the years Magnuson had remained friendly with both men, although lately he had seen them rarely and then only by coincidence. Scarponi he had seen as recently as a year ago when he came unexpectedly to the funeral home where the body of Magnuson's wife was being viewed and was generous with his condolences and grief.

Lately Magnuson had been thinking of those early depression days upon the force, and these remembrances gave him a glint of solace and satisfaction which remembrances of his childhood, his wife and children, his years as a private detective that culminated in his success in both reputation and money could not. Those times when the members of a gang would come to the door of their apartment when he was on duty and attempt to give his wife an envelope of money, and she would refuse and they would then slide it under the door and she would slide it back onto the porch until they would get tired of sliding it back and forth and give up and leave it on the door stoop, and he would then have to report it and turn it in at the station. This happened day after day until, to the disappointment of the lieutenant and sergeant at the station, the gang gave up their attempt to bribe him and came to the door while he was on duty to tell his wife what violent things they would do to him if he didn't take the money or leave the force, and when this had no effect, what violent things they would do to her. Then they would loiter at any hour of the day or night in the shadows of the garage that bordered the empty lot next door, right where those tall scraggly hollyhocks would come up each year, getting taller and more scraggly with each year, and he would set out tin cans in the lot, close to the garage and at the base of the hollyhocks, and when his wife said "Arnie, there's someone in the hollyhocks," he would shoot the cans with his service revolver from his upstairs bedroom window, kicking them up and bouncing them off of the garage and into the hollyhocks with a ka-pow!-ka-bam! until the lieutenant ordered him to stop, allegedly at the complaint of anonymous neighbors. That was when they got Chang, the big chow they walked around the house and lot at night, letting him lift his leg in the shadows of the garage and on the holly-hocks, often hearing heavy, erratic huffing and patent leather foot-steps running down the alley as they approached.

Then the time he and his partner surprised a gang of boys in the act of stealing a car, and when the boys drove the car toward them in response to their command to stop, his partner pulled out his revolver and aimed it at the approaching car, and Magnuson, uncertain if he was aiming at the tires or at the windshield, cursed the man and grabbed his arm and told him not to shoot as he leaped himself onto the running board of the passing car, holding on to the door handle for dear life as they maneuvered at high speeds through city traffic, and censuring himself for the hastiness of his action as a boy in the back seat reached over and stabbed his fingers that clutched the door handle with a screwdriver, and the driver opened his door into him and kicked him from the running board onto the hard pavement and uncompromising friction of the street; for six months he lay in the hospital and then at home with all manner of broken bones, scrapes, and bruises, while the boys, arrested later, were given suspended sentences in the court and released in the custody of their parish priests.

And the time when he and Scarponi were off duty and visiting Scarponi's older brother, who lived in Maywood and had recently been suspended from the police force of that town for beating up a bartender with a rubber hose, when a gang of young dagos drove up to the house and disembarked from the seats and running boards of their sedans with chains, clubs, tire irons, and slats with nails in them torn from crates in their hands, demanding that the three sons of Scarponi's brother, who had beaten up several members of the gang the night before, step outside in the muddy yard and receive their retribution, a command that was instantly obeyed not only by the three sons but by the father and the uncle and Magnuson as well, who, in their eagerness to accept the challenge and be the first out-doors, knocked the screen door off its hinges, with Scarponi's brother actually running through the screen. Magnuson still had black and white impressions of that yard: mud, long deep tire ruts full of gray water, mud-splashed, manure-dirtied chickens squawking and flapping in the mud, sweet peas and pole beans climbing on gray poles and chicken wire, and some mad rooster by himself on the peak of a gray shack and crowing. Remembered how they beat the dagos with their fists and feet and then with the weapons they took away from them, while the muddy, befouled chickens flapped between their feet and over their shoulders and someone was splashing face first into a puddle and coming up gray, wet, and feathered, and someone else was enmeshed in chicken wire and screening and piles of sweet peas and beans, dragging the vines and runners behind him through the mud and looking like some barnyard Bacchus. Then the dagos were hiding under their own cars, where they fought among themselves in the confines of that space between the frame and mud to gain the safe central position between the wheels, while Magnuson and the Scarponis grew winded running in circles around the cars and their feet grew heavy with the mud and they bruised their shins against the running boards and bumpers as they tried, sometimes successfully, to kick the panicking dagos in the head. Then when the dagos had sworn out a warrant for their arrest on charges of assault, their bandaged heads and discolored faces their proof that they had been the ones attacked, the Scarponis and Magnuson had all sat together in the courtroom along one bench and before the judge had finished his opening remarks, they were on their feet, the two Scarponi brothers and Magnuson, shaking their fists and shouting that if this small-time, small-town justice of the peace did not dismiss the case outright they would have him behind bars before the sun went down, and the judge, cognizant in this rare moment of his ignorance of the law and, more importantly, of the political power of the prisoners, voiced his hope for conciliation between the opposing factions and then dismissed the case.

How Magnuson would have liked to reminisce with Scarponi and O'Neil about such things! But that disloyal, drunken O'Neil had showed up in the company of a fourth and uninvited hand: Schneider! Originally he had asked O'Neil to bring along Goldy Goldman, a fellow cop from the old days in the old neighborhood; but O'Neil had informed him when he arrived tonight with Schneider that Goldman had died last year in California, where he had been living for several years. What the hell was he doing bringing Schneider here? He didn't even know that O'Neil knew Schneider, or that Schneider would condescend to accompany O'Neil, and especially to the home of a man whom, Magnuson was sure, he disliked.

He hated Schneider, and his hatred had played his cards all

night. Because the humiliation of Schneider had been his sole aim he had himself played badly, paying more attention to Schneider's play than his own. While Schneider, addressing him in the third person, had called the table's attention to every error he made, once for having failed to meld a pinochle—a jack of diamonds and queen of spades—which he later played. Magnuson, for his part, had called Schneider several times for bad plays and bids only to have the others (including Magnuson himself, to his disgust) agree at the end of the hand that they were well made.

Now in the darkness and quiet of his own room he listened to his own ringing curses, not so much at Schneider for being who he was as at his being here, and therefore not so much at Schneider as at O'Neil, who should have known the man that Schneider was and who spoiled the evening and violated their friendship by bringing him here. His walking out on his guests he justified as being for the best, for he was afraid he would show his temper before them all and curse O'Neil until words could give no further satisfaction and he would have to grab him by the baggy seat of his shiny pants and toss him out the door, when all along he really wanted Schneider, wanted his hands around his throat and the red ash of his cigar poked up into his ear. He hated himself for festering with this misplaced anger at O'Neil even though he thought it justified and reasonable. And he found, as he had throughout his life, that the pain of this self-hatred was somehow a pleasant sensation to feel. It got not only to the deserts but the desires of his soul, and served the proper workings, as he saw them, of the universe.

Suddenly, as if he had at last determined to humiliate Schneider verbally, and failing that, physically, he leaped from the bed with the speed of a man defending himself against an intruder breaking into the room, and bounded for the door only to stop before he opened it.

"So I told the mayor," O'Neil was saying, " 'Tim, you old crook, you and Tubbo'—Tubbo was sheriff then—'you got your fat hands in the pockets of every working stiff in this city and you've got us guys on the force harassing these so-called gangsters that as far as I've been able to tell ain't committing any crimes that are on the books.' And he told me, 'Tip,' he says, 'the papers have put the heat on us. What can we do, pal?' "

"If he ever said that," Schneider said to Scarponi, "he would have been busted and walking a beat on the South Side with the niggers."

"No," O'Neil said patiently, "that was when the *Tribune* was exposing so-called crime. They ran a front-page exposé on one of Jimmy 'The Cod' Fiore's nightclubs out in the sticks, claiming there was gambling on the premises because of all the cars in the parking lot and hardly no one inside the bar and restaurant. But the dummies, when you counted up all the buffaloes working in the kitchen and the waitresses and busboys and bartenders who drove their own cars because the place was in the sticks, that accounted for all the cars. There wasn't any gambling at Fiore's joint and I told the mayor so right to his fucking face."

The subject of police harassment appealed to Scarponi, and speaking passionately, he led it in his own direction. "Look at all them society families the politicians suck around and take their orders from," he said. "Didn't they make their dough running dope and booze and shylocking and paying off the politicians and working dumb foreigners and niggers to death for next to nothing? But that was a long time ago and people forget how you made your dough and only see the dough and the class and the style that goes with it. That's what counts. Fifty years from now the old Italian families with dough will be as good as the old Jew and American families with their dough. My little girl's at Miami U. and my boy and big girl have already graduated from Champaign. Those are good schools, ain't they? You can't be no dummy and get in there, can you? Can you?"

"It never made no difference to me," O'Neil said, "whether a man was white or black or a dago gangster. I gave them all equal protection under the law. No man's alive who can say I did different. But if they broke the law, I want to tell you I done my duty and busted them all alike."

"Come on, deal them pigs' knuckles," Schneider said. "I'm ready to get out of here."

How Magnuson loathed Schneider and all men like him. He knew him around the city for one of those men, not uncommon in Chicago, who had their own clique of male friends that went about publicly abusing and emasculating all other men. He had once overheard Schneider inform a man that the man's wife was a stronger swimmer than he was, and when the man had attempted to assuage the insult by saying that he could swim farther than his wife if you counted the distance it would take him to sink to the bottom, Schneider chose to take him literally, remarking that the man was not only inferior to his wife but was gutless enough to admit it. Schneider was also a great thief, and flaunted his thefts before as many witnesses as possible. When he came as a guest to the Lincoln Athletic Club, where Magnuson was a member, he not only stole sweatshirts, towels, and soap, but called attention to his thefts. Magnuson heard he had even stolen a city lifeboat from a Chicago beach and made his lifeguards lash it, along with the oars, to the top of his car. Magnuson himself had seen him steal something as improbable as a dozen crates of distress flares from a police launch moored at Montrose Harbor, ordering his lifeguards to put them in the trunk of his car.

And his contempt, utter contempt, for any consequence from his thefts or insults suggested that he had great power behind him— the mayor, the aldermen, the superintendent of police—which, if he were ever challenged, he could array against you. O'Neil bragged of his connections but you believed little of what he claimed, although he must have had some power behind him or he never would have reached the rank of captain. But Schneider made no such claim, and yet, because he spoke and acted with impunity, and not only survived but thrived, you knew that in this city he must have some power behind him. In a way he was the typical Chicagoan, as though certain attitudes and tensions native to the city had converged, ultimately, in him, and made him their embodiment. More than anyone else he was the kind of man Magnuson had fought against when he had been on the force, and the kind of man who more than anyone else had made him quit the force.

And yet there was no denying that Schneider was a popular man, and had connections outside politics. Years ago Magnuson had gone to see a baseball game between old-time Cubs at Wrigley Field and was shocked and disgusted to discover that among these hall-of-famers and heroes of his lifetime, Schneider was playing right field, crouching professionally with his hands on his thighs in the white Cub uniform on the outfield grass before the ivy-covered wall. And there was no denying his competence, either. It was a matter of local pride and publicity that no drownings had occurred for a good many years at any of the Chicago beaches patrolled by Schneider's lifeguards. Even though you knew the man for what he was, you still wanted him to like you, or at the very least not to despise you. That was what was so humiliating to Magnuson.

Now Magnuson, leaning in the dark against the bedroom door, saw in a daydream the violent forms of his revenge on Schneider, saw his face blown apart by bullets, saw him lose his car to a head-on collision with a truck, his job to a broken neck, his house to fire, until he realized with some alarm that the only involuntary daydreams he could recall having for some years now never depicted scenes of future hopes or past pleasures, but revealed instead the simple, swift, and involuntary visions of violence. He had only to read in the newspapers or hear on television of the murder of a child to see the murderer torn apart limb by limb by polar bears in the Lincoln Zoo, or of an abuse of an American abroad, or of the American flag, by a foreign government to see the leaders of that country, and sometimes all its citizens, hanging by their throats from their own lampposts and trees. Inside him festered a craving for a vengeance, national in character, that would purge with floodtides of spilled blood all that was unrighteous and unjust in the city, the country, the world, and that craving, which had yet to be satisfied or expiated, could at times devour him.

In the kitchen now, Magnuson heard for the first time what sounded like an opera sung in Italian coming from the living room. Peering out the kitchen door he saw the coatless Scarponi showing Schneider and O'Neil in topcoats out the front door; saw Scarponi lift his hand from his pocket and in a single motion peel off the top bills of the thick roll that was hidden in that hand and pass them on to Schneider, who put them immediately into his pocket. The move was so superbly choreographed that it seemed the bills had leaped magically from one pocket to the other, untouched by hands. "Just in case I'm drowning sometime," Scarponi said.

When Schneider and O'Neil were out the door and Scarponi was at the phonograph, reading the notes on the back of a record jacket, Magnuson shuffled into the room. "I feel rotten," he said. "Must be the flu." Then unable to contain himself and disgusted with his own deceit, he said, "I hate Schneider's guts! And that O'Neil is one son-of-a-bitch for bringing the guy here. He ought to have shown better sense. How can you stand that Schneider's guts?"

"There's a lot of guys like Schneider," Scarponi said.

"So what," Magnuson said. "I can hate every one of them."

"Yeh, but I got to live with them."

"I don't," Magnuson said, hitching up his belt. He pointed to the phonograph. "What the hell is that?" he said.

Scarponi shut off the phonograph and returned the record to its jacket. "I don't care for that kind of music," he lied. "But the people from the Old Country like to hear it on my show." From the little he had heard he was disappointed. The music was too thin, unmelodic, passionless, lacking the blood and thunder and sun-bright, moonlit passion of violent, triumphant song. He would send it on to the radio station and see what they thought of it there.

Magnuson sat down on the Danish couch, lit a cigar, coughed, spit into a handkerchief, and relit the cigar. Hunched over, his suit was almost tight on his bearlike body. His clothes were tailored and expensive, but he wore them so loosely that they looked outmoded and even worn, suggesting the castoffs of some larger man or that the man who wore them had recently lost considerable weight. There was an unhealthiness in the whiteness of his face, which tended to redden easily, especially when he coughed. His hair was also white and tended to yellow. He looked both political and respectable, but a man more of the wards than City Hall: like a Republican precinct captain in a rundown neighborhood who knew he was a solid notch above his Democratic neighbors.

Scarponi sat on the edge of a low chair upholstered with some iridescent, synthetic fabric into which merged the aluminum and chrome quality of his flesh and clothes. "Maggy," he said, "remember when we was both broke, nobodies, rookie cops?" Magnuson came close to silencing the topic with his hand: it was too late to invoke the past to save the evening, too late even to save the man. "Now will you look at us?" he continued. "The two most famous men in Chicago sitting together in this room."

This assertion was probably true. In Chicago Scarponi's liquor stores were virtually synonymous with liquor. When shoppers did their weekly shopping at a supermarket they went almost invariably to a Scarponi's afterward, which as often as not was the store next door, where they could choose from a large selection of liquors sold at discount prices. Scarponi's was as much a household word as First National and A&P, and Chicagoans, instead of saying they were going for liquor, often said they were going to Scarponi's.

Magnuson was famous for the Magnuson Men, an organization of uniformed private guards, industrial patrols, and, in greater numbers, ushers, who were used primarily to handle the crowds at the sporting events of the city's professional athletic teams. This organization had gradually evolved out of his detective agency, the Magnuson Agency, had finally all but replaced it, and was the sole source of his present fame and wealth. Although it was the creation of Magnuson, it was his younger partners, Shannon and O'Bannon, whom he had taken as young lawyers into his agency and elevated to the rank of partners, who had made it into the big business it was today. There was probably not a citizen of the city who had not in some way come into contact with a Magnuson Man. To the public at large the Magnuson Men were as familiar and as symbolic of their city as the Stockyards, the Cubs, the Lakefront, the El.

But the names of Magnuson and Scarponi were well known only through the products that bore their names; neither man would have been recognized along the street, except possibly in both cases by policemen. This was why Magnuson, who saw himself as more alone, homeless, and desperate than a transient on Skid Row, considered Scarponi's assertion with skepticism and surprise.

"I suppose," he said at last, "that might be true."

"I ought to have some Magnuson Men around my places," Scarponi said. "I've had a lot of stick-ups and burglaries lately."

"Take it up with the boys," Magnuson said, meaning his partners, Shannon and O'Bannon. "I don't have anything to do with the Men any more. In fact I never did. Better talk to O'Bannon. He handles that end of the business." But he wondered who, besides kids and Negroes, would be fool enough to rob Scarponi's stores.

"And maybe we can get together in other ways. I use your business, you use mine."

"From now on, I'll buy my liquor at your store."

Scarponi laughed. "That's not what I mean, Maggy."

"I'm not buying any boxcar of gin I'll never drink just because you're using our Men."

Again Scarponi laughed, denying that was what he meant. He sensed the time was inappropriate for broaching the subject of finances with this man who sat with his head almost between his knees, like a drunk sitting on a bench at the station house, waiting to be booked. But he was also convinced that from now on any time had to be a good time, that if he interpreted the signs correctly, time was not only of the essence but his worst enemy. "I want to open up a club in that unincorporated area up in Niles," he said. "Fiore's had his own way up there for a long time and I've got Allegro to back me. It was his idea in the first place. It's a gold mine up there with all those Chicago studs crossing the line."

Any club in Niles, Magnuson knew, would be a striptease joint selling Scarponi's own beer and liquor at unreasonable prices, which would originally be sold to the club by Allegro's wholesale distributors; he also suspected there might be prostitution on the side, the dancers working in the early morning hours out of one of the nearby motels owned by one of the mob. He looked Scarponi in the eye and shook his head.

"I know you wouldn't touch any piece of the club," Scarponi said, "but I want to take money from the stores and put it in the club. The club will be a separate business from the stores. No ties at all. But I need to keep all the money I can in the stores because we're building our biggest store yet up in that new shopping center on the Evanston line." (Now Evanston was a dry town.) "And we got to keep building new stores in these suburban shopping centers. That's where the market is. So I'd take my money from the stores and put it in the club, and you'd put your money in the stores. Both businesses are legitimate, but I knew you'd know the stores were absolutely legitimate."

"If Allegro is backing you," Magnuson said, "why doesn't he put up the money?" And why, he wondered, was Scarponi so greedy as to risk so lucrative and legitimate a business as his stores by investing in the small, shady, and even dangerous business of the club? He had always been amazed at the eagerness of wealthy gangsters to become involved in petty schemes.

"But that's it, Maggy. He wants the club and he's willing to put the muscle and some of the money behind it, but I got to get up some of the money myself. But I don't want him to come out of this deal with a piece of the stores for his putting up all the money. I got to keep him out of the stores. I want you in the stores, Maggie."

Magnuson was confused. Since Scarponi must have had excellent credit throughout the city and any number of prospective investors in so successful a business as his stores, perhaps the share he offered him was made in friendship, and he was giving an old friend the first chance. But he also sensed he was being approached not as an old friend from the old days but as he was now: a wealthy man with a reputation in the city.

"You'd be investing in Scarponi stores and they'd be guarded by Magnuson Men," Scarponi joked. "How could you lose?" Then seriously: "I could have fed you a line that I was going into something more legitimate than the club in Niles. Listen, Maggy, a cut in the stores would be a gold mine. There's no way on earth you could lose."

If Scarponi was telling the truth, then Magnuson concluded, the position he was in, or was about to be in, was perilous. Allegro might have put him up to the club only to buy an interest in the stores, and if so, Scarponi's flirtation with alternate investors came close to a double cross. (And who really had the money in those stores anyway? Certainly Allegro had a piece of them and must have had from the beginning of the chain. Scarponi had seemed to acquire a fortune overnight. One day there had been no such thing as a Scarponi store, the next day they were all over the city.) Then there was the matter of Fiore, who would certainly resent any intrusion into his territory up in Niles and who had a reputation not only for pushing back but for pushing first. In fact, hadn't there been several gangland slayings recently—of small-timers, to sure—along with predictions in the press that new quarrels were brewing in the underworld?

Magnuson wondered if he could believe Scarponi. He knew that Scarponi lied habitually to everyone, but he also believed that Scarponi had never lied to him, and this trust had made him feel select of all Scarponi's friends. How many times had Scarponi, when lying to someone else, turned to him and winked? But now he suspected that he lied, and worse, that he used their friendship to advance the lie, as though over the years he had stored up a backlog of veracity that would make this single false moment into one of unquestionable sincerity. That Scarponi needed money, he did not doubt; but he was not convinced the money was precisely for what he said it was. Perhaps he needed it for gambling debts. After all, the man was a compulsive gambler, and had even wanted them to play pinochle tonight for nothing more than change.

Scarponi read Magnuson's hesitation as the prelude to his refusing him, and to forestall that decision in the hope that he might alter it in his favor at some later date—tomorrow, say—he said, "Think about it, Maggy," and put on his coat and hat. He was certain he had at least until tomorrow to raise the money, and more than likely even longer.

"I will, I'll give it some thought," said Magnuson. As he escorted Scarponi to the door, Scarponi put his arm around his waist. Instantaneously he felt better than he had in weeks, as though he were at last in touch with something masculine and solid that could sustain him. He began to believe in the sincerity of Scarponi's offer.

But when Scarponi was gone, he felt bad. The old depression and anger at Schneider and O'Neil returned, now accompanied by a dissatisfaction with what had just occurred between Scarponi and himself; he felt he had been abused, that he himself had abused, and he felt dirty.

He had recently discovered in a phonograph shop an album of songs by someone called Jimmie Rodgers, the singing brakeman. It was a re-release of old recordings he remembered hearing on Victrolas and radios in the late 1920's and early thirties, and they reminded him of the nights when he and his wife would listen to the "National Barn Dance" on the radio. For several weeks he had played the record nightly, and he played it now. Listening to the high-pitched, nasal, rural voice, accompanied for the most part by a lone guitar, he wandered through his apartment, turning off the lights.

The songs made him nostalgic for the hard times and good humor of the Great Depression, a time in which Magnuson the man had been created, and to which, even now, he belonged more than any other. They complemented and even justified his present feelings of depression and disappointment and soothed him until he felt only sad, although it was a selfish and sentimental sadness. They spoke of homespun tragedies: good boys gone bad through drink and gambling, and old fathers and mothers abandoned by their sons, unfaithful sweethearts begged back with no questions asked or shot down in cold blood in the street, and that lonely migration from farm to city, and that loneliness a man felt among his own kin, knowing that they were more morally upright and faithful than himself. They appealed to the criminal, the hobo, the rounder, the derelict, the black sheep in a man, giving him that lovely sense of manly shame; they made the rounder feel he was better than he was, the solid citizen worse than he could ever imagine himself to be. They appealed to those sweet sentiments of self-destruction in Magnuson's American soul, to that myth of a good man destroyed by a beautiful woman in the fog of his innocent past—a woman who, had she been faithful, could have saved him from a life gone wrong, although it was always more exquisite and manly to lose a woman than to win her; and appealed too to that frontier optimism that said no matter what misfortunes befell a man there were other women, other jobs, new friends, better times and, riding in a boxcar or an open roadster down a dusty road, new and better places down the road. So he thought: I can always leave Chicago. I can always get up and go and that would solve everything. So things can get worse and I can go even farther down in my despair, for I can hold this in reserve to save myself: I can get away.

He pulled back a drape and peered down the six stories through the rain into the street. The sidewalks were deserted. Only a random shade was lighted in the apartments of the Victorian and imitation Georgian townhouses across the street. He felt estranged from what he saw. His building was like a spaceship in the middle of a medieval town, his rooms antiseptic, like the insides of a brand-new enameled pan. Whereas in that world down there of lamplights, brick, stone, and gingerbread, that sense of Gothic and Victorian gargoyles and arches, there was a rich atmosphere of sequestered sin and naked violence. As though rapes and consenting acts of perversion and bestiality were being committed in all the rooms behind the shades, and anyone who ventured out into the streets in such a neighborhood on such a night in such foul weather was out to rape or rob or murder, or would himself become the victim of those crimes.

A black sedan stood in the street before the entrance of the building, the headlights on, the motor running, the wipers working on the windshield. The door opposite the driver was open, and a man stood in the street with his head poked inside the lighted interior, talking with the unseen driver, a package tucked under his arm. Scarponi.

Several taxis swerved around the standing car, tires whining in the wet; several minutes lapsed between their passings. Several times Magnuson wandered from the window and paced around his darkened rooms. By now the record had rejected, and the rooms were still. Then the unintelligible exchange of men's voices and the slamming of a car door. When he reached the window, the car was disappearing down the street, its red taillights reflecting back upon Scarponi walking down the sidewalk. Across the street a man emerged from the vestibule of a building—the very building of green stone with a red door from which, earlier today, Magnuson had seen a youth exit in the company of two detectives, appearing, because of the handcuffs covered by his jacket, to be holding one of the detective's hands. The man paused on the stone porch and put his collar up against the rain. Then with his hands in his pockets he hurried down the steps, only to pause on the sidewalk and stare after Scarponi walking down the street. Then, lighting a cigarette as he crossed the street, staring into the cupped flame as though no other sight concerned him, he got in step behind Scarponi.

A cop, Magnuson thought. Or was he? How could you tell? Then in the corner of his eye he observed an action that had him wrench the drape across the glass, had him quickly from the window and in the darkness of the room where his knees were weak with his depression and his muscles quivered with shame and rage. In a dark apartment across the street a young muscular man had gotten in between the drapes and windows and, facing the street, was moving sideways back and forth, glancing every now and then up at Magnuson. The man was naked and held in his hands his limp, hose-like penis which, by turns, he stretched and waved.

CHAPTER FOUR

THE VILLAGE

In the morning unsettled weather becomes the forecast for the day. Last night's rainclouds have gone east, where they can be seen loitering above the lake, and, as of the moment, the sun is out and shining, warming an otherwise cool and springlike day.

Up in Lake Forest Mr. Frazer Farquarson's estate is like an old-world English village in English weather. Green puddles shrink into the lawn, water dribbles in the rain spouts, glistens on the bark of beech trees, and the brick walks are salmon with the wet. The carriage house, potting shed, guesthouse, and gardenhouse, with their stuccoing, half-timbering, slate roofs, and casements, are like a cluster of cottages around the three-story imitation Tudor manor house with its gables, overhangs, and leaded sash. A high stockade fence of split weathered saplings encloses three sides of the estate, and if this is not enough to ensure the unspoiled nature of the village, high shrubbery grows behind the fence. The east side, however, is open, but only to Lake Michigan. A wooded glen falls steeply to the private sandy Farquarson beach, enclosed at either boundary by a high fence of corrugated steel that extends out into the lake to a spot where the water is over the head of any wader.

Old Tom Thorsen, handyman and gardener for Mr. Farquarson, has been up since dawn, transplanting Swiss yellow pansies on either side of the blue nepeta in the edging before the red City of Haarlem tulips in the spring border. In a long Levi jacket, white around the many tatters, a soft cap the size of a pie, and high rubber boots, he kneels in the damp earth, works it with a trowel, presses in the clumps of pansies piled in the wheelbarrow beneath a soaking burlap bag. This is the time of year he loves the best, when the bloom of one perennial begins to overlap the other, and nature herself seems the gardener. For some time now he has gardened himself into his garden where, unconscious of himself, he works in harmony and grace. The earth shrinks to the reach of his hands.

But now he feels the cold soil caked around his knees and drying in the cracks of the thick, veined fingers of his arching hands, feels all the aches and pains in the joints and muscles of a man who has been a laborer of one sort or another all his seventy-five years, and shows that grumpy temper that has served him all his life in place of disappointment and rage. He stands in the middle of a bed of red and yellow wallflowers transplanted from greenhouse flats only days before and surveys the trampled, broken, uprooted, and imbedded plants, ruined, he surmises with small difficulty, not by any animal but by a man who has left the imprint of his shoes so deep in the earth it would appear he leaped about the plot as high as several feet into the air.

He has good reason to seek the guilty party close to home. Too often nostalgia and infirmity deprive him of his sleep and, homesick and in pain, he roams the better portion of the night through the Farquarson woods and gardens, passing other strollers in silence and even invisibility, his soles like moss, his clothes like leaves. Or else stands still for hours on the lawns and listens to what? The secret tunneling of moles? The germination of planted seeds? To the passer-by he is just another tree.

John Cavan, Mr. Farquarson's nephew, he knows takes a nightly stroll across the lawn but on no random course. Invariably he is drawn to a favorite spot beneath the bedroom window of his uncle's nurse and, coincidentally, always at those moments when she decides to remove her clothes. Naked more often than not, and when not naked, half-naked, she passes back and forth, back and forth, before the lighted window, the shade of which is rarely more than halfway down. Occasionally comes to the window and, naked to the waist, leans out to inhale deeply the ozone of the night air. And sometimes it is as if an inscrutable quarrel has managed to take place between them, the nurse naked at the window but no Cavan on the grounds below or, more frequently, Cavan at his post but the shade on the nurse's room drawn upon the lighted window. Could Cavan in the excitement of what he saw have trampled the flowers accidentally, or in the vexation of what he failed to see, trampled them deliberately?

Or maybe Cavan is not the culprit after all. What about the Moony boy Farquarson hired to help Thorsen with the grounds last fall? Could he have returned last night to renew those midnight meetings with the nurse that took place almost nightly in the fall? That was when Cavan would come outdoors to confront the darkened window of the nurse's room and thereafter would walk aimlessly around the grounds and cough and yawn and whistle and stop to light cigarettes and surreptitiously search the grounds by that brief, insubstantial flame, while the strolling or sitting and sometimes embracing couple kept as quiet as they could until he passed, save for that deliberate, artificial moaning laughter of the nurse when she knew he was close by and the curse from Moony when he would not leave.

But if the nurse and young Moony are responsible for the damage to the wallflowers, they must have coupled—and coupled for the first time, too, he would guess—in some uncomfortable, contortionistic upright posture demanding heroic strength of the man who, alone of the two, left his footprints in the earth. No, this vandalism looks less like the work of lovers than of a gigantic hopping rabbit wearing shoes. No love involved in this, he thinks, but malevolence and spite.

He turns toward the carriage house, his stiff neck, blocklike shoulders, and even his oversized boots all turning together with his head, like a rusty bolt turning with its rusty nut. His back, hunched and crooked just below the shoulders, is balanced in the front by the jut of his almost chinless face from his recessed neck and the outcrop of his Adam's apple on a line with his chin. Standing well over six feet, and with his denim jacket tight on his arms and shoulders and the cuffs of his shirt pulled halfway up his forearms, and, when not in boots, always in black high-button shoes, he resembles the old comic stereotype of the hayseed come to the city.

"Hey, what are you doing there?" he calls. Speak of the devil. Nancy Rhinelander, Mr. Farquarson's nurse, in her nurse whites, backing out of the carriage house and trying to shut the door without making a noise. Challenged, she slams it.

"Looking for a ladder," she calls, approaching across the lawn. The sun shines through her uniform, which is always shiny and thin, and Thorsen can see as if through a milky curtain her underpants, garters, and the chalky stockings on her legs.

"Ladders is my business," he says. "Emptying bedpans is yours. And you was to meet a fellow in there." His accent is Norwegian, his voice high-pitched and sing-song.

The nurse laughs, makes a play of poking him in the shoulder with her fist, then fixes him with the self-confidence of her delphinium eyes. Barely a month returned from a brief holiday in Puerto Rico, she is tan, her face freckled, her short hair unseasonably blond. "Mr. Farquarson wants a ladder," she says. "Put up against the bedroom window."

In the overhang of the second floor, the curtains swinging before the open casements. "What needs fixing?" Thorsen says.

"Him." She indicates the window. "He's afraid of something. Fire. Negroes. Burglars. Your guess is as good as mine. He doesn't think anyone will come to his rescue." She is amused.

"Get out. He's up to his funny business again. He couldn't even walk to the window so how is he going to walk down the ladder?"

The nurse moves on to that subject she has meant to introduce ever since he called her from the carriage house. "Have you ever heard of a friend of Farquarson named Helenowski?"

"I don't know every damn fool he knows. And I don't know no Polacks."

"I'd think he was afraid of this Helenowski," she says, "except this morning's paper said he was found murdered last night in Chicago—in Washington Square."

"Knocked on the head by another Polack."

"Was he?"

"Sure," Thorsen says, "that's how these Polacks do their funny business. A knock on the head. And the boss said he knew him? Get out. He's pulling your leg. Now I got to put a ladder up against his window to keep him happy."

"I was going to get the ladder myself," the nurse says. "Only I couldn't carry it. I thought today was your day off."

"Too good a day for planting," Thorsen says. He takes out a small briar pipe burned down all around the bowl, fills it with burley tobacco, puts it in his mouth, and leaves it there unlit.

"What's the matter, Tom," she says teasing, "no place to go?"

"Sure, I got places to go," Thorsen says defensively. "But I got no reasons to go there. I been everywhere." He begins walking back across the lawn toward the wooden wheelbarrow and bed of pansies, and the nurse, to his annoyance, follows after. "I been to Alaska, sure. South Africa, sure. I been there. I been to all those places. I been a sailor. I been a lot of things. Ever seen them cornices in the Union Station downtown? I done that. I been a carpenter. I don't have to go nowhere. I been everywhere."

"I bet you got some old gal down in Chicago, don't you, Tom?"

"I go to see the fellows in Waukegan when I go out," Thorsen says, getting down on his knees among the pansies. "And stand back or you'll have my head up your dress."

The nurse hunkers down, clasps her hands beneath her thighs, and stares at Thorsen while he works, inches from his face. "Why don't you come to my room tonight?" she says.

"Because you wouldn't know what to do with a man," he says, troweling the dirt close to her polished white shoes and forcing her to rise and move back. "You watch out for me. Maybe I'm not done with it yet. You never know when it comes back to a fellow. When I was a young fellow and sailing on this ship with sails, all kind of sails, there was this old Dane aboard who used to sing them sailor songs, like 'Ho-ho-ho and a Bottle of Rum' and 'Blow the Man Down.' One morning he wakes up in his bunk crying like a baby, and I says to one of the sailors, 'Why is the old man crying?' and he says, 'He ain't had no bone-on in three years and he wakes up with one this morning and he's crying because we're a thousand miles from land.' "

The nurse stares at him skeptically, then begins to laugh, low and almost masculine, the laughter increasing until she has to double over and squat again.

"Sure!" Thorsen says, gradually joining her laughter.

The both of them laughing like a pair of ticklish children. The old gardener on his hands and knees among the flowers as if in imitation of some bony hound and the young nurse squatting beside him in her clean whites, her palms on the ground to keep her balance.

Then the nurse pointing above the tulips at the house. The picture of John Cavan leaning out the open casement of his ground-floor study and searching, with that worried, confounded look recognizable even at this distance, for the source of the inexplicable laughter.

Thorsen on his feet, shaking the trowel at the window and shouting, "You young son-of-a-bitching joker! By Jesus, if you got to be jumping, you do your jumping some other place than on my flowers!"

The confused, embarrassed Cavan withdraws his head.

"Sure, you tease me," he says, returning to those pansies. "But Tom can tease himself. He's an old fellow but he's been everywhere. South Africa. Alaska. He's been around the world. Three times. Sure."

"I've been to Japan and Korea," she says. The profile of the face of a second man comes before Cavan's window. He appears to be standing away from the window and looking at someone or something in the room. The white curtains blow before the face, and when they part, the face is gone. The breeze is suddenly cold along her arms.

"I been there too," Thorsen says. "I been to Vladivostok too. I been to Indochina. And I wasn't no soldier like you."

But the nurse is still watching Cavan's window. "I wonder if the nephew will ever marry?" she says.

"Sure he will. Somebody got to get the money when the boss dies."

"You think he'll get it?"

"Sure he will. Some of it. But the dame that gets him will get most of that."

"Weren't you ever married, Tom?"

"I should hope to kiss a pig I was never married. I liked it in bed with me when I was doing it but when I was done with it I didn't want it sleeping beside me. I got to leave when I was done, too. There's beds for sleeping and there's beds for that kind of funny business. I don't sleep in no bed I done any funny business in. I wasn't no whore in no whorehouse. But I done it with all kind of women, skinny blond women, big black women, little yellow women, even red women and Eskimo women, all sorts, all kind of ways."

"Look," says the nurse. "Someone's in the room with Cavan." She walks across the lawn to the house, watching the damp gray her shoes. She catches sight of Cavan at the study window. She smiles at the thought of the roles reversed. Cavan, embarrassed at first, returns the smile, and even waves.

She is suddenly weary. Weary to death of death. Hospitals. Soldiers. War. How is it that she was first an army nurse and now a private nurse specializing in terminal cases and passing from one house of death to another? Once upon a time she daydreamed on her father's Wisconsin farm of nursing babies, bathing the limbs of crippled children, serving in some missionary jungle hospital.

Old Tom Thorsen on his feet and loping to the mutilated bed of flowers. What an awful thought has just occurred to him! What if the damage is not an inside job after all, but the dirty work of some outsider, an intruder getting through the fence? Who has such a grudge against Farquarson that he would take it out upon his flowers? Or against Old Tom himself? Or is it just a case of unadulterated wickedness? Or, some unfathomable, bad-tempered revenge?

John Cavan, who has been accused by Thorsen of ruining the bed, has left the study window the nurse has seen him at and returned to his desk if not exactly to his unexpected guest. The only nephew of Frazer Farquarson and the only child of the late John Cavan, Senior, and the late Priscilla Farquarson Cavan, both of whom were dead before their son was two years old, he is a recent resident of the Farquarson house. As a minor he only visited here, and then only briefly and irregularly, living elsewhere at boarding schools or with distant Farquarson relatives. But with the settling in of his uncle's illness he was invited to live here last fall, he supposes, because his uncle wished his nearest kin at hand to comfort him and to become familiar with the property that would soon be his. Since his graduation from college, Cavan has led a life of study, travel, and leisure. He has spent more than a year in Europe, served six months in the army reserve, earned a master's degree in anthropology, and has for the past two years taken random courses that have interested him at both Northwestern University and the University of Chicago, while studying and even writing papers on his own in preparation for the expedition to Dahomey he plans to accompany in the fall and the doctoral degree in anthropology he expects to earn when he returns. He has also partied excessively with several "crowds," escorting Myrna Westermann, a steady girlfriend from whom he does not like to be apart for very long.

Last night, however, in those trying hours before he came home in the small hours of the morning drunk, disheveled, and without his house key, only to be greeted on the doorstoop by Nancy Rhine-

lander and her pistol, he and Myrna Westermann had a nasty, hurtful, and even irreconcilable quarrel. Quarrelsome, unreasonable,
and even remote from him in the several weeks since she first suspected she was pregnant, she has informed him that they are
through. This makes no sense to him and contradicts the behavior
he has come to expect of women, since a girl in Myrna's insecure
position should be trying her desperate best to stay in the good
graces of the father. Besides, it seems unfair of her. Immoral even.
What kind of society would allow a woman to go off with a
child in her belly and abort or bear it, keep it or give it away,
without the knowledge much less the consent of the father? He has
also made the disastrous mistake of confessing to her in a moment
of drunken contrition the perverse if innocent window games he
has been playing with his uncle's nurse, a revelation she has treated
with a surprising disinterest or possibly, he suspects, disgust.

At present he is inclined to forget Myrna in sobriety and industry by throwing himself into the revision of the paper sitting
before him that he has written on the origin of several Dahomey
tribes. He is equally inclined, however, to forget her by getting
drunk—if in fact he has sobered up from the night before. On his
desk the red enamel coffee pot covered with a tea cozy and the
oversized coffee mug full of coffee that are always on hand whenever
he works, and in opposition to them, a chilled uncorked bottle of
Moselle and a full quarter-liter emerald-colored wineglass of that
wine. He is so equally torn between sobering up and remaining
drunk that at the moment he is in pursuit of both. In the meantime
his response to his unexpected guest, like the drinks at either hand,
hangs in the balance. Should he remain reticent and discourage him
so that he will quickly leave, allowing him to attack his work, or
should he engage him in conversation, offer him a drink, and use
his company as consolation? Meanwhile they sit in silence, which embarrasses Cavan but does not appear to displease his guest.

The sunlight entering the casement and flaring in Cavan's half-
shut eyes; the breeze ruffling the Princeton cut of his sunlit hair and
the sunlit typewritten pages of the manuscript beneath the sunlit
hands. A large and restful room this study. Faded port-wine orientals overlapping one another on the floor. Heavy port-wine drapes.
An ottoman for resting. Mahogany desks, black leather armchairs,
mahogany bookcases along the walls. Several thousand volumes of
law, history, philosophy, and art arranged in the repetitious morocco
bindings of complete and lengthy sets. A collection a man of wealth

and education and social distinction might possess. An air in the room, of velvet smoking jackets, calabashes, globes, maps, ornamental knives for cutting pages, old brandy warmed in the palm; the aroma of leather, Latakia, ancient dust. A room predicated on the triumph of reason and memory, dedicated to the private and leisurely contemplations of a Western mind upon an anthropomorphic God and the wisdom of Western men.

But what a clashing decor Cavan has imposed upon the place. The skins of lions and leopards, witch doctors' ceremonial masks, dart guns, spears and bows and arrows, delicate flutes and heavy drums, carved tusks of ivory, hand-carved wooden statuettes of gazelles and elephants, ebony phalluses worn smooth by centuries of being gripped in darkened hands, statuettes of obese black women with outrageous breasts and buttocks and pregnant bellies. They take up the open spaces of the bookshelves, are set on desks and tables and on the floor, hang from the walls and ceiling. An air of totemism, superstition, violence, sex, and self-defense, of the perpetual nocturnal fear of jungle and savannah, where everyone is prey and predator and death is never farther than the next heartbeat in the breast.

Cavan himself the synthesis between the two decors is reading the sunlit opening sentence of his manuscript with one freshly opened eye. He must have dozed and dreamed the visitor was in the study. Or if the visitor was really here, surely he must have gone off by now, reading his dismissal in the insult of his host dropping off to sleep. He pours himself a cup of coffee, and just to be sure before he takes the first sip, looks about the room. Sure enough, the man is here! Seated just outside the path of sunlight, somewhere between a pair of drums, his face among a bevy of hanging masks.

How could he forget the man coming up the winding flagged path lined with irises and knocking on the French doors before he opened them himself and entered, saying, "It's John Cavan, isn't it?" Is he so familiar a visitor that he has the freedom of the house? If so he is certainly a man Cavan should know. Or is he merely some door-to-door salesman who picked up his name somewhere as a potential lead and wandered onto the estate? Indeed, he has a battered leather briefcase resting on his knees. He is perhaps fifty years old and has a bony and aesthetic face and a high wavy pompadour of hair streaked chipmunk-like with white combed straight back across his head. Smells like brewer's yeast, Bohemian hops, and pilsner seem to travel from his flesh and the smells of mold and mothballs from the double-breasted blue serge suit with its shoulder pads, pinstripes, and wide lapels that he wears without a tie and with the wide collars of the white sport shirt opened out upon the wide blue serge lapels. An almost East European—or what Chicagoans would call a DP (for Displaced Person)—look about the man, as though he is a Slav or German immigrant and worker in a machine shop dressed up while on the bus to and from his work, a Thermos bottle and a paper sack of sandwiches the only contents of that leather briefcase on his knees.

"A coffee?" Cavan asks, pot in hand, hoping the trick of refreshment will disguise the fact that he has dozed. Although he does get the odd impression that the man has been content to have him sleep so that he could study at leisure the relaxed features of his face.

"Please," the guest replies, receiving the cup and saucer in a hand that travels as far as the wrist into the sunlight and hurries them back into that dark, cluttered corner of Africana. "If I drink coffee, John, it's to stay awake. I can't very well afford to let anyone put anything over on me. I never sleep, you see. Not for a minute."

"Come now, you exaggerate," says Cavan, wondering what it is, exactly, that might be put over on his guest and by whom, but more disturbed at what he remembers now is his guest's tendency to exaggerate, if not to lie. "I'm sorry," he says. "But I don't think you told me your name."

"Isn't the face familiar?" says the guest.

"Yes, it is," says Cavan, truthfully, although for the life of him he can't say why.

"I wondered when you'd get around to asking about the name, though," says the guest. "It's Alvin Raincloud." He stares at Cavan as though to dare or detect any trace of disbelief.

"Is that an Indian name?" asks Cavan. He has studied what he can of the man and discovered little of the American Indian about the bone structure, complexion, and features of his face.

"Is it?"

"Don't you know?"

"Should I?"

"No, not necessarily," says Cavan.

"Perhaps you don't believe me, John, when I tell you that a man like myself could have such a first-rate, pretty name."

"I've no reason to doubt you."

"Why, it's positively poetic, my name. What pictures would you say it brings to mind?"

"Your last name?"

"Everywhere," the stranger says. "I was everywhere."

"That's quite a journey," Cavan says. "When were you there?"

"I was always there."

"Come again?" says Cavan, wondering why any topic of conversation with this man founders immediately on nonsense.

"There never was a time I wasn't there."

"What about now?" Cavan asks, not bothering to disguise his sarcasm and disgust.

"I'm there," says the man. "In spirit. Doing my job."

"I suppose there's a tribe, or a period, or a place you have a special interest in?" Cavan asks, patronizing in tone and much amused with himself.

"I'm interested in all tribes, all periods, all places," the stranger says, giving Cavan that wary look daring disbelief. And thereupon displays a prodigious and even esoteric knowledge of Africa—hidden treasures and lost cities and lost tribes and tribes of Amazons and tribal tortures and snake cults and leopard cults and monkey cults and trial by poison and cannibalism and fetishes and massacres and erotic sexual practices and gruesome puberty initiation rites —all of which astonishes Cavan until gradually it dawns on him that it is the kind of myth and misinformation a man might gather from reading an inordinate number of exotic and often fictitious articles in cheap men's magazines. While he rambles on about his latest trip "in spirit" to Africa, the stranger removes a large monkey mask from the wall and lifts it above his head.

"I prefer you didn't play with that mask," Cavan says.

But the guest has already lowered it upon his head. It makes him half again as tall and makes him look more baboon than monkey. Wearing it he walks about the room completing his impossible and muffled monologue on Africa. "Of course, in the end," he says, "they are all black devils living there anyway." He approaches Cavan, who observes that the man appears to have spent the night in the woods. Shreds of leaves and twigs are caught on his clothes and hair as though in spider webs. His knees are green with grass stains. "I've come to help you get up an expedition to Africa," he says, his voice sounding as though he is in a small closet speaking through a gag. "To search for your long-lost sister."

"I don't have a sister," Cavan says. He is convinced the man is mad, though harmless enough, and he wonders how best he can get him out of the house without creating a disturbance.

"A half sister then."

"Not even that."

"Wrong!" says the guest, pounding his fist on the desk, in fact on a corner of Cavan's manuscript. "You have a half sister who is black, or at least half-black, which is why she's only half your sister. She has, as I understand it, disappeared. Lost in the valley of the moon among the pygmies on the dark continent. After all, I'm a private detective paid to find out these things. You don't have to worry, though. No black blood is in your veins. I know who you are, and everyone knows who I am. And I can tell you that you're certainly not who you think you are."

"Oh? Who am I then?"

"Someone else," the man says, still behind the mask.

"But you knew my name when you came in."

"That," says the man, "is your dupe name. It doesn't mean anything. It just shows they've made you one of their dupes." The blue pinstripe serge arm placed protectively around his shoulder, the monkey mask almost against his face. "You're bound to be the major beneficiary of old Farquarson's will. You must stand to inherit a fortune." Whispering, jerking his thumb toward the door. "I'm not making any threats, mind you. I don't have to make threats. I know who I am. But old Farquarson ought to have his eyes put out. He ought to have his candlepower cut off at the source. Someone ought to put a stop to his electrical interference with other people's moral fibers and brainwaves. He ought to be snapped up in his bed. Admit it, in your heart of hearts you want to see him dead. He has it coming to him. And we have ours coming to us. With that kind of money in your hands you could finance a hundred safaris to Africa to search for your long-lost sister. You could hire a thousand detectives to track her down. Remember I'm on your side in all of this, and believe me you wouldn't get very far if I wasn't. I've got the power. I've got the real thing. I don't dupe people either. I give them the real business." At last the mask is off, his face and hair are wet. "I'll be back. We'll meet a second time. I don't need a plan. Leave everything to me." He is opening the French doors that lead into the garden. "I've always wanted to meet you. To see for myself what the world has made of you. I knew your mother once. They killed her nerves, you know. Just another case of soul murder that went unpunished." At this unexpected mention of his mother Cavan, who has wished the man gone, now tries to detain and question him, but the man has become withdrawn and moody and without saying more steps through the doors.

Cavan watches him as he almost runs down the driveway and passes through the gates of the estate, the briefcase tucked under his arm and his hands in his pockets. Should he call the police and report the man? After all, he did make threats upon his uncle's life. That the man would want to injure another man expected to die at any moment would seem to demonstrate that not only is the man mad but his madness is harmless. He decides he must have met some local character tolerated by the village, out for his morning ramble and mischief. He will ask the nurse or Mrs. Owens or Thorsen about him later.

He tosses down a cup of coffee and resolves to throw himself into his work. But not only the recent visitor but Myrna Westermann and her unexpected rejection of him last night overcome whatever peace and quiet he can muster in his mind. In the face of such unreasonable if not insane behavior the study seems irrelevant: the library seems no more than yesterday's newspapers, the collection of African pieces mere curiosities, his own manuscript an exercise in vanity. He sets down the coffee cup and takes up the bottle of Moselle instead.

Upstairs, Frazer Farquarson, although unaware of the threats against his life downstairs, no longer has the peace of mind to sleep. He has caught the sneaky, squeaky feet on the carpet of the corridor outside his door and opened up a single tobacco-colored eye. He takes consolation in the fact that bare feet do not squeak but thump or patter and that these feet must be wearing shoes. It seems more than just coincidence that he should be wakened by the feet in combination with the climax of that awful dream.

He has dreamed he is living in the tropics, a fact revealed not by the buildings and landscape and flora, which are identical to those of Lake Forest, but by the unbearable heat. He assumes he must be the American ambassador to a jungle republic cr the owner of a large plantation there. From an upstairs window of his embassy or villa, where he has stood only inches from a fan, he spies through binoculars hordes of natives migrating northward from Chicago, running down the winding shady lanes and undressing as they come until the streets and lawns behind them are littered with their discarded clothes. Fascinated he watches them approach but makes no move to sound the alarm within the house. In fact so confident is he that they will attack other plantations, or embassies, leaving his untouched, that he lowers his binoculars and deliberately turns away. But now he can hear, like the distant beat of drums, the thumping of their bare feet. No shrieks or shouts or battle cries, no sounds other than the panting from their open mouths and the massive rhythmical thumping of those feet. Too late he turns around to look. Instead of bypassing his estate, they are making for it first of all! Already the grounds are overrun with naked black men all either the size of giants or pygmies. Terrified, he knows his duty. Marshal the defenses. Protect the house. Safeguard the residents. He leans recklessly out the window, dodging the primitive missiles flying in clouds around his head. He issues commands, deploys the members of the household to positions of safety and defense. But they either disobey him or fail to hear his commands. Helpless, he watches the massacre begin below.

He clamps his skeletal hand to his bony brow. How on earth could he have had such an absurd, terrifying, and childish dream? He is a rational man, he will have his answer. He sweeps away the remnants of the drug and the price he pays for consciousness is pain.

First of all the morphine which made the dream fantastic, and the fever which made the setting of the dream compatible with heat.

Then that ambassadorship to one of the newly independent African nations that the Eisenhower administration failed to give him, selecting career diplomats instead of the wealthy contributors to the campaign. And all those books on Africa he borrowed from his nephew and tried to read more in preparation for any senate hearing on his appointment than to improve his service in that country should he have received the post.

And that damn fool John and his collection of African pieces and that witch doctor's mask he was seen wearing around the house one night when he was drunk, terrifying Mrs. Owens. And come to think of it, what might Lena think if she saw Cavan in the mask? Might she not feel ridiculed? As though the insensitive nephew of her employer was saying in effect: Boo! See who you really are: black magic, mumbo jumbo, and hardly any time out of the trees.

And then that foolish law the village tried to pass several years ago prohibiting the use of the village streets as an evacuation route by the inhabitants of Chicago if and when that city was devastated by a nuclear attack, a law already passed by Evanston, a north shore suburb to the south. Although it was never clear how this law was to be enforced, he supposes he envisioned the building of barricades on the southern town line, manned by village police armed with sawed-off shotguns and submachine guns and facing a panic-stricken mob ten blocks wide and thirty blocks deep in flight from the mushroom clouds overlapping in the sky behind them. A mob that, if it were not stopped at the barricades, bodies piled so high on other bodies that they in turn made new barricades, would trample villagers underfoot in their own streets and commandeer their cars, or prevent, by the sheer mass of their bodies, cars driven by villagers from fleeing north. Persuaded to support that bill he now regrets that support. The bill was not only inhumane but unworkable and silly. By the time the Chicagoans reached Lake Forest (providing anyone was left in Chicago), the villagers (providing anyone was left in Lake Forest) would have already reached the Wisconsin line, and then some. There was no reason to believe that the village police would stay behind to protect the properties of those already fled. The bill was less a fear of nuclear attack than of Chicagoans, black or white.

But although the dream becomes in part explicable and therefore harmless, Farquarson is depressed at having dreamed so violent a dream. Shouldn't a man in his last moments have visions of tranquility, justice, order, along with intimations of immortality? Especially now that he has been converted to a new faith in his fellow man, has himself been reborn as a new man, a good man, a wise man, and, hopefully, a forgiving and forgiven man. Could the dream be a warning that at this late hour all is still not right within his soul?

Even with the death of the man he had most reason to fear, the escaped lunatic Helenowski, he does not feel safe. The joy he felt this morning when the nurse read him the report of Helenowski's death from the newspaper has been shortlived. Evil is being generated not from any source outside the house but, he feels, from within. Didn't he just get a glimpse of its power in the violence of his dream? He is convinced of its presence as surely as if he found his tropical fish floating with their bellies up on the surface of their tanks, his potted plants withered in their terra cotta pots. And like a series of poison pen letters sent anonymously through the mails, the evil disrupts the harmony of the village. Suspicions and accusations are on the verge of being voiced by everyone. All are implicated, all potentially are victims, all potentially are guilty. But where precisely is this evil? And in whom? And where will it first rear its ugly head? Whatever its course he will combat it, overcome it, cast it out, and return the village to tranquility, innocence, a state of grace.

Even with Helenowski dead there is still evil to contend with, a new evil now. Magnuson the detective must be called and directed to get at the bottom of this new affair. Once more he resolves to call him on the phone.

But the morphine makes another march into his brain. He has a cloudy image of himself sitting popelike on a throne and smiling with magnanimity on the mass of men below. Others, to share his wisdom, have only to gaze upon the serenity of his face. He lingers on the image and its accompanying narcotic pleasure. Then he grows confused, has trouble focusing. The evil in his house is crossed with a pestilence in his garden: mites in the delphiniums that dwarf the blossoms and blight the leaves, slugs in the crowns of all his lupines. Now he remembers what he must do: summon Thorsen and command him to examine all the beds, destroy all infected plants. This determined, he surrenders to the morphine and makes another trip, an involuntary scouting of the suburbs of death.

He goes on foot along unpaved streets, past vacant prairies and the random unlit houses. The landscape lit only by the gas lamps at the crossroads. The night air chilly and humid, as if underground. The only fellow travelers the white possum that scurries ratlike from the foggy prairies and into the lamplight across his path, and the lamplighter ahead riding so slowly on his bicycle that the front wheel jerks left and right, the ladder he leans against the lampposts and climbs carried slantwise on his back. The tracks of a streetcar are being laid in the muddy streets and there is a sawhorse and a hole and pickaxes and shovels lying on the shoulders. Above his own footsteps in the damp gravel he hears the echoes of another time and place. Those squeaky footsteps in the hall outside his door. At last he differentiates between the horror of his dream and the evil in his house. He is afraid, and rightly so, not because those feet are bare but precisely because those feet are wearing shoes.

CHAPTER FIVE

THE OLD NEIGHBORHOOD

After a night of little sleep and many violent, involuntary dreams, Magnuson awoke not only to the sunlight pouring through the glass wall of his apartment but to guilty feelings and a sense of shame. His breath was short and he had an aching, circulatory pain. He regretted his suspicions of Scarponi and his misplaced anger at O'Neil. He had himself violated that old friendship he had accused O'Neil of violating when he brought Schneider to the apartment, and he felt a compulsion to right that wrong. This morning he would visit O'Neil. Accordingly, he wrapped in a paper sack one of the bottles of MacScarp's Highland Scotch that Scarponi had given him and, tucking it under his arm, journeyed north on the el to his old neighborhood and the apartment of O'Neil's daughter, where O'Neil was staying. Since he was a man who paid in advance for every service rendered him, who would never allow himself to be in debt to any man for whatever reason, and since it was not in his character to be so open and effeminate as to beg O'Neil's pardon outright, or to admit he wished to use his company to alleviate his own loneliness, this bottle was to be his spokesman and payment of admission.

But there was more substance to his trip north than merely the desire for pardon, company, and conversation. He had finally to go somewhere, to do something somewhere, and he pretended he had no alternative but to rise, dress, and go to see O'Neil. Although he was retired, wealthy, free of all responsibilities, and there was nowhere on this earth he could not afford in time and money to travel to, the place did not exist to which he had to go. And it was this unnecessary and commandless condition of his life that he found degrading and insufferable. His had always been a life of duty, of doing more often than not what he had no wish to do, of going where he had no wish to go, of seeing people he had no wish to see, and he had come to see this duty not so much as a sacrifice for which he exacted from himself, friends, and family the compensation of martyrdom, as the irrefutable machinery of life from which meaning, order, peace, and pleasure, proof of his manhood and even of his humanity could be gained. If he had been compelled to be somewhere, anywhere, at eight o'clock this morning he could have believed that he had saved his soul.

Last week his car had been stolen from in front of his apartment building by a gang of boys, none of whom, he suspected, was over thirteen. They had sideswiped a block of parked cars before abandoning it on the South Side of the city out of gas and, what was worse, out of oil. It was still being repaired downtown in the underground garage of the Lincoln Athletic Club, and Magnuson, rejoicing for the first time at his loss, was forced to take the el. It made him feel common, thrifty, a workingman with humble destinations along the line, a man at one with the vast, dirty, dilapidated city that passed by the tracks and stretched out in either direction like a Russian city built upon the plains.

Even as he exited from the platform down the sooty metal stairway and passed through the cagelike turnstile that resembled some infamous medieval instrument of torture and stepped out onto a foothold of his old neighborhood, he was already in the past. An evening thirty years ago when he had walked out on a guest as he had last night on Scarponi, Schneider, and O'Neil. Herman Goldman who, according to O'Neil, had died recently in California, had called unexpectedly at the old apartment. A hulking friendly blond with mournful blue eyes and a hawk nose, a patrolman out of the same station house as Magnuson, and a bachelor, he was susceptible to chronic fits of loneliness while on his beat, which he remedied by imposing his conversation for hours on end on those listeners accessible to him: unsuspecting pedestrians and drivers who asked the way, storekeepers with businesses along his beat who wept with self-pity at the sight of him entering their doors, and fellow officers assigned with him who bit their lips when the sergeant read the duty rosters, and even lawbreakers unfortunate enough to be apprehended by him and who were softened to the point of confession by the time they reached the station. For what passed for hours Magnuson and his wife sat in their living room pretending to listen to Goldman's monologue, which continued even after they desperately switched on the old Gothic-shaped radio, even after they sneakily inched up the volume as they dialed for different stations, and even after they no longer pretended to listen to that monologue. "You know, Arnie," Goldman would say, "I was driving the buggy past a gas station at Clark and Foster this afternoon on my way to the station and it dawned on me" (here he would slap his forehead with his palm) "that I couldn't remember when I'd changed the oil last. Why, this place is as good as any, I said to myself. So in I drive and say to the mechanic, 'Hey, how about checking the oil?'" For Goldman life had held no relief or texture: it had been a single surface of trivia. A corpse discovered on the beat had no more significance than the simonizing of his car. He had an ability to recall totally and almost minute by minute his day-to-day experiences, coupled with the perverse inability to be in any way selective when recounting them. At some time Magnuson wandered off without excuse as though on an errand that would send him back in seconds. Later, the voice of Goldman droning in the background as though he were himself at last bored with himself and fighting sleep, his wife came into the bedroom after he had heard her open several doors about the flat and whisper his name at each, and there she found him in pajamas, in bed, reading a law book by the night light and fighting with small successes the onslaught of sleep. Out, she ordered. The idea of leaving her alone to suffer his guest. But he refused, pleaded a long day, claimed he had to have the chapter read that night. "What will I tell him?" she said. "You'll think of something."—And evidently she had. When she at last had Goldman out the door and down the stairs and was beside him in the bed, she laughed. She recalled the incident to herself and laughed,

recalled the incident out loud and laughed, and later in the night
she woke him from his sleep by laughing in her own.—

Margey! he thought. Old Pal! They had been close—too close
perhaps, it occurred to him, for the children who, as they grew up,
grew away from them. He had forced her, he supposed, to be close
to him and she had been weak or, as he would like to think, strong
enough, to yield, leaving the children in some ways on their own.

To hell with the children! Didn't they have minds and hearts
of their own? Here he was on foot among streets he knew like a
farmer knew his forty acres. No man returning to the small town of
his birth and childhood could have experienced a more intense nostalgia of homecoming. The very pavement and muddy earth were
consecrated with what was most precious in his life: his past. Going
home, he mumbled to himself. Never left. To prove it, he quit the
streets for the paved alleys that bisected the middle of each block
from north to south, as though he had deluded himself into believing
it was no longer morning but late afternoon, and an afternoon years
ago when, footsore, sweated up, and rumpled, he was coming home
from work down the alley as he did five nights a week, greeting the
friendly but not well-known neighbors in their small back yards
behind the picket or chainlink fences that, along with the hip-roofed
garages, abutted the alleys. Men already home from work and out
watering or weeding or simply meditating in contentment on the
condition of their grounds. And the light he remembered walking
down the alley in the best: that golden horizontal sunlight just before the twilight that made the sunlit walls of the houses and garages
golden and the shadowed walls a bluish-gray. The stillness of the
air then, no gust, no puff, no breath, as though Lake Michigan had
drawn back its offshore winds, and the silent, elusive shifting of the
pastel colors in the hazy, urban sky, and in the distance the faint
noises of that massive aggregation of engines, sirens, tires, horns,
sounding like the ghostly din of battles waged a century ago across
the lake. In a house along the alley a child practiced an accordion.
Sometimes in several houses. Then he would be at his own lopsided,
half-hinged gate, enter through a gooseberry thicket, walk once
around the small lawn to examine the few plants in the border and
gauge the height and greenness of the grass with an eye to mowing
or watering, then up the back porch stairs and into the kitchen, where
his wife would be at the sink and the supper on the table, the evening paper and an open quart of beer at either hand of his plate.

Something foreign about these alleys and back yards, a feeling of Germany or Czechoslovakia. In the spring they were fragrant with lilacs, in the summer roses on rotted, weathered trellises, clumps of peonies and hollyhocks in the yards and morning glories that matted the fences and climbed up strings along the walls of the garages, and in the fall, clusters of Concord grapes on weathered, broken arbors, the grape leaves yellow after the first frost and in that golden horizontal light of the twilight hour of his coming home. When he was a boy, and then again during the Second World War, the better portion of these yards had served as vegetable gardens, with neat rows of tomato plants staked behind the fences, the green and red fruits drooping out between the slats and wire, the scent of tomato foliage filling the alley; chickens and geese had been kept behind chicken wire and, in lieu of cars, in the garages—vicious flocks of gray Toulouse geese that charged the fence hissing whenever anyone passed in the alley, viperous necks stretched, wings raised like weapons; rabbits and pigeons had been kept in hutches; even milking goats had been tethered in the few vacant prairies; and wild rabbits had abounded in the yards and prairies, burrowing beneath the garages.

Several blocks ahead the shouts of garbagemen, the grinding racket of the orange garbage trucks, the deliberate, denting bang of the garbage cans. A block ahead a lone car backed out of a garage, so large a car it could barely maneuver in the alley. Other than this, Magnuson observed to his surprise, the alleys were quiet, deserted. He could hear his own footsteps on the concrete, his own heavy breathing.

What a change from the old days when ironmongers and rag-pickers would cruise up and down the alleys in horse and wagons or those high ancient trucks like ornate indestructible stagecoaches, each man with his own unique, recognizable, unintelligible cry; as would the trucks and wagons delivering coal and hawking whatever fruits and vegetables were in season, produce from the truck farms just to the north and west of the city and not that far from the neighborhood. And the residents themselves, man, woman, and child, would walk the alleys, preferring them to the sidewalks or the streets, using them like a secret network of footpaths and short cuts that traversed the neighborhood.

Scandinavians and Germans mostly, with a strong showing of Slavs, had lived in the neighborhood then. As in most of the older neighborhoods in the city, there was a small tavern every other block or so where many of the local residents drank beer almost nightly, and on almost every block the small grocery store called "a neighborhood store," which was in a house and was where the children were sent daily for whatever was to be eaten that night; and on the nearest main street a Swedish or Norwegian bakery where Magnuson himself or one of the children would go Sunday mornings to wait amid the hot fragrances of yeasts and sugars for longjohns and bismarcks for the Sunday breakfast, waited on by women whose blond hair would be braided like their coffee bread, and the butcher shop run by the Germans in their straw hats and bloody aprons where Magnuson's wife would go Saturday mornings for the Sunday roast, where at Christmastime there would be trays of hogs' heads in the case and in the fall crates of unskinned, slaughtered rabbits on the sidewalks, and the ice-cream parlor run by what seemed to be a dozen adult male Greeks, with its marble floor and counter and tin ceiling, where the whole family might go on Sunday evenings; and a few blocks from the house the brick elementary school with its large gravel yard, like a hundred other grammar schools in the city, where both his children had gone, and the local park and playground with its fieldhouse and shade trees where the children had played Saturdays and after school, and to which he himself had taken them, hand in hand, when they were small.—

If only he could once more be subservient to the timetables and paths of the mundane rituals of walking back and forth from house to bus, from house to school, from store to store on a round of shopping. To frequent familiar places at familiar times! The harmony of life in the performance of those rituals.

Uncertain that he could identify the apartment of O'Neil's daughter from the alleys, he returned to the streets. No cars had passed him since he began his walk. Few cars were even left parked along the curbs, most having departed in the morning rush hour. Several blocks ahead was the only other pedestrian on the street, too far away to tell if it was man or woman. It occurred to him that midmorning on a weekday was an unusual time for him to be about the neighborhood, and would have been so even when it had been his home.

Here the blocks were dominated by large four-story apartment houses of wine-colored bricks. Long conforming rectangles or horseshoes of three rectangles pieced together with a courtyard of grass between the ells, a strong suggestion of a medieval castle in their Gothic arches, bartizans and crenelated parapets along the roofs.

Across the street from these apartments were large two-story frame houses, most of which had been converted into two-family dwellings. Built in the late nineteenth century, there was a Greek influence in their architecture. Although they varied so that actually no two looked alike, they somehow looked alike. All had wooden stairs leading up to the front porch, over which was a roof supported by short narrow columns that rose from the balustrade, and two of these columns flanked the head of the stairs. Below the peak of the roof was a triangular tympanum demarcated by cornices. If the apartment buildings aspired to be medieval fortresses, the houses aspired on a lesser scale to be Greek temples. When the houses had been built there must have been a notion that the home was holy, a place of sanctuary. Forty or so years later when the apartments had been built, the home must have been seen as a castle under siege.

For some reason Magnuson was confident his walk would take him several blocks from his old apartment, which relieved him, for he had no wish to feel the pain and sense of loss he was certain he would feel if he saw the place. When halfway down a strange alley he was passing, he saw it—his old apartment building, even his old apartment. Jutting out among a jumble of back porches and garages, the rear corner of the second floor of a dark brick building, two windows with drawn yellow shades looking down the alley to where he stood confused, startled, afraid. He was not overcome with memories. He did not experience pain or loss. He experienced terror. The building had that bleak, evil, abandoned look of a city apartment house wherein, you have just been told, a brutal and unsolved murder has been committed in the night: a woman raped and battered beyond recognition. The two windows those of the very room in which her body had been found in bed, the windows themselves those through which the murderer entered and escaped. And he saw the windows as though in a photograph in a newspaper, with a circle drawn around them and with dashes up and down the bricks marking the murderer's path. What rooms of his old apartment did those windows look out from? He couldn't remember. Couldn't picture the floor plan of the apartment. As if he had never lived there. As if his past was nothing. As if at this very moment there could be strangers behind those shades with starving children locked in a closet or chained by their wrists and ankles to the footboard of the metal bed. Or some homicidal maniac or sex fiend tramping through the dusty, unfurnished rooms with a bone in his mouth and a half-eaten sandwich in his hand, or sleeping like some vampire with his eyes open, lying fully clothed upon the unmade bed.

When he arrived at O'Neil's daughter's house, he experienced still another shock. Wedged between the grille and bumper of a battered, rusted station wagon parked in the street was a row of a dozen or so rubber dolls, all soiled, some armless, legless, eyeless, hairless, some with their necks half torn from their shoulders. These Magnuson mistook for the mutilated corpses of naked babies. Had the world come to this, he wondered? He began to tremble. He thought his heart had stopped. He was overcome with fear and depression. Even the discovery that they were only dolls brought him small relief. Whoever put them there and drove about the city with them there had to be as perverse and mad as any murderer.

Still trembling he climbed the porch and rang the doorbell beside the nameplate of O'Neil. In answer, a rapping on the window of the downstairs apartment. A corner of the shade pulled up just far enough for him to see the bony knuckles rapping on the pane and a small portion of a woman's wrinkled, wedgelike face, a single lock of blond, violet-tinted hair in a pincurl the size of a baton, and a mouth congested with an overbite of oversized teeth.

"What is it?" he shouted, lowering his head to the window. The hand waved him back, pointed at the door.

A bolt rolled back, a lock released, the door opened but not so wide that the chain was taut. Magnuson pinched his hat brim and lowered his head.

"What do you want?" the woman said in a thick Chicago accent, pronouncing it "Whatch youse want?" Magnuson would not have been surprised if a broom handle poked through the crack and jabbed him in the ribs.

"I'm looking for Tip O'Neil." The name on the downstairs bell said Groeschel. He presumed this was the landlady.

"Who?"

"Mr. O'Neil."

"Well, he ain't here. He's working today."

Working, Magnuson said to himself with envy. Where could he possibly work? He said, "Is his daughter in?"

"What do you want with her?"

"Is she in?"

"She works."

"Lady, I know that."

"Some guys got to work, mister."

"Lady," Magnuson said, "I didn't ring your bell." Dismissing the woman with a disgusted wave of his hand he went back down the steps. He had no desire to be emasculated by a bored housewife whose husband was probably dead or drunk and who spent her hatred on whoever chanced to call at her door. The door slammed behind him.

But on the sidewalk he remembered the bottle of Scotch he had under his arm and, taking out his pen, wrote on the crumpled sack: "To Tip, from a friend." On the porch again he had no sooner set it among some empty milk bottles when the front door was thrown open to the end of the chain and the woman was in the crack shouting, "Hey, you!" If she thought her sudden and bold action would make the guilty Magnuson turn and fly in fear, losing his hat and falling in a swirling topcoat down the stairs, she was mistaken. Magnuson was immediately enraged; his wallet was out of his pocket and flipped open to reveal the badge pinned to the flap, and he himself charged the door.

"Lady, I'm a cop," he lied. "We've had complaints about you, Groeschel . . ." His face looked on fire, his white hair with its curls and cowlicks like smoke. A glimpse of the woman's frightened face, the clacking mouthful of teeth, the slamming of the door, and the bedroom slippers padding through the house.

On the street his rubbers slapped over the wet sidewalk, his wet footprints adding themselves to the block-long abstract mural of muddy curls and treads of other shoes and boots. He looked as if he would embrace or beat to death the first man he met along the street, either act from desperation. What had made him think O'Neil would want to sit around in mid-morning, drink a bottle of Scotch, and reminisce about old times? To O'Neil he would have looked eccentric, desperate, lonely.

The truth was he was ill, and so far this trip was like an unexpected turn for the worse in the night. He was dizzy; elms and brick buildings seemed made out of *papier-mâché,* nudged this way and that by the wind. His legs and back were beginning to ache. If he were to lick his illness alone he had little time to do it in. A breakdown of some kind was imminent, and when it happened, he would have the useless, unwanted help of doctors. He wasn't even certain he could make it back to where he could catch public transportation home, nor was he certain he wanted to. He would have been just as content to drop to the muddy yard he was passing and lie beneath the low barberry hedge, oblivious to passers-by.

If only the depression would assume the symptoms of some disease or injury, a mild stroke, a fractured hip, severe enough to keep him bedded down, helpless, in physical pain. If only it were some ailment that was visible and diagnosable, that could be mended or remedied and, after some period of time, forgotten, then he could have justified the relentless inactivity and sense of worthlessness that plagued him. And although his depression rendered him just as helpless as something visible and diagnosable, he could not justify the depression to himself, much less to others. Even so, he was optimistic enough to believe he could be relieved or even completely cured at any moment. Only the secret of his remedy escaped him. And so he suffered not only from the depression but from the frustration of his impotence in the face of it.

Then he was aware of a woman he had not seen approach passing him on the sidewalk. An old, transient, impoverished, dirty woman, drunk, or mad if sober, the conclusions he drew from the listing and vacillating walk, the sight of the tips of her fingers only, exposed from the sleeve of the cheap worn coat, and trailing in the wet, dirty pavement a dirty scarf which, in her retreats and tacks, she trod on with her own feet. But when she was past him he saw that she was just a girl, probably still in her teens, probably mad and certainly drunk, her clothes torn, threadbare, and lousy (it had been years since he had seen lice), with both human and animal hairs and what seemed to be pieces of plaster clinging to the cloth, her body the dumpy, plump, starchy, breastless body of some prepubescent girl, legs unshaven, her face brutal, inhuman, blank, the small beady eyes set far from the pug, bulblike nose that was turned up and so small it seemed only the vestige of a nose left when the rest was sliced away, a mustache above the lips, an open sore and scabs— venereal, he wondered?—at the corners of her mouth. She was a hillbilly, had to be, recently arrived in the North. And from Magnuson's withdrawn and embittered heart arose an outcry of indignation that was not divorced from pity: she had no business on the street, this street, any street. She belonged in a public institution of one sort or another.

Later he felt envy: envied her courage or cowardice to be drunk before the noon, the justice implied in her down-and-out condition, and wondered why in the several months he had been ill not once had he thought of alcohol. A wild drunk on Bourbon in his bed, or just a bottle of wine at dinner, enough to tranquilize him or transform the depression into melancholia like that which he experienced when he picked up an old waltz on the radio in the middle of the night. Not only had he failed to think of alcohol, but he, who drank moderately, had not so much as touched a drop. Had he feared that drinking would prove an even greater depressant? Or had he somehow been enjoying all along the unrelieved suffering of his despair?

Still later it occurred to him that he should not have been surprised to see the girl upon the street. It was not she who was out of place in his old neighborhood. Poor southern whites had been migrating to the neighborhood for the past decade and it was their presence more than anything else that had finally persuaded him to leave. He had been oblivious to the cars he had passed this morning parked along Broadway with their Kentucky, Tennessee, and Mississippi license plates, and the small hillbilly nightclubs and taverns with their neon signs of cowboys and guitars, places that were dangerous for northerners to enter; oblivious even of the groups of sullen men on the sidewalks, wild clannish men, underdressed for the weather, who had stared at him from their undernourished Celtic and Anglo-Saxon faces, as though to tell him to return at night and they would cut his throat.

The neighborhood belonged to them now; well, they could have it! Unfortunately, Magnuson still belonged to the neighborhood. If the neighborhood could change, Magnuson could not. It was the same with the city as a whole. Chicago had determined him, created him, only to abandon him now to unfamiliar and inhospitable places or, what was worse, the familiar places inhabited by unfamiliar and hostile peoples. He despised the city for this betrayal—after all, he was not one of those who had fled to the suburbs. He wanted, vindictively, to get out of town, as though his desertion could somehow injure the city, decrease it, force it to be sorry. Any idea of flight, however, he knew was fantasy. He was wedded to the city as though to a bad marriage he could not dissolve. Besides, wasn't it more manly to be faithful to your vows and to believe that for better or for worse the contract was your destiny? And yet he suspected that if he could leave the city his illness would disappear.—If only he could go north to Wisconsin or Michigan. Retreat into the strength and solace of the woods and fish some cold lake for walleyes as he and his wife had done each spring and summer in the past, trolling from sunrise to sundown from one end of the lake to the other in a rowboat while the children, left to themselves, fished from the dock, and when older, sat in the cabin reading, and when older still, remained at home in the apartment in Chicago.

Ahead of him was Broadway. Short, squat, robust women shaped like bells were waddling past him in galoshes, overcoats, and babushkas, their rigid arms pinned to their sloping sides and carrying heavy shopping bags that almost dragged along the ground. They knew where they had been, what they had done, where they were going. They had not left the old places or the old ways.

He decided against returning to his Gold Coast apartment and to go downtown to the Lincoln Athletic Club instead and see if his car had been repaired. This time he would not go by el. The sooty iron stairs, the cagelike turnstile, the wait on the platform with its shacks painted that dark glossy green and plastered with advertisements that were torn, mustached, or scribbled with obscene graffiti, the smells of chewing gum, soot, sweat, spit, cigar butts, tar, and creosote, collecting and gathering strength since the Columbian Exposition, the homosexuals that would be clustered in the small toilet, their shoes planted in the urine of the floor, all repelled him; he would have stared at the third rail as a godsend. Nor did he want to ride past the blocks and blocks of packed, ramshackle tenements that lined the tracks and see onto the buckling back porches strung up with laundry, nor down into the grassless back yards of junked cars and furniture, the ground sparkling with broken glass, nor into those kitchens or bedrooms where there loomed behind the dirty windows men in white undershirts and women in white slips, windows so close to the tracks that a hand could reach out and touch the rail. Nor could he have tolerated riding backwards on the el. For the old wooden coaches with their movable yellow cane seats that the conductor at the end of the line switched to face forward again, rhythmically slamming the backs as he went from car to car, had been replaced by metal streamlined coaches with immovable leather seats that seemed always to face backwards no matter which way you traveled, and he would have had the disoriented, upsetting sensation of being propelled helplessly in a direction against his will with unseen and therefore dangerous obstacles ahead, of journeying in the wrong way on an adventure that was not his to make, toward a destination that was not his to reach.

He would take the bus instead. He would face forward, see what was ahead. The coach would be sunlit, he could open a window and get some air. He wanted to see only the surface of people and buildings, display windows instead of alleys, the deliberate dazzle of the facade.

But just after the bus turned onto Clark Street it became stalled in traffic. A crowd had collected on the sidewalk before a restaurant resembling an English pub and had spilled off the curb into the street, blocking cars that would have stopped in any case, the drivers gawking out the windows. In the center of the crowd, seen perfectly by Magnuson from the high window of his coach, was a tall, lean black man handcuffed to the bars of a small basement window beneath the large plate-glass window of the restaurant. This forced him to stoop with one shoulder dipped and one thigh twisted, the manacled hand almost touching the ground. In this posture he resembled less a man apprehended for some crime than a large ape captured after escaping from the zoo. A young policeman stood at some distance from him, his back to the street, hands clasped behind his back and feet apart as though at parade rest. A second policeman was in the doorway of the restaurant talking with a man who appeared to be its owner or manager. He had a yellow pencil tucked behind his ear, was wiping his hands on an apron tied around his waist, and was chewing something, as though he had just been interrupted midway through his meal. In the window of the restaurant, behind the small panes of crinkly glass, a cook in white jacket, napkin at the throat and chef's hat, stared out at the crowd and prisoner with his hands on his hips. Occasionally he would be joined by a passing waitress looming out of the distorted darkness in a black frilly apron and black fluffy cap. Behind them flames leaped from the charcoal grill and, yellowed by the glass, reflected on the glossy, porcine, uncertain, and beef-eating faces of the diners. The siren of a paddy wagon sounded several blocks away.

The crowd gave the prisoner a wide berth and seemed to have done little more than accept out of curiosity this rare urban license to stop and stare. No one seemed so involved that he could not at any moment go on his way. Nothing, so far as Magnuson could hear, was even being said. But something like relief was on their faces, as though the sight of the criminal reassured them of their own innocence and that the machinery of law and order could still be forcibly asserted in the city. Magnuson saw himself among this crowd. His innocence was proven, protected, vindicated. The sight of that black manacled prisoner had lifted the threat of something foul and heavy from his soul. Why, look at the fellow! There, if you will, was guilt. The world was working in the old right ways after all. He was still, as he had been in the old days, on the right side of things.

But then he saw the black man's face, more like the hide of an elephant contorted into something that resembled a face than human flesh. It was lifted to the street with an expression of terror so primitive it seemed the man must have sunk back into the world of magic.

As though he were only days away from chains and slave ships and believed his capture meant a pistol fired at any moment into his head. Of course if he had just held up the restaurant he had been prepared to kill and to be killed in turn, and if he had committed his crime elsewhere and been chased on foot for several blocks he must have expected to be shot at any moment in the back. That could explain the terror and desperation, that soaking sweat, that lightheadedness and breathlessness. Even so, Magnuson hoped narcotics alone explained that look.

Several black men were among the crowd, packages of one sort or another under their arms. Their faces did not appear to condone the man or even sympathize with him, rather they imitated, although with less intensity, the man's confoundedness with his terror. As though they read the futility and indignation of their own lives in his fate. As though they foresaw that day when the whole brutal city would rise up in ritual against them, torturing them with isolation before it brought them down. And Magnuson, catching his own expression reflected in the window of the bus, thought that if it were not for his lack of color, his face at this moment could pass for one of theirs.

CHAPTER SIX

NYMPHOMANIA

In the sickroom of Frazer Farquarson, Preacher and Mrs. Nettles in the company of Lena, Mr. Farquarson's maid, have approached the patient's bedside with the self-importance, suspiciousness, embarrassment, and general uneasiness of serfs summoned to the castle to try their hand at curing the mysteriously afflicted king. Lena, in lilac dress and hat, and smelling like lilacs, has done what Farquarson requested her to do and brought before him the minister of her church. Cognizant that her place in this gathering is not to supplant the preacher or, more importantly, the preacher's wife, she keeps her own counsel in the rear. The preacher himself says little more. "That's right," he intones now and then in agreement with some statement in the monologue of Mrs. Nettles; has said, "My, my," to the more coherent ramblings of Mr. Farquarson; and has boasted several times excitedly, interrupting his wife's exposition of his storefront church with its neon-lit cross and lettering in soap on the plate-glass window, which she aggrandizes into something resembling the Bahai Temple, "In my Sunday school I gives the good children gold stars," a benevolence for which Mr. Farquarson has several times commended him. A big, brown, pursy man in his late fifties with horn-rimmed glasses and flocculent, battleship-gray hair, he wears an almost western shirt with a string tie and black and white shoes with tasseled laces and great, gleaming dancing taps on the heels and toes. A janitor in the post office when he is not a preacher, he is a partner of the mops and brooms he pushes down the aisles between the mail carriers' cases, where the ringing of his taps begins at dawn, and he appears always on the verge of exploding amid the mounds of dusty canvas sacks and the government-green and peeling walls into a noisy dance of windmilling arms above the staccato racket of his feet. Even the drugged and sleeping Farquarson was wakened by those tapping feet as though at the report of a firecracker tossed beneath his bed; was wakened even when they were as distant as the entrance hall and discerned immediately that something exotic and unique was calling at his house, and thereafter followed their ambit through the house, hearing them whenever they departed from the rugs and runners, hearing them even now in short explosive bursts whenever, in the preacher's incessant fidgeting, they step off the orientals in this room. The grand, handsome, and much younger Mrs. Nettles, in fur coat and pillbox hat and veil, is the spokesman for the visitors, behind whom Lena and Mr. Nettles tend naturally to get. She has the nose and cheekbones of a Cherokee and is so black and statuesque in her muscularity and boneyness that she seems carved by an ax from an effulgent vein of coal. Shoulders cloaked in leopard skins, she dominates the conversation. Religions, churches, diseases, hospitals, doctors, finances, drugs, all are in her ken, and she presents her opinions on all to the mumbling, drowsy Farquarson who, if he has any expression on his face, appears to be enjoying the confusion of some silly dream. Charm, amateur psychology, and the positive and aggressive projection of the personality, her manner seems to say, are the keys to friendship and success; an air about her of night courses in theology, philosophy, sociology, and psychology taken at city universities and abandoned before the final grade, of proving to herself and to her audience of husband and Lena that she can at worst handle and at best command every kind of social situation and person, present company and circumstance included. But she is not entirely pleased with the progress of the interview. She alone has been willing to play the superior role of minister to Farquarson's sinner, and she alone, she feels, has sensed the inversion of these roles. Why, it is as if they have been summoned not to aid, comfort, and bless the dying man who, after all, despite his position and wealth, is just another Christian dying man, but to be aided, comforted, and blessed by him, as if they, who are very much alive, are in worse shape than he, who is as good as dead. Why, if they were Catholics they could be at the deathbed of a pope! She almost expects him to proffer his bony hand from beneath the sheets and invite them to kneel and kiss his ring.

"I have been all my life learning the lesson of humility," Farquarson has said sanctimoniously and pontifically. "It was the worst of the many failings in my character." And suddenly transferring this observation of himself to the republic as a whole, as if in himself he has seen the intense embodiment of the nature of the whole, he adds, "It's the greatest failure of the nation! The greatest flaw in the character of the race! But it's what you have, my good friends—not just you here in this room, but colored people everywhere. Humility. And compassion too. There is a lesson in your life for all of us." And Mrs. Nettles, embarrassed at this interjection of race into their meeting, and wondering if by humility he means humiliated, and if humility as seen through her eyes is the virtue seen through his, begins in self-defense the flood of still another monologue. Even so, Farquarson manages to say, "We have eaten the country, my good friends, and now we are eating the world. And eating each other. Thank God I am no longer hungry." Later, "Bless you, bless you," he intones again and again.

Then after Mrs. Nettles's final outburst of commiseration and compassion and the expression of the hope for the arrested course of the disease and, failing that, for the glories of the hereafter, and after the preacher is compelled to pronounce some brief, inarticulate, incoherent prayer, the three visitors depart, having left in Mr. Farquarson's feeble hands and on the table beside his bed pamphlets and magazines on fundamentalism, faith healing, and the wonders of the cancer drug, Krebiozen.

"Get me John," says Farquarson to Nancy Rhinelander, his voice revealing the strain of having masked a crankiness throughout the interview.

Meanwhile the departing guests are marching through the mansion: Lena in her buckling pumps unable to keep up with the preacher strutting and tapping his feet and seemingly on the verge of leaping on some polished tabletop or taking a running start and dancing halfway up the walls, and the triumphant but somewhat slighted Mrs. Nettles striding in the lead, hands on her hips and fur coat thrown back to fly behind her so that she resembles a hustling self-made businesswoman of the *nouveaux riches* who, having just purchased this house for cash and sight unseen, is touring it for the first time pursued by an entourage of breathless and sycophantic architects and decorators. Then the shocked and disapproving Mrs. Owens, the housekeeper, appears in a doorway the visitors are passing, then disappears on a short cut through other rooms and reappears beside the visitors in still another doorway, so that the Nettles, who nod a second time in regal greeting, are perplexed as to whether there resides within this house a pair of identical elderly maiden twins or even, as they pass yet another doorway, a set of stern-faced, flabbergasted triplets, or they are merely walking in circles, lost in the hallways, passing the same woman in the same doorway of the same room.

At the threshold of the library Nancy Rhinelander studies John Cavan in his scarlet dressing gown, sleeping at his desk. A green wine bottle with Rhine castles on the label beside him, a green carpet, the red drapes that frame the open windows and outside the blue landscape of distant trees. She is gladdened by a sudden lust. She sees herself in green tights and executing scissorslike ballerina leaps through dusty sunbeams slanting on the long varnished floor of a white unfurnished room.

But when she wakes him her imaginings are no more erotic than the picture of three black crows perched on the footboard of Mr. Farquarson's bed. She is convinced that Lena is plotting for a portion of the old man's estate. Bringing that suave, phoney minister and his pushy, persuasive wife to work their mischief on the dying lunatic. And how could she protect her patient when for the first time ever he ordered her to leave the room? What she wouldn't give to know what happened in that room! Black intrigue afoot. She feels an instinct, almost more manly than maternal, to protect Cavan who, she suspects, has no nose for money matters nor experience with human greed. She is pleased to view herself as the shrewder, more suspicious, and therefore more worldly of the two. Easily angered by any suggestion of injustice, she feels compelled to take steps to see that Cavan does not lose unfairly what should be his.

But she has also heard stories of lucky and no doubt scheming nurses receiving legacies or even whole estates from the grateful, lonely, or senile men they nursed, and the clumsy maneuvering of the maid suggests the possibility that she herself might receive some small but adequate legacy in Farquarson's will. But scheming repulses her and is, she trusts, beyond her. Farquarson's death is her ticket in the lottery purchased by nothing more than her profession and presence on the scene. Even so she begins to dream of windfalls and to believe she deserves the luck that would send them her way. She is weary of nursing old men and women to their graves and of ending every job by bathing bodies. She longs to lie on sunny, southern beaches, lazy, independent, alone.

In the hallway she informs Cavan of the recent, secret conference between Farquarson and Lena and her two black friends. Not only this, but of Lena's visit with Farquarson last night when she, Nancy, heard Lena steal into his room where she remained for half an hour listening to his whispering, emphasizing in her telling the blackness of that hour; the wifely or concubinary familiarity of such a visit at such an hour to such a room, and implying sinister secrets in the Farquarson family, Farquarson insanity, last wills and testaments dictated from the deathbed, the intrigue of a black Rasputin roaming in a robe behind the drapes with hypnotic rays flashing from the whites of his bulging eyes and a glittering dimestore crucifix swung back and forth before the gaping face. In short, the black mischief of Haiti and the Congo and the plotting of even blacker deeds.

But Cavan finds such familiarity between his uncle and Lena, and Negroes in general, implausible. That they would benefit in any sizable way in his uncle's will, he finds impossible.

"If you don't believe me, ask him about it then," the nurse's hand appears to say as it indicates Farquarson in his room, asleep upon his bed.

As if he has only been waiting for the nurse to leave and shut the door, Farquarson whispers, "John." His hand fumbles free of the sheets and finds his nephew's hand. "I have something to tell you." Then as Cavan leans his ear toward his uncle's face: "When you lay a woman make sure your equipment . . . you know, your organs . . . are cleaned up and in good shape."

But Cavan must reflect his inability to comprehend this advice or else some malicious determination not to profit by it, for the old man continues, increasing the feeble pressure on Cavan's hand, "You must. And if you can't keep it clean, wear a rubber." (Cavan is shocked: it is not a word he would expect his uncle to use.) "I mean, what if you gave her the clap?" (Another word.) "Or the syph?" (A third word.) "And what if you gave her one or the other and she turned out to be a nympho?" (Still another word.) "You've got to keep her in the pink of health. You'll never know for certain who will get to her next. And as far as the next fellow knows she's been left in the best of health. You've got a duty to the woman and to the next fellow."

Cavan coughs into his fist, rubs his nose, and traces a pattern of pears in the oriental at his feet. He seems to be saying something inaudibly. Like "I see." Or "There, there."

"I know what I'm talking about," Farquarson says, "from personal experience. I have a . . . girlfriend. I've had her for years. She gave me the clap because another fellow couldn't look after himself or take her into consideration. Lord only knows where he got it. A lot he cared about her, or me for that matter." He drops Cavan's hands and settles back on the bed, thinking of the girls in the brothels in Waukegan he visited when he was young, driving up on summer evenings in his runabout along the lake. Clean, healthy, horsy girls, fresh from the farm with all the right notions of strong soap and warm water. Why, they would examine your equipment first thing and if you had so much as a scratch on it they would send you out. Concerned with your health, and with their own health, and with the well-being of those fellows who would come after you. And if you passed the test they would take their clothes off right in front of you. And you could watch them do it. They would stand before you naked. Without any clothes on. Naked women. Then the white porcelain washbowl of warm water they held beneath your balls. Soaping your equipment with their hands and rinsing it in the warm water. And when you were done with the girls they would come with another bowl of warm water and once more wash it in their hands. May God forgive him, but he remembers that bowl of water, those warm hands, and that bar of soap and how they felt upon his flesh, and the way the girls' naked breasts looked as they bent over to do the washing better than he does the girls themselves or what they did together on the bed. Better even than he remembers Hope, his wife, or anything much about her. Indeed, he admits, if he ever had a picture in his mind to sustain him in troubled times, to make him tranquil when he was uneasy, it was of those naked girls, their soft hands, the white bowl, the fragrant soap, the warm water. He is surprised to hear his own voice saying, "You should wash yourself, John. It's a matter of trust. Of do unto others." But surely it is something else entirely he has planned to tell John in this dramatic moment. Is it possible that this is the ultimate wisdom he had distilled from the experience of his long and privileged life? This, the final philosophy of that saintly man he would become? Damn the incoherence of the disease and drugs. "That's all I have to say," he says, closing his eyes. "That," he says, opening his eyes, "and what I would have told you years ago if I'd had the nerve. Remember that. Believe that. At my death you're in for a shock. A disappointment I haven't prepared you for. You're no nephew of mine. There, the secret's out. But you're not to worry. I've seen to it that you'll be taken care of. You won't starve. And don't brood about it either. We're none of us who we think we are. Trace any family back far enough and you're bound to find an unfaithful grandmother somewhere along the line that throws the whole genealogy out of whack." He slaps his palms in disgust upon the bed. "I'm too ashamed to tell you more. But at least my girlfriend's husband knows the truth. He knows the whole story. At least I've been able to confess it all to him. At least I've been able to forgive him for what he did to me, and to ask him to forgive me for what I did to him. If you want to know the rest of it, if you want to really touch the bottom of this business, go see Albert Wenzel in Wauconda." His fingertips tug at the sheet to draw it up, and he drops off into a deep narcotic sleep.

Then Cavan is in the hallway, in a state of shock and unable to understand the consequences of what he has been told, while the nurse is showing him the note in Farquarson's handwriting:

If I should meet with foul play Mr. Albert Wenzel of Wauconda has in his possession a letter explaining all.

She has found several such notes since this morning, hidden in his bedclothes or in books beside his bed. "Have you ever heard of someone named Helenowski?" she says.

He shakes his head.

"Your uncle thinks he has," she says. Going on to tell how his uncle said he was an escaped madman who wished to kill him, and how when the madman was himself found dead in Chicago just last night he thanked God aloud for having spared his life. Such nonsense, she claims, reveals how unbalanced he has become. That and the fact that he has written what may be an important letter to a man named Wenzel. A letter he did not have her write, nor have her mail. She lets this sink in, 'then voices her suspicion that he dictated that letter to Lena in the night. And if Lena and her friends have got his ear there is not much, at this stage of illness, they cannot make him do. And once he is gone, and he could go any day, it might be too late for Cavan to undo whatever it is that he has done. "How did he seem to you just now?" she asks.

"He talked a lot of nonsense . . ." But he has yet to be convinced that Lena and the Negroes are a greater threat to the Farquarson inheritance than Nancy Rhinelander, nurse. Her story about the escaped madman has reminded him of that lunatic who walked into his study just this morning and in his fantastic way wished Farquarson dead. "Somebody named Raincloud came here today. I thought he might try to see . . . my uncle. Have you heard of him?"

She shakes her head. "Thorsen said someone was on the grounds last night." She smiles. "Tell the truth, it wasn't *you?*" Which violates the first of the many tacit rules that govern their complex affair, that they do not mention, imply, or otherwise acknowledge between themselves, even though they see each other a hundred times a day, day after day, that she often stands naked in her bedroom window and he fully clothed on the lawn below.

"It wasn't *him?*" Cavan counters, incensed at her violation and embarrassed that she should call attention to his role outdoors in the affair, but ashamed that she could have provoked him into retaliating with a reference to the secret, erotic walks she took outdoors last fall with young Mr. Moony, Thorsen's assistant in the garden.

"It must have been one of *them*," she says, trying to unite them with a common enemy. "Waiting for Lena to pass out the letter. Or whatever else it was she got from Farquarson."

In his turn Cavan, before he has the chance to check himself, violates the most powerful taboo in their affair. He attempts to touch her. And more than touch her, too: to embrace, caress, and stimulate her, pin her roughly up against the wall and send her dress and underthings up around her neck or down below her knees. But when he actually feels her breast give beneath his own he becomes more boy than beast. As though to embrace so young and beautiful and sympathetic a woman is to gain the strength and courage to withstand the horrors of madness, disinheritance, and loss of name and family and disease and death and even murder that have emerged from nowhere to threaten him, or to no longer care if he is delivered to those horrors, so long as he can be destroyed in the consolation of her flesh. "Nancy," he whispers, mumbles, groans, glimpsing in the candescence of the white cloth, blond hair, and tan freckled flesh her pastoral and abundant origins: the red barns and white silos of the green Wisconsin farmland, leaden wedges of fresh cheddar cheese, steins of beer fresh from the brewery, whose heads mushroom until they slop down the sides, leaving a residue of beads, hot milk fresh from the udders and frothing over the tin pail . . .

For a second he seems to be manhandled, to have received some cruel, foul, Oriental blow. Then he is staggering down the hall with his arms outstretched and touching nothing as though he is the blind man in a game of blindman's bluff. The nurse several yards in front of him and backing up, her hair loose and damp beneath her cap, her palms out to fend him off. "Friends?" she says retreating. Like a child who has just struck another child and now wants to make peace before the victim counterattacks and before she herself lowers her guard: "Friends, John? Friends?"

Then Mrs. Owens, the housekeeper, in bathrobe and slippers at the foot of the stairs and calling up the charges of her complaint. "Never in my life," she says, "have I been employed in a household where Negroes could just come in and call like guests. And not even high-class Negroes either. Let me tell you no such thing would have happened in any fraternity I was housemother of. Oh, I know the country is changing and it's probably not right for me to feel the way I do, but that's the way I am and the way I was brought up to be. If the younger people who were brought up differently want to change the attitude and have Negroes in their houses sitting on their sofas, that's their business and good luck to them and so much the better for everyone. But don't expect me to like it."

This subject exhausted, she launches into her second complaint. She has just received another of those obscene calls on the telephone. The same man with the unctuous baritone voice and nervous, noisy breathing not only speaking shamelessly again about where he has his mind and hands but this time threatening her with violence as well, informing her he would come to the house tonight when it was dark and if she told on him to anyone—"if you squeal on me," were his exact words—he would find her room if it took him half the night, break down the door, drag her from her bed and give her a rough pinch on—

"On the what, Mrs. Owens?" asks the nurse.

"Never mind," says Mrs. Owens, afraid she has trapped herself by saying more than she should. "I don't like to say words I don't know the meaning of."

"Well then, Mrs. Owens, what do you think the word means?"

Mrs. Owens gathers her courage. "He said he would pinch me on my . . . big boobs."

The nurse walking down the hall and laughing, leaning against the wall and laughing, turning a corner, still laughing.

Which leaves a stunned and disappointed Cavan alone upon

the stairs. Until now he has had little interest in property or money which, like politics, he has deemed compromising and degrading if carried beyond a certain necessary point. He is a free and uncorrupted spirit, a scientist and scholar, equally at home in the sanctuary of the university and the wilderness of Africa. But now he wonders if he has rejected the pursuit of money only because he could reject it, because he was brought up to believe that it was as natural and unarguable an allotment to his life as was his family and name, assuming, as did everyone else, that he was Farquarson's heir. For just now when he was told he would not inherit the Farquarson fortune he seemed to view the emaciated body of that man he was taught to call his uncle as something resembling a continent sinking before his eyes into the waves.

He gazes at the thin-lipped, wavy-haired, melancholic, handsome, youthful heads of John Cavan, Senior, and Priscilla Farquarson Cavan, their best profiles caught in the glossy, low-contrast, touched-up studio portraits of thirty years ago hanging in the gallery of family portraits along the wall. In their faces Anglo-Saxon orchards, Norman manors, the new towns of freemen, the settlement of New England, the founding of Chicago, and the ventures into meat packing, banks, railroads, real estate, department stores, and the building of the large estates along the North Shore. Something foreign about those faces now. They are like the portraits of two strangers, some recently wedded titled couple in a 1935 edition of the *London Illustrated News.* At last he understands why that secret and compulsive quest he has pursued for several years has been frustrated at every turn, why no birth or baptismal certificate was forthcoming from the courthouses and town halls and Episcopalian and Presbyterian parishes in America and England and Scotland he wrote to, all those places he could be fairly certain his parents had been. And this silence forced him to consider in the middle of the nights he could not sleep and midway through the fifths of wine that he could drink what he must accept now, that Mr. and Mrs. John Cavan, Senior, are no parents of his. How strange that that lunatic Alvin Raincloud should also tell him this morning that his name was not John Cavan. The man appeared to have been right. But how on earth could he have possibly known?

But then perhaps the nurse is right after all, and Farquarson is deranged and babbles nonsense, either on his own, or at the suggestion of someone plotting for a share of the estate. Nor does it necessarily follow that because he is not the son of Farquarson's sister he is no relation to Farquarson at all. He has had a suspicion for years, unvoiced until now, that Farquarson is himself his father.

But who then is his mother? Surely not his Aunt Hope, that madwoman in an asylum, whom he has never seen but supposes he has always imagined as either vegetable or raving beast? She must have been institutionalized several years before he was born, and he doubts that Farquarson had conjugal privileges in the asylum. If Farquarson is his father, and he is still to be disappointed in the estate, it can only be because he is illegitimate. Which means his mother is a mystery woman. Whom Farquarson never married. His girlfriend, perhaps.

He decides to look up this Albert Wenzel in Wauconda and learn, if he can, the contents of that letter Farquarson claimed he sent the man, suspecting that it not only names the man Farquarson foolishly believes would have him killed but the parents of John Cavan, and if not that, the conspirators who would defraud him of the estate.

As Cavan takes his leave, Frazer Farquarson, who could have kept him home had he the courage to confess it all, hallucinates the flesh of several women he confuses into a single image. He steals the eyes of one, the breasts of another, the seductive posture of a third. Then dreams long and hard of what he makes of her. Dreams also of syphilis and nymphomania. Of this woman whose disease, like her love, has its seat between her legs. Whose lovers take death no less than love as a partner in her bed.

Behold the infection raging through the city! Impossible for a computer to keep pace with the complexities of her affairs. Take only Mr. V, for instance. What if he slept with her and, before he died, slept also with Miss X and Miss Y? And Miss X with Mr. G and Master R and Father T? And Miss Y with Miss C and Mr. J? And Mr. J with Mrs. J? And Mrs. J with Captain L, Dr. R, and Professor Z? The proportions are epidemic, a modern plague. At all costs the offending woman must be found and stopped. Farquarson himself will set a detective on her trail. Some man who knows all the nooks and crannies and oily niches of the city and the best and worst—and especially the worst—of all its citizens. Magnuson the detective—the very man for such a job.

Blaze through the city, Magnuson. Shine your spotlight on the doorways of all the rotting buildings, on all the somber rotting faces. Track her down. Laws, customs, natural feelings, subjugate them to the common good. Interrogate your witness with a backhanded slap across the face, your suspects with a pistol pointed at their heads. Shoot all known fornicators. And when you find her, drag her from her infected bed into the street and put a bullet in her head. Pour gasoline upon her clothes. Immolate her corpse. Throw all infected persons in the blaze. Cauterize the city. Purify the race. —An image comes before his eyes: of an indigo sky, and larger by half than that sky a yellow moon like a sunrise, and against that moon the silhouette of the skyline of the city and the monstrous shadow of the detective in hat and overcoat struggling with the shadow of the nymphomaniac in sparse, disheveled clothes until his shadow forces hers upon its knees and plunges a knife the size of a bayonet into its breast.

Purged by this involuntary vision of all his old unwanted malice, and catching the scent of the young nurse as she busies herself above his bed, her body stretched out across him as she tucks him in so that her uniform cracks along his sheet, he goes swimming with naked women in the moonlit lake.

Giggles. Splashing. Goose pimples. Naked Frazer Farquarson floating on his back with water bubbling like a fountain from his mouth. Naked moonlit women floating on their backs in front of him, behind him, on either side of him, performing the intricate maneuvers of a water ballet. Profiles of floating faces, breasts in pairs, and pubic mounds in silhouette against the backdrop of the gigantic golden moon. Naked moonlit women swimming the crawl, the breaststroke, the sidestroke, the backstroke. Women bumping into him. Swimming over him with their flesh against his flesh, momentarily submerging him. Swimming underneath him with their flesh rubbing against his flesh and momentarily buoying him above the waves. Clean slippery moonlit flesh in the water.

—Oh, Mr. Farquarson!

—Call me Frazer.

—Oh, Frazer!

Piggyback in the waves. Naked moonlit pyramids of female flesh. Naked moonlit women knocked down by the waves. Women like alewives in the shallows. Round, moonlit bottoms mounding up as the women dive like porpoises into the waves. Naked squealing women washed up and down the sandy moonlit shore with the water boiling up and down their skins. Large-breasted, long-legged, long-haired, narrow-waisted women that flip and flop about like silvery fish. Sucked back by the undertow into the moonlit source. Washed once again upon the moonlit shore.

The fulfillment, in dream, of a long life's ambition.

The epic skinnydip of the race.

CHAPTER SEVEN

THE
POISON PEN

On Michigan Avenue, Chicago's most fashionable avenue, resides the Lincoln Athletic Club, one of Chicago's most fashionable clubs. In a neo-Gothic building of sixteen gray granite stories it overlooks the downtown lakefront of Lake Michigan and the vast lawns and parking lots of Grant Park. Its entrance is a gilded revolving door beneath a Gothic arch. In that arch is a bronze frieze of youthful athletes in T-shirts and boxer shorts frozen at that supreme moment of anticipation and concentration just before they release the shot or javelin, sprint out of the starting block, jab with a left hand. Firm healthy bodies. Short hair parted in the middle and seemingly colored even in the bronze anywhere from light brown to blond. Handsome faces that have that intense, humorless, ennobled look of those idealized and youthful soldiers who grace the patriotic statuary commemorating World War One. All look to be born from the same womb. All bring to mind the same histories: blazers and boaters, Princeton and

West Point, cavalry lieutenants, Newport pilots, sloops and tennis, the Stock Exchange. All have that same far-sighted gaze upon their faces, but not as though they are glimpsing anything tangible, like distant mountain peaks or the smoke of distant fires, but the glimmer of some abstract and, for them, ultimate perfection that makes unworthy, and even unseen, all objects close at hand. Above them in the arch, a benevolent bronze sun radiating benevolent beams.

On the second floor of the club is the great, high-ceilinged Tudor lounge. Instant old-world age and venerability. A comfortable and respectable distance from peasant immigrations and wild frontiers. A decor demanded by the founders of the club, wealthy men of English and Scottish ancestry who, like the city they ruled, had strong isolationist and anti-British feelings. At present the few men sitting in the lounge, lost in it like some handful of commuters dispersed about the lobby of Union Station, are reading newspapers in the black leather chairs, writing at the large oak tables, staring out the windows, or, as in the case of the narcoleptic man, trying to write and keep from dozing, or, as in the case of Magnuson, thinking and while thinking brooding. They are all old. Sunshine pours through the high narrow oriel windows and ripples on the paneled walls, sneaks into the hearth of the carved fireplace, sprawls across the royal red carpet and floats up to the ceiling where it glistens on the dark oak ribs and beams. Quiet here, like a library of monks sworn to silence. And motionless, as though motions, which often are the cause of sounds, are banished just in case. Only the sunlight wandering along the walls.

Magnuson has just returned from his trip north to the old neighborhood and Tip O'Neil's and looks, sitting in his lightweight topcoat and with his hat on his lap, like a tourist in the lobby of a strange hotel in a foreign country who is resting his feet and summoning his courage before asking someone in sign language if he can have a room. Persuaded after the death of his wife to become a member of the club by several casual friends in the business and political world of the Loop, he was soon to discover that these same men, if they did not die or move to Florida, gave him no more than a passing wave, a hurried hello. He had expected, he supposed, the concern and conciliation of their company, as though he believed they had made a commitment to nurse him into better days. He feels no more comfortable or welcome here than he did in the old days before his fame and wealth, before his name was necessary on the letterheads of causes, candidates, and charities, back when he was a police officer and later a private investigator of small business and less means and was invited to the club to demonstrate his marksmanship on its target range or at its private shooting grounds in Wisconsin. He is, he knows, a man of places other than this club, of people other than its members. But where those people are, and who they are, has somehow managed to escape him of late.

From his wallet he withdraws a thin airmail envelope bearing a foreign postmark and oversized postage stamps depicting zebras, lions, and giraffes. The letter, the creases of which are well worn and beginning to tear, is the last he has received from his daughter, and arrived two months ago. Although she has been in the U.S.I.S. for more than a year he has yet to write her. The letter scolds him like a child for not writing and pleads for correspondence. He'll be damned if he'll write! His eyes, behind the shell-rimmed glasses taken from his shirt pocket, focus, as they always do, on a single sentence in mid-page: "Tomorrow we will leave Addis Ababa and travel overland to Khartoum, which is in the Sudan." Sudan, he thinks, hearing the beat of distant drums and seeing in a cloud of dust on the horizon the shields and spears of Fuzzy-Wuzzies. There is no pain in that sentence; all the others wound. But just what does she mean, *we* are leaving Addis Ababa, he wonders for the hundredth time? Fellow members of the Information Service? Or that boy she writes about and appears to be traveling if not living with? Any news of the boy enrages him. News of her familiarity with the natives which, he suspects, borders on fondness, frightens him. He is certain they will take advantage of her kindness, misinterpret her familiarity.

He refolds and returns the letter carefully, and removes a postcard in its place. Not so worn, it arrived only a week ago. His son Bruce has sent it from Nürnberg, in Germany. Postcards from Bruce arrive on the average of once a month, although they might come daily if he is on a special tour or excursion. As always he studies the photograph on the card, this time not so much to admire it or to see where his son has been but to wonder why his son thought this particular picture would in some way please him. Not a technicolor landscape or a city of medieval buildings but the black and white photograph of a relief in stone on the exterior of a Gothic church, a youthful, sensitive, and Teutonic Christ suffering under the weight of the cross and surrounded by medieval soldiers and burghers. Nürnberg he knows about. He flips the card over. Bruce prints legibly but crams what should have been a long letter into the small space. The note like half a hundred others is without a greeting and is signed only with the letter B. Bruce never gives personal information about himself nor asks for information of his father, but writes instead travel commentaries in romantic language on the particular town he is visiting, the countryside seen getting there, a sunset viewed from some mountain top or cathedral spire, and half the time in any of several foreign languages—in this case several sentences in German—none of which Magnuson can understand. Long ago he concluded that the dutifully sent postcards were written for the pleasure of the son alone. Magnuson cannot write him even if he wishes to, for his son never gives a return address, largely, Magnuson hopes, because he is never in one spot long enough to receive his mail.

Which reminds him. Neither child was at their mother's funeral. It took a week to locate the son in Europe (it was not known whether he was in Portugal or Sweden) and several days for the State Department to locate the daughter (she was in transit between villages, somewhere in the bush). And Magnuson would not delay the funeral. He buried her alone in the deep pain and pleasure of his bitterness. Immediately thereafter the daughter sent several wires and letters expressing remorse and guilt that she was absent and anger at her father for not waiting until she could return, then, in a letter of conciliation and apology, asking him if he wanted her to return, a request he did not deign to answer. The son a brief, impersonal essay on the fate of death in general, referring to death in the specific (his mother) only to say that she was beyond caring or knowing if he came to the funeral or not, that he saw her when she was alive and would always remember her so, and that to have seen her dead (a barbarous American habit, this viewing of the body) would not matter to her and, by inference, him. But, Magnuson thought then, and thinks now, it would have mattered to *me!* "To hell with both of them," he says.

"I beg your pardon," says a voice down the table. A small octogenarian in a thronelike chair, sunlight gleaming on the bald head, the pink and brown mottle of which resembles the skin of a leopard frog; the illusion in the dust floating through the sunbeams of smoke pouring in thin jets from his blue suit and matching vest. A leather notebook before him on the table and a fountain pen held upright in his hand, but awkwardly, as though unknown to him someone has played a joke and stuck it there. His arm crooked around the notebook not so much to protect it as to receive and cushion his nodding head when it falls.

"I wasn't speaking to you," Magnuson says.

"Then," says the man, indicating there is no one else around them, "who were you speaking to?"

"I was praying."

The hand cupped classically around the ear, one eye opened wide beneath an arching eyebrow.

Magnuson dismisses the man with a backhanded wave. "Shut up," he says beneath his breath.

But the man is holding the pen out to him. "Would you mind?" A pencil stripe of white mustache, a gap between the front teeth. "Come closer." Magnuson bows until his mouth is beside the boxlike hearing aid behind the hairy ear. "Close enough." The mood of their portrait in the great Tudor lounge: two Renaissance courtiers plotting treason while other courtiers lurk behind the columns, the balustrade of the balcony, in the shadows of the dark panels on the walls.

"The disease," the man whispers, "is narcolepsy." Magnuson withdraws his head, searches for open sores. "We all suffer from it to some degree."

"Do we?"

"We must. Don't you sleep?"

"If I can."

"When I was younger I often thought if I could only get by with less sleep how much I could accomplish. Continents, so to speak, to be conquered. Frontiers to be opened. There aren't enough hours in the day was my favorite saying. For years I got by on four hours of sleep, often less. Now all that sleep I missed is catching up with me. It's as if the good Lord was determined to take one-third of my life in sleep no matter what. Each day I sleep longer than I did the day before. And what's worse, I'm liable to doze off at any moment, day or night, in any place, inside or outside, standing up or sitting down. The time will come when I'm awake only a few hours out of every day. Then a few minutes. A few seconds. How do you think I'll feel when I'm awake just long enough to think one thought: that I'm about to fall asleep—permanently? A terrible fate to live with, I can assure you. It's not as if I was one of those fellows that collected dust in his life. And everybody I see looks just about as sleepy as I feel. Like they're about to fall asleep."

Still, all in all, thinks Magnuson, better the slow death of catnaps and yawns and the final uninterrupted sleep than to burn yourself up on your own bitterness. "What do you want me to do?" he says, hoping to avoid, if possible, the man recounting his experiences with doctors and hospitals which, he is certain, will come next.

"I'm writing my memoirs," says the narcoleptic man. "A collection of my sayings. My own personal philosophy of life. What I've spent a good solid lifetime learning. If you can't be a man of action, I said to myself, why then you can be a philosopher. Not one of those intellectual fellows no one can understand but the real down-to-earth kind people can get some mileage out of. The great writing, I've always said, is about true experiences and one's own personal philosophy. But I'm a man with a deadline. Why, I'm almost asleep right now. It's hard for me to hold the pen, to say nothing of forming difficult letters. If you'd be so good as to write down in the book what I tell you—"

"Go ahead," says Magnuson, uncapping the pen. The writing on the page before him is in many hands and colors of ink. The most common hand, which he suspects is that of the narcoleptic man, is scratchy and feeble, showing numerous glides across the page where the pen slipped in mid-sentence.

"Write," says the narcoleptic man, " 'Poverty is not the source of crime, but crime is the source of poverty.' "

Magnuson, writing, considers the man skeptically, looking at him down his nostrils.

"Inner poverty!" says the narcoleptic man in reply to such a look.

"Ah. Anything else?"

"Just a minute . . . It's coming to me . . . 'We are like Atlas with the city—the nation—the world—on our backs. If we were to let go, they would fall like the walls of Jericho.' "

"Just curious," says Magnuson, writing. "Who is we?"

"Why, us!"

"We is us?"

"Well, aren't we?"

So, Magnuson thinks, he thinks I'm like him. That I'm one of *them*.

There now follows the slow dictation of the following observations, each one of which Magnuson dutifully records:

—*Any American can rise by his bootstraps if he has the gumption to take hold of the reins.*

—*The wise patriot follows the flag but the stupid patriot follows the man who carries the flag.*

—*The true gentleman is always a gentleman whether in the company of gentlemen or not.*

—*One good man can get more done than any worldwide government.*

—*The only true law, the only true justice, the only true order, the honest man knows, is death.*

—*No man in America gets any more or less than he deserves.*

While waiting for these observations to be dictated Magnuson scans what has been written previously on the page. The man appears to be violently opposed to communism (Godless masters of slave nations), Democrats (Communists), socialism (communism), centralized government (communistic), atheism (communistic), England (since she involved America in two world wars it would be cheaper to transport all her inhabitants to Canada where we could keep an eye on them), Negroes (back to Africa where Lincoln, had he lived, had planned to send them), Jews (they have Israel—send them there), immigrants (keep them out), intellectuals (Communists), taxes (short cut to communism), politicians (crooks), internationalism (Jewish conspiracy), fluoridation (communist plot to turn our brains to jelly), youth (communistic dupes and unwashed savages). A rural and outdated touch to these doctored and confused clichés, as though their author believes that the people of a megalopolis living in skyscrapers and working on assembly lines or with computers and smoking sixty cigarettes a day can believe that an apple a day keeps the doctor away or that early to bed, early to rise, makes a man healthy, wealthy, and wise.

"How do you manage to think all this stuff up and get it down on paper?" Magnuson says sarcastically.

"I can't get some of it down," the man says. "Some I'm sorry to say is lost forever. But I can't help believing that I write with a sense of destiny, that I'm the right man doing the right job at the right time, that anything that's truly good and important I'll remember and write down and that only the second-rate ideas will be forgotten. A kind of divine editing. And that's not as far-fetched as you might think. Some of the ideas I have I know are too good for me and are as much a surprise to me as they probably are to you. Anyway, you should understand the strain I'm under to finish the book.—Oh, I could relax and do nothing. I don't have to write this book. But this country's been pretty good to me, and I owe it something. Especially now when we're in a state of moral decay. When our moral fiber is rotting on our bones. Moral bankruptcy. Look at the youth today. What do you think of them?"

"Not much," Magnuson says honestly, although he does not like to find himself in agreement with this man.

"No responsibility," says the narcoleptic man, yawning. "No patriotism. No fear of God. No taste for work. And look at the colored people. They want to get for nothing what we and our fathers before us worked our fingers to the bones for and increased the intelligence of our minds in the process. And they want to stay hoodlums and criminals in the bargain."

Again Magnuson has to agree in some measure with this observation, although again he finds it distasteful to do so.

"What we need is moral rearmament. Why, the bearing of my book on the immorality of our nation could be momentous. The country's diseased. This book could be the remedy. I'm not saying it will, but it could. I've led a life more than a few men might profit from by imitation. I'm not ashamed to say it. If I didn't believe it I couldn't write my book."

"It's good you can be so sure of yourself."

"But if men like us weren't sure of ourselves, we wouldn't be who we are. It's not the daydreamers and self-doubters that get ahead. It's . . . the bull by the horns!"

A new voice enters the conversation: "You have a message, Mr. Magnuson. Call for Mr. Magnuson. Paging Mr. Magnuson." This is not called out from the middle of the lounge but whispered without warning into Magnuson's ear. The voice effeminate, the accent deeply southern.

"I'm not deaf, man," says Magnuson, and uses his elbow without effect to move the man away. For the messenger is no jockey-sized bellhop, a pillbox with chinstrap aslant on his head, but a great fat boy in the red jacket of a club waiter, a kind of dandified Saxon plowboy, a sissy spoiled by maiden aunts, the unappeasable bully of smaller boys. Blond wavy hair on a prematurely balding head. His bow tie lopsided and fastened by only one clip to his collar; his red jacket too small for his waist. He seems to have trouble standing, for he has leaned against Magnuson who, in order to leave, has to brace his feet and push the man away.

"Did they say who it was?" asks Magnuson. The narcoleptic man has collapsed across his book only to startle awake and raise his head, revealing, before he collapses a second time, Magnuson's handwriting blotted backwards on his cheek.

"No, sir," says the waiter. "The party wouldn't say."

By the time they reach the lobby the waiter is no longer ahead of Magnuson but behind him, huffing and wiping his brow, his pomaceous cheeks puffed up in a pout and imitation of a drawing of a personified and gusty wind. "Please, sir, will you wait up? I'm the one supposed to lead." He catches Magnuson by the sleeve, slows him down, and almost shoves him roughly against the wall. "Sir," he says, "you don't have to answer the phone if you don't want to. I'm willing to tell him I couldn't find you."

Surprised, Magnuson wonders if he should strike the man. He does manage to land a soft blow with his knuckles as he shakes away the arm. "Why wouldn't I want to talk to him?" he says. For the moment he is more puzzled than enraged.

The waiter looks away evasively and grimacing with exaggerated pain rubs his forearm up and down. He seems to be fighting back the tears. "Sir, the man calling you is obviously drunk. I thought you might not want to be troubled, sir. I was only trying to protect you, sir. However I'll certainly know better next time." His voice is childish, whining, insolent.

"But I don't think there will be a next time, sir," he adds. "I'm going out West and become a cowboy. Nothing against you personally, sir, but I'm just fed up with people like you in the city and the gentleman on the phone. I want to round up cattle and break in wild broncos. It's too much for me here in the city, sir. I'm just tired as anything of being a waiter. I guess there's nothing I can't try my hand at doing."

Why, the fellow is mad. Is he ignorant of his own size, softness, and femininity, not to mention what Magnuson suspects is an abhorrence of exercise and the outdoors? Shaking his head, Magnuson enters the telephone booth only to discover that he has closed the door on the arm of the waiter who, inexplicably, has tried to follow him. Even when the arm is retrieved and the door closed the waiter presses his face against the glass, distorting his nose. Does he want a tip? Magnuson will be damned if he'll give him a cent. He motions him off. The man remains. He shakes his fist. No effect. If anyone is drunk, it is this waiter.

"Hello, hello," says the voice in the earpiece, tremulous with weakness and excitement. "For God's sake will you answer the phone?" It is Frazer Farquarson.

"How are you, Frazer?"

"Drunk," says the waiter's lips against the glass.

"At the end of my rope," says Farquarson. Magnuson has heard he is ill, bedridden, dying.

"Stinking," says the waiter's lips, his breath fogging the glass. Magnuson huddles up, his back to the door.

"And how are you?"

"Tired," says Magnuson.

"How can you be tired if you're retired?" Amused by his own remark, Farquarson laughs at his end.

"What can I do for you?" He glances over his shoulder. The waiter is gone.

"You can come out of retirement—if you're not too tired." More laughter.

"It's not something the boys can handle?" By boys he means his partners in the agency, Shannon and O'Bannon.

"Too young. And I don't know them. What I have in mind takes age. Experience. The personal touch of an old friend." A family matter, Magnuson decides, serious enough to have the man on edge. Or not so serious and only magnified by infirmity and age. He has known Farquarson for some thirty years, and although their relationship was sometimes one of more than simply business he would hardly classify himself, as did Farquarson, as Farquarson's old friend.

"Want to tell me over the phone?" Silence on Farquarson's end. "I said, can you tell me on the phone?"

"All right, Wally," says Farquarson, his voice stilted, authoritative, pompous. "Sell if it hits seven-eighths."

"What?"

"Right. Seven-eighths, Wally."

"Someone in the room?"

"Right."

"Is it all that secretive?"

"Indeed, it is."

"A police matter?"

Apparently whoever was in the room with Farquarson has left, for Farquarson is whispering rapidly, out of breath, his hand cupped around the mouthpiece. "I can't tell you over the phone. You heard what happened." Magnuson has heard nothing.

"Who was there?"

"You'll find out tonight. I've made a wonderful discovery, Magnuson. Something apart from the matter at hand. Come out to Lake Forest tonight. Come early. Stay for supper." But before Magnuson can accept or reject the invitation Farquarson's end of the line is dead.

Farquarson sounded eccentric and ill but not drunk. He would like to know what he said to the waiter who answered the phone. The waiter was probably insolent and Farquarson called him a worthless son-of-a-bitch. It now occurs to Magnuson that all the waiters he has ever encountered in the club, with the sole exception of this one, have been black. The fat waiter must be a new man. Which would explain his unsatisfactory behavior and why he was not yet fired. He was certainly proof that Negroes, when it came to some jobs, were superior to whites.

In the lobby Foster the desk clerk, a bald, gray-skinned Negro, is behind the desk. Good-humored and easily amused, he has always reminded Magnuson of a small-town druggist in a white tunic, and struck him as a man children would instinctively call "Pop." "Foster, who is this waiter, this big fat guy—?"

"Oh-ho, that's Bert. Got to be Bert. He's just quit." He points to the red waiter's jacket lying on the counter where, after being turned inside out and wadded up, it has been thrown. "I guess you and him had some run-in. But you don't want to feel you're the one that made him quit. Everybody's been after that fellow. He hasn't done a day's work since he's been here." Here Foster leans confidentially toward Magnuson who, from his side of the counter, leans toward him. "He used to go out every day for his lunch. Wouldn't eat it here at the club where it was free. No, sir, he went to some restaurant that specializes in frying their chicken the only way he likes it. Every day! Fried chicken for his lunch! And the restaurant wasn't even in the Loop but way down on the South Side someplace. He took a cab there and back. Every day! A cab! That's why he was always late punching in after lunch. And that's why, if you ever noticed, his chin and fingers was always greasy in the afternoons." Now Foster's leaning toward Magnuson becomes even more confidential. He can barely whisper through his husky laughter. "You know what he's been telling everyone since he's been here?" Magnuson shakes his head. "That he's going out West to become a cowboy. That's what he just told me was where he was going, what he was going to do. But between you and me—" here he extends his arms to approximate Bert's girth "—I wouldn't want to be his horse! No, sir, I wouldn't want to be that poor horse," he repeats, going to the mail case and handing Magnuson the note that is in his slot.

A notation that a Mr. Scarponi called and will call again soon. No number has been given for Magnuson to call. Just as well, he thinks. Evidently Scarponi intends to make another attempt at persuading him to invest in Scarponi stores. He hasn't expected Scarponi to contact him again so soon. Scarponi's situation must be even more desperate than he thought. He must decide in the next hour how he will answer.

He removes his hat and topcoat and returns to the lounge, sitting down at some distance from the sleeping narcoleptic man. What the devil can Farquarson want, he wonders. At this late hour of his life certainly not a report on some new friend or employee, a favorite request of Farquarson in the past. An outdated last will and testament in the hands of some disinherited party which, if not retrieved, might challenge the valid will and embarrass the rightful heirs? An illegitimate offspring he wants accounted for or possibly discovered so that he or she might be cared for after his death? Magnuson has heard rumors of Farquarson's indiscretions, and Farquarson himself has alluded to complications in his life, along with remote responsibilities. And if Magnuson cared to recall and ponder his past discreet services as a detective to Farquarson he could no doubt infer even more. He is certain that although this might well be a final act of charity or justice, of ensuring order in the transfer of his estate and harmony among his heirs, above all else it is meant to preserve the good name of Farquarson. In any case it is bound to be some skeleton in the closet. Something Farquarson wants desperately to be done.—And come to think of it, Farquarson sounded not only ill and nervous but frightened. Probably frightened without good cause. But frightened best described the way he spoke. Who came into the room and silenced him? Someone who knew Magnuson apparently, knew he was a detective and could be set to work against his, or her, interests.

He is flattered that Farquarson would want him personally to handle what is likely a highly personal, minor, or even menial affair, and for the same reason is peeved at his presumption. For the fifteen years before his retirement he has done little more than serve as part-time administrator and figurehead of his agency with the title of founder and president. A man doesn't call a president out at night to lurk in alleys, shadow girlfriends, rummage through dresser drawers. But I could handle it if that's what it is, Magnuson tells himself. I could go it alone. Like in the old days.

Even before he hung up the phone he had decided he was not up to a visit with a dying friend—an old acquaintance, anyway—and thought he could call Farquarson back later, saying he could not come. Now he decides that he will go. The mystery, and his desire to get the better of it, gets the best of him. His mind, he discovers, no longer feels foggy and heavy but clear and weightless. His spirits rise. Something as trivial as Farquarson's call, and the need and work it promises, is already acting as an antidote to his depression. But he wonders if he would not have gone even if he remained depressed and had no wish to go; if, having given his word in answer to this appeal to both friendship and profession, he really had a choice except to go. He picks up a *Tribune* but finds he is too excited to understand what he reads.

Old Mr. Highland, garbed in his paisley scarf and wine-red robe, shuffles in his leather slippers from chair to chair, searching for someone in the lounge. Magnuson unfolds the *Tribune* before his face. Highland is a boor. He speaks in the thunderous voice of a wealthy man superfluous to the machinery that makes him rich, gives orders where no orders are needed and, as much as the narcoleptic man, if not more so because he is loud and obnoxious, is convinced of the absolute necessity and righteousness of everything he ever said or did. Fifteen years ago he retired (although from what, Magnuson cannot imagine) and moved in with his daughter and her family in their home on the North Shore. The house, although large, certainly not the grand chateau of Highland's day. In such a household Highland found few servants loitering about to command to jump to and perform unnecessary jobs. What orders he did give were overruled by his daughter and ignored by the help. He was expected to eat leftovers, to place his cigar butts in ashtrays and not wherever he liked when he was done with them (often in the refrigerator), and it was even suggested that he lend a hand with the gardening and grass along with the rest of the family and tidy his room and make his bed on the maid's day off. After a few months of this he informed his daughter he would be goddamned if he would do any of these things, that he was retired and after half a century of hard work he would be goddamned if he would do anything other than nothing, absolutely nothing. Immediately he moved into the club, where he has been ever since and where he does as he wishes, which is nothing. The members said that a man who was as active as Highland in his lifetime would be killed by retirement in a year. But fifteen years have passed and Highland still drinks a fifth of Bourbon a day. He is eighty-four and looks sixty. Somehow he has managed all his life, and especially in these twilight years of his retirement, to do nothing with great pleasure, enthusiasm, and activity.

Fingers appear over the top of Magnuson's *Tribune* and slowly force down the page. The shiny, freshly shaved face of Highland. "Found you, didn't I?" The voice even more deliberately loud in the lounge than outside it, although the members over the years have managed to block it out and catalogue it with the rustle of newspapers and the inhuman sounds in the street below.

"I didn't know you were looking for me."

"Well, how are you, Magnuson, you goddamned detective? What are you up to? Still trying to relax? Still trying to enjoy yourself? Been on your best behavior today?" Already he smells of Bourbon, or rather a mixture of Bourbon and the shaving lotion he has used every day for years and that smells—if it could ever be divorced from the Bourbon—like a pineapple stuffed with spices and rum. It has become his smell. "Have you heard from your daughter? Is she still in the Congo with all those killings going on, with all those black savages?"

"She's in the Sudan. She was never in the Congo." This while pretending to read.

"You're a damn fool, Magnuson. She's got a right to live her own life the way she wants. So has my daughter, so have my sons. So have I. I don't need them, they don't need me. That's the way it should be. If she gets her kicks out of dancing with a bunch of naked cannibals around a campfire, what do you care?"

"So I think you've said before."

"You know what you need, Magnuson, to take your mind out of where it doesn't belong?" And when Magnuson doesn't ask, he answers, "A little squat." Both women and the act of sex in all its forms he calls by the peculiar name of "squat," and he seems to be unwilling if not incapable of distinguishing between the two.

"Look," says Magnuson, "is there anything I can do for you?"

"It's what I can do for you." From the pocket of his robe he withdraws a large manila envelope addressed to The Detective, in care of the club. It bears a Chicago postmark but no return address. "Odd," says old Mr. Highland, looking over Magnuson's shoulder, "that it's not addressed to you, just to The Detective."

"I can see who it's addressed to. I just saw Foster a minute ago and he didn't mention any mail—"

"Foster is a lazy, careless, incompetent son-of-a-bitch. Even if the letter did just come in the mail. He asked me who I thought it was for and I said you were the only dick in the club. You have to keep after Foster, Magnuson. Keep after all of them, jump on them every chance you get. I'm the only one left trying to keep up the tone of the place." With that he shuffles out of the lounge, greeting the several members he passes loudly and without so much as looking at them as he passes: "Morning, Harry. Staying out of mischief?—Morning, John. Scotch is poison.—Morning, Martin. Getting any?"

The addressed members wave listlessly or nod silently in reply, peering out at him above their papers and the rims of their glasses resting near the tips of their noses.

Magnuson wonders why he delivered the envelope; he has never known him to do anything for anyone. Perhaps at long last he wanted like everyone else to be useful.

In the envelope are several large folded papers stapled together, the type of paper used for affidavits and wills. They have been professionally typed on an electric typewriter. On the first page there is no date, no heading, no salutation, only:

GOD AND MANKIND

versus

THE DETECTIVE

THE DETECTIVE STANDS ACCUSED

You are a detective. You are not a policeman but the chief of a reputable private detective agency so celebrated in the community it serves that one can safely say your name is better known locally than any man's, including those of the public officials, his honor the mayor's included. Wherever you go you are recognized and treated with respect, especially by those of the more humble classes—newsboys, scrubwomen, shoeshine boys, reformed petty thieves, wayward girls—who visualize you as a man not only compassionate to their existence but one who is always potentially their protector from more powerful enemies, a man whose services are personally and readily available without their having to resort to that degrading and too often indifferent labyrinth of bureaucratic anonymity and dishonest intrigue one finds so prevalent in the public offices. For in the large city of Chicago in which you live and practice your profession the district attorney is a demagogic bungler, the coroner a comical horse doctor, the chief of police a dictatorial idiot, and the policemen themselves not much more than slapstick buffoons. The mayor is not only shanty Irish but an aloof personage with whom you have had few dealings. As he has only summoned you to his office in futile attempts to dissuade you from pursuing an investigation that, he says, might embarrass nameless parties, you suspect him to be nothing more than the puppet of certain secret power interests of privilege and crime. In short, the public officials your duties force you to come into contact with, often to be dependent on, are hopelessly incompetent and ineffectual. For the judges alone you reserve your respect. In those final and tense moments of a publicized trial when the defense at last calls you to the witness stand, the judges listen to your denouements of absurdly complicated plots of homicide—who was where and when and why—with as much attentiveness and excitement as do those in the jury and galleries, and without fail severely and publicly reprimand the stupidity of the public officers in attempting to bring a case against your clients, rarely demanding proof or evidence as to the truth of what you say. In fact, so ingenious and dramatic are these denouements that more often than not the guilty party, who is invariably in attendance in the courtroom, reveals his hand before you have definitely accused him (sometimes when you do not have the slightest notion of accusing him, sometimes when you do not even suspect him), either by leaping up and denying his guilt, and in so doing, committing some verbal inconsistency of deposition that condemns him, or else by breaking down and immediately confessing all.

You see yourself standing on the side of justice, in the company of order, but not always on the side of law. In performing your investigations you have often assumed the liberty to skirt the law, to ignore it entirely, and have even gone so far as to treat it with contempt. This you did whenever you believed it was to the advantage of a client whose innocence you were assured of, or when you feared the law and its officers would impede instead of aid the quest for truth. Yet the public officials whom you delighted in abusing through slight and ridicule, and in their very presence, and in the presence of their subordinates, have allowed you this license with a good will and tolerance you now find difficult not only to explain but to justify. Especially since you have never failed whenever the opportunity presented itself (as it always did) to contrast their stupidity and corruption with your own intelligence and honesty, and publicly too, to the enemies they had most reason to fear, who because of their unscrupulousness and circulation have always the potential to destroy them. This being the press.

But in the last few years you sensed an alteration in the attitude of these officials toward this liberty you presumed was yours. You cannot say how you came to feel this, for you were never charged with any violation nor were you even warned. Perhaps it was only a look someone gave you, a chance remark uttered in your presence into which you read deeper meanings. Perhaps this feeling did not emanate from the officials at all, but from the storehouse of your own conscience, although why this should be you do not know, for you have always felt in your own mind that you have done only what was right. Nevertheless the change in you is definite if, at present, vague. This then is your uneasiness. Your first inkling of the presence in your soul of fear, apprehension, anxiety, guilt.

You have insisted on seeing yourself as some white knight engaged in the lonely, thankless, and, you believe in your darkest hours, futile battle against those human and even cosmic forces of incompetence and injustice if not always evil that are eternally arraigned against you and your infrequent kind. You have seen Death and, with your chest expanded, legs spread, sleeves rolled up on your arms held akimbo, have laughed heartily in his face.

"The Lone Wolf," you have insisted on dubbing yourself, even though you have always had an assistant at your right hand during any investigation. In fairness to you, however, it should be pointed out that these assistants were never really, in your judgment, combatants in that moral struggle you believed it was your destiny to wage. Invariably they were of two phyla: men brave to the point of mindlessness and men cowardly to the point of comedy. What they possessed in common was unquestioning loyalty, a deplorable but amusing stupidity, and, most important of all, a general ineffectiveness that could not help but show you, in contrast, as always at your best. Often they were retired, punch-drunk prize fighters who had illusions of being brilliant criminologists; Orientals who were chatterboxes of confused Confucian sayings; Negroes so cowardly their bones rattled and eyes popped at the least threat of danger.

Now retired from your profession you are for the first time truly alone. You gaze back upon your life with an uneasy satisfaction. But what you do not know—only receive unhappy intimations of—is that at the very nucleus of that life lies a crime you committed before God against man and against nature, a shameful act of inhumanity and ignorance that can only be absolved by contrition and humility and the forgetfulness of death; a crime for which those same judges who once applauded your astuteness and integrity would show you no mercy but in revulsion against your hypocrisy would condemn you not merely to prison and ignominious death but to burn slowly and eternally in Hell. That you were not responsible for the deliberation and total commission of that crime, or conscious even that you shared in its commission, is neither a moral nor a reasonable defense,

and makes you no less guilty nor any more than the lowest scum
of men.

Detective! Your day of reckoning is at hand! The truth will
be known! Destroy your pride! Imitate the lives of saints! Recall your humble origins! . . .

The document continues in this evangelical vein, managing to
accuse him of having arranged an abortion and of shutting someone
up unfairly in a madhouse, and Magnuson, flipping the pages ahead,
finds, as he suspected, that it is unsigned. By now his bewilderment
has turned to rage. An anonymous letter! A poison pen letter! He
has received them in the past, both when he was policeman and
private detective, but never anything as elaborate, intelligent, and
vicious as this. He is the victim of some anonymous revenge. He has
been mocked, caricatured, and falsely caricatured, his life reduced to
the terms of a television show or cheap detective novel. Slander!
He crushes the papers in his fist and throwing back his head so that
his eyes roll back until only the whites show, he imagines that he
opens up his mouth and roars. And discovering that he receives
pleasure and satisfaction in roaring and that he likes the way it
sounds in the funereal lounge of old dozing men, he imagines that
he roars again. And having imagined he has roared, he imagines he
shuts up. Snorting and beating his newspaper against his thighs, he
stomps out of the room.

At the desk he shows Foster the envelope addressed to The
Detective in care of the club. "Why the hell is old man Highland
allowed to play around with the mail?" he demands. "He just gave
me this, just now."

"Doesn't have your name on it, does it?" says Foster.

"It must be meant for someone else," says Magnuson.

"Maybe," Foster says, no longer interested in the question. "I'll
take it back, if you want me to. But as far as I know there's no detective here but you."

"No other detective?"

"Only you."

"No law-enforcement officers?"

"No cops in this club."

"No new man at all?"

"Nobody here, Mr. Magnuson, but you."

CHAPTER EIGHT

FATHERS, SONS, AND MOTHERS

Cavan remembered Al and Bonny Wenzel's Bang's Lake Inn in Wauconda, a tavern on a private beach called Wenzel's Beach, one of several commercial beaches along the shore. On sweltering summer days when the city moved en masse into the country, he had come to this beach with his school friends for a day of swimming and drinking beer illegally. Then cars had lined the highway for half a mile in either direction on both sides of the road and filled the grounds of the beach itself, parking in the open sun and between the shade trees of the small grove and almost to the shore, with only the narrowest passage for pedestrians left between the sun-heated doors and bumpers. Blankets covered the small foothold of beach. Youthful swimmers crowded the water with the density of a mass baptism in India; crowded the rafts, slides, and diving plat-forms until those structures looked like the riggings or the top decks of the pilot houses of otherwise sunken ships and the crowds the frantic muster of remaining sailors. The air popped with shouts and screams that sounded as though they could only be a massive attestation to disaster and appeal for help, while the loudspeakers in the trees amplified the polkas and the rhythm-and-blues played on the jukebox in the tavern. He had been there among this babble and what he remembered as resembling some Bosch vision of humanity playing in the water it was drowning in; had spent whole days in that water (today he didn't even like to swim); had played king of the raft for hours at a time, touching the strange and accessible girls he pushed into the water, touching them as they in turn pushed him, as he fell on top of them, as they fell on top of him, touching them as one and all in one half-naked, interlocking chain of lean young limbs they went beneath the water. And he had tried unsuccessfully to get up the courage to dive from the highest tower and to pick his dark and lonely passage underwater beneath the barrels of the giant rafts.

But now, he felt, Wenzel's Beach was like a deserted battleground, and he a veteran of that battle returning fifty years after. The highway was deserted. His was the only car to park on the beach's grounds. The small lake, ringed with shade trees and cottages with small docks, was deserted except toward the middle, where a lone rowboat contained a lone fisherman hunched up in the stern with a bamboo pole. The rafts, slides, and diving platforms were all out of the water and stored along the shore, looking more gray than white.

He had only seen the tavern crowded with bathers sweating shoulder to shoulder in the booths cluttered with paper plates and empty beer bottles or sweating and standing four deep between the booths and bar, waving bills folded between their fingers at the sweating bartenders who did nothing but pry the tops from bottles and make change. But now the tavern gave the impression that it was an hour before opening time. A man and woman were behind the bar, the woman at the cash register and examining the trays, the man on a stool and spooning a bowl of chili from his lap. Another man and woman sat together at the bar before Pilsner glasses of tap beer. A youth in a leather jacket was playing a form of shuffleboard, sliding metallic discs by hand down a long wooden table to a series of numbered squares. Someone else was behind those green curtains closed on a doorway, behind which the sounds of a slot machine could be heard. (He remembered those curtains and that slot machine.) The curtains were rippling, swinging in and out at the bottom; windows were open all along the booths as though to give the place an airing.

The couple behind the bar were immediately familiar to him. Wenzel he must have seen years ago outside in the driveway in T-shirt, sunglasses, and carpenter's apron, appointing parking spaces and collecting admission fees. But Mrs. Wenzel was so familiar as to make him feel he was obliged to greet her by name and thereafter exchange news of mutual friends. Although he could have seen her here before, as he had her husband, he could not associate her with this tavern. It was somewhere else. To confound him further, the boy leaning over the shuffleboard paused with the silver puck in his hand and peered back over his chrome-studded, scuffed-leather shoulder, showing him the pitted face, the starched hair of the high crew cut, the long sideburns, a face that was even more familiar than that of Mrs. Wenzel. But again he could not associate this face with any specific time or place, much less with this tavern. And most bewildering of all, he could not associate the three people he recognized as being found together in any one place, as though he had met one in California, one in Maine, one in Florida, and now reencountered the three of them together in a tavern in Illinois. He could not be mistaken in his recognitions, for he himself was recognized. Not by Wenzel, who continued to spoon and cool his chili, but by Mrs. Wenzel and the youth at the shuffleboard, who were openly scowling at him as though to tell him they wanted him off the premises as soon as possible. They could not have mistaken him for someone else, since he recognized them.

When he ordered a draught beer the woman sitting at the bar called out in a hoarse, drunken voice, "Hey, Bonny, you better find out if that kid's old enough." This appeared to be a private joke. The three customers laughed and even the Wenzels smiled.

Apparently this provided Bonny with a convenient excuse by which she might be rid of him, and Cavan, who looked nearer thirty than twenty, surrendered his draft card. He noticed now that she was little more than a midget. She managed to look taller because of the wooden platform she stood on behind the bar and because she piled her bleached hair a foot high on her head and wore white toeless sandals with heels so thick and high they resembled the painful footwear of the lame. She also wore white ankle socks with those sandals, skin-tight slacks, and had red fingernails and toenails, and instead of eyebrows a thin line of pencil that arched halfway up her forehead. There was a look about her head of a wig-shop mannequin upon which cosmetics had been applied over other cosmetics and hair had been drawn where not affixed. Everything about her body was small and round and hard. Up close she looked twenty years older than she did from far away. This, he had to remind himself, was Farquarson's girlfriend, the woman who, if Farquarson could be believed, had been diseased.

To read the draft card she put on a pair of glasses with sparkling rims. The boy at the shuffleboard, who could not have been more than nineteen, drank from his glass of beer as though to taunt Cavan, while Wenzel and the man at the bar smiled at Cavan sympathetically. Bonny went to the tap to draw the beer. "John Cavan," she said, nodding her head toward Cavan. The spoon of chili was poised before Wenzel's open mouth.

"Hey, pal," the man at the bar said to Cavan. He had turned on the stool to face him with one eye contemplating the top of the mirror behind the bar and the other the linoleum squares of the floor. He had red eyes, red skin, red hair around a bald spot, and the red stubble of a beard, and he and the woman next to him, who wore white socks rolled down around her ankles and had hair the color of an iridescent tangerine except at the roots, where it looked like blue ink, were huddled together on the barstools, shoulder to shoulder, rump to rump, their heads slouched in unison over the bar. "Don't take it wrong, pal," he said, trying to wink one of the disobedient eyes. "It's got nothing to do with you personally. This colored guy come in here a while ago to give Al here a letter—"

"Say, Al," the woman next to him said, "what was that colored guy wearing, a chauffeur's cap or a mailman's cap?"

"A chauffeur's cap," Al said quietly.

"After he gave Al the letter," the red-haired man continued, "he thought he could hang around and have a drink. But Bonny here asks for his I.D." Here both the man and the woman and the boy at the shuffleboard laughed. As yet Cavan saw nothing to be amused about, although he did recognize that the man was being friendly to him. Then as if the man was forced to explain the joke to Cavan, who had somehow missed the punchline: "He must have been sixty years old, pal! He had a driver's license, but of course he didn't have no draft card. And Bonny said a driver's license wasn't no good."

"How can you tell how old they are?" Bonny said.

"You flattered him, Bonny," said the orange-haired woman. "An old man like that asked for his I.D. He'll go straight home and knock a piece off his old lady. Hey, Bonny honey, why don't you ever flatter me and ask me for my I.D.?"

"You're just a spring chicken, baby," the man next to her said, again trying to wink at Cavan.

"Hey, Al," the woman said, "was that colored guy a chauffeur or a mailman?"

"A chauffeur," Al said.

"Then how come he delivered a letter?" she said.

"Mailmen deliver letters," the man next to her said.

"That's what I thought, too, honey," she said, turning to him.

The man said to the boy at the shuffleboard, "Come on, Skipper, buy your old man and lady a drink." The boy hunched up his shoulder, slid his hand into the pocket of his Levi's, and brought up a handful of change he slammed beneath his palm upon the bar.

Skipper Moony—the boy at the shuffleboard! No wonder Cavan felt he recognized him. No wonder Skipper Moony, with a look Cavan now interpreted as less antagonistic than contemptuous, had in turn recognized him. He had been hired to help Thorsen with the grounds last fall, a job Cavan now suspected he had gotten through the influence of Bonny Wenzel.

And it was this suggestion of sex and place that made Cavan absolutely certain of where he had seen Bonny Wenzel before. At Farquarson's! When he was on vacation from boarding school he had often encountered her inside the Lake Forest house, sitting in a chair in the living room and leafing through a woman's magazine, walking down an upstairs hallway (and walking quickly, too, he remembered, always quickly, and smoking, too, but not puffing but only letting the smoke rise from the ash into her eyes), or in the downstairs hall before the front door in her coat about to leave as he was entering with his bags. Or he would think he saw her as she stepped in or out of some dark car in the driveway, sent to his upstairs window by the shutting of the car door or high heels on the gravel. No one had ever introduced him to her or explained her presence, nor had she ever spoken to him, even in greeting, or even as far as he could remember looked much at him, nor had he, the child, ever dared to speak to her or ask some adult in the household who she was. He supposed that even then he had thought her presence incongruous with his uncle, with Lake Forest, with his uncle's house, and that if he had attempted to explain it to himself he had thought of her as filling in for the less exotic housekeeper on her days off. Often she was dressed carelessly, a knee-length fur coat worn with those high and thick-heeled pumps and ankle-length white socks, her bleached hair in curlers and covered by a babushka, her face free of make-up, all as though she had been called out on some emergency and had left as she was, having thrown the closest coat at hand across her shoulders. Or had he sensed even then something secret and perverse about her presence? He knew he had begun to anticipate with secret, shameful pleasure her mysterious presence in the house at any time in any room. At times he had even doubted that she was real (he had seen her only when both of them had been alone) but believed that she was instead some ghostly grown-up female leprechaun or elf come to haunt the shame and ignorance of his puberty, the creation of his degenerate imagination or of the violent changes—the eruptions, landslides, and mountain building—in the landscape of his loins. Around her he had sometimes constructed in his daydreams a whole mythology of naked or disheveled Amazons, Valkyries, and succubi, a harem at his beck and call of which she was not only the matriarch but in speech and practice the most corrupt. Her diminution made her, the grown woman, seem accessible to him, the adolescent boy. He would imagine her when he was in his bed, and would sometimes go to bed solely so he could imagine her, would undress and arrange the two of them as equals standing eye to eye, the grown woman and the small boy locked in some unfocused, motionless, and thoroughly erroneous embrace, as though to satisfy their lust a man and woman did not lie upon the bed and thrash and pump and slop about in sweat and heat but stood exquisitely close but still, absolutely still, and cold as stone, waiting for that inevitable, unearned, and seedless ecstasy.

Now it was claimed that his uncle, as a grown man and even as an old man, had done to this woman what he had only dreamed of doing as a boy. In rare moments he had allowed himself to wonder about his uncle's celibacy, aware that he had not divorced the wife who had been a patient in a sanatarium for nearly thirty years. His infidelity was only normal. Only his choice of mistress seemed grotesque. He tried to picture the scene of their domesticity. The tall, steel-haired Farquarson in tie and smoking jacket reading his *Tribune* in a leather chair before the fire as Bonny in a dimestore bathrobe was curled up in a chair across from him and filing her fingernails with an emery board or possibly with her bare feet upon a cushion and painting her toenails. The pair of them bickering and squabbling like a couple married twenty years.

Farquarson had told the truth, then: Bonny Wenzel had been his mistress. Had he also told the truth when he claimed that she had given him gonorrhea? And more importantly, that he was no uncle of John Cavan?

If Farquarson was his father, and he hoped he was, wasn't it reasonable to assume in the absence of a wife that Farquarson's mistress was his mother? His mother—Bonny Wenzel? That woman who had immediately disliked him and who was, he judged, intolerant and ignorant and in whose imagined company, God forbid, he had indulged the appetites of his sex-mad puberty. Even now he could imagine her as the desirable plaything of oversexed boys and immature men, her toughness misconstrued by them as sensuality. He could not accept her as a mother, as anybody's mother, surely not as his mother. Especially when for all these years he had found consolation in his often lonely childhood in that mother image of Priscilla Farquarson Cavan, in that soft, melancholic, and silvery inviolacy and aloofness he discovered in her photographs, intensified even further by her early death. He wondered if Bonny Wenzel was old enough to be his mother. In reply he saw the high-school sophomore and the tumescent, thumping belly on her undersized and sticklike frame, the offspring already equal to her in size.—Farquarson his father. Bonny Wenzel his mother. His father with gonorrhea! What was worse, his mother!

Then he was wandering, glass of beer in hand, to the electric organ at the end of the bar where Al Wenzel had gone to play old songs from a small khaki-colored songbook that had been issued by the army in World War Two. He went from Stephen Foster to "*Finiculi Finicula*" to "Boola Boola" to the "Anvil Chorus" and "Yankee Doodle," beginning with the song on the first page and passing on to the next as though it had never occurred to him that he could play any song he wished in the book without first playing all those songs preceding it. The notes and staffs in the songbook were so small and cramped that he had to squint no more than inches from the page. He treated Cavan to a dreamy kindness, nodding his head not merely to the music but in greeting, as though to acknowledge that he recognized him and knew the reason for his coming here. "Anything," he said, "you want to hear?" The countertenor in contrast to the massive sloping shoulders and swollen arms that made it seem he could embrace and raise the organ and play it accordion-fashion if he chose. The body of a professional football player in middle age on which sat the sandy-haired, cherubic, rosy-cheeked head of a youth. A face that might have been unchanged since youth if somewhere in the intervening years the mark of suffering had not been imposed upon that innocence. The kind of face Cavan had only seen before on crippled children, their slumping or tipping shrunken bodies looking not only frozen in their gigantic wheelchairs but frozen at the climactic violence of their throes. "Anything you want to know?"

Cavan was watching the keyboard as though the man were not a heavyhanded and amateur electric organist misplaying simple songs but a jazz pianist of invention, with his own technique. "He told me about the letter . . . He couldn't bring himself to tell me . . . not everything . . . actually very little . . . He told me to come and ask you what was in it . . . I don't understand though why he sent you the letter . . ."

So personal and important a letter, which allegedly revealed secrets of his life that even he did not know, sent to a man Farquarson appeared to have nothing in common with other than that they shared the same woman, he being the husband of Farquarson's mistress, which in itself almost seemed reason not to send him such a letter, not to send him a letter at all.

"To confess," Wenzel said, resembling some tormented pianist torturing out the most melancholic passages of Chopin, his eyes closed and his head cocked so that his ear was only inches above the keys. "To forgive me . . . to ask for my forgiveness . . ." He was playing "Santa Lucia" now.

"What did *he* have to forgive?" It was obvious to Cavan that Wenzel was the injured party.

In answer Wenzel shut the songbook and, behaving like a deaf mute, motioned Cavan into a nearby booth. Cavan could now observe that the man was drunk, and not drunk for just this one afternoon but drunk day in and day out from habit and accumulation. It was amazing he could play the organ. Or even stand. The Moonys at the bar chattered between themselves, cackling and coughing. Skipper continued to send the pucks down the shuffleboard with more violence than precision, for he often knocked them from the table to the floor. Behind the curtains the slot machine discharged a small cascade of silver and a strange man gave out with a victorious cry. Bonny Wenzel broke a cracker above her chili and watched them as they moved from organ to booth. The booth was windowless and in a corner and the high wooden backs like settles shut out the length of the bar. They leaned over their beers in shadows with the sunlight on the floor just beyond their feet and all along the opposite wall.

"He said you would tell me . . . why I'm not his nephew . . .

what my name is . . . who I am . . ." While he wondered: does he really know anything?

"What *did* he have to forgive?" Wenzel said, ignoring the recent questions for that one asked earlier at the organ, and as though he had thought of nothing else ever since.

Then Cavan, cast without warning into the role of confessor with uncertain powers of absolution, staring with shame into his beer while he pieced together and imagined the far-fetched story from the sleepy but rapid speech of the man that sounded in the shadowy, shut-off booth like the drone and mumble of the confessional.

This story. These pictures. A cold-sober Wenzel steeled for the distasteful job ahead calling at the Moony house with a pair of fifths smuggled from the tavern beneath his arms. When one fifth was empty he was in the Moony bedroom and on the bed with Betty Moony—that woman at the bar next to her husband Scotty—who had coaxed and tempted him for years to do what she was now too drunk to enjoy or remember doing. Penetrating after only the slightest rearrangement of their clothes that flesh he must have known—from Scotty's drunken confession of fornication with the wife of a Mexican field hand in the back seat of a junked Ford and of Betty complaining of a female ailment she had yet to diagnose, not unlike his own ailment which he admitted to having treated far too tardily—had to be diseased. The clammy alcoholic lack of passion of the woman, and Skipper the son in his bedroom next door with a half dozen of his friends, playing hillbilly records and drinking the second fifth, and those light bulbs burning without shades above the bed and Scotty himself on the floor, passed out beneath the squeaking bed that sometimes went so deep it depressed his face and chest, his protruding pants cuffs and sockless ankles and laceless shoes visible to Wenzel from where his chin was hooked on Betty Moony's still clothed shoulder.

Then, as Wenzel learned in bits and pieces from Bonny, a furious and incredulous Farquarson learning from his amused and disgusted doctor—the young son of a very old and wealthy friend—the proper diagnosis of what he had taken for a prostate problem appropriate to his age. Thereafter Farquarson's secret and shameful journeys disguised in his gardener's clothes to the black doctor on the South Side of Chicago, where in a bleak office and for an exorbitant fee he felt justified in paying, he was cured in six months of what could have been cured in several days, treated by means of painful and degrading therapies and a spectrum of placebos, pills as small as beebees and large enough to clog the trachea, and rancid salves that seemed to be a blend of hog fat and wild rash-inducing herbs.

But Farquarson had been unable or unwilling to believe that she could have been infected by her husband, preferring to believe instead that they were both the victims of her infidelity. He even had her followed by a detective to discover who the third man was. Or the fourth or fifth. For he could believe that she could be unfaithful and get herself diseased—which did not say much for the type of man he thought she would run around with—but he could not believe that of Wenzel.

He now wondered aloud to Cavan if he hadn't been driven to protest that he was not the silent and saintly victim Farquarson seemed to think he was. Driven to prove that he too was immoral and therefore human. (If so, the strategy had backfired, since Farquarson at first, anyway, could not believe he could be guilty.) If he had thought to punish them, an idea he consoled himself with in his weaker moments, it was only after he had equally punished himself.

To Cavan it was a compulsive confession that seemed to give the man pleasure, to suggest that he might commit evil or even invent it only so as to have the painful pleasure of confessing it. But the joy he received from this confession was equal to the pain, and that joy was small consolation to his general and obvious unhappiness.

By now Wenzel was shaking his head as though to intimate he had reached a point of inarticulation. His lower lip hung slack and his eyes were filmed over. Swaying with beer in hand he returned to the organ, where he sat with his large hands resting at the keys and trying to focus on the music for the next song. He had forgotten about Cavan and all his questions and returned to that private world he apparently inhabited while he played the organ. He even gently dismissed Cavan with an apologetic wave of hand. He had spent himself confiding something other than that which Cavan wished to know. A story that Cavan was not even certain he had heard right, or if he had, that he should believe.

Outside the tavern he felt excluded from the landscape. Felt as though he could have just stepped off the lone passenger car on a freight train at a small town in the middle of a forest in northern Canada, and in his hand was a cardboard suitcase that contained no clothes of his. He was too hungry to continue drinking if he did not eat. Since he intended to drink he went into the small restaurant across the road, stepping into what appeared to be the private kitchen of someone's home. An old white refrigerator, a small white stove with two burners, a counter with only three stools, a pair of ice-cream chairs at each of the two flimsy tables covered with blue and yellow patterned oilcloths. Bouquets of plastic flowers in glass jars on the tables, whole beds of them in planters on the floor, sprays framing family photographs on the walls. Fathers, mothers, sisters, brothers, sons, and daughters all looked out across the room and compelled in him the suspicion he was eating where he did not belong. Even beside the lone box of candy bars on the counter was a recent studio portrait of a boy in an air force uniform, the visor of his cap coming down to his thick, run-together eyebrows, his ears protruding from his shaved skull, a white scarf around his neck. His uniform had been touched with blue color, his cheeks with pink, his lips with red, giving him the appearance of a corpse prettied by cosmetics. The frame was turned so that he scowled at anyone who sat on the stool.

A woman of about fifty entered from the rear of the building—a living room, likely, for he could hear a television—and went behind the counter where, saying nothing, she confronted him with the same scowl as the boy in the photograph. Cavan sat on a stool and looked for a menu: there was none. Only this sign on the wall: Home Cooking—Home-made Pie. He wanted a restaurant with formality and impersonality. Here he felt like a tramp called into the kitchen from the woodpile. The woman seemed to share this feeling with a force that intimated he was at best a not too welcome guest, at worst an intruder. In her face with its pointed nose and suspicious eyes almost crossed behind her glasses he caught glimpses of black Bibles, windmills, canning jars, coffins wrapped in the stars and stripes, a clapboard farmhouse taller by half than it was wide silhouetted against the prairie sky.

He ordered two cheeseburgers and a cup of coffee. She put on an apron, removed a paper tray of hamburger from the refrigerator, and molded two patties in her hands. Then she removed a frying pan from a drawer beneath the stove and set it on a burner. Into it she poured some grease. In agony he watched the time-wasting motions of getting out the cheese, the buns, the dishes. Finally a dented pan of water set on the stove. Instant coffee, lukewarm, into which she poured a minimum of cream. She stood at the end of the counter and watched him eat. The hamburger was too thick and greasy and mixed with onion, the cheese too sharp.

He asked for a piece of home-made blueberry pie in the hope it would redeem the meal. But the crust was raw, the blueberries as sweet as baklava, the sugar unmixed and hardened into crystals.

"This Wenzel across the street," he said, leaving her to complete the thought in whichever way she wished.

Surprisingly this proved to be the opening the woman had been waiting for, although he supposed any other would have done as well. "People claim he used to be a Catholic priest down in Chicago," she said in a voice nasal and monotonal. "But he met this woman—the woman over there—when he was just a young priest, and left the priesthood to marry her. Then they bought this tavern here in town. A funny business for a priest to be running although maybe not so funny when you think of all those stories of priests drinking you hear so much about."

He should have been a monk, Cavan thought, cloistered in a monastery on a mountain top in a cell in which he meditated and fasted and occasionally fed the starlings through the bars. There had been something simple, trustful, and naïve about the man, and something withdrawn and almost monastic too. How far the man had fallen. The shame and degradation and humiliation of his owning such a tavern, of being married to that woman, quite apart from her having been the girlfriend of the wealthy Farquarson, and, if Farquarson could be believed, of contracting a venereal disease from some doubtful quarter and infecting his own wife. Given what the man had been, Cavan wondered if he could have been uncertain of what exactly went on between Farquarson and his wife, suffering with his suspicions for years. From only a glance at his face it was possible to believe that at one time he had thought the best of anyone and anything. If he had ever doubted that there was sex between them though, the gonorrhea passed on to Farquarson had proven the matter once and for all, and a perverse justice had been exacted in giving Farquarson pain where he took his pleasure at the expense of Wenzel's pain.

"They had a son, you know," the woman was saying. "But he was drowned about fifteen years or so ago . . ."

"A son?"

"Drowned in Bang's Lake. That lake out there . . ."

"How did he drown?"

"Caught under the raft. Yes, his swimming suit got caught on a sharp torn piece on one of the barrels. They dragged the lake for days and Mr. Wenzel himself found him when he swam under the raft. That's the very same raft down there on the beach."

Cavan's ears were exploding; his cheeks were puffed; his lungs felt like plastic bags swollen with water; he couldn't breathe. Seaweed and beer cans and a curious perch on the bottom; the distant kicking legs of swimmers on the same level as himself; the sloshing and the booming of the drums above and the bars of sunlight in the cracks between the planks; his own hair rising toward the surface. He was going to pass out; he was about to be sick; he was holding his breath—

"Mr. Wenzel wanted to give the boy a Catholic burial. But they couldn't get a priest to come. I guess the priests around here found out he used to be a priest and left the church and married this woman and had this son and owned this tavern. The boy stayed unburied for three days. And no priest would come. And Mr. Wenzel wouldn't bury him unless he had a Catholic service. He lay three days in the funeral home, until everyone who was going to see him had already seen him, and then they took him down in the basement. But the word must have gotten out because finally this Presbyterian minister from Lake Forest offered to perform the service and Mr. Wenzel accepted, for it was Christian even if it wasn't Catholic. And they buried him that evening. Just about dark. As soon as the minister got into town. And there was no one to the funeral except the Wenzels because no one knew about it with such short notice. Not even his schoolmates who were supposed to be his pallbearers were there—."

The hand of Farquarson! The minister from Lake Forest. But was it an act of compassion and a favor for people who were more or less his friends or was the drowned boy Farquarson's son? Perhaps none of them knew for certain whose son he was. Perhaps the boy had been Cavan's brother, or his half brother. Perhaps either Farquarson or Wenzel had been the father of both, or Farquarson the father of one and Wenzel of the other. Wenzel, the defrocked priest, drunkard, tavernkeeper, and cuckold or pimp, his father; while his mother prostituted herself in the very household into which he, the son, had been sent. Why then had he and not the drowned boy been taken into the Farquarson home and inexplicably given the name of Cavan, Farquarson's own brother-in-law? Or had they reached some compromise, giving Farquarson one of the boys, the choice determined by a toss of a coin, and keeping the other for themselves? Or was it possible that he became John Cavan only because this other boy was dead?

"—Mr. Wenzel was very bitter after that. He wouldn't see or talk to anyone. They even said that for four years he wouldn't speak at all. Not a word. Just point or grunt if he had to. And when he did begin to speak again it was only to swear at people. Then he started to play the organ and that must have helped him some. They say he plays the organ very well. I suppose he must have learned it when he was a priest. I haven't seen him play myself but I can hear him from across the street. He plays some very pretty songs. They sound real nice. And then he started to keep goats and sheep in his barn outside of town, and I suppose that must have helped some. They say some of his animals have won prizes. His wife runs the tavern and he only comes in to play the organ. The rest of the time he spends with his sheep and goats." Here she leaned conspiratorially toward Cavan. "I've heard she's said lately that she wants to sell their place." She paused as though inviting Cavan to supply whatever information he had on the subject. "This morning," she continued, "a colored man called over there and went inside." She paused to allow Cavan to reflect upon the weight of this. "I saw him with my own eyes out that very window. So did other people. Why would that man go inside the tavern? You put two and two together. She's thinking of selling and the colored man is calling. A colored tavern across the road from me." Then prophetically, "The day will come, though. There's nothing you or me can do about it, either. Not the little people."

Cavan was standing, desperate to leave. But the woman, blooming with friendliness, was recounting the story of her childhood in this town, her womanhood on a farm west of here, her return to the town at the illness of her husband who is paralyzed and dying in some inner room of this very house, along with tales of that husband and of her mother and father, whose pictures are on the walls, and of her son, who was in the air force and stationed in Greenland, until Cavan had somehow managed to pay his check and, after a long good-bye, was standing in the road again. Rainclouds, like the smoke from coal furnaces, were blowing above the town and lake, and the water was rippling like a mud puddle in the wind. The lone fisherman was rowing in against the waves that could be seen to chop against his bow. At the gas station next door metal signs were spinning, blowing down, and banging on the concrete. Cavan, in the orphanage of the world, wondering as he had since morning who and where he was.

CHAPTER NINE

THE LOOP

As the medieval European town was defined by its town walls, so is downtown Chicago defined by a rectangle of nineteenth-century elevated tracks called the Loop. Here steel and glass skyscrapers rise from the gray glacial mud and from the rubble of nineteenth-century landfill and of the recently demolished buildings, some of which were architectural landmarks, that they have superseded. Here pneumatic drills break up the old concrete and pile drivers pound wooden pilings with a clang that echoes in the gusty streets. It was here that Magnuson took a brisk walk, hoping to cool with the rigor of his exercise the rage he still felt at the slander of the poison pen letter, for he wanted to be in high spirits by the time he left for his appointment with Farquarson in Lake Forest.

The crowds he moved among were dense and hurried and took up the sidewalks in block-long marches. Against his will he kept

pace with them, competing for time and space. Shoppers and employees of stores and offices on errands and coffee breaks, they
planned their paths a dozen steps ahead and amassed at street corners
in impatient jams that made probes and forays off the curbs until the
light changed and they were whistled across. They walked in silence
and alone, a ruddy lour about their faces that stemmed from the
excitement and friendly arrogance of their own awareness of themselves as Chicagoans, of their cognizance that the whole world knew
who and what and where they were.

At a stamp and coin shop Magnuson paused to study the bulging
packets of stamps clipped to strings strung along the window. In
the cellophane windows of these packets were colorful, oversized,
pictorial stamps of Africa, Monaco, San Marino, Vatican City, the
Soviet Union, and he thought: I could go right now to any of these
places. I could fly to Africa and surprise my daughter. I could fly
to Europe and surprise my son. I could do both. And he remembered
Bruce as a boy sitting on the edge of his bed and sorting through
packets of stamps, which he lifted with a small pair of silver
tongs. Remembered stamps on pieces of envelopes soaking in glasses
of water, and stamp hinges, new and used, scattered over the bed-
spread and floor.

Later he found himself at the western limit of the Loop, shivering on the windy and sunless pavement and looking through watery
eyes at the sunlit, wind-battered crowds marching like regiments up
and down the Madison Avenue Bridge that spanned the Chicago
River, their hands on their hats and skirts, their coats snapping in
the gusts like sails. Across the bridge, Skid Row stretched out like an
underground city of the dead enveloped in lethal vapors and ocher
mists. For a moment, as though listening to the forlorn, inhuman bleat
of homeless men that beckoned and tempted him, he made as if to
walk there. Farther west the city sprawled on a plain to a distant
smoky horizon, where a remote and yellow sun looked like the moon.

But Magnuson headed east instead, back through the Loop and
toward the Lincoln Athletic Club on Michigan Avenue. On the
muddy boards of a wooden roofed sidewalk, a temporary structure
that went into the street and skirted a construction site of a new
building and that had about it something of a frontier-town atmosphere, a man in a flannel shirt, approximately his own age, approached
him with his hand extended, saying loudly, "Well, how are you, you
old son-of-a-bitch?"

The walk was so narrow that many in the crowd walked sideways, and when the man spoke everyone near him turned to look at

him, or at Magnuson who, having failed to recognize the man, answered just as loudly, "How are *you*, shitface?" Which had the crowd looking straight ahead again and catching any steps their feet had missed.

For a moment the man stopped, so that the crowd jammed up and marked time behind him and footsteps went to either side of him, banging on the boards. Then he said, "Gosh, sorry, pal," a surprised and injured look about his face.

Magnuson had assumed the man was drunk and had singled him out of the crowd to befriend or abuse because for some unknown reason he had looked conspicuous. Now he wondered if the man could have legitimately mistaken him for someone else, or even, God forbid, recognized him.

On the open sidewalk again he was accosted by a panhandler. Instinctively he halted and went to his pockets. Even in the depression, when he was a patrolman, he would leave the house with a pocketful of nickels, and if he were assigned to a destitute precinct his pocket would be empty by the end of the day. In the early days of his marriage his wife had berated him for so luxurious a habit, calling him a soft touch. Later she accepted it and even filled his pocket before he went to work, the denomination of the coin progressing over the years from nickels to dimes to quarters.

But Magnuson, who intended to give this man half a dollar, had no change. Resolved to give him a dollar he thumbed through the several hundred he always carried in his wallet and discovered he had no bill less than a ten. "Sorry, pal," he said, walking on, "I've got no change." But the man, having come so close to charity, pursued him, whining that he had not eaten since he had been thrown out of the hospital some days past. For the first time Magnuson looked at the man. He was more beggar than panhandler. He looked as though he had been living in a heap of coal. Gauze was wound around his shins up to his knees, and dirty pus and salve where it was not stiff oozed out between bindings so loose he had to stop and stoop continually to rewind them, tugging at them like a child pulling up a sock. He was a little man with steel-rimmed glasses dislocated by the single strip of gauze wound slantwise around his head. On his feet were muddy socks instead of shoes. Never had Magnuson encountered so wretched a man, certainly never in the heart of the Loop. Such a man would be conspicuous even on Skid Row. He had to be a stranger, a merchant sailor likely coming off a month-long drunk, to have come in this condition into the Loop.

"You can get change in one of these stores, mister," the man whined at his back. He had followed Magnuson for a block, and the passing crowds were turning their invigorated faces to stare at them: the bearlike, white-haired, red-faced, well-dressed, respectable-looking straight man and the small, ragged, beaten clown. When three black youths in deerstalker caps and something like Sherlock Holmes capes turned back to smirk and jibe, Magnuson decided he would not be rid of the man until he made change.

He went into a restaurant and asked the cashier, a heavyset, overdressed woman, to change the ten. To his surprise the beggar, whom he assumed would wait outside, followed him in. "This nice lady will make change, mister," he said.

The woman, however, having looked with indignation and even fear from Magnuson to the beggar back to Magnuson again, now stretched out the bill and, with her black-rimmed glasses on the tip of her nose, examined it, with alternate studies of Magnuson, as though trying to match the engraving of the face of Hamilton with that of Magnuson. "No, we don't make change," she said, handing back the bill.

"But I want to give this fellow something. I've got nothing smaller than a ten." He was certain the woman would relent at this explanation. After all, her philanthropy was less than his.

But the woman looked at him as though he were unreasonable, even dangerous. "We don't make change," she repeated.

"Give me a pack of cigars, then."

"We don't sell cigars to people unless they dine here." She was reaching around Magnuson for the extended check of the customer first in line behind him.

By now most of the diners had turned on their stools to observe the scene at the cash register, their small sandwiches poised in their hands.

Furious, Magnuson said, leaning heavily on the glass-topped counter, "Then give this fellow a meal. I'll pay for it. Then give me my cigars and my change."

In response the cashier waved to a man in a short-sleeve white shirt and black bow tie behind the counter who came quickly to the register. He appeared to be the manager and a Cuban or Puerto Rican. "Are you cashing that ten dollars for him?" he asked of Magnuson.

"I want change for him."

"I mean," said the manager, "is that his ten dollars he got you to cash for him?"

"How," Magnuson said, "would you like me to break your spine?"

On the street Magnuson was again pursued. "Get away from me, pal," he said, shaking his arm as though the man had him by the sleeve. "Look, I've tried to make change and it's no good. Give me a break." He was furious with everyone: that cashier, that manager, the patrons of the restaurant, every man, woman, and child who passed him on the sidewalk, and most of all with this beggar, whom he wanted to kick up and down the street.

Finally he went to LaSalle Street and the bank and trust company where both he and his agency had accounts. Here at least he was certain he could change a ten-dollar bill without incident. He shook his red fist before the beggar's damp nose and ordered him to wait on the sidewalk. But he was no sooner before the teller's window than he caught sight of the beggar stumbling in his muddy socks across the marble floor, beneath that ornate dome that made the bank resemble a Venetian palace or Byzantine cathedral built centuries ago and meant to last centuries hence. A bank guard eased out from behind a fluted marble column and with his hands behind his back strolled in a direction that would eventually take him to Magnuson and the beggar. Depositors and cashiers along the long black marble counter were turned their way. Executives in cages behind the tellers were standing at their desks.

"Can I help you?" the bank guard was saying.

"I'm with this man," the beggar said, anticipating the question and pointing at Magnuson. Magnuson, receiving his ten singles, nodded.

"Good afternoon, Mr. Magnuson," said the bank guard, confused. He did not move off but stood as though to block the beggar from the view of the customers.

Magnuson, resolved to give the man no more than half a dollar, exchanged one of the singles for silver. If the man lacked the dignity and courage to accept the fact that Magnuson had no change and therefore that he was destined to do without, then Magnuson would be damned if he would let the fellow benefit any further from his funk and shamelessness. In the middle of that rotunda of white marble he gave the beggar fifty cents, appearing in the transaction with the dollar bills he had received from the teller not only in his hand but clutched in his fist as though discharging a pressing debt for which he had been hounded. Thereupon he turned and fled, beating the beggar to the street.

On Michigan Avenue he felt the world open up before him. A wide, clean, sunlit, breezy thoroughfare with only green parks and Lake Michigan beyond. Here the wind was warmer and fresher smelling and blowing off the lake he faced and not sneaking out at you from around the corner of a shaded alley or street corner. On the sidewalk fashionable pedestrians who resembled fashion models fresh from Europe and Colorado ski slopes and Caribbean beaches strode briskly, observing their fashionable wind-blown selves reflected in the fashionable display windows of the fashionable stores and in the burnished mirrorlike stones in the street-level facades of the buildings.

But in the Lincoln Athletic Club Scarponi was waiting for him in the lounge, sitting with hat and topcoat on his lap. Magnuson was surprised by his presence; he had thought he would call back on the phone.

Scarponi was full of good fellowship, nonchalance, bravado. "Have you thought about the deal I want to give you in my stores?" he said.

Magnuson had not thought about it at all. Rather than mislead or inconvenience Scarponi any further, he said, "I don't do any investing myself. Not with friends, not with strangers. My money either goes to the bank or the boys in the office invest it for me in the market. This was all arranged some time ago. Except for the agency and the apartment I don't own any real estate or business I've ever seen."

This was true. If he and Scarponi had not been friends, he would have had no interest in the deal, legitimate and lucrative as it might prove to be. However, he decided that if Scarponi persisted in his offer, or confessed he was having financial difficulties, he would make arrangements to get the money to him without necessarily securing an interest in the stores. He was afraid for Scarponi; he didn't like his being mixed up in underhanded ways with men like Allegro and Fiore.

But Scarponi could not bring himself to tell Magnuson the truth. Which was that although he had agreed to put up some of the money needed to invade Fiore's territory up in Niles, he did not have that money to invest. In fact, he had lost much money to Fiore gambling, and owed him even more, which he was paying off on a long-term arrangement from his profits in the liquor stores. This meant he was caught in the middle, in danger from either side. He could not have refused to pledge the money to Allegro without showing an ingratitude and faithlessness that might be revenged, or revealing he had squandered his profits in the stores. Allegro would not trust him in the push against Fiore if he learned of the debt, all the more so now that he had already agreed to the plot against Fiore, and the work against the man had already begun. Allegro would suspect he was working on Fiore's side. Fiore, on the other hand, would see the alliance with Allegro in the move against him not only as an act of bad faith that should be punished, but as a declaration that he, Scarponi, would no longer honor the debt. Indeed, since death canceled all debts, and it could be as dangerous to be owed money as to owe it, especially with men as influential as Scarponi, he might even believe that Scarponi was planning to have him killed in any violence that was to follow the confrontation of the two sides. If he could pay off Fiore he would be rid of an immediate and dangerous enemy, along with removing any cause for suspicions in Allegro that he planned a double cross.

Scarponi had advanced his proposition to Magnuson from the position of an old friend, and rather than make some new offer, or revelation, that would undermine this position, he decided to stand by his original offer and explanation to the end. After all, the time factor that had him up against the wall was not known to him exactly, and Magnuson might be approached again in several days, although he held little hope that Magnuson would change his mind.

And so to Magnuson's confused response of disappointment and relief, Scarponi said nothing more. He waited until convinced that Magnuson had nothing more to say, then rose, fumbled his arms into the sleeves of his topcoat, and dropped a suddenly rumpled hat upon his head. Before Magnuson's very eyes the choreography vanished from his motions, even his clothes lost their crease and fashion. He no longer looked like that cosmopolitan man of finance and intrigue he had shown himself to be as recently as last night, but like a bewildered turn-of-the-century immigrant with his atmosphere of organ grinders, monkeys, tin cups. "It's not often an old friend turns down a favor," he said.

But just who was to do the favor, Magnuson wondered, Scarponi or himself? He said, "I'm sorry I'm no businessman. If the boys in the office had listened to me I'd be living today on my social security."

"Some deals go through," Scarponi said. "Some don't. Sometimes you win, sometimes you lose. Sometimes you get paid, sometimes you got to pay up."

"There's a chance you can't raise the money?" Magnuson said, surprised.

In reply, Scarponi would only smile. In that sad smirk was the sly, smug inference of secret knowledge: I know everything, you know nothing. Magnuson could smell the fatalism on the man, that too quick and easy surrender of the will to what was called a destiny. It was destiny that would see the man through or bring him down. He had observed this surrender in himself and at one time or another in almost everyone he had known in the city, which always surprised him, since Chicagoans as a whole gave the impression they were resourceful and aggressive to the point of belligerence. He had even observed it in someone as selfish, irresponsible, and youthful as his son, who had said, in response to his father's advice that he go on to graduate school or join the reserves before they drafted him into the army, "I might as well get it over now as later." He had been, as was Scarponi now, a victim of this fatalism, this almost Slavic passivity, as though all men were Slavs in the service of Magyars, Huns, or Tartars. It revealed itself in as simple a statement as "You can't fight City Hall," but it went to the nerve center of the spirit. And yet Magnuson acknowledged the good feeling of tragedy in this surrender, as though a man were most a man when beaten and cognizant of the depths of his defeat, as though he could define himself as man only when he reached the limitations of his being, and knew that he was there.

Alone, in the locker room of the club, Magnuson felt as if the soot and shadows of the Loop had fouled his flesh. He decided to take a sauna, a bath he had taken only once before. He wanted his flesh opened and the foulness in him sweated out through his pores, for he wanted to believe his foulness was of the flesh and not the soul. He stripped naked and in his Korean clogs clacked across the tile floor to the shower room, where he lathered up and rinsed, his face in the full force of the heavy spray. But before he entered the bath he went in search of an attendant with a birch whisk. Whisking was an experience he had seen other men have but had not had himself. He knew it was part of the ritual connected with the sauna, and he wanted now, more than anything, cleanliness and order. In a narrow aisle between the green metal lockers he encountered the towel attendant, a stocky Negro in a white T-shirt and baseball cap with a pile of soiled towels draped over an arm and, having just whisked a man, a birch whisk in his hand.

"Can you work me over with that?" Magnuson said.

"Sure can," the attendant said, laughing.

"Good," Magnuson said. "I want to be beaten."

The man's thick lips made a pout that pushed his mustache up against his nose. "Beaten?" he said, suspiciously. "We don't call it beating, we call it whisking. You don't want to call it beating."

"I don't care what the hell you call it," Magnuson said, covering up his own ignorance of the term and reacting to the man's tone of catechism. "I said I want to get beaten."

The attendant looked from the birch whisk to the large naked man with his white flesh reddened by the shower and the massive flabby rolls of muscles on his chest and shoulders, and back to the whisk again, which he shook in his hand, rattling the leaves. He had the sick, disillusioned look of a man whose occupation had been called for the first time into some moral question. "What are you talking about, man?" he said, throwing the towels across the bench and slapping a locker door back and forth against its frame. "I ain't beating anybody. I don't do that kind of thing!" He was shouting and pacing in a circle in the small space between the lockers, his hands on his hips. The birch whisk had been thrown to the floor and was now kicked beneath a locker.

In response to the noise, Tony, one of the masseurs, came running down the aisle, drying his hands on a handkerchief-sized towel. He was a former lightweight boxer and had the impeded speech and disarrayed features of his profession, with numerous scars on his face that looked like silver minnows crushed into his skin. Seeing the anger in the two shouting men and the tension in their muscles, he did not hesitate to step between them. To Magnuson's surprise he seemed to restrain him more than the attendant.

"I ain't going to beat this man, Tony," the attendant kept saying. "That isn't what this business is all about. You tell this man it isn't any beating."

"Why don't you wait for Jimmy to come back, Mr. Magnuson?" Tony said. His palms were in front of Magnuson's chest. "He's on his coffee break. He does the whisking regularly and Louis here only fills in when he's off."

Magnuson, recollecting the slim physique of Jimmy, the other masseur and a former jockey, studied the weight and definition in Louis's shoulders, triceps, biceps, and the upthrust of veins in his forearms and wrists. "No," he said. "I want this guy to do it."

So Magnuson went into the shower room, where he sat on a bench and received, according to his wishes, a whisking at the hands of the muscular black man, whose blows were either too heavy or too light, depending on which mood mastered him at the moment, the defense of his profession or his anger at Magnuson. He whisked Magnuson first on the shoulders, chest, and back, then on his arms and legs, and finally on the soles of his feet. There were moments when Magnuson wished it were not birch leaves on his flesh but leather, and he restrained himself when the blows were light from shouting "Harder!" And when Magnuson, rosy and glistening, headed for the sauna bath, Louis, his head hung and staring after him from the corners of his black eyes, said quietly, a sinister apology in his voice, "Don't you ever call it beating again."

Inside the bath Magnuson climbed immediately to the top platform where he lay on his back on the warm slippery wood, his mouth and nose only inches from the ceiling. He pulled the string that dumped a pan of water on the hot stones; they steamed, hissed, and only seconds later he felt the suffocating wave of heat. Frightened by the shudder of his heart and the apparent inactivity of his lungs he climbed down to the lowest platform, filled an oaken bucket with cold water from a hose, threw a towel in it, and slapped the towel around his face, breathing in the cooler air. He pulled the string again, and as soon as he felt the wave of heat, pulled it again, and again, until there was one incessant wave of dry, withering heat accompanied by the shouts of protests from the other bathers, one of whom, cursing, stomped out through the heavy door.

Now he turned the cold water from the hose upon his body and sat back, the heavy soaking towel plastered across his face. Who, he wondered, could have sent him that slanderous document entitled "The Detective Stands Accused"? Someone who held a grudge against him—but who? And for what reason? Was it someone he had made a report on in his detective days? Someone he had testified against way back in his police days? Some disgruntled Magnuson Man he had never met but O'Bannon had fired? Some citizen who had had a run-in with a Magnuson Man at a hockey match or football game? And why so elaborate a letter?

But perhaps the intention of the letter was not malicious, and only seemed so to Magnuson because of his own ill-humor, a condition its author might not have known existed. Maybe it was a practical joke. Intended to make him laugh at its absurdity and play the game of guessing the identity of its author.

His young partners, Shannon and O'Bannon? Both were lawyers, both wrote well. But O'Bannon was too busy and too mundane to have taken either the time or the pleasure to compose it. He was also an accountant, a manager, a man of computation, and if he had a sense of humor he was most likely to reveal it not in words but in a lengthy and detailed cost sheet laid without comment on Magnuson's desk showing that the company in the past fiscal year had lost a million dollars. Shannon was another sort entirely. Although tall and fair there was something of the leprechaun about him, and he did have a good-natured irreverence for age and authority. He was witty, and loved to write and especially to talk, but his humor was more of the flesh than of the mind. If he were behind a joke, Magnuson would expect a secretary to enter his office not to deliver any anonymous letter in the morning mail but only to reveal that apart from horn-rimmed glasses, high heels, and dictation pad she was completely naked.

Farquarson could have written it! Farquarson had the eccentricity and talent and mischievousness to have written it. That would explain the invitation to his house tonight, the plea for help in some mysterious matter a ruse to get him there and observe first hand the reaction to his prank. Although Farquarson was famous for being a kind of collegiate practical joker who had not outgrown his sense of humor in middle age, Magnuson knew of his playfulness primarily through the stories he had heard about Farquarson and Thorsen, his gardener, that old Norwegian who in his long life had been a master carpenter, sailor, fisherman, streetcar conductor, farm hand, iron miner, and who knew what else, and spent the time he was not employed on the skid rows of the world, including that of Chicago. This was knowledge Magnuson had gathered years ago while investigating Thorsen for Farquarson, a routine Farquarson demanded for all his employees and even sometimes for his friends. Apparently Farquarson had a strange antagonism and respect for his gardener, as though he could not understand this man who came from a foreign country and worked for a living with his hands, yet wanted to, but had no way to communicate his interest except by the peculiar language of his pranks. Months passed, Magnuson suspected, without their so much as speaking, and yet Thorsen, he had heard, was Farquarson's favorite topic of conversation among his friends, where he spoke of him in terms of reverence and exaggeration.

Magnuson could recall the fragments of half a hundred anecdotes. Farquarson suspicious that Thorsen was taking women in the carriage house and in the bushes on the grounds at night ("Young babes, too," he had said, "with that old fart." And winking and warning Thorsen, "I have my eye on you.") Something about mixing up the seeds in Thorsen's seed packets so that flowers grew where supposedly vegetables were sown, and hoes that would fly off their handles with the first hack, and sprinklers that came on mysteriously exactly where Thorsen happened to be working. And someone telling about a competition in vegetable growing that Farquarson waged with Thorsen, each having his own section of the garden, and the sabotage they waged upon each other's plants and soil until Thorsen protected his with chicken wire. If Farquarson could be believed, which wasn't likely, Thorsen not only retaliated but often instigated the pranks. His favorite complaint against him was for the flower bed he had made in the design of the Swiss flag, a cross of red flowers inside a field of white. He was very disappointed in Thorsen for having done this, he had complained in all seriousness, since passengers in an airplane might look down and mistake a gentleman's estate for a hospital.

Magnuson resoaked the towel and threw it back upon his head. No doubt but that Farquarson was capable of sending an anonymous document. But he could not guess why that playfulness should be directed at himself. He also doubted that a man as ill as Farquarson would have the energy or sense of humor to perpetrate such a prank. But if not Farquarson—who?

He left the bath and was about to take a cold shower when he saw the vacant swimming pool. He actually ran and dived into it, clumsily, and the icy emerald-colored water splashed without sensation against his flesh. He swam a length breaststroke, and saw his movements as graceful, fishlike. He could believe he was a boy and in Lake Michigan, swimming in that green water several miles from shore around the water cribs and seeing as he rose out of a trough to the top of a swell the sailboat he had dived from pulling silently away, and then the sails flapping as it tacked. He was swimming a second length when he spotted Tony, the masseur, running alongside the pool and shouting at him, "Watch the heart!" He finished the length and swam another. When he lifted himself from the pool he thought the water ran from his flesh as though from marble. Tony handed him a towel. "You got to watch the heart," he said. "Your skin don't feel the shock but your heart does. You hit that water after the sauna and it's a terrific load on the heart. Especially for a man your age."

In the massage room Tony gave him a sheet in which to wrap

himself. He felt like an old Roman in a toga, a senator, a member of the democratic aristocracy of the city, luxuriating in the restoring waters of the spa. He lay down on the bare mattress of a bed. He felt at once exhausted and refreshed, satisfied and aroused. He had just accomplished great labors and was prepared to accomplish others. He had a wonderful thirst and wanted to drink a pitcher of beer in one draught from the pitcher. His own skin felt more sensual against the crisp sheet than that of any woman his hands had touched. Equally it felt like porcelain. He seemed to fall asleep, awake, and sleep again with his sleep as ecstatic as his wakefulness and with no apparent difference in consciousness between the two. He was aware of the oil of wintergreen, the slapping of flesh, the distant happy conversations of the masseurs and the men who lay upon their tables. He could not move. He had never known his body to be so much at rest. Nor his mind. His body seemed to merge with mind and soul. He thought the condition must be of the womb or grave. Nothing he had seen of life could equal it. He could relax, and forgive himself for doing so, as though he were drugged and had no choice. The sheet was his placenta. Or his shroud. He was in the bag of waters. Or the working earth. He was dead. Or unborn.

Then he saw Schneider. At the head of half a dozen men barging into the locker room like a club of athletes returning victoriously from the field. They were soaked with sweat, in sweatclothes. The bare-chested Schneider snapped his sweatshirt at Tony's backside, then playfully pounded a naked man on a massage table with his fists. The man laughed, obviously pleased to be paid this public attention by a man as powerful and popular as Schneider, called him "Fritzi," and pleaded with him to stop. Tony, head bobbing, was pretending to jab Schneider away. Men beneath the sheets rose on their elbows and smiled.

By now the horseplay had spread through the men and become a rough, good-natured game of goosing. Grimacing, grunting, and whooping men received the open hand in the crotch from behind, the cupped hand in the crotch from the front. Stooped over and with their knees together and turned girlishly to one side, they grappled with one hand while guarding their genitals with the other. The grappling led to bear hugs and headlocks. Fists pounded upper biceps, knuckles rubbed the top of crew cut skulls, sweatshirts were seized at the nipples and twisted to leave nobs in the cloth that suggested large nipples on the men who wore them, towels were snapped at buttocks and genitals. Men were slammed against the lockers, on top of the massage tables. A muscular, curly-haired youth in a University of Illinois athletic sweatshirt, the sleeves of which had been roughly cut off at the shoulders, who had stayed close to Schneider, basking in his boss's popularity, was now playfully attacked by an older man. Shoved against Magnuson's bed, he landed on Magnuson's thigh, where he was momentarily pinned beneath the weight of his opponent. Magnuson elbowed him in the kidneys as hard as he could. The boy stood grimacing and holding his side, uncertain whether he had received the unfair blow from his companion or the red-faced, white-haired man glaring at him from the bed.

Meanwhile Schneider and Magnuson caught each other's eyes. No nod, word, or wave of hand passed between them. Even though Schneider had been the guest of Magnuson just last night in his own apartment, had even been partners in a game of pinochle, they merely looked, acknowledged, and looked away. It was an acknowledgment that no real friendship existed between them and that it would be artificial by even so small a gesture as a greeting to pretend that this was not so.

Later when Magnuson was shaved and dressed he rode the elevator down to the underground parking lot beneath the building. The club's garage was part of a larger and public parking facility beneath Michigan Avenue and Grant Park, a low-ceilinged concrete cave supported by fat concrete pillars, where cars were parked in narrow aisles marked by green and red lights.

In the office of the garage, a brightly lit glass booth, Rosenberg, the manager, sprawled across his desk and stared dreamily out upon the rows and rows of gleaming expensive cars parked beneath the dim fluorescent lights as though he heard music in the echoes of slamming car doors, squealing tires, and horns. He was stocky and tough, a cigar smoker with a fat face and nose and thick lips who looked and acted like an aging, balding, out-of-shape Italian boxer. He never wore anything but sweatshirts, baggy pants, and a cab driver's cap. "It's not ready," he said. "Sorry." But when the disappointed and angered Magnuson continued to stare at him with his hands in the pockets of his overcoat, he said, "We been busy. Smithy's been working on your car three days in a row already and he's even staying late tonight to get it done. Boy, do some guys rate around here. Tomorrow he goes on vacation and what the hell do I do with no mechanic and all the work that's been piling up since he's been working on your car?"

Magnuson said coldly, "You told me that car would be ready by noon."

"No, I'm sorry, Mr. Magnuson. You were to call at noon and see if the car was ready. That's not the same thing. That car was in pretty rough shape. Those kids might as well have totaled it. With what this is going to cost your insurance company you could have bought a new car." Then he approached Magnuson and looked at him slyly. "Those kids would have shit if they'd known it was *your* car. Hey, tell the truth. You going to put your own Men on it?"

Magnuson was surprised. "Why should I? Let the cops handle it. I'm insured. I'd just like to break their spines for causing me this inconvenience."

He wandered outside the office and wondered how he was to get to Lake Forest, rent a car or try to catch a Northwestern train. "Go talk to Smithy," Rosenberg said, following him out. "Maybe he'll have the car sooner than he thought. You know what a perfectionist he is. And you're something of a perfectionist, too, you know, Mr. Magnuson, when it comes to having your cars worked on. And don't think I don't know that Smithy takes special care of you."

Who, Magnuson thought, did he think he was conning? Magnuson was fond of Smithy, respected him, judged him a first-rate mechanic and hard worker, and believed that he did like Magnuson better than the other club members. But if the delay in the repair of his car was avoidable he blamed Rosenberg for putting more favored club members ahead of him on the worksheet.

Two garage attendants, both Negroes, were leaning side by side against the grille of a Lincoln. Usually when they were not parking cars they wandered about with chamois, dusting hoods and headlights. The tall one had a handlebar mustache and wore a yard cap and army fatigues with corporal stripes still on the sleeves. The short one was plump, bald, and probably could have passed for white. Hatless, he wore a grease suit and sunglasses that looked on his large head like the eyes of an insect. Rosenberg had once told Magnuson that this man had been the husband of a Negro fashion model who had been a cover girl for *Ebony* magazine but had run off with a certain well-known Negro comedian and movie star to whom she was now married. Magnuson found this difficult to believe. Although he did agree with Rosenberg that the man's sophisticated speech and polite manners contrasted favorably with those of his fellow attendants.

"How are you this afternoon, Mr. Magnuson?" this ex-husband

of the model said, smiling as soon as he recognized him with a smile Magnuson thought came too quickly and too easily and so broadly it was almost an insipid grin.

"Afternoon, lieutenant," the ex-corporal said. He didn't bother to smile at all but seemed to observe Magnuson with some secret and detached amusement. He had always called Magnuson "lieutenant," and Magnuson wondered what he meant by it. An army officer or a police detective? And in either case why call a man of his age, if he took him for a policeman, "lieutenant" and not "captain," and if he took him for an old soldier, "lieutenant" instead of "colonel"? Was the term meant to flatter him with its implied youthfulness or insult him for the same reason, suggesting sarcastically that he hadn't made much rank in his long life.

"Say, that's too bad about your car, Mr. Magnuson," the ex-husband said. "I hope they catch those kids that did it. You didn't want to use your car tonight, did you?"

Magnuson stared at him and nodded.

"Oh," the ex-husband said, shaking his head. "That's too bad."

"Hey, lieutenant," the ex-corporal said. "Why don't you use your second car?"

The ex-husband beamed. "Say, that's an idea. Why don't you take your Duesenberg, Mr. Magnuson? I've never seen you drive that car since I been here."

"It's not everybody has a Duesenberg," the ex-corporal said.

"It sure isn't," agreed the ex-husband.

Magnuson did have a second car which was, in fact, a Duesenberg. He had purchased it two years ago at an estate auction in Winnetka but had kept its presence a secret from his wife, storing it in a garage on the North Shore and only taking it for an occasional turn around the block. The car was the only extravagance he had ever permitted himself and one of the few secrets he had kept from his wife. For these reasons, along with the possible and legitimate connotation of pretension and the fear of being conspicuous and unique upon the street, he was somewhat ashamed of the car. And ashamed of something else: of the possibility that to him any symbol of his present wealth could not be a contemporary symbol of contemporary manufacture but that of the era of his youth and the depression, when he had keenly felt the insult and degradation of being poor. With his wife dead he had moved the car to the club garage, but refused to drive it except after sleepless nights and then only around and around the blocks of the Loop in the early dawn before the rush hour, when the streets were gray and empty. He had not driven the car for several months. He had almost forgotten that he owned it.

"That Duesenberg's the best car in this garage, lieutenant. Old Smithy will tell you that himself."

"That's right, Mr. Magnuson," the ex-husband said. "I've heard him say so. It's the best-running car here. Better than those Lincolns, Cadillacs, Jaguars, and Mercedes-Benzes."

Magnuson was flattered. But he hesitated to use the car on so long a trip.

"Hey, we going to prove it to you, lieutenant." Here the ex-corporal outlined a plot whereby Magnuson was to crouch behind a car while the attendants got Smithy to come over and tell them, without knowing Magnuson was listening, that the Duesenberg was the best car in the garage. To Magnuson's surprise this plan appealed to the ex-husband, who encouraged Magnuson to get behind the car. Magnuson had thought he would reject the plan and inform the ex-corporal that a man of Mr. Magnuson's age and standing could not be expected to resort to playing so ridiculous a role. Reluctantly he went behind the car and leaned across the trunk, ducking when the attendants motioned him down.

Immediately pandemonium broke out upon the floor. The attendants' high-pitched and apparently foul-mouthed shouts at Smithy who, far down the aisle, stuck his head out from Magnuson's recently wrecked car and answered with his own angry, soprano-like, hysterical screams. This incited the attendants to shout even louder and more obscenely, waving their arms in a confusion of contradictory signals. This answered by Smithy's shrieks and by the threatening wave of a wrench until, as though finally provoked to fight, he scampered out from beneath the car and came toward them screaming in some unintelligible language made all the more so by the echoes of the garage. His grease suit, unlike the ex-husband's, was greasy, and his dark face, the bushy, curly, graying hair, the bandit-like mustache, and the tuft of hair beneath his lip made him resemble a black man in a Civil War daguerreotype, the bandana at his throat heightening this effect.

The tall ex-corporal put his hands on Smithy's shoulders in an attempt to calm him. "We been having an argument," he said. "Which is the best-running car in this garage?"

Smithy looked from one man to the other as though to him both men were mad. At any time he tended to treat the attendants, who were not skilled workers, as he was, nor hard workers, as he was, with impatience and contempt. "We asked you," the ex-corporal added, "because you're the man should know."

Then the explosion of his boundless energy into a fit of jigs and shouts. "Shit! What is wrong with your heads? Shit! What kind of a game do you think I can play when I got my work to do, asking me stupid shit like that?" To Magnuson it was as if he were watching an elaborate and inscrutable ritual.

"I say Mr. Stromberg's Mercedes-Benz the best goddamn car in this garage," the ex-corporal said, folding his arms and leaning back against the car, turning his head to peer back at Magnuson through the windshield and wink.

"Listen, Smithy," the ex-husband said, "I told this fool the Fields' Chevrolet the best-running car. Now you tell him I'm right."

The ex-corporal said, "No, you don't want to tell him that. You tell him he's full of shit."

"You both full of shit," Smithy said. "Why, you don't know nothing about these cars if you can say damn-fool things like that. Old Magnuson's Duesenberg the best car in this garage."

The attendants greeted this answer with one long hilarious whoop, then shook hands and, squatting somewhat, appeared to perform a little dance in a circle. To Magnuson the reaction was out of proportion to the joke which, in his judgment, was not a joke at all.

Smithy, however, was even more confused than Magnuson. "Get away from me!" he shouted, motioning the attendants off with his hands. "What are you laughing at? Crazy people! I don't want you crazy people around me."

"Hey," the ex-corporal said, laughing. "The lieutenant needs a car tonight because you still working on his car. You tell him to take his Duesenberg if it's so good a car. Tell him it's the best car in the garage."

"What are you talking about? There's no Magnuson here. I don't see no Magnuson here. Man, you tell him that yourself." He started to walk back to the greasepit.

"No, you got to tell the man yourself," the ex-corporal said, grabbing his arm and almost jumping up and down in a rhythmical show of impatience.

"He already told him!" said the ex-husband.

"Hey, come on out, lieutenant," the ex-corporal said.

Foolishly Magnuson had no choice but to reveal to Smithy that he had been a partner to the prank. But Smithy, after his initial surprise at seeing Magnuson, instead of sharing Magnuson's embarrassment or becoming angry at the attendants, as Magnuson thought he should, joined the attendants in their wild easy laughter, pointing a finger at Magnuson and then slapping his brow in disbelief. Are they that simple? Magnuson wondered. Are they that easily amused? What am I being left out of? He was both flattered and annoyed that the black attendants should regard him in so friendly and familiar a manner, for he was fairly certain they did not treat the other club members in this way.

Smithy took Magnuson aside. "If you're serious about taking your Duesenberg, you go ahead," he counseled. "It'd do that car good, you know, to get out on the road. Nothing going to go wrong with that car. But if anything does go wrong—not just with the Duesenberg but with your other car or any car you own, you know, even a flat tire you can't change—you call me at home and I'll come and fix you up and get you home. Don't matter where you are or what time of day or night it is." Magnuson was moved by this generosity. Unconsciously he laid his arm on Smithy's shoulder. "Your other car be ready some time tonight. Tomorrow morning me and the family going on our two-week vacation up in Michigan. In the woods of Michigan. Going to go fishing. Going to be the first on the lake and the first thing in the morning. Just me and my boys. Going to be real nice and peaceful there. No noise, no people. Smell the pine trees. Catch some fish. That's living." Gradually his experiences in the Michigan woods grew beyond his powers of articulation and, as far as Magnuson could tell, he made a series of incomprehensible sounds punctuated by the words "you know."

Now the ex-corporal drove the Duesenberg out of its row and left it beside the office, running. Beneath the overhead fluorescent lighting, the great American automobile. A testament to art and engineering. A symbol of taste and wealth. As though all the beauty and power of the best of the republic had gone into its design and manufacture. The American Alhambra, Parthenon, Chartres. The spoked wheels, the whitewall tires, the spares set into the front fenders, the white canvas convertible top, the high polish of the green metallic body, the chrome bumpers, the horns beneath the large headlights and, most strikingly, the outside manifolds, four to a side, running down through the fenders. The car seemed as long as a city block, with the hood so long that the cab and trunk seemed far back in the perspective. Like a magnificent royal carriage used for coronations. Like a powerful, unworldly steed.

The ex-husband walked ceremoniously around the car dusting it with a chamois and shaking his head in the disbelief of his awe and admiration. Even Rosenberg came out of his office and stood with a cigar in his wide mouth and his hands in the pockets of his baggy trousers so that he looked even more pear-shaped than usual and with a look that said, So that's your solution. See, we look after you after all.

"Sounds real good," Smithy said of the loud engine.

The tall ex-corporal bowed in mock formality and, touching his hand to his yard cap, held the door open for Magnuson. "Your car, sir."

"Have a good time, Mr. Magnuson," the ex-husband said, flicking the dust from his chamois and stuffing it into his pocket.

As Magnuson slid into the close quarters between the leather seat and steering wheel he thought the ex-corporal said beneath his breath as he closed the door, "The phantom."

Then Magnuson had the car down the concrete aisles and between the massive concrete pillars of the underground garage, following the colored lights and the arrows painted on the floor, his head thrust forward to stare out the small glass of the windshield and down the long hood and beyond the gleaming zephyrous emblem on the radiator. Up a curving concrete ramp and catapulted into the late afternoon daylight and onto the busy streets of the city. Roaring for the lake and in less traffic and onto a faster road, leaving the Loop and its skyscrapers behind. A feeling of goggles, leather suits, silk scarves. The excitement of an original and wonderful adventure. A journey that would last far longer than just this single night.

CHAPTER TEN

BEER

A day spent on the road as a salesman for Old Milwaukee Grain Brand Lager Beer takes its toll of Herbert "Buddy" Rotterdam. The tie loosened to relieve the rash on the Adam's apple, the sports jacket draped across the back of the seat, and the dusty wrists of the white shirt rolled up the forearms, the socks sunk into the loafers. And that general cheerlessness he must struggle to overcome, especially in the afternoons. Which comes from all those years of calling in day-light and waiting in the heat and overwhelming oppression of dusty sunbeams slanting through the shut-in darkness of empty taverns, the shabbiness of which is not meant to be seen by day and is dis-guised by night; of perpetually intruding soberly upon the act of cleaning up and clearing out last night's hungover party; of doing business in the air of stale beer and smoke and disinfected urinals and with people who are unnatural at this hour and in this light and whom he meets only as they hover above the keys and trays of their cash registers.

The small two-door sedan suffers, too. The ashtray is overflowing and the seat beside him is cluttered with a clipboard, a briefcase so stuffed with documents it cannot close, and a pile of loose papers, half of which have spilled to the floorboard, his small checkered Alpine hat with its green pheasant feather in the band having failed as a paperweight to hold them down. On the back seat several cardboard stand-up displays of a girl in a one-piece rubbery bathing suit, a bottlecap for a hat worn slantwise on her blond head as she tips up a bottle of Old Milwaukee Grain Brand Lager Beer and swallows half the neck inside her heavily lipsticked mouth.

Rotterdam, whose territory is Lake County, is calling this afternoon in Wauconda. His last stop is Al and Bonny Wenzel's Bang's Lake Inn. There he will complete the profitable sale of a new draught beer system he will thereafter service and supply with beer. Even so he does not look forward to the stop. He does his business with Bonny Wenzel and, like most women who have to deal with salesmen, she is suspicious, hardhearted, hostile, and convinced that anyone other than herself who operates a business, especially a business that sells to other businesses, is a cheat. She not only drives hard bargains, she glares, insults, argues, turns her back and walks away to chat with customers, refusing to answer any of his inquiries. As if he has nothing better to do than stand there waiting on her whim, clicking his ballpoint pen, his hat pushed back on his head. A real peasant! A southern German! Or worse—a southern Pole! In any case a hillbilly! It is testimony to his proficiency in his profession that he can handle her. He has only to be polite, patient, and comical, and finally, if all else fails, to manipulate his hands and shoulders like a Jew, and speak like a Jew, which he, a Jew, has to perform with almost the same feeling of remoteness from his model as he would feel if he caricatured an Italian. This never fails to mollify her, as though in order to complete even the smallest sale he must, like some circus dog, perform as she expects him to. He often wishes he could deal with her husband, Al Wenzel, as big and soft a man as his wife is small and hard. An angelic man—which is what is wrong with him. The Al Wenzels are as bad for business as the Bonny Wenzels are good. He respects Bonny, knows that he profits by her efficiency. Wenzel, bless him, would have the tavern ruined in a month.

He also hopes that old Irish drunk, Scotty Moony (to him all drunks of nasty character, pasty complexion, low threshold of violence and anti-Semitism are Irish), will not be there drunk at the bar as usual. (He cannot abide drunks talking to him.) Rotterdam has heard it rumored that Wenzel used to be a priest, has heard Moony call him "Father," and even witnessed Moony once on his knees before Wenzel as he was playing the organ and asking repeatedly, "Bless me, Father," while Wenzel stared at him with a sick, doglike, and dangerous smile. Moony always greets Rotterdam with the same routine, and it is its repetition almost more than its presumption that infuriates him. "Hello, you goddamn Jew!" he shouts as Rotterdam comes through the door. "No one wants to buy that piss-water you sell for beer!" Speaking in that conspiratorial and almost friendly tone that intimates he can get away with insulting you because he likes you, and you like him, and know that he is a good fellow. The greeting followed by the same old deterministic joke: "I may be a goddamn drunk, but when I wake up tomorrow morning I'll be sober, but you'll still be a goddamn Jew!" Although Rotterdam is thick-skinned enough to ignore the man, or at least to pretend that he ignores him, and even at times to joke with him, he looks forward to his presence as much as he would a horse-whipping.

When he leaves the tavern he plans to hunt up Al Wenzel. At this hour he will most likely be at his barn outside of town. He needs his signature on the contract for the new draught beer system. Also, since he has heard that Wenzel raises goats and sheep, and has heard his own new wife, a young woman of Greek ancestry, speak fondly of her family roasting a whole kid or lamb at Greek Easter, he wants to learn if he might buy a kid or lamb from Wenzel, have him or some local farmer slaughter it, and present it to his bride as a surprise. (Having lived in the city all his life he doesn't think he has seen a kid before.) There is about this the suggestion of ancient feasts, rituals, sacrifices. The Old Testament and the *Iliad*. The re-establishing of traditions. (His parents were both high-school teachers, active socialists, atheists, and Unitarians.) It doesn't matter what traditions so much—Thanksgiving and Christmas too—just so long as they are traditions. Israel and Greece. The best of the Mediterranean worlds in the New World. The histories of people he can respect.

When he leaves Wenzel he will stop at his old apartment in Chicago and move out the last of his belongings. Only a week returned from a honeymoon weekend spent in a downtown hotel and at first-run movies and nightclubs, he would race home tonight, except that his wife's former husband, a big, gregarious fellow by the name of Olson, has visiting privileges this evening with his two daughters for the first time since the marriage. Not that he dislikes Olson. He thinks he is dumb, but agreeable. He expects that Olson will take the girls to his own house, or out for a drive and ice cream. But common sense tells him to be away when Olson calls. He likes his stepdaughters, wants them to like him in return, and hopes to start off right with them. He dreads a scene, a cutting remark directed at him by the girls, or at their mother for having married him, and even worse, dreads that their mother will censure them for his sake.

Besides, he has had experience from the other side, and suspects that Olson would feel more comfortable if he were gone. He too has been divorced, has lived as a bachelor for seven years, has a teen-age son and daughter he rarely sees and for whom he pays considerable support. His first wife has long since remarried, and to a divorced man paying support to children whose mother has also married a divorced man paying child support. Even with the good income Rotterdam earns he would have trouble supporting his new household, considering the support he must pay his own children, if Olson did not contribute to his girls' support. Fortunately for Olson he too married a divorced woman with children her former husband must support. Who does all the complicated bookkeeping, he sometimes wonders. Who keeps all the families sorted out? He would not be surprised to learn he is the brother-in-law of every adult and the stepuncle of every child in the city of Chicago, and that all the children in the city are stepbrothers and stepsisters to each other, all related not by blood or marriage but divorce. Disgraceful. What has happened to the family?

His new wife, Sophie. Petite, delicately boned like a small thin bird. Like Nefertiti. Someday, he promises himself, he will take her on a trip to Greece. The girls, if they want, can come along. The Acropolis, heaps of fluted columns in ruins, the Greek Isles, retsina, ouzo. He has managed to save a bit of money during his bachelor years, and if the beer business continues as it has he can expect an even better income in the years to come.

He does have one immediate fear, however. He has heard rumors that the syndicate has bought the controlling interest in the Old Milwaukee Grain Brewery in Waukesha, Wisconsin. That the front for the purchase is Scarponi Liquor Stores, and that the beer will be promoted in the Scarponi stores. That the real owner is no less than Allegro himself, but that his subordinates will operate the brewery while Allegro himself will be employed, on paper anyway, as sales manager, which means he would be Rotterdam's immediate boss. He doesn't want to embarrass his new wife and daughters and shame himself in his new neighborhood by working for a company or a man that has been publicly stamped with a criminal reputation. And he doesn't want to lose his territory, or have it encroached on, by friends or members of the syndicate. But who knows, maybe business would be even better with new owners. They would have influence with, or even an interest in, certain high-class restaurants and burlesque houses where only one brand of beer is sold for a buck or two a bottle. As long as they did no violence and kept themselves quietly in the background he supposes he could live with them. He might even thrive.

He looks forward to living in his new house, actually Sophie's house ("Your dowry," he is fond of telling Sophie jokingly, a term she applies just as jokingly to her two girls), and originally Olson's house. It is fairly new, built of brick, and in the neighborhood of Oriole Park, so far out on the outskirts of the city it is practically a suburb. All his life he has lived in apartments. To live in a house, much less to own one, is an ambition that has never seriously crossed his mind. He will have to buy himself a set of simple tools, and power tools, and a home owner's handyman manual. Wonders if he should see about building a garage. All his life he has parked his car on the street. He has noticed the house has an aluminum combination door but does not have aluminum combination windows, and he wonders if he should look into that. No copper awning above the door either. And the basement could be finished off into a family room. Knotty pine walls, a bar, a Ping-Pong table (Ping-Pong, bowling, and basketball have always been his sports). The girls' friends will be sure to come to the house for a game of Ping-Pong. And he can play the girls a game now and then himself. (He should take them bowling, too.) And some old furniture, another television set, a second-hand refrigerator. When the girls are older and the boyfriends come to call, with such a stepfather the boyfriends will never lack for beer. He will make out a list of what should be done around the house, what he has to buy, and for how much and from whom, what he can try to do himself, what he must pay to have done, and who will do it for what money. He will entitle the list: Projects.

After living for so long as a selfish and fussy bachelor, he looks forward to the rhythm of the new house and family. The supper hour, the sending of the children off to school, of being sent to work himself in the morning and welcomed home at night, the Sunday morning breakfast which he hopes to establish a tradition of making himself (with the girls' help, if they are willing). He wants to spend his Saturdays puttering about the house. Wants to mow the lawn, watch the grass whirl back through the blades, trim bushes. He has always had a fondness for lilacs and lilies of the valley, and would like to have them growing in the small back yard, along with a small rose bush, and a pear tree, if they are grown in the neighborhood, and he suspects that they aren't. Above all else, he does not want to be conspicuous in such a neighborhood. If the house is landscaped somewhat differently from his neighbors, he does not want that difference to show.

But when the girls are older and require more room and become more conscious of their social status and demand an even better house in an even better neighborhood, and he is more familiar with the upkeep and management of a house, and is making better money and is no longer required to support his own children, perhaps they can buy a larger house with more land out in the suburbs proper. A sprawling brick ranch house with attached garage, in the middle of a large sloping lawn, a clump of trees behind it. He and Sophie will choose the site, have the house built themselves. He knows where to get wholesale materials and afterhour labor at nonunion wages: from his own relatives, Sophie's relatives, his former wife's relatives, and all those connections he has made through his own business: bartenders also in the building trades and tavernkeepers with an interest in building supplies, and all those friends of the bartenders and tavernkeepers they can send his way. He would like to have a hand in designing the landscaping himself, visit a suburban nursery and select the evergreen shrubs for the foundation plantings and the lawn of creeping bent.

He also wants to plan the family vacations he hopes they will take by car. Out West, up North. He hasn't fished since he was a boy and has never held a gun, but he thinks he would like to go fishing and hunting, wants to read up on and acquire the equipment and gadgetry necessary for those sports. Maybe he can take the new family for a weekend of fishing in Wisconsin yet this spring. He feels that the secret and happy world of the continent is opening up before him.

At Al and Bonny Wenzel's Bang's Lake Inn, Bonny Wenzel sets aside in a tray of the cash register the cash for Rotterdam when he calls, then ties a red babushka around her yellow hair and goes outdoors in sunlight and breeze to sweep off the tavern steps and keep a watchful eye on a beer truck unloading cases and kegs of beer. She yells at the driver, pointing with her broom. She likes the life of tavernkeeper, and revels in its various roles. Likes the nightly and even the daily rhythm of the tavern. Despite the long hours of tavernkeeping, she has always associated it with jokes, music, games, laughter, escape, and fun. Likes the low, crude humor of men and women of her own caste and turn of mind for whom the frequent attendance at a tavern is in the rhythm of their lives. Even as a small girl she liked to be taken by her parents to a tavern, to be around tables where beer was drunk, and make believe that she would some-day serve beer in a tavern that she owned. Something mysterious, even religious, to her about the business of this beer. Whiskey, wine, other spirits, do not attract her in the same way, and never have. Not that she drinks much beer: a glass of draught at best an evening. But she likes to draw it from the tap, wipe the head, set the glass down on the coaster, receive the money, make the change, and see the silver remain on the counter around the glasses, for she has always equated beer with money. Like a child playing shopkeeper. Likes to wash and polish schooners and the ten-cent tap and Pilsner glasses, to see and touch their shapes. To this day likes to study the effervescence of beer, the settling of the head. Even the color of the beer fascinates her: like a field of grain. And the color of the bottles: brown and green, like a forest. And the labels: Rhinemaidens, posthorns, wind-mills, medieval towns, fox heads, edelweiss, Jack Falstaff, Canadian Mounties, an Indian in a canoe upon a northern lake, sprigs of barley, clusters of hops. She is obsessed with selling a draught beer that is always fresh and of good quality, the secret of which, she tells those customers who praise her beer, is in keeping the beer hoses that run up from the kegs to the tap scrupulously clean.

She was born of immigrant parents who spoke no English, and was raised deep in the North Side of Chicago where the diagonal avenues as they approach the Loop slice through the checkerboard of streets. She has always despised the city. "You couldn't pay me to go back there," she tells her customers, "even for a visit." Hated the dirt and the noise and shadow of the el and that grayness, as though the streets were always full of dirty melting snow. Hated the sight of brick, especially dirty brick. Hated the concrete beneath her feet, especially dirty concrete. Hated riding on streetcars and els. Hated city schools and city churches and city tenements and city factories and city stores: they were gloomy, unnatural, as wrong as prisons.

Hated the machine and assembly-line work she did as a young girl in the factories, hated the smell of oil and grease, the noises of machinery, the constant clucking of the older women she had to work beside, felt debased by the paycheck, the piece rate, the punch clock, the strawbosses, the foreman, the superintendent, the obscene familiarity shown to her by older white-collar men. Her daydreams were not always of men, their bodies and their money, but of northern lakes and forests, landscapes like those in the Old Country from which her family had come but which she herself had never seen. Dreamed of those pine forests where there is no underbrush and each tree is like its neighbor, tall, almost branchless, and perfectly round. Of long, wide lakes full of fish like perch and pike, with sandy and stony bottoms and reeds rising above the water near the shore, ancient babas picking mushrooms in the forest, bears standing up like men on frozen rivers, miles of willow marshes on wide, meandering rivers, barrels of beer set up in a grove of oaks. She could always make believe she heard whoops, yodels, clarinets, drums, accordions, the stomping of feet. Dreamed of men who were fishermen, woodsmen, hunters, mountaineers. Has always felt a mysterious fondness for bathhouses, rowboats, rafts, docks, anything wooden built for water or the water's edge. She has always linked beer and taverns not just with money but with lakes and forests and the north. Has some vague sense of a tavern inside a giant oak tree in the woods that has a shutter window of bark through which she dispenses mugs of beer and receives her money. Dreams of moving even farther to the north now and away from the encroaching suburbs and city, to where the lakes freeze solid in the winter and the snow stays white and on the ground until the spring. Of operating a tavern on an undeveloped lake in the forest and of living in a large log cabin with a steeply pitched roof and a porch that is a dock going out into the water. She would have made the move years ago, would have gladly sold this Bang's Lake tavern with its hard work and crowds of city people in the summer were it not for the amount of money made each summer and her responsibility to the two men of her life, Wenzel and Farquarson, both of whom wanted, each for his own reason, to stay where he was, and demanded that she be close at hand.

Soon, however, her responsibilities will be reduced by half and she will be free to move away. She knows she can expect to inherit a fortune from Farquarson at his death, which will occur now any day. She anticipates that money with what she sees as honest and justifiable greed. She has always expected money from Farquarson.

It is hers! Rightfully hers! "Mine," she says to herself, a word she says often to herself, and that never fails to make her smile. The deepset eyes in the wide face with its high, sharp cheekbones sparkle with suspicion, shrewdness, and a reckoning of plunder. Still, she will believe the money when she sees the money. The actual amount of that money, however, is beyond her interest and comprehension. She could only think of buying a larger and more expensive tavern in an even better place, or a chain of taverns, although the impersonality of this repels her. She likes to do a day's work herself behind the bar, put on the babushka, get out the broom, match wits with the salesman, likes to look at the beer and touch the glasses and the money, likes to watch her patrons drink and hear them talk, likes to sit on her own stool at the end of the bar before a cup of coffee and a cigarette burning in the ashtray and survey her realm.

She is not a warm woman and does not show her feelings easily except to nag and bitch, but that rarely without some cause. Affection, both the show of it and the need of it, is in her either a weak passion or an admission of weakness. She often frowns, and sometimes manages to smile and even laugh while she maintains that frown. As the years pass she grows hard, physically hard, like a small gymnast obsessed with training. She has lost her husband to the beer she daily serves, and her only child, a son, to the lake she sees daily from her windows but only rarely associates with having taken him. Not that she did not want him when he was alive, only that she did not really miss him when he was dead. He was just another child, like all children impossible to speak with or understand. She found it difficult to think of him as her son, of herself as his mother. She had never wanted children in the first place, and after his death, determined she would have no other. She is her own woman. Has always seen herself related to men by beer and money more than lust or love.

And yet for her sake a man has violated a sacred vow of celibacy and left the priesthood of the Roman Catholic Church to become her husband and fellow tavernkeeper. Another has rejected the tastes and judgments of a lifetime and his upper-class society by taking her as his companion and mistress, and is now, apparently, about to disappoint his family by bequeathing her a major portion of his estate. She has never understood either man. Her most common comments to herself concerning them: "I don't get it. What do they want out of life? They must want something."

In the end she has become, she supposes, a kind of companion and even nursemaid to them both, which is surprising, given her lack of interest in conversation and small allotment of sympathy. Originally she must have seen both men in the figure of a father: Farquarson, who still treats her in good measure like some simple-minded daughter, and Wenzel, whom she must now treat like some simple-minded brother, or even son. She has always tended to see them primarily from the perspective of the tavern: Farquarson the financial backer of the enterprise, Wenzel the lackadaisical employee and silent partner. Fitting that she should have met both men originally in a tavern where she worked as barmaid: the slumming millionaire, the drunken priest. Recalls Farquarson in the gray overcoat and hat and gray hair in the interior of the gray limousine with the black chauffeur in the gray uniform behind the wheel, and looking as though he must be the president of the republic; and Wenzel—Father Wenzel then—the sandy boyish priest in the parish church performing in his ornate and rich vestments the mystery of the Mass, rituals which to her were always somehow magical and pagan, not far removed, if removed at all, from worshipping animals and trees. She cannot understand the depths of Wenzel's unhappiness with her, nor Farquarson's solicitous fascination with her, even worship of her. For herself she guesses she is happy. As though having one ambition and daydream in her life, and having fulfilled it, she needs no other. Almost everything else in her life continues to puzzle her, or to draw a blank. "I don't get it," she tells herself, shaking her head, drawing herself a dime draught and sitting at the bar.

Scotty and Betty Moony are also sitting down before their glasses of beer. But no longer in the Wenzels' tavern but at the kitchen table of the farmhouse they rent from the Wenzels. They cackle and slobber and joke and chuckle above those glasses of that cheap beer they drink that has no head and is the color, almost, of ginger ale. This in contrast to the bad humor they showed only moments earlier when engaged in the exasperating game of guessing where in the house they hid the beer. Twice a month Scotty's veterans disability and union unemployment checks come in the mail, and Betty, the more sober and responsible of the two alcoholics, is permitted by mutual consent to meet the mailman first and pay whatever bills and buy whatever groceries she thinks she has to from the checks. In exchange for this privilege Scotty is given money and allowed to buy a large quantity of beer on which he manages to stay drunk for several days. Much of this beer he hides about the house, afraid not only that Betty will take it away from him but also, and with equally good cause, that she will drink it. She on the other hand hides as much of the beer he brings home as she can manage to sneak away from him. She does this to keep him from drinking excessively all at once and from being sent once more to the county workfarm or the county hospital, depending on whom or what he injures while on his spree, and to space the beer out for a few more days and thereby shorten the number of days of sullenness and meanness that always precede the arrival of the next pair of checks, and, of course, to assure some for herself. But this afternoon, having drunk beer at the tavern through the unexpected generosity of their son, they have returned home wanting more only to discover that neither of them can remember where each hid the last cache of beer. Hardly the first time such a misfortune has occurred. Indeed, it has almost become a ritual, as had, before the reaching of their agreement that Betty should meet the mailman first, the stratagems each waged against the other in order to be the first to meet the mailman on those days the checks were to arrive. Betty turning back the hands of all the clocks inside the house; Scotty locking Betty up inside a closet; Betty hiding Scotty's shoes or clothes; Scotty hiding in the shrubbery down the road and waving down the mailman blocks before he reached the house.

Today the treasure hunt has been conducted thusly. Scotty explores beneath the cushions of the chairs he sits upon, moving from chair to chair as though unable to be comfortable, and then beneath the mattress of the bed he throws himself upon in a pretense of drunken sleep, while Betty looks beneath the furniture, muttering how she is searching for a dropped coin. Scotty makes a casual trip to the attic, carrying up the box of Christmas tree trimmings that has sat for months at the foot of the stairs, which gives Betty a chance to dash into the kitchen and feel about the dark among the bottles in the cupboard beneath the sink. "What are you looking for?" the one asks, yawning. "Nothing," replies the other, stretching. For a while they sit down together at the table and, holding their heads in their hands, try to remember. No luck. Difficult to recall the actions of an earlier drunk, especially when they are presently drunk. In his frustration Moony takes a pistol from his gun collection, the one with which he shoots empty beer cans in his own yard and rats at the town dump on Saturdays, and fires it into the old-fashioned lumpy chairs and sofas of the house, adding to the bullet holes already there and through which the stuffing not only shows but spills. He goes from piece to piece, as though in his bleary angry eyes he sees sitting in them stern and sober parsons, prohibitionists who would uncap his beer and pour it down the drains, until from a sofa erupts a foaming spurt not of blood but of beer. A can that has been stuffed through a hole in the cover and worked down between the springs and stuffing. At last a can discovered wedged behind the refrigerator; in the cellar, two bottles just inside the furnace door; two cans outside beneath the porch, a quart beneath the bathtub, and the bonanza, three quarts in the clothes hamper at the bottom of a wadded pile of dirty clothes. Now overjoyed and spilling sentiment with their beer they raise their little glasses and make a toast to their success, now able to see the humor in the hiding of the beer and the frustrating search to find it. "Little mother," he says. "Pa," says she. Oftentimes great camaraderie between them when they drink, other times they only glower.

They are city people who moved to the country just outside the city a few years ago, living first in trailer parks and then purchasing a home in a vast housing development of matchstick houses, a new and self-contained community in the middle of a prairie that in the few years since its construction has already become a slum. No money down and thirty-year mortgages. Ten-thousand-dollar houses that cost fifteen and, after reckoning the interest, cost fifty. They could not meet the payments and lost the house. Betty still misses her old neighborhood in the city. Thinks of herself as an exile in an alien country. The girls of the old neighborhood are still her only girlfriends, and she talks with them daily on the telephone and goes down to visit them whenever she can. She cannot accustom herself to country water and is always praising the virtue of Chicago water, a jug of which she never fails to bring back with her after a visit there. She misses watching cars and pedestrians moving day and night up and down the streets. Likes to be where something is always going on. Misses most the factory jobs she used to have. She likes to leave the house, keep busy all day, come home at night, and at the end of the week have a small paycheck of her own. After all, some of the bills have to be paid. The best job she ever had was in a new, long, one-story factory of yellow brick that smelled of new plaster and new cement and manufactured the materials for do-it-yourself costume jewelry. All she had to do was push a shopping cart up and down the aisles of the stockroom, filling orders from dimestores around the country with the cellophaned packages of beads, sequins, and glitter stored in the bins. She wore a shiny pink smock and could gossip leisurely with her girlfriends as she met them, as though at a supermarket, checking off their lists as they pushed their shopping carts along the aisles.

Scotty spent his boyhood in a small town in Michigan and is glad to be in the country, such as it is, again. He has been a barber and a carpenter and was equally as rough at either occupation, even worked for a time on that housing development he was later to buy a house in, although he was soon fired for absenteeism and drunkenness. ("I had a hand in putting up this piece of shit," he was fond of saying when he lived in that house, "and now I'm having a hand in running it down.") His sole ambition in life now, or so he says, other than never to be found sober, is to live in a shack, an ambition he appears to be on his way to accomplishing in the manner in which he keeps up the Wenzels' house. "There are shacks and there are shacks," he says to his wife across the kitchen table, having gotten onto his favorite subject, which is an enthusiastic description, definition, and discriminating discussion of the architectures of shacks. As though his wife has never heard a word of it before. "A country shack is best," he says. "Out in a field. Or in the woods. Birch trees. Nothing to pay for. Nothing to fix. Nothing to keep up. No worries, just living. And a roof always over your head. Hot dog! That's the house for me!" He fills another glass with that pale, headless beer, two small glasses of which, taken after he has been reluctantly sober for several days, is enough to make him drunk.

His favorite song is his son Skipper's rendition of "Silver-haired Daddy," Skipper having affectionately altered one line of the lyric from "battle of time" to "bottle of wine," so that the song reads:

In a vine-covered shack in the mountains
Bravely fighting the bottle of wine
Is the dear one who's weathered life's sorrows
Is that silver-haired daddy of mine.

"Hot dog!" he will shout when he hears it, slapping his knees and laughing hilariously. "Bottle of wine! Vine-covered shack! Hey, that's me!" Yells in the direction of his son's downstairs bedroom, "Hey, Skipper, old pal, sing 'Silver-haired Daddy' for your pa."

If Skipper hears him, he ignores him. He is sitting on the corner of his bed and amateurishly chording an eight-dollar guitar and trying to memorize the lyrics printed in a country-and-western music magazine as he mumbles them to melodies he remembers from the radio. He has several quarts of beer hidden in his closet, behind his clothes. Although he has drunk several beers at the Wenzels' tavern, and is in the mood to drink more, it does not occur to him that he could do so. Never in his life has he drunk alone. Soon "the guys," as they call themselves, will begin to gather at his house as they do at the end of every week for an evening of drinking beer, singing hillbilly songs, and listening to hillbilly records, and at that time he will drink more beer, but not before. "The guys" are a combination of old friends from the old neighborhood in the city, newer friends from around Wauconda and from the college in DeKalb where he has been a student, on and off, for two years. They arrive after a week of work or school to debauch in the homey, convivial, and degenerate atmosphere that typifies the Moony home. Carrying brown sacks containing quarts of beer in their arms or lugging a full case of quart bottles against their thighs, they are welcomed with effusion and flattery by the Moonys, who like them for their youth, songs, camaraderie, drunkenness, sentimentality, and, best of all, their beer, which has rescued them from many a drought. "The guys" drink until they vomit, fall asleep, or act like lunatics, at which time they prefer to do so in public, in their cars as they drive down the road, or inside some all-night restaurant.

The muffled, drunken voice of his father breaks in upon his song, demanding and pleading that his son sing his favorite song, accusing him of lacking both love and pity. In response Skipper stops singing entirely, and sets the guitar down carefully on the bed. He is once more in revolt against the chaos of his family and this house and equally against that dull order toward which his own life appears to be heading. He has worked hard afternoons, nights, weekends, and summers since his first year of high school. He has been one of those youths who in all seasons and in all recessions has managed to have a job, and a good job at that. He has to his credit the equivalent of two semesters of college, having gone whenever he could afford it, and has been working this spring to save up enough money to go back next fall. He is brighter than most of the other students, and knows it, and knows they know it, and he is pleased by their surprise at his intelligence, since they know he is more impoverished than most and to them must look, dress, and talk like a hoodlum or rube. He has been studying engineering, a profession he has been drawn to not merely because he has always been good in math but because of the good salary he would command immediately upon graduation, and the security and masculine respect that accompanies the job. But even working in a laboratory or, better yet, outdoors, would demand a rhythm to his life against which he feels it is his natural inclination to rebel. It would still be middle-class, nine to five, and somewhere above him would be a boss. And though he would rebel against his

father and the way in which he lives his life, he has always acknowledged the residence of his father's spirit in him, and appreciates his
father as much as he is ashamed of him. He should not be an engineer. He should be a forest ranger. Or a biologist. In any case living
in the wilderness. Off the land. In the Everglades. In a shack. He is
full of erotic and sentimental dreams. Wants to travel, to pick up and
go. Wants to be in love—a pure and perfect love. But wants no less
to lay a woman, any number of times and number of ways in any
given night. He sets an ashtray full of bottlecaps on his lap, rolls up
the sleeve of his shirt to the bicep, and bends the caps one after the
other between the thumb and index finger of a single hand while he
watches the swelling of the veins along his arm. The bent caps he
flicks with his thumb in the direction of the wastebasket. He is
anxious for night to come, for the company of "the guys" and the
license to drink more beer.

In the red gabled barn below the house Al Wenzel has donned
the bib overalls and duckbilled denim cap that hang on hooks in the
milk room just inside the door, and his great rubber manure-heavy
boots, and administers like the good shepherd of the pastorals and
classics to his herd of goats and flock of sheep. The warm aromas of
straw, hay, manure, grain, milk; barn boards banging, the rustle of
hooves in hay and straw. The leap back through centuries of husbandry. The ritual of the chores that must be done: the daily feeding,
watering, milking. The loss of self in the merging of the self with
those rituals. He has transferred his sense of duty and responsibility
and his love from men to animals. As though he has taken literally
Christ's charge to Simon Peter at the end of the Gospel of St. John.
And his livestock thrives. The animals increase out of hand, pack all
the pens, take up all the milking stalls, are even tethered in the aisles.
And they keep increasing. He will not kill them, nor will he eat them.
Nor will he sell them or give them away to be killed and eaten; in the
past he has donated a few lambs to 4-H clubs but because he suspects
they were sold eventually for slaughtering, he will donate no more.
For the sick and old animals he will spend outrageous veterinarian
fees to keep them alive. And so his livestock multiplies, demanding
of him more time, more work, more feed, more money. The goats'
milk he sells cheaply to a few local customers who have allergies or
ulcers, but the bulk of it he feeds to the kids and lambs and the increasing families of cats that live and breed without interference in
the barn. He grows and cuts his own hay in the fields around the
barn but must buy the grain he feeds to the goats and sheep. The
milk he gets he feeds to fatten the kids and lambs so that they will

grow quickly and healthily and wax fat and breed and produce more kids and lambs to fatten with milk and grain. Impossible cycle!

Housing developments, shopping centers, suburban factories, and even brand-new communities have begun to surround his farm and to make his husbandry a hobby and, with the high taxes on land, an expensive hobby. He dreams of a larger farm, acres of wheat and corn, green pastures, and an even larger barn, heaped to the ridge-pole with hay, and full silos, granaries, corn cribs. With the yield of the land, and the space for storing that yield, increasing year by year, along with the size of the herd and the flock, and the number and size of the barns in which to keep them penned. Dreams of moving someday soon to a large farm in southwestern Wisconsin; receives brochures of abandoned farms for sale which he studies nightly. Dreams also of becoming a hermit and living alone with the animals in a small house and large barn, both of which the goats and sheep will have the run of, and a hundred acres or more of fenced pasture and woodland that, with the grass always cropped short and the timber trimmed of its lower branches, will always resemble a well-kept park.

Dreams this as he stabs the pitchfork into a bale of straw and takes a bottle of warm beer from one of the half dozen cases of bottled beer he has stacked against the wall. Uncaps the bottle on an opener nailed to an upright timber and the cap spins down to a pail set beneath the opener, the caps in it having long since overflowed the sides. He drinks a bottle of beer like a thirsty man a glass of water, and when he takes the brown bottle from his lips it is full of sudsy bubbles he watches break. This uncapping and drinking has become as much a part of the ritual of the barn as throwing hay, and he pauses in his chores to down a bottle of beer as other men might pause to take a sip of water. He believes beer gives him strength, that he, a large man, needs it as a food. He has an insatiable and healthy appetite for beer. "My bodybuilder," he calls it affection-ately, and his body, which is big and well developed, if it is not exactly becoming better developed, is becoming bigger. Thinks he can taste the grain and hops in beer, that he is draining a barley field in a single draught. Thinks it is like eating a bowl of cereal. But he drinks also out of habit, and to be numb and forgetful of all but the rhythms of the barn and the company of goats and sheep. Indeed, his problem as a priest was beer long before it was women. He has a special fondness too for the beer bottles he has emptied in the barn. Cases of them are stacked up to the whitewashed boards and joists

of the ceiling, and he no longer even considers the possibility of returning them to their breweries. To him this corner of the barn with
its sour tavern smell is a storehouse where they naturally belong. He
often stares affectionately down the necks of the twenty-four empty
bottles in an open case, or contemplates almost boastfully the stacks
of cases and receives a special physical pleasure whenever he lifts a
new case upon the stacks.

The sunlight passing through the high window in the eaves and
a trumpet-shaped beam slanting across the space make the barn
reminiscent of a cathedral. He has often thought of moving the organ
from the tavern to the barn, into this titanic space, amid the microscopic dust and seeds and chaff floating up and down within the
beam and before the two long naves of animals. Playing Bach, bouncing up and down and bounding right and left about the keyboards,
stops, and pedals. If only he could play Bach. This is his church, his
congregation. Here he has been able to perform those acts of humility and charity he has often in his lifetime confused with degradation, the pursuit of which he can sometimes believe was the reason
why he left the priesthood and church and married whom he did.
But the common humanity he went into the world to serve, or so he
thought, has been replaced by animals, and the city he hoped to
serve in, by the barn. The ritual has changed. He is goatherd and
shepherd. The world that awaited him outside the church has driven
him inside the barn.

Hush. He is gentle here. Soft-spoken, as though whispering
against a coat of wool, a heap of hay. Or as silent as a mute for hours,
sometimes days. The barn is innocent and full of grace. It is timeless.
He could be in prehistoric times. Linked up with the herdsmen and
farmers of neolithic times. The settlements of Jericho. The Anatolian
plateau. The Swiss lake-dwellers. The Danubian people. The years of
surfeit in the Egypt of the pharaohs.

The empty bottle is dropped into the wooden slot inside the case.
A fresh bottle fitted to the opener, another golden cap flicked to the
full pail below and sliding off to join the thousand others mixed in
with the straw upon the floor. He wanders into a pen and sits down
with the bottle among the lambs. The feeling of a peasant tavern in
medieval times. Hush. He is whispering. The animals are silent. They
must be listening.

On the bottoms of the empty bottles the life and death struggles
of the secret world of strings of yeasts, evil-looking flowers of vine-
gar, other bacteria, furry molds.

CHAPTER ELEVEN

THE MAGNUSON MEN

From his high office in the Magnuson Agency, Kenneth O'Bannon, partner of Magnuson and Shannon, oversees the calling up of this evening's requisition of the Magnuson Men. Clerks consult the rolls, draw up the duty rosters, assemble the platoons on paper. Still other clerks push plastic statuettes of sky blue Magnuson Men around the seating chart of Comiskey Park that is spread out on the table, or else pin sky blue Magnuson Men pennants to the seating charts of the Amphitheater and Coliseum that are hanging on the walls.

In several hundred homes the telephone is ringing; several hundred Magnuson Men are answering that call. Out with the ceremonious uniform, kept under cellophane, of the Magnuson Men. The sky blue trousers with gold stripes down the seams. The starched white shirt. The sky blue tie. The already polished black Oxfords given a final buff with the brush. The sky blue jacket with the gold braid around the shoulder. The white cap with the MM stitched in gold on the peak. The white gloves. A uniform that might easily be mistaken for that of an usher in a Byzantine movie palace or, in the case of a bad fit, of a member of a rural high-school marching band, if it were not immediately identifiable as that of a Magnuson Man by anyone upon the streets.

High-school and college athletes, firemen and policemen moonlighting after or even during hours, men on vacations from their steady jobs, these provide the backbone of the Men. Clean-cut, well-groomed, handsome, athletic, lantern-jawed, in the eyes of his employers this constitutes the ideal Man. At the ballpark on a summer day, white-shirted, with his arms at ease behind his back, he should bring to mind the image of a freshman quarterback, a young Irish cop, a youthful minister of the Mormon church gone out into the world to preach in answer to the call.

Models of service given with authority, they work at all the big events—the hockey matches, ice follies, circuses, baseball games—where they are stationed in the aisles like the posts that support the balconies and domes, and to the crowds they serve, no less dispensable or remarkable.—Your tickets, please.—Box seats. (The glove to the shiny visor.)—Yes, ma'am, this way, please.—Just a minute, sir. May I see your stub? . . . I'm sorry, sir, but these are not your seats, sir. The grandstand is back there.

Have a question? Wonder where you belong? How to get there? Ask the Magnuson Man. It's his job to know.

Imagine for a moment an assembly of Chicagoans, or any other Americans, in a public place without the Magnuson Men, or their equivalent, in attendance in force. Fistfights everywhere; burly bleacher ticket-holders in the box seats; beer bottles hurled at the referees; pennies tossed onto the ice, eggs onto the basketball court; fans leaping onto the field to tackle halfbacks in the clear; crowds streaming in the aisles in search of their seats long after the game has begun, stampeding and trampling each other at the exits long after the game is over; pouring onto the field to tear down the goalposts at half time, or to attack the visiting team if it should take the lead; gatecrashers at political conventions sitting without credentials in the legal delegation's seats, or seizing the microphone and nominating themselves for the highest office in the land. It would be chaos, the shameful end of public order.

But another sort of Magnuson Man also receives his orders from O'Bannon. The Magnuson Industrial Patrol and Armored Car Service.

Their navy blue uniforms resemble those of the city police, except that on their cap and breast are silver shields with the double M. Licensed to carry firearms, they perform as payroll guards or as industrial patrolmen, cruising in unmarked cars past those stores and factories that display on their glass doors the shield-shaped sticker with the double M that bears this warning: *This business protected by the Magnuson Men.*

At a time in history when the public police forces are inefficient and inadequate, and the officers themselves demoralized and overworked, and precisely when crimes of violence are on the rise, small wonder that the Magnuson Men are recognized by the business community, the police force, and private citizens alike as providing a service that meets a public need. Imagine the disorder without the deterrent of the Men. Our instincts for lawlessness even closer to the surface than they were before. Armed robberies, car thefts, sidewalk rapes, kidnappings, all committed with impunity, in any neighborhood, at any time of night or day. No safe transportation of monies and valuables, no safe streets or sidewalks, no home safe from the brazen attack of bullies. Imagine the police during such an awful wave of crime. As they risk their lives to investigate a crime in progress a radio call summons them with drawn revolvers to the scene of another and far more violent crime in progress several blocks away, and as they apologetically abandon the site of the first crime and its victims in order to investigate the second crime, still another call summons them to still another crime in progress, even more violent than the second, so that in the end they stand helpless, listening to the reports and orders on the radio and the screams and pleas for help from victims, stopping no one, deterring no one, protecting no one, solving nothing, uncertain which way to turn.

But the ranks of the Magnuson Men are not as thin as all of this. How many men among the crowds upon the streets are Magnuson Men who, for one reason or another, did not receive the call tonight? And how many would have served if they had received the call? Who, if he is not now on the rolls of the Magnuson Men, has served them in the past and, if the time were right, would serve again? Who has yet to serve but is willing to serve, if the call should come? The answers would make an army a dozen city blocks long.

The commander-in-chief of this mighty force, Magnuson himself, has set off on his own errand, having received his own private call. He is in his Duesenberg, motoring up the Outer Drive. The halo of late afternoon sunlight glitters and gilds an outline above the rooftops of the city to the west. The breeze of the lake smells as though it has blown across snow melting on a field of grass. He feels alive, self-confident, sensual. He chides himself for having shut himself up so long indoors with his depression. Why, he deliberately nursed it, there is no other explanation. Merely a drive in bracing weather behind the wheel of the Duesenberg to the home of a friend on professional business is enough to dispel the months of gloom. His car is noticed and admired. From the drivers and passengers of other cars he elicits stares and comments he cannot hear. Sports cars salute him by flashing their beams. Self-consciously he waves back. Everyone on the road seems satisfied and happy and to wish each other well. As though they are not commuting to their jobs but are on a holiday, on the road only to enjoy the city and the drive.

He drives between parks with footpaths, winding roads, and green lagoons. Past blocks of fashionable high-rise apartment houses in a variety of architectural styles that have about them a quality bespeaking wealth and something European, like a row of embassies. They overlook the parks, the Outer Drive, and lake.

Then the North Shore suburbs, the neo-Gothic buildings of Northwestern University, and the beautiful, well-groomed and expensively tailored co-eds who wait to cross Sheridan Road. Mile after mile and suburb after suburb of large landscaped homes and large estates, many showing an influence that is English. Wealth on both sides of the road, and the lake, which he continues to catch glimpses of, just beyond the houses on his right. He is restored by this sight and sense of wealth, and of beauty, so much of it. Grand, like the Duesenberg. He can make himself believe that what he sees is not just a part of the world, and a small part, but that it is the whole world, can believe that these homes and grounds, apartment houses and parks, and the good taste and wealth that lie behind them, extend across not just the city but the continent, making a single garden of that continent. As though the whole nation is living on the shore of a clear freshwater lake of illimitable waters that restores the spirit, and there are no mills, factories, junkyards, shoddy housing developments, or slums. Or if there are, that they will not exist for long. The amount of imagination, labor, materials, and wealth that has gone into the building of just these grand portions of the city and the suburbs along the lakefront that he is passing through, and that in only the past sixty years, staggers his imagination. And to have done it so well, too. "Grand" is the word for it. And so is "good." Why, anything at all is possible! He suspects that everything is, in one way or another, and in the end certainly, and if looked at in the right light, always good. He can believe in the rightness of progress, that in the long run anything that men did, even in their own preferment, was good for the city, the republic, the planet even. Mistakes would be made, surely, but they were predictable, forgivable, and in the long run would only cause small delays. A step backward here and there, to be sure—corruption, pollution, ugliness, whatever—but the direction in that long run again was always forward and therefore good. A direction that injured and embittered some men along the way but in the end benefitted mankind as a whole. That was the difference. And despite the defects and the drawbacks and the defeats, and that bitterness they caused, the democracy was working in the right way after all. Someday no poverty, no slums, no dirty jobs, no ugliness, no unhappiness. The grand creations of man imposed upon the good earth. The whole nation a garden, or at the very least soon to be a garden, given its potential in manpower and resources to be grand and good.

For the first time in many years he feels as one with the life force of this earth—water, wind, greenery, soil, none of it is foreign to him, or outside of himself. And feels equally as one with the brick and concrete and the several million lives that comprise this immense midwestern city. Feels as one with this spring light that is in the air and with the breeze that touches his flesh and with these energetic people smiling at him and waving from their cars. He is overcome with waves of an optimism that is strangely sensual. He is close to love, close to satisfaction. Maybe he is one of those necessary and inconsequential casualties of this world, but there is more to the business of this life than just himself and the small allotment of time and space that has been his. He can even believe that he has contributed in some small way to the direction of this city, the nation, the race of man; contributed to this progress, this growth, this potential to be grand and good. As much as the thousands of bricklayers who laid the bricks in those grand houses and apartment buildings. Despite appearances and even feelings to the contrary, his life has been right. In the long run it has been a wonderful adventure. He is a fool and an ingrate not to recognize what he has done in life, what he has had. Besides, if he has complaints, who is to blame but himself? Hasn't he been the pilot of his life just as, at this moment, he is the pilot of the Duesenberg? Men will make of themselves what they will. He wants to give thanksgiving for this sense of harmony he feels, for this wonderful order that he has glimpsed at work in the good and grand ways of this good old world.

But at this moment a man is loose within the city who has his own notions of order, his own solution to our problems and, for that matter, to his. He is the commander-in-chief of his own private legions, which, at his direction, impose a law and an order that is no less than death. He walks and rides freely among the citizens, none of whom has any notion of the outrageous images that battle in his head. He wants to grow, and he does grow, expands and stretches until several footsteps will take him across the city and skyscrapers are like toys rising up his calves. The most distant stars are mere light bulbs he can spin in his hand. The sun is as close as an orange on a tree, the moon a lemon. For him a single evening is a century, his own lifetime an eternity. And yet he knows how long an evening really is, how long the longest lifetime can be, how far the stars really are from earth— that is, for ordinary men. Spiritually he can extend himself into every building, into every room, into the life source of every living thing in every corner of the globe; and extend himself timelessly, too, for he is everything that has lived and died, that is now living and will some- day die, that will someday live and someday die. From his dark and lofty heights he repeats his name, "the death-maker," and declares this a time of death. Hears himself step as though in heavy, clanging armor to the sound of kettle drums, like a Japanese war god in a dance. Carries crammed in his pockets as another man might carry gumballs or coins, atomic bombs powerful enough to destroy the planet, which he has only to drop and watch burst at his feet. Has extraordinary incendiary matches that with a flick of his nail can incinerate whole crowds as easily as ants. Stores poison gases in the sacs of his lungs that are discharged on his breath and can suffocate whole city blocks with a puff. Carries plague germs on that breath that can disease and destroy in a matter of hours whatever cities and suburbs he coughs or spits upon. His body is a storehouse full of death.

People on the street he views as small, treacherous, and maneu- vering to surround him. He drops to his knees, or imagines that he does, touches his jaw to the sidewalk, opens his mouth wide, and unrolls his tongue so that it serves as a kind of porch, and the long queues of people crowded before the theaters or at the bus stops and traffic lights walk up that tongue, and down that tongue, passing between his tonsils and tumbling down his pharynx into the caves and convoluted tunnels of his viscera. Sometimes he scoops them up and stuffs them into his mouth as just so many handfuls of popcorn; legs and arms, no thicker than hairs, hang from his wet lips and are wedged between his teeth.

Someone in the city is against him. Someone has dedicated his life, which is not without its influence and power, to destroying him, mind and soul. All men are the servants of his enemy, or potentially his servants. He must be prepared to exterminate all mankind in order to be safe. In defense, and no less in revenge, he demands heaps of corpses at his feet. Wants to be the king of a city, a republic, a world of corpses. The ruler over a graveyard of bones. The survivor of the race. The destroyer and therefore the ruler of the universe.

Meanwhile in Lake Forest, Frazer Farquarson on his deathbed and going nowhere at all returns to where he never was: to the heartbeat and soul of this republic, to frontiers, wilderness, revivalist tents erected in the forest, to that primitive world where there is only good and evil and no shades of bad between, to the common people of the country, brother at last to Indians, immigrants, and slaves. He is, in more ways than one, laid low.

But even in death the old ways die hard. For if he is low he sees himself, if not exactly as the leader of the low, then as the man responsible for their lowness. If the American soul is diseased, his must be not only the worst of the lot but that which corrupts all other souls. He is himself the evil in his house. But like the deadly germs of some contagious plague, that evil will be buried with him in his grave. At his death all will be restored to innocence by the gift of grace. It is the ritual of sacrifice that brings salvation from the ashes. He is the father on the pyre.

And so there is new pride in his new humility, as there must always be in humility, no matter how honestly sought, if sought deliberately. His mind is at that narrow band of sundown at the horizon above the prairies. The immobility of sleep. The timelessness of morphine. The darkness of the coma. The candle-snuffer goes from cell to cell. The deathwatch of the soul.

BOOK TWO

THE MURDERS

CHAPTER TWELVE

THE DARK MISTAKE

By the time Magnuson reached Farquarson's house he had passed over into a gray and indecisive world, more night than day. He was unnerved by the lack of wind and color. He didn't like the garage doors being down, the house unlit, the many curtains drawn across the glass, nor the water dripping from the leaky raingutter all along the eavesdrop. At the front door he had second thoughts, had premonitions that he had been followed, that he was presently being watched, and turned around before he could bring himself to knock. The driveway wound in the light of the unseen sun for what seemed half a mile through shrubbery and hedges before it reached the road. The silence and the motionlessness of the Duesenberg when he had parked it on the wet flags, even the intensity of its polish, made him uneasy. It no longer seemed to be his car but to belong instead to this formal landscape and English-looking mansion.

As though its drive along the North Shore had been a journey home to time and place. The lake—the gray open water he could see above the trees—sounded no louder than someone breathing in his ear. Then he saw the man. Across the lawn at the edge of the woods. With an undiscernible face, pushing a wheelbarrow on which a denim jacket had been thrown. At first he mistook the jacket for a second man, riding for some strange reason in the wheelbarrow; then when he saw those lifeless sleeves dangling over the side, for the body of that man. But it was only a jacket, he told himself, and the man, who else but Thorsen?

A nurse let him in, although she kept him a long time waiting on the threshold, looking at him. He could see no difference in the shading of the dusk he stood in on the threshold and that which she was the guardian of indoors. As though the house were facade only and the door opened only on more outdoors. She had seemed moist, as though she had recently bathed and dressed without toweling. Only the dryness of the crow's-feet around her eyes contradicted this impression.

Then she kept him in the hall while she paced back and forth, debating what to do. "Invited to dinner . . . I can't imagine it. The maids have gone home—the housekeeper does the cooking—but she's in bed with a little cold . . . I was just fixing a casserole for myself . . ." Her lazy, reluctant voice both doubted and reproached him. She was with him and at the same time she was elsewhere, as though just beyond his left shoulder she were looking out the sidelights and watching in the distant landscape the black and white details of a man and woman engaged in pornographic scenes.

Magnuson tapped his hat against his hand. Had Farquarson failed to make arrangements for his visit? Could his business here be so important that it was kept a secret? "Maybe he wanted me to have supper with him in his room," he offered.

She laughed at this. "You don't look like you could stomach a diet of dextrose."

"Then," Magnuson said, "my invitation to dinner must have been a mistake. Suppose I just see your patient and get my dinner on my way home."

"But he's just been given a painkiller," she said. "Even if he was awake he wouldn't be coherent. If your visit was important wouldn't he have told us you were coming?" Magnuson, who was being made to feel he had come at the wrong time to the wrong house to the wrong party, thought his visit might well be more important than he had first believed. But he was disturbed at Farquarson for leaving him to his own resources to gain access first to the house and then to the sickroom. "What's your business with Mr. Farquarson?" Again that contradiction in her, the formal speech while she herself seemed relaxed, sleepy, soft.

But now Magnuson suspected she was uncertain of her right to ask the question and that she had cast herself for the first time in the weaker role. "I'm sorry," he said, "but that's none of your business, is it, lady?"

She almost started. She said, "It's not that I don't believe you, but I've no way of knowing if you've been invited here or not. For all practical purposes I'm here alone in charge of an extremely sick man. In a hospital I wouldn't let you in to see him." But then in a sudden show of friendliness she took his arm and said, "But let's ask Mrs. Owens, the housekeeper. Maybe she knows of your visit." Then she escorted him, still in his lightweight topcoat and with his hat in hand, through several large sitting rooms and down a hall. Ahead were the glib, cheery voices of a man and woman on television. Although there was still enough light left to see by it was nevertheless strange that no lights were on.

Instead of knocking on a door the nurse seized the knob and threw it open, revealing a middle-aged woman lying on a bed. Her head was propped up with pillows and her bathrobe pulled up beyond her knees, a heating pad pressed by her hands to her stomach as she watched a panel show on television. She opened up her mouth and prepared to scream.

"It's just us, Mrs. Owens," the nurse said.

"Us?" Mrs. Owens queried.

"I wanted to know if you'd heard anything about a man being invited to the house for dinner tonight. He says Mr. Farquarson invited him." Magnuson had no wish to peer in at the woman but the hallway ended at a wall on one side of him and the nurse was on the other side boxing him in.

"Nothing was said to me," the housekeeper replied, coughing. She reached out and turned down the volume of the television.

"I don't know what to do," the nurse said.

"Is . . . is he here?" the housekeeper asked, staring directly into the face of Magnuson, who stood behind the nurse in plain view.

"Yes. Do you want to see him?"

"No, no," the housekeeper said hurriedly, watching Magnuson. "Is he . . . is he in the house?"

"Yes," the nurse said, trying unsuccessfully to formally present Magnuson, who resisted, by pushing him in front of her. "He got in."

"Got in?" the housekeeper said, sitting up in bed and crossing her hands before her breasts. "He . . . he's not the man who called . . . on the phone?"

"I don't think so. Do you want me to close the door?"

"Of course I want you to close that door."

"But it's so stuffy in here—don't you want some ventilation? You don't look at all well. You look like you've seen death."

Returning through the house the nurse winked conspiratorially at Magnuson. "She got a cold from walking around the house in her slip." Adding, as though he had expressed disappointment in the woman, "She's not as old as she looks."

Farquarson, it would seem, was far more gravely ill than Magnuson had thought. But if he was disappointed he was also excited. He recalled Farquarson's secretive and frightened behavior on the phone. Everything he had seen and heard inside this house indicated the presence of some mystery and disorder.

Apparently the nurse was giving him what amounted to a tour of the house. He wondered if she were being polite and preoccupying him until he could see Farquarson or if she were deliberately keeping him out of the way—but of what he couldn't say. He also feared for her patient since, as far as he knew, she was rooms if not floors and wings away from the sickroom. Wasn't there a bell the patient might ring that she wouldn't hear? She and the housekeeper, she said, were in the house alone, and the housekeeper was indisposed. She seemed confused. It occurred to him that she looked lost, as though her tour was only a ruse to let her search for a familiar door or room. Somewhere he became conscious of the distant rumble of furniture overhead: drawers pulled out and dropped upon the floor and heavy pieces sliding on rollers back and forth across the floor, like the furniture of a ship's lounge broken free of their chains in a storm. The nurse gave no sign that she heard the noises, remarking instead on a potted plant they were observing in the solarium. "Don't you hear that?" he asked.

"Maybe John is home after all."

"Frazer's nephew?"

She nodded and guided him to still another plant, which they both stooped over and examined.

"Does he usually move pianos?"

"Oh, he isn't moving pianos. There are no pianos upstairs."

"Won't the noise disturb your patient?"

She shook her head and laid her cheek against her hands clasped as though in prayer, indicating evidently that Farquarson was fast asleep.

Magnuson now suspected that the nurse's look and behavior were best explained by her having given herself whatever she had last given Farquarson. Morphine likely. Since she walked and talked with reasonable control and did not seem noticeably sleepy or anxious to be rid of him and off somewhere alone, he reasoned she might have taken the drug several hours ago. He was pleased with this suspicion, for not only did it explain her unusual behavior toward him but also provided him with the power to remove her as an obstacle to his seeing Farquarson. It would also exonerate Farquarson, whom he continued to suspect as the author of that anonymous letter, of having any part in the treatment he had received since entering his house. He was willing to bluff an accusation if he had to, but he wanted proof. That nurses, and even household servants, stationed in private homes with wealthy dying patients helped themselves to their employers' drugs he knew was fairly common. He had himself investigated such cases before, hired by the heirs when they were presented with the medical expenses, although in the case of callous or addicted nurses placebos might be given to the patient in place of drugs. But he needed more immediate evidence than the falsification of records or the failure of those records to match with the medicines purchased and used. He was afraid the nurse had taken a pill and not a shot. But since a shot was usually more effective than a pill—at least in the opinion of the addict—he had reason to hope.

"You can come to the dining room now," the nurse said, taking his arm, "and take potluck although I'm not very hungry. Then, if Mr. Farquarson's rested and awake, you can go up and see him for a minute." They appeared to reach the kitchen through the pantry. It was a spacious, brightly lit, old-fashioned kitchen, and the nurse removed her sweater when she withdrew the casserole from the oven. Magnuson, getting close to her and pretending to smell the hot dish she held on heating pads in her extended arms, saw the numerous small punctures in her upper arm. He could not restrain a smile. He would see Farquarson after all.

The casserole, the nurse explained, dishing out his plate, was made from tuna fish and potato chips, a recipe she had cut out from the newspapers and a favorite of her former husband's. Although Magnuson was no gourmet, preferring steak and potatoes and any other food that was boiled, broiled, or fried and that was bland and reasonably tasteless and full of red blood or starch, he found the casserole disgusting. He was also able to sense if not appreciate the absurdity of the scene: the formal dining room with its Persian rugs, mahogany sideboard and buffet, antique side chairs up against the wainscot, the oval mahogany table and the dozen chairs around, on only two of which the diners sat, the guest still in his topcoat with his hat on his lap in place of a napkin, the hostess a servant of the house really, the pair of them eating a tuna fish and potato chip casserole beneath the crystal chandelier. The absurdity heightened all the more when she lit the row of slender tapers in the silver candlesticks centered on the table.

While Magnuson was pushing the soggy tuna about his plate and examining the pattern of heather that lay beneath, and noting that the nurse was not even sampling the small portion she gave herself, John Cavan came into the room, a suitcase in either hand and a bottle of wine wedged in his armpit. Seeing Magnuson he started to withdraw, then stopped, turning to the nurse for an explanation.

"How are you, John?" Magnuson said, rising, grateful under the circumstances to see him.

But Cavan only nodded, sat down, shook his head at the nurse's indication of the casserole, and poured himself a glass of wine.

"Mr. Magnuson, I take it," the nurse said, "is Mr. Magnuson. I ask because it did cross my mind that he might be the man you said came to see you today."

"Mr. Magnuson isn't Mr. Raincloud," Cavan said. "He's Mr. Magnuson. And no one else."

"We had strange callers in the night and again today," the nurse said. "Mr. Magnuson will understand if I was leery of him."

Magnuson was made uncomfortable by this conversation conducted before his face. Cavan, he concluded, was the victim of a peculiar drunk. He seemed on the brink of both exhaustion and explosion. The wine with which he had apparently attempted to sedate his nervousness appeared to have stimulated him instead, so that he now looked at once nervous, emaciated, dissipated, thoroughly reckless, and wide awake.

"Are you moving out?" the nurse said, indicating the suitcases.

"I might."

"To your old apartment on the Gold Coast?"

"I might."

"I thought you sublet it to a friend?"

"He moved out—last week."

"Why were you moving furniture upstairs?"

"I was gathering my things. I was in a hurry . . ." He was staring at Magnuson's topcoat. "Is it cold in here?"

"Hardly," said the nurse. "I took my sweater off."

"I'm not staying," Magnuson said, fingering the lapels of his coat. "I'm just waiting to see your uncle for a minute."

Cavan said, "He's no uncle of mine."

"Oh, dear," said the nurse. "You've quarreled."

Magnuson, who had been recalling a résumé of Cavan's life, said, "You're studying to be an African expert, aren't you?" He had certain views on the trouble in the Congo which he wanted to express and which he hoped would be substantiated by Cavan.

"I don't know about that," Cavan said. "But I'm more of an African expert than a Cavan expert." While Magnuson wondered, Why must these young people speak in riddles?

"My daughter is in Africa," Magnuson offered. "She joined the U.S. Information Service. I get letters from her quite often. She's doing very well, but she seems to find the natives—the local Africans, I mean . . ."

Here he was interrupted by Cavan's uninterested and perfunctory question: "Whereabouts in Africa?"

"In the Sudan."

"Don't know it," Cavan said. "I'm south of the Sahara."

At first Magnuson took this remark as some slang expression he was unfamiliar with, that meant something like "I'm on cloud nine." But when he reasoned that it might be a reference to Cavan's studies, he said helpfully, "The Sudan is near Ethiopia. Khartoum is the name of the capital city."

"I know very well where the Sudan is," Cavan said curtly. "I meant it's not in my area of study. I only wish I knew where I was." Then he turned to the nurse suddenly and said, "I admit I don't know who I am but just who, little Miss Nightingale, are you?"

For a moment the nurse reacted as though she had been physically attacked. Magnuson observed their faces above the candles. He remembered Cavan as shy, unassuming, and scholarly, and was surprised at the forcefulness with which he now challenged the nurse. Something bizarre was going on between them.

"I," said the nurse, cocking her head and smiling at Cavan as though she wished to kiss him the length of his spine, "am nothing." Her smile became bitter.

"You," Cavan said, "are just a pretty face in a window." He

looked through the wine bottle as though it were a spy glass. For a moment the nurse glanced at Magnuson with embarrassment. "I," Cavan said, "am a bastard."

"You are nasty now," the nurse agreed. "But as a rule you're not so bad."

"I," said Cavan, not to be contradicted a second time, "am a bastard."

Despite the nastiness of the private duel the young man and woman were waging, Magnuson felt excitement and pleasure in their presence. He could not recall when he was last in the intimate company of anyone so young even as the nurse, who he guessed was close to thirty. If only he could redirect their conversation and bring himself within it. He desired to talk about his own children. "You went to college at Northwestern with my son," he said to Cavan. "You used to be pretty good friends if I remember."

"Yes," Cavan said, although his attention was given to the nurse. "What's he doing now?" But again the question was uninterested.

"I got a letter from him just the other day. He writes often, especially about where he's been. It's not all wild times and fun for him. He seems to make a study of every city and country he goes to. Writes it all down, too. He's a good writer. You read one of his letters and you feel you've been there yourself. You see that castle, that sunset in the Alps, those old houses along those crooked streets. He's in Germany now, you know."

"No, I didn't know."

"He likes it over there. Seems to know all the languages. He can write in German and French as well as English. He claims the Europeans, some of them anyway, have an appreciation for art and culture that we don't have over here, although I'll bet they're as money-hungry as the next man. He even claims they have a respect for freedom we don't have—can you believe that? I think that summer he spent in Spain turned his brain to jelly. I can't see leaving America myself, or even Chicago for that matter. You can't convince me that we don't have it better in every way over here. Oh, it's all right to visit Europe, I suppose. His great-grandfather came over here to get away from the old country and here's his great-grandson going back to get away from America, if you can believe him." He laughed at what he thought was the irony of this observation.

"Bruce is your son," Cavan said. "He knows who he is."

"But that's just my point," Magnuson said, warming up and

leaning over the table in the direction of Cavan. "I've always thought this European business was an attempt to discover who he was and to get the irresponsibility out of his system. Once he did that he'd come home and settle down. I want to ask you, do you think that's a fair analysis of the young people you've known who have gone to Europe, and of Bruce especially, since you knew him so well at school?"

Cavan had picked up the wine bottle and was studying the label. "Yes, Germany," he said. "Imported by Herr Scarpman. But you're a self-made man, Mr. Magnuson. What is it like to be poor?"

The question injured Magnuson, especially since his own question had been ignored. He settled back in his chair. "No difference," he said finally. "Maybe it was better then."

"Wrong!" Cavan said. "It's one thing to be poor and then rich, like yourself. But it's something else entirely to be rich and then poor."

"Yes," Magnuson agreed, "that's likely worse."

"I don't know that it is," the nurse said. "If you had a choice it would be better to be rich when you're young and can enjoy it. You can be poor later when you're old, and who cares? You can't do anything with it anyway."

Magnuson was shocked at how cruelly he was cut, far more deeply than he would have thought. He felt locked up in a small room. He did not believe, however, that the nurse had addressed herself to him personally. Rather it was another example of the insensitivity and feeling for the jugular that both the nurse and Cavan had shown and which he did not believe could be entirely excused by their somewhat drunken and drugged conditions. But he pondered why the pricking of that tender spot, his age, should have so deeply wounded him. Had he become entranced with the nurse, with her good looks, youth, and that immediate familiarity, almost brazenness, that had put him off at first—responding to her like the patients she must pretend to protect and coddle? He had tried to be objective in the exchanges between her and Cavan, but he had now to admit that secretly, even to himself, he had been favoring her, and that if their argument became obscene or violent he would tongue-lash Cavan and side with her.

"What would you rather have," Cavan said, "money or a father?"

"That," said the nurse, "is a choice that makes no sense."

"It does to me."

"Then money," the nurse said. "Definitely money. Providing you could figure out some way of being born without the services of a father."

"For you," Cavan said, "money is death."

"Not true. Death is the end of the paychecks."

"All right, dying then. It's money in the bank to you."

"Too often true," the nurse admitted.

"What," Cavan said, "does death look like?"

"This is morbid," the nurse said. Magnuson, believing this to be another reference to the worthlessness of old age, agreed. The two were speaking before him as though he did not exist or was of no consequence, like an aged, senile relative given room and board begrudgingly on the condition he be as quiet and invisible as he would be in his grave.

"I'm serious," Cavan said.

"Death," said the nurse, remembering vaguely the outline of one of Cavan's ebony African masks, "is a black man."

"Which black man?"

"Any black man."

"How black?"

"The blackest. Blue-black. Eggplant."

"Not a black woman?"

"A black man." She shut her eyes as though to concentrate upon the image. "He has shiny white teeth. And shiny white eyes. And a scar across his throat. And another scar across a cheek. And he wears a white suit. With wide lapels. And there are sequins, or something shiny, on the suit. And he tap-dances in shiny black patent leathers across a shiny black marble floor."

"Are you serious?" Cavan said.

"I'm very serious."

Out of the bay windows Magnuson caught the almost imperceptible darkening of daylight, the blackening of the overcast and what seemed to be the reflection of lightning flashes in the west, and heard what he thought must be the distant rumblings of thunder from across the lake, from as far away as Michigan.

The nurse said, "Now it's my turn to ask what death looks like to you?"

"I didn't see it," Cavan said. "I heard it. When I was just a small boy alone at the movies in the middle of the night. The last feature was over and I woke up in my wooden seat in a cold and empty theater and it was clapping. For the end of a B-movie. The only hand-clap. Loud, slow, rhythmical, farcical . . ." Magnuson from three seats away felt the fringes of his chill.

"That's almost poetic," the nurse said, clapping. But she too seemed moved. She turned to Magnuson. "But, Mr. Magnuson, what is death to you?"

Without thinking Magnuson said, "The next man I bump into around the corner."

"What will he do," the nurse said, "this man around the corner?"

"He'll be like a woman," Magnuson said, presenting the nurse with a sad, seductive smile he remembered from his youth. "He'll take my heart in his hands and break it."

"It's not the heart the modern woman wants to break," Cavan said. He rose, corked the bottle and tucked it beneath his arm, picked up his bags.

"I won't go to bed until late," the nurse said, the threat of disappointment in her voice.

Cavan seemed embarrassed at this remark, his shoulders sagged and his eyes glanced to the table, where they remained until it looked as though standing up he had fallen asleep. Finally he said, "Be careful, Mr. Magnuson. Nurse Rhinelander owns a pistol. She'll point it at that heart of yours. For me she'd just as soon put out my eyes."

When he had left the room, Magnuson said, "What did he mean by that?"

"A misunderstanding," the nurse said. "We thought someone was trying to break into the house last night. But it turned out to be only John, who'd lost his key. I had a pistol, naturally." But Magnuson wondered, why naturally?

Presently the nurse surprised him by inviting him to accompany her upstairs to visit Farquarson. He was relieved, for he would have been reluctant to confront her with his knowledge that she had stolen and used drugs, although he would have done it, and would have told her employer, Farquarson, too. She left him in the hallway while she went alone into the sickroom but paused before she reached the bed and waved him in. He had grown fond of this nurse. He did not doubt for a moment that she was wicked and irresponsible and possibly perverse but there was something forlorn about her also, some abject quality indicated physically in the weathered, wrinkled flesh about her eyes. As if her attractiveness and strength, which would have made a lesser woman's way in the world, could not make hers, and were to be wasted instead in secluded houses, stuffy rooms, and the company of dying men. The reason for this waste eluded him, unless it was because she was so thoroughly a woman and yet, perversely, wished, in self-destructive ways, to be a man. He decided he would not apprise Farquarson of her thefts. But since it was dangerous to have so irresponsible a woman caring for so ill a man, he would catch her when he left the house, confront her with what he knew, and as sympathetically as he could demand that she resign, promising if she did so that he would tell no one of her indiscretion.

"He's asleep," she whispered. "But you can wake him."

But he hesitated. In the light that came from the overcast and dusk into the room the patient looked far more wasted than he had previously imagined. Perhaps the nurse's concern about his visit was justified. "Frazer," he whispered.

"Mr. Farquarson," the nurse called from the doorway, melodiously, as though speaking to a child. "Someone is here to see you."

Neither the hand or face or foot or knee, each of which Magnuson by turns studied, moved. "Frazer," he called again, moving his face through that natural and disappearing light toward the graying whiteness of the bedclothes and flesh. Before him, the rigid face, the eyes not quite closed, the lines about the jaw appearing to penetrate the flesh deeply to the bone. The gown motionless upon the chest that was sunken and looked like a basin, capable of holding water. But along the arched, emaciated throat, a slow, weak, erratic heartbeat in an artery. Drool from the corner of the gaping mouth, the lips pressed back against the gums. On the face, an expression of immense disgust.

For a moment he was more disappointed than surprised. Nor moments later did he feel surprise so much as rage. The nurse! Careless! Irresponsible! Criminal! It was one thing for young people today to be lax about their jobs and serve incompetently in an office or a bank—but with human life! To leave a dying man unattended to die alone and even now not recognize what he, a layman, could see immediately—the man was dead! Was she a nurse or an impostor? If a man's own private nurse was indifferent, incompetent, or drugged, whom could he trust? He made as though to shout but paused with his mouth open. The nurse was gone. Only the darkness of the hallway beyond the open door.

A table and a small wide-open safe beside the bed cluttered with stamp catalogues and albums; pages turning as though by some unearthly wind, mounted stamps rising on their hinges, loose stamps saltating across the floor. The open casement windows, the curtains billowing into the room, collapsing against the frame and billowing out again until stiff and parallel to the floor, the rails and top rungs of a ladder projecting above the window sill. Leaning his head out the window and peering down the tiers of wooden rungs to the footprints in the mud of the perennial border at the base of the ladder; the vast lawn still green in the menace of the fading light from the sunset behind the overcast; the wheelbarrow abandoned in the middle of that lawn, the man who had pushed it gone, the jacket that had lain across the box also gone; in the glen beyond the lawn the treetops blowing; across the lake the fragmentary flash of lightning no wider than a wire; a toy black freighter on the horizon and trailing black smoke no larger than that from a dying match; and then the solitary and remote boom of thunder; the gust of wind smelling of electricity and rain; the curtains blowing against his face, wrapping around his body, disengaging and blowing free. The washing of the waves upon the shore like the steady brushing of a cymbal. Toward the driveway and the road, only the breeze flapping in the shrubbery. The quiet. The vacant space. As though in the expectation of disaster everyone had gone indoors or underground.

He withdrew his head. Was he imagining that the failing heartbeat still throbbed in Farquarson's throat, a minute, perhaps, apart? What a fragile and failing line of life! A man died in bits, jerks and pieces, and death took its time in all the diverse components, passageways, and parts. What, and when, was death?

A piece of paper blew along the floor among the running, jumping stamps. He picked it up. A note in Farquarson's handwriting, addressed to no one:

> *If I should meet with foul play Mr. Albert Wenzel of Wauconda has in his possession a letter explaining all.*

He read it again; the words blurred; the paper shook between his fingers. He dropped the note, picked it up, reread it, dropped it once again. "Murder," he said. He repeated it, "Murder." The word was full of blood. He wanted to lean out the window and broadcast the news throughout the silent, deserted landscape, roam through the great house and shout it up the stairwells. "Murder!" A primeval urge to share the knowledge of this evil, to warn and indict all within the power of his voice.

But instead, "Murder," he whispered and tiptoed to the door and locked it, then returned to the bed and gripped by calculation and detachment examined the corpse. The cause of death, he guessed, must be pneumonia. But that was natural. Could the nurse, alone or in concert with the doctor, have allowed the man to die, without treatment, of pneumonia, the "old man's friend," a kind of euthanasia by neglect? No signs of violence were on the body, and someone had left the window open. But he could have been given a fatal overdose of drugs. Something in a hypodermic needle or in the liquid in the bottle that hung above the bed and dripped through a tube to the intravenous needle taped to his forearm and still inserted in his vein. But that could be murder as well as euthanasia. Conceivably he could have been smothered. The pillow felt damp and hot. But other means could have been used and the murderer, if he did exist, and if he had escaped through the open window and down the convenient ladder, could have taken the weapon with him. And if so—and Magnuson thrilled at the possibility—the murderer had stood exactly where he was standing now above the victim, had stood here so recently that he might well have escaped down the ladder when he heard Magnuson and the nurse approach the door. Escaped so hurriedly that he did not even have the time to close the window and remove the ladder, concealing his means of entrance and escape. And although he could attest that the nurse had not been alone with Farquarson since he arrived, she could be an accomplice who had kept him from the sickroom by taking him on that absurd ramble through the house and feeding him that preposterous supper until the victim could be murdered, transforming his inconvenient arrival into her alibi.

On such slim suspicions he did not think he could call the police. He would have been averse to such an action in any case. This was not Chicago but a suburb, and the police up here would be incompetent, ill equipped, untrained, certainly unprepared for the subtlety of such a crime. Besides, he despised the North Shore suburban police, who acted too much like the Gestapo to suit him, and who, like the citizens they served, liked to play the moral overlords to Chicagoans. The Chicago police would show him deference. Up here they would resent him . . . But the nurse would call a doctor for a death certificate. And whether this was murder or euthanasia it was certainly one of those unnatural deaths that would likely be recorded through incompetence or conspiracy as natural . . . He would like to see this Wenzel in Wauconda and get his hands on Farquarson's letter. He could drive to Wauconda, locate and interrogate Wenzel, and drive back, all in less than two hours. But if he tampered with time, pushed back the clock so to speak, he would himself be guilty of a crime. Still, that weak, irrelevant, spasmodic throb of blood along the throat . . . He was perhaps not entirely dead. Who was to say the man was dead? . . . After all, he had found the note. It was his note! The note, he was certain now, was meant for him! Farquarson knew that he was coming. And he might even have been murdered to prevent him from passing on the information he had for Magnuson. For why murder a man who was only days away from death except to keep him quiet? Had Farquarson learned about the nurse's theft and use of drugs? Was that what he wanted Magnuson to investigate? "You, Rhinelander!"

When she came quickly from the room next door, he said, "Look at your patient," adding, "nurse," sarcastically.

Confused by his rage and authority she started for the bed only to be restrained along the way. "No, you don't," he said. "He's dead." He drew the sheet across the face.

She shouted, made a lunge at him. Again he restrained her. With his hands in the pockets of his topcoat he held out the sides of his coat to block her way and keep her from moving around him. She stood still, breathless, confounded.

"It looks like murder," he said. "If it isn't murder, he died of your negligence, lady." He found he relished the power he had to impose the punishment of guilt upon her. His spirit was swelling into some intimidating force of righteousness that had its roots in something far larger than just himself.

The nurse continued to try to get to the body and pull down the sheet. Repeatedly he seized her and threw her back.

Good! he thought. At last she looked convinced of the seriousness of this business, demonstrating by her show of fear that she recognized the moral peril in her position. Her fear aroused him, fed his own sense of authority, and cast him in that familiar and satisfying role of the policeman. "I'm a detective," he said, squinting at her suspiciously and backing her toward the door. "Farquarson had his life threatened—maybe you knew that—he called me to investigate that threat. Maybe you knew that too." He showed her the note discovered on the floor. "This Farquarson's handwriting?"

She nodded.

"What?"

"Yes!"

"Who's this Wenzel?"

"I've mailed letters to Mrs. Wenzel. They've been addressed to a tavern on Bang's Lake."

Wauconda and back in less than two hours, he thought. In his mind he was already crouched down in the darkness behind the wheel of the Duesenberg and speeding down unfamiliar country highways through the night. He knew only too well what actions the law prescribed for him in such circumstances. Into a complicated, sluggish, creaking system of law and order he was to commit himself, the corpse, and all his knowledge of the crime. All his life he had been disciplined and even sworn to serve this system; but he had always secretly believed it was inefficient and corrupt and, in the meting out of justice and the quest for truth, more hindrance than help. In fact he had neither used nor defended its procedures so much as circumvented or nullified them, or tried to. Why submit to evil and imperfect forces when he himself was unencumbered and was convinced, in his own heart, that he was right? He knew damn well what he had seen with his own eyes when to a state's attorney, a judge, a jury, it might only be his word against another man's, as if they could have the power to deny what he knew to be the truth. At this moment he made a decision for the individual— himself—and against the impersonal machinery and professionalism of the state; made a choice for the aesthetic and not the ethical; for the loneliness of his own adventure; and he assumed the responsibilities and potential penalties for having made that choice. He had only to doctor time, deny events—but only temporarily and up to a point. Hadn't he seen order violated daily in its own name by its very guardians—legislators, policemen, lawyers, judges? While in the matter at hand order would not be violated but delayed, and delayed not for reasons of self-interest but for truth, for the result of his bold stroke might be the swift and simple discovery of truth that otherwise might remain forever undiscovered or, at best, obscured. This was a terrible and wonderful moment! Before him was the freedom of an endless landscape, outside of time.

"Listen closely," he said. "We don't have much time. I'm going to find this Wenzel and clear this business up. In the meantime, don't notify anyone of Farquarson's death. We don't want his doctor here because this may turn out to be a case of euthanasia—and that's murder—and the doctor may be involved." But he had already decided that if it was euthanasia, brought about by either natural or unnatural means, he would say nothing and give the body to the doctor and the nurse, allowing them to suppress their complicity in so compassionate a crime. "But if the letter suggests murder I'll stop and call the coroner on my way back. It doesn't matter when he gets here. We've already fixed the time of death within minutes. You wait here in the house until you hear from me. No one gets in this room. If anyone asks for Farquarson you tell them he's asleep. As far as you're concerned I haven't been here, you haven't been here, and Frazer has yet to be discovered dead. Let's say, between us, he's still alive."

But reflected in her blue eyes he thought he could see the image of an old, bearlike man in his topcoat bounding down the stairs and no sooner out the door than a nurse running for a telephone. He pounded the brim of his hat upon his palm and laughed. "Don't do anything foolish," he cautioned. "You could be charged with a crime if you interfere in any way. Even if your patient's death was natural you could be charged with criminal negligence or even manslaughter. I could testify to your negligence." He went up to her and tapped her arm. "I know you've stolen and used your patient's drugs. Farquarson told me. That's why he called me out here tonight, to investigate you. And when I get here he's dead. Suspicious, isn't it?" The fear in the nurse's face he had expected, but not the hatred. For a second he thought he might be bitten. He was amazed and pleased at his power to transform and subjugate so domineering and attractive a woman. She could be made to feel him, and although she might despise his weight, she knew when it was up against her. If she thought he was cruel she had only to break down and prove to him that she felt her guilt to see how he could be sympathetic, merciful, kind. He gazed cruelly into her eyes, and in response she lowered hers and handed him the key.

With that he guided her into the hallway, locked the door behind them, pocketed the key, and bounded down the stairs, his topcoat flying.

As he drove down the driveway he saw a small bonfire behind the potting shed, red fire beneath the black smoke pouring up into the evening light, and leaning on a rake beside it, the smoke of a short pipe rising from his mouth, the gardener Thorsen in his timeless and pacific pose. But then the fire was far behind him and he was winding through the hedgerows and out the gate and then into high gear along the curving street, the Duesenberg seeming to race of its own accord.

CHAPTER THIRTEEN

GANGSTERS

In an earlier time the public golf course of Big Oaks on the north-west outskirts of Chicago must have looked like the rolling, well-kept grounds of an English estate set down in the middle of truck farms and prairie. From the teeing knolls golfers in knickerbockers and diamond argyles could have watched farmers plowing their fields with teams or tractors, or spotted the head of an old man in a slouch hat or old woman in babushka bobbing above the prairie grass and heading down the unseen path toward the distant shack enclosed by a weathered fence, a row of sunflowers, and high, wild-growing shrubs. Later, the farms and prairie were given up to miles of new streets and sidewalks, and the golfers looked out across a city without houses, overgrown sidewalks and wavering lines of tar seal-ing the cracks in the white concrete streets, less like a city that had still to be built than one already destroyed, with only streets and sidewalks, beginning and ending nowhere, remaining. Then, as if overnight, houses were built along those streets and sidewalks, one next to the other, stopping only at the high chainlink fence that was put up to enclose the course. Brick, squat, hip-roofed, and solid, these houses are an indigenous combination of ranch house, Chicago bungalow, and something Slavic. They have small lawns of creeping bent mowed so often and so low they are always brown, no flowers, a pair of small evergreens below the picture window, sometimes another window that resembles a porthole, and a copper awning above the glass storm door on which is the initial of the owner's name in aluminum. Already the city has made plans for Big Oaks's doom. New streets and house lots will be laid out on the greens and fairways, and new houses will be built upon those lots. The fences will come down and the streets that were dead ends will join their other halves across the way.

But tonight in the middle of this checkerboard of new streets and houses, of row upon row of street lights and lighted picture windows, lies the darkened country of the golf course. Fieldmice in the rough, possum in the woods, crayfish in the brook, garden snakes in the fairways, boys in the waterhole, feeling for balls lost on the bottom with their bare toes. Suddenly they hush each other up, their flashlights no longer play upon the water, the water no longer purls against their calves. The sound of a car approaching; headlights on the winding road.

Then a black Cadillac races past the darkened clubhouse and caddyshop and halts not in the middle of a fairway as one might expect but on an abbreviated street of half a dozen old frame houses that could serve any turn-of-the-century street in any midwestern town. A street with street lights and sidewalks in the middle of a golf course, a city block divorced from the city, an early settlement that the city for some reason—graft more than likely—failed to take by public domain. Difficult to happen upon so isolated a block as this. And yet at night it becomes as populated as any other block in this area of the city. Cars, many of them Cadillacs, are parked up and down the single street. A small neon sign in the basement window of the corner house proclaims the name of a tavern: The Hideaway.

The off-duty suburban policeman in sports jacket holds the door of the Cadillac open for the four hundred pounds of Jimmy "The Cod" Fiore in the back seat. The car shakes and rocks, the spring sags until the frames hides the hubcap of the whitewall, which momentarily goes flat, and then as Fiore steps out lurches upward on the rebound with a force that suggests it might turn over. As though passing a teacup, Fiore hands the Pomeranian to the driver. "Let her run around," he says, feeling the dog's ribs. "She don't get much exercise in the city." He is inseparable from the little dog. Just an ordinary man, a passer-by might observe, seeing the huge Fiore walking the Pomeranian on a leash about the city, taking the air with a mouse.

As Fiore waddles into the neon lighting at the sunken tavern door his flesh winks along with the giant diamonds bulging from the platinum bands of his unremovable rings. Inside he squeezes into a booth across from the crowded bar, the radium-like quality of his skin lighting up the varnished recess as much as the dim electric candle on the wall. Immediately the bartender nods, prepares a drink, and brings it personally to the booth. It is packed with ice, bronze-colored, oily, enclosed by those wiener-like fingers weighted with their rings. "The Polack around?"

"Upstairs."

"Here," handing the bartender a two-dollar bill, racetrack money.

The Hideaway is a hangout for a younger crowd, a place where by some unexplained mystery the girls come in search of men, and the men come outnumbering the girls. At the crowded bar across from Fiore sits a pair of night students from the nearby junior college.

"The time of the id is at hand," proclaims the one. A battered leather briefcase suggests he is older and serious about his studies.

"It's the great age of the ego," proclaims the second, who lifts his head and searches the tavern for girls, the conversation for him in part a ruse to disguise that search. There is both compulsion and desperation in his eyes.

"There isn't any ego," says the first. "We're all nigger-crazy. Get rhythm and fuck. Like this colored D.I. I had in the marine corps. 'All I want to do in this man's life,' he used to tell us, 'is the two f's: fuck and fight.' It's all superego and id with no ego in between. When the superego goes—pow!—out comes the id. It's like the Middle Ages all over again."

"But I'm telling you everyone's out for himself today," says the second. "He doesn't give a shit about the country or society or anybody else. Gimme the buck. And every guy wants a dame to go down for him, and why? To satisfy his ego. If the dame turns him down he gets kicked in the ego. If he don't make as much dough as the next guy he gets kicked in the ego. And if he ain't driving a fancy new car because he ain't making the dough he gets kicked in the ego and can't make out with the dames."

"But it's not the ego telling these guys to do it," counters the first. "They want dames because everybody else wants dames, or says they do, and they don't want to be left out. They got to conform. That's the superego. What good would it be for most of these guys if they couldn't tell their buddies about the dames they laid?"

But the second student no longer attends to his friend. Bug-eyed, he smiles lasciviously and stretches his neck, hoping to catch the eye of a girl ordering a drink at the end of the bar.

"The same with money," continues the first. "You want it because everybody else wants it, and because everybody else, if they don't already have it, is out to get it. You don't like some guy making more money than you. You can't conform if you're not making money. Picking up dames and making a fast buck is no different from buying a brick ranch house in a neighborhood around here and settling down with the old lady and kids to nights of bowling and television and evenings of sprinkling the lawn. These kids ain't any different from the people living in those houses . . . It's the superego on top, telling you what to do. If the ego could have its say, it would probably get the hell out of the rat race and go fishing in Wisconsin . . ."

The perplexed and indignant Fiore, having overheard this argument, is thinking, What is it with these kids these days? Don't they talk English no more?

A trapdoor opens in the ceiling behind the bar, and the bartender removes most of the bills from the cash register, steps on a footstool, and passes them up to the dangling hand. Next he passes up a round of grasshoppers, pink ladies, sloe gin fizzes. Now the small tidy head of the owner, Romanski, the long cigarette holder clenched between his teeth, pokes down through the door so that it seems he must be standing on his hands. He catches sight of Fiore and indicates by a nod of his upside-down head that he will soon be down. With that the trapdoor closes. The bartender points his finger at the empty glasses he finds along the bar.

But the men have turned on their stools to face the crowds of girls now coming through the door. College girls in toreador pants and college sweatshirts; who hug the men they know along the bar, reaching up to rub their backs; who want to be treated like pals; who believe in fortunes made by popularity, in popularity determined by personality, which to them is a kind of cheerleader's conviviality and pep. Followed in by office girls in their tight knit suits; who will only nod at their acquaintances and barely smile at their good friends (be assured though that they have already taken in the bar and the measure of its men); who want to be treated like ladies; who believe in fortunes made by good reputations, which means keeping aloof—in gossip anyway—from anything scandalous and low.

Here to greet the girls are junior college men who work part-time and live at home. Ashamed of their poverty and school they imitate the full-time students from the wealthier neighborhoods to the north who are also here, home for the weekend from the state universities and the small private colleges in Indiana and Wisconsin. All wear crewneck sweaters and white bucks or saddleshoes; all brag about fraternities, sports, girls. But whereas the junior college men come several to an older car, the college man drives in the family Cadillac alone.

And construction workers are here, the builders of the very homes that surround Big Oaks. Concrete laborers, foremen at most, they drive their own Cadillacs and pass out business cards that proclaim themselves as independent contractors, owners of mythical companies that bear their names. They sleep at most three hours a night, lug cement forms on their backs the next day for ten, then drink and dance and drive in those Cadillacs from bar to bar until the bars are closed. They complain of slave-driving Russian-German contractors and the ignorant DP laborers with whom they work.

And small-time hoods are here too. Apprentices to the rackets and pretenders to that role. Dressed in pegged pants and pink shirts with Mr. B collars, hair in ducktails and sideburns, they arrive in the early evening and again in the early morning, just before the tavern closes. In that thick Chicago accent where "what do you" becomes "whatcha" and "th" of articles becomes "d," and in all other words "t," they refer to the big names in what they call the syndicate with a familiarity that is fraudulent and an awe that is sincere. Their ascent from stick-ups and burglaries to the safety of the syndicate depends less on their own abilities than it does on the patronage of someone like Fiore, who has only to proclaim with his arm around any one of them, "He's my boy."

In fact Fiore, who delights in the munificence of his power far more than he does its destructiveness, has been eyeing just such a group of hoods. He likes a lean boy with dark hair and Roman nose who appears quick-witted, happy-go-lucky but tough, the take-charge guy of any crowd. Who knows, he might be fun. But Fiore is not here tonight to look for favorites. He is here to cross-examine a punk they call the Tanker, whom he was supposed to meet last night in Bughouse Square but failed to meet, and who, unless he has a good excuse for what happened last night in Bughouse Square, will wake up tomorrow morning, if he wakes up at all, in the rough of a distant hole on the golf course, his body bruised and a bone or two broken.

No doubt about it, a dangerous place this Hideaway. Always the expectation of action, the possibility of change. The chance of encountering old friends and enemies; of making new ones; of meeting someone who will change your life or make your night. The risk of baring yourself as a piece of sex and submitting your small hopes to the market place and, in the case of men, of brawling over a girl and being publicly beaten. A market place with an atmosphere of quick easy money earned with long hours and hard labor instead of skill, of lies that promote the image of the liar, of toughness in place of gentleness, of drinking to kill time and give birth to nerve and to disguise and justify one's presence in the tavern. Of a prevalent philosophy that it is not what you know but who you know, that it is far better to be liked than to be bright; of sex that is equatable with money, popularity, physique; of womanhood defined by marriage, of manhood defined by money, work, and sex.

Romanski is fighting his way through the crowded aisle. Not much above five feet and fussy about his clothes, he is dressed in a navy blue serge suit with wide lapels and shoulders. His black-reddish hair rises in piles of waves that appear to begin almost at his eyebrows and are combed without a part straight back across his head; he has a thin mustache of the same color. Handsome like a middle-class gigolo, he would be adulated by most women at an over-thirties dance and automatically despised by the rest. He carries himself like a ballroom dancer, he polkas like his youngest son, he prefers the company of women to men. Everything about him is pointed: nose, chin, shoulders, shoes, even ears. College students call him Mephistopheles.

At Fiore's booth he says, "Let's get a place in the back. I would have come down sooner but the old lady's got her lady friends over to the house tonight." This is a gathering Romanski enjoys attending, not only the sole charming husband present but the sole husband.

They enter a large room with lumpy armchairs and sofas and a few tables and chairs and a row of booths along one bar enclosing an open floor where only a few couples are dancing. This furniture is an important part of the Hideaway. Romanski, once wearying of fighting cigarette fires in the upholstery and pillows in the small hours of the morning after the bar was closed, removed it all to the garage only to bring it back within the month, along with a few new pieces, and to spend the next year in trying to get his business back. He has also gone on rampages of righteousness and checked the identifications of his customers at the door, not because he has any fear of being fined or losing his license, but because periodically he has become incensed by the idiocy of his youthful patrons and been determined to drive them off or at least thin them out and see them replaced by an older crowd that drinks mixed drinks, where the profit is. However, he has discovered that when some leave, all leave. Nor are they replaced by other patrons, either young or old, and the drinkers residing in the other five houses on this isolated city block are hardly enough to keep him in business. If the boys under twenty-one go, the girls, who can drink legally at eighteen, go, and if the girls go, everybody goes.

Since Fiore has already demonstrated he can sit in a booth without destroying it, Romanski seats him in another, the last in the row and hidden partially by an air-conditioning unit.

Fiore says, "You hear what happened last night at Bughouse Square?"

"I heard that Tanker missed you." Romanski, cigarette holder in his teeth and polished, pointed shoes swinging free of the floor, plays with a matchcover he finds in an ashtray. "Bughouse Square would be an easy place to miss someone." Only after he speaks does he realize that Fiore would not be easy to miss in Comiskey Park. "And that there was some trouble there."

"A guy was killed there," Fiore says. Adding, "Murdered." Afraid of telephones, taverns, and parked cars, he thought his choice of Bughouse Square to rendezvous with Tanker had been superb. Wasn't it a public place close to his apartment where one man can meet another man in private and discuss their most secret affairs? Like making the arrangements with this Tanker to kill Scarponi—*the* Scarponi of the famous liquor stores. So what if they were overheard, doesn't everyone talk crazy talk in Bughouse Square? Besides, there he was merely a local resident giving his dog some grass. How was he to know a man would be murdered there, and no more than thirty yards from where he and the Pomeranian waited in the dark?

Now Fiore leans across the table and lays a thick, ringed finger atop the nervous matchbook in Romanski's hand, pinning it to the table. "Somebody messed things up last night," he says. "Maybe you better tell me who."

"If Tanker screwed it up somehow," Romanski says, "don't blame me. You knew you was taking a chance with one of these punks.

They're no pros. I told you that right off the bat, first thing." A reference to Fiore's cashing an old favor Romanski owes him and hiring the killer of Scarponi from the ranks of the young hoodlums Romanski knows and sometimes finances, so that Allegro and his crowd, who will disapprove of Scarponi's execution, will take it for the work of an amateur punk playing a lone hand, and Fiore, although suspected, will keep his enemies to a minimum, especially after Tanker himself is killed, a final twist to the plot the reluctant and frightened Romanski has only guessed.

Fiore stares at Romanski with those sleepy sly eyes that suggest he will pick your pocket in that last second before he falls asleep. "But before you and me have our little talk, Polack, point out this guy Tanker to me."

"What do you mean," Romanski says, stiffening, "our little talk?"

"I mean how come I didn't see him there?" Fiore says. "How come there was trouble there? How come I was there when the kid I was supposed to meet wasn't there? How come I was there all by myself when there was trouble there? I mean only you and me and this kid knew about the meeting down there. If someone was there who wasn't supposed to be there, maybe it was because someone told him to be there."

Confused, but seeing the either/or of this supposition, Romanski says, "Then Tanker did. But why he'd do it beats me."

"Maybe someone mistook the murdered guy for me?" Fiore says.

Romanski, however, cannot get up the courage to state that this is hardly likely. "Well, you know," he says, the reluctant diplomat, "there's such things as odds, for one thing . . . some things you got to take into account, too . . . Different guys got different physiques— you know what I mean? . . . Some guys are kind of stocky . . . they don't look like no one else . . ."

"This Tanker," Fiore says, changing the subject, "want to get him." It is not a question.

Romanski leans out of the booth and manages to catch the eye of Tanker. Dressed in a thin, cheap, charcoal gray flannel suit with a pink pin collar and suede shoes, he stands on the outskirts of a crowd of hoods and construction workers at the bar, talking to an olive-skinned girl with platinum hair.

Tanker takes the seat next to Romanski as directed and pulls a cigarette out of a freshly opened pack with his mouth, showing off his French cuffs and gray cufflinks inlaid with pink anchors. He wears a coronation tie, gray, with the emblem of a small pink crown.

"I been looking forward to meeting you," Fiore says, taking

Tanker's hand and holding it, so that Tanker feels he has poked his hand into a mound of warm, rising dough. "How come I didn't see you last night, kid?"

"I was there," Tanker says. It is a smoky voice coming from a mouth of crooked, yellow teeth. "Waiting on that park bench like he told me." He points to Romanski. "Only this old queer come over and sat on the same bench next to me. I had to get up and pretend I was walking off. I kept coming back but he was always there."

"What did he do," Fiore says, suddenly interested in this digression, "to make you get up like that?"

"He didn't do nothing."

"Didn't he say anything?"

"Nothing much."

"How come you knew he was queer?"

"If you've seen them," says Tanker, "there's ways of knowing."

"So where did you go when you left the bench?"

He was in the crowd, he tells them, listening to an old man speaking from an orange crate. Finding no Mr. Fiore there he was making his way back to the park bench to see if he was there when a crazy woman with a flashlight found a dead man in the bushes. The place was crawling with cops, and he decided, meeting or no meeting, he had better go home.

"Did you tell anyone you was meeting Mr. Fiore there?" Romanski asks, wishing he were upstairs with the women and charming them with small attentions and courtesies and flatteries and elegant movements of his hands and head and with the witticisms he has accumulated over the years for use in just such company.

"Hell, no," Tanker says.

"You're pretty tough," Fiore says matter-of-factly.

"I don't know," Tanker says in all modesty.

"What do you mean you don't know?"

Tanker shrugs. "Sure, I'm tough."

"You got guts."

"Sure."

"You got balls, too?"

"Hell yes, I got balls," Tanker says, uncertain whether he should be offended or amused.

"That old queer," Fiore says, "did he get his hands on them?"

A confused Tanker is on the verge of an outrage he doubts that he should show. He looks to Romanski to learn, if he can, the definition and the intention of Fiore's tone.

"You didn't let him get your balls!" Fiore says, reaching across the table and clapping him on the shoulder. "Good for you!"

"I'd poke him in the mouth . . ." Tanker says before surrendering to emotions beyond the reach or need of words.

Fiore leans across the table. Even with his arms folded he seems about to surround Tanker as he comes forward. "He didn't play with you or nothing like that?"

"I would have poked him in the mouth," Tanker repeats, trembling.

"Tell the truth," Fiore says, winking and leaning even closer, "how come he sat down next to you?"

"You got me—ask him."

"You don't think he thought you were queer too?"

By now Tanker is trying to pretend that he is ignorant of the insult in all of this; he is even trying to pretend it to himself.

Fiore, meanwhile, is recollecting his own unnerving and perverse encounter in the square. With the discovery of the dead man near the bushes, he had been making for the exit when a man in a raincoat had appeared out of the night, walking toward him in long, lilting strides as though springs were on his feet. Seeing Fiore, he had halted, looked behind him, looked to either side of him, then lowered his head and, holding the raincoat together in both hands, strode toward him even faster than before. In answer, Fiore changed his course, angled to his left, only to see the man angle to his right; angled to his right, only to see the man angle to his left. As the distance between them narrowed, he resigned himself to fate and halted in his tracks. So did the man in the raincoat, not ten feet away. Slowly the man opened up his coat as Fiore, anticipating the drawn revolver, thought, Fiore has been fingered, has been set up, for what else explained the man and his behavior other than that the Polack had betrayed him to Scarponi and Allegro, who had sent their own assassin to the square? He put his hands above his head and dropped the leash, which sent the Pomeranian after the man, barking, dragging the leash. And just before the man went down, tripping first upon the leash and then the dog, Fiore saw first the lapels of the raincoat stretched as far apart as they could go, and then with incredulity and relief the pale naked body of the man highlighted by the dark blocks of body hair, a naked body without calves and feet, ending at the knees, and finally grasped as the man fell down upon the squealing, scrambling dog that his suspenders came around his naked shoulders and down his naked body to where they were attached to the tops of his trouser legs, which—no longer than knee socks—were cleverly cut off at the knees.

But now, wearying of his fun with Tanker, and having failed to learn as much about the subject of Tanker's encounter as he wished, Fiore sighs and seems about to fall asleep. "Okay, kid, glad to meet you," he says. "Maybe we'll talk to you later." With Tanker gone, he says, "This kid don't interest me, but I think he's telling the truth." This does not console Romanski. If Fiore believes that Tanker speaks the truth about what happened in the square, but also that someone still is lying, who is there to blame but him?

"What about this guy found dead in Bughouse Square?" Romanski says. He wonders how far he can trust Fiore in what he says. What if Fiore has used him in a manner and within a plot that is other than the one he intimated was being planned? He gets an inkling of the dread he would feel if Fiore, Scarponi, Allegro, and the police were all arrayed against him in an attempt to kill him, a possibility that does not seem that remote.

"That's what I'd like to know," Fiore says. "It was in the papers this morning. The dead guy was a Polack." He removes a clipping from his pocket and turns on the light. "Joseph Helenowski," he reads. "Ever heard of him?"

Romanski shakes his head.

"I just wondered . . . the name . . ."

Disgusted, Romanski thinks: What's wrong with his head? There's more Poles in Chicago than in Warsaw.

"He must not have been in the rackets," Fiore says. "It says here he just escaped from a mental hospital." He turns off the light and gradually his flesh begins to glow. "If someone is pulling a fast one . . ." He halts in mid-sentence. A couple dancing toward their booth, the boy maneuvering the stumbling drunken girl to a spot he must believe, because it is remote and dark, is also deserted. The girl in a dress of rhinestones and with silver hair, her partner a stocky redheaded boy with a crew cut. Afraid the couple will sit down beside them in the booth the two men retreat across their seats until they touch the wall. Instead the girl is pinned against the edge of the table on which she half sits, her round, firm bottom in the sparkling white dress spilling over the tabletop, so close that either Fiore or Romanski, pressed back into the darkness, could touch it in their hands. Passionate, open-mouthed kissing. The scrape and clack of teeth. They seem close to gagging on each other's tongues. The two men sit in their shocked and even puritanical silence, too embarrassed to reveal themselves, much less to move. Thank God the girl escapes—pulling her partner behind her. Out on the floor they resume their embrace, their dance.

Fiore gives an embarrassed cough. "I can't figure what he's up to," he says, unable to recapture the sinister quality of his previous thoughts and feelings. Adding, "Whoever is pulling a fast one." Adding further, "If someone is pulling a fast one." He pauses. Both men watch with apprehension as the couple once more dances toward their booth. "In the meantime," Fiore continues in a whisper, "give this Tanker fifty bucks and tell him to forget he ever saw me. I can't go through with this thing with Scarponi."

The couple has reached their booth in their stumbling, back-pedaling walk that barely passes as a dance, and Fiore reproaches himself for not having turned on the light, and Romanski himself for not having struck the match he has been holding in his fingers to light the cigarette in his holder. Again that white sparkling bottom pushed against and bulging over the table and that heavy kissing along with much rubbing and rhythmic humping, the girl attempting to reach her legs around the boy, which in her tight almost ankle-length dress is impossible, while the two men in the booth feel the tension in the table as it moves back and forth and even bends beneath their palms. "Let's fuck, let's fuck," the boy whispers in her ear. Adding, "In the car." To the relief of the reluctant and disbelieving witnesses, who have been afraid that she was about to be put down on her back upon the table and that they would confront each other across her body and also his. The girl gasps, breaks free, although reluctantly, and again drags the boy by the hand out onto the floor.

"So it's in my interest to see that Scarponi stays healthy," Fiore says, quickly, as though at any moment he expects them to return.

On the dance floor the couple is approached by a black-haired boy the girl has danced with before. He ignores her partner and takes her by the hand, speaking sharply. She seems repentant and willing to accompany him, but the redhead steps between them and puts his arm around her waist. Someone is shoved. Someone says, "Let's step outside." Which proves not only unnecessary but impossible. No sooner is someone shoved than the bar, dumpy sofas, and booths empty of hoodlums, college students, laborers—who can tell?—and a mob already swinging with its fists at anything before it surges toward the redhead who, with his fists up first to fight and immediately thereafter only to ward off the many blows, disappears as though beneath a wave, leaving only the sight of his attackers hammering and trampling a piece of space.

Romanski is on the sidelines giving orders; the pair of aproned bartenders is in the middle of the fray, sorting out the redhead from the windmilling arms and kicking legs. Unable to rescue him, they simply drag him off while his attackers pursue him across the floor, reaching in between his rescuers and landing still more blows on his head. Bloodied, exhausted, his clothes somehow reduced to shreds, he is shoved out a side door onto a darkened gangway beside the house.

"You must be crazy," one bartender says in disbelief, "to start trouble around here."

But the other bartender congratulates him. He says, "You were lucky you weren't killed."

Outside on the golf course Fiore confronts the surprise of the stars and space, a pocket of country night within the city. He ascends a low knoll and sees beyond the silhouettes of shade trees in clumps the plain of street lights and house lights that are the city, so dense in any direction that as they approach the horizons they become a single smoky glow. He smells grass, acres of grass. Is it new-mown grass he smells? Can he actually smell it growing? The off-duty cop who carries in his pocket the blackjack he was told he should be prepared to use tonight has ranged far out on the grass of a nearby fairway and is whistling for the Pomeranian. Fiore joins him, can hear the small dog panting and bounding out there in the dark, halting suddenly only to bark and bound away. "Princess!" he calls. Bends over, claps his hands awkwardly to call her, incite her, to show his own delight, resembling as he does so a Hindu attempting to bow and clasp his hands in prayer. The dog, tiring, approaches, and he pretends to chase her, which means he lifts a foot and sets it down or feints first with one shoulder, then the other. To humor him the dog dashes away from the direction of that footstep, that shoulder feint, but quickly wearying of so unsporting a game sits down and watches him approach. He does so with his legs spread and his arms outstretched as though to catch the dog if she should try to go around him. "I'll getcha!" he shouts out over the golf course, moving those shoulders, lifting those feet. "Look out! I'm coming to getcha!"

Nothing to do now, he tells himself as he picks up the dog and pets it. Better to leave Romanski alone. An old pro, he knows he won't be hurt if he keeps quiet. Probably best to forget about this Tanker too.

Mother in heaven, what can he do now but wait for the first sign of any repercussions? He is a man who would control, if he could, everything he touches. But this affair has passed out of his hands and into other hands. Whose hands, he does not know. Thank God he is smart enough to recognize he no longer has the power to control its course. For this much he can congratulate himself. In such admissions lies that reservoir of cunning that has enabled him to survive his own miscalculations and the treachery of his so-called friends.

Walking back across the fairway he experiences strange desires he somehow identifies with death. He wants to play rough-and-tumble games of tackle, nigger-pile, and wrestling after dark upon the grass. Wants to be called home again through the humid buggy dark, his flesh itching, his clothes cloying with his sweat, those damp, strong-smelling grass stains on his elbows and knees.

CHAPTER FOURTEEN

IN SEARCH OF WENZEL

As he drove westward in the Duesenberg, Magnuson debated how he could best get hold of Farquarson's letter. Tell Wenzel the truth, he decided. Tell him Farquarson was dead and show him the note, minimizing the possibility that Farquarson's death was anything but natural. But what would he do if the letter stated unequivocally that if Farquarson were found dead X should be investigated, since X had threatened his life and had a motive for his death? Give the information to the police, he supposed. He knew he had put himself into a position where he had to protect himself. But he possessed certain powers, certain skills.

In Wauconda at Al and Bonny Wenzel's Bang's Lake Inn he ordered a draught beer from a woman he heard a customer address as Bonny. In her he saw neither small towns nor country but the bowels of the city, Milwaukee Avenue and Division Street, those miles of blocks like a Central European city where English vanished and was replaced by Polish. How was he to reconcile such people as these with a man like Farquarson? And yet not only was there the deathbed letter to Albert Wenzel but, according to the nurse, earlier letters to Bonny Wenzel, the very woman who was drawing his beer.

Four men in athletic jackets, their wet hair combed back across their balding heads, sat at one end of the bar, bowling balls in bags beside their feet. Two Mexican field hands in straw hats and Levi's sat at the other end, speaking Spanish. Someone was playing the slot machine behind the curtains.

"Al here, Mrs. Wenzel?"

She was drawing beers for the Mexicans, her hand on the handle of the tap almost above her head. "At the barn."

"How do you get to the barn, Mrs. Wenzel?"

Shiny folds of hairless brow squeezed her eyes while her penciled eyebrows remained half-moons on her forehead. "You got business at the barn?" she said.

"I just wondered where he was. What he was up to. Him and me used to have some talks in here."

"Yeh? I'm always here when he's here and I don't remember you."

"It was a long time ago." He hoped they had owned the tavern a long time ago.

"I been here a long time, fellow."

"He was tending bar those times."

"He don't tend bar, fellow."

Why was she so antagonistic toward him, and protective of her husband? He was sitting on the stool with his coat open, his hat pushed back on his head. Did he look like a cop? Even so, why should that upset her? At the slot machine behind the curtains the player won some change. "We used to be in the service together," he said, believing the odds favored a tavernkeeper having served at one time or another in some branch of the military. "I was just kidding about seeing him in here before. I haven't seen him since we were in the service, I wanted to surprise him."

"Al wasn't in the service."

"I don't mean military service," he said without thinking, having no idea what he did mean. It seemed improbable that Wenzel had been a houseboy or butler.

Just then Bonny ran out from behind the bar, ducking beneath the gate. Magnuson turned on his stool and saw the curtains before the slot machine pulled apart and quivering, and the front door open. "Born in a barn?" she called, closing the door. "Left his beer, left his change." On the bar next to Magnuson's stool an untouched glass of beer, several coins, a cigarette with a long ash burning in the ashtray. He remembered passing a man when he came inside the tavern. The man was heading for the slot machine as he was heading for the bar. The man had ducked his head and shoulder to avoid bumping into him, and his hand had touched his hatbrim, which had served to hide his face.

Bonny Wenzel behind the bar again was saying, "What kind of service do you mean?" How had he let himself become trapped in his own lies? He was about to confess he was still kidding her when apparently interpreting his silence and discomfort as an answer, she said, "Oh, that service." If he dared it would have been his turn to ask what she meant.

He looked down into his glass and shook the beer around. She leaned confidentially across the counter and stared him in the face with a kind of knowledgeable glee, as though she had just caught him redhanded in a secret and shameful act she herself did not necessarily condemn.

She said, "So you were a priest." He had never in all his life been cast in so unexpected a calling. A cop, a detective, a politician, even a criminal he had often been mistaken for, but never a priest. She would not have dared to make such an assertion unless on the basis of some evidence totally lost to him she had already decided this was so.

"Yes," he said. "I was."

"Did you marry too?"

"My wife died last year." If she did not become exactly friendly, she did seem sympathetic.

"If you're a widower," she said, "can you . . . go back?" Go back to what, he wondered? To being a bachelor?

"No," he said, believing he revealed a certain fatigue and stoicism of spirit. "You can't go back." She nodded as though this was not what she wanted to hear but what she expected to hear, which was all Magnuson was interested in giving her.

But by then he was enough in her good graces to receive directions to the barn: north of town—just behind the house they rented out—Moony on the mailbox—a truck in the drive beside the barn. Then he was in the car again and driving in the open rolling country. Then he was at the barn. The first drops of rain: large, heavy drops that fell seconds and yards apart and broke like eggs upon his flesh and clothes. A farmhouse, not quite yet a silhouette against the late evening sky, the downstairs lighted and the upstairs dark; hillbilly music coming through the walls, a forlorn, nasal, almost drunken voice singing unintelligibly above fiddles and electric guitars. A number of cars parked beside the house. Down the sandy drive to the barn, only the cellar of which was lighted. A pick-up truck in the driveway, in that square of light coming out the open cellar door. From the cellar the pastoral and monotonous clap-clang of half a hundred bells; the bleats of half a hundred goats and sheep pitched from high to low, as incessant as the bells; the banging of barn boards by horns and hooves; the rustle of hooves in straw; already the whiff of animals, the odors heating up the air. Behind the barn, the landscape in the last blue light of sundown, pastures and windbreaks of poplars in the distance turning from green to black, and the silent lights of cars on a highway appearing to blink as they passed behind the trees. Outside the cellar door a pair of dented empty silver milk cans in a wooden cart, man-drawn, its handles resting in the gravel.

Then softly on the straw. A golden quality to the light, reflecting on so much shining straw. Overhead naked bulbs enmeshed in cobwebs that had captured chaff and flies hung all along the whitewashed joists. A long aisle running the length of the barn, pens of sheep on one side and milking stalls full of milking goats, their heads vised in stanchions, on the other; the bags of the does very heavy; some were nannying, others nuzzling up the grain from the wooden troughs. Warm down here, the temperature of blood, with hot pungent drafts from steaming cess, manure, breath. A widespread rustling of hay and straw. The pizzle of urine in the concrete trough below the hindquarters of the does. A ram, slime bubbling in its nostrils, stood motionless and staring at him while, as though unaware of what its body did, steaming feces tumbled to the straw. Somewhere down the line, the horns and heads of does fighting the stanchions. The rich, acidic smell of manure, the oil of dirty wool, urine-soaked straw, gamey hides. The incessant bleating and ringing of bells. Cats running back and forth like pack rats across the aisle. The evil in the eyes of goats, the stupidity in the eyes of sheep, the terror in the eyes of both. Glassy, bulging eyes that saw him sideways, from one eye at a time. Heads trying to back out of the stanchions as he passed, the horns twisted and catching on the boards, the eyes rolling back into the heads. A cat in the aisle ahead, licking an outstretched hindleg that looked bloodied, but slinking off as he approached, glancing once over the shoulder and vanishing inside a pen—

"Wenzel," he called. Instantly the bleating stopped, the bells stopped. The sheep froze in the pens, the ears went up on the does in the stalls. All heads, he felt, were turned to him. Then a random bleat, a clanking bell. More bleats, more bells, until the noise was general. "Wenzel," he called again. Again that instant silence, that sense of timelessness, of the animals waiting intently for him to say more and, giving up on him, once more beginning the bleats, bells, rustlings, bangings. Eerie. Something disordered, out of hand, wild, a sense of ritual disrupted and reversed, of farm animals betrayed and reverted to the wild, as though they were not penned in the sanctuary of the barn but tethered to trees in a forest, and catching the scents of predators traveling toward them through the night.

An open trapdoor overhead between the whitewashed joists, a wooden ladder leading up to it. On the floor below the door, several broken bales of hay, the twine unraveled; one of the bales broken by a fork and scattered. He floundered through the hay, reached the ladder but halted with his foot on the first rung and his hands on the rails. That sound—footfalls on the floor above, muted by the hay? And that—the muted thump of bales or distant thunder? Up the ladder, dust and chaff falling on his hat and in his eyes. His head poked into the loft. Cool here, the only light rising around him from below and falling through the windows high up in the eaves. As though the trapdoor opened into the middle of a small chamber walled irregularly on all sides by those green bales of hay piled like building stones; a smell sweet as clover. "Wenzel," he called, his voice deadened and thrown back upon him by the hay. An unseen bird flying back and forth along the ridgepole, the wings slapping on the rafters, beating against the window, then back again along the ridgepole, against the rafters, upon the window.

He could not bring himself to step up and swing off onto the floor upstairs. He stepped down the ladder, knees and ankles buckling as he took the rungs.

Downstairs again he studied the does that had been given grain but, by the size of their bags, had not been milked, and, by the noise and anguish of their bleats, expected to be milked. Across the way the sheep stood calmly in the pens and chewing, bent hay protruding from their jaws. Fresh straw was spread out on the floor of the sheep pens he forced himself to pass and freshly broken hay filled the feed racks. But in the pens just ahead the racks were empty, and these pens were full of bleating sheep.

The last pen, where the sheep were tugging the hay out of the rack, and he stumbled back, making a small noise, more cough than cry. On the straw inside the pen, between the legs of the sheep surrounding him, a man in blue overalls lying on his side with his back to Magnuson. A pitchfork had passed through his abdomen and the tips of the tines were protruding from his back.

He stepped over the rails, and the sheep, watching him and chewing hay in their jaws, backed up in the pen. Then they crowded along the rails and circled him, going wherever they thought he would not go, one trying to climb over the back of the other in the panic to get out of his way. He put his hand to the dead man's shoulder and began to turn him on his back but was so terrified by the unexpected sight of the handle of the pitchfork rising from the straw with the turning of the body that he released the shoulder and the man rolled back on his side. A big blond man, with a fat, ruddy face, who looked far less like a tavernkeeper than a farmer. The flesh warm, the blood only just begun to clot. Could he have fallen accidentally on his fork? Had one of those ewes butted him from behind when, for some extraordinary reason, he held his fork upside down? Or was this some humble and rural form of Roman suicide? But then, "Murder," he whispered. The man's pockets were turned out and his wallet and papers scattered around the straw, mixed into the bedding by the hooves. He retrieved all he could find, shooing the sheep out of his way and kicking the more stupid or stubborn ones in the ribs. The papers and identification cards were damp and stained and identified the man as Albert Wenzel. An envelope stuck to the lamb's hoof that had pierced it. He isolated the lamb from the flock, chased it, grabbed the tufts of wool on its hindquarters, and braked his feet in the straw in a vain attempt to hold it. Finally he got it by the hindleg and, as that leg pumped in his hand, pulled off the envelope. Torn, covered with manure, the ink wet and blurred. Addressed only to Albert Wenzel. No address. In the upper left-hand corner: From Mr. Farquarson. Nothing else. A woman's handwriting. A woman had addressed the envelope anyway. The envelope had been folded once and had not been sent through the mail. Someone then had delivered it. He took Farquarson's note from his pocket.

If I should meet with foul play Mr. Albert Wenzel of Wauconda has in his possession a letter explaining all.

That letter had been inside this envelope. And the murderer of Wenzel—and the murderer of Farquarson too, for if Farquarson had not been murdered there was no motive for killing Wenzel—was now in possession of that letter that revealed his name and presumably his motive. So the murderer, while he was standing over his victim in Farquarson's room, and perhaps even as he heard the nurse and Magnuson coming up the stairs, had discovered one of Farquarson's notes. But unlike Magnuson he was unaware that it was only one of many notes. He would believe with Wenzel dead that he was safe. The note Magnuson had in his hand, however, would be his undoing. The trail had already been found.

But just how hot on the trail was he? Surely no more than minutes behind the crime. Across the aisle the goats twisting their heads and rubbing their horns on the stanchions, their bells ringing as they moved. He could see through their eyes, slick, bulging, luciferous, transparent balls of yellow glass, and he felt an urge to put his own eye up to one of their own, as though to a peephole, and glimpse behind it the darkened, worldwide landscape illuminated only by sporadic, lightning-like flashes revealing acts of insanity and brutality, a vision given only to the mad. The eyes, pair after pair of them along the stalls, terrified him; all the unexplained, unredeemed, and unregretted horror of the world was in those eyes. They told him: He is here and you will die. Whereas the eyes of the sheep told him: He is here, but stand still so that he will not notice you but will kill the others in your stead. Some presence other than his own and that of the corpse in the bedding at his feet had terrified those eyes. Was the murderer still inside the barn? There—upstairs in the barn proper, hiding behind those walls of bales? Surely that was why he could not bring himself to go up the ladder all the way. In his imagination he saw, dropping out of the darkness of the trapdoor, the masklike beginnings of a face, luminous, white as talcum, the flesh like smoke, as though the man were suspended from his heels. Or was the murderer even closer to him, in one of the pens down the line or even in the pen next door, crouching on the other side of those very boards, having jumped the rail when he heard Magnuson enter the barn? It now occurred to him that he was unarmed, penned in, as helpless as the sheep. But it was likely that the murderer was also unarmed, for he had killed Wenzel with the convenient pitchfork, possibly had even wrestled it from his victim's hands. This, however, was small consolation. He rolled the corpse over so that the handle of the pitchfork stood upright, perpendicular to the body that was arched up beneath it, so that only the back of the head and the heels appeared to rest upon the straw. He wrapped his hands around the handle, which was firm, as though forced deep into a bale of hay, placed his foot on the corpse's ribcage, ready at any moment to pull out the tines and present the fork to anyone who suddenly attacked him. But he soon released the handle, which reverberated and hummed, he had had that tight a hold of it, laid the wallet and papers carefully on the corpse's chest, put the envelope in his own pocket, and climbed out of the pen, pausing to scrape the manure from his soles upon the rails.

He paused again in the small milk room by the barn door, on the concrete floor tin pie pans empty of milk surrounded by wide-eyed, hungry, half-savage cats. Then he moved cautiously out from behind the milk cart and then the truck. Up at the house hillbilly music, a man and woman yodeling Swiss-style above guitars and mandolins. Behind the house the silhouettes of several boys urinating in the grass.

Above him in the driveway a man standing as though waiting to confront him. He called, "Hey, you! How the hell are you, you goddamned Jew?" He appeared to come toward Magnuson, then halt, backtrack, only to come forward again.

Then the porch light of the house came on. A woman passed through the porch and sat down on the outside steps, a bottle of beer in her hand, her head of orange hair almost in her lap. Now Magnuson could see the red hair of the balding head of the man above him, the red unshaven face, the unbuttoned shirt, the unzippered, unbelted pants, the shoes without socks or laces, and then even the finger smudges on his glass of beer. "So," he said aloud in relief, in explanation, "you're—so that's why—you're drunk—"

"So what?" said the man. "In the morning I'll be sober—though I'll wish I weren't.—Hey, Mother," turning to the woman on the steps, "I wish I weren't!—But you, you goddamned Jew, you'll still be a goddamned Jew!" He spoke as though his teeth and tongue had always to contend with a mouthful of saliva.

"You got the wrong guy," Magnuson said cautiously. "I'm not a Jew."

The man stepped forward, squinting; then stepped back in surprise. "Say, pal," he said, "I'm sorry. You're not who I thought you was. Why, you're somebody else.—But that don't mean you're still not a goddamned Jew! Hot dog!" What is this, Magnuson wondered, am I to be taken for a priest and now a Jew?

"My name is Jones," Magnuson said. "Who are you?"

"Me?" the man said, putting on a Scottish accent. "Why, I live here, laddie. That's my home. That's my wife. Scotty Moony at your service, pal. Call me Scotty."

"Who did you think I was?"

"Say, it was an honest mistake, laddie. No hard feelings. I thought you was Bud.—Hey, if you're not a Jew how come you look like Buddy? Your witness, counselor.—But Bud's around here someplace." He looked toward the three cars parked beside the house. Convertibles and coupes that obviously belonged to the boys drinking in the house. "Well, I'll be a dirty drunk but if his car isn't gone.—Hey, but let's forget about that Jew. He said he'd drop by the house for a drink when he came back up from the barn but you can't trust a Jew. Who needs him. Hey, come on in and have a drink, pal."

"Come on, honey," the woman said without lifting her head, her legs spread apart and with her fist between her thighs.

"You won't hold it against me will you, pal?" Scotty said. "Jew or no Jew, I can tell you're a good egg. And that Bud's one hell of a swell Jew. Say, brother, they don't make them any better. He can take a little ribbing. He's got the best job in the world—selling beer! Hot dog! But, hey, I got an even better job—drinking it!" He doubled over and slapped his knee, sloshing beer on the ground. "Jesus, Mother, can you see me selling beer? Hot dog! Put her there, pal." The man had a powerful grip and would not release Magnuson's hand until he had collapsed his fingers.

"We won't bite you," the woman called from the steps, fumbling with a match and a cigarette.

"Where can I find Bud?" Magnuson asked. His hand felt broken.

"Ask Al. Ask Bonny. He sells beer to them.—And, hey, they sell it to me! Hot dog!—But what did I tell you? You Jews stick together.—Hey, come in, pal. Come on. Forget about that other Jew." His voice had become soft, coaxing, foxy. "I got something to show you."

"I was just on my way down to the barn to see Al."

"On your way down?" Scotty said. "You were coming up."

"I was going down. I turned around when you called me."

"Say, brother," Scotty said, scratching his head. "Am I a dirty drunk. I could have sworn you were coming up. Jesus, but I'd better lay off the good booze.—But wait a darn minute! Why did you turn around if you weren't a goddamn Jew? Hey? Hey? Your witness, counselor." This loudly, as though to an audience of hundreds. Then sly and coaxing again. "Say, pal, you can level with me. You're a Jew, ain't you? Ain't you?" Magnuson attempted to draw away, but the man took him by the arm. "Come on in, pal. For old time's sake. For old time's sake." He put his arm around Magnuson's shoulder.

"Maybe I'll stop on my way back up."

"For old time's sake," Scotty repeated, his mind on something else now, his eyes half-closed, crossed and dazed, his hand gently patting Magnuson's back. "For old time's sake." As though he believed the two men shared some past suffering, sentiment, nostalgia.

"We'll see," Magnuson said, freeing himself and observing that the man was without explanation suddenly saddened, embarrassed, injured. He walked back toward the barn, the man urinating in the driveway behind him.

Then the anger of the shout at his back, pursuing him down: "You don't fool me, you fucking copper! When I wake up tomorrow I'll be sober. But you'll still be a crooked flatfoot, you fucking dick!"

Magnuson halted in his tracks. Not because of the unexpected outcry but because from where he was in the driveway he could gaze down through a cellar window of the barn and into the very pen where Wenzel had been murdered. It was like a picture hanging on the night. Although the glass looked almost glazed with cobwebs, fly specks, and dust, he could make out the straw, several legs of sheep, a mass of blue overalls. He could imagine the time a few minutes earlier when there were two men in the stall, one passing before the window and out of sight only to re-emerge as the second disappeared, his back to the window, the face of the other seen above his shoulder; now the pantomime of their arguing, the gesticulating hands, the circling movement of their bodies, one man holding out his hand as though expecting something of the other; confused sheep passing in and out of the scene, obscuring the men up to the waist; then the sheep suddenly leaping and ducking and running for the rails as the man with his back to the window raised the pitchfork so high it seemed that the handle would crack back through the window, then brought it down as the other man gave way beneath it, then leaned on the handle with his feet in the air and his body, almost in an acrobatic flag, perpendicular to the pole. The cry coming above the bleats and bells. Then the face of the murderer, featureless and the color and radiance of a white sun behind a snowy, silvery overcast, at the window as though he had just discovered its dangerous presence above the stall and was peering out into the night, his hands cupped around his eyes to cut down the reflection, to see if he had been seen; his head so gigantic that the face crowded the glass and plugged the light in the barn behind it, making it dark and imprecisely seen.

Magnuson stood just inside the cellar door, staring up at the house. Was it possible that this Bud had witnessed the murder

THE MURDERS ■ 208

through the window as he was walking down the driveway toward the barn?

"Fuck you, John Law!" Scotty shouted as he held the screen door of the porch open, his wife having preceded him indoors. "My booze has been turned down by better men than you." Then the screen door banged, the house door banged, the porch light went out.

Although Magnuson could concede that the beer salesman might have had a motive for murdering Wenzel, it was unlikely he had a motive for murdering Farquarson, the original murder that with the finding of the note compelled the killer to commit the second. Instead, he believed the salesman had either discovered the body or witnessed the murder. But if he had merely found the body wouldn't he have told Moony or, if he suspected Moony as the killer, gone immediately for the police? But the police were not here, and Wauconda was only a mile away. He hadn't notified the police. He was frightened out of his wits. He believed he was in danger of his life. And with good reason too. Through that cellar window he had watched one man kill another. He had watched and panicked. Why else would he try to sneak away and pretend he had never been here when Moony, with whom he had just talked, could place him at the murder scene?

Magnuson pushed the milk cart into the barn, got into the pick-up truck, which he assumed was Wenzel's, released the brake, and let it roll inside the barn. He shut off the barn lights and rolled the barn door closed. So much for that. It would look as though Wenzel had finished with his milking and gone home.

In Wauconda he ran into the tavern and, breathless, impatient, and authoritative, demanded of Bonny Wenzel at the bar the address of Buddy Rotterdam, explaining in bad humor in response to her flabbergasted face, "Al told me about him. He thinks we can make some kind of deal—." He paused. Even so simple a request for information was complicated and demanded the right psychology. He was speaking to a wife who had yet to learn she was a widow.

"What does Al know about it?" she said. "And don't tell me you run a tavern too?"

By now he knew how to respond to those surprising suppositions she made about him. "I'm just thinking about it—."

The four men in high-school athletic jackets climbed off their stools, picked up the bags containing bowling balls, and went out the door, leaving the pair of Mexican field hands as the only other customers in the tavern.

Bonny removed a card wedged behind the cash register. Herbert "Buddy" Rotterdam. Old Milwaukee Grain Brand Lager Beer. His old address, farther away and deep within the city, crossed out, and his new address, on the northwest outskirts of the city, penned in. "He just moved," she said. "Just got remarried. He only gave me these cards when he was in here an hour ago." Her voice appeared to quiver, her hand tremble; her eyes were darting in her head. He would not have thought she could be frightened of anyone or anything.

"Stick around," she said. She had set a glass of beer before him. "It's my round. Bud ain't going to give you that good a deal that you got to chase him and get a heart attack. You want to take care of yourself, guy." Myself, he thought, with that ecstatic bitterness he felt whenever he judged himself as he thought the world had judged him. What do I care about myself? "Al will be here any minute," she said. "As a matter of fact, I wonder what's keeping him." This was not spoken so much as delivered, as though by a stiff actress on the stage, and while she glanced behind her at the clock. —Of course! He had forgotten that Wenzel would be expected home when the milking was done. If he didn't return, and evidently soon, she might telephone the Moonys, go herself to the barn, notify the police.

"Al told me to tell you he won't be back until late—." And why was she shaking her head in contradiction at him and now jerking it in the direction of the Mexicans? "He's staying at the barn."—No, her head said, he isn't.—"Some of his animals are sick—."He was backing away from the bar and toward the door. "He hasn't been able to get the vet yet—." She no longer bothered to shake her head but considered him instead with a look of betrayal and disbelief. Too late he caught the meaning of her jerking head, that she was telling him not only that she was afraid, but of whom. If he left she would be left alone with the Mexicans. He wondered now if they hadn't directed amused and even studious looks at the woman and himself, and especially at her, as though their continuous and rapid talk in Spanish was pretense, or even jibberish, and their real business in the bar was in the meaning of those looks. If only he knew what they had said and were saying now. For all he knew they were insulting his manhood, his looks, physique, age, were even coupling him and the woman in degenerate postures that revealed that he was impotent and his flesh obscene. But although he could not understand them was it possible that, unknown to them, she did, and therefore knew from their own mouths what precisely, when she was alone with them, they planned to do? He glared at the Mexicans as though to tell them that for two cents he would rough them up and run them in. A short fat man with a round pockmarked face and Oriental eyes. A short thin man with a rodent's face and a mustache like the whiskers of a rat. As if they were not men at all but a pair of quaint animals dressed in human clothing and encountered in the illustrations of a children's book. But in their faces was that serene evil of those from whom good has never been expected. And who have learned that to fear and to be feared in turn is the only way of life.

Yet he couldn't allow himself to be kept here by a frightened woman. Maybe she had an irrational fear of Mexicans or of anyone who wasn't white. And even if they did rob her at gunpoint, what was the loss of a day's take in a small tavern compared to the justice and retribution that would be gained from the expedition on which he was engaged? And how could his presence deter them from their crime, or protect her, when he was an old man and was himself unarmed? They might injure him or lock him up in a back room from which he would not be released until morning, preventing him from pursuing the salesman to Chicago. They might even kill him, destroying entirely his knowledge of the crimes. Difficult as it was, he knew where his duty lay. "I'll get you next time," he said, dismissing the glass of beer and regretting the fear of doom he read upon the woman's face. He wanted to tell her that as far as the world worked tonight she was on the small end of the scale, but that the odds were still way in her favor and that her fears, more likely than not, were unfounded.

Then he was pulling away in the Duesenberg from the neon-flashing sign perched on the roof of the tavern, peering through the slow, erratic action of the small windshield wipers on the chopped windshield as the tremble of the exhaust reverberated in the rolling hills and he raced southward through the sudden rainstorm and darkness toward Chicago.

CHAPTER FIFTEEN

BLACK NEWS

No-Man's-Land. A stretch of North Shore beach where no township has jurisdiction, and accordingly a lovers' lane and Bacchic party site. Lightning above Lake Michigan and distant thunder. As yet no rain, although Cavan puts up the top of his MG, snaps on the side curtains only to open Myrna Westermann's door and say, "Come on." Since she herself introduced him to this beach in summers past she must know he means to take her there when a thunderstorm is imminent, just as she must have known that to stop precisely here to rainproof the car was no coincidence. To his surprise she comes.

But with this stipulation: "Will you promise not to come to-night?" She means to the small party for a girlfriend celebrating her divorce and to which she has already asked him not to come.

"If that's what you want . . . really want . . ." What he wants though is to get himself reinvited, foreseeing in the balance more than just the loss of an evening's company.

He goes first down the steep sandy slope, she follows. Light-ning in a crazy network that zigzags north and south across the sky. Bolts that stab the lake. Flashes flung out from the horizon. It could be a war between the planets. The demolition of the universe. Or the genesis of life.

Bonfires burn up and down the beach, the flames leaning land-ward as though about to rise into the gale and blow away. Huddled around them, parties of teenagers, their drunken shouts and ukuleles wind-blown and drowned in waves and thunder.

On the beach Myrna sinks to her knees with a heaviness that proclaims she will not go farther. She lets sand fall through her fin-gers while Cavan hunkers down and weighs that same sand in his palm. "If you're pregnant," he begins awkwardly, "I'd marry you—I'd want to marry you." A repetition of his position in their argu-ment last night. He has heard the call of responsibility, self-sacrifice, has been touched by a moral sense far greater than just his one selfish human self.

"Oh, you would want to," she says, wondering if he can catch the anger in her voice. The insult in being married only for the child he has put inside her womb! "Funny, in the three years we saw each other I don't recall your mentioning marriage before." Imme-diately she regrets having sidetracked their "having it out" with this remark. She wants this hurtful business done with, this man before her pushed back into the past. Hereafter she will suffer in silence the wounds she will receive from his attack.

"I thought it was understood between us," he says in his own defense, pacing back and forth now, pushing sand around with his instep.

"If I was pregnant," she begins thoughtfully, "I suppose I'd have to tell my parents—they say you should tell your parents. My father would want to know—he would have to know. He would know what to do about this sort of thing." She is thinking of abor-tions.

"You're only twenty-four," he says, unable to hide his injury. "You only have a master's degree in art education." Her father is the president of a company that manufactures a popular electric blender advertised by pitchmen in the early morning hours of tele-vision. And before that the sales manager of a furnace company infamous for its "heating engineers" who removed or destroyed im-portant furnace parts during "free furnace inspections" and terrified the furnace owners with the report that the furnace would fail in midwinter if it did not explode first. Cavan has always thought the man *nouveau riche,* selfish, uncultured, mercenary. He eats steak every morning for breakfast and drinks old fashioneds in which he floats pinches of small and evidently digestible golden stars. He is even the chairman of his alma mater's alumni fund. What would be the fate of Cavan without the Farquarson wealth or even family, if and when he became the son-in-law of such a man, dwarfed by the name of Westermann, dependent on the earnings of that miracle blender, and even living for a time in that sprawling redwood ranch house with its pool and porches in a wooded setting in Highland Park? That she would choose to huddle with her father and determine what to do about his child infuriates him with its injustice. "So you wouldn't ask me," he says. "Or even tell me."

Both mask their injuries, Cavan because he does not want to hurt his chances with her, she, who gives him no chance, because she does not care enough to show her anger.

"You can stop worrying," she says. "I'm not pregnant." The garden of her body is, as she has felt all along despite the evidence to the contrary, unchanged.

"Thank God for that," he manages to say, although he is surprised to learn he is not relieved by this news. Now he has no moral claim upon her, now there is no unbreakable moral bond between them, and he is all the closer to losing her. It is as though a wife and child could prove somehow that he exists; that he leaves his mark; that he is a man of kin, future as well as those unknown generations who are his past. "I shouldn't have told you about my window games with my uncle's nurse," he says bitterly, for he would still convince himself that this alone explains her rejection of him. "I should have kept my mouth shut. It was a mistake to try to be open with you. You don't know how to handle honesty. You want only lies—the facade—the role." How can he know that she merely found his confession a convenient moment to prepare him for the blow of breaking off with him by confessing in her turn her own dark secret, that she recently met a man named Bradford McCarthy and that between them there is even more than just attraction at first sight? She has mentioned Bradford McCarthy again tonight. But Cavan wants to block Bradford McCarthy from his mind. From her mind too. He cannot believe that Bradford McCarthy can be the cause of their separation. "I should have lied to you," he adds.

"That had nothing to do with it," she says truthfully.

"Of course not. It was the 'sledgehammer affair.'" Throwing

back at her her confession of last night that the first meeting between her and Bradford McCarthy affected both of them "like a blow from a sledgehammer." He is well aware that it would be manly to be stoical and understanding. But what a weak and puny thing he is! Just look at him! Listen to him! Quarreling in the language of a soap opera in the face of this panoramic, storm-tossed sky. Disgusted with himself, he strolls away.

The bottle of Moselle he has brought along to celebrate their reconciliation he buries up to the neck just where the frigid water boils farthest up the sand. Then he wanders to the ruins of No-Man's-Land—the Casino—a jumble of broken blocks and slabs of concrete that spill out into the lake. In lightning like indecisive daylight, he leaps from rock to rock, avoiding pools and puddles. Ahead of him waves splash against the upthrust stones. The water must be deep out there. Someone told him once that the Casino had burned down back in the 1920's. The implication had been that the owners were gangsters and the fire arson, a skirmish in a gang war. It must have been a watering hole, a pleasure dome, a miniature Monte Carlo, a cabaret for café society. Small yachts and sailboats with their running lights moored along that pier. Strings of Japanese lanterns. Gangsters in double-breasted tuxedos. Society people strolling on the concrete veranda, looking out across the lake between the urns of geraniums positioned along the balustrade. Frazer and Hope Farquarson arm in arm. John Senior and Priscilla Cavan. Inside the French doors the huge gaming room with roulette wheels and dice tables lit by chandeliers. Prohibition liquor in every glass. The hot dance music of a clarinet, banjo, a tongue-slapping saxophone. The bright world of his past. Now this rubble. He could be standing on the ruins of an ancient fortress of a vanished people on a continent as remote as Africa.

He no longer lives among people he recognizes or knows. Where has he been prepared for the reckoning of such a day as this? Strangers did not tiptoe into your house to tell you that you had a mulatto sister and then attempt to persuade you to act as an accomplice in the murder of your uncle; that same dying uncle did not confess that there were no blood ties between you, and that his wealth would not be yours, nor insist you would be well-advised to keep your privates clean; priests even if they did marry and own taverns and have unfaithful wives did not contact gonorrhea deliberately and then infect others, premeditating that somewhere along the line they would lay their victims low. And now on top of all of this Myrna denying to his face that affection she has felt for him these past three years. (He recalls the old ballads where the man walks the pregnant girl down to the water and drowns her there to avoid marrying her, whereas he, who wished to do the right thing, is sent home.) The nurse with her compulsive drama before her windows was proof enough that the play was less upon the stage than in the dressing rooms below. Why, the man across the street looking out his window could know more about a woman than the husband who shared her bed.

Suddenly a vision of Africa opens up before him, its darkness a sea of diamonds refracting light. The Dahomey tribe he planned to live among and study and whose history and culture he has prepared himself to record. Doesn't he know more about them before he even goes to Africa than he knows about himself? He does not know his name, parents, age, even nationality and religion if it comes to that. Knows only by the visual confirmation of his body that he is male and white.

He resolves to go to Africa. Not in the fall as planned but as quickly as he can. And not with any camera and microphone to set before those dark people who, unlike himself, know who they are and where they have come from if not exactly where in this modern world they are going, but to lose himself in their primeval world, where past and present are still a single moment and a man's life is dictated by millenniums of customs and taboos. To lose himself to find himself, simplified, ennobled, savage, the lone albino member of the tribe.

On the beach again he cannot find his wine bottle in the sand. He removes his shoes and wades on the fringes of the icy water, digging with his feet. The bottle must have been dug loose by the backwash and carried out into the dark, spinning in a wave. He rolls up his pantlegs and steps into a wave, alarmed at how quickly he goes so deep and even more at the power of the undertow. To be pulled in and taken down, spun in a wave, sent like a torpedo to that deep chamber where the lake inters its own. Floating underwater on his back in that storm-tossed lake. That wilderness of thunderlight. That water charged with energy and light. Lightning and lake. Life-givers and destroyers. To be drowned like Wenzel's son. Who might have been his brother. Who might have been himself. He is terrified of the lightning, the darkness, the indecisive daylight, the wastes of dark water. For the first time in his life he is afraid of death, and equally for the first time is tempted by that fear.

Myrna Westermann, meanwhile, who can fall asleep at any time in any place, is sleeping soundly on the beach. She has a dream. A

parade is passing through her village. She is at the head of that
parade, a little drum majorette with gold curls poking out from her
shiny cardboard shako. She prances in her oversized white boots,
twirling the silver baton she sometimes drops. Her father marches
behind her, in his Uncle Sam suit. He is so tall and thin he seems
on stilts. Behind him come the drum and bugle corps, the bagpipes,
the phalanxes of tasseled and pom-pommed shakos, the barrels of
the rifles, and the flags, those great wind-tossed flapping flags, and
the thunder of the ragged beating of a big bass drum—

"We ought to go," she says, yawning. "They're expecting me."

So that is how it is now, Cavan thinks, standing over her, *me*
and no longer *us*.

Her shirtwaist dress has slid up from her knees and the luminous and silver patch of panties shows between her thighs. Just
how innocent is this, he wonders? Perhaps it is the sign he has been
looking for. He leans across her without touching her. A child-
woman for whom he has always felt protective, and sexual in that
feeling. The simple sensual pleasures she has given him he can only
savor now. All those sunny, windy afternoons he would pick her up
after her classes at the Art Institute, waiting in the MG on Michigan
Avenue until she came tripping down the steps between the twin
stone lions in her smock and colored stockings, her hair in a pony-
tail, beneath her arm those canvases and sketchbooks that he always
struggled so to fit inside the little car, sometimes driving with a
canvas on the running board and held there by his arm. The paint
and chalk on her hands and beneath her nails that spread to her
smock and even face. To his Gold Coast apartment for a drink where
in brassiere and half-slip she would wash herself in his sink. Then
on the streets to window shop and grocery shop and eat supper. And
always with their supper, white wines or rosés. The wonder of opening the front of her dress and sliding his hand inside her brassiere,
freeing her breasts. Or his hand feeling the moisture on the inside
of her thighs and the smoothness to her panties when she was wet
beneath. If he could go into her now he might keep her, might cement her to him and make a pact of touch and seed that would have
a moral gravity. And if he kept her he might begin to know his name.
He is encouraged that she should look sleepy, permissive, worn-
down, and more guilty than imposed upon. But her flesh is cool, and
he suspects she will not resist him if he enters her, but neither will
she respond, but will lie cool and detached, paying the penance for
having hurt him and freeing herself from him forever.

At the beach party several hundred youths have made a ragged conga line that winds like a dragon around the bonfires, giving the illusion that some of the dancers are consumed in flames. They chant a combination of rhumba and rock-'n'-roll and a hodgepodge of lyrics like *"La Cucaracha"* and *"Tutti-Frutti"* and *"One-two-three-four Conga!"* Elsewhere lone couples embrace in firelight, arms of sweatshirts tied around their waists and necks. Two boys wrestle in the sand, rolling between the fires. Someone is in the water fully clothed, shouting he will swim to Michigan. Cries to rescue him. A line of rescuers holding hands and wading out into the waves. Cries warning of the undertow and lightning. Commands to bring him to the fire and warm him. To remove his clothes. To catch him before he falls or throws himself into the fire, one of which he is in the act of doing. To Cavan they seem the youth of another race of people, far removed from here and now. A Stone Age tribe celebrating in a thunderstorm the fetish of lightning. Or salvagers of the merchant ship their beacons on the beach have lured upon the rocks.

"Marry me," Cavan says, unable to guess at the firmness of her determination to do no such thing.

For the close call of her pregnancy has taught her what the three years of going with him did not: that she would lose her happiness and her self—her real self—with him. And what an awful irony to discover she does not want him only when—and only because—she is in danger of being forced to have him. And wouldn't it have been awful to have had him forced upon her just when it was her destiny to meet Bradford McCarthy, the new man who is himself further proof that Cavan has been all wrong? Life isn't habit, she tells herself. It isn't security—although in time, she concedes, she will probably want these things. She marvels at how dangerous life is—how unfair!—and compared to many women how lucky she has been. She has escaped the trap life has set for her in the guise of this man who leans across her. Has escaped with her youth, her freedom, the new man's love. She has always believed in the power of her luck. She has always known she was not born to suffer. "O storm!" she wants to shout. She wants her hair tossed in the fury of the wind, her face stung by the violence of the spray.

"We'll go to Africa," he says.

She turns her head away to hide her laugh. Africa indeed! Africa to her is jungles and Negroes and heat and snakes and bugs and parasites and sickness and poverty and wilderness. If she goes anywhere on a honeymoon it will be to Paris and Provence, the haunts of the Impressionist painters she admires. And she will go on the arm of the new man. In France she will speak the language, know the culture, appreciate the art, and the new man will be dependent on her knowledge. He will listen to her, let her go her own way when she pleases. Which in her vague definition of the roles of the sexes is as it should be. She has always suspected that Cavan's interest in culture, even though it was scientific in its perspective, infringed upon her rightful role.

"I see," he says, catching her laugh and rising. "The 'sledgehammer affair.'" He acknowledges a passing urge to shake some sense into her head.

"What can I tell you?" she says, almost happy with herself. She has only come here with him because she judged this much to be her duty, suspecting, and rightly, that he would become so weak and spiteful that her conscience would allow her to break with him without fear of further guilt. She is free. She is herself. Just who did she think she was these past three years?

"The 'new man,'" he says, picking up that term now and throwing it back.

Then in the car and heading for Chicago, determined to go with her to the party no matter what she says, he suddenly discovers that he too can be a new man. It is so simple, really. He can learn, if he wants to, who he really is. If the nurse was right, then the letter Farquarson sent to Wenzel had to have been dictated to Lena when she was in his room last night. Which means that Lena knows as much about that letter as did those men. Then Lena knows more about his identity and history than he knows himself! Why would Farquarson entrust such secrets to a colored maid when the nurse and housekeeper were in the house and could have just as easily taken down the letter? The world is topsy-turvy, crazy.

Despite Myrna's complaint that she is already late for her party, he stops in Evanston at a drugstore, calls home to Lake Forest, and learns from a nervous Nancy Rhinelander Lena's address in Evanston.

The neighborhood is in the colored section. Neat, residential streets away from the lake and close to the elevated tracks, the houses smaller than in other neighborhoods, and the shade trees not so full and tall. On the corner of her block a chicken-and-barbecue restaurant in the lighted plate-glass window of which is the pantomime of the black cook in white ducks and chef's cap and several black customers waiting at the counter. A man with a shopping bag disappears down the sidewalk and the block is empty. A feeling of curfew in the air. Of something alien, exotic, and even dangerous, as though Cavan is in the middle of a Johannesburg slum. The lightning flashes like heat lightning, rain ricochets through the trees. From a gangway three boys on bicycles without fenders or reflectors fly out upon the sidewalk and standing on the pedals fly past on either side of him, shouting something above the clunk-clunk of the manual bicycle bells that he does not catch but suspects has been addressed to him. Something ivory in their faces, eyes or teeth. He tells Myrna to lock the car, to blow the horn if there is any trouble.

Lena's apartment is on the second floor of a small house with a small yard. Lena and her husband, Max, the former Farquarson chauffeur who now chauffeurs in his own car several retired doctors and lawyers whenever they have to travel from the north shore to the Loop, are sitting at the kitchen table. Max reads a library book, and Cavan recalls he is an avid if indiscriminate reader, a habit he must have picked up waiting those long hours in the Farquarson limousine. Lena plays solitaire, writing her scores down as she has for the past thirty years into the latest small spiral notebook. "Sit down, won't you sit down?" says Max, rising. He makes a slight formal bow, and no joint of his body moves except his waist. His hand indicates the living room. For a moment Cavan is confused. In the kitchen the Formica table and matching set of chrome chairs, the white enamel cabinets and bronze-colored garbage pail, the checkered linoleum upon the floor, the sunburst clock above the refrigerator, the ceramic wooden shoes and windmills along the window sill in which grow African violets, Swedish ivy, tiny cacti; and in the living room the matching upholstered furniture, the television console, the floor-length drapes. He has expected nothing so typical as this. It is more his apartment than theirs. Even the radio on the kitchen counter is playing what sounds like Mozart. He recalls his boyhood summer visits to Farquarson's and Max in T-shirt, gray pants, and suspenders washing the limousine in the driveway and listening to the radio, to the White Sox game if it was on, otherwise to operas and symphonies. Even now Max is dressed as he remembers him, in that white T-shirt and those suspenders, like a fireman, or barracked soldier of the last century. Bull-like, he has at seventy the physique of a man of twenty who works out with weights. The skin lies in tight folds and furrows on the bald dome of his gigantic, Prussian-looking head. Is his name really Max, Cavan used to wonder, or is it a nickname given to him because of his Prussian look, those Prussian manners?

"Is anything the matter?" Lena says. "You want some coffee? I can make it."

He doesn't want any coffee—he wants the truth! Shaking his

head he collapses at the kitchen table and tries to tell his story of the sickbed revelation of Farquarson, that he should see a man named Wenzel if he wanted to learn who his real parents were.

"That man at Bang's Lake?" Max interrupts. "I went out there to see that man, just this morning." Then to Lena, "I told you about him. You know, that business with his wife."

"He was too drunk to tell me anything," Cavan says.

"I can believe that," says Max. "You say something to that man and all he can do is smile at you. He could hardly open that letter I had to give him."

Cavan, grateful for this opening, says, "I know about that letter, Lena. I know you wrote it. I want you to tell me who my father is." He is desperate, and knows he looks it. That she will not tell him what he asks is a possibility he does not consider. She has always been understanding and sympathetic, if at times cantankerous, and when he was the small visitor to the Farquarson house he must have been something of her fair-haired boy. Besides, she is a Negro, and from his limited experience they are more compassionate than whites. What choice will she have but to recognize and ease his suffering?

Even though Lena has dreaded just such a question ever since Cavan came through her door she is nevertheless caught off guard and flustered. "I don't know if I can tell you that," she says, laying out another game of solitaire.

"But Lena," he counters, "you don't know what it is not to know who your parents are, where you came from, not to know who you are. If you could only put yourself in my place—" He pauses, exasperated with himself. What an unforgivable *faux pas!* Weren't Max and Lena more than likely themselves grandchildren of slaves who were unable to name their fathers for generations back? And given the propensity for illegitimacy among Negroes, might they themselves not know who their fathers were and have reconciled themselves long ago to never knowing that? But if they are aware of the insensitivity of his remark they do not show it. His embarrassment is not theirs. He can say no more. He puts his trust in her humanity which, he is willing to acknowledge, is deeper than his own.

But Lena does not believe this is any of her business. How the responsibility for this dirty work of telling Cavan all about the Farquarson skeletons has been passed down from Farquarson to this man Wenzel to her is beyond her. She has only been a duped and reluctant intermediary between Farquarson and Wenzel and, by

Farquarson's own definition, divorced entirely from the contents of that letter and the business of his estate and death, hired as the stenographer of that letter by the sole reason of that understanding—*his* understanding. Did he believe that the shame of his secret corruption would fall without effect upon her subhuman senses and that his sins could be absorbed inconspicuously within her black soul? Or did he choose her not because she was not quite human but because she was so degraded a human that his crimes, embosomed in her, were at last at home? No wonder he wanted a black minister of the Gospel of Jesus Christ to administer to him and forgive him on his deathbed: only a black minister was equal to the corruption he wished to pass on from his soul. And then to buy her silence on this business—her humanity—for fifty dollars! She is not inhuman, neither is she so low or lost that she can absorb without shame his sin within her soul. She smokes with indignation and injury. She couldn't care less, or very little, for young Mr. Cavan in this moment. But she must demonstrate, if only to herself, that her humanity cannot be bought for money, that she will not accept in silence this levy of white sin upon her soul. "Your father's name," she says, "is Helenowski." There —it is out! She doubts that she feels better for having said it and suspects that later in the evening she will feel even worse.

"Helen who?" Cavan says, believing she must have given him his mother's name. He has expected to hear the name of Farquarson. Possibly of Wenzel.

"I didn't say Helen who," she corrects. "I said Helenowski. All one name. Helenowski."

"Helenowski," Cavan repeats.

"Helenowski," she repeats. "That was your father's name."

"But you can't be sure?" says Cavan, rising.

"I'm not sure of nothing," Lena says. "What I'm telling you, you understand, is what Farquarson said in his letter."

"And my mother's name?" It is a question he thought he was too afraid to ask.

Although Lena has resolved to tell him everything—his mother's name and the place and circumstances of his birth—the shock the relevation his father's name has given him makes her have misgivings about saying more. Her indignation cools. "I don't know about that," she lies. No, she could never bring herself to say that name.

She doesn't fool Cavan, though. He knows that she is lying, and concludes that she must have good reason to do so, that the rest of his secret is that perverse. He is certain now that he is illegitimate

(Male Child Helenowski). He no longer wants to know his mother's name, no longer has the stomach to learn the worst.

Overcome with a gratitude that is more sentiment than passion at having learned his father's name at last, he stammers, "You were very kind to tell me. I knew you would . . . You've been . . . very good to me, most considerate, really . . . most kind. I'll repay you somehow . . . someday . . . I promise you."

But in the street he breaks down and weeps, leaning with the key in the lock against the door as the locked-in Myrna points at her watch and then south toward Chicago. In all his imaginings on the subject of his origins he has never once doubted his ancestry was anywhere but somewhere in the British Isles. But Poland? A Pole? How is he supposed to look? act? dress? think? feel? Johnny Helenowski. It is the name of a machinist, a gym teacher, a tavernkeeper, a professional bowler. It is a name he associates with boilermakers, pinochle, polkas. Who would he have to be today if his name had been Johnny Helenowski from birth? Who would be his friends and family? He looks at that glow above the buildings that is Chicago, thinking of the steel mills and those stinking marshes to the south.

Then he recalls the name of the dead man in Bughouse Square.— Helenowski. According to Lena, it is also his father's name. According to Nancy Rhinelander, Farquarson was frightened of a man with such a name. Who had escaped from an asylum just before he was found dead in Bughouse Square. And not merely dead, either, but murdered. Could he be the son of such a father? Whom Farquarson knew and feared? If so, what bizarre and violent origins were beating in his veins! Small wonder they were keeping secrets from him. Small wonder Farquarson and Wenzel and Lena could not bring themselves to tell him everything they knew. His past is made out of madhouses, not mansions.

But why on earth had Farquarson adopted him as his nephew? What connection could there possibly be between them? Why, he was little more than the monstrous creation of Farquarson, who had said, Lo! let there be a John Cavan. And there was a John Cavan. He was made of flesh and had a heart and tongue, and he breathed. And Farquarson said, Let him have the best of everything. And he had the best of everything. And Farquarson said, Let him believe the best of everything. And it was as Farquarson said, he believed the best of everything. Then one day Farquarson said, Let there be no more John Cavan. And poof! John Cavan was gone. And poof! Johnny Helenowski was in his place.

CHAPTER SIXTEEN

IN SEARCH OF ROTTERDAM

When Magnuson approached the outskirts of Chicago it was in a heavy rain and through the fragments and construction of super-highways that detoured abruptly at barricades of flashing lights. Without any warning that he had seen, the surface beneath him changed into gravel, or into a narrow potholed blacktop demarcated, as were the deep ditches in the shoulders into which the tar of the roadway itself was crumbling, by smoke pots and flares. What had been divided highway became heavy with two-way traffic, a fact brought home only when the blinding headlights bearing down upon him passed him at the last possible moment safely on the driver's side. The center line he focused on in order to stay upon the road ended as though at the edge of a cliff, delivering him to a prairie of darkness, or else, fading, curved off in a false and dangerous direction onto old and unused roads. Unlit sawhorses and barricades of barrels loomed up in the headlights as though placed for no other purpose than to be knocked down; signs as wide as the road were suspended overhead, mysteriously wrapped up in canvas or, if visible, giving in their reflecting letters directions that as yet were meaningless and commands that were impossible and even dangerous to obey. Meanwhile seen vaguely in the landscape all around him, massive white concrete bridges—steel reinforcement rods projecting from them like the nerves and veins from the stumps of severed limbs; blockaded cloverleafs and figure eights and stretches of concrete road that as yet began and ended nowhere, impossible to get to, or if there, to leave; sections of huge concrete viaducts lying in rows beside the road like the vertebrae of unearthed dinosaurs; rows of idle bulldozers, trucks, and cranes; the eroding clay of the countryside bulldozed into the artificial moraines and valleys that had become the countryside. Here, he was certain, there had once been truck farms, barns, and silos, fields of onions and corn, shade trees, roadside vegetable stands. Now he felt lost in the incomplete and fantastic future. Even when he reached the city limits and drove down the quiet residential streets a feeling of nightmare and destruction pursued him, as though he expected the search for Rotterdam to take him along unfinished, cratered, and dead-end streets, with whistling air-raid wardens and policemen suddenly before him, fire reflecting on their soaking uniforms, waving him around the broken mains and hoses lying in the streets.

But he found the house easily. He went to where he reasoned it should have been and it was there. How could he have doubted where he was? He knew Chicago, knew that it was impossible to become lost on its immense but logical checkerboard of blocks, where a man needed only to know the number of the house and the number of the closest perpendicular street to pinpoint the house on the map with the certainty of fixing a position by degrees of latitude and longitude. Chicago was the most logical of cities. He calmed down, took comfort, felt reassured. As if on these streets he had returned to rules, reason, common sense.

A residential section called Oriole Park. Wine-colored brick houses built just after the war, which seemed suburban and faintly Georgian. Here it was only sprinkling. Adjacent to Rotterdam's house was a park, a large field ringed by trees and bushes and a few arc lights, which were on. Boys were playing softball in the rain; a bat thumped against a ball, someone cheered. At the entrance to the park several small boys in oversized baseball caps and gym shoes straddled bicycles around a cement drinking fountain the size of a birdbath, as a gang of teen-age girls in leather jackets and Levi's swaggered past smoking cigarettes. A sudden altercation, a girl overhearing a whispered insult or splashed with water from the fountain and shoving a boy in a clatter to the grass beneath the bicycle he had straddled, along with the boy sitting on the handlebars. Then the boy on the bicycle and pumping down the street, chased by the boy who had been riding on the handlebars, while the girls with their arms around each other's shoulders vanished among the shrubbery of the park. Down the street a woman called out her back door for her child to come home. The cry echoed by a second woman down the block. One of the children answered from blocks away. The lone voice of a man shouted from his back porch for his son. A group of boys stood below a back porch and called for another boy to come outdoors. "Yo-o, Chuck!" A feeling on the street of gas lamps and fog, and in the people of excitement and animation, like getting in the hay before the storm. In the back yard of Rotterdam's house a man smoking a pipe was playing catch beneath an empty blowing clothesline with two young girls. Both man and girls were wearing hardball gloves.

Then Rotterdam's wife, the young dark woman in sweater and toreador pants, her jet black hair blowing as she leaned out the aluminum door, stood before him. Her husband was not at home but was expected any moment.

She let him in, reluctantly he thought, and left him on a plastic-covered sofa in the small living room while she went into the small dining room and returned to the sewing machine, where she was piecing the material of a girl's dress. She had a broad, olive face and a classical nose originating above the eyebrows. He saw her as a Jewess in biblical Palestine, as in a colored illustration of a Sunday school lesson, attired in robe and sandals, a veil across the lower portion of her face, an earthen water jug upon her shoulder. The decor of the room, however, was Greek. A large technicolor photograph of the Parthenon with a special lamp illuminating it, wallpaper with a pattern of the Ionic design, and ashtrays and vases in the classical Greek black and tan, with Greek lettering and the classical figures of piping or spear-carrying men and dancing maidens. Above the vase on the coffee table he caught the gray flicker of the television set, which unconsciously he had been watching. The sound was on softly but there seemed to be no dialogue, only the agitation of the atonal music in the background and the sound effects of gunfire, horse hooves, cattle hooves, wagon wheels on bedrock, and the whoops and screams of stampede or slaughter.

He fled to the window and sights of the approaching storm. Boys and girls were fleeing the park, some pausing in the downpour to circle and examine the Duesenberg and calling to those who had raced on to return.

Mrs. Rotterdam was in the kitchen calling out the back door for the man and two girls playing catch to come in out of the rain.

Inside, the man collected the baseball gloves and put them in a closet. The woman leaned toward him and whispered something Magnuson could not hear. But the man appeared to glance in his direction and nod.

"Pa," one of the girls said. "You're not going, are you, Pa?"

The man had taken a jacket from the closet and was putting it on. "Yes," he said. "I've got to go now."

"But why, Pa? How come you got to?"

"Pa," the other girl said, "you were supposed to fix my bike before you go."

"Your father's got to go now," the woman said.

"Girls, I got to go," the man agreed.

"But, Ma," the girl said, "he has to fix my bike."

The man opened the back door and Magnuson jumped up to pursue him only to sit down again when the man returned, wheeling a bicycle into the kitchen. He set it upside down on the floor and adjusted the chain and sprocket with a wrench he took from a drawer. He relit his pipe, drank the last mouthful in a quart of beer, and began to whistle. A fleshy man with broad hips and sloping shoulders, he looked as if he had once been a sailor, happy-go-lucky in his whites, and was now the foreman of a loading dock or shipping room. Facially the girls resembled him, and their physiques suggested his, but whereas he was fair, sandy-haired, and freckled, they were like their mother, raven-haired and dark. The mother, meanwhile, returned to the sewing machine.

Magnuson sat stunned, insulted by their audacity. Did they think he was so doddering and feeble that they could pretend that Rotterdam, who was parading before his very eyes, was not at home? The man obviously lived in the house, was the father of the children and the husband of the wife. Did the man really believe he could dress to leave, announce his intention to leave, then dawdle fixing children's toys and finally leave without Magnuson deducing who he was? What a reckless but self-possessed man was this Rotterdam.

He certainly wasn't acting like any panic-stricken witness to a brutal murder.

The man finished with the bicycle but instead of leaving came into the living room to watch the last of the western on the television. The girls sat on either arm of his chair and laid their heads on his shoulders so that the three of them made the triangular portrait of a plump man flanked by cherubs. The man resembled a beer salesman less than he did the driver who delivered the cases from the truck. He didn't look Jewish either.

He nodded to Magnuson. "What do you think of Bud?" he said.

"I think," Magnuson said, convinced that some confrontation between them was being forced, "he's got a lot of nerve."

The man thought about this. "You mean because he's a salesman?"

The telephone rang and the woman answered it. "I'm sorry but Mr. Rotterdam's not at home . . . If it's important you could try his old apartment at Fullerton and Clark. He was supposed to stop by there to pick up some things before he came home tonight . . . Yes, that's right. The old address on his business card . . . I think the phone is already disconnected there . . . He ought to be on his way home by now, though . . ."

What a cool customer was this Rotterdam. Not once had he taken his eyes from the western on the television while his wife was telling lies into the phone. Magnuson wondered why they had let him in the house, why she hadn't lied to him at the door and sent him on a wild goose chase as she had the caller on the phone. Only the presence of the children seemed to guarantee his safety.

Then Rotterdam kissed the girls, who managed to cling to his neck for a moment even after he rose. He said good-bye to the woman and was about to exit out the front door when Magnuson seized his arm. He said, "Do you take me for a fool?"

The man reddened, turned to the woman.

"Maybe you'd better tell me what you're trying to pull, lady?" Magnuson said. He pointed his hat at the man at the door.

"What's he talking about?" the woman said. The man shrugged.

"You're Bud Rotterdam," Magnuson said, continuing to point with his hat.

Both the man and woman were embarrassed. Then the man laughed, nervously. "He's not Bud," the woman said.

"What are you, a process server?" the man said. "Because you've got to be somebody who never saw Bud before."

"I'm not a fool," Magnuson said. "I saw you tonight up in Wauconda. At Bang's Lake." He came up close and gazed with recognition into his face.

"You may have seen me before," the man admitted. "But you couldn't have seen me anywhere but here tonight. You've got the wrong guy. I'm not Bud. Are you a cop?"

"What do you think?"

"I think you're a cop."

"What's your name, lady?"

"Sophie Rotterdam. You see, before . . ."

"And yours?"

"Gerald Olson."

He knew without asking that the surnames of the two girls Olson had left half-asleep in the easy chair were Olson. Knew even before the woman informed him that she and Olson were divorced, that Olson was the father of her girls, that she had remarried Rotterdam, and that Olson had visiting privileges tonight but had not taken the girls out anywhere because of the storm nor to his own house because his second wife would not have them inside the door. (This last whispered with her back to the girls.)

"Then Bud is at his old apartment?" Magnuson interrupted, looking at his feet.

"If he did stop there . . . and if he's still there."

The couple looked embarrassed, ashamed. To Magnuson they had secrets that were lascivious, passionate, corrupt. He suspected that their marriage had not entirely ended with their divorce, and that Olson might well have cuckolded Rotterdam on the pretense of visiting his children.

Magnuson was at the phone, trying to call Rotterdam's old apartment. But the phone was already disconnected.

"You were right," Magnuson said, putting on his hat and making for the door. "I'm here on police business. Your husband isn't in any real danger or trouble to speak of but I've got to see him right away. If he isn't at his old apartment I'll call you back. If he comes home while I'm gone tell him not to leave the house or talk to anyone until I return. In fact you ought to lock your doors."

Then he was in the Duesenberg and heading against red lights and buses across the city in the direction of the lake, had already gone deep into the checkerboard of those long, equal, and recurrent blocks before he remembered that an expressway he had never used had been built recently to cross the city at an angle from the Loop in the east to O'Hare Airport and those superhighways and tollways that were now being constructed in the west, and that if he had taken it the time of his trip would have been cut by two-thirds. But he would have been unfamiliar with the expressway turnoffs, and did not know where that expressway was in relation to where he was now, and besides it was much too late to change his course, for he was mired in that monotonous and somber checkerboard of streets that were never broken by any curve or diverted at any rotary or square. He felt like a pawn moved logically but inconsequentially from square to square. Block after block of low buildings, dirty yellow brick apartments, two-story factories, and disused stores whose display windows seemed to show only a few dusty, outdated, and inexplicable pieces of plumbing or dusty, yellowed girdles, nurses' uniforms, and mismatched artificial limbs, the people gathered in the streets at the bus signs and kiosks. The blocks contradicted the power of the Duesenberg and his own sense of urgency and duty and even destiny with a terrifying montage of grotesque and guilty images: Bonny Wenzel robbed at knifepoint by the pair of Mexicans who, the contents of the cash register in their pockets, hold the knife blade against her throat and force her on the tabletop of one of the booths, the fat, pockmarked Mexican first upon that hard rubber-doll body, while his thin, rat-whiskered friend stands behind him holding a small high-heeled foot at arm's length in either hand; and Nancy Rhinelander, disgraced by his discovery of her theft and use of drugs and despondent that her incompetence should be responsible for her patient's death, flooding her veins with a lethal dosage of those drugs, or poking the barrel of that mysterious pistol she owned into the tan, wrinkled, freckled socket of a turquoise eye and blowing that eye back into the brain of her blond head; and Frazer Farquarson not dead after all but still very much alive as that faint throbbing in the vein along his throat had attested and trying to breathe beneath that sheet Magnuson has stretched across his face and which he is too weak to remove himself; and the drunken Moonys staggering out of the cellar of Wenzel's barn with blood, hay, and manure on their hands and screaming, "Murder!" above the bleats and bells.

Then at last the city ended and Rotterdam's stone and brick apartment house rose before him like the tower of a Norman abbey. Beyond the apartment the landscape of Lincoln Park, the zoo, the string of headlights on the Outer Drive, and finally the lake. He left the Duesenberg doubleparked in the street. In the vestibule rows of bells and mailboxes, all with names except one on the sixth floor. The door from the vestibule into the building was unlocked; the small carpeted lobby was deserted; the elevator, according to the needle, was on the sixth floor; he rang, but the needle remained on six; rang again, leaned on the button, but with no more success, for the needle remained on six and he could hear no cables moving up and down or swinging in the shaft. Of all the times for the elevator to be out of order. He found a stairway, carpeted and dark; holding on to the bannister he ran up the stairs, two at a time, holding his heart. When he reached the landing of the fifth floor he heard the cables humming and clacking in the shaft and on an impulse he turned down the corridor of the fifth floor, ran to the elevator, and pressed the down button; but by then the elevator had passed, the arrow indicating the third floor. He waited until he heard the elevator doors open in the lobby.

On the sixth floor the door to Rotterdam's apartment stood open, the lights on. The living room was bare. Only several cardboard boxes stacked beside the door, along with several six packs of beer; a pile of dusty phonebooks beside the dead phone on the dusty floor. The muffled music, applause, and voices of television sets in apartments along the line. He leaned out an open window, saw the street lights in Lincoln Park, marking the lanes through the zoo, the headlights of the traffic on the Outer Drive, the darkness of the lake, heard the distant sounds of tires and horns.

Footprints in the dust that led across the floor to the bathroom, where water was running from the tap and down the green stain in the sink. He shut it off and crept to the shower stall and pulled apart the tattered plastic curtains beaded with drops of water. No one was in the tub, but a bloody towel was soaking on the drain. Footprints led through the dust back into the living room and into the bedroom.

An army cot and on the floor beside it an ashtray full of cigarette butts, a half-empty bottle of beer, an open paperback book. The body was on the other side of the cot, where it had rolled after the head was battered by the blows of a bloodied and unbroken bottle of beer that had rolled across the floor. The man was dying. Papers in his wallet identified him as Rotterdam.

The third murdered man that Magnuson in a single night had discovered. A coincidence impossible to dismiss as chance. Dazed, he dropped to the cot and saw himself as the police would see him, the prime and even only suspect. Was he mad? Was he having sick moments, momentary and passing spells of amnesia, in which he blacked out, sleepwalked, stepped out of time, went contrary and berserk, when the purpose of that crusade he was embarked upon tonight and which he had made the moral center of his life became inverted, and he was transformed into his opposite? Had he deluded himself into believing he was preventing murders and chasing a murderer when in fact he was himself the murderer and pursued no one but his mad, malevolent, violent self? In those brief moments just after the nurse had left him in the sickroom and just before he called her back to confront her with the corpse, had he found Farquarson alive, asleep, and snoring or, God forbid, awake, alert, and raising a weak hand or even able to whisper his name in greeting? Had he slipped the pillow from beneath his head, placed it atop his perplexed and frightened face, and leaned with all his weight upon the hot struggling feathers until the bed was still and the air smelled of dead chickens plucked from boiling water? When he found the note in Farquarson's handwriting, had he gone to Wauconda not to discover the identity of the murderer but to silence Wenzel, whom he feared had learned his name from Farquarson, who had somehow managed to suspect him? When he wandered into the barn, his presence hidden by the bells and bleatings and rustlings, did he have a second spell of sickness just as he encountered Wenzel alive and spreading straw about the pen? And when Wenzel set down the fork to attend to a troubled sheep, had he stormed the pen, snatched up that fork, and when Wenzel, surprised, confronted him or even perhaps pleaded for his life, thrust the tines home into his stomach, then returned to the barnyard, where he recovered from the spell, re-entered the barn, and discovered Wenzel's body? And having learned from the drunken Moony that a beer salesman named Rotterdam had been at the barn and might have seen the murder through the window that looked down into the pen, had he pursued the salesman into the city and in a third spell of sickness picked the lock to his apartment, picked up a beer bottle from those stacked inside the door, rushed the bedroom, and surprised the man on the cot and smashed in his head only to leave the apartment, awake in the hallway, and re-enter to discover him?

Then he was up and creeping through the rooms, shutting off the lights. His fingerprints and footprints were everywhere. What did it matter? He set the catch so that the door locked when he closed it. Just then a man in a sweater came out of the apartment next door, carrying a paper sack of garbage. He glanced at Magnuson, dropped the garbage down a chute, returned to his apartment, and slammed the door. Further down another door opened, keys jangled, the door locked, the pattering of a dog on the carpet and the jangle of its chain and the floor creaking and someone coughing until around the corner came an Afghan followed by a woman in slacks and fur coat. Doors began to open not only on the sixth floor but on other floors as well, letting out a confusion of music, the dialogue of television, and the far less ingratiating voices of domestic quarrels, and closed as suddenly as they had opened, muffling or stifling those sounds. The elevator cables clacked in the shaft. The overturned chair beside the elevator—had it been used to prop open the elevator door? He set it upright against the wall. Footsteps and whispered greetings as others joined him and the woman with the Afghan at the elevator, followed by the self-conscious silence of people at a funeral. When the elevator came it was already crowded. He stared at the inside of the elevator door, the brim of his wet hat pulled down all around the crown. His hands shook in his pockets, so did his arms in his sleeves; his knees gave way with the descending floor and he leaned against a man who objected and considered him with disgust. Fragments of conversations in the hallways coming from beneath the car, then from just beyond the door, and finally from above, as though the elevator were stationary and the unseen speakers beyond the door were floating up. The same with the soprano voice of an older woman practicing scales off pitch, and a man's lusty, self-satisfied laughter.

In the lobby a fight broke out between the Afghan and a poodle. The owners strained on the leashes and lifted the forequarters of the snarling, snapping dogs off the ground. A man shouted, "Lady, call off your dog!" A solitary flash of lightning and the almost simultaneous heavy thunder and tropical downpour of rain. The crowd clustered at the vestibule, adjusting raincoats and poised with half-open umbrellas. In a dark, fountain-like recess in the lobby Magnuson found a pay phone and struck a match to see the dial. He called Mrs. Rotterdam. ". . . I'm at your husband's old apartment. I ran into him just as he was going out the door. He asked me to call you and let you know that he's upset with your ex-husband hanging around the house when he's gone. I guess he doesn't believe he's just seeing his kids. He's hurt, Mrs. Rotterdam, kind of jealous. He didn't even trust himself to talk to you on the phone . . . He's going off by himself for a few days, to think things out for himself. He thinks it's best that he doesn't see you for a while. He doesn't want you to try to get in touch with him. He'll call you when he's ready."

In the receiver the intake of disbelief and injury. Then her

"Oh," like a moan. As though her most secret and irrational fear had just come true. "Did you . . . what did you tell him? . . . Because it's silly . . . it's not that at all . . ."

"Good-bye, Mrs. Rotterdam," he said. "I'm sorry. I told Buddy I didn't want to call. It's not my business, even though in my line of work I'm used to these kind of jobs. It's best to let things work out by themselves. You'll see for yourself, it will all work out in the end."

Only when he hung up did it occur to him that Rotterdam was dead. He had believed his own lies, that the temporary separation of man and wife might in fact help the marriage. He turned around and was confronted by a stepladder on which perched a janitor in a gray uniform screwing a bulb into a ceiling socket. When it came on in his hand it revealed a second man in hat, scarf, and topcoat with a newspaper under his arm and with his foot planted on the first step of the ladder. Both men were Filipinos, small khaki-colored men with mouths full of teeth and heads like skulls. They seemed posed beside the ladder, immaculate, redolent, and even arrogant, like a pair of Spanish caballeros or dons. As Magnuson put his hand to his hat and passed them they gave out with sly, inappropriate, incorrigible laughter of an Oriental culture so inscrutable and remote as to sound, in his ears, inhuman.

In the car and driving north his head cleared. He was no homicidal maniac, no amnesiac. His arteries weren't hardening, synapses weren't snapping in his brain. Someone else, a butcher who would stop at nothing to keep his identity a secret, had killed those men. He, God knows, was the detective. Good was embodied in his quest if not exactly or always in the man himself. Only his competence explained his presence at the murder scenes only moments after the crimes had been committed, those quick, clear-headed deductions and those speedy and decisive and correct actions he had taken in support of those deductions, when a less experienced or gifted man would not have dared to make the chase alone, nor even have seen that Farquarson's death was murder. And mere chance did not explain his presence, so much as fate; as though the series of so-called coincidences added up to what was no more or less than his appointed destiny.

It now occurred to him that he had trapped the murderer only to let him get away. He must have been in Wenzel's barn when he was there, hiding upstairs in the loft behind the bales of hay as he had sensed he was. When he left the farm for Wenzel's tavern, the killer must have come out of hiding and learned from the drunken and gregarious Moony the identity of the man he had seen loitering about the barn as he was killing Wenzel. He must have gone to Wenzel's tavern to get Rotterdam's address from Bonny Wenzel after Magnuson had been there. Then Magnuson had beaten him down to Chicago, had actually gotten ahead of him only to let him get ahead again. While he was at Rotterdam's house, mistaking Olson for Rotterdam, the killer must have seen and recognized the Duesenberg in the street outside, and called Rotterdam's house from a pay phone, learning from Mrs. Rotterdam that Rotterdam was not there but might be at his old apartment. Then it had been the murderer who called on the phone when Magnuson was there. He had been in Rotterdam's apartment bashing in Rotterdam's head as Magnuson had entered the vestibule, had ridden down in the elevator as Magnuson had labored up the stairs.

If the murderer had killed Wenzel because of what he had learned from Farquarson's letter and killed Rotterdam for being in the vicinity of Wenzel's barn (and Magnuson wondered what he had been doing in his old apartment, hiding from the murderer or merely waiting until his wife's former husband had left the house in Oriole Park?) and was that desperate and determined to keep secret his identity and obliterate his tracks, why, then Moony and Mrs. Wenzel and who knew who else were also in danger of their lives. He had not killed them on the spot, as soon as he had gotten the information he wanted from them, because of the gang of boys at Moony's listening to the hillbilly music and stumbling outside the house, urinating against the clapboards and yodeling, and at Wenzel's tavern the pair of Mexicans at the bar (had the presence of the very men Bonny Wenzel feared actually saved her life?).

And what desperation the murderer must be feeling now with Magnuson in the Duesenberg breathing down his neck. He must know that at every turn he had been pursued. Surely the Duesenberg had become a familiar and puzzling presence. At Farquarson's, Wenzel's tavern, Wenzel's barn, before Rotterdam's house in Oriole Park, and doubleparked before Rotterdam's apartment house in Lincoln Park. (And since he must have known that two strangers were at Wenzel's barn, he must have gone after Rotterdam and not Magnuson because Rotterdam, unlike Magnuson, had seen him, or witnessed the actual crime.) Given his logic and ruthlessness, the man would have no choice now that he knew he was pursued but to retrace his route and silence those who had seen and spoken with him earlier and could place him at the scene of the crimes, and perhaps even to attempt to waylay and murder Magnuson himself somewhere along the way. Indeed he could be certain this would be so. Hadn't he demonstrated his power to react and reason exactly like the murderer? Confronted with the same obstacles and reversals, hadn't they come upon the same solutions and pursued the same course, the one killing and the other trying to stop him from killing and to keep others from being killed? Small wonder Magnuson could believe in a weak moment that he was himself the murderer. The only difference was the gulf between good and evil. And that was all the difference in the world.

Since Magnuson could not be in all places at once protecting everyone, he had to make a choice. He did not worry about Mrs. Rotterdam since she had only talked to the killer on the phone; and less about Moony, since the driveway before his house had been dark and the murderer must have seen that he was drunk, than he did about Bonny Wenzel, who had seen him in her lighted tavern at least once and more likely twice, the first time when, like Magnuson, he learned from her that Wenzel was at his barn, and knew that Magnuson had asked after her husband, who was dead, and later after Rotterdam, who was also dead. As it was in the murderer's interest to kill her before any of the others, so was it in Magnuson's interest to get to her before the murderer and keep her alive, for of those who were endangered she could best describe and identify the man. Therefore he headed for Wauconda and Mrs. Wenzel.

The notification of the police was even more out of the question now than it had been before. The bureaucratic incompetence, contradiction, confusion, and conflict of jurisdiction there would be now! One police force would be enemy enough, but not only were the Lake Forest, Wauconda, Lake County, and state police forces involved but the Chicago and Cook County forces as well, along with the Park District police, since Rotterdam's apartment was close to Lincoln Park, and who knew, perhaps even the FBI. Even if he provided them immediately with all his information and suspicions, hours, days, and even weeks might pass before they would be willing to connect the murders to a single man, when perhaps no more than seconds had in the case of both Farquarson and Wenzel been the difference between the escape and capture of the killer, and for the victim, of life and death. The time that would be wasted in the paperwork of reports, conferences, interrogations, all of which would be duplicated and then reduplicated, not just in one police force but five; and the further delays caused by jealousy, rivalry, and incompetence, one officer withholding information from his fellows, a town police department withholding information from the county police, the state police withholding information from both. While the murders would be featured daily in the newspapers, traveling from front page to last until the readers, like the police themselves, would weary of them, and the pressure outside the force and the dedication from within the force to solve them would diminish and finally disappear, and the crimes would remain unsolved and the murderer undiscovered and, what was worse, unpunished. But he, Magnuson, alone held the thread that linked the three crimes as one. Contained within the rules and boundaries of his mind was the emerging pattern of lines and times, names and places, opportunities and motives. He had to keep it there. One man alone, if he believed that, despite his many drawbacks and deficiencies, he was good and honest and stood tall in the good graces of truth and justice, could with a little luck solve the mystery before the night was out. Indeed, it appeared it was his destiny to do so.

Convinced of his own innocence and competence, he assumed the responsibility for everyone and gave himself entirely to the chase. The exhilaration of that competence. That innocence. The awesomeness of that responsibility. That destiny. The thrill of this cross-country chase, of sweeping aside the wind. The power of those cylinders beneath the polished hood, the miracle of that instant acceleration beneath the foot. The glamour of the passing headlights and the lighted skyscrapers of the Loop retreating behind him, as though taken by the turning earth that, miraculously, did not take the Duesenberg. The spaces of darkened concrete eaten up beneath the white wheels. The sense of passing everything and leaving everything behind. As though on a superhighway that crisscrossed the nation and in a car that traveled at the speed of jets. Past small towns, farms, other cities, other suburbs. All encountered in a split second and left behind. Wonderful adventure! Lonely crusader of the cause. The mood of headlights like searchlights, sirens, figures crouching on the running board, drawn revolvers out the windows, tommy guns and remote roadhouses on the no-man's-land of moonlit lakeshores or among the woods of lonely moonlit country roads. And somewhere on the road ahead the secret enemy speeding through the same vast, changing landscape of moonlight on an errand just as desperate as his own. But it was not so much a man that Magnuson pursued as it was a force. The evil, natural, ultimate force of death. But not so much a force as the working out of Magnuson's own spiritual destiny, which was in the end himself. Which was in the end no more or less than death.

CHAPTER SEVENTEEN

THE AIRPORT

At the moment O'Hare Airport is a combination of futuristic space terminal and frontier town. Rising on flat farmland on the outskirts of the city, it is, as it has been for years, in the process of being built. From the parking lot where thousands of cars are parked in ruts and puddles, passengers and visitors pick their way on muddy planks set out upon and sinking in the mud and on muddy board sidewalks enclosed by temporary wooden fences, past work shacks and tarpaulin-covered machinery, then onto stretches of newly finished and already muddy concrete walks, an occasional kerosene lantern hanging from a sawhorse to light the way. Ahead rise the blocklike terminals with their neon airline signs. Some completed, some unfinished, some rising perversely from their own patches of mud and as yet unconnected with the complex as a whole. Overhead, the jets, outlined by their colored, blinking lights, descend and rise immense as skyscrapers. What a show of power! What a glamorous sight! Surely they can ferry nothing shabby, nothing ordinary, only sun-tanned million-aires, furred women with lapdogs, foreign diplomats, a private cham-pagne party of Hollywood and Manhattan personalities, and can travel only to exotic islands and the distant financial capitals of the world. To the file of people tramping through the mud there is a quickening of heart and foot. Hurry! they tell themselves. It is al-ready happening! The moment is always now! From the glassed-in observation tower and the rain-swept observation deck they look down upon the file of wind-blown passengers going to and from the idle planes, the inconspicuous but efficient labors of the ground crews, the noisy but effortless takeoffs and landings of the heavy planes; share in the glamour of the pilots, stewardesses, and passengers, and in that instantaneous and glittering mobility that has become the hall-mark of their lives; share even in that catastrophe they more than half expect, when the silver plane will fail against the sky, and they will witness that public theater of sirens on the runway, towers of flames and smoke.

The plane from Miami carrying Allegro, the alleged overlord of Chicago crime, and his companion, Lazzaretto, a retired captain of the Chicago police force, has just touched down, and the two men midway in the file of passengers have disembarked down the portable stairway and onto the runway shiny with the rain. They have walked past the friends and relatives of other passengers waiting behind a thick rope, as though for a table in a fashionable restaurant, and among the long loose crowd down the long concrete corridors, have waited in line for their baggage to arrive on the freight escalator, have carried their own bags through the terminal and down the silver escalator somewhere in the long line of soldiers, sailors, marines, and airmen with flightbags and duffel bags, salesmen with sample cases, executives with briefcases, suburban women in slacks and sunglasses meeting their husbands, the two men greeted by no one and no more conspicuous than anyone else. Everywhere this public and exciting light, like the popping of flashbulbs or the play of spotlights at the premiere of a movie.

Outside, the two men stand patiently beneath the roof of the curving sidewalk before the terminal among the comings and goings of pilots and stewardesses and the black baggage handlers attired like white pilots, and the dashes of executives and salesmen. Every-thing out here in the night and the wet seems to jump and snap and glitter. A procession of taxicabs and private cars comes up the wide, curving lane, discharging and taking on passengers during a hurried and nervous stop, as if calling at the Pump Room, the portico of a foreign embassy, the first night at the opera.

A Lincoln Continental pulls up for Lazzaretto, and for the first time the two men relax, satisfied that their conspiracy to sneak home unannounced has worked; no cameras, microphones, or reporters have appeared to greet them, and their hands loosen on the hats they have carried ready to put up before their faces. Unfortunately, with the discovery by the Chicago newspapers that the city's most famous criminal and a former captain of its own police force were on a holiday together, they have had to cut short their long-planned vacation in Florida. Daily reports have informed the public when they sat side by side in cars and restaurants, when they had adjoining hotel rooms, and in some instances adjoining beds. Editorials have condemned them; featured articles have presented detailed investigations into their private lives. Reporters and photographers have observed and obstructed their every move, even hired a fishing boat to trail the boat they hired, with undercover agents from the local Florida police and, allegedly, investigators from the Chicago police, dispatched by the commissioner himself, always in the background. They have been surrounded, hounded, mobbed, blinded by flashbulbs, provoked to respond angrily while, unknown to them, a microphone has been snuck under their chins. Their photographs, the tanned faces behind the dark glasses—Allegro usually looking confused, embarrassed, and in the act of sneaking away, and Lazzaretto outraged and as though in the act of attacking the camera—have become common sights on the local television news shows and in the daily papers. The fatigue and disappointment of their ordeal still registers on their faces. Now the driver of the Lincoln, who is Lazzaretto's son, reaches across the seat and holds the door open, while the two men embrace and exchange farewells, both grateful that the ordeal is over. Lazzaretto utters some final indignation at the press's treatment of his friend, whom he sincerely believes has been slandered and has had his privacy invaded even though he has committed no crime for which he can be convicted. "You're a martyr, Frank," he says. Allegro utters some final apology and regret. Then Lazzaretto is gone in the car, leaving Allegro alone, waiting with his leather bag in hand like the tall and slightly overweight and tanned president of some new, enterprising, and successful corporation; with his pressed raincoat and dark hair silvery at the temples he could even pass for a model in a men's fashion magazine.

A Cadillac pulls up against the curb and the small man who is Allegro's uncle jumps out of the front seat beside the driver, greets

Allegro affectionately, then climbs back in, leaving Allegro to open
and close his own door into the back seat. The door shuts silently,
and in the plush and private darkness of the roomy, airy, and brand-
new-smelling car the glamorous technology and dramatic facade are
left to the world outside the windows. Immediately the Cadillac is
racing down a superhighway, past the neon-lit luxury motels, hotels,
and nightclubs built on the no-man's-land outside the airport, a new
city of sorts existing solely for the airport and its wealthy, far-flung
transients. Races through the suburbs of new houses with their check-
erboards of streets under high arching street lights, jockeys among a
crowd of other speeding, gleaming cars for the best opening in a
given lane, headlights and taillights reflecting on the wet pavements.
Now the outskirts of the city pass below the expressway on either
side, neighborhoods dense with houses, stores, and factories built
low to the ground; and in the distant Loop ahead the lighted skyscrapers appear unconnected to this landscape, as though rising on
an island in the middle of the lake.

Allegro's uncle is turned around in his seat beside the driver. He
looks ancient, withered, weathered, like a dwarfish Sicilian peasant;
wears large horn-rimmed glasses the color of ox blood, a fedora that
appears to be held on his bald head by his ears, and a chesterfield coat
that appears too large for his height and frame. He has himself just
returned from wintering in the Argentine, where he has both interests
and relatives. A former dentist, he is still called "the Doctor," in fact
insists on being called "the Doctor," and manages—in name anyway
—a nightclub that exists, chiefly, so that vast sums may be invested
in it and, allegedly, lost in it, sums that might otherwise be paid in
taxes. "You got some bad press," he says.

"I don't want to talk about it," Allegro says, aware that his uncle
knows that he is brooding. "I just hope Lazzaretto don't get hurt. I
heard there was talk about taking away his pension. I don't see how
they can do it, though." He wonders how he could have been so
naïve as to fail to see that the press would go after the pair of them,
Lazzaretto especially, even though he was retired from the force and
legitimately an old boyhood friend whom he had kept in touch with
for years. He should have known that the police would have to respond to the pressure of the press. The truth is he often forgets, or
finds it impossible to believe, that he is the notorious public figure
the press makes him out to be. He feels ashamed, as though he, personally, has let Lazzaretto down. What is worse, this was a trip both
families had planned for years, and the two men were to have been
joined later by their wives, who are themselves old friends.

"We just got a call from a guy named Romanski," the Doctor says. "He runs a place called The Hideaway out on the golf course we sell beer to. He says Fiore was out to get Scarponi and was trying to use some kid Romanski knew to do the job."

Allegro starts forward, drops back, nods. He hasn't known of any bad blood between Fiore and Scarponi. He wonders if it has to do with that matter of Scarponi and a few others—with Allegro's blessing if not exactly backing—initiating what might be construed as an intrusion into Fiore's territory in an unincorporated area near Niles.

"But Fiore's called off the job and he told Romanski he done it because he suspects Romanski told someone about the job. Romanski's scared Fiore will come after him."

Allegro removes his eyes from the city passing below the expressway, the house lights, billboards, and factories stretching to the bruised smoky horizon, and settles into the cushioned corner of his seat, his legs stretched out and his hands in his raincoat pockets. "He's smart to be scared," he says. "Still, I'd like it a lot better if this kid had called to tell us Fiore was out to get Scarponi." Only after he has spoken does he realize the implications of this desire. He removes a brown hand and contemplates in the shudder of the passing street lights and the headlights of other cars the manicure of his nails and the oversized diamond ring on his finger.

"This Polack says he didn't know Fiore planned to use the kid to get Scarponi," the Doctor says. He glances apprehensively out the windshield at the taillights of the speeding traffic just ahead and then remonstratively at the impassive driver, who tends to tailgate and, when he has to, suddenly but skillfully apply the brakes. "He only found out what Fiore was planning when he accused him of fouling up. Anyway, that's what he says."

"So how come he calls us?" Allegro says. His voice is deep and resonant, friendly but authoritative, the voice of a sales manager of a thriving firm.

"Protection. What else? And according to him just in case in the future Fiore changes his mind and goes after Scarponi again. But we don't have to buy that. Maybe he figured we wouldn't want Scarponi out of the picture, knowing how we feel about him, and knowing how we feel about Fiore. If you want my counsel, Frank, that's the way I'd figure it."

"Maybe," Allegro says. And later: "I don't know why those two guys can't get along. Maybe we ought to try to get them together." Privately he has wanted to remove Fiore from the world for a long time, to read about him washed up on a beach of Lake Michigan like a baffling, stinking whale. His grievance against him is past, present, and, more importantly, future. This is because Fiore is by instinct selfish and a loner, independent, if he can get away with it, from any organization. He cannot be trusted or predicted. (What kind of a guy is it who would do such business with a small-time Polack hood?) He is more a continual threat of trouble than a great danger, and Allegro could probably order him executed and suffer no recriminations. It would not be likely to coalesce the supporters of Fiore into an alliance against him, nor alienate any supporters of his own. But such an action would be too gratuitous and might well be construed as a deliberate show of indiscriminate, despotic force unsupported by any reasonable motive or by the counsel of the other sources which, as far as they know, have always been consulted up to now. Distrust, deviousness might well result. Phone calls from the small-timers like Romanski might no longer come his way. They might feel they could no longer trust the judiciousness of his actions, a man like Romanski afraid he might be punished for having, no matter how innocently, participated in a plot against Scarponi. These were not necessarily ruptures and suspicions he could not repair by good words and deeds, but why risk uncomfortable moments and expending time and energy simply to repair without return? He has an image, he knows what his image is, and so, he thinks, does everyone. He knows this image is not necessarily the man himself, but he is not certain that others know this. He is unhappy at the thought of being viewed by others, or even by himself, as performing in a different role. It is dangerous to destroy the image; it confuses people, makes them nervous. How much more comfortable for himself, and orderly for everyone, if he could present to all concerned parties after the fact of Scarponi's murder a legitimate excuse for Fiore's execution. He feels that an opportunity has been lost before it has been presented to him. "Scarponi's got a son, doesn't he?"

The Doctor turns around and throws his arm across the seat. "A good kid, Frank. He's graduated from college."

"Scarponi's got him managing one of the stores, doesn't he?"

"On Central Avenue. We sent him to Europe to learn about wines, Frank. He knows all about wines. Zinfandel, that's what he advised me to drink for a table wine. It comes from California. Don't drink that cheap French stuff when you can drink Zinfandel, he told me. He's the wine buyer for the company."

"Didn't he try out for the Cubs once?"

"I don't know, Frank," the Doctor says, somewhat disgusted. "I don't know nothing about that kind of stuff."

"Yeh, he did," the driver of the car says from the corner of his mouth, his eyes still on the road. "He was just a kid. He never played professional or nothing. Lots of kids used to try out for the Cubs. They used to have a special day for it."

"Hey, hey, hey," the Doctor says to the driver, looking back over his shoulder out the windshield.

"Hey, what?" the driver says.

"You're going too fast. The road gets slippery when it's wet. You ought to know that." In response the driver speeds up, and the Doctor jerks his thumb at him as though to say to Allegro, Will you get him?

"What did he play?" Allegro says.

"Second base," says the driver. "Good glove, weak stick. I used to go with Scarponi sometimes and watch him play sandlot when he was in high school."

"I remember now," Allegro says. "Scarponi used to talk him up."

"What do you want to know about Scarponi's kid for?" the Doctor says.

"His name's Scarponi, isn't it?"

Concrete overpasses and a series of large green road signs with white letters flashing by.

"It's not like we got to change the name of the store," Allegro says.

"You're thinking about who'd take over the stores if Fiore had gone through with it?" the Doctor asks.

"No," Allegro says.

By now the expressway no longer sweeps over new streets and new houses but neighborhoods of old dilapidated congested factories and houses, offset by occasional red brick churches, so incongruous with the expressway that it seems so modern a road could not have been built to take motorists to these streets but only to speed cars through them as quickly as they can travel. And the enlarging skyscrapers of the Loop no less incongruous with these neighborhoods, dominating them like a cathedral over slums, but appropriate to the expressway, the logical front door at which it should end, the castle at the end of the rainbow.

"It's not like we got to change the labels on the bottles," Allegro says.

He would prefer to be rid of Fiore at less expense than this, would like to be rid of him at no cost at all. But are the consequences of his plan any different from what they would have been had Fiore not changed his mind, and Romanski failed to make his call? An opportunity, costly as it is, has been presented to him, and how can he tell when he will get another? To persuade him even further in his plan it occurs to him that Fiore's murder of Scarponi might well have been intended as a personal warning to Allegro, that Fiore intended to say, in effect, I could have killed you as I have killed him. All along it is Allegro whom Fiore really wants to kill. Only he does not dare to kill Allegro! The murder of Scarponi was to have been an act of respect, a confession of fear. He, Allegro, has had a close call and at the same time no close call at all. He is delirious with the fact that he is alive. He celebrates and marvels at his power to escape the threat of death. Until now, in this matter of sacrificing Scarponi he has been merely thinking out loud, at most testing a scheme. Now the fate of Scarponi, whom he can make out to be in one sense already dead, is sealed.

He leans toward his uncle and places his hand on the driver's back to indicate he is included in what he says: "My idea is to call Romanski, quick as we can." The driver swerves into the right lane and without reducing speed turns off onto the next exit ramp. "Get him to tell this kid of his that Fiore wants to go through with the contract on Scarponi after all. Tell him if he does that for us he doesn't have to worry about Fiore."

The Cadillac doubleparked and idling before a small tavern on a corner with a stop light, only a block from the expressway but already deep into the city. Middle-aged men, hands in the pockets of their jackets, and old men in long overcoats, troop by. The Doctor already out of the car and leaning his head back in through the window. "I don't know, Frank," he says.

"Where can we set him up?" Allegro says.

"We could get him over to Angelo's, I suppose."

"Then you or Angelo ought to be there to talk to him. Have Romanski tell his kid to pick him up there. The closer to closing time the better."

"He don't usually get to bed before sunrise," the driver says.

In the air the high pitch, expectancy, and explosive energy of creation.

"We get him to Angelo's to warn him Fiore's coming after him," the Doctor says. "We tell him we just got tipped off by Fiore's friend Romanski. And if he can't arrange to protect himself we'll have one of our guys traveling with him tomorrow, for his own protection."

Allegro lays his hand on his uncle's forearm and squeezes it with respect and admiration. "If you can get in touch with Scarponi," he says, "go ahead and set it up for tonight. We got to do it quick."

"You go ahead," the Doctor says, starting for the tavern. "I'll take a taxi home if we can't set it up, I'll take one out to Angelo's if we can."

The Cadillac on the expressway again above the rooftops of the houses that stretch to the horizon on either side and again among the force of racing cars and meeting across the highway another inexhaustible force of cars, pair after pair of headlights, side by side, one after another, curving, descending, rising, as though engaged in a futuristic race against the night. Out the rear window the size of the lighted skyscrapers in the Loop decreases, as once more the outskirts and suburbs with their evenly spaced houses and street lights are encountered. The destination, the airport again. Allegro's daughter is coming home on a plane scheduled to land in approximately an hour, and he has decided to surprise her and meet her at the gate. Indeed, it has suddenly become a good thing for him to advertise his presence at the airport, to spend that hour waiting in a public crowd. She is on vacation from Penn State, where she is a senior in elementary education, and has just written to him while he was in Florida of the job she has taken for next year teaching first grade in a western suburb, and more importantly, of her engagement to a medical student, a member of an old wealthy New Jersey family of American descent, an engagement she wants her parents to announce formally. Inexplicably he is overcome with affection and the need to give protection: that image of a father hugging tightly his small frightened child. Another man out there in that night and continent to the east! And for her, another life! Who knows how it all will end? But he can identify with her enough to know her joy as his own, even though he will take her leaving as his loss.

He knows he will not be able to watch her plane approach and touch down, that his fear and sense of helplessness will not leave him until the plane taxis on the runway, at which time he will know relief and joy. He anticipates the surprise her beautiful and professionally cosmeticized face will show when she spies him in the crowd, the feel of her weight against him as they embrace, the long walk arm in arm as he carries her flightbag down those long, well-lit corridors through the crowds of well-dressed, well-to-do, important, even famous people. Then through the modern and luxurious and functional decor of the terminal and in all that public and alluring light, her father sharing in the public broadcast of her charm. Who could fail to notice so expensively tailored, well-groomed, and glamorous a girl? It is as though a spotlight follows her, and her personality projects like starlight from her eyes. Soldiers and airmen as they light their cigarettes stare above the flame, saleswomen at the gift shops peer out through the glass walls, pilots take their eyes from the stewardesses they accompany, while passengers give her double takes and tap the shoulders of their friends. Then to sit beside her in the privacy and comfort of the car and listen to her news of her fiancé and her first job teaching school. Speeding down superhighways in their journey over and under the city home. His daughter. Who knows? Perhaps the last time she will come home to him alone.

Scarponi, he recalls, has a daughter the same age as his own. They have mutual friends and sometimes attend the same parties. She goes to college too and must be flying home for her vacation. She might even be a passenger on one of those planes circling the airport overhead. Scarponi himself might be at the gate already or, even like Allegro, driving through the city on his way to greet her. "Scarponi's daughter goes to school somewhere in Florida, doesn't she?" he says.

"University of Miami," the driver says. "She's a cheerleader. Hey, remember when we were watching that football game on television last winter and I kept pointing her out. She was shaking pom-poms and jumping up and down. Toward the end of the game they had that real nice shot of her on the sidelines crying."

Besides, Allegro consoles himself, why was Scarponi stalling in the scheme against Fiore? Where was the money and connections he was supposed to bring? Something was wrong somewhere. Maybe he thought he would be protected behind Allegro in the move against Fiore, and lost his nerve when he discovered Allegro had him out in front? What in hell had Allegro built him up for, if not to get behind him at convenient times?

Allegro is fatalistic about it all. Everybody's time has got to come around. Everyone is mortal. And Scarponi, like those men who have made contracts with the Devil, has had a note he knew was always on demand call. His family was provided for, far more than most. And Scarponi had done far better than most men. He was rich, famous. He was somebody! What else was there anyway? How many good men—better men than Scarponi even—made that much of themselves? He has basked in luxury and limelight and, unlike the more reclusive Allegro, has known what it was like to cabaret.

And so Scarponi who was, for reasons beyond his knowledge or control, saved from execution by his enemy Fiore, who had originally sentenced him to death, is sentenced to death a second time, this time by Allegro, his good friend.

CHAPTER EIGHTEEN

THE MASSACRE

Fog in the low spots of the fields between the rolling hills and looking like a chain of lakes. Fog in the dips of the slick blacktop, blunting the headlights of the Duesenberg.

Then Wauconda, and the emerald letters of the neon beer sign in the window of Wenzel's Bang's Lake Inn reflecting on the long green hood of the Duesenberg. Rain on the steaming gravel, plunking in the puddles of the potholes, the warm engine hissing beneath the hood. Only a pair of lights on inside the tavern. Closing time, or so Magnuson would have thought if the door were not wide open. He hesitates. No other cars parked in the lot that he can see. Surely, having overtaken every car he saw upon the road, he has come here first. Surely the ambush is his to make.

Inside, empty stools and empty booths. No one on the floor behind the bar. "Mrs. Wenzel," he says. An open window beside a booth and raindrops streaking across the table and dropping to the floor. He approaches the curtains closed on a doorway cautiously. Throws them apart violently, forgetting in his panic that the flashlight he switches on is not a gun. The slot machine, a dead-end empty hallway. Two empty washrooms behind two doors.

Outside on the gravel he studies the apartment above the tavern where, he supposes, the Wenzels live. Throws the light upon the darkened windows, anticipating the face of someone pressed against the glass. Only lace curtains framing the drawn yellow shades. Walks behind the tavern into a kind of grove and is halfway up the white exterior stairway to the apartment upstairs when he hears the distant sound of something being dragged across the ground and, in the sudden gust that blows the rain against the clapboard wall, what sounds like heavy breathing, and the groans and snorts that remind him, oddly, of raccoons. Turns off the flashlight and bounds down the stairway, heading for the lake. Feels his way between the trees, stumbling on the roots. Can hear the rain falling on the water now. Stops to listen. The dragging sound has ceased. A light splash, like a small animal entering the water. A purling, as though someone is wading and water laps his legs. Then feet stumbling on the bottom of a beached aluminum boat, something heavy dropped into that boat, a sound like a can sucking in and popping out its sides. Another splash and the boom of concrete against the boat—the anchor—the echoes seeming to come from across the lake. The creak and bang of an oarlock and the bang of an oar against the boat. The scrape of the boat along the shore. The ripple of the water against the bow. The movement of feet upon the bottom of the boat; the wobbling of the boat upon the water.

He dashes for the shore only to find himself in darkness among a maze of beached diving towers, slides, and rafts. Picks his way among posts and crosspieces until he comes to sand and almost as immediately to water. The beam of his flashlight cuts through the drizzle and strikes only a few yards from shore the first of the clouds of fog rolling on the lake and a rowboat poled by a figure standing in the stern above a second and shrouded figure slumped across the seat. Slowly the oarsman plies the oar until the bow is lost to fog. But the boat lingers at the point of vanishment as though the clouds keep pace with the oarsman and separate just enough to let him through. Then the stern vanishes, and the beam of light is sent back by the fog. Boat, ferryman, and passenger crossing into another region, another world. The hereafter. The lake of death. While Mag-

nuson on the bank makes a foray into the water in his shoes and helplessly returns. From the fog beyond the useless beam the boat rocking, footsteps on the metal bottom, the metallic bang of oarlocks,
wood against metal, the alternating creak of oarlocks, the dip, purl,
splash, and drip of oars.

He runs down the shore flashing the light until at a private dock
he finds a boat with oars; throws in the tin can of concrete which
serves as anchor, pushes off, leaps in, and with a dozen forceful poles
and strokes is in the fog, deep inside the fog, surrounded by the fog,
cut off from shore by fog. He lifts his oars and listens through their
dripping for the other boat. He can barely see the end of his oars, or
where his boat begins and ends. Fog passes over him, through him,
clings like smoke to his clothes, rolls over the surface of the water
and gives the drifting boat the illusion of moving at a high but silent
speed. Which way can he reasonably row? He fears he is already
lost, drifting for all he knows back to shore. He pulls weakly only to
brake his own advance with his oars, watching for the other boat as
it might glide from the fog across his stern or bow or collide midships
with his own.

A thunderous splash close by! A massive weight that made a
great ker-thump followed by a ker-plash that must have sent the
water six feet in the air. So loud a splash for an anchor? It has come
to his right and he pulls with his left arm until he sets his course and
then rows hard, stern first. He thinks he sees the outer rings of the
concentric circles made by the splash. Hears the feet on the bottom
of the boat again and raises his oars to listen. Hark! The creak of
oarlocks, the dip and plash of oars. Hush! The man is rowing. He has
thrown something other than the anchor overboard. Magnuson rows
a dozen strokes then drifts. Leans his head over the side and shines
the flashlight down into the water, going quickly from one side to
the other, rocking the boat. The water gray and green and black and
not so deep that he cannot illuminate the beds of black speckled
weeds that rise like human hair and wave with the running of the
water. He rows with one oar in a circle, pausing after each stroke to
shine the light into the water. Nothing.

Silence. Lost upon the waters. Amid the fog. He sees fog and
water in a new way, as unearthly elements of an alien atmosphere on
another planet. Dips an oar timidly into this cold, glassy, oily, smoking substance, pulls one way then another, then raises his oars and
drifts—bewildered, confounded, alone.

The rain has stopped. Muted thunder. Frogs croaking. Occasionally he thinks he hears the creak of oarlocks and the wash of oars and pulls hard in their direction only to raise his oars into the silence and even denser fog. Listens less for the sounds of the other boat now than those that would denote the shore: a car, a shout, a door slamming. Searches less for the other boat than for a break in the fog, or a light that will lead to shore. If he can find the shore, he has only to row along the shoreline until he comes upon the tavern. He chooses a direction at random and rows in it until he has to rest, his stomach cramped, his wrists locked, the boat surrounded by the fog and water. Surely he has been so close to shore that a single pull upon the oars would have beached the boat, only to have angled off until he reversed himself, heading back out upon the lake. Now he stands and dips an oar into the water to measure the depth and to gauge, if he can, the distance from the shore. But poke it from one side to the other as he may, he does not touch bottom. Then something seems to seize the oar and drag it down, bending it beneath the boat. He wrestles with the weight. Caught in muck? He levers the oar against the oarlock and brings it up. A dripping mass of black weeds is wrapped around the paddle. He scrapes it off against the gunwale and it falls back into the water, a sinking, muddy, primeval heap. He lies up in the bow and drops the anchor overboard to test the depth, feeds the damp, slimy rope between his hands so that the weight will enter the water without a noise. It does not appear to reach the bottom. Unnaturally deep. He must be drifting above a hole.

He panics. With the murders of Wenzel and Rotterdam and possibly Mrs. Wenzel, won't the killer continue to work backwards to cover up his tracks and as soon as he can get off the lake return to Wenzel's barn to kill the drunken Scotty Moony and, if he has to, whoever else is there? His oars beat the water, slapping on the surface. Again he rows as powerfully as he can in one direction, gritting his teeth in expectation of the violent scraping on the bottom or the collision with a post or raft. Only to lift those oars and drift hunched over like an exhausted skuller at the finish of a race, still on the calm water, still adrift among the blowing fog. He consoles himself that the killer must be equally as lost. Indeed, hasn't Magnuson even gained on him, the fog having erased his small but powerful advantage of time and made them equally at the mercy of their luck?

To his left—a light! Watery and greenish rays that radiate as though through smoke from some blunted, smothered yellow source, looking like a miniature aquatic borealis. He holds his breath, suspends the oars. The rays do not reach him and he can see where ahead of him they are stopped against the fog. Illusory, extraplanetary light. As though down a tunnel of fog this is the distant opening. Too steady for a flashlight, too stationary. He dips a single oar and circles the light, keeps it centered just above his stern, a phosphorescent hypnotic eye. He fears that it is searching for him, then decides it must be in the distance, the lighted picture window of a cottage on the shore. But no more than two pulls upon the oars and he is upon water streaked green and yellow and bearing down upon the light, which is no more than ten feet away. He comes as close as he dares, braking the glide with his oars. A lantern hanging from the bow of a rowboat in which a man looms up like an apparition against the green fog blowing across the bow. A yellow slicker on his back, his head bent forward and hidden in his hood. He could be an ancient Indian wrapped in a blanket before a fire. The greenish rays are more distorting than revealing. A light to see by but not meant itself to be seen. The light of burglars, grave robbers, treasure seekers. But why sitting here with a light in fog? Unless it is a trap, and the light the bait.

He has one hand midway down the shaft of the oar and the other on the bow of the strange boat and holding the two boats side by side. He is ready to smite the man or rock the boat and send him overboard, or even, if he has to save himself, push away into the sanctuary of the fog.

He feels he has traveled down roadways and waterways to a region not of human flesh but of human souls. An underworld of mephitic marshes and mazes of narrow channels overhung with willows where the man in the silent boat is the spirit of a dead man or even nothing of a man at all but that which comes to every man. A journey he has been making, and a quarry he has been chasing, all his life. Now the end of that ultimate pursuit and on the verge of that ultimate discovery and capture. Trembling with fear and righteousness he rocks the other boat. A cry of "Whoa" or "Hey" or perhaps only an inhuman and monstrous bellow. The man grabs hold of either gunwale for balance. Then looks back over the yellow shoulders, green smoke rising into the green fog from the yellow pipe stuck in the yellow mouth. Face to face at last. With his own death no less than all the others. Deaths. Destiny. The ultimate revenge. The ultimate justice. The end.

Wait! His hand steadies on the bow. The lantern. The anchor line cutting the glassy water at an angle: the boat is not adrift at all.

The open tackle box on the seat full of a hundred battered plugs and spinners. The bamboo fishing poles propped up to fish from either side. And floating out from beneath the shadow of the boat and into that greenish water beneath the lantern, bullheads swimming up and down a stringer. Then the incredulous and frightened face of the man yellowed in the fog and lantern light, the white mustache and the white crew cut beneath the hood, as he creeps drunkenly but cautiously toward the bow, his eyes glittering in the heavy humid air and his mouth open and emitting dreamlike, underwater sounds.

Magnuson hears his own voice as though it comes from underwater and through walls of fog. ". . . They saw you from Wenzel's tavern . . . all the people . . . then the fog . . . you were gone . . . they worried . . . they couldn't see you . . . they said someone should go out in a boat . . . I said I'd go . . ."

The man is still wary, still frightened. "The tavern," he repeats. "You were drinking there?"

"Yes, drinking. I've put down a lot."

"But why didn't you just holler from the shore? I would have answered."

"We didn't think of it."

"The goddamn fools!" he cries, still feeling the shock of his first sight of this old man in the soaking topcoat and fedora as he appeared in the middle of the lake and night and fog to seize his bow without warning and rock his boat. He is quick to add though, "Not you, mind you, but those guys who got you out here.—Bill wasn't one of them, was he?"

It wasn't Bill.

"Not Charley, was it?"

He doesn't know any Charley.

"A little fog can't hurt me," says the fisherman. "I could have gone in if I wanted when it first came up. I've got the time to wait for it to lift." Now he is telling Magnuson that he is retired to the cottage—all knotty pine inside—he designed and built with his own hands on this lake, that he has wanted all his life to be able to do what he wants—which is what he can do and is doing now. This, in his opinion, puts him ahead of most men in the game. He likes bullhead meat, likes it for breakfast. If he knows one thing well in this life it is where and when on Bang's Lake the bullheads feed.

Something suddenly familiar about the man. Those evasive movements of his eyes and the belligerence with which he presents those shoulders has Magnuson wondering if he could be an old classmate he hasn't seen since he quit high school. He can't recall the name, only that he apprenticed to a carpenter.—But good God, he was about to dump him in the lake and beat him on the head with an oar until he drowned. He interrupts the man—"Which way to shore?"

The man throws out his arms as though to indicate and embrace the fog. "The tavern?—Over there, probably. But I wouldn't count on it. I'd stay put until the fog lifts, if I were you. You don't want to get in any trouble, not if you've been drinking." He pours coffee from his Thermos into a plastic cup he offers Magnuson, the smoke rising like a frothing potion into the fog.

For Magnuson the temptation of waiting here, of clutching that hot cup in both his hands. But his own desperation is only magnified in the face of such human patience. He must get off this lake, must get to Moony first. Instinctively he lets go, watching the gap of fog and water grow between the boats.

"Hey!" the man calls. "Come on back! You're soaking wet. Anchor your boat. Or say—get into mine! I'll probably have better luck rowing you in . . ."

The lantern withdraws into the night, the patch of fog it touches like a room lit by a dying candle. That light a beacon for a haven that is silence, insignificance, happiness even. The voice calls from behind the blanket of fog, "Give a yell to shore . . ."

Then he is lost upon the lake again, surrounded by the fog again. He has the premonition he is being watched. He shines the light over the side and catches in the beam a green frog floating close by the boat and staring at him. Only the top of the head up to those bumpy eyes above the water, the legs spread apart and motionless. He moves the light around the water. He is surrounded by frogs. Frogs are everywhere, anywhere he puts the beam.

Hark! The purl of oars, the creak of oarlocks, the glide of a bow against the water. He lifts his own oars. A boat passing nearby in the fog. (Take care, though, he knows how sounds can be carried across the water.) Feet shuffling on the bottom of an aluminum boat. Ragged rowing, splashing. The grunts and heavy breathing of the rower. As though muttering to himself beneath his breath with every pull upon the oars. The sounds farther away now. How close has the boat passed to his own? Twenty feet or a hundred? His hands are frozen on the oars.

Then the ramming out there in the dark and fog, the aluminum battering of wood, the splashing, the shouts of surprise of at least two men. Followed by a momentary and unnatural silence. Then more shouting, this time of fear and anger, and the banging of wood, the heavy splashing of something heavy in the water, the thrashing of a swimmer, a man's cry of help. The persistence of that cry. The smacking of not only water but something solid.

Magnuson is rowing in the direction of that clamor he no longer hears. Look you! The light off to the right again, the greenish rays radiating from the yellow lantern, the rays broken and returned by fog. He brakes and waits. Unless he himself is drifting backward the light is sailing toward him through the fog. The boat bears down upon him and he oars off to the side to let it pass. It is drifting, the rope of the anchor severed just above the waterline. In the green water streaked with the dusty yellow rays beneath the lantern on the bow, the bullheads, like the silent engines of this silent ship, swim up and down their stringer.

He leans over and shines the light into the passing boat. An overturned tackle box and can of worms; colorful fishlike and buglike plugs intermixed with knots of living earthworms. One oar missing, and only one bamboo pole, trolling off the stern. Water splashed along the sides. He lets it drift by, drawn on by its team of ghostly fish until the light fades and vanishes behind the fog.

The fisherman is drowned. He has been mistaken for the man in the Duesenberg, the only man who could catch the killer and prove his implication in all the crimes. But Magnuson lives! And for good reason lives! His sense of destiny is reconfirmed by such good fortune. The strawman is on the bottom of the lake, strings of bubbles exploding from his flesh. Overhead the keels of passing rowboats, bubbling oars, the light of the lantern, the stringer of bullheads.

Impossible lake. Something bumping broadside. Against the bow. Now against the oar. A log? The oar lost from the other boat? It catches on the oar and drags it down. Something floating out there. A hard pull upon the oar and the thing is forced off. Now it is beneath the keel, bumping against the boards beneath his feet. It will not come out. He rocks the boat, rows back and forth, but he cannot get off the thing. He wonders if he could be caught upon a shoal. Then the thing resurfaces alongside and bumps broadside again. He pushes it away with the oar only to have it float back and bump broadside again. He puts the flashlight on the water and beneath the green and yellow fog a floating mass of something dead in the center of which is something like flesh, like a face, something—dear God— that is a head! In shallow and weedy water a face just beneath the surface, eyes with no irises and yellow hair loosened and graying and bound up with weeds as it swirls and writhes around the head, parting long enough to reveal the rope knotted around the neck that disappears in the darker, muddy bottom where the anchor lies. The corpse rising on its rope like some strange, dead, and tethered fish. The feet floating much lower than the head, the water running beneath the clothes, and the white blouse pulled up over the hard naked midriff and wadded just below the breasts. He puts the oar over again and pokes the thing away. Bonny Wenzel. He is sure of it. The man has killed her after all. Must have thought himself so far ahead of his pursuer in the Duesenberg that this time he could take the extra time to hide the body.

He poles through a bed of lilypads and beaches the boat at last, he knows not where. Docks and darkened cottages in the flashlight beam. Barking dogs. A man in a flannel shirt standing at his picture window and thumbing through a magazine. He walks around the shoreline in and out of water. He stumbles against docks, climbs over boats, falls face first once in the water until far sooner than expected the emerald neon sign glimmers through the fog, advertising beer.

He switches off the lights inside the tavern, the neon lights outdoors, shuts the door, locks it with the key he has found behind the bar, and hangs a sign on the doorknob: Closed. Into the Duesenberg and racing on the country road across the fogbound hills and valleys, the lights of the town withdrawing in the distance, and ahead the enlarging outline of a barn, silo, and narrow farmhouse in which every light in every room is on. The red convertible with the foxtails and mudflaps no longer in the driveway; nor any other car; a long peel-mark left in the gravel. No hillbilly music; the damp dripping from the eaves onto the leaves of the bushes in the eavesdrop. How long has it been since he was here last? Passes through the screen porch, raps once on the half-open door, and enters, certain of what he will find. In the kitchen smells of kerosene, flat beer, and something like creosote: paths worn in the linoleum and the reddish brown substance showing beneath the pattern that has itself been painted over. The oilcloth pulled from the steel kitchen table and onto the floor among the brown beer bottles, sudsy glasses, spilt beer, spent shells and cartridges, and the bloody pools and gore of the bodies of a man and woman—Moony and his wife—shotgunned to death at close range. Walls, sinks, chairs, and cabinets are splattered with the blood. Tufts of tangerine-colored hair blown about the room and, with the door open, still blowing. Steps back and into a spill of blood like half-dried paint emanating from a larger pool in which has been scratched the word DEATH. A shotgun leans nonchalantly against the wall, the bloody barrel of which has been used to write the word. Written with the innocence of a child scratching with a branch in the damp sand of a beach.

In the living room he drops into a chair. He is repelled, sick in spirit and in flesh. Even so he admits to the presence of a certain satisfaction and elation. Aren't these murders further evidence that his own safety and innocence are guaranteed? For all those persons who could place him at the scenes of murders, as they could also place the murderer, and who could give evidence against him are dead. And admits also to a feeling of loneliness, as immense as space: the loneliness of being marked, set apart and chosen, a condition proven by the fact that, having done what he has done, he is innocent, and knowing what he knows, he is alive and safe.

Wanders through the three floors of this narrow house, anticipating the discovery of other bodies. He finds none. In each room shuts off the light. An arsenal of guns and ammunition discovered everywhere. Rifles and shotguns stacked in corners behind doors, on gun racks on the wall, in gun cupboards, bookcases, in closets, and piles of pistols, like old pipes, in drawers. Finds an old unused refrigerator the shelves of which are stuffed with boxes of shells and bullets. An inordinate amount of firearms. He wonders if the man could have been the leader of a private right-wing army.

The room of Moony's son. A phonograph, piles of old 78 rpm records, mostly hillbilly, some of which are broken, having been sailed across the room against the wall, a few 33 rpm records, oddly mostly classical, empty quart beer bottles of the cheapest brand of beer, barbells, piles of weights, a pair of dumbbells, handgrips, a chest expander, overflowing ashtrays, and more rifles. What is suspicious: dresser drawers pulled out and emptied on the floor, others still in the dresser or on the bed but empty; empty hangers in the closet and on the rumpled bed; discarded suits and jackets on the floor; no suitcases in the closet; as though a hasty and indiscriminate act of packing clothes has just taken place. On the dresser the gray photograph of a nineteen- or twenty-year-old boy posing with a cocky smile beneath a pompadour of hair, his lips and cheeks touched up with pink. Takes the picture from the frame and slides it into his pocket.

A den with a worn linoleum floor, more firearms, and, on the knotty-pine-wallpapered walls, a collection of calendars from the past ten years showing busty, bare-breasted, idealized pin-up girls in color, and wooden plaques and postcards with dirty jokes and poems and double meanings, their pictures and topics outhouses, honeymoons, traveling salesmen, pregnant girls, lazy hillbillies, all what a Sunday school teacher might term pornographic, all popular in the 1940's, the postcards sold along with picture postcards at vacation places and drugstores. But also truly pornographic snapshots in black and white. Piles of them scattered about the chests and tables as casually as this month's magazines on a coffee table. He cannot reconcile the cheapness and mild bad taste of the calendars, plaques, and postcards with the deep pornography of the snapshots. It does not seem probable that a man, if he liked one, could like the other. Perhaps the plaques and postcards appealed to the taste of Mrs. Moony.

In the Moonys' bedroom still more of these pornographic snapshots, on the dresser, in the drawer of the nightstand, and inserted all around the mirror. They are put down everywhere, and in the open, as casually as change emptied nightly from a pants pocket. Small, soiled, grayish, blurred photographs taken by amateurs, often cracked like crinkled glass. The women in a hair style and underclothes, where worn, of twenty or thirty years ago. Women who look like housewives, barmaids, and whores in pathetic imitations of the exotic poses of movie starlets and fashion models. A few of girls so young they are without pubic hair, others of women who must be in their fifties. If they are accompanied by a man he is usually faceless; more often only a penis is shown inside a mouth or a vagina, or as it is about to be put there. He shuffles through a handful and halts shocked before a woman he recognizes. The flabby, ivory flesh, small breasts and great thighs and buttocks, stockings rolled up just above the knee, and beneath the folds of the stomach hardly any pubic hair, so that she seems an absurd and timeless combination of pubescent girl and grandmother. The same face as in the photograph of the bride in the silver frame on the dresser. The same face as the dead woman in the kitchen. Mrs. Moony. She is in other obscene photographs stuck fondly to the mirror. Did both husband and wife think she was beautiful? Moony must have shown them to his friends. Surely their son must have known that they were there.

Outside he notices the silence of the barn, the light from the windows dulled, dissipated, and turned back by the fog, lights he himself earlier shut out. No bleats or bells. Frogs in distant ditches.

Cars on distant roads. Who finished feeding the livestock and milked the goats? He forces himself to go down. Approaches the barn door with caution, peers around the corner. Even his worst premonition has not prepared him for this. Sheep and goats slaughtered in their pens and stalls, shot to death or butchered, their throats cut or simply stabbed. Rams and billies, ewes and does, lambs and kids, indiscriminately. Fallen does with their imprisoned heads twisted in the stanchions, their eyes open and tongues protruding from the bloody mouths, their nostrils thick with blood. Pens strewn with dead sheep, their wool looking as though smeared with ruddle. The heat and steam of blood and open entrails. The straw red from one end of the barn to the other. Even the cats have been shot down in the middle of the aisles. A halfhearted attempt has been made to drag the corpses from the pens and stalls and heap them in the middle of the aisle in several pyramids, sheep and goats intermixed, what appear to be alive but wounded animals buried beneath the dead. On top of one of the heaps has been thrown a black cat without its head. Rifles and pistols set down or dropped throughout the barn as though the murderer brought an armful of weapons from the house and after emptying each discarded it as useless, ignorant that it could be reloaded and refired. How long it must have taken him to pass methodically amid the bleats and bells, from stall to stall, up one side of the aisle and down the other. Miraculously the wounded and even unscathed survivors, staring at nothing straight ahead, or at Magnuson, or at the open doors. At his feet a dying ewe, and reluctantly he removes the wooden bar of a gate and clubs it repeatedly about the head. But the animal will not die, and he gives up in desperation, drops the bar, and leaves the animal still not dead.

Indiscriminate slaughter of dumb brutes, as though the killer's quarrel is not with certain men, nor even with mankind, but with life. Against the very nature of the act of life. Unnatural. Unspeakable horror. The work of a madman. A madman who has crossed over into a bloody landscape from which he cannot return. Who, hereafter, unless he has glutted himself on murder and becomes shy, mild-mannered, ordinary, will kill without motive, and massively, whenever that urge he cannot master overwhelms him.

Again Magnuson shuts off the barn lights, again slides the barn door closed. He sits in the Duesenberg with the door open to the mist and night. He no longer cares to apprehend the murderer. No longer believes it possible. Clues only lead to new murders with clues that only lead to still newer murders. In a world of three bil-

lion souls it is a chain that is all but inexhaustible. He can imagine
Thorsen already banged to death with the back of a spade, Mrs.
Rotterdam stabbed to death with a darning needle, Mrs. Owens
strangled with her dressing gown, the man in the apartment next
to Rotterdam's forced down the garbage chute where Magnuson
saw him dump his garbage, the Mexican field hands who were in
Wenzel's tavern hacked to pieces with their own machetes, Farquarson's nurse injected with a fatal overdose of morphine. But perhaps if he stopped now and no longer gave chase but sat idle in his
seat behind the wheel, the murderer would also stop, would be pet-
rified even as he stood poised above Nancy Rhinelander's arm, thumb
to syringe. It seemed as probable as certain other happenings of
this evening. Indeed, why shouldn't the murderer stop if he stopped?
Until the slaughter in the barn, didn't they reason identically? As if
the murderer is a twin who would obliterate the truth he would
discover, and destroy the people he would save. Each time the murderer discovered a new and human obstacle in his path, didn't he
understand immediately the implication of that obstacle, as did
Magnuson, an obstacle that was for Magnuson the path? Why, Magnuson has only to wish to interrogate or save a person for that person to be discovered dead. As if he alone is the lethal force behind
their doom, as if his compulsion to solve the crimes is the motive
that compels the murderer to commit them, his compulsion to save
the people the murderer's compulsion to make certain they are dead.

But why should he alone be chosen to shoulder the responsibility and share in this complicity? As though when once in a mil-
lennium a comet passes by the earth he is the sole man in the world
at the telescope, trying desperately to focus the milky lens. Again
that sense of destiny. But now no longer chosen so much as cursed.
The depression he suffered before the exhilaration of this evening
returns a hundredfold. His worst moment is at hand. He is no longer
convinced that good and justice will prevail, or that they are working on his side. He can even admit to that awful possibility that his
errand is without hope, his errors without redemption. Who is he
to make himself responsible for justice? How can he be the caretaker of what is good? But he has been committed to the battle for
too long a lifetime to do otherwise than wage his war. Even if he
fails utterly, even if he works evil instead of good, even if in the
end he is not merely destroyed but damned and doomed, he cannot
do otherwise. Even this, he tells himself, is destiny.

CHAPTER NINETEEN

CATACOMBS AND BEER GARDENS

Among the Gothic-looking universities and hospitals along the Chicago lakefront can be found the Germanic-looking Varsity Inn. Upstairs an empty bar with oaken booths. Downstairs a rathskeller of brick and plaster walls between half-timbering on which the seals of midwestern universities hang like medieval coats-of-arms on shields. In that rathskeller a Dixieland band of heavyset white men with gray hair and business suits is playing "When the Saints Go Marching In" to the young crowd that packs the booths and bars and aisles. Junior advertising men, interns, nurses, small-town girls who are students at the charm and modeling schools, army reservists home on leave, husbands-on-the-make, wives-on-the-prowl, divorcees, high-school students with false I.D.'s, and any number of secretaries and members of fraternities and sororities, along with John Cavan, who has just discovered that his father's name is Helenowski, and Myrna Westermann and the impromptu party for Kay Wanda that celebrates her divorce from one Pete Pfister, a divorce granted earlier today.

"For the first time in four years I feel like me," says Kay Wanda, who was Kay Pfister just this morning. "Now all I have to do is discover who that is. Because I was certainly not me when I was married to him. And I'm certainly not who I was before I married him—."

"To the new you and your new life in the East," says Trixy Ekstrom, saluting with her stinger and referring to Kay teaching kindergarten in a suburb outside Boston in the fall. Trixy has long silken hair with bangs, and cheekbones so high that her eyes look squeezed and slanted. She looks at once beautiful and ghastly.

"And to yours in the West," returns Kay. Trixy may move to Los Angeles, where she would share an apartment with girlfriends already there and work for an uncle who breeds, trains, and boards poodles.

"I don't want to disillusion you," says Vollmer, "but Los Angeles is smog over a thin veneer of health and happiness over a thin veneer of tragedy over a thin veneer of veneer." A flight engineer with an airline that works a steady run to Los Angeles, he makes his home here instead of there. A big man with short arms, hair like an Indian, and the suggestion of something like a dowager's hump, he sometimes wears joke-store glasses an inch thick when he boards his flight, bumping into passengers and asking them the way to the cockpit.

Listen to Motluck, another native Chicagoan, counsel Kay against the perils of the East, which to him is New York. Which to him is a particular apartment house in Queens. Where everyone was unfriendly and obnoxious and pushy and loud and Jewish, and his own passive and pleasant nature became so paranoid and misanthropic that he barricaded himself in his apartment and only ventured out to lose himself among large crowds, where he could anonymously trip, elbow, and otherwise jostle New Yorkers as the fancy took him. His return to Chicago after a year of New York is described in terms of returning simultaneously to Civilization, Eden, and the Womb.

"But Chicago just doesn't give me the feel of a city," says an instructor of drama, a plump anglicized Texan with the head of a lion. "Not a real city. Downtown is just so dead at night. It's just another small town. Except that it's bigger. The only cosmopolitan cities, the only real cities, that have real personalities all their own, are San Francisco, New York, New Orleans . . ."

"And Milwaukee," adds Vollmer.

"Really? I've never been to Milwaukee . . . Still I would have hardly thought . . . Really? Milwaukee?"

"The dilettantes go east," Motluck says. "The phonies go west. It's like we got a sanitary canal leaving in either direction." Curly-headed, frowning, and chain-smoking, Motluck looks out at people like the self-portraits of van Gogh.

The Dixieland band playing "Tiger Rag" and the crowd clapping and whistling and chanting *Hold that tiger.* Striped ties, blazers, plaid vests, crewneck sweaters, Peter Pan collars. A rush of conversation, the gift of gab and patter the young men give to the girls they have just encountered. A healthiness and heaviness of flesh about the people, a lifetime of dumping good beer and noodles and beef and sausages into their good midwestern flesh. The men look like football players fresh from the shower. The girls like the cheerleaders for the team that won. Sex, at once repressed and flaunted, is in the air with the strength of choking fumes. If only some means could be found to harness all that sexual energy fomenting and dissipating in all that flesh, another wilderness could be cleared, another great city built along the lake.

"At least you can be thankful you got out of it without children." A cliché from Burkhardt, a former schoolmate of Cavan's, who has it on his mind to take Kay Wanda to bed tonight if he can. A former Big Ten wrestling champion, he disguises his premature baldness by keeping his head almost shaved.

"They say divorce is like a death," says Kay. "A divorcee is like a widow . . ."

Myrna Westermann whispering her experience in divorce court this morning to Trixy Ekstrom. "I didn't have to testify that I saw him actually hit her, just that I saw the marks on her after he hit her." There should have been outrage in the courtroom at the bruises she catalogued with some exaggeration and no certain knowledge they were caused by Pete Pfister. Instead of pathos, or tragedy, there was uninterest, and an air of eye shades, cigar butts, spittoons.

"When the rhymes aren't coming," Burkhardt tells Cavan, "you practice your combinations on the old lady." Pete Pfister, Kay's former husband, has pretensions to being a poet.

An amateur comedian imitating the jokes and deliveries of several popular television comedians for the benefit of the girls while he watches the smoke spiral from the tip of the cigar he uses as a prop. He can be the stand-up comic who insults his audience, the storyteller in dialect of his city boyhood, the witty host of a talk show. "You ought to watch television sometime," Vollmer says, moving on.

A habitual liar mentioning in passing that he has a Ph.D. in nuclear physics from Illinois Tech, has the hobby of catching rattlesnakes, holds the record for the longest ski jump at Fox River Valley. When he describes in an aside to the wide-eyed and open-mouthed Motluck how he laid a girl in a Piper Cub while in mid-air over Pistakee Lake, Vollmer, himself a pilot, is incited to attack. "She probably sat on the stick and thought she was on his prick, and he had his hand on his prick and thought he had it on the stick."

"Then that means," says Burkhardt, "that she flew the plane with her —."

"Which means in turn," says Vollmer, "that he fucked his fist. Now that's entirely possible in the cockpit of a Piper Cub."

Protests at such language from Trixy and Myrna and the feminine end of the table in general.

From the liar words to the effect that they would "step outside" if it were not for the black belt he holds in judo, which requires him to register himself as a lethal weapon with the police of any town he enters and lays him open to the charge of assault with a deadly weapon if he were ever foolish enough to hit anyone. On the excuse of going for a drink, he disappears. "Wooden planes and iron men!" Vollmer calls after him, a favorite cryptic saying of his that covers all situations and means all things, usually something like "sticks and stones may break my bones," but which originally referred to the one great disappointment of his life: that he was born too late to fly the planes of thirty years ago or even to have gone to Canada to fly for the RCAF at the outbreak of World War Two.

"What beautiful lies!" says Motluck. "What an actor. Before you could think about one lie he piled on another. What technique. What dodges and wiggles. Think how screwed up he is. A living bundle of insecurities and pressures and complexes and tensions. A haunted man, driven by demons. Did you notice he was so small his feet were swinging off the floor? And how his clothes were scruffy and his fingernails dirty? And those suspicious, terrified, tiny black eyes?" Motluck not only identifies with cripples, freaks, harelips, speech impediments, idiots and outcasts and misfits in general, he hero-worships them, savoring and recounting his more memorable encounters for years.

"My real goal in life," Trixy Ekstrom confides to the instructor of drama, "is to understand other people. I want to see through their games and defenses and into the real motives behind what they say and do." She sees philosophy, literature, and most of all psychology as a means toward this end. She is hardly alone in this. Such an understanding of other people is to give her power and wisdom, whether to help or exploit those people she can see through is not always clear, for the salesman and social worker are alike in having this ambition. Paradoxically her interest is solely in herself, a person she has no wish to know, but nevertheless her favorite topic of conversation. Like many girls she refers to herself quaintly as "me." It is an important word with her, and is an object without a subject.

"They say after six months," Kay Wanda says, "you're ready for . . . new relationships."

"I wouldn't think so long," says Burkhardt, deadly serious. "If the dead are supposed to bury the dead, why not let the divorced bury the—" he frowns, confused. What he is about to say is nonsense.

As Vollmer, who is quick to seize on any weakness, is quick to point out. "You mean the divorced can divorce the divorced. Burkhardt, even when you get it right you don't make a hell of a lot of sense."

Myrna has pushed through the crowd until she is touching Cavan. "Oh, look now," she says. "I asked you nicely not to come, remember?"

"Well, I did tell Burkhardt I'd meet him here. And I wanted to see Kay before she goes. I've always liked Kay the best of all your friends. I always thought she liked me, too."

The band playing "Mama Don't Allow No Banjo Playing Around Here," and a pair of young athletes with fat faces and choking pin collars screaming out the lyrics while their hands imitate the instruments.

"You could meet Burkhardt anywhere. And you don't care about Kay or what she's been through, and don't pretend you do." Then a final pleading admonition, taking his sleeve: "Be nice."

He soon understands why she has collared him. A man is squeezing in next to her, and she is introducing him to everyone but Cavan. Bradford McCarthy. "I hope Myrna's friends will be my friends," he says. "I'm sure you've all been very good to Myrna." As though they have done their duty by her, and he is taking over from them now. As though he has come to take her away from all of this. The "new man." He has lost her to this country club life-guard, insurance broker, marine lieutenant, halfback. A man who has always worn a wristwatch and a silver identification bracelet on his wrist, and has always called his father sir, and has been called in turn by his father, son.

Cavan feels more fooled than betrayed. All her years in art school and Myrna Westermann is not the artist and bohemian she pretended she could be. All those long conversations spent in deni-grating her own father for his mercenary values and lack of culture and humanitarianism in its simplest form and then to fall in love with a man who is surely his youthful counterpart. And she must have viewed his own dedication to science as the same passing fancy as her own interest in art, anticipating all along that he would someday tire of the game and return to the mercantile ways of his fathers as she intended someday to return to hers. She is, and has been all along, a Westermann. A child of that miracle blender of her father's manufacture. A suburban housewife masquerading in a painter's smock. A little girl who will become a suburban matron with no perceptible steps during the transformation, like the turn-ing of her hair in time from blond to gray.

Trixy Ekstrom, caught between injury and indignation, seeks in Burkhardt her champion. "Did you hear that? He said I'm one of those women who go around castrating men."

"Correction," Vollmer says. "I said you like to cut their nuts off."

"Don't pay any attention to Vollmer," Burkhardt says. "You know the sort of fellow Vollmer is."

But Trixy is not to be consoled. "Motluck, tell your friend here if you've ever seen me act that way."

"I have never seen you act that way," says Motluck as though reading awkwardly from a piece of paper.

"The hand," says Vollmer in falsetto, "is quicker than the eye."

Cavan wandering away, pushing through the crowds. Several bars down here and all are crowded, all look alike. Candles in Chianti bottles on the tables. Rooms off of rooms. Arches of brick vaulting that lead into bricked-up cells. Others into what appear to be tun-nels. The feeling of the Roman catacombs, the Paris sewers, the cellars of cathedrals and castles. Of torture devices, skeletons, hid-den pits, chains. Men and women kissing and dryhumping in the darkness against the walls, becoming fewer along the way. As though going back into a grotto. Back to a brick wall and the cauliflower of a candle burning from several hundred pounds of multicolored wax, the drippings of ten thousand candles. It is like a shrine. He anticipates the manifestation of a priest in vestments, a nun in habit, the celebrants of a Black Mass. The impulse to go down on his knees. As though he has arrived at the secret holy place of his culture where some oracle will speak to him . . . Will tell him who he is. Where he is. Where he came from. The reason for this wayward world as he finds it . . .

Then he is journeying through the rathskeller in search of a girl. He tells outrageous lies, brags about himself so that the girls will honor him, deprecates himself so they will pity him. He is a jet pilot who strafed an orphanage by mistake, a best-selling novelist in search of local color, the black sheep son of a wealthy family, and the despicable but sweet mistreater of wonderful women. When another man speaks he says, "He's a bullshitter." Or, "Don't listen to him, he's lying." In the end he is refused and ignored and insulted by the girls and threatened and in some cases manhandled by their escorts.

Then on the sidewalk outside the inn in a party that includes Burkhardt and Kay and Trixy and Vollmer and Motluck and Myrna and Bradford McCarthy and waiting for the cars to take them elsewhere. "Well, if it isn't Joe Epic," a boy of no more than eighteen says, squaring off before him.

"That's the guy," says another. There are four boys. Maybe five.

"We want you to apologize for calling us Polacks in front of those girls."

"His name isn't Joe Epic," Trixy says.

Cavan recalling a table where he said something like, "Hi, girls. My name is Joe Epic. And get away from this bunch of Polacks." Or was it, "What are nice girls like you doing with this bunch of Polacks?" He is confused. He cannot fathom their anger with him. "What can I say?" he says. "If you're a Polack, you're a Polack. My saying you're not a Polack won't change—"

He is struck a glancing blow, only the knuckle of the index finger catching his lip. Before he or anyone else can retaliate the boys have jumped into the car that has been idling at the curb and driven off. A trickle of blood from the corner of his mouth that Kay is dabbing with a handkerchief. He is bundled like a sick person into a car.

He falls asleep with his head out the window, wakes to the argument between Vollmer and Burkhardt in the front seat. "Nurses are too worldly, Burkhardt. They have to wipe guys' asses and give them sponge baths all over their bodies and catheterize their—you probably don't even know what they have to do when they do that."

"That's what you mean by 'worldly'?"

"That's what I mean and I wouldn't marry one."

"What about stewardesses?"

"What about them?"

"What do you think of them and are you getting any?"

"Burkhardt, you're the only guy I know who is a living testament to Freud. Every word you speak, every gesture you make, every thought you think, is motivated by sex. You can say, 'Pass the mashed potatoes, Grandma,' at Thanksgiving and say it because you think for some reason it will let you tie up some naked dame to a tree in the woods."

Burkhardt appears not to know whether he has been complimented or insulted. "Better than your queer ways, Vollmer. I know all about your little games. How instead of planking dames you beg them to jerk your meat . . ."

"Wooden planes, Burkhardt. And iron men."

They disembark at a restaurant called the Sherwood Forest, where Vollmer has insisted on taking them. In the lobby more stucco walls, artificial half-timbering. Suits of armor in glass cases. A crowd waiting for tables outside a dining hall larger than a gymnasium and with a high vaulted oak ceiling. Shields and broadaxes and crossed swords and spears on the walls. Hundreds of tables crowded with large families and conventions and office parties served by waitresses in uniforms of Lincoln green with laced peasant bodices. A fountain with a large spout in the center surrounded by a circle of lesser spouts on which colored spotlights are playing. With the heavy clatter of knives above the prime ribs and steaks it sounds like a thousand swords battling at a rushing brook. The rear wall entirely covered by a tapestry, two stories high, depicting in various hues of green the stiff figures of Robin Hood, Friar Tuck, Little John, Ivanhoe, King Richard the Lionhearted, Maid Marian, all of whom have about their faces that imprecise and even crude look often seen in Occidentals drawn by Orientals.

The bar of the restaurant has the odd name of Hell, and is entered off the dining hall. A narrow passageway dark except for the flashlight of the young man waiting to escort them. "This way to

Hell," he says. "Kindly watch your step." No sooner said than fun-house monsters are lighting up in the walls ahead, the rubber or *papier-mâché* faces of the skeletons and devils telescoping behind the dusty wire of their cages, the machinery whirring and clicking. Worn recorded voices: "Welcome to Hell, ladies and gentlemen." Followed by fiendish laughter. Jets of air shooting up from the floor and making the girls' skirts resemble inside-out umbrellas. Burkhardt laughing and pinning Kay's wrists at her breast. In the yellow light of a skeleton craning its skull toward Cavan he catches the face of the girl beside him. A beautiful face. That promises to be the master of him. He blames it on the lighting, the drink, the sentimental mood, all of which favor the looks of women. A railroad bandana on her head that may be blue or red.

Into a small elevator lit only by a pair of red light bulbs. The guide pulls a lever and the elevator shakes and rattles like a cart on cobblestones. When the motion stops the operator opens a door on the other side. They have gone nowhere at all. It is a phoney elevator. They are on the same level as the vast dining hall which is, in fact, next door. The atmosphere of a deep and dark and dank cellar, more catacombs than rathskeller. Lamps in the shape of torches on the walls. Arches, passageways, nooks, alcoves. Long oaken tables and benches. Waiters and bartenders dressed in red. Swizzle sticks shaped like pitchforks. Flames on the bar napkins.

"In the name of God are those bones in the wall?"

The courses of brick interrupted with various-shaped bones set in the mortar to make a variety of designs and arches.

"Clever way to dispose of a body."

"More likely that the mason when he was through with his lunch—."

Cavan the anthropologist feeling the bones in the near-dark. "They're not human," he says. Thoughts of Helenowski, his murdered father, the relics of his mortality, the body in the morgue.

A mousy girl celebrating the boyfriend she dances with at the Aragon Ballroom. Showing Motluck a write-up on him, complete with photograph, in a clipping from the *Daily News*.

"When she first told me she had a boyfriend who had a sequin suit," Motluck says, passing the clipping on to Vollmer, "I'll be frank with you, I didn't believe her."

"It's not a suit you'd see on the racks every month of Sundays, Motluck."

"He had his suit made especially . . ." she says.

"If I had me one," says Motluck, "I wouldn't wear it just for dancing. I'd wear it everywhere. To the office. On the street . . ."

"Let the sunlight with all its little angles and refractions play off it with all its subtle little changes of mood," Vollmer suggests.

"But he just dances in his . . . I don't think you should . . ." unaware that she is being ridiculed.

A girl at the next table giving the Latin names for the bones in the wall, identifying them as the shanks and hocks of cows. Cavan suspects it is the girl with the bandana whose beauty struck him in the passageway. Myrna and Bradford McCarthy with drinks in hand sneaking off to a small table in a darkened alcove. The bride and bridegroom ducking out on the wedding party. A light comes on above the keyboard of a piano and a piano player in a red velvet jacket plays Broadway show tunes and popular ballads, his hands rising and falling on the keys like triphammers. Music incongruous with the atmosphere.

"Froggy Moore," Motluck is saying. "I saw him at the freak show of a carnival when I was just a kid. He wore a green frog suit that was skintight and spotted and bumpy and wrinkled just like a real frogskin. He had big frog feet and a big frog head and he could wrap his froglegs around his thick frog neck. And when he opened up that big frog mouth there was this tiny head of a sweating nigger with his eyes rolling back in his head. Froggy Moore! What I wouldn't give to have a name like that, wear that frog suit, bend myself up like a pretzel . . ."

"Wooden planes, Motluck, and iron men. That's the way the world works and don't you ever forget it."

Kay Wanda, down in her cups, showing a touch of temper. "They're all divorcees." She indicates the alcoves and nooks and corners and whoever is huddled in them out there in the dark. "Married men and divorced women. Secretaries and bosses. What is it with these bones and bricks? It's a cocktail lounge. The sons-of-bitches bring the wife and kids out there in that gymnasium for dinner and then sneak in here the next night with some divorcees—"

"I don't think they're all divorcees," says Burkhardt, always the diplomat. "You don't know that for a fact, Kay."

"But can't you see it's dark because they don't want to be seen, that they're huddled together because they want to hide their faces? It's all secret sex and mixed drinks and flashing rolls of money. It's so middle-class. And they're all divorced. It's one hell of a place to take me to tonight . . ."

"Shameless about its shamelessness," Vollmer says. "That's my city and I love it."

Kay trooping out of Hell, pursued by Burkhardt, with the rest of the party following after. In glass cases at the cashier's desk in the lobby souvenir stuffed dolls of Robin Hood, Friar Tuck, Maid Marian, and Ivanhoe are sold. Motluck saying, "What's she got against the middle class? It's given me a car and kept me in beer and pocket money and lets me fry my eggs in butter . . ."

Outside, Cavan observes that Myrna and Bradford McCarthy have stayed behind. Then it is over. He can admit it now. To his surprise he discovers he is no longer in love with Myrna. A passionate moment, this falling out of love. He is overwhelmed with freedom. He does a little dance step, kicks his heels, gives out with a little whoop. "To fall out of love, you know," he says, putting his arm around Burkhardt, "it's wonderful. Exhilarating. A thing of joy, Burkhardt. Compared to falling in love, which is so painful, this is breathtaking."

Arguments among the party as to where to go next and with whom. Cavan in the back seat of Burkhardt's car spies the girl with the bandana debating with her girlfriends whether to go with some medical students to the Gold Coast or with Vollmer to the amusement park at Riverview. It is a blue bandana, and he would not be half so much attracted to her somehow if it were red. Her decision is too painful to observe and he puts his hands across his eyes. But the girls are climbing into Burkhardt's car after all, and the girl in the bandana herself is sitting in the dark upon his lap. In the rapture of freedom of his newfound lovelessness he is almost for ordering her to sit on someone else. She smells as girls did when he was a teenager and they were heaped upon him in the back of crowded cars. Subtle natural smells, like milk and fog and water in a thawing brook. She is growing warm upon his lap. A forced and embarrassed silence between them he is determined not to break. Stubborn fellow. She studies the passing lighted display windows of the stores. Turns once to him, smiling in the dark. As though she understands his reticence and will, in the end, defeat it. If so, God help him, he is lost. A girlfriend in the front seat has called her Sonja.

Over the low flat rooftops of the sprawling city appear the tops of the roller coasters and that city landmark, the tower of the parachute jump, where a tiny human figure rises along invisible guide wires to the very top and then is dropped, the parachute exploding silently against the evening sky and the figure floating down upon the dusty, smoky plain.

Inside the gates of Riverview the party becomes separated in the crowd of families and teenagers and organized factory outings. The feeling of a World Series victory celebrated in the streets. Burkhardt shouting back that he is taking Kay on the Bobs, the most infamous of all the rides, and will meet the others later at the Beer Garden, a place Cavan has been dissuaded from visiting first thing. "To the freak show!" cries Motluck.

Carnival posters painted in one color and in that ornate but primitive technique and with that perverse air of tattoos. Men with the heads of wolves, the torsos of snakes. Women with the legs and trunks of elephants, with naked bodies entirely covered with hair. Inside, the one-man band—accordion, mouth organ, and foot cymbal—who says in a Polish accent that he will play "O Susanna" backwards and then proceeds to put his back to the audience and play it. A man in full beard removes his shirt. His arms and torso are covered with what appear to be hairy warts the size of small pancakes, one no more than inches from the other. He turns around as though modeling a sports coat, and informs the crowd that they are not infectious. He is the Human Alligator. In an almost weary monotone he presents into a hand microphone a memorized lecture, scholarly and scientific in vocabulary, on the history of his affliction and the various treatments he has received at the hands of various bewildered doctors. He has been married for twenty years to the same woman, was in fact afflicted when he married her, and has two children, normal in every way, and is at present permanently under study at the medical center of a local university (unnamed). He has dedicated his life to science. Next, he separates drapery to reveal a headless woman sitting in what resembles an electric chair. The life-sized rubber body of a woman in her twenties, with several tubes penetrating the bandaged wound of her severed neck. She wears a strapless evening gown twenty years behind the fashion and her flesh is dusty. Her breasts rise and fall mechanically in the simulated act of breathing. The man with the warts gives a weary and almost apologetic lecture on her medical history while he buttons up his shirt. The crowd stares, as it has all along, in polite but embarrassed silence. A placard says she lost her head in a train wreck in Belgium in 1938.

As the crowd files out a woman mutters that they are the ones without heads for paying money to see that crap.

"She was real," Motluck says. "I saw her breathing."

"People would complain to the city or something if there was a phoney in the show," Vollmer adds.

"A couple of dumb bunnies," the woman says.

"I suppose you'll say next those warts were just pasted on that bearded guy's back?"

"Or that guy wasn't playing those three instruments. He was just miming them to a record."

"Hicks in the big city," the woman says, nodding toward them.

"A wife," Trixy says, lost in her own thoughts. "And children."

Cavan watches the crowd exit behind him. The girl called Sonja is not among it. Vanished into the masses of Riverview. The will of fate. So be it. All for the best, considering the circumstances. If she were meant for him he would have seen her in the crowd. Better yet, she would have followed him into the freak show, stood at his side.

The midway again and calliope music and microphone voices and the roar of roller coasters and the splash of a ride that descends a ramp at high speed into a pond and the shouts and screams of the riders. In the sky the tiny figure of the man in the harness is hauled up to the top of the tower where the panorama of the city expands before him with an endless checkerboard of light, and then is dropped upon the city, which flies up to meet him as it shrinks in size until the parachute opens and slows his fall.

According to Vollmer, who has it straight from a man whose father is one of the owners of Riverview, there are numerous deaths here each year that are kept out of the papers. He conjures up the sight of bodies flying head first out of roller coasters, or a whole train jumping the tracks, the seats of the Ferris wheel breaking, the cables of the parachute jump snapping. Kay and Burkhardt meet on the midway on their way to the Beer Garden, Burkhardt smiling foolishly and Kay somewhat disheveled and damp and toting a middle-sized panda. Motluck pausing to watch monkeys in pillbox hats race little cars around a circular track beneath a canopy.

Cavan wandering over to a game called the Baseball Dip. A pair of much-dented wire cages in each of which a Negro in mechanic's overalls sits on a swing suspended over a tub of water. Outside each cage is a circular target connected by a rod to the swing inside the cage which, if struck by the baseball, releases the seat and drops the man up to his waist in the water. Having a go at the targets are a variety of southpaws and country arms and sandlot stars complete with leg kicks and windmill wind-ups. The balls that miss thump against the padded backstop and roll back along the canvas to the counter. The Negroes hold on to rods at their chest and swing their legs back and forth above the water. One of them sullen, quiet, glowering. The other a constant chatterer. "Hey, man, you can't hit nothing! What's wrong with your arm?" In he goes! He picks himself up and dripping water from the waist down hoists himself upon the swing and refastens it. In he goes again! Small waves leap up and slosh around the cage. For a split second he looks defeated, chagrined, even profoundly embarrassed, only to return immediately to the smile and insolent chatter. In goes the other man now! For a third time in goes the chatterer. As he returns to his seat he mockingly salutes the heavyset blond man who dropped him.

The barker, wearing a carpenter's apron, extending three balls toward Cavan, all of which he is able to hold in one hand.

"I'm looking for a job," Cavan says, perplexed as to why he should say this.

The barker continues to confront him quizzically. "Good for you."

"Have you got a job?"

"You want my job?"

"I want to work in that cage. Wear that suit . . ." He is aware of Vollmer and the smiling Motluck pressing at his back.

"Son," the man says, "that's a black man's job."

"You could give me a try . . ."

"I might—if you were big and fat and out of shape with a big mouth and a sunny disposition. Or if you had a look that was 'nigger-mean.' And in either case if you were black. Son, that isn't you."

"But you should see the way he can fall off that seat," Vollmer says.

"And get wet too," adds Motluck.

"You could put up a sign, 'Dunk Chauncy D'Arcy Ethelbert III,'" says Vollmer. "Think of all the people making under ten grand a year and with only two cars in their garages who would like to dunk a rich playboy type who has never worked a day in his lily-white life."

"Maybe you guys got something there," the barker says, amused.

"Look at him," Vollmer says, presenting Cavan. "That Ivy League haircut. That supercilious mouth. Those haughty eyes. That degenerate posture. Everything about him bespeaks insincerity, privilege, wealth. I'd like to wipe that smirk off his face myself."

"He could wear a feminine-looking tuxedo," Motluck suggests. "Tight at the hips, double-breasted, wide lapels, huge carnation."

"You're appealing to race hatred," says Vollmer. "Why not make a pitch for class hatred and double the take?"

"He could shout something from the cage," says Motluck, "like

'My father could buy and sell you bunch of niggers.' Or Polacks. As the case may be."

"He'd have to say it, though," adds Vollmer, "like he's got an olive in his mouth that's been dipped in shit."

"I want to get in that cage," Cavan says, trembling.

A young black man in the company of two girls, one of whom holds his jacket, is throwing at the targets. "Man, you can't hit nothing," the chatterer in the cage cries. "Hey, you throw just like a girl. You ain't got no arm on you at all. You let one of them girls throw. They built better than you." Thereupon he whoops and hollers, making happy and insulting noises. The man misses all three balls, buys three more, misses those, and when he puts on his coat to go a look of understanding passes between him and the man inside the cage. "You got two girls, man," he calls in consolation. "You don't want your brother in the water too." The small man laughs and waves. So do the two girls. Even the sullen man in the other cage is smiling, although sinisterly. A group of Negro high-school athletes in their Negro high-school jackets are at the counter, firing at the targets. Their aim is deadly.

"You can get other jobs, son," the barker says. "You don't have to do this for a living."

"Hey, what are you standing there for all this time, young man, without taking no pitches," the chatterer calls from the cage. "Ain't you got fifty cents?"

"I'll give you ten dollars," Cavan says. "Let me take a turn in there. I'm going to start somewhere . . ."

"Not here you aren't."

"Twenty dollars."

"You're getting as weird as Motluck," Trixy says.

"Don't be so disappointed," Motluck says, leading Cavan away to the Beer Garden. "You can't very well start at the top. By which I mean the bottom, since the bottom is top."

"I was born at the top—"

"At the bottom," Motluck corrects.

"I want to start at the bottom—"

"You mean the top."

The Beer Garden, roofed and with a front porch opening on the midway, is crowded, noisy, hot. Tables with red and white checkered tablecloths wet with beer and pulled halfway to the floor and crowded with empty pitchers and glasses. An incredible odor of sweat and spilled beer. Sawdust thrown on the beer spilled on the floor. Puddles of beer on the chairs and tables in the center of which sometimes rests a dirty rag. Heavyset, sour-smelling, sweating beermaids, ruddy-faced and often lame and toothless, lumbering and trudging in shapeless shoes and dirty aprons, their hair hanging wet and stringy and their glasses smoky and smudged. They remove only as many empty glasses as they need room for new. Two pitchers of beer to Cavan's table. Vollmer flags down another waitress and orders two more. Elbows and cuffs are wet with beer—Motluck could wring out his shirtsleeves—soles are heavy with sawdust.

Enter a group of girls who were with them at the Sherwood Forest, taking a table close by. Sonja is not among them. Lost. Or picked up by some guy along the way. Fate, Cavan consoles himself, drinking directly from a pitcher he holds in both hands. Thank God.

Burkhardt whispering to Motluck that he is taking Kay to a German tavern he knows about. "Ask Trixy and come with us. We all know you like Trixy."

Trixy Ekstrom, who resembles a glamorous movie siren and concentration camp victim all in one, up to her old tricks again. Dribbling beer down the front of her dress. She is so messy, a gracelessness that drives Motluck wild.

"Trixy's a typical Chicago girl," Motluck says. "Attractive, self-centered, insensitive, and dumb. Who treats men like they've got dogshit on their shoes . . . Besides, if she did come with me then I'd have to decide if I can make out with her, and that would ruin my evening."

Burkhardt nudging Cavan. "Pick up one of those girls at the table over there and come with us."

But a look about those girls that suggests they will not easily forgive any man who had a hand in bringing them to the Beer Garden and Riverview. They sit as though they anticipate that at any moment beer will be spilled down their backs. They talk of chartered flights to Innsbruck for skiing, dancing to steel bands in Jamaica, their fathers' and boyfriends' cars . . .

"I'm free," Kay says, her hair loose and her eyes sleepy. "I can do anything. And, buster, I'm interested in me."

"As you have every right to be," says Burkhardt, sweating and pouring them both another beer. "Considering what you've been through."

"I supported him so he could finish college. And then I supported him so he could go to graduate school. So then what did he do for me? He worked just long enough for me to get my degree so I could get a job teaching to support him while he stayed home and wrote poetry full-time and, I suppose, found himself. That was when I said, Buster, I'm through. He wouldn't let me be a part of his career . . . he wouldn't let me have children . . . he wouldn't let me have a career of my own . . . I was him. I didn't exist. It was a houseful of him. He pushed me up against the windows and I was fighting to keep from being pushed over the window sill. How long is life anyway? Not long enough to be pushed around and suffocated. We all have to have the chance, somewhere along the way, to be ourselves . . . Sister, I said, you better find out who you are . . . because I am someone . . . in my own way . . . maybe no one so very important . . . But I am unique . . . I am me . . . don't you see, I have to be . . . don't I?" She shakes her head, frustrated as though Burkhardt contradicts her.

"I'd think marriage would have to be a two-way street," Burkhardt says, sighing. "It's got to be give and take, based on something like mutual respect."

"And it wasn't as if he was a good poet," she says.

"'Chicago is a big black buck rapist stalking a black alley at midnight,'" Vollmer says. "A line from one of Pete's poems. He was passing through a Sandburg stage."

Burkhardt nudging Motluck. "You could make Trixy."

"The most passionate love affairs of my life," says Motluck with dignity, "have always been with girls I never even kissed, never mind the other stuff. Believe it or not, sometimes with girls I never even talked to."

"That's an awful lot of pussy, Motluck," Burkhardt says. "By those rules you're fucking everybody."

Which for some reason enrages Vollmer. "Burkhardt, you're one of those guys who are going to end up hanging out in taverns and telling other guys like yourself about the girls you almost laid."

Which hits home to Burkhardt who, unable to better the insult, seizes Vollmer around the neck and shakes him.

While Cavan is thinking: Motluck is right. Those have been my greatest love affairs also. Since childhood. With girls and women all over the city, from all walks of life. Of all ages. Why, the whole world is a harem. A wonderful world. With all combinations possible. And it is love, and it doesn't have that much to do with sex at all.

Vollmer and Motluck now engaged in their favorite drunken confabulations. Get-rich schemes and the dream of approaching people and being able to say, "Hello, I'm rich. I can do anything. I can buy and sell you." Tonight they have something to do with smuggling and gun-running and kidnapping of millionaires and commandeering and ransoming of Vollmer's airliner by Motluck in disguise and defrauding insurance companies by crashing a plane from which both men have parachuted earlier, assuming new identities and disappearing once upon the ground.

"Why don't you guys get on a plane with a bomb and blow it up," Burkhardt says, "after you've made out your insurance policies to me?"

Then Cavan spies her on the midway. Sonja. Miraculously apart from the crowd that surrounds her and delays her as though not only a head taller than everyone else but with a halo above that head. Then she spies him, and the crowds in the Beer Garden and on the midway blur before his eyes. The blue railroad bandana, the leather purse on her shoulder and hugged against her hip, the leather sandals, the brown and faintly muscular legs. Blond hair sticking out from the rear of the bandana hiding her hair entirely above her forehead. The high cheekbones, the brown eyes. She is smiling and sweating lightly with her walking. He is rising as though bidden by a mesmerist's hand and could be knocking over his chair behind him and glasses and pitchers from the table with his elbows for all he knows or cares. Now picking his way through the tables and possibly doing some damage there, and around an Amazonian and unmovable waitress. She squeezing through a crowd of teen-age boys who give way and look after her in sullen admiration and disbelief. Each fixed upon the other's eyes, both smiling. He knows she has walked alone about the park in search of him, with him solely on her mind, promising to meet her girlfriends at the Beer Garden later. And he has been here all along! So much time already wasted needlessly. Life is not long enough to tolerate such foolishness. He is lightheaded, heartsick, happy. He takes her hand. He is speechless. She cocks her head and bites her lip. Her eyes are watering. If he could just see through the water of his own eyes he could be sure. It is so good he wants to tell her. So good it must be doomed, for he cannot tolerate the intensity and goodness of this moment, nor will the times that follow ever equal it. He is at such a pitch that he would have an orgasm if she touched his arm, and yet he knows it is not carnal. What exquisite pain!

Vollmer joining the girls at the nearby table, saying, "Hey, you babes, move over," as he forcibly parts their chairs to make room for his own. Leaning forward and wagging his finger he apparently asks a question of the table that is so unexpected and shocking and obscene that the girls are gasping and grabbing for their purses and rising in their chairs and making remarks like "How dare you?" and "You pig!" with Vollmer calling after them, "The girl I marry has to be a cuddly dimpled dumpling of a honeypot of a little teddy bear of a pussy cat!"

Cavan and Sonja and Burkhardt and Kay are gone to a small German tavern called the Ulmer Stube. Brightly lit, ruthlessly clean. Again the red and white checkered tablecloths; tubas and posthorns and stag racks on the gray stucco walls; rows of heroic clay beer mugs with pewter tops behind the bar, no two alike. An ancient piano player and violinist with the faces of Teutonic medieval bishops but the sad eyes of Celts, playing a medley of German drinking songs, light classics, old American favorites. A lame bartender. Blond waitresses in red skirts and white peasant blouses with laced bodices who can barely speak English. Customers greeting each other, often in German, and with heavy handshakes and slight bows, their red beaming faces bursting with their smiles, making room for the newcomers at their tables. A few older men alone at small tables and reading a newspaper with their late supper. Young couples with a European look to their hair style and fashion in clothes who must be newly immigrated. Here and there a leather coat, a leather hat, carved wooden buttons, a green Bavarian coat. Above the bar a pair of large paintings done in that cartoon style popular in Germany before the First World War. They dominate the tavern. In the first painting a peasant in Tyrolean hat and *lederhosen,* with mustaches and bulging eyes and bulbous nose and swinelike face, refuses to pay a fare for his goat on the train and ties him instead to the rear platform of the last car. In the second painting the same peasant is slapping his head while the conductor and passengers with their swinelike faces are grouped around him, pointing and holding their sides with laughter; at the end of the rope in the middle of the railroad track is the decapitated and bloody head of the goat, eyes bulging and tongue hanging out. "Barbarians," Burkhardt says, nodding at the paintings.

Customers have put tables together to make one long table. The strong chords of the piano and the vigorous bowing of the violin. *Ein prosit!* The singing of beer-drinking songs. The patrons at the large table linking arms and swaying left and right. *Mein*

Hut der hat drei Ecken. The familiarity and friendliness between men and women, old people and young people, old hands and newcomers. A dominance of redness, as though everything is seen through a red expansive light.

Cavan and Sonja with their hands folded and elbows on the table and looking at each other. They are speechless. They ask the waitress what she wants a minute after she has spoken to them. They don't know what they order. Steins of dark beer are set before them, schnapps glasses of *Steinhager*. A dish of *brat* herring before Cavan. A thuringer and rye before Sonja. Still looking at each other, still smiling. As though his hand belongs on the body of someone else, Cavan is crumbling her rye bread on the tablecloth, looking at her eyes.

The piano player smiling at their table and nodding, apparently recognizing Burkhardt. He is playing selections from *The Student Prince,* which pleases Burkhardt until he blushes. During an intermission Burkhardt sends the musicians a glass of beer. They stand and toast him; the violin player with a handkerchief folded on his shoulder tightens his bow. Burkhardt and Kay drinking a bottle of Moselle, he with his arm around her shoulder. A man with a cigarette holder has set a pair of mechanical dogs walking along the bar. Customers and the lame bartender crowd around him, exclaiming at the dogs. The man turns on his stool to Sonja and Cavan, smiles, invites them with his hand to watch the dogs.

Cavan tries to speak. He cannot. Sonja tries to speak. She is just as helpless. They squeeze each other's hands in their happiness and frustration. They try to eat. They cannot. Cavan is afraid he will be sick, that his sickness will ruin everything. His stomach is an exquisite tangle of improbable knots. They try to drink. But the beer is already warm and will not go down easily. They can only sip. Sonja licks the brown foam from her lips.

The waitress smiling and saying something in her heavy accent. They cannot hear her. She is so far away. At another table. In another room. In another tavern. Her hand appears to indicate the beer, the food. "No?" she says, laughing. "You don't understand what I say?" Laughing, she goes away.

A taxi driver in baggy pants and with his license pinned to his cap enters to pick up his fare. As he leaves he pauses at the door of colored, crinkled, leaded glass and sings in a good but trilling tenor a verse of "Galway Bay." The piano player accompanies him. Finishing up the driver removes his cap, bows, throws kisses, waves to all, and escorts his passenger out the door. A woman in furs and a hat skewered by a feather leans over from the adjoining table and whispers to Burkhardt, "You know we used to have places like this in New York where I come from, but not any more." She leans closer still, whispers conspiratorially, "The Jews."

The marvelous polish to the brass horns on the wall. The medieval green and red colors in the pair of paintings above the bar. Cavan pats Sonja's hand, repeatedly. Now and then she takes his hand in both of hers. They press their palms together, interlock the fingers and unconsciously wage a struggle that is fierce. She is surprisingly strong. Only after a mighty effort can he force her hand down to her lap. He bangs the table with his fist. They both seem on the verge of crying. She takes a letter from her leather purse. It is airmail and bears a foreign stamp. Without taking her eyes from Cavan she tears it into tiny pieces, which she drops carelessly in an ashtray. He knows it is a letter from some boyfriend, a soldier or student, knows it without asking or examining the letter. She has said so much. People at the other tables are staring at them, commenting on them and laughing. The young German couples nod and smile as though they would like to meet them. An older man with an accent comes up behind them, claps them on the back, squeezes their shoulders, puts his face close to theirs. "It's so good to see young people in love," he says. "So good—bless you." He seems overcome. The owner of the Ulmer Stube, Herr Willy, short and fat, comes out and greets his guests with a nod. He seems to know Burkhardt. "Look at these young people, Willy," the man behind them says. Herr Willy, not easily given to smiling, smiles, and buys them a drink. The man notices the wound in the corner of Cavan's mouth, the sliver of dried blood. "What happened to you?" he says. "Sweetheart, you did not hit him already, did you?"

"No, no," he says. "These Polish kids . . ."

Before he can say more the man puts up his palm and delivers a brief lecture on the inferiority and barbarism of Poles. There are Polish machinists and German machinists in the plants where he has worked, both in this country and in the Old Country, and believe him, the German machinists are better, in all ways. Crude work, that is all the Poles are good for.

Cavan and Sonja saying such things to each other as, "Do you know . . . ?" with the other answering with a shake of the head. Or, "What do you think?" Again answered with a shake of the head. "What can you say?" he begins, uncertain as to what he is referring to, as she shakes her head again. "What can you say?" she says later. "Nothing," he manages to say.

Kay sobbing despite Burkhardt's repeated assurances that the world works well and the consolation of his arm around her shoulder. "I used to love Pete," she says into her handkerchief. "I used to think he was the only man for me. I want him to become a poet—a wonderful poet.—I wasn't out to destroy his poetry, was I?"

"I don't think there was all that much to destroy."

"And I wasn't trying to cut off his precious balls."

"Who said that?"

"Vollmer."

"Don't pay any attention to Vollmer. He says that to all the girls."

"I had to leave him," she says. "I had to. But I feel wicked about it. . . . and alone . . . and unhappy . . . I feel like a failure . . ."

Ein prosit! Good cheer to all. The tavern stomps and rings. Martial beerhall singing. Heels and fists and elbows boom against the floor and tables. Poltergeists blowing the posthorns and tubas on the walls. The violin transformed into a brass band. The piano into accordion and drums. In the world of the gnarled tree roots and hop vines on the clay beer mugs along the bar, friars are winking, black cats arching, Rhine maids combing, peasants playing cards and smoking, milkmaids dancing. Beer drinkers' faces puffed up and flushed like the bottoms of newborn babies. A round of drinks for Cavan and Sonja from a man at the bar who salutes them with his glass and tells them they are wonderful. And excuse him, he is not being impolite, but he just likes to look at them, they are so happy. "You are not hungry?" the waitress smiling with a secret knowledge, pointing to the thuringer, the brat herring. Sweeping up the rye crumbs, the shreds of the torn envelope. "Shame on you," she says. They shake their heads.

Kay drunk and demanding more to drink against the counsel of Burkhardt. Suddenly she throws back her head, shakes her hair, and slams her palms down on the table. "Fuck Pete," she says. It is not quite a shout but the words are drawn out and insistent with an emotion that comes from the gut.

"*Was ist das,*" says a grandmother type at the adjoining table to her middle-aged son, "*diese* 'fuckpete'?" The middle-aged son has turned in his chair to glare at Kay.

Burkhardt's head shrinks into his oversized neck and his hands would turn up his collar if it were not buttoned down. "Snap out of it," he says, hoping to shame her. Keeping an eye on the other tables and afraid she will attack with a flurry of elbows and nails if he so much as touches her hand. She grows pale, grows sick, wobbles to the washroom where Burkhardt waits foolishly outside the door, listening to her wail and retch. A pair of young immigrant Volkswagen mechanics are laughing at him brazenly. Their hair already worn like Chicago hoodlums. "Hey now look here, man," one says to Burkhardt. "You got to be a daddy cool now, you know," and snaps his fingers.

Burkhardt stares them down, jangling the change in his pockets. When Kay comes out at last, drained, gasping, coughing, he whispers, "We shouldn't have come here. My mistake. We don't belong here. Barbarians. A Bund meeting. Cabbageheads." He stumbles at her side, no less drunk than she.

Cavan squeezing Sonja's hand and dreaming not of sex or women or even of love as he has known it but of some unfocused feeling of sustenance and consolation he cannot fix inside his mind or senses, much less define. The recollection of a night he is certain he has not recalled before, that until this moment he has had no inkling has been saved within his memory. He is drunk and wealthy with allowances and without home or family and brawling with his college roommates in the street and breaking glass and screaming and then chased through back yards and into bushes and over fences and down alleys by the police when shots are fired—warning shots in the air? (They actually fired their guns!) Then alone and lost in a strange and hostile town at night in the wilderness of his savage and lonely youth when everyone, including friends, is an enemy. The refuge of a truck stop where an old man takes the stool beside him and drinks his coffee and dunks his doughnut and tells him of his daughter and grandchildren until Cavan is finished with his plate of eggs and he says, "Well, we better take you home."

Home. Dear God, yes. Take me home.

The man taking him in his car to the dormitory where Cavan tries to give him all the change he has in his pockets and the man says, No, no, he is a policeman of sorts and it is his job to round up all his drunken boys and see them safely home at night. And what he felt then for that man and for himself for feeling it and, yes, for the very world itself, he is feeling now. More than gratitude. Closer to reassurance. Even hope. A glimmer of grace. Sonja, you are like that old man. He will not tell her this but knows he could tell her if he wished, that unlike Myrna, who would miss the feeling and see with outrage the comparison only to something old and male and low, she would understand and blossom with the compliment.

"I was searching for someone else tonight," he admits.

"She ran away—"

"No, no. I was searching for me."

"And you found me?"

"Maybe that's another way of saying I found me."

"You're a new life to me," she says. "You're new days." She touches her lips to his knuckles. The sensation of a kiss on the inside of the thigh.

This newness. This unexplained and undeserved happiness. This immediate affection. Before them the adventure of a long life. Endless time.

She withdraws from him, frowning as though she knows that to let him touch her is to surrender herself totally and for far longer than just the moment.

Sonja Maki, she tells him, is her name.

John Helenowski, he says, is his.

CHAPTER TWENTY

ESCAPE!

Old Tom Thorsen has long since left his lawns and gardens for his potting shed where, seated on a tulip crate, his muddy boots propped on a wooden box of potting soil, he is fast asleep. Leaning back inside a wheelbarrow from which it would appear he has been dumped, he looks for all the world like the model for a drawing out of Mother Goose. Around him, stacks of clay pots, seed trays covered with brown paper, plain packets of seeds. Smells of moist earth, damp roots in even damper sawdust, bleached vegetation, the musty inference of something new, something green. Why, the shed could be inside the earth, could be a chamber inside a mound of grass—sod roof, sod walls—for all the dark smells of earth and damp.

What a pair of hands the old man has! The knuckles resting on the brick floor, the cold bowl of his briar still cradled in his palm. In comparison to his arms and wrists they look as large as baseball gloves. They are hands that have been shaped by tools, enlarged by tools, calloused for the grip of tools. Hammers, axes, saws, trowels, ropes, knives, all fit neatly into their own molded pockets of those hands where they become, as it were, extensions of flesh and bone. With a tool in hand he could be an exorcising priest holding a crucifix for all the awe and mystery he feels. That moment in prehistory when for the first time an ape brought home the branch he used to knock an apple from a tree would be for him the be-all and the end-all of man's creation. Nothing more elaborate than tools define the species man. Sleeping in the potting shed among his spades, grubhoes, and turning forks, he could be a Viking entombed in a barrow with all those treasures he has favored in this earthly life and will want beside him in the world to come.

But his dreams range far beyond the shed. They are as far-flung as the farthest reaches of the globe. Green fjords and fjelds. Wind-jammers with white sails. White steamships. White glaciers and blue oceans. Emerald-tinted icebergs. Sandy roads and railroad tracks. Wheatfields—fields of flowering mustard—of goldenrod—with the bluish peaks of mountains in the distance. Against the prairie cloudscape, a yellow threshing machine. A green tractor. Then a city and the backs of red brick buildings. Red wooden streetcars with yellow cane seats—the street sign says Van Buren Street. Horses pulling red and yellow wagons full of coal. And there—in the sun-light on the sidewalk a tall blond youth in a straw hat, bow tie, tight unpadded jacket, and cuffless trousers ending six inches above the black high-button shoes, a cardboard suitcase in his hand. There you are again, he thinks fondly in his sleep. You little vagabond, you little bo, you funny young fellow. Suddenly he is impatient to be awake.

He stirs, his damp joints aching even in his sleep. He stretches with the feeling of breaking through a tent of cobwebs. Why, he could have slept the winter for all he can remember of the last time he was awake. There it is—that same urge that overpowered him in his dream. He wonders that at this late age and after all these years in one place he should again feel that instinct of migra-tion and self-interest that tells him it is once more time to set out upon the sea, the rails, the road.

With a spade on his shoulder he pauses at the doorway in the dark, staring at the darkened Farquarson house. "You ain't my home," he says.

For Mrs. Owens, inside the Farquarson house, there is no thought of escape. Not even in her dreams. Feverish from her cold and dazzled by the "cold serum" the nurse said would make her comfortable, which to her surprise the nurse injected in her arm before she could says yes or no or ask for a definition more precise and Latinate than merely "cold serum," dreams of moles, graves, buried treasure, the sounds of digging. And at night too. And a rainy night at that. And in a thunderstorm. There it is, the spade forced into the earth, the careful turning of the soil upon a pile, the scrape of the spade against a stone. It is enough to make her open up her eyes. A frequent but distant lightning, as though a neon light hangs just outside her room. She is calm, invulnerable, unable to move an eye, never mind a leg. Even so, she rises and drifts in swirling swathes of nightgown to the French windows in the room next door.

A lantern in the rhododendron shrubbery between the evergreens. It must be hanging on a bough. The man takes shape within that light. There he is, ghostlike, sinking into the earth, disappearing up to his knees, planting his boot upon the spade. Digging himself a hole. Digging it deep. She thinks: the man with the foul mouth and breathless voice who calls me on the telephone, come at night to dig a tunnel beneath the distance of the open lawn from the shrubbery to the house. She can see his spade break through the cellar floor and the man himself surprising her inside the house, placing a dirty hand across her mouth.

Now he lies down upon his stomach, stretching himself out as though attempting a rescue on thin ice and, with the lantern held aloft, peers down into the hole. It could be an opening into a bubbling inferno inside the earth. A smear of light flashes across his lascivious, leering face. Thorsen—his face. But why working in the garden at such an hour?

Now he thrusts his arms up to the shoulders into the fire and smoke within the hole and pulls from the earth neither roots nor bones but a small chest from which he scrapes the dirt. In the lightning man and box glimpsed as though imposed only on every hundredth frame of film. Rising and hugging the box to his breast as a father might his threatened child.—Sitting on the pile of dirt and smoking his pipe as he contemplates with satisfaction that same box set before him on the ground.—Midway in a stride of a dash toward that box.—Squatting on the ground, pipe in mouth again, and peering into that box, the lid of which he holds up in his hands. A green light explodes up into his face. Into an oafish face full of selfishness and greed, as though the gardener is by night black-mailer, kidnapper, miser. Even his flesh turns green—money-green. Behold the green face, the pair of huge green hands. A green man fills in the hole, stomps on it with his big green feet, then sidles off with that box tucked underneath his arm, swinging his lantern. Later in the potting shed a low light comes on that bespeaks the secret rituals of outlawed cults, and the long green face, all nose and chin, looms up in the distortion of the little leaded window, the long green fingers stroking one another before they begin the slow tally of the money.

Hush! The telephone is ringing. A cruel nervous ring that won't take silence for an answer. In the dark study she makes out the white uniform in the middle of the room: the nurse already there and listening to the phone. "It's him, isn't it?" she whispers, close enough to catch the demonic, theatrical, masculine crackle on the line. She doesn't want to hear the words, doesn't want the nurse to hear them either, doesn't want her to know what she has had to listen to before.

Then—"You swine," says the nurse as Mrs. Owens tries to clamp her hand upon the mouthpiece. "You impotent swine," adds the nurse, elbowing Mrs. Owens away.

Please, Mrs. Owens's eyes implore, do not encourage or dis-courage (which is merely another way of encouraging) this sick man.

To no avail. The sardonic laugh of an amused woman feeling pain followed by the several taunts Mrs. Owens does not under-stand: the pair of tweezers the man behind that awful crackle must be using—oh, he isn't using tweezers? Then he should be careful or hair will grow on his hand. And thereafter her response to his, "You wouldn't dare!" She even manages to repeat the challenge several times before Mrs. Owens can tug the receiver from beneath her ear and hang up on the floodtide of fantasized acts of flagella-tions, sodomy, and spankings her challenge has set loose.

Then the long silent time spent by both women staring at the silent phone in that dark room.

"What was it . . . ?" Mrs. Owens begins as the nurse guides her toward her room. "I mean what did you dare him to do?"

"Don't worry," says the nurse. "He won't come here. He gets what he wants by himself, at home."

"That's very well for you to say," says Mrs. Owens, probing her head with her fingertips as though it is a membrane-thin, blown-up balloon into which is being pumped still more air, "but it's me he called, and if he comes here it's me he will do those nasty things to—thanks to you." Says later as the nurse pulls back the covers of her bed and guides her in, "Maybe he recognized it wasn't my voice that said it. Maybe he won't take it out on me because he knows it wasn't me that said it. Maybe your voice scared him off—I mean he hadn't heard it before. You could have been a policewoman for all he knew."

"No," says the nurse wearily, "he was just all done."

"You're right about one thing, though," says Mrs. Owens. "He is a swine."

"No," says the nurse. "He's just a man."

"Don't wake me," Mrs. Owens says, settling in her pillows, "don't let anything disturb me. I feel so weak, so strange. I'm awful lazy . . ."

Asleep, her sleep made easy by yet another shot of that "cold serum" administered to her by the nurse, she doesn't see the headlights flash through her room. She doesn't hear the car come up the driveway.

The nurse hears it, though. Hears the yodels, too. Then that shout above the honking of the horn, "Help me, nurse! Help!" A car door slams to laughter. Footsteps on the gravel. A heavy knocking on the front door.

She slips her pistol in the pocket of her uniform, peering down into the driveway below. A cherry red, highly polished convertible ten years old. Hanging from its windows the arms and legs and heads of half a dozen drunken boys. Skipper Moony is alone at the door. "No one's home," he says at last and starts back for the car only to be greeted with boos and catcalls and again that drunken call, "Help me, nursie! Only you can help me!" A conference at the car interrupted by laughter and commands for silence. Two factions, one that would be soft-spoken, well-behaved, and foxy, the other loud, bad-mannered, and brazen, each convinced its course will achieve the common goal. Then the shout she hears before it can be stifled, "Nancy, sweetheart, come out wherever you are and lay me in the garden!"

They know my name, she thinks, along with all the drunken fantasies that he could think to tell them.

When she looks a second time she catches Skipper on the ivy of the wall, climbing toward the only lighted window of the house —Farquarson's window—the window he mistakes for hers. Below him a boy strums a badly tuned guitar. Up and up he goes, climbs around the window of Mrs. Owens, who doesn't see him rest his foot upon her window sill. He pauses, holds on to the vine with one hand, throws an arm dramatically above his head, leans away from the wall, and breaks into song. It is a breathless, embarrassed voice that wavers with his fear of heights, singing what sounds like "Red River Valley," skipping lines and whole choruses whenever the climb is rough. Bits of leaves and vines rain down upon the boy below.

"Go on!" shout the voices from the car as Skipper reaches up to touch the window sill of that single open lighted window.

She runs down the hall, pausing just long enough to reach inside a room and switch on its light. Runs down the stairs, still switching on the lights, frightened that they should be here when the detective and the police might arrive at any moment. While singer and guitarist are dumbfounded by the windows lighting up before them, one coming on after the other, all down the line.

Downstairs she switches on the outside flood lights, steps out upon the flags. "Now," she says, "what's all this?"

The guitar player, holding the guitar before his face, runs for the car. Skipper leaps from the wall, starts for the car also only to change his course and limp toward her self-consciously, grimacing and rubbing his knee. At the door he stands slouched and hunched with his hands slid in the front pockets of his tight jeans in the popular pose of nonchalance and indifference of the day.

In the car the posture of the passengers worsens until the seats appear crowded with midgets or sullen sleepers with knees and arms before their faces. Like a bunch of rebels who have come to the castle armed with knives and revolvers to kill the king and having been ordered by him to wipe their feet and not make so much noise, wipe their feet and stop making noise. The woman they have until now imagined as a mannequin has come before them in the flesh of an older woman, an attractive woman, a bold woman, any one of which intimidates them.

Skipper mumbles something about going off to Florida, of coming here to say good-bye. While she considers him in a silence that is meant to tell him he is a fool. Finally she says, "Good-bye."

But he cannot lose face before his friends and allow himself to be so immediately rejected by so attractive an older woman, who resides in so grand a village and in so grand a house, throwing into doubt the veracity of all those tales he has told or implied concerning her. He overcomes his bashfulness and places his palms on the door above her shoulders, pinning her up against the door without touching her, like high-school sweethearts saying good-night. It's a spur-of-the-moment decision, he tells her, this trip to Florida that will be made in one mad dash of twenty-four hours across Illinois and the southern states. He and his pals were drinking tonight and someone dared him, dared all of them to drop everything and get up and go, and by God, he saw the sense in that dare and he got up, and everyone else got up, and they are all going. He has quit his job, dropped out of school, taken the car, and left no note at home. He no longer wants to be a civil engineer and work in an office with a suit. His feelings have always been for travel, nature, beauty. He will get a job in fruit orchards if he has to, and if he likes it and takes to it, who knows, maybe he'll buy himself a citrus grove or two. He will get a job as a merchant seaman on a Caribbean run. He might stay in too, and work up to mate, which is an officer, he explains. Or he might buy himself a boat and charter it out for deep-sea fishing expeditions. Or run guns to Cuba. Or become a lifeguard and marry some wealthy dame. He wants to travel, to see the world. Chicago and Illinois are ruts! He will write to her and he hopes she will write to him. He used to like her a lot—still likes her a lot, he corrects himself—and will always remember what they had together. He hopes she will understand why he has to leave. By now he has worked himself up to a pitch of manly self-pity; doomed romanticism hangs heavy in the air, a sense of impending tragedy that belies his own bursts of optimism; his eyes are wet.

"Good luck," she says, and supposes she must mean it. She is amused by his bad theater, although to him, she acknowledges, it must be genuine enough. There was never anything between this boy and her. Whatever she satisfied in their affair she satisfied cerebrally. It was an experiment, the dramatization of an idea that in such things as youth, brawn, menialness, and even ignorance and insensitivity and possibly innocence too there is to be found excitement, eroticism, and the natural domicile of sex.

He glances back at the car as though to open up the conversation to that ashamed and silenced audience. Asks with reluctance and nonchalance, and the attempt to sound seductive and even obscene, "Why don't you come with us?"

She wonders if he is joking, and if he is not, if his drunkenness is sufficient reason to excuse him. "Us?" she says.

He is willing to put it differently. "Come if you want. It's up to you."

She knows from her army days how some boys tend to see all women as being either queens or whores. Knows also in which camp they have quartered her. But do they actually think for one moment that she will join them on their drunken, makeshift odyssey across the continent? Is that what her friendship and flirtation have meant to him and, as a result of his public boasting, what they mean automatically to his friends? Why, he must have told them he could make her come with them all for no other reason than that she was sexually insatiable or insane or had no alternative but to satisfy his whim. The not unpleasant nor unwelcome sense of humiliation that he has made her feel.

"If you don't want to go all the way to Florida," he says, "just come out for a while and say good-bye to me—and the fellows." But now he speaks as though he jests. And having satisfied some challenge to his manhood and audacity he becomes more ingenuous, although no less impossible. His eyes glisten with his own high spirit of adventure, romance, the limitless possibility of himself and everything. "I could get rid of them," he stammers. "I will, if you come with me." He leans forward protectively, his hands still placed on the door above her shoulders, so that he resembles in his posture some young, gigantic dog standing on its hindlegs. "Pack a bag—I'll come back."

For a moment she is tempted. The nocturnal magic of cross-country motoring at high speed interrupted only by the higher speed needed to pass another car, of nonstop and sleepless driving when miles, like your own past, race behind you in the starlit and continental night. The images she remembers of other journeys south: the towering fires of the Gary steel mills, the smell of mown bluegrass in Kentucky, the red clay and Spanish moss of Alabama, the flat, tropical countryside of northern Florida, the sensual and sultry night motored through with the top down on the convertible, her arm out the window and scarf blowing on her head, the small American flag on the aerial flapping with the speed, and the bodies of exotic tropical insects breaking against the windshield. That voluptuousness of racing through a countryside without knowing or caring what is out there in the darkness of either side, of the wheels rolling over unseen stretches of the continent, while in contrast to that speed and darkness the drowsy mind dreams of erotic joys with future lovers in the prismatic splendor of future places. To pick up and go on the spur of the moment and say good-bye to those conventions and responsibilities that are the anchors of your past; to push the machine to its limits of speed until the new self rises from the body of the old and is catapulted like a rocket down the road, while the old self is jettisoned at some forgotten roadside already out of sight.

"I'll build a cabin in the Everglades," he says. "The two of us in the middle of nowhere." Conjures up for her the picture of a life that is strangely sexless and innocent, a shack built on stilts in the middle of a steaming jungle and over the hot black water of a swamp; a wilderness of deadly snakes, rare birds, and alligators he will observe, study, and ultimately befriend; the same with the local Indians—Seminoles by name—who will in turn befriend them; of fishing from canoes, eating mangoes, battling hurricanes. And she imagines the torn and tattered clothing, the network of vines they use for inland transportation, the animals that are adopted members of the family, whose language they speak and understand, their own speech reduced to grunts and monosyllables. Only another morphinic dream that would be all the worse for being real. She smiles as he talks on, and shakes her head.

"Then if you don't want to go to Florida," he says, "I can get rid of them and come back alone. And you can say good-bye alone." Injured, he is on the edge of nastiness. For the real risk for him all along has not been in asking her to go away with him and all his friends but to go away with him alone. She sees something else about him too, that he lacks the courage to embark on his adventure all alone, and must go with someone else or not at all. So young and already afraid of loneliness, she thinks. How often in her own past, in her own blundering, unhappy ways, has she struck out alone—has she been forced to strike out alone—in the middle of the night for places unknown? And where was that romance, and those adventures, she asks bitterly, that she found either there or on the way?

"Write," she says, opening the door.

He stands dazed, indignant, suffering that romantic and now tragic wound to his manhood and youth that has been sentimentally self-inflicted. "Then I will go to Florida," he says.

"Yes, go—quickly."

"We won't meet again."

"You're right, we probably won't."

"I'll never meet another woman like you."

"Not exactly like me, no," she says, resisting the temptation to add, "And luckily for you," which she knows would only be stepping into the melodramatic role his own role has offered her.

"I'll never love another woman like I loved you."

She can only shrug this off and resist the temptation to say, No, you'll love her (or all of them) better, which she knows would sound maternal. She is touched by this willingness to believe his life—or any life perhaps—is capable of tragedy, adventure, high romance. A strange mixture of troubadour and vandal, with little or nothing in between.

Suddenly he leaps toward her, crooks his arm around her neck, and dips her back as though giving the final touch to an old-fashioned waltz, then kisses her roughly on the mouth and releases her in so sudden a dramatic gesture that she would have fallen down had she not fallen back against the door. Then he is off in the car, spraying the gravel of the driveway onto the lawn and into the hedges while beer cans ricochet off Farquarson cars and trees as curses and drunken war whoops fly back at the nurse and that intimidating house, cries less of insult than of the boys' relief to be leaving this woman who embarrasses them and this house where, despite the democratic birthright that insists they are its equal, they feel they have about as much business as in the inside of a bank vault after hours. "So long!" someone shouts up from the road. And except for the one or two of them who will lose their nerve and ask to be let out before the journey is begun in earnest, they are on their way to Florida. To hell with their dreary jobs. Let them hire a new laborer, gas jockey, shipping clerk. Setting out with no more than the few dollars in their wallets, a piece of hose for stealing gas, and the numerous tire irons they plan to use to defend themselves with, if necessary, from the violent and backward people of Kentucky and Tennessee when they are passing through those states. So what if in a few days all, or nearly all of them, will be back broke, unshaven, unwashed, weary, back on the job or looking for a new one. Until then a long night and a continent of roads they have yet to try is opening before their headlights.

She, however, shuts herself up with a sick woman, a dead man, and herself. No youth or wilderness, no open road inside this house. Only blackmail, more drugs, and death. And shuts herself in with something else besides. That man there in the center of the darkened room, his head hung like a hanged man. Who hasn't moved now in the several minutes she has been watching. It is one of the boys, she thinks, the worst of the lot, who has stayed behind. Or that awful man she challenged on the telephone, come as he said he would. Something wet about this man, some quality that has turned the air wet in the room, there—the sound of dripping, the smell of rain, marshland, wet clothes. A drowned man that has materialized inside this room to strike his dreary, contemplative pose. Or Death himself, come from the deep.

"You there," she calls.

In answer he lifts his face. No, not Death, but familiar all the same. Magnuson, the detective. "You live dangerously," she says, fondling the beaded butt of the revolver she has been squeezing. "You should be careful."

"You should have been careful all your life, lady," he answers. She cannot tell whether he is depressed or just indifferent. Only that he has been purified by an icy and gloomy instinct until he has become like some caricature of puritanical retribution and revenge. He looks as if he has been skulking all evening on an ung021uttered eavesdrop in heavy rain.

"How did you get in?"

He laughs, throws back his head and laughs, repeatedly.

"Did you talk to him—to Wenzel—about the letter?"

But he will only give her that policeman's smug look of authority. It says that what he knows is a secret she has no right to ask about, much less to know. Still wearing that expression he goes upstairs and unlocks Farquarson's door.

—What a fool he has been! Although he locked the door he left the window open, the light on, and the ladder up against the window. Why, anyone could have entered through that window! Fortunately as far as he can tell Farquarson's room is as it was before. The body seems undisturbed, the face unchanged. As he lets the sheet fall from his hand he imagines he detects the feeble signal of a final spark in the artery along the throat.

He wants to drop in a corner of the floor and sleep for days. Instead, he forces himself to do his job. He stoops to the small open safe beside the bed. Stamp albums and an unlocked cashbox full of money. Robbery is not the motive. Nothing else of interest except for a leatherbound, pocket-sized ledger wrapped up in a dozen rubber bands, and stuck in the farthest recess of the top shelf, and inside, of all things, a cigar box. The secrecy of its location makes him suspicious. But instead of accounts of money on the green and red ruled pages there are what appear to be notations in code. Two columns run down each page, one under a heading marked W, the other N, and every entry is either a KO, TKO, or D, with a number anywhere from 1 to 15 after it. To the left of each entry is a date, the dates often a week apart. Page after page of such notations, the dates going back a dozen years. A strange code. Strange records to have kept in a secret locked place for so long. Obviously something to do with boxing; KO means knockout, TKO technical knockout, and D, he assumes, means decision, while the number refers to the round the fight ended, and the date to the day of the bout. Was Farquarson a minor gambler? Or was he involved in the fixing of numerous and even major prize fights? Were Rotterdam, the beer salesman, and the Wenzels, the tavern owners, and Farquarson all mixed up in some illegal liquor business with illegal betting or the fixing of prize fights on the side? It seems more probable and reasonable, however, that the boxing abbreviations are a code for something else. But what? He feels certain he has a promising clue.

He will study it later.

He is shivering, soaked to the skin, and from Farquarson's closet and dresser drawers picks out a complete set of Farquarson clothes, including a hand-tailored, conservative blue suit. He strips naked beside the corpse and puts on the dead man's clothes. The fit is close enough. He even finds a pair of shoes that are not uncomfortable, along with a hat and raincoat. He cannot find an overnight bag in which to stuff his own clothes and he drapes them across the dresser and chairs to dry instead. If he cannot safely return Farquarson's clothes he can always burn them in the incinerator of his apartment building. This time he shuts off the light and locks the door.

He wonders why the nurse should startle so as he comes toward her down the stairs, why her surprise should yield so quickly to a look of horror. He even looks back to see if it isn't something behind him that causes such alarm. Only when he reaches the foot of the stairs does he notice her fixation with his clothes, suspects that if she could be certain of what she sees she would back off, screaming, "But you're dead!" and then when he is even closer to her she would point at him and say, "It's only you—but in his clothes!"

He begins to question her. No need to be ruthless, though; in reply she tells him everything. About this Helenowski, that escapee from an asylum who kept Farquarson in terror until he learned this morning that the man was found murdered last night in Washington Square; the visit of Lena, the black maid, last night to Farquarson's room; the second visit early this afternoon of Lena to Farquarson, this time accompanied by the Nettles, a black minister and his wife; the mysterious visit of a man named Alvin Raincloud whom Cavan

claimed to have received this morning in his study; the obscene calls
Mrs. Owens has been receiving lately, the most recent just tonight.
And come to think of it, Cavan may have gone to see Wenzel in
Wauconda earlier today—and oh, yes, Cavan called just after Mag-
nuson had left and asked for Lena's address.

"Let's see the housekeeper," he says, thinking to inquire first into
those obscene calls.

"She's sick in bed. Sound asleep. Under medication."

"Cavan," he says, thinking about that mysterious visitor he had
this morning and about his interest in Wenzel and the black maid.

"I haven't seen him since you saw him at supper. He didn't
say where he was when he called."

"Thorsen then." Thinking he may have seen someone go
down the ladder.

"Disappeared," she says, recalling how she saw him in the house
as he snuck past the doorway of the room, wearing a straw hat, ill-
fitting and tight suit jacket and shrunken cuffless trousers, high-
button shoes, and carrying a battered cardboard suitcase wrapped
up in rotting leather straps, looking like a passenger aboard a sinking
ship sneaking for the lifeboats before the command to abandon ship.

"Disappeared," he echoes, fearing for the worst. The old man
lying in the shrubbery, hacked to death with a hoe. Is he never
to have a witness to interrogate?

He produces the photograph of Skipper Moony for no better
reason than at the moment he has no other lead. He is astounded.
She has recognized the face and is surprised that he should have
the photograph in his possession. At last something that definitely
connects these disparate people and disparate places. "How do you
know him?"

Quickly she determines that he must have been here when
Skipper was here, perhaps even hiding in the shrubbery and eaves-
dropping on their conversation at the door. Therefore he knows she
knows him before he asks. How he came by the picture, though, per-
plexes her. "He worked here last fall. Helping Thorsen with the
grounds."

"What, worked here?" he echoes.

It is the connection between Farquarson and the Moonys he has
been searching for! The one missing link that binds together all the
murdered parties! What good fortune! "And you saw him last?"

She evades his eyes. "A half-hour ago."

"He was here!" he cries, revealing his ignorance of Skipper's presence here. He is on the verge of a meaningful discovery. "Why here?"

"He was on his way to Florida—"

"Yes, in a red convertible with a white top." He says this almost to himself, confusing the nurse who seems about to ask, How do you know? "Was he alone?"

"His friends were with him—some boys."

Yes, thinks Magnuson, a gang on their way to Florida. Which explains the clothes missing from his room, the signs of hurried packing. He was running away—but why? And why stop here?

"Did Thorsen go with him?"

She looks surprised.

He explains: "You said Thorsen was gone. You said Thorsen and this Moony had worked together in the garden. He came to see Thorsen, didn't he?"

"No, he came to see me." She hesitates, finally explains, "We used to be friendly . . ."

"What do you mean friendly? How friendly?" But immediately he guesses all. From his gloom and weariness and the concession of his defeat rise sparks of bewilderment and rage. What was wrong with people? Could they only exist like Chinese puzzles, interlaced, intertwined, interlocked, intermixed, interknit, complexly and unreasonably if not always immorally, and were they to repeatedly drag him into their maze but never so completely that he could be certain of what he saw, never mind the complications and implications? Why couldn't they leave each other alone? They expected him to understand them, to protect and even at times avenge them, but how could he stay clearheaded and act on a firm footing amid the flabby and filmy messes they made of their lives? People lead simple lives. He believes this despite all the knowledge to the contrary that he has acquired as a policeman and private detective. Believes he has lived a simple life. He is, he tells himself, a simple man. He squints in pain at the square youthful face in the photograph, the smugness in the smile and the sensuality in the eyes that declares he is cruel and without innocence. He resists the urge to tear up the photograph and toss it in the nurse's face or at her feet. If only he were the murderer!

He interrupts her explanation. "I don't want to listen! Maybe your boyfriend was here earlier too. Maybe you two murdered Farquarson, although it beats me what your motive was unless you were just out for thrills. Maybe you murdered Farquarson yourself— to keep him quiet about your stealing drugs." She protests but he waves her to be silent and continues to impose upon her what he judges to be no more than the natural burden of her guilt. "And I was stupid enough to show you the note that told me Farquarson sent a letter to Wenzel. You must have known you were named in that letter. Smart of you to tell me on the spur of the moment that you'd seen the note before, lots of them. Then you relayed the news of Farquarson's letter to your boyfriend up in Wauconda. He and his pals were on the scene to do the rest. Although they had to chase down into the city to take care of Rotterdam. Maybe your boyfriend stopped by just now not only to tell you he was clearing out to Florida, but that he had got hold of Farquarson's letter to Wenzel and destroyed it, and murdered anyone else he thought could place him at the murder scenes. But I wonder if he told you how he blew his parents—his own mother and father—to pieces with a shotgun. I'll bet though that he told you how he drowned that old fool Magnuson who was hot on his heels, who was closing in. But I'm not so old—I'm not so great a fool as all of that. And you know better, besides, don't you? Look at me closely, honey. Do I look like I've come off the bottom of the pond? Use your eyes. Magnuson is here before you. He is alive. He lives!" He wants to push her against the wall, hold his hand across her mouth and force his knee between her legs. Wants to give her the back of his hand, or a hard kiss, on the mouth, her lips cool and tight until from her own free will she opens her mouth.

"Other murders?" says the nurse in disbelief. She has been saying it all along.

"Farquarson was only the first—but maybe I'm wrong about the boyfriend. Maybe you're only playing him for a sucker. Maybe you've done all the killing by yourself. Maybe your mind's been turned to jelly by the dope, your morals turned inside out until you don't know right from wrong. Maybe after you murdered your boss you left the house right after I did, passed me on the road, got to Wenzel first. You could have been out there all night, driving up and down the roads—how do I know? Maybe you only got back inside the house before I got here myself—and you made up this story about Moony being here to give yourself an alibi." He checks himself. He cannot bring himself to believe his own charges, they are that absurd. Although he suspects that the truth, whatever it is, will prove no less absurd. His hands shake, he has to fight to keep his voice from cracking. "You could have been such a fine woman . . . such a good girl . . ." He wants to put his arm around her, touch her, treat her like a pal. "Or maybe there's a madman on the loose, honey. A clever fellow killing everyone in sight, and no one, not you, not me, not anyone, is safe." He wipes his eyes with his hand. "You've got to trust me. You don't know what I know . . . what I've been through." Foolishly he expects her to yield to that warm instinct of her sex, to attempt to cure and comfort him, to drown him in the consolation of her compassion; he expects her to have no choice. But she is too drugged or shocked, too deeply inside herself to extend herself to him. Not only this, but he sees now what he failed to see before, that she is pointing a pistol at his chest. He slaps his palms against his thighs in disappointment and resignation. "So that's how it is," he says.

"You're sick," she says. It is the clinical indifference of the voice that injures him. "You were up there alone with him, you killed him then. You found the note—you went after Wenzel. If other people have been murdered, you must have killed them—"

"It's not true, sweetie," he is quick to reassure her. "I'm on the other side—"

"Now you've come back," she says, "to the scene of the crime. To destroy evidence—it must be that." She indicates Farquarson's clothes with the barrel of the pistol. "You're a deviant—a maniac."

"Don't make me tell the police about your stealing drugs," he cautions. "And about your negligence in your patient's death. I don't want to turn you in. I don't want to threaten you. I want to save you —I can save you too, save you from yourself. I'm the only one who can save you, sweetheart. You've got to trust me. You have to see you have no choice." He wants to take her in his arms, kiss her forehead, stroke her hair, wants her to put her arm around his back.

"You put me in this mess in the first place," she says, her trembling hand in contradiction to that steady coldness in her voice. "Someone has to stop you."

"Yes, stop me," he repeats. "You can stop me."

"Stop you . . . " she repeats.

"You can kill me," he says, wanting to shout it, "that's how you can stop me . . . Come ahead! . . . You can do it! . . . Do it! . . . Let me have it!"

He cannot believe it is his fate to die before the search is ended, no matter how shameful and disastrous that end will prove to be for him; surely he is invulnerable until then. Or is he? Isn't it more in keeping with the bitterness that up to now has been his fate in life for him to be frustrated with death before the adventure can be finished, justice enforced, innocence revenged? And most absurdly of all, to be shot to death by a woman, a drugged and frightened nurse? He could believe such was his destiny. Could welcome it. How easy and sweet an ending to his frustrations and failures. Wouldn't it corroborate that vision of life as being doomed and inconsequential that has always been a basic and cancerous portion of his nature, quarreling with his more demonstrable optimism and wish for happiness? Kill me, he wants to shout, baring his chest to receive the bullets. Says instead, "I don't care if you kill me—I wish you would. It will tell me something either way. But you'll be tried for murder if you do. I don't really think you're involved in this madness, and I'm probably the only one alive who can tell the police so. And if you kill me there's an outside chance—and only an outside chance— that you'll be responsible for killing other people I might have been able to protect."

The nurse is paralyzed; the only action she sees as being open to her, if she will not trust him, is putting the pistol to her head. Stumbling with the revolver held limply in her hand she follows as he walks away from her and goes from room to room, finding telephone wires and ripping them from the walls. He is haunted not only by this woman with a pistol at his back but by a vision, if she fails to kill him, of her calling the police as soon as he is gone. "It's to protect you too," he says, giving a wire a yank. "I don't think you're in any danger, but you can't afford to let yourself get careless. If you can't face up to the danger, take another shot of morphine and lie down behind a locked door. I won't blame you. If anyone tries to break in, or you spot anyone prowling around outside, you've always got your pistol. Don't be afraid to use it."

Then he is out the door and running down the driveway toward the Duesenberg. He steps into the darkness. She hasn't shot him! His fate is settled. He is to see the adventure to the bitter end. Once more alive! Once more saved for the thankless job ahead.

As he goes from one Farquarson car to the next, letting out the air from all the tires, the nurse stands in the open doorway with the useless pistol hanging from her hand. "You son-of-a-bitch!" she shouts. It is a shout that both pleases and cuts him to the heart.

CHAPTER TWENTY-ONE

MOTIVES

Then Magnuson remembered Solomon Chandler, Farquarson's lawyer. He lived in Kenilworth, a suburb Magnuson had to pass through if on his aimless drive he headed home. Wasn't it possible that Farquarson in his last days had contacted Chandler on the same matter that he had contacted Magnuson on, giving Chandler more information than the nothing he had given him? Chandler would also have knowledge of Farquarson's will, and in the provisions of that will might lie the motive for the murder, or murders, and the identity of the murderer. But in order to learn of the will Magnuson would have to take a chance and acquaint Chandler with the fact of Farquarson's death. Despite the lateness of the hour—what hour exactly, he could not say—he was resolved to call on Chandler. It was possible that Chandler was now his only hope for further clues.

A winding, wooded residential road and a brown rustic shingle with the name of Chandler carved in it nailed to a tree. An asphalt drive that curved and turned to cobblestones not much beyond the small iron gate, and he was before the darkened house of red bricks between imitation half-timbering, and narrow gables, resembling an illustration of a castle, in miniature, out of *Ivanhoe*. No lawn here, only shrubs and trees, all evergreen. Evergreen needles lay in mats around the trees, were strewn across the cobblestones and steps, were even on the window sills; they came down with the rain that dripped from bough to bough.

He hammered the brass knocker against the door, put his fists to the panels. Finally the leaded coach lights came on beside the door, along with a dim light inside the house that revealed the crinkly window panes. For a moment he could believe that this was not Chicago and America, but Scotland or England, and the time a century in the past.

"Who is it? What do you want?" From behind the still closed door. Chandler's voice. Frightened, too.

"Arnold Magnuson—you know me. I've got to see you, Chandler. I've important news, important business—."

Then the open door and a wide-awake Chandler in bathrobe and pajamas. He was short and portly, with a round, red face, and although of an old Chicago family that had migrated from New England, he resembled a German Wisconsin dairy farmer more than he did any Brahmin of Beacon Hill. Recently he had all but retired from his law practice. In the hallway he said, "What on earth is it?" Magnuson's excitement had become his own.

"I've just come from Frazer Farquarson's house," Magnuson said. "He's dead—he died tonight."

Chandler laid his hand on Magnuson's arm, and squeezed it. He said, "It's a shock to me, Magnuson. I know it was expected, that it's the best thing for the poor fellow, since it was hopeless, and he must have been in awful pain . . . But we grew up together, went to school together." He could not look Magnuson in the face. Considering the fees he would receive as the executor of Farquarson's estate, Magnuson could not believe that he received this news as being entirely bad.

"Frazer asked me to come and see him tonight," Magnuson said. "But by the time I got there he was dead. He died only minutes before I was supposed to see him."

Chandler seemed lost in thought. "Odd, isn't it, how these things happen," he said, "but when I first saw you, before you had a chance to say anything, Frazer was the first thought that came into my head. It must have been one of those premonitions . . ." He shook his head and frowned, searching for an explanation. Magnuson observed that he was staring at his clothes—clothes, he remembered, that were Farquarson's. What was he on the verge of recognizing? The suit? the tie?

"Do you have any Bourbon?" Magnuson asked, diverting his attention.

Chandler led him into his large study, book-lined and with a sunken floor, and switched on only the fluorescent lamp on the desk top. Although the embers of a recent fire were in the fireplace, the room felt damp and cold, as though affected by that shade outdoors. The two men sat down in easy chairs some distance from the light and desk, as though at this hour they both preferred the near-dark.

When Magnuson had his glass of Bourbon, he said, "Do you have any cigars?" With a cigar in his mouth, he said, "Farquarson wanted to see me tonight not just as a friend, but as a detective. According to him, I was the only one he could trust. What he was so frightened of, I don't know."

Unknown to Magnuson, Chandler felt slighted by this news. The implication was that Farquarson had not trusted him, an old friend, his own lawyer. He was also puzzled that Farquarson would call Magnuson and not himself.

"It was a personal or family matter, you can be sure of that," continued Magnuson. "He wouldn't talk about it over the phone. Did he get in touch with you recently on any important private matters?"

Chandler shook his head. "I know in the old days he used to have some work done through you, and your agency, but lately any investigations he wanted done he did through our law firm. The fact that he went to you does make this business seem important—different, anyway."

"Can you give me an idea of what he might have had in mind," said Magnuson, "taking into consideration that he was dying?" And when Chandler continued to shake his head, he added, "Something in the provisions of his will . . . What he wanted me to look into must have had something to do with his will."

It was apparent to Chandler that Magnuson was shattered by the death of Farquarson. What else explained that look of shock, that nervousness and fatigue? The man seemed on the verge of a coronary. He assumed this was in good measure due to the frustration Magnuson felt at having death cancel a responsibility that a good friend (but were Farquarson and Magnuson all that friendly?) had wanted to impose upon him. He poured Magnuson another Bourbon, reached over and relit his dead cigar. He said kindly, "It's too late for that to matter now. You haven't made the investigation—you don't even know who or what he wanted you to investigate—and Frazer is not around to act on your report in any case. There is a will, of course, but as far as I know right now there is nothing to alter its provisions, or to invalidate it."

Magnuson sensed in this a reticence to reveal Farquarson's affairs; he determined to be forceful with the man. "As you can see, Chandler," he said, showing him his shaking hand, "I'm very upset. This was a personal request—a dying request—a last request—from a man I was fond of, and I'm not about to neglect him just because he's dead. Besides, I have a suspicion that he made a new will—or tried to make it, anyway. His nurse claims a maid went to see him in the middle of the night last night and wrote something down for him. What, exactly, she didn't know. It was all very secret."

To Chandler a new will was not good news. His reputation would be severely damaged in the business community if Farquarson had made a second will with someone other than himself (a maid, no less), although since he was retired, with his best days behind him, he could tolerate such damage. And although he was himself a wealthy man, it would be more than just disappointing if someone other than himself had been appointed in any new will as the executor of Farquarson's estate. The fees from the estate would constitute a fortune. He had counted on those monies for years; so had his partners in the firm. And since it had first become known that Farquarson was fatally ill, he had set in motion plans to set up trust funds for his grandchildren, and scholarships for underprivileged students at his alma mater, Princeton, in the name of a son killed in World War Two. He said, "A new will? I don't believe it." But added quickly, "But if he did do such a thing, you can be sure it was for some goddamn idiotic reason he took with him to the grave. I know enough of Frazer and life and death and wills and old men and inheritances and disinheritances to safely assume that much. Frazer was a damned good friend, but he was an eccentric the like of which will not soon pass our way again." Then a new thought came to him: "This maid who saw him in the night? Was there anyone in the room with her when she saw him?"

"The nurse said she went alone."

Here Chandler, much relieved, made a mistake. He said aloud:

"There you are. There could have been no witness to any new will— if in fact a new will had been made."

Magnuson, having failed to foresee this implication, now rose to the occasion. "But the maid and a strange man and woman saw him privately this morning. They were in there with him for some time. The nurse wasn't even allowed in the room." He let Chandler frown over this for a while, then said, "I'd like to know whatever you can tell me. I have my reasons."

"I hope you will acquaint me with them," said Chandler quickly.

"Trust me," said Magnuson.

Chandler took this as an indication that a bargain of sorts had been struck, so he said, "You asked about Frazer's will. It was made some time ago and hasn't been changed basically since. The estate was to be split up among a number of beneficiaries, both individuals and institutions."

"Who was the largest beneficiary?"

"A Mrs. Albert Wenzel. She lives in Wauconda." He stared at Magnuson as though to ascertain how much he knew.

Magnuson had to force himself to close his mouth. The importance of this news was incalculable! The link then was not between Farquarson and Al Wenzel after all, but between Farquarson and Bonny Wenzel! And what a powerful link it was, too. But what was the nature of that link? And why was Farquarson's letter sent not to her but to her husband? "Is she a relative?" He could barely talk.

"No, no relative," still staring at Magnuson.

"Is a Mr. Wenzel mentioned in the will?"

"No. Is there a Mr. Wenzel?"

"I don't know," Magnuson said. Then remembering that Bonny Wenzel was already dead, he said, "Who was to get her portion of the estate if she died before Farquarson?"

"It was to be divided among the other heirs. The children of a cousin were to receive the largest share."

"Who was to get the house?"

"Cavan. Although the income he'll realize from the rest of his inheritance won't let him keep it."

Magnuson was again surprised. "Wouldn't Cavan expect the bulk of the estate to come to him? He was Frazer's closest living relative."

"But he wasn't. Three second cousins were. I'd have to see the will to give you their names. Cavan was no blood relation to Frazer."

"He was no relation," Magnuson repeated, convinced that at

last he was onto information that would go far to solve the mystery.

"Unfortunately after the will is read it may have to come out in the open in court. Frazer had a flock of distant relatives and by the law of averages alone there ought to be a greedy one among them." Having said this much, Chandler decided to say more.

"About thirty years ago Frazer had his wife put in a private sanitarium. Notice, I say 'put' deliberately. He set it up so that she would be taken care of even if she survived him—which she has. She's still alive, still in a sanitarium. Oh, she was discharged a few times, especially in the early years. She stayed with her own relatives, or with a hired woman, but she always went back. Her name is Hope. I used to know her—Hope—knew her well." He paused, unwilling to go on. As Farquarson's lawyer he had taken part in the legal arrangements necessary for her committal, and for a reason he either could not or would not make himself articulate, he was unhappy with that role. He knew only that when she came to mind he felt something close to shame and guilt. Thirty years and she had yet to be cured or permanently released. He had been a reasonably young man, she a young woman. Her life had been wasted, and he suspected he might be in part responsible for that waste.

"Several years after Hope was committed," he continued, "she had a child. Conceived and born in the sanitarium. This was John Cavan. Apparently she fell in love with another patient. Romance in the asylum. These places are never properly staffed, and a good deal must go on inside them that just cannot be stopped. However, there was some evidence that members of the staff had allowed this affair to continue. Frazer claimed this was because they were sadists or voyeurs or bribe-takers or whatever, but I shouldn't wonder if it weren't done out of indifference, or even compassion. In the stink that followed, some people were fired. Cavan's father I know absolutely nothing about, although I always suspected Frazer knew quite a bit about him. I always assumed he was from a wealthy family. It was an expensive sanitarium. A pathetic story."

In Magnuson memories that connected him in ways he could not yet understand were surfacing. Years ago he had been hired by Farquarson to investigate his wife—he was sure of it. That would have been before she went to the sanitarium. A copy of his report along with the notes he would have used to write it from should be in the personal files he still kept in his office.—And hadn't Farquarson also hired him to investigate a man in a sanitarium? That must have been several years after his investigation of Farquarson's wife. The man must have been Cavan's father. He was certain to have a record of that, too.

"Frazer took the pregnancy surprisingly well," Chandler said. "In a strange way he even seemed relieved. Of course he was upset with the sanitarium and had her transferred elsewhere."

"And what happened to her baby?" Magnuson asked.

"Frazer took him. I advised against it, although my own feelings went against my own advice. Originally he gave the boy to his sister and her husband, who were childless. The husband's name was Cavan. He was killed in a plane crash in Holland. Frazer's sister died a month later in a car crash up in Scotland. Frazer took advantage of these tragedies and passed Cavan off as his sister's son. Frazer never saw much of the boy. He shuffled him back and forth among distant relatives, boarding schools, and foster parents. His upbringing must have been pretty unstable. Occasionally he visited Farquarson between school terms but it was only in the past year or so that Frazer took him permanently into his house. I must say if Frazer didn't exactly love the boy or want him around him, he eventually did reasonably well by him. A good many people had their suspicions of John's origins. But Frazer wisely kept him out of his own society. To this day I doubt John knows who his parents really are. I always advised Frazer to tell the boy the truth—not the absolute truth, mind you. As a matter of fact I advised him to do so . . . the last time I saw him. The will lets the secret out in any case."

"Did Cavan, or any of the heirs, know of the contents of Frazer's will?" Magnuson asked.

"I doubt it," Chandler said. "I can't see Frazer doing that myself. Although in his last days who can say how his mind was affected, and what he might have said, and to whom? After Frazer had Hope transferred to a second sanitarium she became pregnant a second time. As in the first case there wasn't any question of abortion since it wasn't discovered that she was pregnant until she was much too far along. This time Frazer was furious, but he couldn't very well blame the previous patient who fathered Cavan, because he wasn't there. The baby—it was a girl—confirmed that the poor fellow wasn't responsible anyway. The father was a Negro. There were no Negro patients at this sanitarium but there were male Negro orderlies and the assumption was that one of them either raped her or else took unfair advantage of her. Even today I find it depressing to think a man could take advantage of a sick woman he was supposed to help. Still, nothing human surprises me. And maybe the orderly was in his own way as sick as his patient. They never discovered which one was the father but I believe all male Negro employees were fired. Frazer, of course, sent Hope off to a third sanitarium. Frazer would have nothing to do with his second child. He got angry with you even when he asked you for your advice. She was sent to a state institution and presumably placed up for adoption, although I suspect adoption wasn't likely, since mulattoes, as I understand it, aren't much in demand. What has happened to the girl since then, I don't know. Frazer never mentioned her, and he made no provision for her in his will.—But come to think of it, Magnuson, that explains something." He jumped up and poured himself a drink from the bottle he had taken out for Magnuson. "About a year ago—around the time Frazer first became ill—he contacted me about having a young woman investigated. He wanted a résumé of her whole life, where she had been, what she had done, where she was now. I referred it to one of our younger lawyers. He told me once in passing that the investigator he had worked through had been able to trace her through foster homes, reformatories, what have you. Finally she was located somewhere in Texas. She was working in a bar—a twenty-six girl, or prostitute—something like that. The investigator described her as a light-skinned Negro in her early twenties. It must be the same girl."

This remembrance and discovery made Chandler all the more depressed. He was overcome with distant and distorted images of Farquarson's wedding: the summer garden party and a great green and yellow striped canopy set up upon the lawn; silver service in the hands of maids and dispensed from silver carts and trays; vases stuffed with white and yellow daisies; the young couple arm in arm, face to face, the bride handsome but pale, looking like a cloistered medieval maiden in a white gown of lace on lace, her corsage of orange blossoms and baby's breath held in her hands between her breasts as though it belonged there, would always be there, as though she were herself her own portrait in a painting. Something magical—Arthurian even—about the idyll of that day. But what a source of misery that moment had proved to be! The poor brown baby girl born in a madhouse. And how was it that Cavan should receive the best and his sister the worst of life? Something more than fate explained it. As if the girl could be held responsible for her father's color and his lust, or for her mother's madness. What did a child care if it was conceived in love or lust or boredom, legitimately or illegitimately, by sane progenitors or mad? It lived—it lived as itself!

"How did Frazer react when you gave him the report?" Magnuson said.

"I've no idea. We gave him the information we had and asked him if he wanted us to follow it up. But I never heard any more about it."

Surely, Chandler told himself, on the very night of the death of an old friend there were pleasant memories one could, indeed should, recall. He wanted to be alone in the darkness and among the leather of his study with his own remembrances and thoughts. But his memories, even before he had learned of Farquarson's death, had been unhappy memories of Farquarson and of this very unsettling business he was recounting to this man. Only today he had received in the mail a lengthy and anonymous document that had accused him of malpractice in his profession as lawyer, and alluded to his culpability in the commission of one or more unspecified crimes. From the style and tone and presentation of certain knowledge he suspected the author must be Farquarson. But because of Farquarson's illness he decided he could not approach him and ask him the meaning of so libelous a piece of paper. He wanted to dismiss it out of hand. But it troubled him and wounded him and made him thoughtful nonetheless.

He said to Magnuson: "I don't see why Frazer would have contacted you to investigate Hope's girl. Since our firm had already had her traced it would have been easier and faster to follow up that information with us. In fact, if it was a secret there was every reason to contact us, and only us, especially if he did wish to make her a beneficiary in his will. The matter he wished to take up with you must have been something other than this unfortunate girl, something we weren't acquainted with or equipped to handle.

"One thought puzzles me, though. Why did you come so soon after the death and at such an hour of night to see me? You knew I was Frazer's lawyer, but was there another reason?"

Magnuson grew tense. He had not expected so direct a question. The dangerous moments of the conversation were beginning, and he would have to be on his guard if he were not to be discovered.

"The nurse who was with him at the end," he said at last, "thought his last words were directed to me."

Chandler could not believe that deep friendship alone accounted for Farquarson's choice of Magnuson to hear his final words. As far as he knew from what Farquarson had said over the years, Magnuson was at most a remote business acquaintance, and in that capacity only, a friend. But something intangible about Magnuson reminded him of Farquarson. "What were his last words?" he asked.

"She thought he said, 'Tell Magnuson to look up Chandler.' "

There followed an embarrassing but electric silence. For the first time Chandler considered that his suspicion of a new will in which he was no longer named as the executor of the estate might not be so far-fetched after all.

"But goddamn it all," he boomed, "it's . . . theater! Last words . . . mysterious last words . . . Good Christ!"

To Magnuson this was a much stronger response than he had anticipated. "She was positive he said Magnuson," he said. "She was less certain she heard him say your name."

Chandler, however, chose to believe the worst. "Did he leave you a note of any kind?" he said.

"Nothing." Magnuson would have said more, but fortunately he was interrupted.

"What about his papers? If there are strange goings on in his household, or a second will somewhere, I ought to go over there immediately and seal his papers."

Magnuson, alarmed, resisted the urge to seize him around the chest and pin him to his chair. As calmly as he could he said, "There aren't any papers around the place. I looked. They're all in the safe."

"But he kept his important papers in a locked box in his desk," Chandler said. "He kept his stamp collection in the safe."

"This morning he had the box removed from the desk and, along with some papers he had in his bedroom, placed inside the safe."

"He must have been afraid of someone in the house," Chandler said. "Or someone who had access to the house." He restrained himself from adding, or someone who would have access to his papers. He closed his eyes and clasped his hands as though in prayer, his fingertips touching his nose. "For the sake of hypothesis," he said, "let's grant that Frazer did make a new will last night or even this morning. Then he calls you, Magnuson, and plans to ask you to investigate something important, something secret. A new will means a new heir, or heirs, or at least a new distribution of the estate. Since by making a new will he has already made up his mind to discard the original will, he must have wanted you to investigate something to do with the new will. The question is, what? A new heir or heirs obviously. Was he persuaded by these new heirs to change his original will while his judgment was unsound, and then in a moment of clearheadedness does he have his doubts about them and want them investigated?—You see, I don't know. You said in the beginning, Magnuson, that you had your reasons for wanting what information

I could give you. It seems to me the time has come for you to tell me what those reasons are."

Magnuson observed that Chandler, who was capable of bullying him, showed no inclination to disbelieve him. "I suspected," he said, "that Frazer's death might have been unnatural." He felt as though the barrel of a rifle were in his mouth. He could feel the vibrations of the shivers of Chandler, and shivered himself. It was as cold and collective a response as if both men were sitting in the same wintry draft.

"But you don't suspect that now?" Chandler said, leaning over the table so far that he appeared about to scramble across the top of it to Magnuson.

"Less than I did before."

"Had you any evidence?"

Careful, Magnuson. He wanted to justify his coming at this hour to interrogate Chandler, and his receipt of the information Chandler had given him. But he did not want to arouse his suspicions to such a degree that Chandler investigated this business on his own. At all costs he had to keep him from the house. "No evidence," he said. "Only a feeling. The urgency of his call to me. His fear of someone in the house. The visit of the maid in the middle of the night. The visit this morning of the maid and her two friends. His locking up his private papers. His last words on his deathbed. The fact that he was dead before he had the chance to tell me what he wanted to. It was all circumstantial. I can see that now. It was foolish of me."

To Magnuson's surprise, Chandler said, "I'm not so sure. That list is impressive. And I trust your judgment, Magnuson. If you suspected something amiss, perhaps there was." Magnuson had seriously miscalculated. He had expected a smile, a pat on the knee, to be told his suspicions were absurd.

"You didn't call the police?" Chandler said.

"Not on the strength of what I've just told you."

"And the doctor—"

"He's been there. He signed the death certificate—in my presence."

"That means nothing," Chandler said. "Frazer had been incurably ill for over a year and was expected to die any day. Unless he was lying there with his throat cut, any doctor—and his own doctor especially—and especially that goddamn fool son of Ev Archer—would assume he died of that illness. He didn't give the body a thorough examination, did he?"

Magnuson could not deny this and not arouse Chandler's suspicions. "He checked the vital signs. He may have made other superficial examinations—"

"Precisely," Chandler said. His tone and manner were those of an attorney in a courtroom. "You mentioned a visit this morning by the maid and two other people. This the same maid who saw him in the night?"

"Yes. The only thing I know about her so far is that she's a Negro."

"A Negro?" Chandler said.

"She's gone to St. Louis to visit relatives," Magnuson said. "No one knows the address in St. Louis. She isn't expected back for several days."

"Now that is very strange," Chandler said.

Magnuson had to look over his shoulder at Chandler, who had stood up and walked behind him.

"And these two people who accompanied her on the second visit?" Chandler said. "Who were they?"

"A man and a woman. They were also Negroes. I don't know their names yet. No one in the house had seen them before. The nurse thought the man was a preacher and the woman was his wife."

"Not a lawyer?"

"She said a preacher."

Chandler dropped into the chair next to Magnuson and slapped his thighs with his palms. The mystery of this affair, once unraveled, would resolve itself not in high tragedy but comic opera. Legally a man should be considered dead when his mind was dead. He had a vision of Farquarson, in his final moments, turning to the solace of some primitive, mystical, faith-healing, holy-rolling religion that promised him, by his faith alone, salvation from a brutal Hell. You could never be certain when the hellfire of crazed Presbyterians was in the blood, and you could never be certain with Frazer Farquarson in particular. In conjunction with this conversion he had a vision of a colored storefront church in the middle of the South Side Chicago slums, its name advertised on a neon sign or even painted or soaped on the dirty plate-glass window, and endowed with the Farquarson millions, a black preacher decked out in diamond jewelry and an ankle-length chinchilla coat, accompanied by a fleet of Cadillacs and a harem of black and white women attired in angelic robes.

Then a bizarre possibility revealed itself to Chandler. Could there be a link between the Negro maid and her two black companions and the mulatto daughter of Frazer's wife that Frazer had recently investigated? Magnuson, he observed, was frowning, and he guessed that he was entertaining the same thought. Unbelievable was the word whispered on his own lips.

But as Chandler exhausted himself on the weight of the night's news, Magnuson, despite the bloody landscapes he had witnessed, recovered if only momentarily his spirit and energies. "The maid and her friends may have tricked Frazer into making a new will," he said. "Later he may have thought better of it and wanted them investigated. That would explain why it would be in their interest to kill him before he had the chance to talk to me. Other than that I can't see who could have had a motive for killing a man who was as good as dead."

"I wonder," Chandler said, shaking his head. "Maybe we're making it too complicated. If he was murdered, and if he had not made a new will but planned to, and the visit of the maid and her friends was then harmless, the motive would lie with an heir in the original will, someone Frazer wanted investigated with the idea of disinheriting. If you want a guess—and only that—of who this heir might be, I would have to say Mrs. Wenzel, the largest beneficiary of the will by far. This business with her was probably the most secret and delicate of all Frazer's affairs. I will say no more since Frazer never really confided in me on this matter." He shut his eyes and slumped back in the chair. Any further advice he gave would be given only from a sense of duty, like a doctor who has left his own sickbed to make a wintry midnight call.

Magnuson sensed his stupefaction, and, determining he had obtained as much information as he safely could, now resolved to calm those suspicions he had himself aroused, and to get himself out of the house. He was alarmed at how much time he had allowed to pass here. "Until you have a chance to examine Frazer's papers," he said, rising, "I think it's best to put your mind at ease about this business."

"Magnuson, Magnuson," Chandler said, laying his hand on Magnuson's forearm and guiding him back down into the chair. "We can't just drop the thing like this. The combination to Farquarson's safe and the key to his strongbox are in a safety deposit box in the bank. And I won't be able to get to the bank before Monday. Now you had an original enthusiasm to look into Frazer's death, and I believe that enthusiasm was morally sound. After all, you did know the man. He wasn't a stranger. He did want to charge you with some responsibility. Why couldn't you continue to investigate the circumstances of Frazer's death? As you say, there may be nothing in it. But we should know one way or the other. Find out what you can about the maid and her friends. Check up on the members of Frazer's household and family. You already have information and an access to the house that another investigator wouldn't have. You were willing to accept a responsibility from Frazer. Well, accept a responsibility from me—in Frazer's name, so to speak. Who knows, in the end it may turn out to be the same favor he would have asked of you had he lived. Let our law firm be your client."

The offer surprised Magnuson. For his own purposes it was perfect. It satisfied a moral and professional need. But was his hiring also perfect for Chandler's purposes? What had he revealed to him that had made him alternately excited and depressed and finally frightened? Hadn't Chandler been pumping him for information just as he had been pumping Chandler? "Put that way I can't very well refuse," he said.

"Good," Chandler said, patting his arm. "Now, what should we do first? Get hold of Farquarson's doctor and find out what we can about the cause of death?"

"Don't you do anything," Magnuson said quickly, certain he had the upper hand. "I want you to stay out of this. How do we know the doctor and the nurse aren't involved in this business? Don't do anything until you hear from me."

Promising to be in touch with him and to see him at Farquarson's funeral if not before, he dashes out of the miniature castle into the miniature forest and onto the carpet of cones and needles. He must brush the needles from the windshield of the Duesenberg. He glances back through those crinkled gold-tinted windows at Chandler leaning on the desk in his study like a crippled man who needs it for support. It had been too easy to fool Chandler! He is convinced of the man's guilt, but for what, exactly, he cannot say. Is he somehow involved in the murder of Farquarson, the secret power behind the crimes? Or is he only involved in a crime against Farquarson, like the robbing of the estate, that the death of Farquarson threatens to expose?

Magnuson can almost wish for daylight. At last he has a client, a list of motives, any number of leads.

CHAPTER TWENTY-TWO

THE DEATH OF SCARPONI

In Chicago there was half an hour of heavy rain. Underpasses flooded, water roared black and white along the gutters, and the streets and buildings gleamed as though shellacked. Throughout the city the name of Scarponi spelled itself repetitiously on the neon signs that hung before Scarponi's liquor stores, reflecting in fuzzy, elongated, and glaring green, red, and white letters on the slick black pavement of the streets. Cars splashed through the colors, took and bent the letters momentarily on their trunks and hoods. Pedestrians who crossed the street stepped into an O, waded through a P, took the colors on their rubbers and the domes of their umbrellas. Like spilled gasoline, streaks of color ran in the flooded streets. Inside the Scarponi stores, which were the size of supermarkets and like great technicolor billboards set out against the night, drowsy clerks stood in the aisles between the shelves of bottles and lines of empty grocery carts with their arms folded across their chests, or they leaned upon the counters by the cash registers, pencils tucked behind their ears, staring out through the downpour that rolled down the plate-glass window at the bedraggled, floundering pedestrians and the creep and glitter of the traffic in the streets.

It was tonight that the Tanker, who was not a professional killer but only a young car thief and burglar of far less experience than he liked to claim, was to kill Scarponi. In fact he had been hired to kill him not once but twice and, although he did not know it, by two different men. On the shortest possible notice he had been ordered to follow the skeleton of a plan and to improvise the rest. He had received these orders from Romanski, who had allegedly received his from Fiore but actually from the Doctor, who had received his from his nephew Allegro, and he now in turn entrusted the first step of the plot to kill Scarponi to Ralph Borman, a boyhood friend. They had grown up together in the old North Side neighborhood of narrow, odd-sized frame houses often shingled in asphalt and in various stages of decay and expedient repairs, with no two of them on the same street the same color, looking as though they had been saved from demolition and moved to their present lots from somewhere else. It was a neighborhood that smelled of machine oil and the tannery on the river, that was traversed day and night by big trucks, where someone was always working on the engine of his car in the street and boys were interested in cars and jobs and money and left school at sixteen to apprentice to a trade. Both Tanker and Borman still lived in this neighborhood. Tanker knew that Borman needed the fifty dollars he had promised him if he would steal a late model Oldsmobile and leave it with the keys on the front seat at a designated hour in the parking lot of a restaurant in Edgebrook in the northwest section of the city. Friendship alone determined his selection of an accomplice. If Tanker had a favor to give, he gave it naturally to a friend. That Borman, in his opinion, was weak, unlucky, and incompetent only gave him, the stronger and more competent if not exactly always the luckier of the two, all the more reason for helping him. He felt responsible for his old friend.

At present Borman was under indictment for armed robbery but was out on the bail Tanker had arranged through Romanski. He had held up a cab driver who, as his luck would have it, was a moonlighting cop. Upon hearing the childlike and apologetic voice at his back demanding his money and observing that the pistol pointed at him was made of plastic with a seam running down the center of the plugged-up barrel and the color of the plastic a kind of mauve, the policeman had taken his time in removing a thick piece of hose from the glove compartment ("I always carry an extra piece of hose with me," he was later to tell the press, "because you never know when the hose to your radiator might spring a leak"), had taken his time in locking both rear doors, and taken his time in clubbing Borman unconscious in his seat. Tanker had first heard of it on the news on his car radio and had shouted out loud in surprise at the mention of his old friend's name. It was typical of Borman's destiny that the announcer treated robbery and robber with amusement, as did the newspapers in the morning. It was the light side of the news. Tanker had been puzzled by Borman's resort to robbery. He thought he held a steady job as a bartender in an old-fashioned tavern in the old neighborhood. Located on a residential street corner that even the local residents rarely passed, it had large unwashed windows, steps you had to walk up to enter, and a musky air that smelled like beer thrown on the embers of a wood fire. Borman had stood behind the bar in a white apron and soiled white shirt, with his pale, fat, frightened face and his blond hair slicked down along his sideburns, looking as though he were afraid of being robbed, fired, or ordered to make a drink he had not heard of before. Even his numerous tattoos did not suggest military service, manliness, or evil so much as his having been held down forcibly by sadistic friends and mutilated.

Unlike Tanker, Borman was married and the father of two frightened, sickly children, the older of whom he had fathered at the age of sixteen. Tanker believed the children's unhealthiness was the result of Philomena, Borman's wife, keeping the heat in their basement apartment at 90 degrees. In the worst of winter Borman would sit bare-chested in the living room while Philomena, in short summer shorts, ironed clothes. Philomena looked at most seventeen, was built like a sparrow, and wore horn-rimmed glasses too large for her small pointed nose. A kleptomaniac, she made her obsession her profession and supplied the family with many of its needs, especially the children's clothes. She could be induced to steal on assignment for a friend, for which she asked no payment, and Tanker had acquired from her an electric razor and a transistor radio. She had a habit of undressing behind open doors, just out of sight of visitors, peeking out at them through the crack as she threw her clothes out onto the floor. This offended Tanker greatly, and he could explain it only by the fact that she was crazy. When Borman enlisted in the air force, mainly he confessed to Tanker because he wanted to get away from Philomena, and went to Florida for his basic training, Philomena became so lonely in Chicago that with the help of her sister, Pearl, she stole a convertible and with her two children drove to Florida and picked up a reluctant Borman from his base. They spent several weeks touring both coasts of Florida, living off the fruits of the land and Philomena's kleptomania, Borman because he had no other clothes always in his air force uniform, and always frustrated in his attempts to seduce his sister-in-law. When they were finally captured, the AWOL Borman was given a dishonorable discharge and Pearl was sent to prison for the theft of the car, while Philomena because of her size and sickly children was never considered to be anything more than an innocent passenger. Recently Pearl had been released from prison and on her first night home Tanker and Borman had taken her in Tanker's Cadillac for a ride around the city, Borman having earlier confided to Tanker that after being in prison so long without getting any she would really want it now. They parked in Grant Park where by turns, or together, since one was on either side of her in the front seat, they attempted to remove her clothes. She neither resisted nor helped and at last explained her indifference by confessing she had become a Lesbian in prison, which did not surprise either of the men since she was wearing a short-sleeve man's shirt rolled up to her armpits and had somehow developed biceps the size of a weight lifter's and acquired on a triceps a small tattoo of a cross or dagger. She seemed unhappy about her transformation, and the two men commiserated with her and offered to try to put her right. Dubious, she agreed, and with that same indifference she had greeted the petting in the front seat she now greeted the therapy she received by turns in the back. No one, however, felt very bad about the failure. The two men had laid her less from a desire for sex than as a show of camaraderie, not between themselves and the sister-in-law but only between themselves, and not for the immediate thrill either—which both would have admitted was very little—but so they could acquire a mutual experience worth recollecting. It was to be enjoyed in the future as a recollection of the past.

So it was not surprising that Tanker, when he drove up on time to the parking lot of the restaurant, did not find among the many cars the Oldsmobile he had commissioned Borman to steal. It occurred to him that Borman had probably never stolen a car before and that his first attempt had likely met the same fate as his first armed robbery. Still, he might not have been able to get the Oldsmobile and had stolen another make instead. He walked around the lot, checking all the cars, but found no car that was unlocked with the keys on the front seat.

The restaurant was called the Pie Prince and was in a neighborhood more suburban than city and probably the wealthiest section of the city proper. Whereas the new homes in the developments to the west were identical, or nearly so, and built one next to the other out on the prairies, with few if any trees upon the block, the new homes built here were more expensive, reflected a variety of styles from ranch to something faintly English and Germanic, and were often on large wooded lots on the borders of forest preserves. For some reason the lower middle class built on prairie and the upper middle class in woods. Here, amidst the country darkness the long lighted windows of the restaurant that faced the road and the floodlights in the shade trees of the miniature golf course next door with its windmills and miniature castles and handful of golfers in heavy Irish sweaters and the fluorescent lights of the modern gas station across the road where brand-new cars pulled in and out of the pumps as though at a fashionable pit stop in a glamorous race and the headlights of the cars on the roads in this neighborhood where every family had several cars gave Tanker the excited and erotic sense of visiting a futuristic but wooded town at night. Sex and money, inseparable, co-inhabiting, slicked together and tightly locked, as though money were the man and sex the woman of a fornicating pair. He felt it in the lights, the darkness, the woods, the cars, in the speed of the cars and in the people who drove them. He felt it in the high-school girls who drove up in groups in their own convertibles. Blond girls who looked German or Scandinavian or Jewish and wore loose leather jackets and tight Levi's, their lips and eyes and teeth turned purple in the downfall of the street lights. Money in their faces and a leanness and toughness to their bodies, a kind of boyish masculinity to their femininity that made them all the more desirable. They reminded him of forests, bonfires, and of fall and winter, as though he could imagine them only when the days were short, overcast, and cold. He longed to be alone with one in her wealthy wooded house and lay her in her own bedroom in her own bed, or in the den of a neighbor's house where she was baby-sitting. He imagined her as lying cool and hard beneath him, or else hot and soft on top of him, either of which, depending on his mood, aroused him.

Deciding that Borman might be late he went inside the restaurant. The booths were crowded with families, parents and teenagers alike, and the long S-shaped counter with groups of those high-school girls and boys. Everyone seemed cheerful and to know each other. The silliness and innocence of their remarks disgusted him. He felt all the patrons of the restaurant, young and old alike, hadn't lived, would never live. They were outside experience. And yet he ached for that world of sex and money he believed they had made their own private province, and was attracted to that very falseness of their lives he claimed to see through and despise, for he also saw that falseness as success and glamour. The specialty of the restaurant was pies, some thirty varieties of which were baked on the premises. He ordered a cheeseburger and a piece of apple pie, liked both of them along with the coffee, and left the thirty-year-old waitress, whose shiny robin's egg blue uniform he thought he could see through, a dollar tip. He did not like to eat in restaurants or drink in bars alone.

Outside, he made another check of the parking lot. Still no Oldsmobile. He checked his watch. He was already forty-five minutes late. He called Borman from a telephone booth outside the restaurant and talked with Philomena, who informed him in her scatterbrained and seductive fashion that Borman was out, she didn't know where, didn't know when he'd be back. He did not believe her. He could see Borman bare-chested in that superheated living room before the television, drinking a can of beer. Now he was angry. Borman had not only let him down and possibly gotten him in trouble but had failed to use the favor he had given him. He was willing to concede, however, that Borman might have thought he could be lackadaisical about the job, especially if he had trouble finding an Oldsmobile he could easily and safely steal, since Tanker had not informed him of the serious purpose for which he planned to use the car.

Tanker drove his Cadillac several miles south of the restaurant and parked it among other cars along the street. He waited for half an hour at a bus stop beside a stretch of woods he finally discerned were the grounds of the city tuberculosis sanitarium. Once he suffered the indignity of having a car full of boys slow down beside him and shout, "Get a car!" He was the lone passenger on the bus, a large, brightly lit coach that lurched and swayed as the humming driver raced it recklessly through the night. At the restaurant again he was further delayed by the presence of cars packed with boys in athletic or leather jackets cruising slowly up and down the street, faces at the windows; groups of these boys were also in the restaurant, looking out the window. They were nervous, sullen, posturing. Of all the luck. Apparently the word had gone out that the Pie Prince was to be the site of a gang fight tonight. As soon as he could he stole the first unlocked car he found with the keys left in the ignition. He turned down a side street, pulled off the road onto a small trail that went into the woods between two remote ranch houses, the picture windows of which he could see between the trees, and replaced the car's plates with those from a junked car, the registration for which he still possessed, having carried them on the bus tucked uncomfortably beneath his shirt.

He headed for a nightclub and restaurant on Harlem Avenue called Angelo's, which was across the street from the Chicago line and was conspicuous for the blood-red neon sign of a lobster that hung in front of it. Scarponi, he had been told, would be there tonight, probably, he suspected, because someone involved in the killing had lured him there. He was to abduct Scarponi when he came out to his car in the parking lot and take him elsewhere for the killing; under no circumstances was he to do the job at Angelo's. He had two alternative sites chosen for the killing, the Forest Preserves and a railroad yard.

He drove as fast as he could within the speed limits, but because of the delay Borman had caused he did not think that Scarponi would still be there.

He felt neither frightened nor excited about what he was to do, nor did he think about the danger he might be placed in during the commission of the act, nor about the consequences which might come his way, if he were successful, from any of several quarters. He did feel secure and powerful in that trust and protection given to him by powerful friends. Other than that he was impatient and slightly numb. He had always anticipated a life of adventure and a youthful death as the consequence of the adversity of that adventure, and he took a sentimental pleasure in the anticipation of his end. He had no expectations, and no vision of himself as a man of twenty-five, much less of fifty; it was as if in his own mind at those ages he did not exist. It was not so much that he lived for the moment—although he did—as that he believed, at his young age, that he had seen everything of life, and that he was world-weary with those sights. He thought of life—real life—as beatings, rapes, whores, queers, bribes, pull downtown, robberies, and total drunkenness, all of which he was in one way or another familiar with and in some cases familiar with in several ways, and which most people, he believed, and especially those false and deluded people back in the restaurant, were to be denied. Small wonder that when he and Borman or any of their other friends from the old neighborhood got together over a case of quarts of beer, they only talked about what they had done in the past; "the old days," they called it. Life was already behind them.

Tanker did want to make a lot of money, and he wanted to make it soon. But he would not have used this money to leave his old environment but only to raise himself within it, for the most part by spending it quickly and lavishly and on those tastes and pleasures that were already his. If he could have spent ten thousand dollars in one of his favorite taverns on his old friends in a single day he would have gladly died on the next. He believed that you drank only to drink as much as you possibly could, that you screwed only to see how many times you could screw in one night, and so that you could talk about it afterwards, and that money was to spend and give away as fast as you could. In his own special way he knew he was as much a loser as his old friend Borman.

When he reached Angelo's, Scarponi's car was no longer in the parking lot. The restaurant portion of the nightclub had already closed, and groups of happy black cooks and dishwashers and sullen white waitresses were coming out to their cars. For several minutes he smoked and debated entering the bar to learn if by chance Scarponi was still there and, if not, if he could receive new instructions from someone who was, the man who had invited Scarponi here. He thought this would be unwise. He had no wish to know too much, or even to appear to wish to know more. He also did not wish to admit his bungling so quickly. He had a vague premonition that if it were known that Scarponi had gotten into his car unmolested and driven away, he would be in trouble. There was nothing left for him to do but drive to Scarponi's house in River Forest and see if Scarponi's car was there.

But before he could turn back onto Harlem Avenue, and even after he did manage to turn onto it, he was held up by the traffic of a drive-in movie theater that was letting out down the road, discharging what seemed to be miles of alternately stationary and crawling headlights, policemen in the middle of the road shaking flashlights beside their thighs and shouting at the passing cars. From the grounds of the theater came the noise of hundreds of cars revving their engines and honking their horns. The gigantic movie screen with its gray admonition seemingly projected on the night: Please Drive Carefully. Tanker seemed to be caught bumper to bumper for half an hour and for the first time he panicked, shouting out his window at the cars ahead of him and at the policemen with the lights, who he thought were treating his lane unfairly, and at those cars honking behind him, "You dopes! You big dummies!" while he himself leaned on his horn.

The neighborhood of River Forest where Scarponi lived was entirely residential, new red or yellow brick ranch houses landscaped with a few shrubs and fair-sized lawns. When Tanker reached it the streets were empty and the houses dark. In the picture windows he could catch the faint flicker of gray light coming from the unseen television, the only light in the house. But a loud party was in progress at Scarponi's ranch house. Every light was on, including those in the basement, and outside at the front door and in the garage. The driveway was crowded with cars, as was the street in front of the house. This confused Tanker since he had been told that Scarponi himself would be out. Actually it was a party given in the knotty pine basement by Scarponi's daughter, who had just come home from college. It was attended by her local friends, most of whom had gone to high school with her and now attended college themselves, and by their friends, and as the evening wore on, by the friends of their friends. The ebullient and drunken conversations of a hundred youthful voices came from the house, as did the music of a collegiate Dixieland band, and from the open cellar windows, seen in the escaping light, so much cigarette smoke it appeared the house was burning. This party sealed Scarponi's doom. Had the driveway been empty he would have driven directly into the garage and sent Tanker, who could not find his car on the street or in the driveway and had concluded it was already parked in the garage, in frustration home. As it was, Scarponi, who now came home, having stayed out tonight much later than he had intended because of his daughter's party, had to park on the street at the end of a long row of cars, and at some distance from the house. He no sooner locked his door than Tanker, who been smoking and slouching down in the car ahead of him and looking up into the rear-view mirror, leaped out of his car and confronted him with a pistol.

Scarponi sensed that he was not immediately to be shot down. He raised his hands and obeying the nod of Tanker's head got into Tanker's car, in the front seat beside the driver as he was bidden.

He knew he would either overcome this danger or he would not. He knew that if his affairs were as bad as in his worst moments he saw them, he was doomed, and therefore that the power of good fortune was limited whereas the power of time was not. When his luck ran out time would reassert itself and that foreordained direction would once more propel him toward his destruction. Had this assassin who confronted him now failed tonight he would have succeeded on the next, and if not him, then someone else.

Flight or even self-defense was to him as alien an alternative to his destruction as was suicide. He could even believe from Tanker's appearance and actions that all this had not been initiated from that source he feared, but was instead the coincidental work of a reckless and amateur lone wolf intent on shaking down or kidnapping the wealthy owner of a string of liquor stores. In fact he came to this conclusion, and even managed to relax. He would talk smoothly to the fellow and work something out as soon as he too got into the car.

Tanker, however, had no sooner put Scarponi in the car than it occurred to him in a moment of panic that he could not very well drive the car with his victim conscious, untethered, and seated beside him, nor could he reseat him in the back seat where he would then ride behind him, nor could he make him drive; and it occurred to him that even now Scarponi could slide across the seat and drive off since not only were the keys in the ignition but the motor was running, and that if he walked in front of the car to get to the driver's side Scarponi might drive over him, and if he walked around the back of the car Scarponi might back over him or simply drive away. So Tanker fired through the open window two shots in the area of Scarponi's chest, killing him if not instantly then very soon thereafter. It would be impossible to determine how many and what fears, injuries, and confusions were momentarily satisfied by the firing of those fatal shots. He experienced the same high pitch of satisfaction and exhilaration he would have felt had he been victorious in a street fight. He had performed a manly job, entrusted to him by manly men. He would have felt much the same had he been a bridge builder, dynamite handler, war hero, sandhog. He regretted only that his action necessarily had to be unwitnessed; as he fired the shots he would have liked to learn how he looked. Not that he liked doing what he did; but that was the way the world worked, and he was one of those privileged few who could admit it and act upon it, and who had the experience in life to know that it was so. Only after the shots were fired did he recollect that his original plan had not called for Scarponi to be put in the front seat but in the trunk, from which he was not to be released until they had reached that isolated spot where he was to die. He had fouled up incredibly!

That he could now stand frozen in the street for several minutes with the gun still in his hand, watching and listening for any sign that someone had heard the shots, should have been an indication to him that even worse errors were to come. But no window opened, no one came outdoors, no light went on in any darkened house; the party continued as before. Later someone came up from the cellar to urinate in the dark back yard; a boy and girl from the house walked down the street in the opposite direction from Tanker and got into a car the engine of which did not start up; a group came out onto the porch above the basement stairs, and a boy perched himself on the railing only to topple backward on the lawn where he was immediately surrounded and helped to his feet by his friends. Finally Tanker got in beside the corpse, propped him up in the seat to make him look asleep or drunk, and peeled away so swiftly that the corpse's head banged back against the seat, rebounded against the dashboard with eyes and mouth open as though it felt the pain, then slumped beneath the dash and crumpled up against the firewall. He had to stop, drag out the corpse, and rearrange it on the seat. Thereafter he drove more carefully.

He decided to take the body to the old neighborhood and throw it in the river from the safety of a dark alleyway behind a factory that ran no night shifts. As much as he could he kept his eyes off his passenger, although he had to see to him whenever he failed to make a green or yellow light and had to stop for a red. He tried to make all the lights. He was recalling the time a few years ago when he and his friends drank beer in a funeral home in the old neighborhood where Perdido, another old friend apprenticed as an undertaker, performed the embalming, among other things, and served as caretaker, sleeping in at night. They would drink in the embalming room in the basement sometimes as Perdido worked, and as the night wore on would range upstairs into the viewing rooms and chapel. They sat and even slept in the coffins, examined and poked corpses, which Perdido treated fearlessly and with contempt. Even Tanker thought Perdido strange, ghoulish in behavior and deathly in look, as he did all undertakers, and suspected him, again as he did all undertakers, of necrophilia. They had stolen from a storeroom in the attic dark capes and plumed cockhats that were the funeral regalia for the Knights of Columbus, and worn them with their engineer boots on their motorcycles, and in the hushed and gloomy funeral parlor where they bombasted about the heavy rugs and drapes like bad actors in a bad historical play. Once they had lifted a young and beautiful but wasted woman from her coffin in the viewing room, carried her in all her shifting softness to Borman's coupe where, unknown to Borman, who had passed out downstairs, they set her upright in the seat beside the driver.

Only when he was deep in the dreary blocks of the city, driving through the sparse night traffic, did it occur to Tanker that having shot Scarponi in front of his house he should have had the sense to have pushed him out of the car onto the street and driven away alone. But instead here he was with the strongest possible evidence against him beside him on the front seat! What was he doing, driving through the city with a corpse at his elbow, falling into it every time he made a left turn, and taking it, of all places, to his own neighborhood? He was terrified that he could be so stupid! He would turn off on the next side street, cut down the first dark alley, shut off his lights, and push Scarponi out into the street.

But before he could make his turn he became so rattled that he ran a red light and was immediately trailed by a policeman on a three-wheel motorcycle. He would have made a run for it down side streets and alleys with the headlights off, since he had done this often in the past and always successfully, the police concluding finally that he was far more reckless in eluding them than they cared to be in chasing him, except that a pair of police cars, their blue dome lights spinning, were parked in the street just ahead of him. Several cops were standing in the street, and the crowd from a closing tavern in which there had likely been a disturbance congregated in small groups on the sidewalk, their shoulders hunched and their hands in their pockets, and looking underdressed and cold as though the weather had been much warmer back when they first entered the tavern; the radio in a squad car could be heard above the shouts and laughs they gave each other which resounded in the early morning darkness of this vacant street. Since Tanker could think of no other alternative, he pulled over to the curb. His position was not yet hopeless. Most cops had a sense of tolerance and camaraderie about them at this hour of the night, especially with youthful drunks. In all the times he had been stopped for traffic violations only once had he received a ticket from a Chicago cop, and that for a lesser offense than the one for which he had been stopped, and only once had he had to give a bribe. But he believed this was due more to his own cleverness than to any compassion on the part of the cops. Be polite, he counseled himself, show him you're one of them, a good fellow.

The officer left the three-wheeler idling beside the car and walked over to the driver's window as Tanker, feeling with his right hand, made certain Scarponi was upright in his seat. The officer was in regular uniform, without helmet or boots, which seemed incongruous with his assignment on a three-wheeler. His face was square and shiny, and he looked about thirty years old and Italian.

"You must be color-blind," he said. The voice was unfriendly and carried the threat of rubber hoses, but Tanker knew it was a bluff, a part in a game they had to play.

"I guess I fell asleep for a second," Tanker said. "I ought to get off the road for a while. You don't know of some place around here that's open where I can get some coffee and some bacon and eggs?" He tried to sound innocent and only slightly drunk, and more tired than drunk.

In reply he was asked to show his driver's license. He fished in his wallet and sorted through the cards in darkness, afraid to turn on the light. The cop took the license into the headlight of the three-wheeler. "This is a Wisconsin fishing license, Stanley," he said. (Stanley was Tanker's Christian name.) The cop was proud of his sarcastic wit and reluctant to let this opportunity to exercise it pass. "You can't even fish with this in Chicago," he said, "never mind drive a car. You can't even fish with it in Wisconsin. It's three years old. Don't you clean out your wallet, Stanley?"

Finally Tanker located the driver's license. The fishing license had been a legitimate mistake. He saw the cop was amused.

"You guys been drinking?" the cop said.

"Just a few."

The cop smiled. "Just a few," he said. He examined the driver's license, then asked for the car registration. Tanker had it ready. Again into the headlight of the three-wheeler. Then with the registration in his hand around to the back of the car. "This is not a Cadillac, Stanley," he said. "You've come down in the world. This is a Chevy. You want to step out and see what it says all over your car? You see, it says Chevrolet here on your trunk and up there on your grille . . . and even if it did say Cadillac, Stanley, this car would still be a Chevrolet."

"I just traded cars," Tanker said. This was a legitimate excuse.

There was a grace period of a week or so between transferring old plates to a new car and registering that car. To calm his nerves and to appear natural he lit a cigarette, carefully cupping the flame. To his surprise a foul burned taste was in his mouth and the tip of his cigarette was crackling as though he had just lit a sparkler. As he looked cross-eyed down the cigarette at the inexplicable site of those small explosions at the tip, the cop peered in the window and watched him, so close their faces almost touched. The cop was now extremely amused. He had lit the filter tip!

"Just a few," the cop said, unable to restrain himself and bursting out laughing. Another legitimate mistake, and it was working in his favor!

Then the cop said, "What's the matter with your friend?"

"He's asleep," Tanker said. "Guess he can't take it. He ain't got my ability to hold it."

"Your ability to hold it," the cop repeated with good-natured disgust, shaking his head and making a noise that sounded like tsk-tsk. "Let's see your title, Stanley." This would be difficult.

Again from the headlight of the three-wheeler: "This isn't no-tarized, Stanley. And the guy you bought the car from didn't put down a date for the time of sale. You're in a lot of trouble, Stanley." This final judgment meant one of three things: you were in a lot of trouble, you were now supposed to offer a bribe, or you were not in any trouble at all and the policeman was only playing out the part for his and your amusement. Tanker could tell that the cop meant the last. He was safe! He wouldn't even get a ticket.

"The dummy didn't even put down the date?" he said incredulously.

But now the cop was saying, "Stanley, there's blood on your title and you got blood all over my gloves." He got a piece of paper from the three-wheeler and was taking his time wiping the blood from the paper. Now he was approaching the car and shaking his hand as though something were sticking to it, like a piece of tape, that he could not shake off. Tanker reached over and pushed Scarponi so that he tumbled with his head tucked down against the door. "What have you guys been up to?" the cop said.

"Nothing."

"What do you mean nothing?"

"The guy here fell down. On the sidewalk."

"Fell down, shit, Stanley. You guys were probably in a fight. What did you do, get into a fight with each other?"

"No, we're all right, officer," Tanker said. But the cop leaned in the window, reached around Tanker who obliged by ducking, and shone the flashlight on Scarponi crumpled up against the door.

"Now, Stanley," the cop was saying, "you're in no condition to know if you're all right so how can you know if you're in any condition to know if your buddy's all right? Get out of the car, Stanley."

In desperation Tanker tried to hand him a five-dollar bill. The cop put the light on it and handed it back. "Come on, Stanley," he said. "Can't you see there's other cops just up the road ahead? You don't want to get me in trouble. And you don't want your buddy to bleed to death." But Tanker could tell that he would not have taken the bribe even if other policemen weren't just up the street.

Tanker stepped out of the car. One of the two police cars parked ahead drove off with its blue light no longer flashing. The crowd on the sidewalk and in the gutter began to break up, shuffling and staggering down the sidewalk alone or in pairs, their hair disheveled and their shirttails out, pausing to light cigarettes and shout back at each other. The cop kneeled on the seat and leaned across to Scarponi. "Hey, buddy," he said, shaking his shoulder. At this point Tanker shot him three times in the spine. In the quiet and deserted street the shots rang out and echoed like weak firecrackers in an alley.

Then Tanker ran. Across the street. Down a sidestreet. Down a passageway between two buildings. Over a low picket fence. Across a yard. A side street and into an alley. Crawling beside a house beneath a row of darkened windows. Another alley and he put the pistol in a garbage can. He hid behind a garage when the headlight of a three-wheeler came bouncing down the alley. From several directions he could hear the drone and crack of the deep, monotonal voice on the police radio. He hid in shrubbery when a police car cruised down a side street. He could see headlights in the alleys and on the streets.

He was able to sneak through the underpass of the expressway, then through the darkened yards of a block of factories, and climb a chainlink fence, and make it far enough north and east to come upon the Northwestern Railroad tracks, the safest place at night in the city. Let the cops beat the streets and alleys, stop cars and search garages. He walked alone in the darkness of the tracks, high up on an embankment enclosed by the backs of factories. He could look down on the lines of street lights along the streets and on the roofs of the old frame houses, interrupted by Romanesque- and Byzantine-looking churches. He had always liked to walk, especially at night, alone with his thoughts, or in company and talking with his friend, and he had liked to walk for long distances and for the whole night. On moonlit nights he had often walked these very tracks from his old neighborhood out into the northwestern suburbs, or the other way, down into the Loop. But now his legs quivered, he stumbled over the rails and ties, and he could not walk without bending his knees. Ahead the skyscrapers of the Loop rose like a fabulous silver city of the plains. He had made it! He had done it! Gotten away with it! It was all over. It had been easy!

But then he felt as though he had been shot. Not in life so much as in a dream. He sat down on a rail and watched through the grimy windows of a factory down below women in babushkas and slacks working at large, black, and clicking machines. He folded his arm around his eyes and cried into his sleeve. He had to be wrong! It had to be a dream. He checked his wallet. He even lit matches, every match he had in his pockets. Left behind in the hand of the dead policeman was his registration, title, and driver's license, each of which bore his name.

But the world worked as it worked, he told himself. He knew the penalty the city exacted from the killer of a cop. They were going to kill him. They would have to kill him! The flesh he felt in his fingers—only so many pounds of cool, worthless meat. His spirit, mind, soul, whatever that spark was called that was him, the Tanker —all for nothing! The sleeping city stretched before him like a cemetery, the houses like repetitious and limitless rows of tombstones. The headlights of a lonely car easing out of a garage in an alley of factories below and passing out into the deserted street were like the lights by which to dig a secret and unhallowed grave.

CHAPTER TWENTY-THREE

THE DEATH
OF THE
DUESENBERG

Magnuson in the Duesenberg and roaring up and down the roads with everywhere and nowhere his destination. Northbound and swerving onto a turnoff and rapping around a cloverleaf until he emerges southbound and on his way to Oriole Park and Mrs. Rotterdam, convinced that she more than the others is most in danger of her life. Only to brake suddenly and bound and bump dangerously and illegally across the median strip of grass and roar onto the northbound lane again, convinced that the nurse at Farquarson's is most in danger. Only to turn off and take an underpass back onto the southbound lane and head southeast toward the downtown of Chicago, convinced that the nurse is involved in the plot and Mrs. Rotterdam is already dead and that the man in the apartment next door to Rotterdam's who came out into the hallway carrying a bag of garbage, along with the Filipino janitors of Rotterdam's building, are most endangered, having seen and even talked to the murderer and being able to identify him. While beneath the hood ominous noises are in the valves, tappets, lifters, and what is possibly the knocking of a rod.

Dangerous and drawn-out dreams that have the complexities and casts of epics and novels occur in those instants that his eyes are closed, and he starts awake to find himself behind the wheel of a speeding car that is miraculously still upon the road. He talks to himself to keep awake, knows he is dreaming when he can no longer hear his voice. While along the shoulders of the highways, seen from the corners of his aching eyes and in the outskirts of the beams, what seem at one time to be gray howling dogs bounding alongside him at a speed equal to his own and at other times simply stationary mounds of slaughtered horses. He seems to see his dead wife, too. In the rear window of a car that overtakes him, her face drawn like the red taillights into the darkness of the road ahead.

Automobiles like balls of light speeding through the night of space. Speed that sends him off the earth and into the laws of that universe within his dream. No longer in a world where there is any place for chance or innocence. But here where all coincidence is the consequence of plot, and all innocence the masquerade of guilt. No lone murderers in this landscape, only lone detectives and infinite theories of conspiracy.

The conspiracy of Negroes who champion the claim of the long-lost and wronged mulatto daughter of Farquarson's wife and milk Farquarson's desire to do good deeds before he dies, persuading him to write another will in favor of the girl (which means themselves), then killing him by laying a large hand across his face that stuffs up his mouth and nose with blackness before his relatives or lawyers can change his mind. Then the discovery that Farquarson has sent a letter to Wenzel and in the consequence the death of other whites and the unleashing of a savage and insatiable appetite for blood, as in a dog that has once killed and eaten portions of a deer or sheep. Human sacrifices, cannibalism, blood rituals, the legacy of Africa that has always pulsed within that flesh beneath the European clothes.

And the conspiracy of youths. Skipper Moony and his makeshift and raggle-taggle gang, aided by his girlfriend Nancy Rhinelander, and hired by John Cavan to murder Farquarson to keep him from carrying out his threat to disinherit Cavan of the Lake Forest house in another will. Then Moony and the gang, drunk and high on the drugs the nurse has given them, dispatched on a cross-country murder spree,

slaughtering anyone even remotely connected with the affair, especially Bonny Wenzel (whose death Cavan believes, erroneously, will
increase his share of the estate) and even including the father and
mother of Moony himself. (Didn't boys go berserk every day and shoot
down their parents with shotguns and high-powered rifles?) Youths
who are selfish, self-righteous, narcissistic, insensitive to life, ruthless
and mindless in a gang rebellious to anyone in a position of authority
or older than themselves. Who begin to murder for a lark, or profit,
but end up killing for sadistic and ritualistic fun.

And a third conspiracy of businessmen, politicians, and lawyers,
given naturally to intrigue, with Chandler in the role of chief con-
spirator. Murdering Farquarson to control his millions or to recover
some politically damaging document in his possession and stationing
the unwitting or corrupt employees of the government about the
landscape to silence whoever they suspect has knowledge of the
men or motive behind Farquarson's death. The conspiracy only
one cell of an even larger conspiracy that is the secret power behind
both government and industry, a notion that appeals to Magnuson
and confirms that suspicion he has always nursed, that all politicians
are corrupt and all governments opposed to freedom. And how can
anyone uncover such a conspiracy, never mind bring it to justice,
when it has the power to handcuff and corrupt judges and police?

And how can a law-abiding informer be certain that the officer
he confides in is not himself an agent of this financial-political conspiracy? And with so many blacks jammed together in the city slums,
who can be certain that the black he investigates is not a member of the
black conspiracy? And with so many youths jammed together in the
colleges and bohemian neighborhoods, who can be certain that the
youth he interrogates is not a member of the youth conspiracy? Who
besides the detective on the road even suspects that such conspiracies
exist?

The citizens of those suburbs beside the highway, who are
barricaded in their homes as though in the blockhouse of a frontier
settlement in the wilderness that is nightly under the threat of
Indian attack. Dr. and Mrs. Horowitz sleeping side by side in their
bed at the foot of which the prowler stands, shining a pencil-sized
flashlight on their faces. Mrs. Swanberg up to open windows now
that the rainstorm has passed discovering an open window she
cannot remember opening, and through which a prowler has already
crawled; Mrs. Osucha wakened by the sound of coughing in the
children's bedroom about to give her surprisingly peacefully sleep-

ing son a teaspoon of powerful expectorant when she hears from a remote quarter of the dark house more coughing and someone stumbling against a chair; Mr. Richter asleep in his clothes in his armchair before a television set tuned to a station that is transmitting the shrill signal of its having gone off the air while the intruder is in his bedroom and in his bed, on top of Mrs. Richter, holding a knife against her throat; Mr. Oliveri awakened by the obscene call he thought had to bear the news that someone close to him was dead, groaning and belching in the dark, nursing his ulcer with a glass of buttermilk; young Mr. Frankovitch wakened by a nightmare in which he and all his family are murdered in their beds and on top of Mrs. Frankovitch who has drugged herself with sleeping pills; young Mrs. Newman, awakened by noises she thought were made by prowlers, on top of Lieutenant Commander Newman, an action witnessed by the peeping tom standing on the eavesdrop outside their bedroom window, fingertips and nose resting on the window sill; Mr. Whiting awakened by the fumbling at his front door and the tiptoeing across the living room and taking one of the several loaded pistols he has hidden strategically about the house in case of housebreakers or rioters and shooting his teen-age daughter who, unknown to him, has been out tonight and is returning secretly at this hour. None of them aware of the conspiracies afoot. Blacks. Youths. Gangsters. Agents of big business and even bigger government. Secret societies that are determined, if the need arises, to see them dead. Which of them alive today will die before tomorrow? Which of them has learned today from one of the victims killed tonight a piece of information that, unknown to them, betrays the existence or membership of these conspiracies, which means that they too are marked for death? Nor do they know or even care that at this late hour on the highway and among the traffic they have conditioned themselves not to hear there is riding in a grand and failing car the guardian of their lives, the defender of their faith. Whose defeat is close at hand. Banging and knocking among the rattling and tapping beneath the hood, the smell of smoke and oil, the sight of smoke, the feel of heat; the needle of the oil pressure gauge is at rest on zero.

Ahead the lights of a restaurant and gas station loom up like a lighted space station fixed upon a flat disc that floats through space. The restaurant spans the highway like a bridge, the traffic flowing directly underneath its lighted windows, while the gas stations flank either side. The Duesenberg on a concrete field with numerous safety islands and gas pumps, only one of which is lighted. No other cars. No other people. Plastic pennants on long sagging wires strung from one island to the other flapping like tethered birds that cannot fly away no matter how they beat their wings. Smoke pouring out from beneath the car. From the office of the small lighted service station that seems blocks away, the lone attendant reluctantly sets out. A large, rural, wind-chapped man in white coveralls and white visored cap that make him resemble less a filling station attendant than a pilot on an aircraft carrier. He tells Magnuson that his engine is hot and his oil full, and that his lack of oil pressure indicates some mechanical trouble he, who is no mechanic, cannot diagnose, much less repair. A mechanic, however, is due in the morning. Then after he has watched Magnuson stare dumbly at the hissing car, he adds, as though to weight the choice in favor of Magnuson's going away, that he doubts if parts can be found for so unique and antique a car.

But there must be a mechanic or garage close by to which he could be towed! "Call them up!" he shouts. "Get them out of bed if you have to!" He stomps his feet, seems about to seize and shake the man, or circle behind him and cut off the path of his retreat. But the attendant only picks his teeth with a fingernail and continues to contemplate him with a wary but uninterested skepticism, as a sleepy polar bear might some furious fox. Then he wipes his clean hands on the clean cloth he carries in his pocket and makes his long, lumbering walk through the pumps and safety islands back to his lighted office, where he stands staring out the window across the concrete field at the headlights speeding up and down the highway and above them at the stars appearing in the sky. Then leaning back against a rack of road maps he reads a newspaper folded commuter-fashion, glancing up only to watch the old-fashioned car as it lurches and smokes through the long rows of pumps.

In the parking lot beside the restaurant Magnuson stares glassy-eyed out the small windshield, unable to get out from behind the wheel. In his dazzled mind he is speeding down the highway among those cars he hears. He falls asleep, or thinks he does, and in that sleep is once more speeding down the highways, his head hanging out the window to catch the air, his hand upon the horn. Awakes to the roaring of cars and trucks behind him on the road and the flashing of their headlights passing through his car, and panics, believing he has fallen asleep behind the wheel of a car speeding down the roads. But the car is parked, he is sitting quietly behind the wheel, which he grips in both his hands, and in his mind, he is still racing down the roads. At last he leaves the car, staggers toward the restaurant ahead, and in his mind is back inside the car, racing breakneck down the roads behind the vanguard of his beams. Stranded, he thinks. Beaten. Out of the race. Finished.

The immaculate and brightly lighted restaurant that spans the road. Sections of the dining room closed off by unfolded and plastic-looking partitions; sections of counters roped off. Philodendrons, the waxy leaves of which look artificial, climbing the shiny latticework of a room divider. Shops enclosed by glass walls selling boxes of candy, jars of jam, immense multicolored lollipops, life-sized or even larger stuffed animals and dolls. Luxury, efficiency, consumption, light. A man in white mopping reflective water across the marbleized floor, another squeegeeing water from the glass doors. Everything glass or polished like a mirror. Cooks and waitresses, rural people who look out of place in their antiseptic and corporate uniforms. The silverware muted as though wrapped in napkins; the suggestion of meat sizzling on a grill. The few customers, freshly awake or sleepy, whispering or silent, their systems un-settled by this lack of motion, like men ashore after months at sea. Groups of them sit at tables, looking dazed, dumbfounded, nervous, as though fresh from a room in which they have been interrogated and tortured. When they walk they appear elongated, limping, transparent. A black man alone at a table with his glasses off and pinching the bridge of his nose as a waitress sets before him a menu as large as a newspaper. He consults his watch, winds it, shakes it, holds it up against his ear. What is he doing here? On this highway? In this restaurant? At this hour? Where can he pos-sibly be going? A pair of youths at the counter joking with the counter help whom they apparently know. They chain-smoke ciga-rettes with their coffees, spin on their stools, legs apart, heels up against the post, hands folded between their thighs, studying the restaurant behind them. They appear to have been here for some time, to be in no hurry to leave. Local boys likely, out for a night of drinking or thieving. But how does he know? Haven't they studied him at some length at least once, just as the black man has, replacing his glasses to do so? A state trooper in campaign hat and pea-green uniform enters, pauses in the center of the floor as though searching for someone in particular, then sits down on a stool. Magnuson slouches over his coffee, which he spoons like soup.

He leans his head against the window. Traffic approaches through the night from miles away and disappears beneath him. He feels he is down upon that road, that he has circled back upon himself and is watching himself pass by on the road below. Feels inside a lighted spaceship sailing through the night of space, gazing out a large porthole at the steady and curving stream of meteors passing beneath him. America! Where on earth is it going? Everything shaken loose and rolling. Insane, sightless, dangerous, racing down superhighways with the riders in the cars and trucks and buses of no more consequence than the impulses transmitted down the telephone wires strung, like the roads, across the continent. Speed and distance the only destination, the only message. Nothing seen along the way at such a speed, nothing remembered, nothing gained by reaching the destination. The means to travel, the means to speed, the compulsion to travel great distance at great speeds, with the destination always whatever open road lies just ahead. But toward what blind unhappy fate is it compelled to speed? He sees a precipice where all highways converge and end, as though where the planet Earth leaves off, the planet Pluto, a thousand feet below, begins. Down there, heaps of burning cars and skeletons stacked up like cordwood. A limitless plain of moon craters and the blasted landscapes of the no-man's-land between the trenches of World War One. The sky the color of a dead fish with a single worldwide ocher stratus cloud at the horizon, and behind it, the top half of a green moon, larger than the earth, that does not rise or set or even move.

Then he is on his feet. He recalls the promise made to him by Smithy, the mechanic in the underground garage of the athletic club, to come and fetch him home or repair his car if he should encounter trouble on the road. Promised him this very evening as he prepared to set out upon his journey. Guaranteed the indestructibility of the Duesenberg. At the telephone, the ringing in his ear violating the tranquility of distant sleeps and dreams. The sleepy, high-pitched, and smoky voice of Smithy drawling in his ear in that accent that is Chicagoan because it is Mississippian, a rural voice unequal to the demands imposed upon it by this city of the North.

"I wouldn't have called," Magnuson begins. "Not at this hour, anyway." Goes on to catalogue his desperation, helplessness, loneliness, sense of urgency. Explains the problem of the car, reminds him of his promise, tells where he is. On the other end a silence that suggests the listener has fallen asleep or has just calculated the great distance between his house and Magnuson as he has simultaneously discovered the lateness of the hour. He stalls, fumbles an apology (Magnuson is certain he is scratching his head or neck), suggests alternatives, none of which is comprehensible to Magnuson; recalls that he must leave at sunrise with his family for two weeks' vacation fishing in Michigan, adding a brief, repetitious, and again incomprehensible discourse on his, and especially his wife's, passion for fishing: a cabin, a stove heated with pine slabs, pine trees circling a small lake in the middle of which is a rowboat with him fishing from the bow, his wife from the stern, the half a dozen children in between, poles and lines extending from the boat in all directions. He doubts he would be able to get back in time to leave. Nevertheless he says in good humor, wide awake now, having mentioned something about coffee and a plate of eggs, "I'll be there. Hold on. I'm on my way."

But now that Magnuson has the offer of this man's help he discovers he does not want it; wants only to know that in these days of indifference the offer of this man was made in good faith, that the old ways of an older world are not entirely gone. "No, stay there," he says with the begrudged gratitude of the stoic. "Go back to bed. Go to Michigan in the morning. Just tell me what's wrong with the car." He is told the oil pump to the valves is broken and that he should wait where he is and have it fixed, or else have the car towed into the garage at the club, or anywhere else they can do the work. "But I can't wait!" he cries.

In that case if he has to drive it home tonight he can stop every five miles or so, remove the valve cover, and pour oil in by hand upon the valves. "But listen here," Smithy says, "if you want to change your mind and have me come and get you—."

But Magnuson is back upon the road with a case of oil beside him on the seat. Trailer trucks and doubledecker buses bearing down behind him as though their accelerators are stuck to the floorboard and their brakes are gone, pushing up his own speed, their blinding headlights a few feet from his trunk, and then blowing him halfway into the breakdown lane with their blast of wind when they finally pass. Ahead, a red flare and a man, his body reddened by that flare, squatting dangerously out in the lane as he changes a flat tire. Headlights approaching him head-on! But he is on divided highway, the two lanes he is traveling on are both one-way—his way! A limousine flies past in the other lane, and in its windows, half a dozen well-dressed old ladies are sitting in their seats as though cups of tea and saucers are on their laps, one of them with rigid, extended arms behind the enormous steering wheel. Northbound, they must have wandered onto the southbound lane, mistaking it for a two-way road. How long have they been speeding suicidally and murderously through the night? Suddenly he loses whatever sense of direction he has had. Is it possible he has gotten off onto some two-way road, or good God, is he still on divided highway, southbound but in the northbound lane, or northbound but in the southbound lane? Who then is destined to have a head-on collision with an innocent car on the road ahead, the old ladies or himself? He imagines the screeching tires, buckling metals, shattering, raining glass, the explosion of gasoline.

He stops on the dark shoulder to remove the valve cover by flashlight and pour a can of oil upon the smoking valves. Rainbows in the oil oozing across the gun-gray metal. On the road again a siren and then the spinning dome light of a police car pursuing and passing him; later that same cruiser parked behind a second car beside the road, the light no longer spinning, both cars dark and no sign of life. Farther on a man walking beside the road, waving him to stop at the last minute, an entreaty he ignores. Flares ahead, and a policeman with a flashlight in the road to slow him down; tow trucks, ambulances, police cars, a semi down in the ditch and several totally wrecked cars. Farther on, out in the darkness of a field, a car is burning by itself, an accident that he, apparently, is the first to notice. He stops to pour more oil upon the valves, and the burning car is behind him now, the red flames against the blackness snapping like wind-blown sheets, muffling what might be human screams. Then as he races through an underpass where a man is flattened against the wall and sticking out his thumb the knocking begins in earnest beneath the hood. In the fragmentary dreams he has behind the wheel he can believe it is his heart he hears or the knocking of police upon his door. Convinced the car will see him home he puts the accelerator to the floor and holds it there. A single loud knock: the heart breaking and the man collapsing or the door battered off its hinges and the uniforms trooping in. The immediate freezing of power in the engine, the movement of a glider, the silence of a mountain top. The Duesenberg parked beside the road, mud-splattered, oil-splattered, smoking. Small secret dying noises—pings and hisses—from its various parts. The magnificent machine abused, worn out, broken down. The end of the adventure. He is on foot and far from home.

In the rough beyond the shoulder he runs and stumbles in the dark and when he forgets his panic slows down, staggers, sleep-walks, falls. The suspicion of impending dawn. Of a light that will reveal by imperceptible degrees out on the darkened fields beside the road the ripped, charred, and still smoking pieces of armor destroyed in a savage battle waged in the night. The eerie feeling that out there at the horizon where the light is low and gray, legions of ghosts are being driven with whips across the prairies. Bones and sheets in masses. Tribes of Indians, blocks of slaves, wagon trains of settlers, regiments of soldiers, their bodies leaning forward as though dragging a heavy weight or battling a mighty wind, small white flags with red crosses flying aloft. Beyond them the blood-red reflections in the sky of a hundred burning towns. He stops. Holds his breath. Listens. In the wind the sound of whips, moans, chains, tramping, drums, the minor-key singing of a martial song.

Ahead a gas station like a lighted platform floating through the darkness. A phone call made by the attendant into the local town, a taxi ordered. Magnuson trying to wash the oil and grease from his hands in a black, grainy sink. No soap and now no towels. He slumps in the oily leather chair beside the cluttered desk and falls asleep. A local police car pulls up, an officer enters. "He's Okay," the attendant says. "Car trouble down the road."

The cop addresses Magnuson: "Did you lock up?" Magnuson nods. The cop asks the attendant: "Drunk? Sick? Sleepy? What?" The attendant shrugs.

When the car leaves the attendant says, "They're watching out for me. I got held up last night for two hundred dollars." He pulls the twenty-two target pistol from the pocket of his coveralls. "Now I got this." The ringing of bells as cars pass over the hoses at the pumps. The attendant departs, returns, sits on the desk. "You know how I could tell you were all right when you walked in here off the road? The way you're dressed. Now if you were dressed like some bum or hood I'd have been suspicious. That call I made wouldn't have been to no taxi company but to them cops. Only you wouldn't know nothing about it because I'd pretend I was talking to the taxi company. It would be a kind of code between me and the cops." The bells again. The attendant returns, showing him a wad of bills the size of a softball, which he keeps in his pocket. "They held up a guy some place down in Chicago last year and left him tied up in the john with his pants around his ankles and a bullet in his head."

The suburban taxi is at the door. Magnuson is helped into the back. The driver writing on his clipboard. "I want to go to Chicago," Magunson says, and falls asleep.

The attendant chasing the taxi and shouting, "What do you want to do about your car?" as the taxi pulls onto the divided highway in a direction it cannot reverse for miles.

Magnuson's head bounces against seat, windows, doors, lolls from side to side. He dreams that the Duesenberg is resurrected. That he is once more behind its wheel, tearing up and down the roads. Suburbs to city and city to suburbs he crosses indistinguishable boundaries only to backtrack and recross them, passing from ramp to expressway to ramp to highway to side street to boulevard to ramp again as though searching by chance alone for an exit from this megalopolis that will take him into wilderness and space. The ghostly convertible, racing through the fog swirling in its headlights and over the smears of taillights and neon signs reflecting on the shining streets, running stop signs and stop lights and passing every car upon the road. The top is down and the seats already crowded with all those people he does not dare to leave behind for fear that in his absence they will kill or themselves be killed. Nancy Rhinelander and Mrs. Rotterdam and her former husband Mr. Olson and their two daughters, and Mrs. Owens and the two Mexican field hands and the four men with the bowling balls from Wenzel's tavern and the two Filipinos and the man with the sack of garbage from Rotterdam's apartment house among at least a half a dozen others. They sit like acrobats on each other's shoulders, stand on the running board, hug the spare tires, lie across the hood and fenders, sit inside the trunk. "I can't be everywhere at once," Magnuson has explained to them, waving his revolver. "You've all got to come with me if I'm to keep an eye on you."

Thereafter he kidnaps at gunpoint any suspicious-looking or frightened-looking persons he encounters on the streets, commandeering other cars to hold them all. He welcomes them aboard with the proclamation that there is always room for one more, that a wonderful adventure awaits them all in the hour and landscape lying just ahead.

Now the caravan of cars speeds through the crowded city, making for lonely country roads. Looking like a funeral procession racing for the graveyard before it closes. The spirit of a dangerous holiday among the passengers. The thrills of a high-speed death-defying chase—the shooting out of the tires on the cars ahead or the swerving into them to force them off the road—combine with the atmosphere of a drunken college or country club party that has taken to the roads.

The Farquarson mansion, looking more prison than palace, looms up ahead, and Magnuson brakes the Duesenberg and flags down the cars behind. Scrambles onto the shoulders of his passengers. Takes off his hat and waves it along with his revolver so that with his coat open and flying around him he resembles a hero of a revolution in a classical pose. "We'll all be safe if you follow me," he shouts. "There's no earthly reason why we have to be beaten by these injustices and deaths. Everybody, no matter who or what he is, gets to go on ahead. As long as I'm in charge, no one's left behind!" Cheers, the honking of horns and flashing of headlights.

A spacious living room inside the Farquarson house, reminiscent of a lounge in an English country hotel. Worn but comfortable armchairs and sofas, vases of chrysanthemums, fruitwood blazing on the irons, a wall of bookcases in which all the books are novels, and mostly mysteries, whose jackets reveal they were published at least thirty years ago, and a wall of French windows that open out into the garden and through which the party enters, far more people it seems to Magnuson than could have possibly been transported in the cars. The men sprawl on the armrests of chairs or lean on the backs of sofas on which the women sit. Some warm their hands before the fire, lean back against the mantel. Someone is picking out a show tune on the grand piano. Several couples are dancing. Drinks have been obtained from somewhere.

"I've called you all together," Magnuson begins from the center of the room, "because you are all suspects in a series of very clever and brutal murders. In fact, the murderer is one of you in this very room." Gasps of surprise, fear, outrage. Followed by forced smiles, self-conscious jokes, gallows humor, and suspicious studies of all the faces in the room.

"Well, go on," a man says impatiently, at the pitch of breaking. "Tell us who it is."

"Not so fast," says Magnuson. "First let me show you my deductions step by step." Like a gunshot: "Mrs. Reed, when General de LaSalle was murdered in his cabin cruiser off Montrose Harbor you were not in Mrs. Hart's apartment on Sheridan Road with Sandy Bitters as you claimed you were. Would you mind telling us where you really were? And with whom?" Panicking and thinking as he speaks, Who in God's name is Mrs. Reed? Mrs. Hart? General de LaSalle? And who is Sandy Bitters, man or woman? He has never heard of any of them before.

"That's a lie!" shouts a woman who must be Mrs. Reed, or possibly Mrs. Hart, or Sandy Bitters, in any case not the woman he faces accusingly.

"Is it?" says Magnuson, although for all he knows it could well be a lie, as he tries to confront the real Mrs. Reed who, because she no longer speaks, is no longer distinguishable in the crowd. "And Miss Gerardi," spinning about to confront a mass of faces, one of which he hopes is Miss Gerardi's, and discovering that a jam of people are in the garden and crowding against the French windows, with more joining them from across the lawn. He is speaking names, more unfamiliar names, and dates that to him are meaningless (he has no recollection of November 19, 1956, much less of August 3, 1942) and places he has little if any knowledge of (he is certain he has never been to Fond-du-lac! Nor to Sioux City!).

"That's preposterous!" cries the young woman who must be Miss Gerardi.

"Do we have to stay here and listen to this nonsense?" demands the young man on whose arm Miss Gerardi rests. Murmurs and nods of agreement among the crowd.

"I didn't accuse you of being the killer, Miss Gerardi," says Magnuson. "Only of lying to me the first time I questioned you." (Good God, he thinks, I never talked to her before.) "I admit your lying had me puzzled. It led me down the garden path. Once I took into account the possibility that everything you said was an outright lie all the other pieces of the puzzle fell nicely into place."

"It's a trap!" someone shouts.

"Of course it is," says Magnuson. Then in his best bullying manner: "Perhaps Mr. Cohen will now be kind enough to tell us his real name, and what his relationship really was with the deceased."

"You'll never prove it!"

"You're bullying us!" shouts someone else.

Magnuson pacing back and forth, juggling names with dates and places in his brain and measuring the drama in the pauses in his speech until he sees all aspects of the plot and has all its parts arranged. The moment of revelation that will force guilt and evil to reveal its hand. "The name of the murderer," he says, extending an index finger and spinning it around the crowd of faces with the accuracy of a man playing blindman's bluff, "is—"

Off go the lights. Darkness. Women screaming. The cry: "Look out! He's got a gun!" Feet shuffling, bodies wrestling. Grunts and groans and breathless remonstrations, like "No, you don't," and "Easy, easy," and finally, "Everyone, get down!" And then the inevitable, anticipated, and chaotic violence: the firing of those shots. Flashes of light cutting diagonally across the dark, as though from floor to ceiling. Hysteria. As though the women are holding their ears, jumping up and down in place, and screaming. The clatter of shattered glass. The shout: "He's getting away!"

"No one move!" orders Magnuson in a voice icy with authority. "Everyone stay perfectly still. Don't you move an inch until the lights come on." A brief spell of silence punctuated by coughs and sobs. Followed by the noises of people creeping in the dark, like stagehands moving furniture between scenes about a darkened stage. Someone strikes a match; several matches; someone has found a candle; fragments of frozen faces glimpsed in the small flames flickering with the natural wind of so many breaths, a cheekbone, an eye, a tip of a finger, a cleft chin; someone else has found a flashlight; the beam roams around the room like a spotlight, passing from face to face, and lingering for several seconds on each, the faces looking talcumed in the light. Suddenly the lights come on, revealing a complicated tableau: a crowd of people none of whom, Magnuson is certain, was here before, frozen in uncomfortable, unnatural, and even compromising positions which they abandon only after blinking with the light and as though waking from a sleep. The furniture seems rearranged. Several of the French windows are open, the panes of one are broken. Who, if anyone, has left? Miraculously there appears to be no corpse. Although he may be pinned upright in the crush of people concentrated against the walls and will be noticeable only when the crowd thins out and he is allowed to fall. Or he may be one of the many people with the frozen wide-open eyes sitting upright in their chairs, the blood of the wound not yet observable to those he sits beside. And perhaps the shots were only a ruse, an attempt to mask the real means of murder—poison, a cord around the neck, a knife.

A man in his shirtsleeves and with his tie loosened comes up from the cellar. "Someone removed a fuse," he says, brushing his hands.

"Who are you?" asks Magnuson.

The man opens his mouth to speak. "Never mind," says Magnuson, pulling out the pistol. "Get back down to the basement. And the rest of you people, follow him." If he locks them up, he tells himself, no one gets in, no one gets out, and everyone is safe. He can't watch them all at once. At last he will be free to go about his business without worrying about the people he has to leave behind.

"But you're shutting us up with a maniac!" someone complains, shouting up the dark and narrow stairway to the basement he is being forced down with the others, his voice muffled by the underground room and the crushing crowd.

"Only one of us is guilty!" says someone else.

"We're unarmed. He's got a gun!"

"You're condemning all of us to death!"

"He'll get rid of us one by one!"

He has to push the last of them down the stairs, closes the door on arms and legs, and puts his shoulder to the panels. Wonders as he draws the lock if the murderer is indeed among them. Wonders if he will choose and isolate his victims one by one, lead them, under the guise of helping them to escape, to coalbins and lonely corners, like a boy choosing a girl at a basement party and leading her off to be kissed. He can make out in the darkness of his mind heaps of corpses in those corners.

But then the dream is gone and he is awake to the reckless ride he is taking in a rattling taxi, the wheels more off the road than on, and down highways, back roads, and alleys that surely cannot be found on any map.

The brakes are slammed and Magnuson is thrown against the front seat. The taxi driver leaning out his door and shouting. A man in the middle of the road and between the beams of the headlights and waving. On the shoulder a gray car with the hood up. The feeling of a warning of a bridge washed out ahead, a city burning. Rain again, drumming on the roof, splashing in the rivulets already running darkly down the road. The driver leaning over the seat and shaking Magnuson. "You mind if he rides with us?"

Magnuson, falling asleep again, waves his hand. "Take him where he wants to go."

"Chicago," says the man, getting in. Between the sweeps of the windshield wipers and through the distortion of the sheets of rain upon the glass the skyscrapers of the Loop rise up like rocket ships about to blast off for the moon.

As though only passing from one dream into another Magnuson starts up awake, convinced the man beside him has been whispering in his ear. Starts up awake again, convinced the man has been on top of him with his bony arm around his shoulder and his bony hand clamped on his thigh and grinning at him from a bony face that has been knocking with every turn and bounce of the jostling ride into his own. He shoots forward and takes the driver by the shoulder. "Where are you taking me?" he cries.

"Sit back," orders the driver. "You're all right now." He nods toward the windshield and the lights ahead. "We're just taking you home."

BOOK THREE

CLOSING IN

CHAPTER TWENTY-FOUR

COPS

Magnuson was in the woods. He was standing in the door of a cabin, on the shore of a northern lake. The sky was cloudy and the wind was up. The black water, clear as glass, was lapping over the shallows of dark pebbles, and the few reeds were blowing above the choppy waves. A rowboat moored to the dock was rocking. He was wearing high-top laced boots, a red and white checked flannel shirt, a red and white checked wool cap. He was smoking a cigar. Then he went behind the cabin into the woods, the ferns parting against his thighs. He went deep into the darkness of the trees, among the incense of pines. In the forest his spirit would be safe, here it would begin the journey home.

Then he was wide awake in his bed and suffering with the fear of execution, the guilt of murder, the shame of rape, the disgrace of public exposure, and the gloom of knowing he could not undo what he had done. He had already forgotten the woods, and his escape there, and he could not be certain whether the crime he had committed that caused those feelings was real or only dreamed. He now realized that the ringing of the buzzer and the voices outside the door had wakened him. Daylight and the windows of his Gold Coast apartment were open to the sun. A man he knew instinctively to be a policeman was at the threshold of his bedroom, his fingers drumming backhanded on the open door.

He was short and stocky, with yellow, oily, almost hairless skin. He was young but looked ageless, as though he would look at sixty as he had at fifteen. The loose fit of his almost old-fashioned clothes, and his glasses with their plastic rims yellowed with age, made him seem a weight lifter masquerading as a clerk. He introduced himself as Detective Machak. Other voices in the apartment or, if the door was open, out in the hallway. Police voices, loud, irreverent, inconsiderate, detached. Magnuson was certain they had come to arrest him, that they would make him dress himself and go with them in handcuffs to the station. He was certain he would lie to them, and equally certain that they would catch him lying. He feared being exposed and degraded. Inexplicably he also feared a beating. Machak was looking through the wallet he had picked up from the covers of the bed. "Did you have any money in this?" he said. Magnuson, examining the wallet, nodded. "Your door was open when I came in. Did you lock it last night?"

"I forget sometimes . . ." His own voice sounded intimidated to him, even frightened. He remained lying in the bed, his head on the pillow, the covers around his waist, his forearm across his forehead.

"You'd better lock it from now on," Machak said. Then he left the bedroom with the wallet and returned with a second policeman, also in plainclothes. He introduced him as Lieutenant Goetz. They both stood in the doorway staring brazenly at Magnuson on the bed, Goetz, hat on his head and fists on his hips, nodding his head as though in his wisdom he understood this situation. Machak was showing him the wallet.

"So you're this guy Magnuson," Goetz said. He was taking a long look at Magnuson. "I wanted to see you anyway. I'll be back."

When he had gone Machak said, "Your building had a robbery last night. Just down the hall from you. I didn't come here on that call, though. Did you know your friend Scarponi was murdered last night?"

The name but not the deed surprised Magnuson. Was it meant

to? He had expected any of a dozen others. The news in his present confusion and shock did not surprise him. He felt no loss or grief. If anything he felt the possibility of relief, a double-edged relief, of postponing punishment rather than escaping it. He put up his hands helplessly as though to tell the young cop that given who Scarponi was, and who his friends were, to think this would not happen someday would be naïve.

"When Scarponi was in your apartment two nights ago," Machak said, "Fritz Schneider and Captain O'Neil said he stayed behind with you when they left. Did he say anything to you about someone wanting to kill him?"

"No."

"Was he in trouble in any way?"

"He didn't say he was. He didn't talk about such things." He wondered if this line of questioning was legitimate. He was suspicious and even frightened of this Machak. He would have to be careful and cunning.

"Did he bring up the name of anybody in the syndicate?"

"No."

"Maybe he mentioned a guy named Stanley Buddecker? Or Tanker Buddecker? Or just Tanker?"

"No."

"Have you got any suspicions yourself?"

"Not a one."

"How would you describe Scarponi when you saw him? Was he scared?"

"Happy-go-lucky."

Unable to contain the news any longer Machak said, "This Tanker also murdered a young patrolman named Carbone who stopped his car when he was trying to get rid of Scarponi's body." He was exhilarated with his consciousness of himself as an actor in events that were already history. "The clown was driving around the city with the corpse in the front seat beside him." His face suggested it was impossible to imagine the stupidity and effrontery of these hoods. He spoke to Magnuson as one comrade to another. It was, like the death of Scarponi, news he thought Magnuson should know.

Magnuson could feel the waves of righteousness and vengeance. It was the duty of every officer now to find the killer and, if possible, kill him in revenge. It was to take precedence over all other duties. The cop-killer would be shot down in an alley, in the front seat of a parked car, at the intersection of a busy street, in a surrounded and stormed apartment, a hundred slugs and shotgun pellets sent through his body, as though as many policemen as possible had to share in the ritual of his death. Even this stolid Machak was swept up in the electricity of the search, and expected Magnuson, whom he knew to be a former policeman, to share in the grief and rage.

"You'll get him," Magnuson said, thinking of the cop-killer in his hideout.

Machak, his apparent purpose at an end, now engaged Magnuson in small talk about the force, waiting for Lieutenant Goetz to return. But Magnuson wondered if this wasn't itself a subtle interrogation, or if he were being disarmed in preparation for the interrogation of Lieutenant Goetz. He thought he should get out of bed and get dressed but he lacked the strength and courage and was afraid that Machak, for some reason, would not let him. The best he could do was sit up in bed.

The death of the policeman had caused Machak to wax philosophical. It was apparent that to him men were basically corruptible, faithless, and without redemption, and that this was an attitude he had arrived at from his experience on the force. He had probably always been suspicious and mistrustful but now he was also disillusioned. Originally he had wanted to become an accountant or a lawyer so that he could become an FBI agent. Now he wasn't so sure that he shouldn't have stayed in the neighborhood grocery store he had helped his mother run when he was a kid, even though the chain stores had ruined their business. "If I'd known then what I know now," he confided to Magnuson. He seemed to accept Magnuson as a man not unlike himself. If he was tough and shrewd he was above all else a loner. He would have worked every hour he was free from school in his mother's store, spoken Polish to the customers, worn a man's hat and shoes when he was fifteen, and treated his younger brothers like sons, which meant he would not have hesitated to beat them. In high school he would have played no sport, belonged to no crowd. He would not have been bright or rich, and never young enough to have gone to college. The taste of power could not corrupt him nor could the fraternity of the police force ever sway him more than momentarily from his natural allegiance, which was to himself. If he was not noticeably intelligent or even efficient he was hardworking and uncorruptible. He was a man Magnuson could admire and in his own day would have tolerated and even welcomed on the force.

But Machak was now his enemy. It frightened him to realize

that his affinities were not with Machak but with this unknown Tanker who had murdered his old friend Scarponi and a policeman, a man of his own profession and on the same side of the moral line as himself. But somewhere during the night he had crossed over to the other side. Like the Tanker he too would be hunted, was perhaps being hunted even now, and was aware, as he thought the Tanker must be aware, that he could only postpone his end. He did not doubt that the city would exact the punishment of shame and even death from him, or that there was, as in the case of Tanker, some code that would demand that he be destroyed in compensation or retribution for the cost of his presumption and especially of his failure. He already felt as if the bedroom was his prison cell and Machak and Goetz were his jailors and eventual executioners. It was the kind of feeling he was certain Tanker must have felt when the police officer stopped him as he was driving through the city with the corpse of Scarponi beside him on the seat. "You've got to get him," he said suddenly.

"Tanker?" Machak said, surprised at this interruption to the anecdote he was telling.

"You've got to," Magnuson repeated.

When Goetz returned he had apparently learned of Magnuson's identity and connections, for he treated him with that begrudging show of deference he had perfected from necessity over the years. He would tend, Magnuson observed, to bluff and bully, a master of drawn-out pauses and sharp retorts. But he was probably capable of kindness and mercy, although less from feelings of compassion than of futility, indifference, and even disgust. "What difference will it make ten years from now?" was his favorite comment upon someone's lengthy tale of woe.

"Your watchman or glorified doorman downstairs says you entered the building last night in the company of another man. What time did you come in last night?" He was irritable, and was affected by the murder of the policeman in the night even though he was not on the case. He was aware, however, that it gave him a certain license to be irascible in his own assignments if he wished.

"I don't know," Magnuson answered, thinking about it. He was alarmed at this piece of news. Surely they were trying to trap him. He could not even remember returning home, only vaguely speeding in an other-worldly cab across dark, desolate back roads and bright but desolate thoroughfares, the aura from the lights of Chicago always in the distance.

"You don't know," Goetz echoed. "Who did you come in with?"

"I don't know that either. Unless it was the cab driver helping me in—"

"Helping you in?" Goetz said, seizing on the expression. "Were you hurt?" He couldn't hide the sarcasm.

"No, I wasn't hurt."

"You weren't drinking, were you?" This asked with an expression of mock seriousness on his face, and delivered loudly as though to an old man who was not only deaf but senile.

Magnuson made a bitter and disgusted smile, and almost snorted. Both officers smiled. "If the man in the lobby says somebody helped me in—"

"He didn't say he helped you," Goetz said.

"I thought you said—"

"No, you said that."

By now Magnuson had managed to take himself to the edge of the bed, where he was sitting in his undershirt and wrinkled, unzipped trousers in which he had slept, his bare feet on the floor. He wanted to rise, excuse himself to the policemen, and continue the interrogation as he was getting dressed. But he was afraid that if he stood up he would somehow reveal himself, or would be struck down. Goetz's technique was by now apparent to him. He managed to put himself at a distance from the man he interrogated. He listened to him sideways, grimacing as though he could not quite believe what he heard him say, and as though he had only to devote a small portion of his thoughts to what the man was saying. He was a man accustomed to having and using almost unreasonable powers and, at the same time, of suffering at the hands of those who wielded greater power, great indignities.

"In any case—" Magnuson began.

"It isn't any case," Goetz corrected.

"The man who didn't help me must have been the cab driver."

At this Goetz almost laughed. "What time did this guy leave the apartment?" His head indicated Magnuson's apartment, the whole place.

"How do I know when he left when I don't even remember him coming in, regardless of the time?"

"Okay," Goetz said, retreating from Magnuson's first push. "The Fishbein apartment down the hall here was robbed last night. A guy in a Hallowe'en mask, a pumpkin with scars and an eye patch—if you can believe it. This joker tied up the good doctor and his wife, gagged them, and set them up against the wall like they were a couple of dolls. That's why we been out there in the corridor."

Magnuson had seen the Fishbeins often in the hall and in the elevator. A dwarf-like couple who spoke with a strong accent, neither much more than five feet tall or weighing over a hundred pounds. He was a retired urologist who wore sandals and polo shirts; she had been an executive in a cosmetics firm and often wore sunglasses and pale blue slacks. They seemed to be in Florida more often than not.

"I don't suppose you heard anything last night in your condition," Goetz said.

Magnuson shook his head. He wondered if he hadn't heard a woman pleading, even screaming, in some remote landscape of a dream.

Goetz was holding the wallet. "How much you have in here?" He asked this as though Magnuson had quoted him a figure earlier he had since forgotten.

Magnuson shrugged.

"Did you give the guy the money?"

"What guy?"

"The guy that came in with you last night."

"If I didn't know he came in I didn't know I gave him any money. Besides, what would I give him money for?"

Goetz nodded as though this was a truth he had not foreseen. He was staring at the empty wallet, at the unmade bed, at the man in wrinkled undershirt and slacks sitting on it. "Well, for cab fare, for one thing. I don't know—for helping you to your apartment when you had one on. For services rendered. What do you make of it?" But before Magnuson could answer he asked, "Do you live here alone?" And when Magnuson nodded Goetz nodded in turn as though he understood. "Is it possible this guy came in here and spent the night?"

Magnuson could see through the doorway policemen wandering through his apartment, examining things, leaning against his kitchen counter and conversing about a baseball game, coming in to look over Goetz's shoulder at the man he was interrogating. "Well," Magnuson said, impatient with the game that Goetz was playing, "if some guy came in here without my knowing it, and I just woke up when young Officer Machak here woke me up, I suppose it's possible somebody slept here, especially if the door was open like you say. Look around, you're not short of manpower. See if any of the beds or couches been slept on."

"We have," Goetz said. "Yours is the only bed slept in."

"That ought to tell you something," Magnuson said, only momentarily enjoying the feeling of vindication. For suddenly he saw that Goetz was attempting to discover if he were a masochist or homosexual or pervert of some sort and if he paid out of his wallet for certain services received or given, or if because of his vulnerability he had been blackmailed or been the victim of a robbery he dared not report. The insult! Did he think a man, some young boy perhaps that Magnuson had had to pay, had lain in this very bed with him last night in some perverse embrace? Was that the picture he was composing in his mind? The boy defiling him with urine? Semen? Feces? Or beating him? Did he look that dissolute, degenerate, guilty? Had he not been Arnold Magnuson he was certain Goetz would have made a direct inquiry and even risked an accusation. As it was, Goetz had directed the interrogation in such a way as to allow Magnuson to explain the loss of money and the presence of the man accompanying him into the building without actually confessing to perversion. He was outraged, and only his sense of danger and a deeper sense of the beginning of a destined series of indignities— deserved indignities—prevented him from being violent. Instead he sat still, stunned, embarrassed, and ashamed, pretending he did not understand the officer's implications.

"I'm trying to learn if this theft of your money is really a theft," Goetz was saying, "and if it is, if it's related to the Fishbein robbery. What I think might have happened is this: the thief robbed, and planned to rob the Fishbeins, and when he left them and saw your door open he snuck in and robbed you too."

The implications of what might have happened in his apartment finally came home to Magnuson. Had the cab driver or the passenger they picked up in the rain escorted him in and robbed him quite apart from the coincidence of the Fishbeins being robbed almost simultaneously on his own floor? Or had the Fishbein thief actually been in his room while he slept, shining a flashlight in the dark and removing the wallet from the pocket of the pants he was still wearing, a knife or pistol in his hand, ready to kill him if he awoke and shouted? He seemed to recall a beam of light no wider than a pencil shining on the dresser, the wall, up and down his back and legs, and a rustling in the dark. Then the white fingers of a glove entering the beam. He was awake, his eyes open, and he was lying motionless and breathing regularly in the hope the intruder would think he was asleep. A hand was touching his thigh, was somehow going up beneath the bedclothes. Then the light was in the kitchen, silent and relentless, playing on the corners of distant walls.

"Either that," Goetz was saying, "or he came in with you last night. You were, to put it mildly, indisposed and he pretends he's a pal of yours to the doorman and that he's helping you in. No one else got past the doorman who didn't have any business in the building. But then again the guy had the mask and must have cased the Fishbein apartment beforehand. It's not a spur-of-the-moment robbery. Maybe the doorman is in on it. Either that or the guy was already in the building."

"If he got in he'd have to get out," Magnuson said.

"He can get out any time he wants to without anyone taking notice," Goetz said. "Maybe it's somebody visiting somebody that lives in here on a semi-permanent basis. Maybe it's someone that lives here himself."

Magnuson was surprised. The co-operative skyscraper was a fortress against the neighborhood in which it had been built. It was meant to keep mischief out. The black neighborhoods that were creeping toward the lake from the west, the kids that hung around the streets of Old Town, the drug addicts on the Gold Coast itself, and the young burglars, dope peddlers, and pimps that blended in with the students and young office workers and junior executives. The owners of the apartments had banded together to keep this world out.

"These are all co-operative apartments," Magnuson said, as though providing Goetz with information he did not have and that contradicted his theory. "You've got to have money to buy in here. You've got to have money to keep up the place."

"More money sometimes than maybe you're making," Goetz said. "Listen, you've got some young people living in this building and maybe they've got expensive habits and are living over their heads. The Gold Coast isn't exactly the best neighborhood for meeting the right people and picking up inexpensive tastes. Maybe the guy we're after is walking out your front door right now. Looking like a million dollars. Like a movie star. Blond, wavy hair, sunglasses, paisley scarf, cigarette holder, and a herd of Afghans or poodles. And your doorman is touching the visor of his cap and calling him sir. You probably nod to him when you see him in the elevator. If he is someone inside he's not going to be easy to catch— he's not even going to be easy to stop."

Everyone living in the building then was at the mercy of the thief. Everyone was potentially a victim, and everyone was a suspect. They were shut up with a criminal. It would have been safer to have stayed on the street. The watchmen at the series of locked doors, the intercoms, and the buzzers had only served to lock the criminal in.

"Lock your door," Goetz said.

Then after Magnuson had stumbled through his apartment at Goetz's request and discovered that nothing else was missing, the police left.

Immediately Magnuson dressed and went downstairs to get the morning newspaper. In his apartment again he tore through the paper standing up. In a small column on the front page was the last-minute extra in darker print reporting that an unnamed policeman had been shot early this morning on Western Avenue and that the killer had escaped. Inside the paper was a story with photograph on the murder of a man named Behnke, a sergeant on the police force Magnuson had known slightly. It was improbable and melodramatic: he had been murdered by his wife, a woman Magnuson had met several times, who had been a school friend of his wife. Apparently Behnke had been running around with another woman. While he and the divorcee were in a tavern, his wife, who had followed them, hid herself in the back seat of the car. When they parked in the street before the divorcee's house, she had jumped up and shot her husband fatally in the face. She was being held for a psychiatric examination. Magnuson remembered Behnke as a big man, six and a half feet tall, with a thick waist and big feet. He had been slow and sloppy and there was nothing of the Lothario about him at all. He and his wife must have been in their mid-fifties at least. Ironically, he had been a sergeant of homicide and had specialized in task forces investigating sex murders. His son was himself a policeman, and had been an end on a University of Illinois football team that had played in the Rose Bowl. Other than the death of the policeman, the murder of Behnke was the only murder reported in the paper. At the time the paper had gone to press last night none of the murders Magnuson had discovered had been reported to the police. For a matter of hours, perhaps for even as much as a day, he was probably safe from discovery. The police knew nothing then, and he was still free to pursue the murderer. Indeed, he had no choice. He did not know whether he should rejoice at this news or not.

He took several thousand dollars he kept loose in an unlocked bedroom dresser drawer and left the apartment as quickly as he could since the police, when they came for him, would look there first. He planned to go immediately to the Magnuson Agency downtown, consult the old records he had on Farquarson, and conduct what he could of the investigation from there, for as long as he could.

He told the doorman that if the police came looking for him he was driving north to his cousin's house just outside Minneapolis and that he probably wouldn't arrive there until some time tomorrow night. The doorman obediently wrote this down. "I forgot her address," Magnuson added. Just outside Minneapolis, he thought, that ought to confuse them. He thought he had a second or third cousin somewhere around Minneapolis, but it would probably take him longer to find her than it would the police. On a hunch he asked the doorman to describe the man who had accompanied him in last night. But this doorman had not been on duty then.

In the mail was a card from his son Bruce. The colored photograph showed a small medieval-looking town in Czechoslovakia: lopsided, gingerbread houses with steeply pitched roofs, a small church with an Oriental-looking spire, narrow cobbled streets, and window boxes of flowers. As usual it was a carefully printed note crammed into the small space and signed as always: B. The town on the photograph he claimed was the birthplace and home of his mother's family, a place he had always planned to visit. He had found tombstones bearing his mother's maiden name, had talked to old-timers who remembered the family, had actually located some distant cousins. He had made a mystical return to the place of his origins, had returned to where the bones of his ancestors lay buried. "At last," he wrote, "I am beginning to know who I am. The search has begun in this obscure village."

Magnuson read the card on the sidewalk before his skyscraper apartment house of glass and charcoal steel, standing under the cantilevered roof above the glass doors. He was aware that he would probably never return to this building. It was just as well; he had never felt at home there. He had the impulse to get away, to lose himself swiftly and irretrievably in the sanctuary of city streets.

CHAPTER TWENTY-FIVE

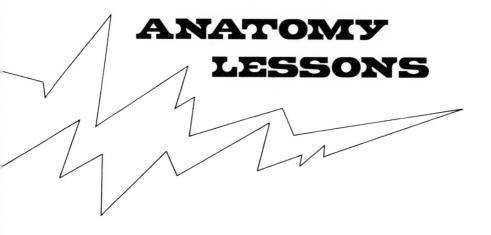

ANATOMY LESSONS

Cavan awoke with good feelings. Despite the late carousing of last night that ended up in the Ulmer Stube he was clearheaded, light-hearted, rested up. The combination of breeze and sunlight coming through the open window beside the bed—so close he could stick out his arm from where he lay—tempted him with happiness, as though the world by this sign promised him good news. Even the noises of the Gold Coast section of the city below, including the clanging of a pile driver, sounded as homely as the hubbub of a barnyard.

He awoke in Sonja Maki's apartment, in Sonja's bed, in Sonja's arms. Naked they looked like fatigued wrestlers who had fallen asleep during their most violent effort to pin each other in a con-fusion of holds. The heat of her flesh was that of blood and organs. He felt his body was surrounded and engulfed by hers, like a smaller organism by an amoeba.

She stirred, rolled off him, and sprawled on her back, entangling one of her legs with his. He lifted the sheet and looked down the length of her body. At once muscular and soft, it was a body for loving and dancing and child-bearing and working with a pitchfork in the fields. A peasant queen.

When she awoke, he said, "You have a wonderful body."

She yawned, stretched, arching up so that it seemed only her heels and shoulders touched the mattress. "Would you like me if I didn't?"

"Not like this."

"Is my face radiant?"

He nodded. "Do you have a secret?"

"You're my secret," she said, taking his hand and holding it up against her cheek. "Have you noticed how touching and loving other human skin makes your own skin come alive? Skins take from each other. It's a theory I have." He was disappointed. He thought she beamed because she was so much in love with him. Now he supposed any skin of any age and sex and color would have done as well as his.

She was up on an elbow, looking him in the eye. "Would you like me if I was ugly?"

He shook his head. Her face was at once innocent and sensual, her features broad and sharp. She looked like the offspring of Slavic peasants and German princes. But he was somewhat taken aback at her own admission that she was beautiful. He didn't know whether to admire the candor or mistrust the pride. He supposed that she could dare to acknowledge her good looks to men since there was little risk that they would accept her only as an object of the flesh. She had told him last night that she was a medical student at Northwestern who would intern next year and a graduate of the University of Chicago. He guessed she had been one of those child prodigies with a high I.Q. who had gone on to the University of Chicago without first finishing high school. She could be confident that intellectually she would be the superior of almost any man she met.

"If you go to Africa, would you take me?" she said suddenly, revealing that he must have told her something of himself and his interest in anthropology and Africa in the night.

"I'd not only take you, I'd stay home if you wouldn't go."

"Would I like it—Africa, I mean?" He noticed she phrased her questions in the English manner with an English inflection that was both feminine and pleasant if not entirely free of affectation.

He shrugged.

"While you dig up the dead I could keep the living from being dug under.—Let's go to Africa, John. Say you'll take me."

He was flattered and even a bit frightened that so soon after meeting him she would want to go far away with him, subordinating her profession to his. But he would never go to Africa. He was embarrassed even to think of Africa.

"Oh well," she said, seeing him hesitate, "let's stay in bed then."

"There's more for me to find here, in you, than in Africa."

"And for me in you," she said, taking his nose between her lips. "You look so intellectually handsome. And you look so rich."

"I'm penniless."

"How can you be penniless when your hair is straight and combed straight over and curls aristocratically around your ears?"

He was afraid that she would be disappointed in him if he were impoverished and was about to confess that not only was he not penniless but was really fairly well-to-do, when she said, squeezing his pectoral muscles, "You have a nice build."

"Not really," he said, half-truthfully and expecting to be contradicted.

Instead she said, "You do have the beginnings of a beer belly."

"A man's belly ought to shed the rain, Sonja."

She was rubbing his sternum with her fingertips. "If you're an anthropologist do you have to know a lot about anatomy?"

"You're supposed to. My interest was cultural, though. I wasn't much on the physical side of it. Even if I was, only the bones would be left of the people I'd see. And then only a skullcap, a molar, maybe a fibula—."

"What's this?" she said, placing his hand.

"A clavicle. A good clavicle, too."

"And this?" Putting his hand on her chin.

"Mandible?"

"Very good." Now the hand put beneath her back.

"Vertebrae."

"Yes, but which?"

"Lumbar—but they're all equally good."

"And?" Reaching beneath to move the hand.

"Coccyx."

"Shall I show you some of your muscles?"

"I only have one."

"This is your gracilis," she said, giving his inner thigh a mighty squeeze. "And your adductor longus. And—" moving her hand up so rapidly that he jumped "—if you're interested in tendons—"

"I am."

"—this is your lingual ligament—"

"I think you missed something," he said, sliding her hand back down.

"That is your *ab*ductor longus."

"It doesn't seem so long . . ."

"Ah, but last night . . ."

"Oh well, last night, Sonja . . . everything looks bigger in the dark . . ."

She was reaching her hand beneath his buttocks. "This is your gluteus maximus. And this your fold of nates."

"It sounds like the sheep farm of a Jew in the Old Testament." He felt he was straining for humor. Worse, that he had to please and entertain her. Without warning he put his hand between her legs.

"And what's that?" he said.

"I think," she said, closing her thighs on his hand, "that's called a vaginal fornix."

"It's never for *nichts,* Sonja." He squeezed a breast in both hands and put the mushrooming salmon-colored nipple in his mouth. Then he bit her gently on the shoulder, the other breast.

"Omophagist."

"Anthropophagite."

"You're eating me alive."

"I wouldn't want you dead."

"You wouldn't? I'd want you to."

"What good is the wanting without the getting? And necrophilia is not one of my vices. Is it yours?"

"It's a bit awkward with male cadavers," she said, laughing. "In fact, come to think of it, it's impossible!"

"But dead females are more accommodating?"

"One would think so . . ."

He paused with his mouth open against her throat, about to make a joke about a vampire. In a second he had gone from sensations to thoughts, from sex to death, from the material of Sonja's body to the spirit of his father. He had had a dream here in the night. In the heat and weight of Sonja's arms. In this best of places. He could recall it now. He was standing at sunrise on the shore of a large lake. If it was Lake Michigan it was in a world, or on a continent, in which there were not yet men. The air was touched with frost, the pebbles on the beach were rimed, and ice floes floated in the green waves. Down the beach a dog was barking around a fire tended by a figure in a blue cloak. When he approached the fire he saw that the dog was more jackal than dog, and that the figure's face inside the hood was that of early man, almost more ape than man. The figure pointed into the fire, pointed with a bone. There human bones were laid out in a crude circle that enclosed a human skull. The bones had been cracked open, the skull smashed. In the flames and smoke and heat waves he had intuited the presence of his father's ghost beating upward, a spirit without face or flesh. The dream had been more philosophy than nightmare. It had pointed to a lesson in the past instead of prophesying the future. Nor did he believe that the vision could have come even in this fantastic form from the storehouse of his own experiences, but rather had surfaced from a common pool of racial memories recollected only in the images of dreams.

"You're no better than a corpse," she said.

She had climbed on top of him, where she leaned over him, naked, her breasts swinging, watching his eyes as she scooted her sex back and forth across his soft penis. Above all else he wanted to be aroused, to be deep inside her. But his own body attracted him far more than hers, and he observed for the first time how the passive position of a man beneath a woman resembled that of a corpse upon a table. And as he had just recollected his vision of his father's spirit, he now imagined his father's body, looking like his own. Except whereas the son was beneath a woman, his father was beneath a sheet—in the County Morgue. Perhaps his body was still there and it was his duty to go and claim it and arrange a burial, preventing it from being shipped to a medical school for preservation and dissection. And even if the body were already claimed, might he not discover new members of his family in discovering who had claimed it? If he could never know his father, nor so much as talk to him, he could at least look upon his face. "What's a morgue like, Sonja?"

"I wouldn't go there at midnight."

Odd, he thought, that even professionals should have this primitive fear. "You wouldn't get used to it?"

"To death, yes. Corpses, yes. The morgue, never."

Arms at his side, legs together, feet turned out. Unconsciously he opened his palms. Opened his mouth. This girl astride him had cut open bodies like his own. Like his dead father's. Cut them open and cut them up. Even now some portion of her was capable of seeing him as just so much steaming, pulsing viscera inside something like untanned leather that was sliced and clamped and swabbed. "You don't mind the dissecting labs?"

"I don't care for the gallows humor. The cadavers don't bother me." Suddenly she got off him, leaned across him, and pointed out the window. "Do you see him over there?"

"Who?" He stuck his head out and confronted across the way the rows of windows reflecting sunlight and into whose apartments he could see no more than a few feet. "Where?"

"He's gone now," she said. "But there are others in the other windows. Most of them are married men, too. Disgusting, isn't it? They've got binoculars you could see Pluto through. Little bourgeois sex fiends. All-American boys with their intellectualized and naughty sex. Sometimes I think they set their clocks by me. Well, they can't get hurt by just looking."

If Cavan felt himself placed in the company of those unknown and censured men across the way he was more disturbed to think that those same men with high-powered binoculars could be studying Sonja and himself right now. In fact, since the shade was up this morning when he awoke, they could have studied them last night. Since Sonja made no move to draw it even now he pulled it down instead.

When she left to take a shower, he stayed in bed until he heard the sound of water, at which time he got out of bed on tiptoes.

She did not seem surprised to see him join her in the shower. Nor did she seem pleased or displeased either. She put her back to him and offered her face to the full force of the spout and warm water boiled out of the corners of her mouth and beaded on her flesh from which it rolled as though from marble. He decided that the most beautiful part of her body was the curve of her backbone from shoulders to buttocks. He took the soap from her and lathered her from neck to feet, going on his knees. What a magnificent woman! What a work of art was the human body! What passion he was putting into his job of lathering. When he surrendered the soap he received in turn a weak soaping of his back, and no more, and that with a washcloth. When she took down the douche bag and hose that hung on the white tile wall, he thought it proper to leave first although she made no attempt to shoo him out. As he toweled himself he noticed the antiseptic cleanliness of the room. As though the white walls and floor had been washed with something that not only cleansed but killed. The room was stark, too, with no toilet objects on the back of the toilet or on the sink but shut up apparently in that surgical-looking medicine cabinet on the wall, fogged up by steam. As he watched the silhouette of her douching behind the white plastic curtains he wondered why she would have a douche? For reasons of feminine hygiene? Or did she need it for the purpose she used it now? "You'd better be careful," he said, playfully. "I've heard you can make yourself pregnant by douching. It forces the sperm that otherwise might not have made it right up into the ovaries."

She was shocked to learn this and momentarily stopped both douche and shower, demanding to know if he was joking. Above the sound of dripping water he assured her he was not, surprised that she, a medical student, had not heard of such a thing before.

In the bedroom again he dressed himself. His clothes smelled of smoke and beer. It was especially noticeable in the apartment where there was that same antiseptic cleanliness he had noticed in the bathroom. White walls unadorned except for a few reproductions of medieval icons, some on wood, and Icelandic runes. Only one shelf of books, medical textbooks and numerous books on Slavic languages, Russian mostly, and he guessed that this must have been her undergraduate course of study. It seemed a large apartment for a single girl, and he supposed she could afford it because it was on the fringes of the Gold Coast, with a more rundown neighborhood just to the west.

She came naked into the bedroom and dressed before him without any trace of shyness and with a bold sense of parade that slightly angered him. Just the presence of underwear on her body made her seem simultaneously elegant, athletic, sensual. She put on blue sailor slacks and white sandals and walked out into the living room buttoning up the front of her blue sweater. There Cavan, who had been sitting on the edge of the bed watching her, caught up with her.

He had recalled the passion of last night. The sweetness of her sex (for the first time he understood the meaning of the sexual metaphors of "sugar" and "honey"), the pressure of her pubic bone, his body wracked like a woman's as he came down upon her. The privilege and wonder of that body he had lathered with his hands in the shower moving beneath his own. What a wasteful and impotent fool he was! He had just had that body naked in bed with him, and then naked in the shower with him, and he had not made love to it. He was now removing the same clothes he had just watched her put on while guiding her to the narrow couch in the living room. Her nakedness however did not make her seem receptive so much as vulnerable. She returned his kisses but appeared fearful of his passion, uncertain as yet whether she would respond or fight. He began to remove his clothes. Her body seemed to be in the act of cooling beneath his hands. She smelled like nothing, not even of soap. "No, not now," she said, pecking him on the lips.

Meanwhile the telephone was ringing, loudly and at length. Although it was only a few feet from the couch she made no attempt to answer it. By the time it stopped ringing she was sitting up and putting on her brassiere while Cavan, his head hung, was noticing that he was no longer aroused.

He followed her into the bedroom, where she sat on the bed and brushed her hair. She seemed both in pain and distracted. "If a man knows something about a woman," she said, "something that might hurt her . . . even if it is true, should he tell it to her?"

"I don't quite know what you mean, Sonja."

"If he tells you something that's a secret—or should be anyway—I mean even if he is right, doesn't it reveal a kind of cruelty on his part?"

Cavan was confused. Her evasion was maddening. But he was curious to learn the secret that this other man knew about her. "You're still not very helpful."

"Yes, but what do you think? I can't say more than that." The brush tore furiously at her hair. Electricity flew around the bristles.

"Well, I wouldn't think he should say it—not if he knew it would hurt her." He felt compromised, for after all the unknown man he censured could well have been in the right. At the same time he was injured that she could not bring herself to tell him everything.

"I know this man, you see. Who is writing a book—a novel, actually, and I'm a character in it—or he says I am—or someone very much like me—the main character, actually—and he says these things about me. Not just in the book but to my face too. Look, what would you think of a man like that?"

He was intimidated by the authority of her beauty, and had intimations that he would always have to come to terms with it. "Well, it's fiction, isn't it? . . . Even so, I guess I wouldn't think very much of him." He had just lost some portion of his integrity in his own eyes, and was convinced that in time he was bound to lose respect in hers.

In the efficiency kitchen she set about making breakfast. She was herself efficient and he guessed she was a compulsive housekeeper, a good cook, a woman who had to plan and program her day and keep herself busy. He could imagine her in a medical smock with her hands in her pockets, confronting a patient and the chart at the foot of his bed. There was no orange juice in the refrigerator and she asked him if he would mind running down to the store and buying some. She would not think of having breakfast without orange juice, for which she apparently had an inordinate fondness and appetite, for her garbage sacks were full of empty orange-colored cartons.

He ran down into the street, taking the sidewalk in the sunlight with what he saw in his own mind was the speed and grace of a champion miler. He felt tall and athletic and very handsome. Everyone on the street was happy and smiling at him. He bought two—no, make it three—quarts of orange juice from the Greeks and bounded back down the street and around the corner.

When he bounded like a kangaroo into her apartment singing in bad German an aria from a Viennese operetta he encountered a young man sitting at the breakfast table, drinking a cup of coffee, smoking a cigarette, and nibbling on an unbuttered triangle of toast. He was short and dark and so thin he looked emaciated, with hair that was long and curly. He looked like a Puerto Rican or Cuban. Sonja introduced him as Carlos but gave no explanation for his presence. There was more embarrassment than tension in the air. Sonja would look at Cavan but not at Carlos, while Carlos would look at Sonja but not at Cavan, and Cavan, who was willing to look at both, looked at his plate instead. He wondered if Carlos lived across the hall. Or if he was a fellow medical student of Sonja's, a foreign student perhaps. It seemed more likely, however, that he was a laboratory technician or assistant. The truth was he resembled a busboy. Cavan believed that Sonja was innocent of the fact of his presence, that she was as disappointed with it as he was. He suspected that Carlos had a crush on her, or at least enjoyed her company, and that she was merely compassionate toward him. If this were so he felt sorry for Carlos, the woman's lover having suddenly arrived on the scene to spoil his moment in the sun. He was also embarrassed for him, and was willing to forget the annoyance he had felt at his ruining the private breakfast he was to have had with Sonja. There would be a thousand such breakfasts in the future for him. He could give up one.

With an awkward nod to both Cavan and Sonja, Carlos soon left in the hurry of someone late for work. Cavan decided this was none of his business and that he would say nothing about it. Besides his silence on the matter would demonstrate a certain toughness and nonchalance, qualities he would need in that battle he expected he would have to wage against the authority of her beauty.

A plate of fried eggs and bacon was set before him on a place mat shaped like an orange, along with a large glass (decorated with oranges) of orange juice. She drank her own glass in one draught, as though it were medicine, and poured herself another. When he complimented her on the eggs and bacon, which were cooked perfectly, a rare skill for a woman, she responded with enthusiasm. "Why don't I make a great gourmet dinner for you!" She was like a little girl, clapping her hands.

"I'd love that," he said. But he detected something vaguely ominous in her offer. He was not certain that she meant it, or if she did, that she would remember it an hour from now, or that she wasn't bribing him with it, for what exactly he was afraid to guess.

"Good," she said. "Now, what have you got to do today?"

"I don't know . . . I was thinking I'd see my father . . ."

"Why don't you do that? I have to study some and then go to my job at the lab."

"I've got a better idea. Why don't you stay home?" He would give up seeing his father in the morgue if she would stay.

She smiled. "I can't," she said. "I have experiments to update. And I need the money. I'm not almost penniless. I am penniless."

"Please." He took her hand. "It's only for today. For me."

She continued to smile.

"Why don't you get off early, then?"

The smile again, which he interpreted, because he wanted to, as that in this she would acquiesce.

He helped her wash the dishes, which she cleaned immediately, along with sink and table, scrubbing them until the soap raised a lather. She then went to a butterfly chair, taking a medical book and glass of orange juice with her. He looked over her shoulder at the diagram of a cross section of some unrecognizable portion of the body that fascinated her. He felt increasingly awkward in the apartment, and in her presence, and on an impulse he kissed her once and forced himself to stride out the door.

As he rode the bus across the sunlit city on his way to the County Morgue, Sonja's reticence and the haste of his own departure troubled him. His feeling of foreboding deepened. She had promised him that fantastic gourmet dinner—but when? He had assumed for tonight, but might it not be months from now on a date of her own choosing? And what time would she come home from work tonight? And if she did come home early, what time would that be? What time should he be there for dinner, assuming he should be there at all? He assumed he would see her tonight, indeed that he would again spend the night with her, but not only had they made no such arrangement, they had made no arrangement to see each other again at all. How could she have let him leave the house without a date fixed between them?

He also wondered if it might not have been Carlos calling on the phone when he lay with Sonja on the couch. Had she expected Carlos for breakfast, which would go far in explaining her reluctance to make love this morning?

The County Morgue was in the compound of the Cook County Hospital, itself a large decaying city set in a section of the city of similar decay. Here the patients were poor and mostly black, and attended to by blacks, and suffering from almost every known disease and injury in overcrowded environs that proclaimed that same futility and ugliness they had known at home when they were well. If the wards and rooms and even corridors of the hospital were crowded and noisy and often dirty and not unlike the streets and tenements just outside, the morgue was clean, uneasily quiet, and with its crowds kept out of sight. Its bright lights instead of erasing a degree of fear and gloom about the place seemed to heighten it. The air smelled perpetually of formaldehyde. At the moment three corpses were on tables on the floor, one inside a zippered plastic bag and apparently only just arrived; the other two were wrapped up in green sheets and were both black men, one of whose face was exposed, apparently yet to be replaced in trays after they had been viewed and presumably identified. Neither body was wasted with an illness but looked muscular and healthy, suggesting a death that was sudden and even violent. The power in the bodies contradicted the rigid pose, and it seemed the men had been brought here only until they recovered from anesthesia.

There was an unnaturalness about the morgue. Of some unreasonable expectation of life or afterlife. Here the dead were above the ground, on the same plane as the living, in the same quarters as the healed, intruding upon the territory of the living, as if there was still some uncertainty as to whether they were completely, or even really, dead. The corridor outside where Cavan waited was unusually crowded. The bodies of Scarponi and the murdered police officer had been brought here early in the morning, and the doctors and staff had been busy with the autopsies. Several small groups of uniformed policemen and men obviously policemen but out of uniform stood about conversing among themselves and with members of the murdered patrolman's family. There was about these men a hushed bravado and reverence and that fearlessness and insolence that preludes a justifiable and certain revenge. Close by them stood several of Scarponi's friends and relatives, a pair of younger men consoling a woman. There was about them all a beaten, surprised, and angry look. One of the men was Scarponi's brother, a former policeman himself, and he conversed familiarly in a hushed voice with a pair of policemen. He wore a large overcoat and gesticulated with his hat. It was as though in this instance, if not in others, there was a common and collusive bond between the Scarponis and the police. On the opposite end of the corridor, with Cavan alone and in between, two separate black families were gathered, grief and fear upon their faces, a tall man consoling and at times restraining a short fat woman who was hysterical and swearing in foul language when she was not walking aimlessly up and down the corridor, her hands beating against her thighs.

When the attendant came for Cavan and escorted him into a smaller room for viewing, Cavan did not know how to tell him that he only wanted to see the face of the dead man and that he could not identify him even though he was the dead man's son. Somehow he thought the authorities would find this unacceptable and refuse to let him view the body. Therefore he said nothing. The remains of the man tentatively identified as Joseph Helenowski were soon wheeled in by a black orderly and Cavan at last looked upon his father, albeit his remains. But the foreignness of the face made him startle no less than if he had actually known his father all his life and could say that this was not his face. He came close to informing the orderly that he had brought the wrong corpse to the room. If he had ever manufactured an image of his father's face, this face in no way nor in any feature resembled it. Certainly its features were far different from his own, and this difference astounded him. It was the face of a man who might have been stung to death by bees.

He tried to infer the nature of his origins in this single moment from the face of this man already dead. He knew that he was low and common but even so, he had to admit, not so much as all this. It was the face, all in one, of slave, criminal, and victim. What waste and shame and degradation the man had suffered, and the seeds of that same brutishness and anonymity and destruction were not only working at this very moment in his own cells but were stored up in his loins, linking him up with those men on either side of him. Indeed, the very remoteness of that face from any resemblance to his own forced within him an acknowledgment of his connections not only with what had been this man, but with all men, and he was overcome with a wonderful sorrow for all men, for this man before him and no less for himself and his own sons, if any, that were to come. "Father," he said, staring at the gaping mouth, the milky eyes. He placed his hand on his brow and seemed to totter toward the corpse, threatening, or so the attendant thought, to embrace it.

The deputy coroner had been set to enter the room when he caught sight of the grief upon the face of the young man inside, the tears and the shudder of the body with the sobs the man would not let out, that intense ritual of bereavement and recognition, and in deference and sympathy he paused on the threshold. He looked at the attendant and observed that he too was studying the man, only with something like awe and suspicion on his face, as though he were expecting him not to faint or even scream so much as spirit off the corpse, believing he could bring him back from the dead by carting him head and foot out of the morgue. When at last the deputy entered, Cavan was holding his handkerchief in a wet wad against his face. The deputy placed his arm on Cavan's shoulder. "This is your father?"

"Yes."

"Joseph Helenowski?"

"Yes."

The deputy now discovered why the attendant was staring at the young man in such a way. The man looked Ivy League, north shore, monied, whereas his father looked like the worst of Skid Row bums.

"What's your name?" he asked.

"John . . . John Cavan . . . that's my father . . . My mother . . . remarried," he lied.

The deputy thought this might explain it. On the other hand the face of the dead man not only did not resemble the face of his son, but did not look Polish. Rather, it seemed the face of a dissipated Mexican or Indian with possibly some Negro or Oriental mixture, who had suffered at one time from a severe skin disease that had left the face, which was now puffed up, pitted. It seemed to the deputy, who was himself a Pole, that not only was the dead man not the father of this Cavan but no man named Helenowski had been the father of the dead man. A couple of unfaithful wives, he wondered? Still there were those Poles with Mongol blood in them, who had dark skin and Oriental features. "Are you positive of your identification?" he asked. Adding, "We have to ask that of everyone when they're upset."

"Yes. He's my father." Again the sobs, this time as the man sat down, handkerchief in hand, in a nearby chair.

Now Cavan signed papers in which he identified the body as that of his father, and promised to make arrangements for the body to be sent to a funeral home when the city was ready to give it up for burial. The deputy informed him that because his father had been a victim of homicide an autopsy had been performed on his remains. Also the police would want to speak to him soon. "How was he . . . ?" Cavan began, his handkerchief around his mouth.

"He was strangled," the deputy said.

With this Cavan shook hands with both the attendant and deputy and took his leave, leaving both men with troubled thoughts.

Only minutes after Cavan left, the doctor from the sanitarium from which Helenowski had escaped arrived to make the identification. Since no living member of Helenowski's family that the coroner's office had been able to locate had seen him in thirty years, with the exception of his parents and brothers, all of whom were dead, the coroner had asked that someone from the sanitarium come down to the morgue. The doctor was a young woman, a psychologist in residence and an assistant to the psychiatrist who had been treating Helenowski and who was to have come himself yesterday but still could not come today, and had sent her in his place instead. She was not that familiar with Helenowski but would certainly be able to identify him.

The attendant had no sooner put the corpse away than he was told to bring it out again. "In and out," he mumbled to himself. "Come on, old man, we're off again."

The psychologist looked from the face of the corpse to that of the attendant and deputy coroner as though to determine if they were playing her a joke. "This isn't Helenowski," she said.

"It's not?" the deputy said, his worst fears confirmed.

She showed him the photograph in the folder of personal and medical information on Helenowski she was to surrender to the police. The man on the table and the man in the photograph were as different as a Bantu and a Chinaman.

"But we just got a positive identification," the deputy said. "From his son."

"I didn't know he had a son," the psychologist said. "I've been through his records and there's no mention of his being married. There's no mention of a son."

The attendant laughed. "I knew something was wrong," he said, shaking his head. "If that guy hadn't fooled me by crying like that and carrying on like that—"

"Quite an actor," the deputy agreed. Adding, "What do these guys do, walk in off the streets and play practical jokes on us?" He still wanted to believe that this was just another Skid Row homicide. He also wanted to believe that the man called Cavan had somehow managed to make a legitimate mistake.

At this point the chief pathologist and a police detective in plainclothes who was routinely assigned to investigate the deaths of derelicts and was assigned now to investigate the murder of the man tentatively identified as Helenowski entered the room and quietly joined the conclave that had lapsed into a stunned silence around the corpse. The pathologist complained to the psychologist that they had held up the postmortem until last night, thinking that someone from the sanitarium would come, while the detective peered over and examined the corpse's head.

The detective next attempted to interpret the various marks upon the body—in this case on the throat and head—while the pathologist evaluated his deductions, pointing at the corpse with his fountain pen and referring to the autopsy report which the detective held open in his hands. It was a game they often played, the pathologist treating the detective with amusement and superiority but pleased with his interest in anatomy.

The pathologist lifted the head delicately from behind with his fingertips while the detective peered beneath at the wounds and bruises.

"I'll bet somebody was banging his head on something while he was strangling him," the detective said.

"Possibly," the pathologist said. Suddenly he threw off the sheet, snapping it, and pointed at the stab wounds in the corpse's thighs and calves. "Interesting, isn't it?" he said.

"How did he get those?" the detective said.

"All I know," the pathologist said, "is that they didn't kill him."

"If he was in a fight, it's hard to figure how he got stabbed so many times down there, and just down there—"

"I told you it was interesting. They were made with a serrated knife of some sort. A bread knife, a steak knife, maybe a knife for cleaning fish."

The psychologist interrupted, "Did you know I can't identify this man as Helenowski?"

"Not only that," the deputy coroner said, "but we just had some clown come in here claiming to be this Helenowski's son and he identified the corpse as Helenowski."

The detective studied the photograph. "Boy, this sure isn't him, is it?" he said, passing the photograph on to the pathologist.

As the detective had earlier played pathologist, the pathologist now played detective. "If this Helenowski's identification was found in the pockets of the deceased, then this Helenowski must have murdered him and placed his identification on him."

"You may be right," the detective acknowledged. "It could be as simple as that." He turned to the deputy coroner. "Could this guy who came in here and identified him have been this Helenowski?"

"He was too young. He might have been his son, though, covering up for him or something. There could be some resemblance to the photograph."

The detective did not look convinced. He said to the psychologist, "Is Helenowski homicidal?"

A mood of excitement and tension came across the group. The psychologist said, "He wasn't my patient—"

"He wasn't your patient, lady?"

"I mean I'm not a doctor. He did have paranoid tendencies. Delusions of grandeur—"

"Who did he think he was? Napoleon?"

"He thought," the psychologist said, "that he was Death."

A shiver went through them all. "When he was playing he was Death," the detective said, "was he dangerous?"

"I suppose he could have become dangerous—"

"Could have become?" the detective echoed. "You'd better find out, lady."

After a lengthy silence during which serious looks were exchanged and heads were shaken, the deputy coroner said quietly, "Well, as far as this poor fellow was concerned he was Death all right."

"If we got a homicidal maniac running around loose on the streets we'd better find out," the detective said, clicking his tongue in disbelief at the sanitarium's incompetence. "We'd better check up on this guy who identified him, too." He considered the corpse. "But if this ain't Helenowski, who is he?"

The pathologist shrugged. He said, "What any fool can see he looks like—a dead Indian."

CHAPTER TWENTY-SIX

THE DETECTIVE AGENCY

Magnuson was on Wells Street, in the shadow of the elevated tracks, heading as he had daily in years past for the detective agency that bore his name. If the streets of the Loop had their own hierarchy of prestige, Wells Street, the western boundary of the Loop, had to place near the bottom. Its shops and offices were in the Loop but just barely. And the elevated tracks, the raw riveted steel uprights that rose through the pavement and supported that bleak canopy of raw steel beams and tracks and creosoted boards and timbers overhead, let no man forget where he was. No sky here, and no sun, only that late afternoon gloom of winter at every daylight hour of every season. And the wind once it got down into the street stayed there, chilled in shadows. It was that coldness that Magnuson remembered, when the newsdealers stamped their feet beside the fires they had in barrels on the sidewalk and the traffic policemen, surrounded by the steam of cars and manholes and bundled up in overcoats over jackets over sweaters, looked like fat, awkward man-shaped balloons. And the noise, and not only the roar of the trains but in the street the blatant laying on of car horns and the shiver of police whistles and the enraged, impatient police shouts that were commonplace but surprised like revolver shots in alleys. Here there were bricks and windows that had not seen the sun in this century. And the people who did their business here—in the tobacco shops, liquor stores, and stamp and coin shops that were common here—lived as though beneath a bridge. It was a street at the crossroads: a block to the east the beginnings of the wealth and hustle of downtown, but just across the river to the west the languorous smoky boulevards of Skid Row.

As Magnuson approached his office he noticed that the enclosed stairways leading to the elevated tracks were blocked by gates, and instead of newsdealers at the foot of those stairs there were only padlocked steel boxes. He had yet to hear a train pass overhead.

He almost failed to recognize the building that housed his office. Built of brick late in the last century it stood for the first time that he had ever seen it all alone, the buildings gone from either side of it, as though they had been demolished and hauled off in the night.

In the small lobby empty cardboard cartons were piled against a battered wall. The lone elevator was small and padded and carried freight as well as passengers. As always Ginsberg, the operator, was perched upon his stool. Toadlike, jaundiced-looking, he had been the operator long before Magnuson had come here with his fledgling agency, and Magnuson had never heard him called by any name but Ginsberg. Always in shirtsleeves and tie and baggy trousers, he gave the appearance of merely filling in for the regular operator who had gone to lunch, when in fact he had spent a quarter of his life inside that elevator, which not only smelled of those green cigars he chewed and spat and sometimes smoked but in which he performed with the same lethargy and obstinacy as the machine itself, his own pace conforming over the years to that creaking, clanking cubicle he captained. He often accompanied the reluctant and querulous noises of the elevator with his own "Sons-of-bitches . . . dirty bastards . . ." As always he neither nodded nor spoke to Magnuson.

Along the slow passage up, the elevator stopped for a man in gray work clothes and the dolly he pushed out of an oily shipping room; stopped again in what seemed minutes later to discharge man and dolly on the next floor. Automatically Ginsberg reached out for the gate and let Magnuson out on his own floor.

But despite his turns up and down the corridors Magnuson failed to find the name of his agency lettered on the white frosted windows of the half a dozen doors. Wisconsin Pulp Testing, Ace Novelty Co., Great Lakes Import, but no Magnuson Agency. But he was on the right floor! He was standing before the right door! The tapping of typewriters, the chattering of machinery as though something were being stitched.

He entered the Windsor Laboratories, where he was convinced his agency should have been, and asked the secretary, who sat with her shoes off behind the oak desk piled with reports, where the Magnuson Agency was located in the building. She seemed surprised that her office should have a visitor and called to a man who came in a white and inexplicably bloody laboratory smock from a room Magnuson was certain should have been his office. He held a silvery sounder-like instrument in his hand. In the dirty window behind him an el train passed, unfocused and somehow remote, as though it were not a part of this scene. "Not in this building," the man said. "Didn't you check the directory downstairs?"

"Wait a minute," the secretary said, getting up in her stockinged feet and placing her hands on her hips. "They had an office in this building about ten years ago."

"You couldn't prove it by me," the man said.

"The Magnuson Agency," the secretary said. "I seen that over on LaSalle Street. It's lettered up there on one of them windows."

But the man in the smock studied her skeptically, as though it was his opinion that the Magnuson Agency did not exist.

Out in the corridor Magnuson stood dumbfounded and ashamed, his hat held in both hands at his breast as though he stood before an open grave. He had come to the wrong building, the old building where neither he nor the agency had had offices for years! Had come when he had so little time to waste! And Ginsberg had taken him to his floor as if those ten years ago were yesterday and did not exist. It was like being shown his tomb.

Even his old office had appeared unchanged. Plaster walls still that glossy green and smooth with the many coats of paint, and the white streaks where the wall had cracked and been patch-plastered but not repainted. The dirty windows painted shut, the soot along the window sills. The metal filing cabinets, the wooden floor without covering or varnish and showing where furniture and even machinery had been bolted in the past. The same smell too, of oil in contact with hot metal, cigars, glossy paper, ink.

When he had resigned from the police force, not the least reason for which had been the failure of the department to promote him to sergeant even though he had scored the highest mark on the examination, he founded his own detective agency on the money his wife had received in inheritance from the sale of an apartment building her father had owned, renting his first office in this building. In those days before the creation of the Magnuson Men, when the agency had been a detective agency and only that and he was the only person working in the office, this building had been the proper setting for his calling. The shabbiness and grimness, the sense of slumming and participation in a shameful and secret action for which one was justified in feeling guilt, was in his judgment only fitting. His profession did not mean space, fresh air, comfort, light. It dealt with shame, weakness, meanness, dirt, and more often than not with spying on unfaithful wives and husbands with a prejudice to proving infidelity. In his office neither he nor his clients were allowed the luxury of forgetting the demeaning nature of their business.

If Magnuson had had his way they would not have moved from this building, nor off Wells Street. But with the expansion and volume of their business, and the increase in employees and the prestige of their new clients, Shannon and O'Bannon had sought more fashionable and convenient quarters. In their new offices on LaSalle Street they were among banks, brokerage houses, railroad, steamship, and airline offices, an address with prestige. Here their clients were no longer ashamed or aggrieved private persons but credit bureaus, law firms, corporations, banks; and their investigatory business was by far secondary in importance to that done by the ushers and industrial guards called the Magnuson Men. Indeed, Magnuson suspected that the better portion of the investigatory branch, which was supervised by Shannon, did little more than industrial and even political spying, employing manpower far less than sensitive electronic cameras and microphones.

On LaSalle Street the crowds were not so dense as elsewhere in the Loop and were comprised mainly of gray-haired men in gray homburgs and gray overcoats unbuttoned on gray suits. They walked in groups of twos and threes, conversing good-naturedly and greeting those passers-by they knew. They were in no great hurry and they paused to shake hands and introduce their friends. The street seemed to be their own private inner courtyard enclosed by gray walls of several hundred feet in which they could stroll, as though in a garden, and take the air.

Up the swift crowded automatic elevator to a floor above the city and the carpeted office of the Magnuson Agency, where he was stopped by a teen-age receptionist sitting with her hands folded at a large glass-topped desk on which sat nothing, not even a telephone. She looked like a high-fashion model. She did not know him, and when he identified himself did not believe him. When he showed her his identification (he had the honorary Magnuson Men badge Number 1 pinned to the inside of his wallet) she apologized and let him pass.

The main office was large, with three rows of ten desks each at which sat clerks and secretaries. Several men in the Magnuson Men uniforms were sitting uncomfortably in chairs, waiting for special assignments or pay envelopes. Magnuson hoped to slip into his office unnoticed, but he encountered O'Bannon immediately as he was coming out of his office in his shirtsleeves, a folder of papers under his arm. O'Bannon with his black curly hair, white freckled skin, and blue eyes that glittered gave the impression that he was both bookish and pretty, and resembled less the chief of this office than he did a minor clerk. Both he and the third partner, Shannon, were graduates of Notre Dame and of John Marshall Law School at night. Whereas Shannon was a public man, O'Bannon was private. Shannon had even been a policeman for a few years mainly to gain experience and make connections, and Magnuson suspected he someday aspired to a political career. But O'Bannon had always worked in law offices in capacities that never took him near a courtroom. If Shannon was the agency's public relations man, O'Bannon was its manager. Apparently the agency, which functioned efficiently and profitably, required no other leader in any other capacity.

O'Bannon was surprised to see Magnuson and wagered that he had not been in the office for at least a year.

"I came in to get some work done," Magnuson said, almost apologetically.

O'Bannon put his arm on Magnuson's back in what Magnuson interpreted as an awkward attempt to patronize him and led him over to the water cooler, where he put the folder of papers up before his face. "You must have heard about Scarponi," he whispered. "What was he up to that he could come to an end like that?"

Magnuson shrugged.

"I wonder what's going to happen to Scarponi's stores?" O'Bannon said. "Maybe now we'll find out who really had the money behind them, although I bet they put up another front man."

"Maybe," Magnuson said.

Feeling rebuffed, O'Bannon said, "Let me know if you need anything." Inside his private office, Magnuson found a pair of teen-age girls with cigarettes in their mouths sorting papers into piles that were strewn across his desk and chairs and even on the floor. O'Bannon was at his heels apologizing and explaining that since he no longer used the office he sometimes allowed the girls to use it. The girls were flustered and kept dropping the thick sheafs of paper they picked up and hugged against their breasts. Girl file clerks in his office. Sorting papers.

Alone, he shut the drapes upon the city. He was suddenly overcome with desperation. The bodies would be discovered. The police would come for him at any minute. Gradually his spirits rose, at least enough so that he felt that he could function. If he had to, why couldn't he direct and co-ordinate the investigation without ever leaving here? After all, he had thousands of employees at his beck and call, and telephones and files of information. He began to feel the power of the office, the agency, the street, the city behind him. This was the new age. Here in this office with the information and power of the city at his fingertips, and not in a car on a lonesome chase at night, was where he had the clear advantage over the murderers.

The mysterious notebook found in Farquarson's safe, with its peculiar notations in boxing abbreviations. TKO, D, KO. The two-column headings on each page, N and W. He studied page after page but could make no more of the code than he could last night. He was wasting time in trying. He still had the intimation that this might well prove to be the most important clue he had. He gave the book to a file clerk and told her to go to a newspaper office and check the sports sections of old papers to see if boxing matches had taken place on the listed dates. If they had, she was to write down the names of the fighters and the round and manner in which each fight had ended.

He thought of calling a garage and sending them out to locate and retrieve the Duesenberg but decided against it. The car didn't matter to him now. He also decided against calling Mrs. Rotterdam. There was no reason for her life to be in danger.

Farquarson's nurse had claimed that Farquarson had been frightened of a man named Helenowski, a recent escapee of a mental hospital who had been found murdered in Chicago the night before last. Something familiar in the name of Helenowski, and in connection with Farquarson, too. He called police headquarters, identified himself, and learned from an officer who showed him deference that Helenowski had indeed escaped from a mental hospital and that a man carrying his identification had been found dead two nights ago in Washington Square. It was a case of homicide. The body was presently in the morgue and as far as the officer knew had yet to be positively identified but an autopsy had been performed and death was due to strangulation. He promised Magnuson that if there was a positive identification of the body or an arrest of a suspect he would let him know as soon as possible. If Magnuson could believe the nurse, then the one man Farquarson had been frightened of was already dead when Farquarson was murdered.

He found the Farquarson folder in his private files. Among the copies of correspondence and reports, including drafts and even notes, for Magnuson could never bring himself to throw away anything he had committed to paper, was a sub-folder entitled, to his surprise and satisfaction, Helenowski, Joseph. More than twenty-five years ago Farquarson had ordered an investigation of this Helenowski and his family, and Magnuson himself had personally conducted all aspects of the investigation. No reason for the investigation, apparently, had been given.

The Helenowski family had owned a one-story yellow brick factory, on the northwest side of the city next to the Northwestern Railroad tracks, that manufactured the partitioned plastic trays in which drugstores displayed their gum packages and candy bars. He had not interviewed the mother and father, neither of whom apparently spoke much English. A sister was in a convent. There were four brothers in all, two of whom were the president and vice-president of the factory. He saw from his notes that he had interviewed one of them, Chester—the president, he guessed—at the factory. He had maintained that Joseph was not mentally ill but was suffering from a nervous breakdown, adding that Joseph had always been bright and sensitive and should have been a professor or priest and that he could recover and be home with the family and in the factory any day now. But Chester Helenowski and the time and place and their conversation remained cloudy to Magnuson.

He remembered the second brother, Eugene, the vice-president, better. A bitter winter day and his car, with chains on the tires, had been parked beside a huge mound of snow. He had engaged the brother in the snow outside a milk store without revealing he knew who he was. The man had been a giant, wearing a Russian fur hat and a fur-collared coat, and Magnuson could clearly recall him standing with a gallon jug of milk in either mitten, the smoke pouring from his mouth. According to the notes, he had in the course of their casual conversation spoken vehemently against Negroes and Jews, denounced a sister-in-law who had just divorced one of his brothers as a "German Pole," later as a "Southern Pole." Had spoken with ridicule of low-class peasant immigrants from the Old Country. And against Germans, especially "Russian Germans." He had claimed that Poland, translated, meant "Land of the Poets." That he had a younger brother so sensitive he was in a sense a poet and presently in a rest home for artists who, as everyone knew, had a problem with their nerves on top of having delicate health. Also that he and his family were descended from counts and princes in the Old Country and possessed a coat of arms which he would show Magnuson if he called at the factory. He and his brothers were factory owners, he explained.

The third brother, Zigmont, reported to be a playboy, ballroom dancer, gambler, heavy drinker, and ladies' man, and to have something of the honorary position of sales manager in the factory. He had told Magnuson not to believe a word his brothers said about their family. Why, the family wasn't Polish at all, but Austrian, the "old man" having been born in what was then the Austro-Hungarian Empire. His mother's maiden name was even German—Teuscher—didn't it sound German to Magnuson? (Magnuson recalled that one of the brothers—and he wondered which one—had been elected to congress a dozen years ago or so as a Democrat but, since his district was usually Republican, had only served one term.)

Magnuson had interviewed Joseph at the private and inexpensive hospital where he was committed, and Magnuson guessed that it had been a matter of pride among his family that they had been able to keep him there. It appeared that Farquarson had used his influence in some way to contrive the meeting. Now from the pages written in his own hand a quarter of a century ago he tried to resurrect the man from the pages. The thin face with high cheekbones, the high waves of chestnut hair brushed back, the white shirt with a large pointed collar open at the throat. During the interview the man had claimed to be a descendant of a Polish prince: the Polish eagle was on his family coat of arms; claimed to be a wealthy industrialist, a "captain of industry" at a frontier of industrial discovery and production; further asserted that he was not Polish at all but a Polish-American, later that he was simply an American; that he possessed extraordinary powers of destruction; that he had been imprisoned here so as to be purified and to prepare himself for the day of his release, so that all his powers would be potent, wholesome, and intact; on the other hand, he wasn't imprisoned at all but was merely being protected in an impregnable fortress; he was here to be kept safe from his enemies, who were watching him and would kill him if they could; he was also here because of the grand design and destiny that was to be his life; he was simply to wait here until a new identity was revealed to him. He asserted repeatedly that he was very optimistic for the future and that he could do anything he wanted, including walking out the gates of this marvelous fort; he maintained he had done nothing wrong and that he had been unjustly imprisoned; on the other hand, he considered the hospital a just punishment for his sins which, he claimed, were many. Cosmic forces were to reveal his new identity; he would save America and destroy it; he could do this because he was the best of the Americans; his destiny was to become a great American patriot; Poles were wonderful people; on the other hand, Poles were barbarians; he sometimes believed he and the nation were doomed by God and would soon be destroyed; if that were ever the case, he speculated, he thought he would be God's instrument; he was waiting here in this marvelous fort for that historical moment when his country would summon him to save it and he could then fulfill his destiny.

Magnuson had left with the impression that he was full of nonsense and contradictions. He appeared intelligent; although he had attended Loyola University briefly he seemed self-educated, and frequently misused words. Magnuson had concluded he was probably insane.

But now he saw that this Helenowski must have been the father of John Cavan, Hope Farquarson's child conceived and born in the asylum that Solomon Chandler had told him about last night. It would explain why Farquarson had wanted Helenowski investigated in such detail. The time of the investigation must have been just before or just after Cavan's birth. Perhaps his report had even had some bearing on Farquarson's decision to take Cavan in as his nephew. He had simply put down most of Helenowski's long-winded chatter without comment. He now wondered if Farquarson had actually believed the nonsense about being an industrialist and super-American and related to counts and princes and had concluded that Cavan had been sired of satisfactory stock.

How much Magnuson had learned! He could understand why Farquarson might have feared for his life when he learned that this Helenowski had escaped. After all, he had had a quarter century to nurse his grudge against Farquarson for having separated him from Farquarson's wife. But how did Helenowski's death contribute to the solution of the mystery? Was it possible that father and son had conspired together against the dying Farquarson but that Helenowski, having been used in some way necessary for the preparation of the crime, had been silenced before the actual murder?

Then the sub-folder on Hope Farquarson, which contained a copy of the final report he had sent to Farquarson, along with his own daily reports and the small handwritten notes of that investigation he had made of her some thirty years ago. Separated from Farquarson, she had gone down to Chicago where she moved nightly from one hotel to another, the hotels varying in quality from the two Ambassadors to small cheap hotels for pensioners and transients. From his own unfamiliar handwriting the lanky, attractive woman and the Chicago streets that for ten straight days she walked and he pursued her down came alive inside his head. Very white and blond and delicate and with her blue veins visible erotically within her flesh she had given the impression of having suffered a recent illness, tuberculosis perhaps, and having just left a hospital or even prison. Every day she had walked those streets, beginning late in the morning and stopping only late at night when she would pause on the sidewalk to massage her feet, leaning against a lamppost or even fire hydrant; walked in the same white pumps and wrinkled summer skirt and blouse with a button or two usually left unbuttoned and the tuck loose from the skirt, the same off-white summer coat carried over her arm and with that small white suitcase in hand, looking always as though she had just arrived in the city and was amazed at what she saw. Often in the heat of her walk her face and underarms would sweat. Her distraction was such that he soon discovered he could follow her with impunity and grow so bold as to stand beside her as she looked into a store window. Often he was not the only man who followed her. For she seemed to send off in her wake some stimulating fragrance that suggested she was helplessly indiscriminate in her taste of men and as agreeable and placid in bed as though bound and gagged and sleeping. Old men, teen-age boys, black men, well-dressed businessmen, and tramps

were all equally attracted and emboldened enough to approach or
speak or follow or at the very least to stop and stare, mistaking, perhaps, her distraction for sensuality and her air of helplessness for
liberality with sex. Men seemed to fall out of doors to get in step
beside her, and in reply to their invitations and flatteries and filthy
suggestions in filthy language, as far as Magnuson could tell, she
would only smile. She was oblivious to the men, or else she misunderstood them, as though she saw them in her head as tipping their hats
and saying, "Madam, good day." She passed through the hot streets
and breezy parks of the city with her head high, her face confused
but smiling good-naturedly at all she saw, oblivious, Magnuson would
have wagered, to fires, explosions, and toppling buildings until the
most persistent of the men who accosted her gave up with fatigue
and dropped beside the way in anger and confusion, as though they
believed she had accosted them only to reject them, making them
ridiculous in their own eyes. She seemed driven to go daily into the
city in search of something, as other people in those times went out
in search of work.

She had stayed one night at the Edgewater Beach Hotel and
in the morning had gone out on the marshy beach to swim, changing in one of the cabanas that had been there then. She emerged
beautiful but pale and still looking confused and ill, childishly delighted with the sun, the sand, the water, her chair immediately
besieged by the few men and boys on the beach. Something careless even in the way she wore her fashionable swimming suit, for it
seemed tight where it should have been loose, and loose where it
should have been tight, and Magnuson suspected that if he were
close to her he would see her pubic hair and the tops of her nipples.
For hours she dived into the breakers and rode them to the shore,
splashing like a squealing girl. Later she swam in deep water back
and forth the length of the beach and up and down on the incoming
waves, her head often disappearing from his sight.

Another night she led him out onto the horseshoe pier that went
out into the lake at Montrose Beach. She wandered past the tower
with its blinking light and the smelt and herring fishermen and their
lanterns fishing off the inside of the pier and facing the city and
stood at the very end of the pier, on the lake side, where the wind
blew and the water was rough and the night was black and there
was no horizon or light to be seen. She stood there with her shoulders hunched and her hands in her pockets, her hair wind-blown.
Sometimes during that long night he thought he could see her step

forward and he felt he could tolerate it no longer and would have to go up to her and grab her and drag her back. Only with the coming of the dawn did the night watch end.

He often wondered if she knew that she was being followed, especially when, because of her distraction, he tended to grow careless, sometimes deliberately so, as though daring her to acknowledge that she knew that he was there and, perhaps, why. He began to suspect that her innocent behavior was for his benefit alone, and that her perpetual smile mocked him. He began to predict and anticipate a total breakdown into perversion and immorality, like a weekend drunk after a month of hard work and abstinence. She would explode before his eyes or within his hearing, would fill her room with Negro drummers or punk kids. Even now, he had reasoned, she must do something abnormal when she was beyond his sight and hearing and in the privacy of her hotel room, like taking drugs or masturbating excessively and unusually, something she did alone. For despite his taking rooms next to hers, where he put his ear against the wall, or a room across the street, from which he stared into her window, the shades of which were never drawn, or standing in the street and looking up at that window, or loitering in the lobby and observing who went in and out, in the ten days he watched her she did nothing that he could say was wrong.

But the peculiar facts he had chosen to set down in his notes. They contradicted or at least distorted his present memories of the affair. And what strange conclusions he seemed to have reached in his report to Farquarson, the copy of which he now studied. He had implied a judgment or, what was worse, had appeared to have attempted unsuccessfully to conceal some degenerate or unstable habits of her character. Surely there were missing notes or some knowledge he had kept in his head to substantiate these veiled but apparently unfounded innuendoes and conclusions. Or had he simply failed to be fair and objective and let his own suspicions and even frustrations concerning that woman intrude upon her character and impose themselves upon the impartiality of his report? If so, he had been incompetent. How could he have been so unfair? Was this what his profession, his life, had been all about? He must have been a different man then, as the unfamiliar handwriting attested. And if his later report on Helenowski had influenced Farquarson's decision to take Cavan into his family, he wondered how much this report had influenced Farquarson's decision to have his wife institutionalized in a sanitarium.

Also in her folder was a handwritten memorandum concerning an inquiry he had made into the credentials and reputation of a Chicago doctor named Lopko, who performed abortions. He had been in contact in this matter with Farquarson's doctor on the north shore, a man named Archer. But he could not recall this investigation at all, even though by the date it was made only two weeks after he had sent his final report on Hope Farquarson to Farquarson.

He went out into the office to look up the address of the apartment on the Gold Coast that Cavan had said last night he was returning to, and encountered Tip O'Neil at the paymaster's window, in a baggy, shiny, navy blue uniform and the badge and cap of the Magnuson Men Industrial Patrol. His daughter's shrewish landlady had said he had gone to work—working, as it now turned out, for Magnuson. That was only yesterday morning. It was only the night before last that he had played pinochle with O'Neil and Schneider and the murdered Scarponi in his apartment. How much had happened since then. As if that night were in a former lifetime, lived a century ago. O'Neil, the retired Chicago police captain, the former police sergeant and academy instructor of Magnuson himself, now a Magnuson Man.

"I'm one of your Men now, Maggy," O'Neil said. He seemed embarrassed by the uniform. "I thought I'd pick up some spending money and keep out of mischief while I was up North."

Magnuson was about to berate him for failing to tell him the other night that he was working as a Magnuson Man so that he could use his influence on his behalf in his own company, when it occurred to him that O'Neil had already done for himself whatever Magnuson could have done for him. He had no doubt bragged to Shannon and O'Bannon and whatever Magnuson Man captain he was assigned to of his close friendship and influence with Magnuson himself, and had been given in response an easy and even meaningless job and was now picking up his pay prematurely so as to have immediate cash for liquor.

"Christ, I almost didn't come to work for you today," O'Neil said, his breath sour and his face red. "The milkman left a bottle of Scotch at my door yesterday and I thought I'd better have the empty for him to pick up this morning." His mood quickly grew darker. "It was Scarponi's brand of Scotch, too. I think he must have left it there or sent one of his boys over to deliver it. What a guy! Who would want to kill a guy like that? What a shame! Why, I was just playing pinochle with him the other night. He was my partner, too." He seemed to have forgotten already that Magnuson had also been there, that the game had been held at Magnuson's house. "And it's a shame about that young patrolman getting killed by the guy that killed Scarponi." His eyes watered and he let fly a string of obscene words until, discovering the girls at the desks laughing, he covered his mouth, laughed himself, and apologized to all, exercising his Irish charm as he explained to them about the murder of Scarponi, his good friend he was playing cards with just the other night, and the murder of the young policeman, and that he was himself a former police captain and instructor of rookie patrolmen, one of whom was now Maurice Comiskey, the superintendent of police. He hoped that this explained and justified his anger and inexcusable language in front of women.

It now occurred to Magnuson that if he could bring himself to use agents wherever possible he could multiply his efforts, could, in a sense, multiply himself. After all, he had the whole agency and the political and financial arms of the city at his disposal if he needed them. His search for the killer, and what was at stake behind that search, he decided, included far more than just himself. He took Tip aside. "I think I've got a lead into Scarponi's death," he said. "Which means a lead into the death of that cop, too. I don't want to let the police in on it until I'm certain of the facts. I don't want to look like a fool." If he could keep O'Neil sober he could, by extension, be in two places at once. He asked O'Neil if he would get out of his uniform and spend a few hours trailing one John Cavan who had an apartment on Goethe Street on the Gold Coast. He was to record where he went and with whom and everything he saw him do or overheard him say. Magnuson would call him up for the information later. In the absence of a photograph of Cavan he gave O'Neil his description.

"I don't know," O'Neil said. "If you got anything you ought to tell the detectives—"

"I think this kid Cavan may be involved in the murders," Magnuson said, his voice as passionate as O'Neil's had been earlier. "But he has connections and I don't want to make any accusations until I'm sure. We ought to be able to handle this, Tip. We used to be policemen. We can still do our jobs."

The most O'Neil would promise, however, was that he would look in on this Cavan on his way home.

Back in his office Magnuson looked through the afternoon papers. Still no reports of any of the murders of last night. Miraculously he was being granted still more time in which to act. He reasoned he would be safe for at least the night. Wenzel's tavern was simply closed for the day, as the sign he had left on the door proclaimed. The bodies of the fisherman and Bonny Wenzel would stay on the bottom of the lake and although he was certain they would drag the lake for the fisherman, since his empty boat would have been found floating on the lake, unless they hooked Bonny's first he would be safe, for they would believe the fisherman's death was accidental. Skipper, the Moonys' son, was on his way to Florida, and if anyone did call at the Moonys they would merely assume no one was home. There was no reason for anyone to investigate the barn where Wenzel's body lay, since his truck was not in sight and the livestock was silent. Rotterdam was locked up in an empty apartment, while his wife believed he was hiding from her deliberately. His one weak spot was at Farquarson's, where there was Farquarson's corpse and the two live women who were themselves possible suspects of the crimes, potential victims of the murderer, and potential informants against himself. He wanted to be certain that the nurse, despite his threat of blackmail, did not escape or notify the police. More importantly, he wanted to honor his commitment to protect her and to ease his own sense of failure and inadequacy by doing so. Although he could discover no reason why her life should be endangered.

Next he asked O'Bannon to recommend the best man available in the agency for a discreet and difficult assignment. O'Bannon after consulting the files came up with a Chicago policeman named Meyer, presently on vacation, who had received a number of bonuses as a Magnuson Man and numerous citations as a police officer.

When Meyer answered the phone Magnuson imagined him before the ballgame on his television set, weeding the back yard, working with a wood lathe in the basement. He was flattered that this assignment came from no less than Magnuson himself. Magnuson informed him that this was to be a job of special sensitivity for which he would receive extra compensation, and directed him to Farquarson's estate in Lake Forest, where he was to stand guard all night. There were woods and outbuildings he could lurk behind, although Magnuson could see no reason why he should not show himself. Only two women and a seriously ill man were inside the house; he was there ostensibly to protect them, and it would be easiest to protect them if they could be prevailed upon to remain indoors. In other words, he was to do everything possible to keep them inside the house, although he suspected he would only have to identify himself as an agent of Mr. Magnuson to convince them to return indoors. He was to go armed and was to prevent anyone from entering the house that he could, and was to be on special lookout for a gang of youths in a red convertible and a group of Negroes. With either he was to use caution. If a John Cavan came to the house he was to let him enter but not exit again, and he was to notify Magnuson as soon as possible.

The battle plan then was this: O'Neil would follow Cavan on the Gold Coast, and Meyer would watch the Farquarson house in Lake Forest, while Magnuson himself investigated Chandler, since he would have easy access to the people and information of his world. But first he had to secure the services of someone to investigate the possibility of that black conspiracy of Lena and her chauffeur husband and the mysterious Preacher and Mrs. Nettles and possibly even that illegitimate daughter of Farquarson's wife. It meant trips to both the Evanston and Chicago colored sections and he was wise enough to know that a white man could not acquire information readily from the people living there.

He decided to contact Maynard Robinson, a Negro and former employee of the Magnuson Agency, whom everyone had called by his nickname, "Lucky." He had been something of a glorified office and errand boy, and might deliver money to the bank or be sent out for coffee. Occasionally he served Shannon and O'Bannon and more often Magnuson as a chauffeur on business trips around the city. Sometimes he was sent out to make minor investigations in the black neighborhoods. With Magnuson's retirement he had been kept on temporarily at the insistence of Magnuson, who had originally hired him and often protected him from both Shannon and O'Bannon, who were adamant in their judgment that he was worthless and should go. O'Bannon would not have him or any other Negro as a member of his office staff and Shannon would not have him as one of his investigators, and all other positions in the agency were only part-time. Finally, seeing no future for Robinson in the agency, Magnuson had used the considerable influence he had to put Robinson on the Chicago police force. Since then he had lost touch with him, had neither seen nor thought of him for more than a year. He was certain Robinson would help him. He was the Negro Magnuson knew best, and he owed Magnuson many favors.

He called Captain Gaughan, an officer he knew vaguely and who also owed him a few favors, at police personnel. After consulting his records the captain informed him that Robinson wasn't stationed anywhere. In fact, he wasn't even on the force. "Him and another jig were kicked off the force six months ago," he said. "Some jitterbug took their service revolvers away and sent them back to the station with nothing but their hands in their holsters."

Magnuson was shocked. He wondered what Gaughan meant by "jitterbug." He had a picture of a drunken or doped-up black man in zootsuit forcing Robinson and his partner, both in uniform, to perform a softshoe on the sidewalk before an audience of hundreds while he held their revolvers, one in either hand, upon them. He was hurt to learn that Robinson had not acquainted him with the difficulties he had had on the force and allowed Magnuson to use his influence to protect him. Perhaps considering all that Magnuson had done for him he was too ashamed.

"How come you're interested in this guy?" Gaughan asked.

"He used to work for me," Magnuson said. "I put him on the force."

"Well, Jesus Christ, you didn't say nothing about it to no one at the time," Gaughan said defensively. "I didn't know you were recommending him." The implication was that had he or the department known Robinson was a favorite of Magnuson's, or had Magnuson brought pressure to bear at the proper time, the man would still be on the force. Because Magnuson had not, the implication continued, he had only himself to blame. For his part Gaughan seemed genuinely sorry and even angry that Magnuson had not used his power as he should have, for how else would anyone know the man had power behind him? He certainly shouldn't hold this business against anyone, least of all Captain Gaughan himself.

Magnuson's disappointment, however, was shortlived. For his purposes it was far better that Robinson was no longer a policeman. And better yet that he had known dishonor.

The office girl now returned from the newspaper office where Magnuson had sent her to learn what she could about the mysterious notations in Farquarson's notebook. He compared the information she had taken down from the newspapers with the notations in the notebook. He was onto something all right! Farquarson had not used the terminology of prize fighting as a code for something else, for there had indeed been boxing matches on the dates listed in the notebook and the outcome of each fight corresponded exactly to the notebook, both the means of victory and the round in which the fight had ended. Everything was explainable then except the heading of the fighters (there were no names), each of whom was either N or W. Over the years the N fighters had gotten the best of the W fighters, for a running score had been kept after each fight. What was the key to those abbreviations? He studied the names of the boxers who had participated in the matches Farquarson had listed and which the girl had written down on her sheet. He recognized most of the names. And then the truth came to him with a surprise that nearly had him rising in his chair and pounding his desk in rage. It was unbelievable! This was to have been the most important clue he had in the solution of the murders! N stood for Negro, W for white. In every case where he recognized the name the formula held true. It explained why the weeks were not consecutive, too, since on many nights the two boxers had been both black, or both white, and Farquarson had only watched and recorded fights that were confrontations between black and white.

In a fit of rage he threw Farquarson's notebook against the wall. Was this what Farquarson had done over the years in his leisure moments? The week-long anticipation of the fight and the disappointment when the boxers were of the same race but the secret excitement and glee when they were not and he sat before the television with his fists clenched and the secret notebook on his lap. The joy that must have been his when the white boxer won. The frustration and disappointment when the victor was black. The notebook wrapped up in rubber bands and hidden in the deepest recess of the safe beside his bed as though it were not only his most valuable possession but the most shameful. When he had so little time to work in was this how the clues he had would resolve themselves, in nonsense that related to the crimes in no way at all?

The telephone of Robinson, he now learned, had been disconnected. He gazed out the large window of his office at the smoggy evening settling on the skyscrapers of the city. Lights were coming on in the windows of the buildings on the darker streets, as were the headlights of distant cars. He feared the night, and another night like last night. As though summoned he would have to leave this office and go out into the city; would have to do first thing tonight that which he had most hoped to avoid doing; would have to go in the alien and dangerous neighborhoods of Negroes, not in search of the black conspiracy but of Maynard Robinson, whom he wished to send in pursuit of that conspiracy. He dreaded the possibility of further justice in even greater dishonor and deeper degradation, although he still held on to that faint hope that he could save himself and realign himself with what was right.

CHAPTER TWENTY-SEVEN

THE GOLD COAST

In the history of the world another son in search of traces of his father. John Cavan walking through the Gold Coast on his way to Bughouse Square, driven to look upon his father's place of death as he was driven earlier to look upon his father's face. Like a clairvoyant who receives impressions of a man by merely laying hands upon his clothes, he is driven by his need to feel and to intuit as much as by his need to know.

A woman with dwarf-like legs that look like stockings stuffed with sawdust pushes a hurdy-gurdy the size of a small car along the gutter. Beneath the canopy of a nightclub a navy captain with silver sideburns in the company of men in homburgs and women with silver hair in silver furs waits for a taxi as a passing homosexual with his hair curled in a poodle-cut and waddling his large, high-waisted buttocks says, "A fucking admiral no less." Along an iron fence a

394

sidewalk exhibition of canvases of out-of-focus gypsies, sad-eyed clowns, smeary matadors, attended by a middle-aged woman in Levi's and cowboy shirt and a bearded boy in a poncho and a stocky pig-tailed girl in a sweatsuit smeared with paint. Here someone takes Cavan by the sleeve. "This world around them," Kay Wanda whispers, indicating the neon of the nightclubs, the glitter of the taxis in the streets, the swagger of style and opulence and industry and indolence along the crowded sidewalks, "not to mention themselves, and they paint . . . this. Although I admit I'm a sucker for anything, no matter how bad, of clowns. They must figure that people picture themselves as one of the three. The free gypsy. The sad clown. The brave mata-dor." She looks lonely and exhausted. Her face so white it is almost blue, but rosy just beneath the surface of the cheeks as though flaring with some recent exhilaration or exercise. She makes an open and apologetic appeal to him for company. He feels he should not allow himself to be used in this way, that he should be watchful of his new-found freedom and wary of those who would clutch him by the knees.

They walk together onto residential streets with shade trees. Victorian townhouses converted into apartments. Deserted sidewalks. Unlit windows as though the residents are on the streets of other neighborhoods. A lingering twilight as though the sun has stopped not far below the horizon in the west. A hot-dog vendor in the gutter beneath a locust, sitting in a white apron on a folding chair beside his wagon. A storklike man bounding down the front steps of the building, a paper sack in hand and his face hidden behind the open book he is reading. A car at the curb with its hood up, a man pro-truding, from the waist down, from the engine, his feet off the ground, looking as though someone has stuck him there. Suddenly she takes Cavan's hand; her hand is cold but moist.

"Is something wrong?" he says.

"Wrong?—What do you mean wrong?—Do you feel it too?"

"Feel what?" he asks, alarmed.

"That someone is following us?"

Only empty sidewalk at their backs. Across the street something taking form between a tree and a mailbox. A face or only a branch of blowing leaves? Someone in a window or gangway whistling. The distant narcotic twang and whine of a sitar.

Ahead lies Bughouse Square. An exhaust haze in the air in-congruous with the presence of a wind. On the corner the silhouette of a church more like an abandoned warehouse than church. In the lighted windows of the Newberry Library, the faces of readers among the stacks of books. "Wait here," he tells her at the entrance to the square. "I have to see someone."

The hallowed and mysterious ground of the square. A sense of something historical and ancient, of a graveyard underfoot, of being linked up with the bones and spirit of the past. This is where his father walked before him. And the murderer of his father. Where his father met his death. As though this happened centuries and even millenniums in the past. Street lights along the path and yet so dark. Old men on the benches and yet so empty. Dark suits, high-button shoes, suspenders, slouch hats and caps. He interrupts the recollection of an epic pinochle party at some lodge hall decades in the past. "The man they found murdered here—do you know where they found him?"

Counsel taken among the men. "Over by Clark Street, Bill, wasn't it?"

"I think Clyde said it happened right behind that bench there—right over there."

Enter the bald man in the polo shirt and sandals with the physique of a weight lifter, Mr. George, the itinerant dishwasher and master of ceremonies and sergeant-at-arms of Bughouse Square. Why does the young man want to know?

"He was my father."

Surprise. Condolences. Apologies. The word passed along in whispers: "Fellow says he's the dead man's son."

An entourage of old men and Cavan with the dishwasher in the lead, trooping across the lawn. "There," says Mr. George, pointing to a patch of trampled grass, hard-packed earth, plantain gone to seed. "Around the roots of the tree. He was on his back. From where we are, his face would have been upside down." Several students who have come from the library join the crowd; so do men walking dogs and taking a short cut across the square.

"They say that's the murdered fellow's son."

"Do they know why the guy was killed?"

"I don't think they know."

"Sure they know, they're just not saying."

"He must have been sleeping."

"These days they'll kill you for the price of a cup of coffee."

The canonical voice of some self-appointed detective in the background giving his interpretation of the crime: ". . . He must have been drunk . . . Either that or he knew his killer. Because there was no sign of a struggle and no one heard him yell . . . How do I know the motive was robbery? His pockets were turned inside out, pal . . ."

A sense of evil in the air. No less of danger. As though the murderer himself has chosen this same moment to return to the scene of his crime and is one of the faces in the crowd grouped around the tree.

Smoke rising from the murder site like steam from a catch basin. The face of his father in the morgue imposed upon the roots. Disembodied, the cheeks gray and pockmarked, the mouth gaping, the eyes closed as though sewn. Followed by the rest of the corpse dressed up in clothes. Followed by a man in a trenchcoat and slouch hat strangling the corpse. As though Cavan comes alive at the moment of that death. Born somehow from the released spirit of his father. As though where his father's breath was smothered, he catches his own. As though where the trial of his father ended, his begins. His origins are here. Bughouse Square: John Helenowski's place of birth. Suddenly that spot of smoke he watches takes—or else gives off—a light. "The ghost," he says, stepping forward.

"Ghosts?" repeat several voices in the crowd, which steps back.

The beam of a flashlight has streamed through the smoke and fallen upon the plantain and roots. "The woman," says Mr. George, "who found your father."

The red beret, pleated skirt, and stockings rolled down below the knees that Crazy Mary has worn for years, that flashlight and a shopping bag from which protrudes soiled clothing intermixed with the flagged and dirty tops of unrecognizable greens.

"You found him?" Cavan says.

"That Indian—"

"Indian?"

"Merciful Jesus, but didn't the Son of Darkness call him home to do his dance?"

"Was he already . . . dead?"

"One of the boys of light." Her voice rises. "Murdered in a world of thieves and murderers. A son of sin. Tenting tonight on the happy hunting ground of Christ." Then moaning and singing: "Boys, while you have the light, believe in light, that you may be the boys of light. Hallelujah! A world of light!" Raising the hem of her skirt and dancing, shining the flashlight on the crowd of men.

Mr. George is at Cavan's side. "Forgive me," he says, "but I can tell you are a young man of education. You are supposed to be intelligent and eloquent. But maybe you are also a man of strong feelings—a man of real passion. Perhaps you will come back to us when your grief for your father is not so great and tell us your thoughts and feelings on all this violence and what you think we must do about it." He is setting up the orange crate. The barbershop harmony of "Let Me Call You Sweetheart" sung by men with foreign accents inside the square.

"Don't look now," Kay says, joining Cavan and putting her arm in his. She indicates Peter Pfister, her former husband and would-be poet, standing on the steps of the library he pretends he has just come out from and staring off into space only a few yards to the left of Kay and Cavan. "I wondered if he was following us. Before we were married he used to follow me—but only when I dated other men."

"He doesn't seem to be behind us now."

Back through the Gold Coast, the art, youth, nightclub, and wealthy quarter of the city all in one short and narrow stretch along the lake. Nightclubs with canopies and doormen, crowded bars that resemble English pubs, antique shops that feature English and Oriental pieces, small foreign restaurants, small groceries that deliver gourmet foods, art galleries, numerous crowded and expensive short-order restaurants. On the sidewalks crowds of out-of-towners nightclubbing, art students, young men in advertising and television, playboys and girls with private means, young professionals, young Greeks and Iraqis, gangsters, homosexuals, celebrities, salesmen entertaining clients. It is the only neighborhood in the city where walking is considered fashionable.

"Where's your Sonja?" Kay says. "Why isn't she following you?"

Cavan is defensive. "She had to work tonight."

"And you didn't want her to go?"

He looks at her with respect. "You're pretty wise," he says, grimacing as he recalls his childish attempt to persuade her to stay at home with him, especially since it was in vain and must have cost him something in whatever respect she has for him.

"It wasn't Sonja you saw in Bughouse Square?"

"No," he says, unwilling to tell her who or what he did see.

Then in the window of a shop selling Oriental basketware Bradford McCarthy and Myrna Westermann exclaiming over a straw lampshade as he lights her cigarette and then his own. They could be posing for an advertisement in a magazine. Kay says, "Do you want to say hello?" In reply he takes her hand and runs away.

"Myrna will be married in six months," Kay says, catching her breath. "She invested a lot of time in you. She doesn't have the patience to invest it a second time. Divorcees have to be even more careful. Of the rebound."

"Burkhardt?"

"I don't think so."

Into an espresso coffeehouse. A short wait behind a red rope. Rossini overtures and Vivaldi's *The Four Seasons*. Red walls. Paintings in ornate gold frames of Mediterranean landscapes, Riviera villas. Highly polished coffee urns, espresso makers, samovars. Art equated with luxury, consumption, the baroque. Prices no struggling artist could afford. He has a Russian spiced tea (the menu says a favorite of the czar), she a Viennese coffee, topped with whipped cream. He tries to persuade her to have a slice of *le marquis au chocolat*. She tempts him with a wedge of Camembert. The room is crowded with well-dressed couples. It is the place to come to exchange critiques after seeing one of those austere, grainy, black and white subtitled films.

He reaches for his tea and his wrist goes limp. His hand falls. It looks lifeless against the tablecloth. He becomes obsessed by the knuckles, digits, hairs, wrinkles.

"Where does your father have his greenhouses, Kay?"

"Lake Zurich."

"You must have had flowers around the house."

"All the time."

"Flowers make you gentle, I suppose?" He is thinking of flowers, heaps of them.

"I suppose they do."

"You don't often hear of florists going berserk in their greenhouses and murdering their plants." Still staring at the hand.

She laughs. "Some euthanasia."

"And your mother's alive?"

"She's the foreman of the greenhouses."

"Brothers or sisters?"

"An older sister. She's married to a ski instructor, lives in Colorado, and has three boys. The whole family skis and mountain climbs. Even as far back as when she first went to college she planned to marry that kind of man, live in the Rocky Mountains, live that kind of life. She even wanted three little boys. She's probably the only person I know who is completely happy."

"Who do you look like, Kay?"

"Did you ask who I looked like?"

"Yes."

"My father mostly."

"Handsome man."

The fascination of that hand on the table before him. All the homes of Farquarson friends and distant relatives and hirelings, and the boarding schools, summer camps, and private academies he has lived at in his life. An orphan of wealthy institutions. The small boy sneaking out at night or getting his own way through tantrums and alone at the movies and sleeping in the wooden seat with the voices on the soundtrack of the last showing of the last feature of the double feature cracking like pistol shots against his ears. The only patrons a handful of old men and women in overcoats, their shadows visible in the light of the flickering of the frames upon the screen. Then the voices replaced by the swell of music and The End flashing behind the transparent curtains drawn across the screen and just before the house lights are turned up and the wooden seats clack against their wooden backs, from somewhere in the all but empty theater the lone, loud, slow, rhythmical, almost farcical handclap that echoes through the nightmare of his sleep and the midnight of that emptiness he feels within his soul. The clapping of death. The sound of death. Death: something he has heard but never seen.

"Is anything the matter?" she says.

"There must be a great deal of unhappiness in the world. I was thinking about what you said about your sister."

"Is something the matter with your hand?"

"As a matter of fact there is. I don't seem to be able to take my eyes off it."

"Then why don't you move your hand out of your line of vision?"

"I can't seem to do that either. It's paralyzed and has me hypnotized all in one. I feel a bit foolish about all this. It's like I've got my finger in a bottle. Or my foot in a pail. I've just been looking at my hand and it appears it doesn't belong to me. Not that it belongs to anyone else, mind you. But on a lizard. Because of the wrinkles, I suppose. Or on a Martian. It's like some kind of a tentacle. What I'm trying to say is that it doesn't look human. I'm sure I can even see the tiny cells that make up the tissue. It resembles plant tissue. If I didn't really believe in evolution before I certainly do now. I know what I come from all right. On the other hand it looks like it's cut off and just lying there on the table. If I rolled up my cuff there would be an inch or so between my hand and wrist. It looks, you know, like meat. Like it could rot . . ."

She lays her hand on top of his, and then the other hand, covering his entirely. He feels the urge to tell her everything: his new name, the mad and murdered father in Bughouse Square.

"I think I want to go outside now," she says. She calls for the waitress, pays for the check from her own purse.

Shady side streets and on their way, he guesses, to Kay's apartment. Rowhouses of Georgian architecture with wrought-iron balconies, and stone townhouses intermixed with steel and glass co-operatives, some in the process of being built with signs already up advertising efficiency apartments. An elegance and sensuality in the air that is almost southern.

Her face in the street light. A childhood scar continuing the line of her lips. Her front teeth gapped and slightly crooked, and her upper lip twisted up so that it seems almost split. Something sensual about the crookedness of both teeth and lips, and about the presence of that scar. He guesses she is an erotic woman.

A folksong fest in an apartment they are passing, students around a guitar and singing Border ballads and labor songs. "I think we're being followed again," she says. Footsteps behind them from several quarters.

"Did Pete really beat you?" he asks, hesitatingly.

"Don't be so Russian," she says. "He slapped and kicked me. But I suppose he gave me no more than he got."

A street violinist playing *"La Paloma"* offkey, the cuffs of his trousers in heaps around his shoes. They pause before her apartment, a small Victorian building of green stone with a bright red door and bronze knocker. "If I don't see you again before you go East," he says, "good luck. If I ever come East I'll look you up."

He would loiter on her doorstep, when it occurs to him that she is concerned with time and wants him gone, that she must have another engagement for the evening. He parts with her reluctantly, would use her if he could to kill still more time until Sonja returns. More than this too. He has the apprehension that it is risky to love a girl like Sonja, that he is vulnerable having committed and revealed himself to her. It might be wise to fill the hours away from her with the company of someone else. A place to go immediately if he is ever hurt or, God forbid, turned out. Besides, he has felt an ease with Kay—perhaps it is no more than an equality—that he wonders if he will ever feel with Sonja. Indeed, he entertains an image of Kay he is certain he has not recalled before. He is standing on the shaded sidewalk in front of Georgian rowhouses and looking across the street at the dappled playground of the small school here on the Gold

Coast where Kay teaches kindergarten. Behind the iron picket fence she is in a pale blue smock and German stockings, her almost gray-colored hair held back by a blue and yellow headband, leading the chanting children as they circle hand in hand.

Several times he passes Sonja's apartment on the chance that her desire to see him is such that she has come home early. But the windows are always dark. Something ominous in that darkness. Shouldn't she be home by now? Could she have come home already and gone immediately to bed? He calls at Vollmer's apartment to invite him out for a drink, along with Motluck if he is there, but Vollmer is not at home. Then outside a restaurant specializing in shish kebab he comes face to face with Pete Pfister. Both men are surprised. Pfister carrying a small bag of groceries under his arm which unconsciously he presents to Cavan as though to justify his presence on the street. Cavan pretending he is ignorant of Pfister following him, Pfister that he is unaware of Cavan having been with Kay.

"I hear you're divorced," Cavan says.

"Am I? Then I'm the last to know. When was it?"

"Yesterday."

"I've been divorced for two years. The only things that kept us together were sex and guilt."

"Well," Cavan says, trying not to show that he is offended at this revelation, "that's certainly very American, isn't it?"

Pfister laughs. "Stronger ties than love and understanding, Cavan. These days anyway." They walk on together.

Pfister is large, sandy-haired, freckled, with horn-rimmed glasses, and is wearing a sweat shirt and Bermuda shorts. An odd mixture of athleticism and aestheticism, an intellectual snob with the build and coloring of a lifeguard. An all-state athlete in high school, he went to college on an athletic scholarship he was to lose as soon as he discovered the wonderful worlds of philosophy and poetry, and surrendered to them his body as well as his mind. The Spartan disciplines of his youth he dismisses with disdain, ridiculing all sports as brawn and no brain and bourgeois besides. To him athletes are "goons" and athletics are "a bore."

A used bookstore crammed with stacks and crazy tottering piles of books, displays of dusty literary magazines in the window, the doors wide open to the street. Bearded and barefoot men, some bare-chested, and a woman in denim overalls, grouped reverently around a game of chess played on a desk between a giant Negro with a van-dyke beard and a little white man with yellow skin. They are playing by candlelight, a bottle of sherry between them. "Goddamn dilettantes," Pfister says loud enough to be overheard by those inside. "Literary phonies. Coffeehouse intellectuals. Weekend artists. *Schwarze Bohemienen.*"

"How is the poetry coming?" Cavan asks when he is certain no one is coming after them.

"Jesus, I don't know. I haven't got command of the language yet." Later he says, "So the divorce went through. I thought these things took years. So just like that I'm free. It's the push I need to pick up and get out of here. Out of the university most of all. I'm getting tired of those freaks in the quadrangles with their mismatched socks and a copy of Camus under one arm and Dylan Thomas under the other."

"I hear Kay is going East," Cavan offers.

"Well, I'm going West. The university is dead. It's monastic . . . medieval. It's out in the country where the real poetry is. I used to write that kind of poetry where every other word is in italics because it's in a foreign language, and in some complicated form like terza rima, and the subject matter and the metaphors are all taken from Greek and Roman mythology. God, how I hate myself for it. And the poems were so safe! And correct! And so coy! So flat!" He snorts, speaking passionately. "The other night I criticized this graduate student's poem at our poetry group because every other word was so Latin or Greek you had to look it up in the dictionary. He wouldn't use them unless they had ten syllables. And the Anglo-Saxon words he used had been dead to the language for a thousand years. And the Norman words—he used Norman words—had something to do with heraldry and castles, what we're really concerned with today. And this guy answers my criticism by saying that perhaps the proper place for poetry in our time is in the university. I tell you, Cavan, everybody who is alive and healthy and willing to be fresh and work is going West." Then confidingly, "I've got this idea. I think I have this vision. But I need more time before I start to put it down on paper. I've still got a lot to learn . . . I want to go out and live with the Indians for a while, study their language, learn their poetical forms, their speech patterns, their special rhythms. I'd like to try to blend them with their European English counterparts—our own present tradition, you know—and see if somehow what I come up with isn't something truly unique and American. Not to mention valid. After all, what original literary form has America given the world up to now except the detective novel?"

To Cavan this in itself sounds pedantic and falsely scholarly and certainly not the stuff of poetry, although he does not doubt the man is genuine, but he refrains from saying so.

They pass an old, dirty, stunted man with the beard of a rabbi, wearing an overcoat tied at his waist with a piece of rope and shoes that look as though they could separate into twenty pieces at any step. A common sight along the Gold Coast, he is never without a manuscript of at least a thousand pages, dog-eared, yellowed, soiled, and wrapped up in numerous strands of string, which he unties sometimes in restaurants when he eats a muffin and scribbles with a pencil, glaring at the other customers suspiciously, as he glares at Cavan and Pfister now. "I wonder what he has in there," Pfister says. "An epic poem. The great American novel. The definitive study of the English language. Poor old geezer. What's a worse fate than becoming a fifty-year-old bohemian and living in a place like this?" His head indicates the Gold Coast. "The greatest fear I have for myself, and for my adventure, is that it is only a kind of insanity and vanity, like his is, and that I'll waste my life on the task, getting nowhere, ending up like him." He shudders as though reckoning the miles he will travel, the Indian languages and customs he will study, the countless manuscripts he will write, all of which he can already condemn as worthless. All his sacrifices for nothing. A bearded and lonely middle-aged man exercising to regain the muscles of his youth. And Cavan suspects that his loss of Kay is also in some way part of the sacrifice he is making for his art.

At Pfister's door, Pfister looks down the street behind him. "I've had the queer feeling someone's been following me," he says. Is this a test to learn if Cavan knows he has been following him? Cavan doesn't think so.

"Good luck on your quest," Cavan says in parting. He realizes he would not have wished him well even a day ago, or if he did he would not have meant it as he means it now.

Once again he goes to call at Vollmer's house, only to catch Vollmer coming out his door in the uniform of a flight engineer, a flightbag in hand, looking sober and efficient, as though he has, for this flight to Los Angeles anyway, entered into so different a role that he would not even recognize his good friend Motluck if he met him on the street. Motluck himself Cavan encounters a little later promenading down Rush Street with his hands in his pockets and his head lowered to watch the footfall of his shoes, and in the company of Trixy Ekstrom, that glamorous skeleton whose bones seem always on the verge of bursting through her skin, and who just last night Motluck deprecated and dismissed. Reluctantly, Cavan goes alone into a nearby bar. Quiet and cool and dark and almost empty, an air of contrivance and insincerity. They give tokens in place of change. Three girls overdressed and overweight in low-cut dresses, wearing false eyelashes and net stockings. There is about them a kind of sullen and even nasty sexlessness. They are being courted by a pair of salesmen young enough to be in college. It occurs to Cavan that he does not like bars—and certainly hates this bar in particular—and does not care to drink alone, perhaps does not even care to drink at all, in bars or anywhere, or with anyone.

An older man in shirtsleeves takes the stool beside him and orders a double whiskey and a beer, complaining about the price and demanding silver in place of tokens. He is weary and sweaty and complains of being footsore. He looks as though he would be more comfortable in a neighborhood or even a Skid Row tavern. He makes small talk with Cavan, explaining that he lives in Florida and that he is just about as hot right now as he would be down there and that down there he would drink his beer with a dash of salt. "But I'm glad to see you've got the right idea at last," he says, toasting Cavan and ordering the bartender to give Cavan another drink and not to try and give him any more of those tokens. Adding, "You're quite a walker."

"Why do you say that?"

"Why? Do you ask me why? Jesus Christ, man, haven't I been following you for several hours and a dozen miles? Up and down. Up and down. This way and that way. You don't mean to say you haven't seen me tailing you?"

Cavan is surprised. "I thought someone was following me. Why on earth were you doing that?" And why, he wonders, would you confess to doing it?

The man introduces himself, if he can be believed, as Captain Terence "Tip" O'Neil, a retired police captain of the Chicago force, and shakes Cavan's hand. "I've been tailing you on police business of a sort. As a favor to some of the bigwigs I know." He scratches his neck. "I had nothing to do today so I said I was willing. Besides, you get a bit rusty being retired and it's always good to find out you can still do your job."

"What kind of police business do you mean?"

"I hate to admit it, Johnny, but it was on the suspicion that you might have had something to do with the killing of Scarponi—a good dear friend of mine who I was playing pinochle with just the night before last—and also with the killing of that young patrolman named Carbone."

Cavan is speechless. "But that's . . . nonsense." He wonders if he should laugh. "I don't know those men."

"Of course you don't." O'Neil putting his hand on his shoulder. "You and I know that but do the bigwigs know it? After seeing you for so many hours and blocks, and now after talking to you, Johnny, I know you're a clean-cut kid. The bosses made a mistake, don't ask me how. But they ain't always too bright upstairs. And don't think I won't tell them they're off their heads, too. And that wonderful girl you were walking with, too. Beautiful girl. Beautiful legs. Moves like a lady. Not like these pigs over there." He indicates the girls at the bar. "Look, I been in this business, which is another way of saying I've been a student of human nature, too long to be fooled."

Then the drunken and belligerent O'Neil leading the drunken and submissive Cavan a few blocks west to Clark Street and a neighborhood of housing projects and apartment houses inhabited by retired men, Puerto Ricans, blacks, hillbillies. Here there are burlesque houses with glossy photographs of the strippers in the dusty windows, and bars with prices, atmospheres, and clientele more to O'Neil's liking. O'Neil playing the father and mentor to Cavan's innocence and youth. Cavan killing time until Sonja comes home and hoping to discover why the mysterious "bosses" should suspect him of murdering a cop and gangster. Who do they think he is? Who do they have him confused with? He has never heard of so improbable a suspicion. But as the night wears on, and the drinks go down, both clock and mystery are forgotten, while the loquacious O'Neil addresses the bar at large as much as him.

". . . And Lou Costello—remember him?—when he come to town always asked for me to be assigned to him. We'd be out eating together in a restaurant and he'd say, 'Come on, Tip, let's go back in the kitchen and squeeze the waitresses.' And I told him once, 'Lou,' I said, 'for Christ's sake, watch out for these guys that are managing you and looking after your businesses and flattering you with a lot of bullshit because they're out to bleed you dry.' And if he'd taken my advice he wouldn't have had nothing like the trouble he had . . . And Jolson—remember him?—I said to him once, 'Al, you may not like what I'm going to say to you but if I can't speak plain to you who the hell can? You ought to marry that little woman and you're man enough to know it. She loves you, Al, and you'll never find a truer dame, and the least you can do is make an honest woman of her . . .' And boxers, too, Billy Conn, a hell of a fighter. He'd always call or wire on the daughter's birthday. Always wire. And Max Baer. Good old big Max. I knew them all. Knew the best of them. Well, down the hatch."

Later he says, "But it's all over for me, Johnny. My work's finished and I can't help wondering about a lot of things I've done. But you've got your work ahead of you. You're a man without a past. You're nothing but future, with all your options open to you." He leans toward Cavan sympathetically. "You know, you ought to be a cop. The force needs men like you. What's your present line of work?"

"It used to be . . . anthropology."

"Well, what's police work but the study of man?" O'Neil counters, surprising Cavan with his knowledge of the term. "What's your interest in that subject?"

"Africa."

"Africa is it? What about a beat on the South Side? Why, that's Africa. Talk about Africa. And you don't have to cross no deep and dark water to get there. You could do all the human relations work you want down there—that's what police work is. Human relations. Young lawyers, criminologists, sociologists, they become cops when they're young and starting out. It's the best education in the world. I used to be an instructor at the academy before I took command of a station and I can tell you got it in you to be a first-rate cop. You're an honest man. Innocent but honest. And you're a humanitarian. The study of mankind, for Christ's sake. How can you beat it?"

"I couldn't . . . become a policeman . . . I don't know . . . I never thought . . ."

"Not good enough for you, with all your education? Well, probably right. Lousy money. Lousy hours. No prestige. Always dangerous. Maybe it would be a waste considering what you could do with your life."

"It's the . . . I suppose . . . the violence."

"Goddamn it, you got to bust heads now and then, Johnny. But if you're smart you learn when to let up and not step on no toes. Now, I sold out. I don't mean I was dishonest, I just looked the other way. But you, Johnny, you won't have to sell out. You learn humility. It's not just pushing tough guys around. It's service. Well," observing Cavan's hesitation and patting his hand, "think about it."

John Cavan a policeman. Never in his life has he entertained such a possibility. But why not? Who is he anyway? Anything is possible. Patrolman Helenowski.

"You ought to think of marrying the beautiful girlfriend you saw home," O'Neil says, "and settling down and joining the force. Worse things could happen to you. And I think you ought to know that that tall guy in the shorts you were talking to after you took the girlfriend home was following you before you ran into him."

"Pete," Cavan says. "Her ex-husband."

"It's like that, is it?" Then whispering: "You lure him in an alley, say you got some dirty pictures to show him or something, and I'll be hiding in there and when he comes in I'll whack him in the head with a baseball bat. That'll teach the son-of-a-bitch to follow you and your sweetheart."

Cavan is shocked. "She's not my sweetheart."

"Are you saying there is nothing between you, Johnny? You could have fooled me."

Recalling Kay, Cavan recalls Sonja. She should be home by now! Should have been home long ago. His heart misses several beats with fear and anticipation. What is he doing, wasting time with this fool loudmouth of a retired policeman? At least Sonja has not found him waiting on her doorstep or pacing up and down her street. At least by coming late he can demonstrate he is not that dependent on her, not that deeply in love with her. He tries to take his leave of O'Neil.

But O'Neil won't hear of it. "Come on home with me, Johnny," he says, "and meet the daughter. And say, if you're not engaged to that pretty girl, what's the matter with my daughter? I'll fix you up. You can join the force and marry into a captain's family. She's as ugly as a city sidewalk, and I'll admit it even if she is my own daughter. Red hair, and if that isn't bad enough, she dyes it orange. Thirty-seven years old and the temper of a tiger. And dumb too. The nuns couldn't teach her nothing. Awful girl—always has been. I wouldn't wish her on anyone. Still, you ought to meet her and decide for yourself. What do you say, Johnny?"

Cavan says thanks and good-bye, backing out the bar as O'Neil pursues him and pumps his hand and in parting warns him that someone other than just this Pete has been following him tonight. Why, to hear him tell it a whole army has been spaced out along the sidewalk behind him, following him up and down the Gold Coast streets. "Be careful," he says.

A dark and deserted block. Sonja's gloomy apartment building of bulging brownstone laced with fire escapes. The lights are on in her windows! His heart quickens, beats erratically, his loins ache, and he sweats as though he has run for several miles. She has not gone to bed after all. He pauses on the sidewalk, overcome with a terror in league with waves of joy. An eroticism, uniquely urban, merely in the presence of those lights. What should he say on entering? Something sweet and clever and exactly right. But what if she doesn't expect him to call this late, much less spend the night? Isn't he presumptuous in his certainty that an arrangement for tonight, if not for all nights, has been made between them?

She is not surprised to see him at her door. She is in her slip in the efficiency kitchen, ironing. Her beauty, although he has tried to recall it a hundred times today and failing that to imagine it, is still different, still fresh and startling. He smiles. As before there is nothing he needs to say. He kisses her once lightly on the cheek, once lightly on the lips. He does not feel he must do more. He moves a chair closer to the ironing board and sits in it. Watches the iron go back and forth, watches it rested on its end, hears the sprinkle from the beer bottle on the clothes, hears the hiss, feels the heat, smells the hot humid smell of ironed clothes. Observes with an exquisite and almost voyeuristic pleasure that the blue railroad bandana is among the pieces ironed. A pile of medical tomes and notebooks on the kitchen table. The stark white plaster walls of the apartment. The inside here like the outside of a whitewashed cottage. A feeling that walls and floor have just been hosed down. Every now and then she looks up from her ironing and smiles. The ironing board is creaking.

He slumps in the chair. His weariness is neither physical nor mental but emotional. He is drained—utterly. All the shocks and madness of the past few days have come back at once to take their toll. But come with such incomprehensible and undeserved tranquility.

"Would you like to go to bed?" she asks.

A wonderful question which he can answer best with his body. What a sleep he will have tonight in the foreign and sweet-smelling luxury of her bed. Between white sheets like these walls. Although he fears he may be too tired not only to make love but even to sleep. But in the morning she will be beside him when he wakes. He wants to seize her like some Sabine, proclaim she is his salvation, his serenity, his sustenance. Wants even at this late hour to celebrate into the small hours the miracle of that sustenance.

He stumbles down the hall with its white walls and sees in the open door of a small bedroom he must pass to reach her bedroom, a door that was closed this morning, the worst of his unspoken apprehensions. Sees it even though he does not turn his head, or stop, or even hesitate, and without commenting on what he sees. Carlos, bare-chested and in Levi's, his back to him, seated at a desk made from an unpaneled door and working beneath a fluorescent desk lamp, an open book beside him, a sheaf of papers, a yellow paper in the portable typewriter, the novel, Cavan knows in a flash, that Sonja told him this morning someone she knew was writing and in which she was the main character if not exactly the heroine. And the clothes hanging in the open closet, the rumpled beds, the board and brick bookshelves lined with paperbacks and phonograph albums, the cameras, tape recorder, high-fidelity phonograph, and on the wall the several large matted photographs of Sonja posed against various backgrounds of the city. A room lived in for months, if not for years. Carlos with his narrow brown back and hunched shoulders and black curly hair on the back of his head lives here, has lived here, and still lives here, lives with her. Cavan catches it all in passing and understands it all. But he cannot make himself pause at the open door, or once past it, to pretend a double take and turn back, asking Sonja for some explanation. Instead he continues down the hall as though he has seen nothing, closing the bedroom door behind him. What can he do now except throw open the door and with his hands hiding his face make a mad dash without speaking through the apartment and out the door? Or pretend first that he must use the bathroom and then that he discovers Carlos for the first time along the way? Impossible alternatives! He has trapped himself, placed himself in an intolerable situation. Heartsick, he undresses in the dark and climbs into the bed. A street light yellows the shade. He cannot sleep. Or cannot stay asleep. A weight and weariness of body he has not known before. But accompanied by such a weightlessness and exhilaration in his spirit! Whose room will she sleep in tonight, Carlos's or her own (where he is himself bedded down, which in itself must portend something, or so he consoles himself in his obsession with this question)? Or some chaste compromise on the couch, perhaps? He anticipates the bedroom door opening, Sonja entering on tiptoe and undressing in the dark, the bed depressing beside him. Or else the line of light beneath the door vanishing but the door remaining closed. Even so he does not care! There is more to being someone in this world than merely she and he and I and them and this night and bed. He is possessed of strange powers to see and feel beyond himself, as though his wild-eyed spirit has left the sick heart and weary body and gone abroad above the rooftops. He understands, forgives, sympathizes. How much more there is between the two people in the apartment beyond that door than there ever was between him and Myrna Westermann. Far more than there is between him and Sonja now. Perhaps more than there can ever be between them. He can only guess at those feelings between them that are too complex to disentangle, too warped to be made wholesome, and yet in the end too safe to abandon for the risk of new faces, new adventures, new injuries. How naïve of him to think that other people are as nameless, footloose, and dustless as himself, that they would not be bound up with themselves and others and with the circumstances of their lives and could at the first embrace pick up and go, eloping, as it were, in the middle of the night.

He lies absolutely still and listens: no sound of conversation. The faint hissing of the steam iron. The creaking of the ironing board. A chair pulled back. A tap turned on. A book thumping closed. How irrelevant in the sum of things is her traveling by his side. And how selfish even of him to desire to have her. He is part of a vast and timeless human force, full of the unspoken explosions of its understanding and compassion.

He is out of bed, tottering and hopping in the dark in his delirium as he dresses. The honorable course of action, he decides, is flight. He puts his eye to the lighted keyhole. Sonja at the kitchen table and reading from a medical book, a sweater thrown over her slip. Carlos with his back arched against a doorway, one foot planted on the jamb, drinking from a coffee cup, a sheaf of yellow papers in hand. As though waiting for Sonja to finish her chapter so he can present these fresh pages for her approval. No talk takes place between them. This is intolerable. Heartbreaking. He has to leave! He could almost make that undignified dash between them and out the door. But instead he opens the window, steps onto the fire escape and, after hanging by his hands and involuntarily swinging for what seems several minutes, during which time he is observed by an Oriental woman in hair curlers and brassiere in a window across the street who fetches a man with bright yellow hair and an Oom Paul pipe to join her at the window, he drops painfully to the street.

Instead of to his own apartment he walks with a noticeable limp to Kay's. He acknowledges she is a kind of consolation prize, and he is pleased with himself only by reason of the candor of his admission. But he fears the jealousy and pain of loss he suspects he might well feel for Sonja once he is sober, clearheaded, rested-up. The windows of Kay's apartment are surprisingly lighted, the sash open, the curtains pulled apart and blowing. The flushed and swollen face of Burkhardt above the pin-collar shirt, that head almost shaved to disguise the premature balding, his mouth open with speech. Turning now to gaze out the window and abstractly down into the street. He strikes a match, rises, disappears momentarily only to emerge holding a flame to Kay's cigarette in the next window. Cavan can see the length of one of her pale arms, bent at the elbow, and the white linen short sleeve of her blouse and a silver ornament on her slim wrist. Kay in a pantomime of laughter. The remote, muted, and incomprehensible patter of their speech. They are sitting at least ten feet apart. She on a low sofa of green and blue stripes, he in a yellow butterfly chair. He admits he is stimulated, even somewhat aroused just watching them. So he has lost out here too. Still, he goes into her small vestibule and writes a note saying he stopped by, that he appreciated her walking with him, that he would like to see her again before she goes East for good.

As he turns down the sidewalk he catches the face in the doorway watching the windows of Kay's apartment, just as he was moments earlier. He lowers his head, determined not to embarrass the man with a look or speech. But the man, unable to resist the power of his venom, speaks anyway. "You have to wait in line, Cavan."—Pfister! But Cavan walks on, neither frightened nor angered. What can he do but present Pfister with the possibility that he has not heard? He forgives him—he has to. Knows him well enough to know he will regret his words, and suffer for them.

The playboy in the townhouse next door to his own small rooms across from the Ambassador Hotel is flying his cocktail flag above his doorway upside down tonight, whatever that means, and the bay window is crowded with bleary bachelors in ties and plaid jackets and Bermuda shorts, drinks in hand and examining the jackets of phonograph albums and still looking now and then with expectations out into the street.

In the bed of his own room he is again too tired to fall asleep. Or to stay asleep. A vision of Sonja discovering her bed empty and the open window out of which she pokes her head and spies the fire escape and sidewalk below, and then with her bathrobe thrown over her slip running barefoot into the night and knocking at any moment upon his door. Or Kay finding the note in her mailbox as she ushers the unhappy and rejected Burkhardt to the door, and then passing that same bewildered Burkhardt on the street, clacking in her high heels along the sidewalk and rapping any moment now upon his door. Or heaven help him, both of them at his door at once!

Slats of light angling through the venetian blinds and lying like bars across the bed and floor. A boisterous, drunken conversation down in the street. A lot of bragging, name-dropping, backslapping. He recognizes the loudest voice as that of Von, the city's most famous gossip columnist (Vonny's Windy City), who must be standing in the street, and the other of a famous comedian and movie actor who must be inside his limousine and leaning out the window. The conversation is interminable and often obscene. Later the city seems, to city ears anyway, as silent as the country.

At last the knock comes upon his door. A demanding knock. A knock of passion. It won't take no for answer. It is meant from the start not only to summon the host but wake him up if he is asleep. And not only wake him, but scare him. Cavan leaps from his bed and still in the darkness throws open the door to the light from the hallway and the pair of shadows at his door. A pair of men. Policemen who want him to come down to the station and answer some questions.

He invites them in as he dresses to the nightlight above his bed. They are glad to find him home, they tell him, having called several times tonight already.

"I suppose," Cavan says sleepily, remembering O'Neil and making conversation, "it's about that nonsense of me being involved in the killings of Scarponi and that policeman—what's his name?"

Both policemen become attentive, wary, one who has been sitting down springs up. Only to sit down. "What makes you think that?" one of them says, pretending indifference, looking at the other man.

Cavan catches their surprise. "Of course," he says, remembering the corpse he identified in the morgue as, still barefoot, he buttons up his pants. "It's about the murder of my father."

"It's about," the policeman says, "the murder of Alvin Raincloud."

CHAPTER TWENTY-EIGHT

BLACK ANGELS

The South Side of Chicago. A slum so expansive and impoverished it seems impossible to believe it could be in Chicago, or America, or anywhere in a part of the world that calls itself New.

Blocks of warehouses and abandoned factories, the walls papered with the posters of boxing matches and political campaigns of a decade ago, and abandoned stores and tenements, boarded up and dark, inhabited by homeless families as much as homeless men. No cars parked on the streets and no pedestrians on the sidewalks, only a man sprawling in a doorway, drunk or dead, and the possibility that other shadows in other doorways are also men, and the only light from street lights, half of which are dark, their bulbs shattered in the streets.

Then excavations penned in by walls of battered doors, and blocks of the rubble of demolished buildings interrupted only by a gutted building without steps up to its doors or glass in its windows and in the distance a new high-rise building of the housing projects, blocks away from its identical neighbor and as yet without a planting of grass and trees, as alien to the landscape as a spaceship on the moon.

Then blocks of brick tenements often faced with gray-faceted stones, a locust tree, a striped awning over a window or front door. The faces of black women at the often broken windows. Black men congregated on the front steps and on the fenders of parked cars and outside the taverns that have rusted and unlit neon signs and inside the bright windows of barbershops where they are talking, laughing, smoking. Black children skipping rope or playing hopscotch on the sidewalks or sent out on errands to the small basement groceries, the doors and windows of which are patched with battered soft drink and cigarette signs.

Here Magnuson parks and locks his rented car, then goes on foot. Faces float before him only to fade back into the lesser darkness of the night. He searches among them for the face of Robinson, the former policeman and employee of the Magnuson Agency he has come here to seek. And searches in his more fantastic moments for Lena and her husband, Max; and the mysterious Preacher Nettles and his equally mysterious wife; and the vanished mulatto daughter of Farquarson's insane wife. Faces, none of which he has ever seen. The futility though of searching for a murderer among these faces. Here there is murder in every face. Here, at least, the nature of his search is at last at home.

An apartment house, once a mansion, takes up half a block ahead. Standing in the middle of several flattened blocks of rubble it could pass for an eccentric, bombarded castle on the moors. Behind the matchstick iron of the broken fire escapes that hang as though by threads along its walls, a full moon has begun to rise. A feeling that the light behind the window shades is moonlight, that the rear of the building has been demolished, exposing the honeycomb of flats. A number that matches the last-known address of Robinson is chalked on the bricks beside the door.

Inside the vestibule along the broken mailboxes and buttons a hundred illegible penciled and taped-on names, no doubt of tenants from decades in the past. In the lobby an architecture that seems Moorish or Egyptian: tiled walls and floors, and wide squat arches on which pineapples and coconuts are carved, and heavy columns with capitals of palm leaves on which the paint has curled. A wide stairwell and stairs that climb dizzily overhead; corridors that lead through the arches in all directions and are lined with doors. Everything lit brilliantly, like a prison. Voices loud and excited and so distorted by echoes as to sound not only unintelligible but inhuman. In distant chambers children chanting, feet and rope tapping on the floor. Strange sounds, or the lack of them, which he realizes is because there is only the humming of voices. The overwhelming odor of urine and garbage. Black faces along the bannisters overhead, like sailors at the rail, their faces growing smaller with the elevation. He continues to look up and expects to see that the building is roofless, bombed out, open to the moon and stars. A high dark hand reaches over the rail and lets something fall that increases in size until Magnuson must step back and the thing explodes with a squashed liquid sound beside his foot, splattering his shoes. From above, bursts of childish laughter. Garbage underfoot everywhere, orange peels and fruit mostly, and he is reminded of the litter on the floors of cages in the Zoo. Plaster on the stairs. He peers at the marks left where numbers used to be on the battered doors. People pass him almost on the run, heads lowered, eyes averted, hands in pockets, along the corridors and stairs.

Then high up in the building, as though at the top of a cage, he finds a number on a door, or thinks he does, and counts down the hallway from door to door, passing apartments in which the doors are open or gone and the rooms wrecked and strewn with whiskey bottles, with holes chopped in the floors, until he reckons he has come upon the apartment of Robinson. Two men and a woman are standing outside that door, leaning back against the bannister. One of the men looks like a heavyweight boxer and wears a woman's purple bathrobe that is pinched up on his shoulders and ends above his knees. He is barefoot like the others, and holds a highball glass and cigarette in the same hand.

"Hey, that my door," the man in the robe says as Magnuson pounds heavily upon the door. "What you want there, old man? Those people don't want you in there."

"Maynard Robinson," Magnuson says. "Isn't this his apartment?"

"Maybe he's with those boys?" the woman says to the man in the bathrobe.

"That man don't live there," the man says. "I live there."

"They call him 'Lucky' Robinson," Magnuson says.

"Don't make no difference what he called," the man says. "I still live there."

"Kids come and steal them numbers and move them around, you know," the woman offers. "What number is it that you looking for?"

Suddenly the door before him opens almost to the limit of its chain and he nearly stumbles in surprise through the narrow opening and into the white youth with terrified and threatening eyes standing as though to block his way, wearing a T-shirt but no pants, his genitals and pubic hair lathered with sweat and semen, the blade of a switchblade grasped in his hand at the level of the penis as though to protect it most of all but by some optical illusion appearing to replace it; and in the light inside the room that seems no more than moonlight shining through the faded, ragged shades of a single window he sees beyond the boy's right shoulder the white back and the buttocks snug in a pair of jockey shorts of a second youth urinating on high piles of dirty dishes that fill the ancient sink, and beyond the left shoulder the lean white naked backside of a third youth on the bare mattress of a bed and on top of a brown woman whose brown legs rest listlessly on his almost luminous hips as he moves upon her. "Get away," the boy hisses, and feigns a lunge with the knife at Magnuson's bowels, and Magnuson clutching his abdomen staggers backward as the two black men rush forward as though to help and the woman retreats down several stairs as though to run away.

"Why don't you listen when I tell you something, old man?" the man in the bathrobe says. Shaken, Magnuson wanders down the hall, leaving the men and woman to dispute among themselves as to the identity and whereabouts of someone named Lucky Robinson while he searches for that number that will prove conclusively that he has found Robinson's door.

A small man and heavyset woman (grandfather and grandmother?) stand in the hall beside a closed door (their apartment?), the man leaning over the railing and smoking while the woman bounces on her breasts a crying baby (their granddaughter?). From behind the door men and women (their daughters?) laughing and complaining and the squeak of beds. Magnuson cannot bring himself to go past that door, and the old man, suspicious perhaps that he is stimulated by what he hears and intends to enter, motions him away.

He retreats back down the hall just as the three boys now dressed exit from the room followed by the brown girl, who hands the man in the purple bathrobe a dollar before she races ahead of the boys, flying down the stairs. One of the boys is drunk and supported by his friends. He says good-naturedly, as though expecting the company to commiserate, "I couldn't come."

"That's your business," the man in the robe says. He extends his arm and like a good host ushers his small party back into the room from which they had earlier adjourned, drinking from the highball while the cigarette smokes in his hand. Then Magnuson like everyone else is racing down the stairs, one hand in his pocket, his face averted from all other faces, passing through an arch that dwarfs him and takes him out into the night upon a different street.

Ahead a busy intersection beneath a neon haze, where the pedestrians scurry like frightened animals and the cars cruise like invulnerable predators. A liquor store with white managers and black clerks behind the counter, where black men and women file in and out. A bar in an English basement where black and white Lesbians dance together, and boyish-looking white sailors sit at tables with girls with long hair and dresses who dance with the Lesbians more often than with the sailors.

Two men sit on a stone step, observing the passing life of the street. They could be in beach chairs, looking out to sea. But as Magnuson approaches, the younger man seems on the verge of sneaking off. The face beneath the dirty cap paler than Magnuson remembers it, and plumper, and the mustache heavier—"Lucky!" Magnuson cries, placing a hand on his shoulder and searching for a hand to shake. A million blacks packed into this stockyard of a city and he happens by chance on the first of a thousand corners on the very man he seeks (although is the coincidence really so great, since Robinson allegedly lives in that building less than a block away?). Magnuson no longer alone and conspicuous in this black underworld of violence and conspiracy, but with Robinson in his disguise of darkness as his guide. "Robinson!" he says now, shaking the man as though he has found him fast asleep and in great danger. Up! he wants to shout. Put your arm in mine! The impoverished clothes, the perverse and rundown neighborhood: the completeness in so brief a time of his fall from favor to destitution and degradation. Redeem yourself, Robinson! No longer down and out. Here before you stands your second chance. But in the face of the man he holds he discerns that puzzlement and caution black men show before the mystery of white men, when their drunken eyes flash like starlit ice and their bodies are hair-triggered for violence.

"My name's not Robinson," says the man at last, neglecting to say what his real name is.

Impossible to have made a mistake. "But don't you recognize me?" Magnuson cries.

An old flat-chested woman in slippers grabs a younger woman with haywire, mannish hair and no front teeth and introduces her to the white youths she has been parleying with with the words, "This girl sucks cock." The woman admits she does indeed, but not in cars. "This girl don't suck no cock in cars," the older woman says helpfully, as though the woman has spoken in a language incomprehensible to the boys. The boys decide to rent a room. "Only one in the room at a time," the young woman insists, apparently recalling past dangers and indignities. But the boys balk at this restriction and enter the Lesbian tavern instead, where they can be seen querying the black barmaid who serves them beer.

A flash of recognition (or is it cunning?) on the face of the man Magnuson has identified as Robinson. "He must mean Pimpy," he says to the old man beside him in the hope, apparently, of confirmation. But the old man in his dusty black suit and hat is looking off into the distance as though to inform Magnuson that he knows the man beside him no better than a stranger on the subway, and that in this matter of handling crazy white men he is on his own. "Everybody thinks I'm that man Pimpy," the alleged Robinson says, turning to Magnuson. "If he looks like me, then you're looking for Pimpy."

"Pimpy?" Magnuson repeats. If the man before him is not Robinson—and he is not willing to say he is not, although he knows of no reason why the man should lie—then unless his memory has gone completely, he is Robinson's double, and the man called Pimpy is Robinson then.

"Say, isn't Robinson that Pimpy's name?" the man says, once more attempting to enlist the support of the old man, who continues to look elsewhere, disdainfully smoking his long cigarette, too proud or frightened or wise to get up and move away.

A white man in a rumpled seersucker suit and brown and white shoes, with a mane of white hair and glasses so thick they seem to magnify his eyes tenfold, steps from a taxi and approaches the thin black woman in the housedress who has been slapping up and down the sidewalk in her slippers. They seem to know each other. He no sooner whispers to her than they step into the taxi that has been waiting at the curb, a large bored black man at the wheel. The white man has looked like a minister or professor.

"Young white boys always beating me up," the man mistaken

for Robinson, alias Pimpy, is saying. "One time I was in the Cook County Hospital with this jaw all wired up and four of my ribs broke." He grabs his side and winces in remembrance. "See this nose? Didn't always look like that. That's been broken two times just as I was walking along these streets. All on account of that Pimpy." He shivers only to laugh, as though he sees the humor in those terrible inconveniences and dangers that are his fate because he has a look-alike. "Just the other night these white boys jump out of their car and say I took their thirty dollars and didn't meet them on the corner with some white girls like I said I would. Well, you can believe I told them they wanted old Pimpy. But one of those boys puts a pistol right up against my head." He puts his finger to his temple. "He says if I don't give back the money by the time he counts three I'm going to be one dead nigger. I don't blame him one bit, I tells him. I'd feel the same way myself about this Pimpy if he played me a trick like that. He deserves anything they going to give him. Only one thing, I tells him, I'm not Pimpy. But you see that only make him madder. And if those other boys didn't grab that pistol and put him back in his car—." He shakes his head. "If only I could get myself out of this neighborhood and go somewhere else where there ain't none of this Pimpy business. Or if Pimpy would just get himself killed. Or arrested. Or just go live somewhere else." But his self-pity and indignation sound theatrical.

"Robinson—a pimp," Magnuson repeats in disbelief, realizing that the man before him has assumed that he too was naïve enough to give this Pimpy money for a prostitute, and that Magnuson will beat him if he does not give it back.

"That man's no pimp," the man says. "Worse than a pimp. A pimp has got a product to sell and peoples to look after. He's got to deliver the goods. But Pimpy take your money and don't give you no girl. He don't put no girl to work and everybody is dissatisfied. Everybody, that is, but him!" Laughing. For the first time the old man beside him chuckles and even darts a quick look at Magnuson.

The white boys emerge from the Lesbian tavern in the company of three black teen-age girls. They run hand in hand, beneath the moon, heading for that Oriental-looking building where Magnuson earlier began his search.

"If you're looking for Pimpy," the man says, "just walk around like you wanting something. He ain't far away, that's for sure!" Laughter from both men. Adding, "That man ought to be in jail where he belongs!" Hilarious laughter.

But that sly glint of superiority in the brown eye that searches Magnuson for his response. Almost fooled! The man before him is Robinson. Is also Pimpy. Why won't he acknowledge his former boss?

Or is he Robinson? He holds his head in his confusion, pushing back his hat. No longer able to recognize a face. No longer able to tell if a man is telling him the truth.

He can receive no clear picture of Robinson in his mind. Remembers only that he was well dressed, polite, reasonably efficient, that he was loyal and trustworthy (or so he thought), and only absent or tardy or lethargic on the day after payday. He had expected him to make a superior and model policeman, a credit to his people.

On the step more talk of Pimpy, from which Magnuson seems excluded even though he himself introduced the subject. The streetwalker who would not get in the car with the white boys has joined them. A man with a paper bag of beer bottles beneath his arm stops and says, "Who you talking about? Old Pimpy?" Even the old man is speaking.

"You know where Pimpy carries his money?" the man who looks like Robinson says. "In his asshole! Rolls his bills up until they nice and thin and sticks them up his asshole. That's so when he gets drunk like he does and the womens rolls him they can't never find no money on him. But one time when Pimpy's drunk this man has his clothes off and is turning him this way and that way and standing him on his head and he can't find no money and his woman—she used to be Pimpy's girl—said, 'Why, that's Pimpy. I know where that dumb cocksucker keeps his money. Look in his asshole.' Because once when he was staying at her place she seen him with his pants down and bending over and feeling of himself up behind. So they turn him over and get a flashlight and a pair of tweezers but they couldn't get it out. Then they give him all this medicine, you know, Ex-Lax and milk of magnesia and stuff like that, and that did the job all right!" Uproarious laughter, from everyone.

What good is Robinson to Magnuson now? How can he be so publicly debased and devious? Small comfort for Magnuson to learn from the outrageous fate of Robinson that his own humiliation is by no means as deep as it can go. Now he discovers he needs to find Robinson not so much to have him investigate the black conspiracy of Lena and the Nettles and the daughter of Farquarson's wife as to learn for himself in the cunning and corruption of his former troubleshooter's dark face just who Magnuson has become. No longer to pluck victory from the ashes. Only to gaze upon the depth and meanness of his defeat.

A gang of boys is all over his car, is even inside it. They look like ants tugging at a much larger and lifeless prey. They vanish into the night as he approaches. His hubcaps are gone; a wing window is broken.

A girl walks alone along the sidewalk, swinging her purse. She pauses before the window of a store that has been closed for years. Magnuson no sooner blinks his lights than she is in the car beside him. The powerful aroma of jasmine and of something like dried salt fish. The light dress hiked up just below the hips, legs like glazed earthenware. Her hair in an oily Cleopatra cut. "Old folks," she says, "you going to be some fun." Her accent is only months away from Mississippi.

She directs him down an alley between the steel uprights of the elevated tracks and has him park midway in the block in that coal-black darkness beneath the el. In all the city where is there a more brutal place than an alley beneath the el at night? And Magnuson recalls the recent newspaper account of a woman murdered in an alley beneath the el as she walked from her apartment to her garage. Literally torn apart limb from limb, as though by an enraged gorilla, the most savage crime they had ever encountered, the police officers said. The girl's voice in the darkness beside his ear: "How much you want to spend, old folks?"

He can barely discern his hands among so much night. He fumbles with the wallet he suddenly remembers contains thousands. "Here's five—but not for what you think—."

"What you want me to do, daddy?" From her presence in the dark the sensuality of hot, humid, rural nights and the rank vegetation of stagnant back-road ditches and lush, moth-filled hedgerows.

"I'm looking for a man they call Pimpy—" he hushes her before she can reply and freezes in his seat. Someone is in the dark outside the car. The careful and almost measured placing of feet upon the cinders. He becomes aware of small gridworks of lesser darkness that may be the residue of moonlight falling through the tracks upon the cinders and steel uprights and girders. He searches among them for the passage of some portion of the shadow of a creeping man. Has the girl led him into a trap where he is about to be robbed and beaten?

Then just as the man out there bumps against something metal in the dark, a piece of junk perhaps, which scrapes along the cinders as he cries out in pain, Magnuson is distracted by the uncomfortable sensation of being touched which, like his hearing, is heightened in the dark. The girl has opened his fly and put her hand upon his privates, has had it on them for some time and is stretching his penis up and down in the movements of masturbation in an attempt to make it erect as she maneuvers on top of him, her dress hiked above her hips. Her pubic hair like a wire brush against his genitals, the pressure of her hand painful as she tries to force his flabby penis inside her where she is tight, dry, abrasive, succeeding only in bending it against her thigh. "No, no," he says, seizing the wrist of the hand that has hold of him. "Tell me where Pimpy is, that's all I want—"

"Old folks," she sighs, "I ain't never had a man like you."

Then the man at the window beside Magnuson, his dark face no more than inches from Magnuson's, a suggestion among the dark of a panama, shirt collar, fingernails of a hand holding the five dollars, proving that the man has already been at the other window and taken the money from the girl. "What's taking you so long?" he says, looking past Magnuson, scolding the girl.

Magnuson feels hemmed in by the girl, the steering wheel, the el overhead, the tenements on either side, the darkness. He flails out at the night as though it is coal smoke that will suffocate him if he does not disperse it with his arms.

The girl says, "It ain't my fault. It's old folks."

The man whines to Magnuson, "I don't like this girl fucking for no five dollars." As though to impress upon the girl that he has her interest at heart. "Ain't you got some change in your pocket?" Magnuson feels among a handful of change for quarters. "That's all right," the man says, "I'll take it all." He does take it all and disappears into the darkness until Magnuson makes him out beside a girder in that dismal gridwork of urban moonlight, squatting on the cinders like an Oriental and smoking a cigarette. Is it possible that this man could be Pimpy? The Pimpy who is also Robinson?

He is on the verge of calling out and opening the door when the girl beside him opens hers, saying, "Goddamn sons-of-bitches ruining my business because I won't give them none of my money—." She flees into the doubtful sanctuary of the darkness, calling back over the clatter of her footsteps down the alley, "You be all right, old folks."

The headlights of the squad car parked behind him pass through his own car and out the windshield and travel down the alley. "Get out of the car, Pop." The policeman is at the window with a flash-light. He is almost as old as Magnuson himself. A second and younger policeman, also white, stands behind him. As Magnuson slides off the seat the flashlight is shined upon his open fly. "Put them in, Pop. And zipper up. Now put your hands against the car." Magnuson with his hands on the roof while hands move up his legs and thighs. A cry of alarm as they pat his left pants pocket. "What's that? Turn around!"

The younger officer picks up the cry. "Turn around! Keep them up! Turn around!" When Magnuson turns around he faces a drawn revolver and a frightened cop.

"What's that?" the older officer is shouting, pointing at the pocket. "Take it out of there! Take it out! Take it slow! I said take it slow!"

While at the same time the younger officer screams, "Easy! Easy! Take it out!"

"Slow!" the older officer says. "I said slow!"

Slowly Magnuson removes the cigar and lighter that together have conspired to create a shape inside his pocket resembling that of a small pistol and displays them in his open palm. The police are crestfallen but relieved. "Open up that lighter," the older one says in an attempt to save face. Next Magnuson is ordered to show his driver's license. To his relief the name of Arnold Magnuson means nothing to them. They do not want him in connection with last night's murders. Nor are they out to shake him down.

"Look, Arnie," the older officer says, "you don't want to mess around with the girls down here." His concern is genuine, as though he sees his true duty is to counsel, caution, and protect. The younger officer glares at Magnuson with stern paternal disapproval. "They'll give you a good dose of syph or clap. Or a case of crabs. They'll roll you for your bankroll and cut your throat for a quarter. Why, even the colored themselves won't have anything to do with the people around here. Do you think we'd be down here if it wasn't for our jobs? Aren't there any white women up where you're from, Arnie? Go up to the Gold Coast, look around, ask a cab driver. If you got something special going for you with dark meat maybe they can even fix it up with some high-class colored dame. How would it look if we brought you into the station and booked you for what you've been doing and your old lady or the kids had to come down and bail you out? I'm surprised at a guy your age and with your kind of background being interested in this . . . stuff. We're going to let you go this time, Pop. Get in your car and get out of here. Go home."

But Magnuson drives deeper south into the black neighborhoods instead. He is too conspicuous. He will never find Robinson. Much less those blacks implicated in the murder plot. All this time wasted not on the search for the conspiracy but merely for the man to make the search. He decides to give up on Robinson and the black conspiracy and move on to the investigation of Chandler when he thinks of Two-Gun Washington. Why hasn't he thought of him before? He stops at a phone booth and learns from police headquarters the address of Washington and the surprising news that he has retired from the force. Which is even better for his purposes. Who knows the black underworld better or is more feared by it than Washington? While a plainclothes detective stationed on the South Side he was reported to have killed seven men in the line of duty, all black, although some claims put the number nearer thirty, again all black, many of these never reported much less investigated. Big, broad, bald, and black, his neck the size of a thigh and piled in folds above his collar, and always in that large fedora with its wide brim turned up all around the crown and loose-fitting suit without a tie, and smoking a cigar, he pounds on doors, shouting, "Open up, nigger! Two-Gun Washington is here and your time has come in the name of the law!" Then without waiting for an answer he shoots off the lock or shoulders the door off its hinges and with a service revolver in one hand and a sawed-off shotgun in the other bursts into the room with both of them blazing. Or so legend has it. Stories are also told of his beating confessions out of black prisoners. Of his being so rich from his extortions of black businesses that he owns numerous liquor stores and half the real estate of Jamaica. Allegedly he can walk into any South Side tavern and before the song he plays on the jukebox is finished the tavern will be cleared out. Although never publicized by the newspapers he is famous within the police department, infamous on the South Side, and legendary throughout the city as a whole.

Magnuson driving down the broad Midway of lawns and colonnades of shade trees, past the blocks on the moonlit Gothic buildings and towers of the University of Chicago. He finds the address easily, stumbles up the stairs, passes the open door of an apartment crammed with blond furniture where a large woman sprawls in an easy chair and perhaps eight children and teenagers sit in a row on a bed, watching a quiz show on television.

In the doorway of his apartment Washington awaits him, leaning on a cane, looking in his black bathrobe like the shadow of a gigantic and wrathful minister. He knows Magnuson when he identifies himself, recollects having done some "special assignments" for his agency in the past, and won't Mr. Magnuson come in? The only light from the television tuned to the baseball game, gray White Sox players standing motionless on a gray field. Washington passes through the reach of that gray light on the cane and a single stocky bowed leg which he hops on, springing forward almost from a squat and landing on his one foot with a noisy force that shakes the floor and rattles distant dishes, using his cane only for balance after landing. As though each step is a standing broad jump made with only one leg. "As you can see Two-Gun has only got one of his legs left," he says, puffing, setting himself for another hop. "He has got Berger's disease. That, as you may recall, is why I had to retire from the force and for no other reason. Some people have been saying he was shot in this leg, and that is how he lost it. But I know the truth about that leg, and now you know it too, Mr. Magnuson. He dropped a pistol on the big toe of that leg, of all the foolish things to have happened to him, and the sore never healed." He uses first person singular and plural and third person singular interchangeably when speaking of himself, as though in his head he is enough man for several men and is best approached by several points of view, or else, being a living legend, is himself confused between the myth and man. "We went out to the Hines' Veterans Hospital and they sawed off his leg. Like he was a turkey. I am not allowed to smoke or drink." But as Magnuson becomes accustomed to the weak and flickering light he makes out numerous empty beer bottles on the tables and cigar butts in the ashtrays. "And they are cutting his leg higher and higher. Someday there will be no more leg for them to cut. Only his hipbone. And then his guts."

With only one leg, Washington is worthless, and Magnuson has no choice but to fall back on Robinson. He asks Washington if he knows his whereabouts, claims that is why he came here, that Washington, if anyone, would know where to find the man.

"You have come to the right man," Washington says. For a while he leans forward, watching the White Sox have their turn at bat. The noise of the crowd buzzing more than cheering in the background. "That man a policeman somebody took his gun away from?" he says finally. Strong disapproval expressed. And contempt.

"He also goes by the name of Pimpy."

"Does he now," Washington says. Adding, "I don't know about that—." Doubtfully as though to tell Magnuson he has been misled. "There are lots of Pimpys."

"This man is supposed to be notorious."

"They are all notorious, Mr. Magnuson. But they cry like babies when they see Two-Gun coming after them. They are nothing but scum, them pimps. They all belong in jail or in the electric chair." He leans toward Magnuson confidentially. "The trouble with them is they are all cowardly and only violent with the women. They do not give you any excuses for shooting them down in the line of duty, you might say. But I know about this Robinson fellow. I know all about him." He is rocking in his chair and appears almost to be asleep. Magnuson suspects he knows nothing or only very little about Robinson but does not wish to show his ignorance. But then Washington starts forward in his chair, seems about to jump up on his one leg, leans his huge head into the path of the light coming from the television. "Some folks might say I know nothing about this man," he says. Then settling back into the chair, "But you and I know, Mr. Magnuson, the truth whereof I speak." A muted roar from the baseball crowd. His eyes are closed, and he laughs to himself, remembering perhaps the pleasure of beating or killing some pimp in his past, his voice as deep, Magnuson decides, as any human voice can get. Thick ridges of scars stand up on his knuckles, throat, chin, and cheeks, caused apparently by tremendous knife slashes and bullet wounds.

Then shouts from the street, lights flickering against the windows. "The police," Magnuson says. Below, patrol cars and a paddy wagon line up before a small hotel, with stone turrets, Victorian gables, awnings, and resembling a French chateau. Brown men and women file out beneath the bean-green canopy and disappear into the paddy wagon. A wailing ambulance pulls up to the curb. In the open window of a new high-rise and fenced-in dormitory of the university, Indians in turbans indicate with their bottles of soft drinks the hilarity of the scene below. The same scene in which Magnuson can read his destiny.

Washington hops to the window on that single leg, takes up the large pair of binoculars resting on the window sill. "They are always raiding that club," he says. "They got gambling. And whores. And dope. And they are always fighting." With what nostalgia, Magnuson wonders, is he recalling other raids on other nights and the battering down of barricaded doors with those arms and shoulders that have been made to break and splinter and send things flying, followed by his pitching a cowering man head first out the window, dropping to one knee and shooting in the back a second man in flight; then relishing the clutching of his knees and pleas for mercy from women who are naked or in nightgowns and who know him by reputation if not by name and sight, before beating a man with his fists in the back of the windowless wagon as the driver takes the long way to the station. "Ha-ha-ha," laughs Washington. Repeatedly. His head with the binoculars like the head and eyes of some large insect. The man identifying with his old comrades in blue below. A man who could break human limbs on his knees like other men break kindling. With teeth that could bite into human thighs, tear live meat from the bone. A man-killer. A man-eater. A cannibal who has killed real men. A hundred men. With real bodies. With human hearts and eyes and thoughts and feelings. Men put to death by the brutal but sanctioned violence within this man. This evil outside the law employed by the forces of good in the name of order. Magnuson is terrified of the man. He is inhuman. He is alive with death. He is swarming with it.

Washington is seated in the darkness now. Only his one big toe, which pokes into the path of the light from the television, is visible. Looking like a dismembered toe. Magnuson is fascinated by that dismembered-looking toe. He cannot take his eyes from it. "This Robinson may be at the Klondike Tavern," Washington says, pulling the toe back into the darkness. "He is one of that crowd that hangs out down there. We would go with you ourselves—"

"I know you would," says Magnuson, rising. "I understand about the leg—"

"Oh, not the leg. Why, I can get around on one leg better than most men can on two. He cannot run like a deer but he can hop like a rabbit." Then confidentially, "The trouble is, I have no clothes, and I will not have any clothes until tomorrow morning when I can get someone in the building to go to a clothing store and buy me a suit of clothes." He leads Magnuson to a closet and a wardrobe that resembles an aisle-long rack in a department store, hanger after hanger of immense double-breasted suits slashed and shredded by a razor. "See what she did to her black angel?" he says. "She did it just before she left, and for nothing but spite. And she took all my shoes, too. I expect she is going to sell them. Why I had over a hundred pairs of shoes. Of course I did not have any use for the left one any more. I used to shine shoes when I was a little gentleman and I have been buying shoes, the best there is, all my life.

She must have given some young man a dollar to put them in big boxes and carry them down the stairs. Then she must have taken them off in a taxi. If she ever comes back here, Mr. Magnuson, her black angel is going to beat her black and blue.—I mean he is going to beat her white and some other color. She is already black and blue." He laughs as if this is a joke, clapping Magnuson on the shoulder. Then adds at the door in a low voice of masculine collusion, as though Magnuson must know exactly what he means, "I am thankful it was just my clothes she cut."

Thereafter the neighborhood of the Klondike Tavern and the cosmopolitan South Side. A busy business intersection beneath the elevated tracks, noisy with car horns and music. Cars everywhere, doubleparked and cruising. Taverns, small nightclubs, palatial and Oriental-looking movie houses, department stores. The capital of the black city within the city. Men and women arm in arm and window-shopping and promenading. A crowd pouring out of a theater, an all-black stage show advertised on the marquees. Plastic and leather coats. The feeling of people who like to swagger and make themselves known along the street. Who work hard and have meat to eat and beer and whiskey to drink and tobacco to smoke and overtime to work and big checks to cash. Money is cars and clothes. Dreams are of even bigger and grander cars and more expensive clothes. And of speedboats with outboard motors and golf clubs and spinning rods and color television sets. A feeling that they are better men than black men elsewhere, and most white men anywhere. That if asked who they were they would say they were Chicagoans before they would say they were Negroes or Americans or anything else.

The plate-glass window of the Klondike Tavern blackened to the street, but inside it is well lighted with no hint that anything is secret or sullen and with the door open to the sidewalk. Crowded with middle-aged mustached men in sport shirts and fishing and golfing caps. Several-deep at the bar, and humming with the talk of men just off the afternoon shift of a payday at the plant, or fresh from the ballpark and a baseball game. The loud rhythm-and-blues of saxophones and electric guitars from somewhere in the rear. Magnuson orders a beer at the bar, and the bartender and the men pressed around him glance at him only once and thereafter ignore him as though he is not there.

He has another beer. And then another. He is among happy sweating men who seem to touch and shake and slap each other

often with their hands. Robinson is forgotten. He feels the fellowship in the air, is foolish enough to think that he belongs within its
solace and protection. If he were in blackface he would be safe.
The absurd possibility of charcoal. Special dyes . . . After all, he
would only have to do his face and neck, his hands only up to the
wrists . . .

The large young black man standing next to him is staring at
him through the smoke. He is the color of a bruise, and the most
handsome man that Magnuson has ever seen. He leans against Magnuson, leans hard. Pushes him and pins him by slow degrees up
against the bar. Stares hypnotically into Magnuson's eyes for what
seems minutes without blinking, his face fixed with a frown of hatred
and suspicion and outrage and challenge that strangely does not
seem unfriendly, as though his feelings are at once theatrical and
real. Magnuson returns the stare if not exactly with a look of hatred
then with the information that he will not be intimidated and will
accept all challenges, will meet violence with violence, receiving, if
he must, the worst of beatings. He is amazed that everyone is oblivious to his danger, that among this cluster of laughing men draining glasses such a silent and private confrontation is taking place.
By now the pressure on his chest is so great he can barely breathe,
nor can he reach back to pick up the beer bottle to defend himself,
for his arms are pinned against the bar. The man towers over him,
his head craning toward him like the head of a serpent, so that Magnuson must turn his head first one way and then the other to avoid
being touched by his face.

"I can see in your bonny blue eyes," the man says at long last,
smiling, "that you hate my guts." At that his face relaxes, and the
pressure is removed from Magnuson's chest. The black man leans his
elbows back against the bar. "Don't I know you from some place?"
he says suspiciously. "Sure I do. You are bad luck. You the man in
the Uncle Sam suit pointing his finger at me. You are daddy death.
We going to put you in the ground, daddy death, and walk on top
of your head." He is still smiling, even friendly.

A man close by in the crowd says to the black man, "Say there,
my man. Why don't you leave that old man alone?"

Magnuson's tormentor, still smiling, eases into the crowd and
disappears.

Magnuson looks after him and catches in a break among the
crowd of heads and shoulders a portion of a distant face. Robinson!
Or the man called Pimpy. Or the man on the street corner who

claimed he merely resembled Pimpy and was or was not Pimpy, was or was not Robinson, or was some other and third man entirely. But the Klondike is a long way across town from the neighborhood of the man who resembled Pimpy and Robinson's old address. Now that face seems to sort out Magnuson's face from brown and black and show an astonishment that could only come from an unexpected recognition. Because the face he sees is white, or is the face of Magnuson? Because he knows he is discovered? Or knows he is pursued? Then the man is no longer at his table but discovered elsewhere in search of some avenue of exit, or escape, ducking where he has to and taking men by the shoulders and forcing them apart as though opening sliding doors. Magnuson keeping his eyes on that bobbing head as he squeezes himself through the men along the bar. "Robinson!" he calls, afraid the man will make good his escape, his finger raised in the air to reveal his presence in the crowd.

Then an altercation of shoving, radiating outward through the crowd from some undetected source and preceded by noise of argument, as though the fight is occasioned by a mute insult, like someone stepping on another's toes. The crowd surging to assist someone attacked or to flee the fight, and Magnuson lifted from his feet and carried even deeper into the crush. Finds himself in the rear of the tavern pinned up against a small stage and peering down into the well of a brass bass saxophone, larger than the saxophonist who is on his knees and leaning backward, his cheeks puffed out, his eyes closed, the veins exploding in his head. The calls of foghorns interspersed between the rapid phrasings, the force of which he feels against his face. The monotonous feverish complaints of an electric Hawaiian guitar, the bar flying up and down the frets. A bartender beside the stage and shouting, "Louder!" The small band playing, if possible, even louder. Then the crowd, which he thought was working in a secret concert to keep him from the man called Robinson or Pimpy until that man could escape, now separates enough to reveal in a pocket in the crush ahead two black men flailing at each other with razors in a duel to cut and not to kill. Shirt fronts sliced, buttons missing, sleeves plastered to the arms by blood. Blood sails through the air in a string of drops, and, as though handfuls of it are being thrown, splatters against the shirts and faces of the retreating bystanders, who are shielding themselves with their hands, almost more afraid of being soiled than cut. Chairs and stools are overturned, glasses broken on the floor, and among the shards and spilled beer another man is crawling on his hands and knees while a young woman with her handbag underneath her arm like an airline stewardess is swearing and trying to get through the crowd and turning to kick at the head of the man on the floor with a wicked-looking high heel.

Magnuson outside and running down the block as an el overtakes him with a roar on the tracks overhead. Instinctively, before he can gauge the danger to himself, he flags down a police car cruising in the street and waves the black officers inside the tavern.

Blocks later and Magnuson cannot remember where he parked his car. What is he doing here in the middle of the night searching for a rented car? What is he doing here searching for Robinson? How far he has wandered from that original path down which he pursued the murderer, predicting and then discovering his crimes. So far that he doubts he can ever find his way back. How on earth did he come to be here in this black South Side city ghetto when his duty lay among the lawns and woods and lakefront mansions of Lake Forest? Protecting the Farquarson household if nothing else.

And what is he doing here when he has overlooked the most important clue he has in his possession? The envelope that contained the letter Farquarson sent to Wenzel was not addressed in Farquarson's handwriting! He removes the envelope from his pocket. He is right! It is not in the handwriting of the boxing notebook but in a woman's hand. Then whoever addressed the envelope presumably also took down the letter from Farquarson's dictation. And presumably this was either the nurse or the housekeeper, Mrs. Owens. One of whom knew the contents of that letter which named the murderer. That letter which was now in the hands of the murderer himself. Then the secret has been in Lake Forest all along! Why didn't he quiz the women about that letter when he was there last night? And why didn't they volunteer the information themselves? And what was to keep the murderer, now that he was no longer busy chasing about the countryside to silence witnesses, from discovering that the letter in his possession was not written in Farquarson's hand but in a woman's hand, and most likely a woman in the Farquarson house?

A telephone booth like an upright glass coffin on the empty street. It is carved and battered and with a light inside that will not go on when he shuts the door. He calls the Farquarson house to learn the name written in the letter and to warn the women of their danger. The name of the murderer only seconds away on the other end of the line. But a busy signal. A busy signal repeatedly. He has the operator try with no better luck. Then he remembers why. He himself ripped the Farquarson telephones from the walls. What a fool! Fortunately he recalls the Magnuson Man and Chicago policeman, Howard Meyer, whom he assigned to watch the Farquarson house tonight. He was not so great a fool that he had failed to think of that. The women are safe after all, as safe as he can make them. So is their secret.

Meanwhile he still cannot find his car. Where to now, he asks himself? If he is not yet wanted by the police he will be shortly. With his white face he is hardly safe upon these streets. It is as though he runs the gauntlet for miles with all the doors he passes closed to him. If only he were black. If only in this time of defeat and outlawry and insanity he could lose himself among these people, justifying and protecting himself amid the refuge of their black faces. To lose himself in anonymity and worthlessness. To be lost where it is possible to be at once lost and at home.

He finds a consolation he acknowledges as unreasonable: the farther he wanders from the trail of the murderer, the closer somehow he comes to the sources of the crimes.

CHAPTER TWENTY-NINE

SHADES AND CURTAINS

Mrs. Owens, housekeeper to Frazer Farquarson, is secluded in her room, suffering with her flu symptoms now that the morphine the nurse has given her is wearing off. As if to prove that her ailment is national but remediable a commercial on the television showing the profile of a sneezing, sniffling, aching man whose body is divided into numbered zones, like a butcher's diagram of a side of beef. Pills tumble down the throat zone into the stomach zone where they don infantry helmets and bayonet bugs that resemble centipedes with Chinese faces. Zone by zone the body is liberated, and the man slowly turns his smiling, pain-free face to the viewer, only to be replaced by a distinguished doctor with a mirror on his forehead who says, gesticulating with a tongue depressor, "It's no crime to be sick. The truth is, anyone can be sick. But science has shown conclusively it is downright silly not to make yourself feel better when you are sick."

"Of all the nonsense," she says, managing to switch off the set. "Who do they think we are, fools?" But the silence of the house disturbs her: underground rivers flow through underground caverns in her ears. So large a house and so few people living in it. She recalls with fear the sexual threats and invitations of the anonymous caller on the telephone. (Did men actually do *that* to women? She has heard they only did *that* to other men.) Why, without men or even so much as a man in the house he or anyone else could break in, rummage through the drawers, and ravish the women in their beds. She is accustomed to a large house, but a house that is, if anything, overcrowded and noisy at all hours with the horseplay of young men. For two years she, who never bore a child and was married late in life to a bounder who deserted her within a year, was the housemother of a college fraternity of eighty sons. She can still recall the name and face of each. Mom, they called her. Up until the day they "let her go." A mother sent packing by her sons.

To the charge that she was too permissive she might agree. After all, they were her boys, and boys would be boys. They rigged the telephone so they could call anywhere in the country free of charge and when the man from the telephone company came to investigate they went up to the roof and dropped paper sacks full of water on his head. They projected a color slide of a naked girl with her legs spread apart from the upper story of the house onto the front lawn of the sorority house next door. They kept drunken girls, and sometimes high-school girls, all night in their rooms. She knew all this and more, far more than the boys thought she knew, but she neither criticized nor reported them.

If her permissiveness alone were the reason for her dismissal she could acknowledge that the boys had had to make a difficult and manly decision, as critical of themselves as they were of her, and soothe herself with the balm that she had been so good to them that she had been bad for them. But there was more than this. Before the first year was out she could overhear the boys referring to her in such esoteric and slangy terms as "cipher," "zilch," "clod," "nonentity," "stereotype." She began to suspect she was also becoming something of a private joke among the girlfriends and real mothers and even the members of other houses on "frat row" which, considering the pride a house was to have in itself, must have hurt the boys most of all. That there was competition between the fraternities she was well aware, but did it exist on so trivial a battlefield as housemothers? They became ashamed of her, at first in public and then even among themselves, and solicitous of her welfare ("Why don't you go to your room and rest now, Mom. You look all in.") but only so as to keep her out of sight. They avoided her whenever possible and when they passed her room looked vaguely guilty or disgruntled. They flagged and quarreled and took to moping. Even the morale of the house as a whole dipped as though an evil influence dwelled within the walls, sucking at the spirit. It was remarked that during the tenure of the old housemother the house had not known such evil days. How was she to blame for such unhappiness? The twenty-year-old president, when he fired her, had criticized her image. Her own as a housemother, and that which she gave the house. With the woman herself and with her work they had no quarrel. Her "image"! Why, it was her image that was at fault. As if she or anyone else could do anything about that. What on earth was it, anyway?

She recalls the freshman boy some of the boys took down into the basement on rush night for a game of Ping-Pong, isolating him from the other prospective pledges. "A dog," they called him among themselves. At the time she thought it cruel but necessary perhaps, and more kindly certainly than telling him to get out which, since it was a private house, they had every right to do. After all, it had been unpleasant for the brothers too, since they would have much rather been upstairs drinking beer in better company. Only later did she realize how the boys kept her from girlfriends, parties, and prospective pledges by engaging her in conversations in her office, oftentimes delegating the responsibility to the newest pledges as part, perhaps, of the trial of their initiation. She had even been encouraged to speak of what was most precious and private to her, her childhood and parents and the older brother who died when just a boy. She might as well have recited phone numbers for all it mattered to her bored but smiling boys. And why is it, she wonders, that she can recall that freshman boy down in the basement, missing the Ping-Pong ball and slamming his paddle against the table and the side of his head, with greater vividness than she can any of her eighty boys?

But enough. Bad times are not to be dwelled on. She resolves that flu or no flu she will rise from bed. But the nurse is there again, administering despite her drowsy protestations more "cold serum" in her arm. Flu, "cold serum," heating pad, mercifully begin to take their toll, and she surrenders to her forty winks.

Suppertime. The basement of the fraternity. Candlelight. A dozen tables. Eighty boys in ties and jackets standing behind their chairs. The president seating her beside him at the head table. Delphiniums "bella donna" in a vase before her place.

"*Bon appétit,* Mom!" the boys shout in the gleeclub harmony of their eighty voices. She smiles and nods in regal and maternal recognition, as though to tell them they may take their seats. Eighty chairs scrape along the floor, eighty boys sit down, eighty chairs scrape forward. Waiters in white jackets hurry into the candlelight, emerging from the dark.

Nancy Rhinelander, who has managed to get downstairs and give Mrs. Owens another shot of morphine, now manages to get back upstairs, where she collapses across her bed. She imagines herself awake and at her desk, writing a letter to her former husband, an airline pilot she met for the first time in Korea when he was a fighter pilot and she an army nurse. "Dear Dick," she writes. "I am writing this as I squat naked on the couch, smoking a cigarette." She pauses to sort out her opinions on the proximity of love to hate, and their application to the failure of their marriage. But as with the real letters she has attempted to write him in the past two years the pen even in her sleep and imagination falters. "You motherfucker!" she writes instead. The same insult that once caused him to slap her face, that caused her to threaten him with a carving knife, that caused him, after first revealing the cowardice she always knew was in his heart by turning from her and trying to run away, to wrestle the knife away and punch her in the jaw. She crumples up the imaginary letter. Don't beat a dead snake, she tells herself.

Then she imagines herself in the bed of the apartment in which she lived when she was married and waking to find a man asleep beside her. He is naked beneath the sheet, his face buried in the pillow. A heaviness to the flesh and freckles along the back. She isn't certain that she recognizes the body. She studies the length and breadth of him, listens to the power of his breath expended against the pillow, strokes the heavy hairs along his skin, smells the bitterness of his flesh, tastes the sweet salt of his shoulder with her lips. What could be more perfect, she reminds herself, stretching, than to lie beside a sleeping man in the morning when neither has to rise and go to work and when she herself is only half-asleep?

Later she sleeps. Fantasies of dogs digging in the garden. A hand rapping on the window. A man with a spade on his shoulder strolling across the lawn and whistling "Jesus Loves the Little Children."

How many days and nights have passed since the man called Magnuson was here? And since that night when he was here has it ever been day? An interminable night. The night of a patient who has been given gas. Sometimes she thinks: It is only an hour after sundown. Other times: It will be sunrise at any minute. Where is Magnuson? Where are the police? The doctors? Where is anyone?

Footsteps in the gravel of the drive below. Pacing back and forth and the scraping of feet, as though toeing the gravel to learn what surface lies beneath. She is at the window. No more pacing now. She catches him directly beneath on the eavesdrop with his face against the glass. Thorsen? Magnuson? Skipper? Cavan? Or someone else? On the shore waves that sound like wind. Like someone breathing in an iron lung. The feeling of an island. Of being alive inside a house where everyone else is dead. She removes the pistol from her drawer, where it is wrapped up in a pair of panties, only to replace it. If she could bring herself to fire it the man called Magnuson would be wounded now, or dead. Unarmed she steals downstairs. She picks up the phone—but even if she could have called who could she call? She cradles the dead phone against her ear. Magnuson, she remembers, has cut the wires.

Upstairs again and at the window she sorts out the man from the clump of trees below in which he hides. Then a match is struck, the small flickering fire illuminating the cupped hands and the upper half of the face. Now only that red circle of light from the ash of the cigarette in the darkness. A single fiery eye. The signal from Cavan that tells her he is there and that if she is willing, the game begins. Cavan to whom she has confessed through the glass the depths of her loneliness and selfishness and secret cowardice in the face of men with feelings in the flesh and the weakness of that savage necessity of her woman's sex which she must satisfy alone and for which she feels corrupt. How can there be anything good and natural between them when he knows all this?

She fears the urge to succumb to the safe eroticism of the pattern. Addicted to the ritual as much as to the lust; excited by the game and even by the very idea of perversion as much as by the thrill of setting free the spirit of the animal in her sex. She surrenders almost against her will and with a sense of hopelessness, judging in her guilt and danger and proximity to death that she is down and down to stay. With nerve-wracked pleasure she steps into her role. Opens up the window and adjusts the shade at a level not far below the top. It is the signal in reply that she will play. Switches on the dresser lamps, making her window the only lighted window in the house, then paces back and forth before the window, watching that glowing cigarette from the corner of her eye and pausing now and then with her arms folded across her breast to glance out the window as though to beg the man to go away and not to drive her into doing what he knows she has no choice but to do. Back and forth, shaking her blond hair about her head. Fingering the buttons on the front of her uniform and then unbuttoning them, but absently, as though her thoughts are somewhere else. Now out of range of the window and hoping that flashes of the uniform as she removes it can be seen in the outskirts of the window frame. Suddenly and brazenly before the window again, walking right up to it and then retreating, this time in her slip, which is also white, examining and brushing with her hand the uniform she hangs on a hanger in the closet at the rear of the room, only the upper portion of which, because of the angle, is visible to anyone below. Back and forth before the window, pausing several paces from the window sill where she slides the straps of her slip off her shoulders and lets them hang around her waist, revealing the glossy and white brassiere and the tan flesh that swells against the confines of the edges. Facing the window she removes the brassiere, reaches behind her awkwardly to unclasp it, then slides the straps down her length of arms, and her breasts, full and long and with nipples that are red, fall free. She places an arm across her breasts and scratches an underarm. To remove the stockings she must get as close as she can to the window if the man below is to see her legs above the knee. Hikes up her slip and, bending over so that her breasts swing before her waist, unfastens the stockings at the hip. Immediately they collapse and lose their shape along her legs. She goes to the window, yawns, fiddles with the open window and with the shade without changing either, then places her hands firmly on the window sill, throws back and broadens her muscular shoulders, lifting her breasts, and breathes in the air. Holding the slip bunched up around her waist she walks in the disarrayed stockings over to the bed where she sits down and rolls the stockings down her legs and off her feet. Carries them to the closet and, while in passage across the floor and directly before the window, lets the slip fall from her waist to lie around her heels. Picks up the slip and in her panties carries it to the closet. While there, with her back to the window, she hooks her thumbs inside her pants and pushes them off her buttocks and to the floor where she steps out of them, one long leg at a time. Picks up a hairbrush from the dresser and, naked now, walks back and forth before the window, brushing her hair. Back and forth nervously, letting the abandon build within her loins. When out of sight of the man below she touches her vagina, stiffening and her head jerking back as though in pain. No more than several strokes and her limbs would jerk, her nerves jangle, and she would double up and come. At the window and gazing directly and drunkenly and even sadly at that intense red eye. The game is about to end with the drawing of the shade. But the surge of will to put an end to the obedience to the pattern, the cowardice, the intellectual and lonely sex, the pleasure found only when pleasure is combined with torment. Smash the glass! Down there is life. Cavan for all his faults and failings and her own unwillingness to love him is still a man. With knees and armpits and ribs and pores and hairs and the beginnings of a pot belly. Made of the elements. Full of salt and sweat and semen. Who is here on the worst night of her life. She leans out of the window into the night and beckons for the first time with her arms for him to enter, meaning by it house, bedroom, woman. The red circle of light sailing through the darkness, as though the cigarette is thrown, and moments later disappearing, stamped out beneath the unseen foot. She has done the thing at last. She throws herself backward with a force capable of injury, and reaching out shuts off the light, hoping that her action and her arm were seen.

They were. As well as all that came before. By Howard Meyer, the Chicago policeman on vacation and Magnuson Man dispatched by Magnuson to watch over the Farquarson house and protect, if necessary, its occupants from danger. Stopped in his tracks by the single square of light among the darkness as he came out from behind the potting shed where, unseen from the house, he paused in his silent and unseen rounds to steal a smoke, his hands cupped around the cigarette just in case. Holy mother! What an unexpected and erotic sight! The lovely woman prancing in her shiny underwear that was sometimes silver in the light, sometimes gold. And then to show her ass! And then, climax upon climax, a triangle of honey-colored pubic hair! He could not believe his eyes. His heart a single heartbeat, his mouth dry, his knees unhinged, his breath short, hands delving into his entrails as though kneading dough. A family man with seven children and a recent grandfather for the first time, he cannot easily believe that the performance in the window was anything but accidental. In a place as private and secluded as this she must not be in the habit of drawing shades. And how would she know that a prowler, albeit legitimate, was on the grounds below? It was improper for him to have looked. He feels ashamed that he is aroused. It seems unfair that he should be so at her expense, as though he has somehow managed to take advantage of her innocence. He holds his breath, hoping the erection will go down.

Still, her actions did suggest she was playing some deliberate and erotic game with herself. Even so, that was her business—certainly not his.

But then again her motions at the window might have been a signal for someone down below to enter. Has he been noticed after all? Or did Mr. Magnuson tell her that he would be down there? As a policeman he has certainly had such invitations before, none of which he would have ever thought to accept. There was that society dame in Rogers Park who went after policemen in uniform, trying to make them lay her in squad cars and showing them the dildo she carried in her handbag.

Still another possibility occurs to him. Unknown to him, is someone else upon the grounds, someone whose presence is known to the woman in the window? He had best have a look around. He hurries across an open stretch of lawn, pauses behind a spruce, slides into a clump of rhododendrons, moving to a place beneath the now darkened window of that naked woman.

In the room she waits with her hands spread open on her stomach, fingertips where her pubic hair begins. Aching in the dark, eaten up with urges. She waits so long she seems to fall asleep and dream of urges. Seems to hear outdoors, as though from the farthest corner of the estate, the interchange of men's voices, scuffling and huffing, a cry for help, a noise like a deer breaking through underbrush, and then as though someone is chopping kindling. But no one comes inside the house.

Whistling outdoors. Of a kind that is a signal to come out or open up. Of course! Cavan has lost his key! She steals through the darkened house, inexplicably bringing the sheet with her, which she clutches at her breasts and drags between her legs, and unlocks the door, then runs back upstairs anticipating the door flying open at her back and his bounding after her up the stairs, catching her on a landing and throwing her down upon the runner or pinning her up against the wall or newel post or balustrade, or failing that, catching her in time to throw himself upon her as she throws herself back upon the bed. But she is not chased up the stairs, and when she falls into her bed she falls alone.

Downstairs the door opens only after the lock has been fiddled with and the doorknob rattled. She pictures Cavan on the threshold with the doorknob in hand, that worried, confounded, and lately desperate look upon his face, the frown above the mouth opened perpetually in surprise, wondering how the door has suddenly become unlocked, who has unlocked it, and what it means. She bites the back of her hand to keep from laughing. But no Cavan bounding up the stairs, three stairs at a time. In fact, no Cavan on the stairs at all. She thinks she hears a distant refrigerator door opening, the clank of bottles, the scraping of a kitchen chair. Cavan, she tells herself, that's who. Searching for a bottle of chilled wine and a pair of wine glasses to bring upstairs.

Then the pounding on a distant door. Heavy with authority and the threat of brutality. The police at last! The man's voice: "Open up!" Not the voice of Cavan. Nor the voice of Magnuson. But of a man not to be trifled with.

The remote and frightened voice of Mrs. Owens, as though coming through a dozen doors ten floors below.—What is it that she said?

The answer, "Death."—What is the question she has asked? Who are you? Who is it please?

Then another answer, "Life!" The voice enraged, amused, breathless.—Dear God, has she asked him what he wanted?

This followed by Mrs. Owens's high-pitched voice again, this time suddenly crystal clear, as close as the room next door. "But I didn't say that on the phone!"

"No phone," says the voice. "That letter—you wrote it!"

"I don't . . . I didn't . . . What letter do you mean? . . . I didn't write you any letter . . . I don't write letters . . ." It is a whimper that threatens to become a scream.

What sounds like the smashing of an ax into the panels of a door, the splintering of wood. Mrs. Owens making noises as though winding up to sneeze.

Death, the nurse repeats, listening to him go about his business. She has always known he would be masculine. Something with a mustache and a crew cut and wearing boots. In the uniform of an officer. Or the overalls of a farmer. Or the flashy white suit of a black tap dancer. What a relief though—what good luck!—that he has come only for Mrs. Owens. But what guilt too, for, as she well knows, Mrs. Owens is innocent of the crime for which she must be punished. Unquestionably a dreadful mistake is being made. But such are the injustices of life, the tricks of destiny. Mrs. Owens—your time has come! You are a drop of water that has reached the bottom of the waterfall, the last calorie of heat to leave the sun. Even so, she should not have let poor Mrs. Owens take the blame. She will be punished for that, she can be certain of that, she knows that. Mrs. Owens is quiet now. It is all gone out of her: breath, color, the five senses—everything! No more thumping and knocking about downstairs.

Then those kitchen noises again, as though the man has returned to eat. Later subtle changes in the darkness of the hallway outside her door. Lights in distant parts of the house are going on and off one at a time, as though a search is being made of all the rooms. The man is speaking to someone in what she thinks at first must be a foreign language, later a language that is unintelligible and that he makes up as he speaks, talking to himself. He has had his victim. Now he will have to leave.

The stairway light comes on, traveling down the hallway and penetrating the threshold of her room. The light switched off again. Footsteps on the stairs. If she is quiet and very good and very still and goes to sleep he will have no choice but to go away. If he does not, then she will know it is only a morphine nightmare taking a turn for the worst.

She intuits his presence in the doorway. He says nothing. He does nothing. He neither enters nor goes away. A breeze blows across her nakedness. The curtains billow out into the gloom like ghosts that would escape but are tethered to the window. The silhouette of her own breasts rises and falls against the lighter background of the window and the starlit night beyond. The lake is washing on the shores of another planet.

"That letter," he says softly, as though in explanation of his charge against her. "This conspiracy." He whose work she has seen on battlefields and in sickrooms and hospitals. Who has been clinging to her nurse whites. Who has been her soft-spoken adversary in a thousand battles. Who has known all along that he would triumph in the end. Who comes as a stranger, and as her death and lover all in one. He is no better and no worse than those who came before. He is only what comes next.

The engine of his breath above her, his mass cutting off the breeze, the starlit sky in the window. The heat and reek of horses. She reaches out to embrace him and repulse him and takes the first blows on her arms.

Bloody, her murderer goes downstairs into the bathroom and cleans the ax in the toilet bowl, where he leaves it, the handle sticking up above the seat. He sees the futility of washing his hands in the sink, strips naked, stuffing his clothes in the hamper, and takes a shower. The water beats against the plastic shower curtains he has pulled around the tub. He does not dry himself but like a creature that has just crawled naked from the sea walks through the house, dripping water and leaving his damp footprints across the floor. In his hand he carries the Magnuson Man badge shaped like a shield and emblazoned with the double M and the Chicago policeman's badge he has taken from the body of the man he has just killed outdoors.

He returns to the kitchen and the jars of pickled pigs' feet and dill pickles he has found in the refrigerator and sits naked at the kitchen table with the stiff propriety of a Prussian officer. He eats by the light of the open refrigerator door. He breaks a large pig's foot into several pieces with his hands, then takes the pieces into his mouth where he sucks the jelly and grinds off the flesh between his teeth, expelling clean nuggets of bone and gristle upon his plate. The dill pickle he slices paper-thin with fork and knife. In the refrigerator he finds the carcass of a huge turkey covered by tinfoil. He brings it on its platter to the table and picks at it with his fingers, stripping the flesh from the almost translucent bones. With one bare hand he digs into the body cavity, penetrates his arm up to the elbow, and brings out a handful of stuffing, which he eats from his hand. He rinses the dishes in the sink, scrubbing them with his fingertips, shuts the refrigerator door.

He finds the door to Farquarson's bedroom locked and instead of fetching the ax to chop it down he goes outdoors and walks naked across the lawn, stepping over the body of the man he left upon the grass. He climbs up the ladder that still leans against the house below Farquarson's still open window, and enters through the same window as he did on the night before.

The wasted shape of the corpse beneath the sheet upon the bed. The triumph he feels at beholding his archenemy laid low. His eyes sealed by death, and the death-dealing rays he could deliver from them when alive shut up inside his head. He gloats and grins above the corpse, puffs himself up. Puts his hand around his penis as though upon a magical and potent staff that protects him from his enemies and destroys whoever he points it at while rubbing it like a stick that starts a fire. Farquarson, the soul-murderer, unmasked and made a subject of his realm. Farquarson, who imprisoned him in a madhouse where the doctors, nurses, orderlies, and other patients were Farquarson agents engaged in a conspiracy to convince him that he was mad (How better to make a man crazy than keep him in a madhouse?) and deprived him of his right to vote so as to prove to him that he was not an American citizen but a foreigner with a foreign-sounding name, brainwashing him into accepting the dupe identity of an impoverished and impotent incompetent. While Farquarson himself from the safety of this very house sent his murderous rays through the prison walls to burn his mind and rot his nerves and blight his seed, attacks he resisted by lying absolutely motionless for weeks on end, pretending to be a corpse and therefore invulnerable to the damage of the rays. He was like a man tied to a tree, at whose eyes someone was throwing darts, until he heard that voice talking to him in the night and was resurrected and made his ascension over the walls and above the clutches of the soul-murderers below and shed his dupe identity and became transfigured, regaining his power and destroying his oppressor. Along with that network of myrmidons and minions Farquarson organized to spy on him— and interfere with him—and conspire against him—Farquarson dupes who are his enemies. A vast conspiracy that surely must include all living men. He is afraid that at this rate his work will never end.

He decides to hide his nakedness in the magic of Farquarson's clothes. Underwear, jacket, trousers, and hat are strewn across a chair, a pair of shoes and socks are on the floor. As though thrown there when Farquarson undressed some months ago and climbed into his bed. Odd that they should be wrinkled and stiff and muddy as though only recently wet and dried.

He backs down the ladder and, in the stiff, pinching shoes and flapping jacket and beltless trousers he must hold up with his hands, having paused to pin the Magnuson Man badge to the inside of one lapel and the Chicago police badge to the other, he runs off into the night.

CHAPTER THIRTY

THE DEATH
OF TANKER

As the news of the murder of the policeman traveled through the city the mood in elevated trains and on elevated platforms and on buses and in movie theaters and on the streets became electric. The excitement of a tornado watch was in the air. It passed from one person to the next and created in all a single consciousness of what had happened and an apprehension of what was to happen next. Like the solemn and incensed policemen they studied for an insider's insight into the depth of the prevailing passion, they became obsessed with the killer, read the sensational stories of his prosaic life in the newspapers, checked the newsstands for extra editions of further news, searched for him in the face of every stranger of a comparable physique and age, daydreamed of discovering him and participating in his capture and even death. It was simultaneously high drama and the hellfire of history. They believed the killer could be detected at any moment and shot down on their own street, in their own building, before their own eyes. While some killers of policemen had managed to live long enough to be executed and in a few cases only to be imprisoned, enough had been shot dead for Chicagoans to believe it was a tradition of the city and a code among the police that they themselves avenged the killing of their own. Citizens not only believed this, they sanctioned it. It appealed to their sense of the just and irreversible working out of fate. The crime had set in motion a ritual beyond the control of police, murderer, and citizens alike. Only the death of the murderer could satisfy it. He had made the city conscious of itself as a city, and had become the property of the city as a whole. He was one man with the whole city set against him, if with no other weapon than the resignation to see him dead. To many people he was like magic, and they claimed special knowledge of him. If they did not know him personally, they were the friends or cousins of someone who did; invariably he was described as very ordinary and even a "nice guy" who because of some injustice in the past at the hands of the police had become a "cop-hater." Every street and neighborhood was anxious to claim his presence, which meant equally his death.

He had been sighted everywhere; he had already been shot down by the police in any of a hundred locations, including—a rumor popular among blacks—an apartment on the South Side, although why a white man would hide out for his life in a neighborhood entirely black the informants did not explain; he had killed a second and even a third policeman, always the most prevalent rumor, and one that further charged the electricity already in the air. In addition there were those two inevitable rumors, that the underworld in order to demonstrate its own innocence and outrage was secretly co-operating with the police, and that confessions had just been beaten out of suspects with rubber hoses in the basement of the jails.

Meanwhile the weight of the moral concern of the city was on slender shoulders. Despite rumors to the contrary, Tanker had made it safely back to his own neighborhood on the morning of the murders of Scarponi and the policeman and there he had remained. He was in a third-floor apartment of an old frame tenement on a street of like tenements interspersed with small frame houses often covered with asphalt shingles that could have passed for miners' housing in a West Virginia town. This apartment had always been rented to some member of the Baumgartner family, a large clan of second and third cousins to his good friend Ralph Borman. Through Borman he had learned of the availability of the apartment, and unknown to Borman he had rented it only a week before the killings. The name on the mailbox said Baumgartner as it had for more than forty years. He gave the landlord the name of "Mr. LaChance," no first name, only that, a name he thought up on the spur of the moment and of which he was very proud. Here in his old neighborhood if he had the disadvantage of being easily recognized he had the advantage, momentarily anyway, of an animal in his own territory. It was the first place the police would look for him, and yet all in all it was still the safest place for him to hide.

The apartment had only one entrance and exit and that was the wooden back stairs, which looked tacked on to the building. On the front above the street was a porch enclosed with windows on which the shades were always drawn. All the floors were covered with well-worn linoleum and tilted one way or another. The whole apartment smelled of cabbage, not sauerkraut so much as fresh cabbage allowed to rot, mixed with the smokiness of kielbasa and thuringer. There was the sour smell too of a large, heavyset family's sweat in a summer heat wave, or of clothes that have dried improperly in humid weather. All the plumbing was rust-colored. Two empty cases of beer quarts were beneath the sink. At times Tanker admitted to himself that this apartment was not only his prison, it was his tomb.

The only person who knew that he was here was Della Nakowiecz, the young girl he was living with. She had been the main reason for renting the apartment a week before the killings. She had told him she was eighteen, which he had interpreted to mean that she was sixteen, only to have recently discovered to his disgust that she was only fourteen going on fifteen, and that having flunked at least one semester of high school, she would only have been finishing her freshman year had she not run away. It meant that back when he and Borman picked her and her girlfriend up on the street (they were both cutting school) and drove around the city in broad daylight drinking beer from quarts, the two girls on either side of Tanker in the back seat, each with a hand around his erect penis, and Tanker with his arms outstretched shouting out the window to passers-by, "I am Jesus Christ!" she and the girlfriend were only thirteen. This depressed him; he did have scruples.

She liked to stay indoors in the apartment and listen to the radio, and play 45 rpm records on her small phonograph, and set her hair, and paint her nails. She wanted to be grown up, to play house, to become overnight exactly like her middle-aged mother, and to do so with that incompatible sense of rebellion and adventure. Sometimes he wondered if she didn't see the days she spent with him as in a movie. She did not seem to understand yet the futility of his situation. Just this afternoon she regretted that her girlfriends could not come over and meet him and see her house. Thus far she had been devoted to him, called him "My guy," and had done whatever he asked of her. Once he even sent her out to buy rubbers at the drugstore and quizzed her at length on how the druggist had reacted to her. What had he said? She said? How had he looked? She was creating a wealth of anecdotes for him to tell "the guys" about. It was too bad, he reflected sadly, that he would not have the chance to tell them.

He thought of sending her home, for he believed this would ennoble him. But he thought her stupid or naïve or possibly retarded, and he did not trust her not to reveal his identity and whereabouts in the neighborhood. After all, her old man and old lady might beat hell out of her until she told them where she had stayed and with whom. He also wanted her and believed he deserved her company in the evil days that lay ahead. Without her he would have to go himself into the street. Instead he could send her out for the hot dogs and tamales and roast beef sandwiches with hot peppers sold at the local stands. She did not know how to cook, nor did he, nor did either of them know much about buying groceries. But they could always eat, as they had today, canned soup and potato chips.

According to the radio the police were already conducting house-to-house searches in the neighborhood but so far they had not come to the door. Tanker had been terrified to overhear two old ladies in his building discussing on the gangway below his window how a pair of policemen had searched and banged around in the basement that morning. He recalled hearing the noises, the belligerent voices, but had taken them for the work of the janitor. Della had been instructed to tell any stranger at the door that she was Olive Baumgartner and her mother was not at home. To the landlord, or anyone in the other apartments, she was Mrs. LaChance.

Already Tanker was desperate for money. He was afraid to send Della out to look for work because she looked too young and might be recognized as a runaway. He was reluctant to call either Fiore or Romanski for fear it would not be in their interest to acknowledge that they knew him, much less to give him money and help him to escape. He suspected that if Fiore knew where he was he would have him killed, and that if Romanski knew, he would tell Fiore.

Besides, after he killed the policeman it ceased to be anyone's affair but his own. He might injure them, but where was the sense if he condemned himself in an attempt to ruin them? And why should he attempt what was futile when he had the courage and the common sense to admit to himself that he had come to his unfortunate but logical and even justified end?

He had only change left, and this he emptied from his pockets on the kitchen table. He gave it all to Della, along with a shopping bag and instructions how to get to a tavern several miles away where he was certain they would sell her liquor. There was enough money for carfare and six quarts of the cheapest beer. If asked she was to say she was nineteen, and if asked for identification to say she had none. If she still did not get the beer, she was to leave. She was also to save a dime and call Ralph Borman. If Philomena his wife answered she was to hang up. If Borman answered she was to tell him where he was and that he was to come tonight and bring all the money, no matter how little, he could get his hands on. He knew this was dangerous, but it was either contact Borman, the only man he believed he could trust, or go himself into the streets. He was certain the police had questioned Borman but that if they followed him here tonight they would think he was only going to his cousins' house, where he had gone often in the past. He who had dreamed of coming by money easily and spending it lavishly and indiscriminately now dreamed of the miracles he could perform with five dollars. If he could just get a few dollars out of Borman he would try to sneak out of town. Summer was coming and he could go to Wisconsin and live in the woods beside a farm, sneaking out at night to rob the fields of vegetables. By fall the search for him might not be so intense, and he could come out in the open and go elsewhere.

When hours passed and Della did not return he started to watch the street, pistol in hand. When she finally came she was carrying the shopping bag, which had torn under the weight and the wetness of the beer bottles, by the bottom in both hands. She had forgotten his directions, missed her stop and ridden the bus to the end of the line, and had to return, so that there had been money for only five quarts. She had been embarrassed, she said, because the bag had broken on the bus and the brown necks and bottoms of the big bottles had protruded and everyone had looked at her. She had called Borman, he had sounded frightened and wanted her to hang up, saying over and over again in a loud whisper, "Are you nuts?"

and had made no promise to come. "What's going to happen to us, Tanky?" she said.

"Nothing," he said. He went into the living room, sat in a dumpy chair with an open quart of beer between his legs, and listened to the top fifty hits on the radio he had had Borman's wife steal him on assignment. It occurred to him that Borman was at heart a coward and too much in trouble with the law himself to dare to come. Still, he was an old friend and knew what that demanded of him. But then again since Tanker's present difficulty derived in good part from Borman's failure to do his job and steal the car Tanker needed for the killing of Scarponi, he might be too afraid of Tanker to come. Tanker however did not hold grudges or nurse grievances and had already forgiven Borman, resolving to say nothing about it to Borman if he came. In fact, considering how Borman's failure corroborated Tanker's notion of his character, or his lack of it, he found it exactly right and amusing. Something to tell "the guys" about later.

When night came and still no Borman he wandered out onto the back porch and leaned over the railing. He thought he saw a nighthawk across the alley, gliding above the roofs and wires. Several blocks away the spire of a Catholic church where he had taken his first communion, and the glow of a distant expressway, and the remote noises of tires and horns. Then he had somehow run down the stairs and gone into the alley to the edge of the shady street before he realized, as if waking from a dream, that he was about to set out on foot into the city. He froze. The night was balmy, erotic, holding the promise of adventure on distant streets, a time to be out on sidewalks beneath blowing elms. The natural and powerful desire to walk blindly on a tramp that would last all night and take him through the blocks of strange neighborhoods or along the railroad tracks as far out as the suburbs. To make a sandwich and wrap it up in wax paper and put it in his pocket, as his grandfather had done almost daily in the years after he retired and before he died, setting out on foot into the streets, calling Tanker's father from some remote neighborhood to come and get him when he became too lost or tired to go on. It was a practice Tanker had imitated since he was a boy, even after he owned a car and it was fashionable to drive out into the country or cruise the city streets. But how terrifying to imagine doing such a thing now, never mind actually coming as close to doing it as he just had! He hurried back to the apartment. The simple life of driving cars and walking was in the distant past.

Later that night Borman came plodding up the back stairs accompanied by his two children, the six-year-old boy and three-year-old girl, whose presence Tanker assumed was meant to throw the police off the track. Borman carried a sack containing two quarts of beer and laid seven dollars, mostly in change, on the table, claiming in his shy sleepiness this was all he had. His forearms and face were soaking wet, and it was apparent he wished to leave as soon as possible. But Tanker was so grateful and glad to see him that he made him sit at the kitchen table and drink as he did from an open quart of beer. Thereupon he described for Borman how he had killed Scarponi, slapping his forehead and laughing when he explained how he had foolishly bungled the disposal of the body. He also described in precise detail his encounter with the cop he shot, including the lighting of the filter end of his cigarette before the cop's eyes, which again had him laughing at himself. He was aware that he was giving an oral history which he hoped would be repeated later. He expected to be talked about with fondness and appreciation by Borman and other friends for years to come. He regretted killing Scarponi, he said. But since Scarponi had likely killed men himself, or had them killed, he regretted most the killing of the cop. He had been a good man and that was the way it was in this world with all the rotten cops there were that when you were backed into a corner and had to kill a cop it had to be a good one. He wasn't excusing himself by any means but he was not the culprit so much as was the stupidity of fate. Someday Borman was to tell the cop's widow or mother that Tanker was sorry for what he had to do, and he was to try to tell her what Tanker was really like, just a guy, not all that bad. He rubbed his eyes as he said this.

During this report Borman's son, wearing a Cubs baseball cap too large for his small head, sat in a chair beside his father, his face intimidated and rigid. The girl sat on the kitchen floor, her back stiff and legs apart like a plastic doll, and played with nothing. Her eyes were small and pink, like a rabbit's. Both children seemed to have spent days and nights on end whimpering. Tanker had always suspected Philomena, who he believed was crazy, of slapping them around if not of tortures far worse. Borman, he knew, was too weak to interfere or complain. Neither child had ever looked as though it would survive childhood.

Borman had taken the boy to the Cubs baseball game that afternoon in Wrigley Field. Tanker had listened to the game on the radio, and they talked at length and with animation about the game, and the state of the Cubs and the course of the season in general.

Borman then told of his recent troubles, the thwarted attempted robbery with a toy pistol of the cab driver who had turned out to be a moonlighting cop, and his subsequent beating in the back seat of the cab. Small bruises, scabs, and patches where he had been stitched could still be noticed on his fat, pretty, childlike face. His blond hair was stiff and wet-looking and he habitually shook his head to send his forelocks away from his eyes. He was wearing a soiled short-sleeve shirt with the sleeves folded carefully almost up to his shoulders, the butchered execution of his savage blue and green tattoos revealed along his arms.

Della was grateful for this opportunity to demonstrate her womanly affection for Tanker to a third party, the first she had had since setting up house, and she remained close to Tanker, sitting at his side with her elbow on the table and turned sideways to gaze into his eyes as he spoke. Later she stood behind his chair with her arms around his shoulders, staring at Borman to see how he responded to this. When Tanker rose to open another quart of beer she came up behind him and grabbed him around the waist as though she would not allow him to escape, while he continued to converse excitedly with Borman and, oblivious to her presence, dragged her back and forth only dimly aware that his mobility was in some way encumbered. In the meantime Borman, who got drunk easily, relaxed and smirked sleepily from a face that became soft and red.

Sooner or later the two men began to recount, as they always did when together, stories and anecdotes from their past, as though what had happened to them only a few years ago had happened in some remote and golden age. They were of incidents they had told each other many times before. Both knew exactly what the other would say. Sometimes one would add information, often with excitement and laughter, that the other left out in his telling. There was to be no new insight into the remembrance, or alteration of events, or even if possible no change in the very words, down to the dialogue quoted. It was as if they were trying to demonstrate that the stories were committed to memory, repeatable at any time.

Tanker again recalled the funeral parlor where their friend Perdido worked when, after drinking in the coffins and while wearing the capes and plumed hats of the Knights of Columbus, Tanker and Perdido placed the corpse in the front seat of Borman's car. Borman laughed but could also be seen to shudder at the thought of the beautiful but dead girl beside him on the seat. "Such a waste," he said as he always did at this moment in the story. Tanker was recalling at length his screams and flight from the car. Then Tanker wondered if Perdido, who was strange and therefore to be appreciated if not admired, had ever done anything with the dead bodies of good-looking women. It was a question he would not have dared to ask before. Borman offered the opinion that Perdido had. Their remembrances then centered on the days when they had hung out at a shabby neighborhood tavern near the tannery and river called the Golden Trumpet. It had been frequented by Lesbians, good-looking girls who were prostitutes, and their butches, and the men who sought them out. It had been at this time, Borman remembered with a shudder of distaste, that he had first been AWOL from the air force and had been hiding out in the apartments of one friend after another and had finally been forced to make money to support himself by letting himself be picked up by queers. Tanker next recalled how they used to play poker at Philomena's house when they were kids, and Philomena's mother would take a quarter from every pot for the house, which she used to buy her beer. If they had a fish in the game they sat him across from Philomena's mother who, because she dressed and sat carelessly, would distract him with frequent sightings of her pussy. After almost sliding to the floor in laughter Borman next recalled a youth they called Wild Mustard. Small, intense, and handsome he went out of his way to pick fights with policemen, gangs, and big men. One night they had all gone to a roadhouse on a lake just over the Wisconsin line where Mustard had been approached by two middle-aged, wealthy, and athletic-looking queers. They had then devised a plan whereby Mustard was to go with the queers in their car and the others were to follow in Tanker's car, and as soon as the queers parked in some dark field or wood they were to pull up alongside, jump out in force, and shake the two queers down for all their money. A perfect plan, Borman explained with laughter, but with one exception, and that was that they had lost sight of the queers' car! But what was even funnier, Tanker countered, shouting above his tears of laughter, was that when Mustard returned some time later to the roadhouse he did not seem that upset that they had lost the car, and although he had been reticent as to what had taken place between the two men in the front seat he did not appear displeased. Both men by this time had a laughing fit. Della, who had paid no attention to the children, now went into the living room and listened to the radio. The boy continued to stare silently at his father and then at Tanker. Once he whispered in his father's ear and was taken to the bathroom. The girl on the floor looked at the floor, walls, ceiling, looking like a bewildered dwarf who could not stand up and did not know who or where she was.

Tanker now outlined a plan he had for getting out of Chicago and eventually out of the country. He leaned across the table and spoke low and confidentially to Borman. He would disguise himself and make his way to California and from there he would get a job as a merchant seaman on a freighter. He wanted Borman to join him there, and get a job on the same ship. They would jump ship in the South Seas somewhere and find some remote island where there were only natives and where they would be treated like kings and would in fact be made kings by the natives. He asked Borman what he thought of this plan. But this change in the conversation had brought Borman from the safety of the pleasant past to the uncertainty of the dangerous present, and he became noticeably uncomfortable and afraid. He pointed out reluctantly that one of the Baumgartner cousins was a merchant seaman (the family never saw him) and he knew for a fact that the coast guard had to give you a merchant seaman's ticket before you could get a job on a ship and that meant they fingerprinted you. Upon hearing this, Tanker suggested the possibility of stowing away, while Borman got the job of merchant seaman on the ship. Borman could sneak him aboard, bring him food, and they could still jump ship in the South Seas. Borman smiled, scratched his throat, and silently picked the label off his quart of beer.

Fortunately, Tanker had now been led onto a different topic. He recalled that night when he and two friends decided on the spur of the moment to go to California on their motorcycles and look up Wild Mustard, who had gotten married and moved there a few months earlier. Borman was not pleased with this remembrance since not only had he not been one of the two friends but Tanker, who had no motorcycle of his own, had borrowed or stolen Borman's, and had returned it a year later without compensation, apology, or explanation, thousands of miles the worse for wear and almost worthless. The two friends had turned back in Kansas but Tanker had made it all the way to southern California, where he stayed with Wild Mustard in a tiny Spanish-style house with a tile roof until Mustard finally took him aside and informed him that he had changed his ways and was not the wildman he used to be and that his wife was expecting a baby and did not much care for Tanker hanging around the house all day when her husband was off to work selling cameras nor for her husband coming home after work to spend the evening drinking beer with Tanker. In short, Tanker was breaking up his marriage.

So Tanker borrowed some money from Mustard and alone on Borman's motorcycle headed home. He was already out of money and living off the land (by which he meant thieving) when the motorcycle broke down on an Indian reservation in New Mexico. Fortunately he was befriended by the local chief, who was also the local sheriff, and he let Tanker sleep in the jail and feed with the prisoners, most of whom were weekend violators of the laws against peyote, while he waited for the shipment of the motorcycle parts the chief had loaned him the money to buy. The chief was amused by his urban cockiness and took pleasure in being charitable to him. Later he took Tanker into his own home and treated him like a son. The chief also owned a construction company and building supply yard, indeed had a monopoly on those businesses as he did on a number of others on the reservation, and he gave Tanker a job driving one of his trucks and soon thereafter the position of managing the yard. Here, Tanker claimed, he had instituted the procedure known as the "kickback," a business method that, to Tanker's surprise, the Indians had not heard of before. Yes, Tanker said, he had gone Indian, worn Levi's, cowboy boots, a straw hat. This was a story Borman had not heard before. To his surprise he saw tears forming in Tanker's eyes.

Tanker now told how he dated and laid Indian girls. He claimed to have initiated them in the skills of oral-genital love, a form of lovemaking they had not practiced before, and which the young men of the reservation, after dating the same girls later, had much to thank him for. He had dated the chief's daughter and become engaged to her with the chief's blessing. She was a senior in high school and had been chosen the Indian beauty queen at some Indian festival or other. He took a newspaper clipping encased in plastic from his wallet and showed it to Borman, whose mouth opened in admiration and surprise. This was certainly a dark area in Tanker's life. The girl in the photograph was beautiful. Dark, full-lipped, in a white dress with a rose corsage pinned to her breast. Written in ink across the clipping: To my Tanker, Love Josie. Tanker said he had planned to marry her and remain on the reservation forever, the manager of the construction yard and a deputy sheriff of the local police. She had even been pregnant with his child. But one night they had been making love in a new house her father was constructing and she had stepped out the front door in the darkness, unaware that the concrete steps had not been put in yet beneath.

In the fall she lost the child. Broken-hearted, Tanker suddenly began to long for Chicago until one night, drunk and on the spur of the moment, he took Borman's motorcycle, or rather stole it once again, this time from a shed behind the jail, where the chief, fearing perhaps that his favored son-in-law-to-be might do just what he was doing now, and not wanting him to leave him, or his daughter, or to injure himself on the motorcycle, had locked it up.

He left without so much as leaving a note to anyone and drove straight home. He still owed the chief the money for the motorcycle parts, along with the several hundred the chief had loaned him in cash. Borman interjected that he remembered that when Tanker arrived home his flesh had been black and peeling and his hair bleached snow-white. Tanker, his eyes wet and trying to hide it, continued to speak at length about the Indians, New Mexico, and the girl with longing and regret. He could see now, he claimed, that he had belonged there, that he had found his rightful home there, and if only he could he would return there and lose himself there and never leave there. On the other hand, he said, it did no good to regret the past. He had apparently done only what he could have done. He had all his life, he claimed as he opened another beer, only asked people, girls especially, to accept him as he was.

This conversation and Tanker's new mood cast a melancholia upon what was already a sentimental meeting at an unhappy hour. Tanker went into himself and sat glassy-eyed before his quart of beer. He was greatly moved. He was feeling waves of an affection and even of a romance that he had never felt before. Despite his firmly held belief that he had lived to the fullest and that in quitting this world he had no regrets, he now had mournful, chilling intimations that he had missed everything and regretted all. The mood around the table in the kitchen became that of a visit by the friends of a condemned man in the death cell in the last hour before his execution. The movements of the men became heavy and slow and in the air was the weight of fear and grief. They took a farewell that was tearful at the door. They pressed each other's hands, shoulders, biceps, thumped each other's backs. Tanker choked and repeated, "Thank you," over and over again. He then said, "It's all been . . . splendid!" The word surprised even him, for it was a word he was certain he had never used before but which described exactly that feeling he wanted now to proclaim. "Splendid!" he said again and again, pleased with himself. So Borman left, drunk, sentimental, silly, sleepy, and fearless in the face of his forgotten danger, almost on the verge of breaking into some nostalgic song.

On the sidewalk Borman could have presented the classic picture of the flushed, beer-bloated, and whistling father sauntering his way home, helped along by the two small starving children, except that his son shuffled along behind him and he carried his daughter, who was crying, in his arms. A block from Tanker's apartment he was accosted by several men. One took the girl from his arms, another seized him by the front of his jacket so fiercely that it was pulled up into a kind of sling in which he was suspended. He was then pushed backward into a low barberry hedge and slapped repeatedly across the face. He could feel the branches give and break beneath his weight. Someone on the sidewalk was saying, "Take the kids home." A voice coming from a darkened car he now noticed parked beside the curb was saying, "Get them out of here!" Saying it over and over again hysterically. "All right, Borman," the man holding him said. "Where's your friend Tanker?"

For the rest of the evening police officers massed silently in the alleys of the neighborhood around Tanker's apartment. The wind hummed with their whispers. They crept forward like an army in the night, block by block, house by house, apartment by apartment. Moving people out, moving themselves in. Later, streets and alleys were blocked off. The event was so much larger than the man.

Della slept in a small windowless bedroom and Tanker on the porch above the street on an old armless sofa, covered by an army blanket. On such a bed on such an unheated porch he had slept during his childhood and youth, attuned even in his sleep to the night sounds in the street below. The night turned cool and windy, and he could see from where he lay on his back, in the inch or so between the bottom of the shade and the window sill, clouds blowing across the moon that made the moon appear to move, and move rapidly, while the clouds stood still. He was traveling with that moon, moving fast. A beer sleep. Beer dreams. Wind along the wires. Dust. Cornfields. A man in a leather suit and goggles riding a motorcycle at night in pouring rain. The lone headlight bouncing. That street light across the street and almost on the level of his window: New Mexico, the reservation, the desert, the west, Josie, fatherhood, marriage. As close as that. To escape to open spaces and the alien ways of another race.

Below him footsteps sounding oddly wet, as though the sidewalks were puddled or at least tacky with dew, and the whisper of voices that seemed to emanate from the blur of the street lights. He woke suddenly. In the apartments of the building next door people seemed to be moving in and out, creeping down the back stairs from porch to porch as though unwilling to wake anyone with their noise. Or were those sounds in his own building? The buildings and streets were teeming with careful footsteps and whispers. They filled the dark, coming from all corners, until he thought they were coming from inside his room. He felt his way through the apartment. He was barefoot, wearing a T-shirt, slacks without a belt, the fly open. His hair was thick with cowlicks and was in his eyes. Della was asleep in bed. Absolutely quiet. Absolutely motionless. Her hair in curlers, her face cold-creamed. He could make her out in the light of the radio she had left on, tuned to a station that was off the air. On the porch again he turned on the small light and had no sooner removed the pistol from beneath the pillows of the sofa when all the windows around him blew in as if from the concussion of an explosion. Glass shattered across the floor he threw himself upon, and splinters of wood, chips of plaster, and the stuffing of the sofa he had been sleeping on flew about his head. They were firing at him from an apartment in the building on his left and from a window across the street. He seemed to have miraculously escaped these murderous volleys, although he had no time to determine if this were so. He was confused and even angry. He thought the police had to forewarn him before they fired like this, had to break down the doors and rush him, lob tear gas through the windows, or call over a microphone from the street for him to come out peacefully with his hands in the air. All hell was not supposed to break loose like this. With the cessation of the firing from across the street into the porch bullets immediately ripped through the back door, sending splinters through the kitchen and leaving holes larger than the bullets in the panels, while the door itself came off its hinges and down like a besieged drawbridge to a castle. Not only came down but came forward, like a shield, forced down finally by the crowd of men trampling on it with their feet and scrambling into the room literally in a cloud of dust. All leaning forward and looking top-heavy and managing to squeeze between the jambs. Men in shirts open at the collar and fedoras with the brims turned up, with five o'clock shadows and thick, hairy forearms and fat frightened faces and bulging blue eyes, firing from revolvers and shotguns at the dumbfounded Tanker standing with his pistol held like a carrot in his hand. And one of the scrambling men holding very clearly in his hand a set of handcuffs and reaching toward the Tanker as though for some strange reason he believed those extended handcuffs would reach Tanker before all those bullets.

CHAPTER THIRTY-ONE

IN THE GROVE

Magnuson had spent the night in his private office in the Magnuson Agency, slumped over his glass-topped desk, the black fountain pen he had never used slanting like an arrow into the slab of marble at his ear, the lights of the city at his back. He had not expected to see the night through alone. He had considered suicide, and would have submitted to it, if he had not known that he could bear up under punishments of even greater shame. This, and not suicide, was for him the worst of penalties. It was also his fate. It was also justice. He was tough enough to take it—take anything! He was too old to escape and alter his identity, or lose himself in the vast spaces, or among the many peoples, of this continent, although he had considered that too, and the smoky boulevards of Skid Row with their wasted and haunted men had loomed up before him like a vision of the grace of God. There, if you would, was justice! As much justice as you please! For the most part he saw visions of his late wife. Her presence filled the darkened room. He saw her best at the dawn of a gray day when the sun, behind the blankets of overcast, did not look strong enough to burn the mists away, out on a lake in a rowboat, fishing. She was standing up in the stern, wearing a man's hat and windbreaker, casting with one hand in her trousers.

When the police contacted him it was on the telephone in the person of a Sergeant Dopke calling for Captain Gaughan to report that one Joseph Helenowski was not a homicide victim in the County Morgue as had been reported to Magnuson yesterday by Captain Gaughan. Instead, the body was that of one Alvin Raincloud, an American Indian and war veteran of no little fame, having won the Congressional Medal of Honor in Sicily, who, under the auspices of the federal program to integrate Indians into the society by moving them off the reservations and into the big cities, had been recently settled in Chicago. An alcoholic, he had become a vagrant on Skid Row. This mistake in identification was due to an unexplained delay in the receipt of fingerprint identification from the FBI office in Washington. Also to the preliminary identification of the corpse as Helenowski because Helenowski's identification was found upon the body, and to the positive identification of the corpse as Helenowski by a man named John Cavan, who may or may not turn out, upon investigation, to be Helenowski's son as he had claimed, but in any case having never seen Helenowski before had no business identifying the corpse. Since a man had visited this same Cavan two days ago and identified himself as Alvin Raincloud, and showed identification to this effect, they suspected that that man was Helenowski and that he had murdered Raincloud and exchanged wallets with him.

"Then where is Helenowski now?" Magnuson interrupted.

The sergeant acknowledged that this was a good question, and that the department had put an all-points alert out for his capture. With the killing of that cop-killer Tanker, he had become the prime concern of the force. His doctors at the hospital had now come forward with the information that he was psychotic and potentially dangerous and that he had lately taken to masquerading as some personification of Death, in which role the staff and other patients had humored him, information they had felt no compulsion to bring forward earlier, since they had thought he was no sooner discovered to have escaped than he was discovered dead. However, there was reasonable hope that he would be captured soon. Over the years he had demanded to be released on national holidays, and on the Fourth of

July and Columbus Day most of all, and also whenever there were Polish-American picnics in the Forest Preserves. Such a picnic was being held today out on Milwaukee Avenue in the Caldwell Woods, where the police were dispatching a special detail to watch for him. But with a turnout of over a hundred thousand people predicted, even if he were there they did not hold out much hope of finding him. He was alleged, however, to have a mysterious and even sinister affection for the woods, sneaking into the groves on the hospital grounds whenever he was let out of doors, and lately he had been telling attendants at the hospital that he planned to attend this particular picnic along with looking up his son, perhaps this Cavan whom he had in fact looked up in the guise of Alvin Raincloud. They were trying—unsuccessfully so far—to reach Mr. Frazer Farquarson in order to verify Cavan's assertion that he was really Helenowski's son.

"You won't be able to reach him," Magnuson said. "He's out of town . . . the house is locked up . . ."

When the sergeant had hung up, Magnuson had only to sit at his desk with his head in his hands for a moment to know everything. The man named in Farquarson's letter to Wenzel as the man he feared was Helenowski. And Helenowski had escaped the hospital not only to attend a picnic and see his son but to kill Farquarson. And those murders that came after Farquarson's had not been the work of a conspiracy but of one man, the madman Helenowski. Paranoid and susceptible to suspicions of conspiracies, he must have deduced wrongly from the note and letter and possible witnesses at every murder scene that there was a mass conspiracy at work against him.

And Magnuson had made mistakes no less terrible in their consequences. But how could he expect to cope with madness? Immorality and evil, yes! They could be destroyed by honor, morality, selflessness. But madness? And hadn't the police themselves been careless and inefficient? After all, how could he have suspected a man the police had told him was already dead?

Now while he sat here alone and waiting to be arrested the police were closing in on Helenowski. If only he could get to Helenowski first! Get up from the depths of your humiliation, he urged himself. Make this final effort. The last chance to redeem some small portion of your self-respect. He had no more illusions that he could apprehend the man alone, and accordingly he devised and set in motion a plan to search for him utilizing all the help that he could muster. This was to dispatch a contingency of Magnuson Men to the Polish-American picnic in the Caldwell Woods.

These woods were in a belt of public forests along the river bottoms on the outskirts of the city. Indeed, the whole area in and around the city abounded in parks and groves and forest preserves. Like his fathers from the Old Country—the Scandinavians, Germans, Slavs—the Chicagoan had an almost mystical attraction and affection for the woods. Mountains, deserts, seascapes, rural or pastoral landscapes did not bewitch or beckon him with the promise of returning to him some ancient and unnameable portion of himself. To him such words as vacation, holiday, picnic were all synonymous with woods, and any notion of the good and peaceful life called up visions of a forest. He spent his summer vacations in the northern forests of Michigan and Wisconsin, and his lunch hours, weekends, and evenings in the Forest Preserves, where he may have done no more than pause to draw some strength and consolation from the presence of so many trees.

Later in the day the Magnuson Men began to gather in the woods at the base of the toboggan slide as Magnuson had ordered. The day had turned out to be one of those unseasonably hot and humid midsummer days that Chicago often experiences in the spring, and the Men even though they stood in shade were already sweating. Since Magnuson had been forced to choose their names at random from a list of men who had declared themselves available for duty today, they were a mixed lot of ushers and industrial patrolmen who in their full-time occupations were policemen, firemen, schoolteachers, students, factory workers, clerks, even pensioners. They numbered twenty-five in all. All were in street clothes with the exception of a high-school student and all-city basketball center who, having misunderstood Magnuson's orders, wore a Magnuson Man uniform, the sky blue pants with the gold stripes, the sky blue jacket with the gold braid, the white hat and gloves. He looked embarrassed and ill at ease while the others gawked up at him, this freak by reason of that uniform upon that height.

From the woods around the Men, into which families with shopping bags and picnic baskets and children on bicycles were filing in wide, fast-moving crowds, the Men could hear the muted squeals of clarinets and the steady pounding of the foot pedal on the bass drums in the many polka bands, and the whoops and hoots and shouts and the happy voices speaking Polish in the microphones. It seemed as though some sport or spectacle was about to take place before a massive crowd in the forest, a football game or a speech delivered by a Central European dictator, and that at any moment there would be explosions of applause and cheers. Listening to it, the Men experienced the excitement and fear of reserves about to be sent into a mighty battle. This tension increased with the arrival of Magnuson. Nervous himself, he greeted each Man individually with the sentimental gratitude of a field marshal for underlings he is about to ask to die for him. He briefed them breathlessly upon their duty. They were searching for a man named Joseph Helenowski, he said, and gave them the description he had received from the sergeant on the telephone. He was a madman, an escaped mental patient, and was considered dangerous. If asked he would more than likely give the name of Alvin Raincloud, and even possess identification to that effect. He also was under the delusion that he was Death—he was a maniac, remember—and he might give that name also, which sent a chill among the sweating Men.

Magnuson now circulated the hastily drawn copies he had made of the map of these woods he had found in his office. The Men themselves he divided at random, seizing them by the arms and shoulders and forcing them physically into groups of threes and fours. Each group was assigned an area on the map for which it was responsible until summoned or ordered elsewhere. Each Man received a whistle from the box of them Magnuson had found in the office, and they were to be blown only when someone sighted Helenowski and required help in subduing him. Magnuson himself would act as the co-ordinator between the groups, checking in on their posts by turns. Now Magnuson took out his wallet and counted out three thousand dollars in hundred-dollar bills, which he held up for all to see. He said, ruffling the bills like a deck of cards, "This goes to the Man or Men who bring him in."

At first the Magnuson Men had been reluctant to believe that the old man before them was really Magnuson. He was unshaven, carried himself like a drunk, and his clothes were so rumpled it seemed likely he had only just come out of the woods where he had spent the night. Now with this display of money, which increased their excitement even further, they accepted him for who he was, reasoning that because he was famous, powerful, and rich he could also be eccentric if he wished. After all, who were they to know, much less say, how such a man should act?

Around this same time John Cavan and Kay Wanda entered the woods at the end of the bus line, where the extra green trolley buses were lined up, disgorging picnickers, emerging at a large grassy clearing where there were wooden platforms for the polka bands and wooden pavilions with counters and shutters where sandwiches and beer were sold. Polish was spoken everywhere. A hundred thousand Poles were everywhere. Grouped in families, neighborhoods, clubs, friends. Men drank beer and played pinochle on folding tables and picnic tables. Women dipped into their cardboard boxes and shopping bags for sausages, hams, and breads, and cooked on the smoky grills. Here and there were red shirts and red hats with feathers, and Polish flags, and Polish eagles, and American flags, and men and women in the American Legion–style caps of their own Polish clubs and legions, and wizened old men with slouch hats and canes and long mustaches, and lame old women in babushkas and long black skirts, and even two men in the bemedaled uniforms of World War Two Polish officers.

In the woods beyond the grassy clearing, the picnickers lugged sacks and baskets and babies down the trails between the oaks and elms. Ahead were smaller clearings where men and boys played softball or pitched horseshoes. Kegs of beer were set up in the shade. A fair-haired man, his shirt open to the navel, sat in the sun, playing an accordion. A priest in a clerical collar and steel-rimmed glasses was drinking a bottle of beer. Back in the brush, a woman with a switch was screaming at her children in broken English. A fat man with silver teeth, a panama hat pushed to the back of his head and wearing brown and white shoes, was mopping his brow with a folded-up handkerchief. The heat was oppressive, swamplike, like the worst of an arctic summer. Behind them, the polka bands and the murmurings of the crowds.

How strange it seemed to Kay that she should be here with this man, trying to keep up with him as he hurried despite the heat, searching every face. With the discovery of the note he had left in her mailbox in the night, she had stopped out of courtesy to see him on her way to breakfast, and he had told her everything as he sat exhausted in his underwear on the edge of his unmade bed, of his disinheritance and false identity, his humiliating interrogation at the hands of the police from whom he had been released only within the hour. From the police he had learned that his father was not dead but alive, that the corpse he had viewed in the County Morgue had not been that of his father but of his father's victim, that Bughouse Square had not been the place of his father's death but of his victim's. Assuming of course that this man Helenowski was his father, a fact the police had yet to prove. "I'm not the son of the victim," he kept repeating, shaking his head, "but of the murderer." The police had also told him that his father might attend the Polish-American picnic today and even suggested that since he could identify him he should go there. He had been anxious to go not so much on the chance that he would see his father as to be among those foreign people who shared his origins, and among whom he might begin to discover who he really was. He had asked, and even pleaded with her to accompany him, maintaining that although his quest was personal he no longer felt that he could go on alone. She had acknowledged that she had come in part because of the thrill of being close to murder and madness and even danger (what would happen if Cavan *did* see his father in the crowd?) and to a man on the verge of dreadful discoveries, a ghoulish appetite, in short, for the first-hand sensations of the front-page news. But she was also drawn by a curiosity of a different sort, which did not preclude the possibility of affection and compassion.

He had changed, as the kindness and concern for her that was so apparent in his note had attested. She had always thought him intellectual and aloof, secretly proud of his name and money and connections, although his knowledge of anthropology seemed to please him far more than either high society or money and was in his own eyes that which set him most above the mass of men. And she had thought him soft and self-indulgent, too satisfied with that pattern into which he had steered his life, with the companionship of Myrna Westermann, in comparison with whom she had always favored him (although she conceded this might be no more than her natural inclination to prefer men over women and certainly in any conflict to give the man the benefit of the doubt), and with his avowed profession of student and scholar of Africa that so often even at the best of times and in the best of company took him into the monkish solitude of his thoughts as it someday promised to take him distant geographically. In her own unhappy marriage she had judged herself inferior not only to his apparent satisfaction with himself but to his upper-class standing and wealth (after all he was a Farquarson on his mother's side, *the* Farquarsons), especially when it led him not to indolence or business but to a selfless and scientific investigation of man. But now he had been brought down, and she could see and almost define her own strength in comparison with his weakness. She had to fight her inclination to detest him for his weakness, which in any form in any man she intended to interpret as a symptom of something vaguely unmanly, even though she believed, or wanted to, that it was in the nature of this very weakness, which was no more than his sensitivity to reveal and doubt himself, that a man was manly. Although they were both confused, rootless, and on their own, she could not identify with him entirely. Whereas her decision to be free had been made over a period of several years, the living of each day moving her that much closer to making it, his freedom had been thrust upon him overnight and was the result of no decision of his own but of merely discovering what, unknown to him, had always been. Indeed, his special suffering did not come from turning his back upon the past, as did hers, but from discovering it. He had come here to find something of himself, but he looked lonely, helpless, isolated from the crowds they wandered through, as though he were at a crowded party where everyone knew everyone else and no one knew his name.

"All these people," he said suddenly. "Until today they would have given me claustrophobia. I've never been a joiner, never wanted to be a member of a crowd or club. Somehow I felt I would lose something of myself by being in a crowd. I never pictured myself inside a crowd. If I ever pictured myself anywhere it must have been in a big empty house. Where I was sitting by myself in every room. Where I talked to myself. I must have been pleased by what I heard. If I'd ever really thought about it I probably wouldn't have allowed for the existence of more than a dozen people in the world besides myself. I mean people with intelligence and taste. There were all these bodies, of course, but I couldn't begin to imagine that they were alive. Not like I was alive anyway. They were like so many mosquitoes. Like trees. Now it's like I'm in Calcutta. On the streets, Kay. Where I'm no better and no more significant than the old man dying in the gutter. The reality of every person at this picnic overwhelms me. It's like looking at the stars.—And it's not a bad feeling, this being in Calcutta—"

She felt the need to impart some wisdom she had learned from the unhappiness of her own experience. Instead she took his hand. He, remembering when she placed her hands on his in the coffeehouse last night, put his other hand on top of hers. In the pleasure of this action she put her other hand on top of his, so that when they paused beneath a large oak, he in his white shirt with the sleeves rolled up and she in her white blouse, they resembled in the dapple of sunlight shining through the heavy boughs the classic picture of young peasants plighting their troth beneath an ancient oak.

Hand in hand they went deeper into the groves. The polka

bands receding in the distance and blending with the beat of the bass drum, the hillbilly whoops, the thump of a softball, a horseshoe ringing on a stake. They came to the river bottom and a small, shallow, and polluted stream where the humidity hung like smoke. The banks were muddy and messy with footprints. Couples had chosen spots among the tree roots. A woman lay entirely on top of a man, as though they had decided only his backside would get dirty; she was kissing him passionately. Another couple lay side by side locked in each other's arms, sleeping. In a dusty beam of sunlight off in the woods a grinning woman slapped a fat-cheeked and complaining boy back and forth across the face. It sounded like someone breaking branches.

Meanwhile the Magnuson Men had been unable to locate their stations in the woods from the maps provided them by Magnuson. Arguments broke out when one group found another group already on what it regarded as its territory, and much time was spent in consulting, comparing, and interpreting maps. Some groups gave up and ignored the maps entirely, stationing themselves where they pleased. Others in a desire to earn the bonus by themselves split up, each Man going his own way, while two Men who were police officers, having little faith in Magnuson's paying out the money or in the possibility of discovering Helenowski, and having worked a shift last night, went off into the woods and fell asleep. To add to the confusion the description of Helenowski that Magnuson had provided appeared to fit several thousand men in the woods today, and the men wondered why they had not been provided with a photograph. This forced them to interrogate any number of men.

The plainclothes detachment from the police department had the advantage not only of photographs of Helenowski but of two orderlies from the hospital from which he had escaped, who could recognize him on sight. They were backed up by a contingency of uniformed Park District policemen who were on foot and three-wheel motorcycles and on horseback, no larger a force than would normally be assigned to patrol an outing of this size, but all of whom were alerted to the search for Helenowski.

The day was filled with rumors. The report that the police had cornered and shot down the cop-killer Tanker this morning was a popular topic of conversation in all corners of the woods, and was later verified by radio reports and early afternoon editions of the papers. Another rumor was also circulating, whether originating from the police themselves or the radio was never clear, that the police were searching for a man who became known, as the word was passed along, as the "Mad Polack," a maniac escapee from an asylum and a murderer of such brutality that he would stab to death anyone he managed to get alone. As this rumor spread throughout the day many people began to look upon the normal detachment of uniformed police as something special. Added to this were the observations and reports that police in plainclothes, who were in fact Magnuson Men, were interrogating men left and right, which made many believe that the police were mingling with the crowds, busy everywhere.

Later two young girls and a boy, all around ten years old, reported to some adults that while on a path some distance from a clearing a man riding a bicycle had stopped, spoken briefly with them, then exposed himself and ridden off. Apparently this had happened some time ago, but the children for some reason had only dared to report it now. The adults in turn flagged down a three-wheel motorcycle and had the children repeat their story to the policeman. A crowd gathered. The women were mean-looking and excited, hugging their elbows. The news spread that a man was exposing himself to children, was attempting to attack children, had attacked children, had murdered children. In many minds, including those of some of the police, the man was linked up with the "Mad Polack" rumor. In the course of the afternoon more sightings of the man, or of another man entirely but equally as perverse, were reported by both children and women. He was sometimes on a bicycle, at other times standing behind a tree close to the brush into which he would then disappear. He now seemed no longer satisfied to merely display himself but was seen masturbating. Because they were searching for a psychopathic killer the police took the man far more seriously than they might have otherwise, although the detectives in charge of the force doubted that he was their man. They warned as many groups in the clearings as they could, not to let their children go unescorted into the woods, and dispatched three-wheelers down the forest lanes to remoter clearings to warn the families there. Groups of children riding bicycles through the woods were stopped and queried by police on horseback. The rider could be seen in his spit-and-polish uniform and leather leggings and sunglasses leaning down to the guilty-looking children straddling their bikes, who sometimes pointed or shook their heads. News of a lost child caused far more concern and effort on the part of the police than was usual. By the time all the sightings of the pervert could be co-ordinated in some fashion it appeared that, after exposing himself at one site he must have dashed pell-mell to another, for he had been sighted from one end of the preserve to the other, oftentimes with only minutes separating the sightings.

At the same time the police had to be busy elsewhere, on other matters. There were eleven cases of heat stroke, one perforated ulcer, and three coronaries, including a man who died. There were also reports that a man was on the roof of the women's outhouse peering down through the boards, that two boys on motor scooters were rifling cars and, as the drinking increased through the day, of numerous fistfights. The considerable sale of beer, especially to teenagers, many of whom were not Poles but merely boys from the local neighborhoods taking advantage of the willingness at the pavilions to serve anyone, went unnoticed through the day. Gangs of drunken teenagers roamed through the woods, singing and leaning into each other, brown bottles of beer in hand. In the main they were only loud and lewd. Three boys had managed to climb to the top of the toboggan slide, down which they rolled their empty beer bottles, and from which they shouted and screamed until the police waved them down, collared them, scolded them, and let them go. There were at least two reported instances of men discovered urinating in the woods being mistaken for the exhibitionist. Both men were manhandled by an impromptu mob of vigilantes. One man was badly beaten, dragged in by either arm, with his eyes full of blood and his forehead swollen. In both instances the men were released by the police.

Otherwise the picnic continued as normal. Polkas and softball and pinochle and beer drinking. But here and there was an undercurrent of fear, of an evil being searched for in the woods that was equated not just with danger but with death. Women sometimes looked up at the cloudless but hazy sky with apprehension, as though wanting to pack their baskets and leave before the coming of the storm.

The frequent blowing of whistles above the crowd noise confused the police, who sometimes tried desperately to answer them, shoving through the crowds, thinking they came from fellow officers who had spotted the pervert or murderer. Actually they came from the Magnuson Men, who blew them whenever a man resisted their interrogation and they required help to subdue him or bring him back. These men were often manhandled and sometimes beaten. Usually their friends let them be dragged off and mistreated while they stood by dumbfounded, mistaking their attackers for the police, often because the attackers identified themselves as such. If his friends came to a man's aid, skirmishes developed with shouting and pushing and slapping of hands with the Magnuson Men usually outnumbered and driven off. During one of the brawls the police themselves interfered, and a fight took place among the three parties, none knowing why it was fighting the other two.

A man bearing a resemblance to the photograph of Helenowski had been stopped by a pair of officers, who were leading him behind the bandstands and through the dancers to their sergeant for questioning when they were set upon by several men with whistles around their necks. One of them was a youth the height of a basketball center and dressed in the immaculate uniform of a Magnuson Man usher. They surrounded one of the officers and, to the policemen's surprise, demanded to know if he was Helenowski. When the officer resisted and attempted to identify himself as a policeman his interrogators attempted to drag him toward the woods. When his partner came to his aid the suspect they had escorted between them broke away and vanished in the crowd. A fight ensued between the officers and the Magnuson Men, with the police prevailing only when they drew their revolvers and their attackers took to flight, the police not daring to risk a shot in the crowd. They did manage to capture the conspicuous and gawky youth in the Magnuson Man uniform and they brought him back to the sergeant as a kind of freakish prize, where among the clutch of police officers he looked like a giraffe browsing above the treetops. Both of the officers were now convinced that the man they had had in custody was Helenowski. The more the day wore on without success the more convinced they became of it, swearing, kicking the turf with their hands on their hips, and spitting, listening to the unbelievable story the kid in the Magnuson Man uniform was telling to the detectives of why he was here and had done what he did.

A report came in from a young man and woman, neither of whom spoke much English, and it took some time before the police could locate someone they could trust who spoke Polish, and even longer to locate the orderlies where they had been set to roaming through the crowds. The couple had encountered an old man far back in the woods on one of the lanes, carrying a wrinkled brown paper sack, greasy as though it had contained doughnuts, in which he said were mushrooms he had collected just this morning. He had tried to persuade the couple to take a bite of the piece of mushroom he offered them. The young man did not know much about mushrooms but he thought this mushroom might well be a poisonous variety. In addition the old man had said that the mushrooms would put them to sleep, that he had put thousands of people all over the world to sleep with his mushrooms. They were "Death-in-a-bag," and he gave out the "mushroom sleep." In fact people who had eaten of the mushrooms were sleeping all over the woods right now, under a blanket of leaves or with their backs against oak trees. He had pointed to people who appeared to be sleeping or at least lying upon the ground with their eyes closed, but the couple did not believe these people were dead. He had called himself the "sleep-maker." The couple had politely refused the piece of mushroom and after debating for some time between themselves whether to report the man finally went in search of a policeman. The orderlies were excited by this report. One of them even recalled a time when Helenowski returned from a stroll in the sanitarium woods with his arms full of toadstools of various sizes, shapes, and colors which he delivered to the cooks to prepare for supper for the staff and patients, a meal which he would excuse himself from if they didn't mind since he had a touch of the grippe and wasn't up to eating. This in turn excited the police, although the couple's identification of the photograph was far from positive, and they were further frightened that a madman might be giving poisonous mushrooms to children, and a call was sent out for reinforcements. Some policeman, however, thought the old man was probably innocent, and that the couple, who did not know English well, had merely misunderstood him.

Any doubts that Helenowski was not here were soon dispelled. A detective had encountered a man whom he thought strongly resembled the photograph he had seen of Helenowski, and he had approached the man only to have the man laugh and identify himself as a policeman, showing him his patrolman's badge and a Magnuson Man badge as well. Now with the photograph of Helenowski in his hand the detective would swear that the man with the badges had been Helenowski. A mood of dread touched with melancholia fell upon the group of policemen.

"How did he get those badges?" someone asked.

"Not another one," someone else said, shaking his head, referring to the recent murder of the young patrolman Carbone by the man called Tanker.

Later a report came in that someone had been observed in the Indian Grove Woods on the other side of Caldwell Avenue, although there was some confusion as to whether it was Helenowski, the exhibitionist, the man with the bag of mushrooms, or someone else entirely. A complement of police was transferred over there. Three-wheelers sped across the clearings and down the forest trails, raising dust, and the mounted officers cantered on their horses, rising and falling in the saddles as they passed through spots of sunlight that slanted between the trees. Squad cars pulled out from where they were parked in shade between the trees, their blue lights spinning. Here and there in the woods it looked like the small army of a small country ordered forward to meet an army that had invaded its territory on a quiet Sunday.

Magnuson, meanwhile, was like a general who, reduced to acting as his own messenger, still could not find his army. The master map was worthless. It did not appear to correspond to the layout of the woods at all, and not one of the groups of his Men was found at the station to which he had thought he had assigned it.

Any man who chanced to remind him in some way of that patient he had questioned in the mental hospital almost thirty years ago he stopped and attempted to interrogate. Because he looked dissolute and drunk, if not half-mad, these men dismissed him out of hand or else listened to him with a polite embarrassment. He implied, and more often stated, that he was a policeman, showing his badge. But it seemed that half the men he questioned replied to him in Polish, shrugging. People would point at him as he stumbled through the crowds, ask him if he was lost, calling him *"Pan,"* addressing him in Polish.

He was convinced that a man with sunglasses and a pair of binoculars around his neck was Helenowski. But when he attempted to question him, the man smiled and walked away. Magnuson followed after, told him he was a policeman. This time the man laughed and shoved him lightly in the shoulder before he walked away. Again Magnuson followed, collared him, called him Helenowski, dared him to deny it. The man broke away and Magnuson seized him by the sleeve. The man protested and scuffled with Magnuson, fighting him off with his hands. "Get away!" he said. "Someone get this old guy away!" By now Magnuson had followed him out of the woods and through a crowded parking lot and onto the concrete walk beside a large public swimming pool, fenced in and at this time of year empty of water. Magnuson pinned him up against the chainlink fence, held him by the strap of the binoculars and, to see him better, slapped the sunglasses from his face. "Help!" the man shouted to the passers-by, who were numerous. "This guy's a madman!"

"You're Helenowski," Magnuson said, shaking the man, twisting the binocular strap at his chest. "Admit it. You're Helenowski!"

A gang of swaggering drunken youths, bottles in hand, were

among the passing crowd, and they stopped to watch the two men wrestling against the fence. Amused, they cheered on one or the other, offering advice as to the success of certain blows. Finally they took hold of Magnuson and pulled him off. They wore Levi's and Levi jackets and boots and their hair was long and their faces broad and pale and their eyes almost closed with a drunken sleep. On their mouths were the traces of ironic smiles.

A crowd began to form, people jamming up against those who had stopped only seconds earlier and asking of men as ignorant as themselves what was going on.

"I don't know. Maybe it's the 'Mad Polack.' "

"Hey, they got the killer."

"Who did he say?"

"Those kids got the pervert."

"Hey, they got the guy was fooling around with them kids in the woods."

"That must be him," the man with the binoculars pleaded to the crowd, showing his broken sunglasses. "He just comes up and attacks you. Someone ought to get the cops." A young man did, on the run.

"Boys, don't let him get away, boys."

"All these cops around and a bunch of kids catch him."

The boys had made a ring around Magnuson and were standing with their legs spread and their knees bent, their guard down but with their hands in fists. When Magnuson attempted to force himself between them they merely leaned against him and pushed him back. Sometimes they pushed him up against the fence, or back and forth between them, as though passing a basketball. The crowd stuck their arms into the ring and shook their fists and rolled-up newspapers and beer bottles, shouting in heavy Chicago accents, laced with Polish.

"You goddamn no-good filthy son-of-a-bitch!"

"They ought to lock you up."

"They ought to kick his fucking head in."

"Guys like him ought to be fed to the polar bears in the zoo."

"Let's see you pull it out and show us what you showed them little kids," one of the boys said, pushing Magnuson.

"He ought to have his business cut off him then he don't get in no trouble and nobody get hurt!" a woman shouted.

One of the boys had a set of keys on a long chain fastened to a loop of his belt. He swung the chain in an arc so that the keys at first grazed and then struck Magnuson in the genitals. "Come on, you old fucker, take it out," he said, swaying and staggering, leaning back with his knees bent, swinging that chain.

"Hey, you better cut it out," another boy said, "he'll get a hard-on."

The boys were discovering that somehow they had been put on the same moral side as that society they rebelled against and bullied. The sanction of the citizens of the city was behind them, and they began to go berserk with the fresh intoxication of this power.

"Wait for the police," someone said, sensing something in the boys' eyes or in the tenseness of their muscles that suggested trouble. "You're doing right. Just don't let him get away."

"That's it," someone else shouted above the persistent insults and threats. "Wait for the cops. Let them handle it."

But Magnuson was struck full force without warning by a fist on the side of the nose, and although nothing but the nose was struck, he was lifted bodily off his feet by the blow and onto the ground as quickly as if someone had kicked his feet out from under him. Immediately his face bloodied. He attempted to pick himself up, certain that it was his duty to rise and attempt to hit at least one of his attackers, and was kicked by another youth who had stood over him with the force and follow-through of a soccer kick, the foot catching him miraculously only on the skin of his testicles and although less painful than a direct blow, still painful enough to make him scream. He grabbed his groin and dropped to his knees. Someone straddled him and cupping both hands beneath his chin pulled up on his head as though baring his throat in preparation to having it stuck. When he was released he was kneed in the face and knocked back against the fence. A fist hit him on top of the head as though it was pounding on a table, and he fell head first to the ground, his chin striking first. Someone dropped to his knees and struck him in the open eye as he was rolling in pain on his back. Before he could cover his head he was kicked in the right ear and it filled with blood. To protect his ears he exposed his ribs, and he was kicked there, on both sides. On his stomach he kept his legs together and was kicked repeatedly at the base of the buttocks, the toe of the boot attempting to force its way between his thighs and get at his genitals. Someone took a running start and landed with both knees upon his back. A herd of feet seemed to be stepping on him, as though he had fallen in the middle of a busy footpath or among a marching crowd. His fingers felt broken from all the blows his hands received from the feet that were trying to kick him in the head. He could no longer sort out any one pain from the whole, nor in his state of shock did he really feel the pain. His only thought, and it ran through his head repeatedly, was that he was an old man, that it was all up with him.

The crowd on the concrete wall moved back in fright, and many turned and fled for fear of becoming themselves involved, and those that remained did so from shock, looking on with horror and indignation or else laughing involuntarily with secret shame or pleasure. "Wait for the police!" some men shouted, outraged but keeping their distance from the boys. But the boys set upon them, and, as they braced their feet and begged to be let free, pulled them by the arms toward the fence, where they were shoved and struck and tripped. A girl even threw herself among the boys and tried to pull them off Magnuson, but they laughed at her and pretended to protect themselves from her ineffectual blows until at last she ran hiding her head and crying to her boyfriend, who had been standing on the edge of the crowd with his arms extended, trying to summon her back. During all of this the boys were sullen, sleepy-looking, pleased.

Finally the policeman, led by the man who had gone to fetch him, came limping on the run down the needle-covered path beneath a stand of spruce. A watchman for the pool and toboggan slide, he was a Park District policeman in name only. A year away from retirement he was lame, had a milky eye, moles on his face, bushy eyebrows, and hair in his nose and ears. He carried a revolver he had never fired in the line of duty and which he had never liked. Once upon the scene he could only limp nervously toward the beleaguered Magnuson and then retreat, return and retreat, like a man trying to rush up and snatch something from a fire and being forced back empty-handed by the intensity of the heat. Once he did manage to get Magnuson by the foot and called for the bystanders to come and help him, only to have the boys set upon him and drive him off.

Then without cause, unless it was the blowing nearby of a whistle, the boys dispersed, ran roughly through the crowd, and fanned out into the woods, a maneuver executed with such lightning speed that it suggested they had practiced it before. The policeman asked someone to help him get Magnuson on his feet and to take him elsewhere, for he could not be certain that the boys would not return, especially since he saw no reason for them to flee; but the crowd looked upon the beaten man as though he were a leper. A young man in a red T-shirt and softball pants finally came forward, and with Magnuson supported between them, the two men took him to the locker room of the swimming pool, where they set him down on a wooden bench beside a row of army green metal lockers. The locker room was a labyrinth of these benches and lockers and was cool and dark, with what light there was seemingly filtered through something dark and medicinal, like iodine. It smelled of chlorine, hygienic soap, adhesive tape.

The policeman told the man in the red T-shirt, who looked as though he would hang around, that he could go, and gave Magnuson his handkerchief to hold against his bleeding nose. Then he went through the Dutch doors into his office, where he had been reading a newspaper at the desk when the breathless man had burst in to fetch him, and returned with a towel soaked in cold water and a can of Band-Aids. With the towel he dabbed the blood and dirt from Magnuson's face, and determined from his superficial examination of the wounds that although the man had been brutally beaten he was not as injured as he had thought. However, he had witnessed very little of the actual beating, and none of the worst of it. He could not know that besides the many scrapes and bruises hidden by his clothes Magnuson had a concussion, a broken nose, a broken jaw, a punctured ear drum, bruised ribs, and several dislocated fingers.

"I guess you learned your lesson," the policeman said, applying to the facial wounds Band-Aids that would not adhere to the wet skin and curled up all over Magnuson's face or else hung there as though by a thread. "I guess you got what you deserved . . . I don't see that there's much reason for you to suffer more . . . You got a car parked in the lot?"

Magnuson nodded, although he had come in a cab.

"Think you can get to it?"

He nodded.

"Think you can drive?"

Again he nodded.

The policeman had known nothing of the search conducted in the woods today for the suspected killer Helenowski, nor had he heard of the rumors of the "Mad Polack" or the reports of exhibitionists. The citizen who came to fetch him had blabbered something about a homosexual assaulted by a man he must have made obscene suggestions to, and that he was being detained by a gang of tough-looking kids. The policeman was not one for making out reports and becoming involved in police matters if he could in any way help it. He was also something of a secret homosexual himself, and liked to have long talks with the lifeguards and older boys alone in his office, in which he attempted to learn about their sexual successes with girls and, if possible, their masturbatory habits, and liked to loiter in the locker room and at the side of the lifeguard, who was stationed where he could make certain that all the boys ran naked through the gauntlet of sprays of icy water that made them high-step and squeal, before they could don their suits and go into the pool. Unlike the poor devil before him he had always been careful. He sat down on the bench beside Magnuson and turned to him those moles and bushy brows, that hairy nose and milky eye. "Those punks will get theirs in jail someday," he said, placing his hand on Magnuson's shoulder and shaking it reassuringly. "Now I've got to call a squad car to take you to a doctor. After that they'll probably take you down to the station. I suppose you could beat it while I was in the office making the call and lose yourself in the crowd. You could make it to your car and drive to a doctor yourself. Sure, a bunch of guys jumped you in an alley. A young cop would probably handcuff you to the lockers while he made the call, but nobody expects an old-timer like me to keep on my toes." Adding, as though to convince himself of the justice of his compassion, "You didn't hurt no one."

As soon as the policeman had shut both Dutch doors of his office, Magnuson staggered to the door, leaning where he could against the lockers. He moved so slowly that the policeman had time to come to the doorway and watch as he went from tree to tree, losing himself among the crowd before he disappeared into the woods.

By late afternoon Cavan and Kay came up from the river, where they had slept on the ground, and wandered into the main clearing, where they drank beer at one of the pavilions. They were among half-drunken happy Poles. Tall thin Poles with hatchet faces; short stocky Poles with bulbous features; Poles as fair as Swedes, as dark as gypsies; who looked more Germanic than Slavic, and more Oriental than either. A timidity about the older men, a pomposity about the middle-aged, a belligerence about the younger, a shrewishness and toughness about the women.

"Hey, I got the dough," a little man called Stan said as Cavan tried to buy a round of beers. "I'm popping. I got money all over the joint." Stan and his wife, whom he called Lady, resembled a pair of circus midgets with curly blond hair. There was something gold and white and well scrubbed about them, and a feeling that they ought to be in costume. Stan was smoking a cigar.

"*Dziekuje!*" said Kay.

"Hey, nice, thank you," Stan said in his midget's voice.

"*Jak sie masz,*" Cavan said, showing off what he knew.

"Very nice language," Lady said.

"*Dobrze, pan,*" said Stan.

"Hey, let me give the kids a boilermaker," a man called Popeye said.

"*Owszem, chetnie,*" Cavan said.

Popeye was a friend of Stan's and wore an orange hat that was a combination porkpie and mountaineer's hat, with Popeye written in silver glitter on the crown. He poured Bourbon from a pint into Kay's and Cavan's paper cups of beer.

At twilight the western sky above the woods was rosy, and there could have been a prairie fire for all the haze. The great crowd had been reduced by more than half, and picnickers streamed out of the footpaths, laden with folding chairs, shopping bags, and baskets, resembling refugees fleeing with their possessions. Rumors pursued their flight, of mass murder and bodies discovered throughout the city and the surrounding countryside. There were no lights in the clearing. The air was muggy and smoky, and as darkness fell clouds of mosquitoes ascended from the river. Two of the polka bands still played from their platforms, although carpenters were already busy with their hammers tearing down a third. More and more couples danced the polka in the trodden grass before the platforms. Younger men shouted in good-natured imitation of their immigrant elders: "Everybody have a good time! Everybody whoop it up!"

"Say, Lady," Popeye said, "do you stick out your can?"

Lady gave him her hip and swung at him with her purse.

"I mean," Popeye said to laughter, "for the garbageman?"

"And for the milkman, coffeeman, meterman, all those guys," Stan said.

Popeye sang:

Lady stick out your can
Lady stick out your can
Lady stick out your can
Here comes the garbageman
Lady stick out your can

To applause Kay stuck out hers, shaking it. Cavan slapped it, and then got behind her, holding her by the hips.

"Holy smokes," Stan said, "don't bang the can."

"Hey," Popeye said, "where can a guy hose the lawn around here?"

"Hey, I got a hell of a hose," Stan said. "Does nice job." He pointed at Lady. "I water her lawn every goddamn night. She got nice lawn." He hugged and kissed her.

"Listen to the big shot," Lady said. "I make the guy get on his knees and beg me for it. It gives him big headache, he says, if he don't get nothing—."

"When I'm on my knees," Stan said. "I'm on my elbows. Making honey in the flowers."

Cavan dropped to his knees before Kay, throwing out his arms.

"No, no," Lady said, taking Cavan seriously. "Don't give him nothing, honey. Wait till you married. You might get baby—." Then as Cavan held his head as though it hurt, "Get up, Mr. Smarty." As though fearing that Kay would not only accede to his plea but do so there and then. "You make him marry, honey. Make him give you big diamond."

"You don't want to marry no pretty lady," Popeye cautioned. "You go to the tavern and six other guys come from all over the city to sit in the house."

He sang:

We left our wives at home
We left our wives at home
We left our wives
With six other guys
O we left our wives at home.

"Hey, don't listen to the guy," Stan said. "You keep the car in the garage and no other guys are going to park there. Holy smokes, what kind of Johnny are you? With a pretty girl like that it's worth it for the honeymoon. The priest told us guys anything goes on the first night. In the bathtub, up on the piano, on the radiators, you guys the boss, he said.—Just don't hose out the can, *kielbaso.*"

"You get married and you both get T.B.," Popeye said. He pointed at Stan, "Tavern belly." And then at Lady, "Tremendous behind!" With that he broke into a song in Polish that seemed, from the good-natured objections of the women, to be obscene.

There at long last was the hooting Cavan, who could not polka in his sock feet, dancing in the crowd before the platform with Kay, who could, following her as awkwardly as a stag prancing on his hindlegs, unable to get the rhythm of the hop and skip. Stan and Lady hopped by with an effortless but flashy grace, Lady bouncing primly while Stan looked down behind him at his heels as he kicked them up. "You're looking good, Johnny," he said. Only to wince and shake his head as Cavan tripped over his own ankles and fell to the ground, bringing Kay down beside him.

They stayed on the ground, panting in the dark, fighting off the mosquitoes, with the feet of the dancers flying past their heads, listening to that snakelike clarinet and beat of the bass drum and the talk in Polish that buzzed and sang around them, all those z's and j's and w's interspersed with vowels. "Time out," he said, taking her hand. "Stay put," he said as she got to her knees and lay her arms upon his shoulders. He kissed her cheek as he pulled up his socks. Then sweating, half-drunken, laughing, she was against him, kissing him on the mouth. An incredible kiss, of heroic warmth and openness. Instantly all the bones dissolved inside his head, which then entered her mouth, followed by the boneless and caved-in rest of him. He was completely inside her, standing on his head. How was he to reconcile such a sensation with this woman who, like no other woman he had ever met, put him at his ease, was his comrade, his confidante, his good friend? Was it possible that friendship and kindness did not negate erotic feelings in him, as he would have thought they would, but generated them instead? Why, he could rise and polka Kay through the crowd and into the dark woods where they would dance between the trees, spinning and hopping and kicking up their heels until they fell in each other's arms upon the roots and leaves.

Magnuson, meanwhile, had been hiding on the edge of the woods, beneath a small footbridge that spanned a small, polluted brook no more than a few feet wide and a few inches deep, the current so sluggish it could be seen to move only where it purled against an oily branch. Having got this far he had been afraid to go farther while it was still daylight. He had passed out with his aches and pains and slid partway off the muddy bank, one pantleg in the water and the water trickling over his shoe. He had attempted to wash his wounds, and his face was muddy from his splashing. He was not well hidden, and was sighted several times by the few people who used the bridge. One boy paused with his bike and said, "What are you doing? Taking swimming lessons?" A high-school student said, pointing over the side, "*Die Lorelei*," and his girlfriend laughed.

The brook bordered a golf course, and in the distance were the soundless golf carts, a man posing with his driver draped over his shoulder, another man holding a flag, other men walking and vanishing behind knolls, their heads and caps the last to go. Nearby in the woods a high wire fence could be made out among the trees, and behind it the green buses of the end-of-the-line bus yard as they pulled in and out and parked, their electric arms gliding with silent sparks along the wires overhead. In the distance those clarinets, bass drums, the clang of horseshoes, the owl-like hoots of the dancers; and close by the occasional hooves of horses.

Around twilight, as a yellow haze seeped from the fairways of the golf course into the woods, Magnuson thought he could make out a policeman coming down the footpath that paralleled the brook. Weakened by the pain he crawled up the bank, calling, "Hey you . . . Help . . . Hey you . . ." The man came running, and Magnuson stared at the worn black shoes and white socks, the baggy shiny navy blue pants on the bow legs, the silver coin-changer on the belt, the lunch bucket in hand. The man was a city bus driver, taking a short cut home from the bus yard. "Not a cop," he said.

The motorman stepped back. He was flustered, frightened, he could see no one else in the woods around them. That yellow haze had reached the brook, where it settled, reaching for the bridge. "I'm the police," he said. "You just go on about your business. Don't give me any trouble."

Magnuson managed to crawl a few paces toward him. "I can't make it, pal," he said.

But the motorman picked up a branch and shook it at him. "I'm the police," he repeated. "Go on. Or I'll run you in." Still shaking the branch he backed down the path until it curved behind some trees, at which time he turned and ran, the change in his coin-changer jangling.

CHAPTER THIRTY-TWO

CHANDLER
DISCOVERS

As far as Solomon Chandler knew there had been no report of Farquarson's death in any of the Chicago papers. He could understand how it might not have made yesterday's morning edition, but it should have been in the afternoon edition and certainly in the evening. What was more surprising, it was not in this morning's *Tribune* either. Surely a man as important and well known as Farquarson had been in the business and social communities warranted a photograph and a lengthy column in the obituaries. Was there some plot or conspiracy between Magnuson and the newspapers, or among the newspapers themselves, to keep his death a secret? He called Magnuson but got no answer from his apartment, and his office said he was not there, nor was he expected later. Desperate, he telephoned Farquarson's house, calling several times, but the line was always busy. Perhaps the phone was out of order. Or the receiver deliberately left off the hook.

He was confused and depressed, and feared for the worst, although he had no clear notion yet of what the worst might be. He was convinced that the poison pen letter he had recently received, and which he suspected was authored by none other than Farquarson, played no small part in the mystery. It was certainly the fountainhead of his depression. On its pages he stood accused of all manner of deceits and malpractices in his profession of attorney; of advocating the cause of evil as indiscriminately as that of good; of collusion with opposing counsels and even judges to the injury of his clients and the mockery of law and justice; of milking clients of their hard-earned savings by making lengthy and foredoomed appeals; of owning slum properties. His character was described as mercenary, equivocal, hypocritical, and stinking with moral funk. He was also accused of being an accomplice in certain unspecified crimes, including what sounded very much like murder—crimes for which he was now at this late hour to be brought to account, even if he had been ignorant of their commission, a possibility the document had conceded. In terms often theological, often Calvinistic, he was scourged and flayed and burned and doomed and ordered to make a confession and a sincere repentance and advised to throw himself upon the mercy of Almighty God and the good feelings of his fellow men. Although the document appeared to be the work of a deranged, self-righteous fanatic, Chandler was nonetheless uneasy to know that someone could think so ill of him. Although he could not say why, he suspected that the document, along with Magnuson's suspicion that Farquarson had been murdered and those Farquarson skeletons he had himself dredged up two nights ago, somehow all went hand in hand.

Typed expertly on legal paper, the document had arrived in a manila envelope bearing a Chicago postmark. On a whim he now telephoned Farquarson's office in downtown Chicago. He was amazed that the secretary there, with whom he had dealt for years, had no knowledge that her employer was dead, speaking instead of his failing health, and he decided to say nothing to the contrary. She admitted freely that Farquarson had sent not only one document down to the office to be typed on legal paper, but three. She had had the girls type them, so she herself knew nothing of their contents. However, she thought they might be a joke of some kind, not uncommon with him, because they were to be mailed out without return address and were to be addressed only with the addressee's occupation and not his name. Yes, one of them had been sent to him, addressed only to The Lawyer. "The other two," she said, "were addressed to The Detective with a Lincoln Athletic Club address . . ."

Magnuson!

"And to The Doctor, with a Highland Park address."

Everett Archer!

Archer had been Farquarson's doctor for years, as he had been Chandler's. He was now semi-retired and both Farquarson and Chandler were attended to by his son. Chandler had intended to call Archer in any case. If anyone would know of Farquarson's death, he would. He now asked him to come over to the house and have a listen to his heart and a long drink while discussing an important matter that had just come up concerning Farquarson. To his inquiry after Farquarson's health, Archer said, "There's no change. Son" (the word never preceded by pronoun or article) "plans to stop by today. I thought I might go over with him." But hadn't Magnuson, Chandler recollected, said that the doctor had already been there (and that was a day and a half ago) and signed the death certificate? And hadn't he said that the doctor was Archer's son? Either Farquarson was still alive and Magnuson was lying, in which case he had a perverse sense of humor or was criminally insane, or Farquarson was dead and Magnuson had managed a mass conspiracy among his household and doctor if not his good friends to keep it a secret from the world, perhaps as a cover for his own investigation.

Chandler was lucky to have found Archer in the country. His one passion in life was to take long cruises to remote ports of call on small foreign freighters in the company of his wife or cronies. His service as the chief surgeon of a hospital unit in World War Two, with the rank of colonel, had been the most memorable and pleasant period of his life, and his manner was still militaristic. Even now he liked to wear lightweight, loose-fitting, but highly pressed khaki slacks and tan jackets, with light tan shirts that accentuated his tan flesh and white hair so that with his English-style mustache he gave the appearance of some staff officer just home from service in the tropics. Chandler had always thought him to be one of those arrogant, insensitive, and even ignorant men who automatically assume authority in any situation and are automatically granted authority by everyone else. Archer just did not doubt himself, nor was he pretending when any reasonable man in his place would have second thoughts and he had none. And yet he was an example of that breed of doctor who is competent in his profession even though he lacks, totally, kindness and compassion. He was candid with his patients, if he felt like it, candid to the point of cruelty, and if he didn't, there was no moving him to talk.

"There's no need for you to examine me," Chandler admitted first thing. "I asked you over here for other reasons." He handed him the anonymous document.

"Oh, so you got one too," Archer said, his nostrils shrinking up as they often did, giving him the appearance of inhaling snuff.

"Do you know who wrote it?"

"Farquarson." He handed the document back without looking at it.

"Do you know that for a fact?"

"I don't need any facts, Solomon. I read mine. Yours looks like mine. I know he wrote it."

"Well, I need facts. And I've got some. I called his secretary. He also sent one to Arnold Magnuson."

Archer seemed to view this bit of detection with amusement, as though Chandler had gone to unnecessary lengths to discover what was obvious. It was clear that he did not treat the document as important.

"Can I ask what your letter accused you of?" Chandler said.

"It's easier to say what it didn't accuse me of. I have violated my Hippocratic oath. I am guilty of malpractice. I am autocratic, militaristic. I lack humility. I deny my guilt. And I had better be ready to answer to my maker for all crimes."

Although he was obviously impatient with these accusations he was also amused by them, and certainly did not take them seriously.

"What made you think it was Frazer?"

"Well, I'll tell you," Archer said. "The letter hinted rather heavily at some wrongdoing I was supposed to have committed as a doctor. Even if by some stretch of the imagination they were crimes, they were Frazer's crimes, not mine."

"You're speaking now of Frazer's wife?"

Archer seemed on the verge of complimenting him. "If you could come to the same conclusion from your letter, that proves I'm right about mine. So does the letter to Magnuson. He was just as mixed up in that business as the rest of us."

"By 'that business' I take it you mean Farquarson's sending Hope to the sanitarium and the illegitimate children she had there?"

"That and the abortion she had before she was committed. All three of us must have been involved in that. Magnuson made an investigation of Hope and sent Farquarson a report that was a bit damaging. Farquarson thought so. I thought so. I know you thought so too, Solomon. I know we got together and decided on some action after we read it. But I can't recall now whether Magnuson's report was just after the abortion or just before, and so I forget whether our decision then was to commit her or to have the abortion. Which came first, eh, the chicken or the egg? Whichever one it was I know that report of Magnuson's had some bearing on our decision. I don't care what Frazer hints at in his letter, I didn't perform the abortion—I wouldn't touch a thing like that— but I did help with the arrangements. I can even remember the abortionist's name. Lopko. He looked like a Tartar. You must have been involved in the legal—or illegal—end of it."

Indeed, Chandler had been involved, and had a vague recollection of talking to the man named Lopko once or twice on the telephone. Somehow he had managed to forget all about the abortion; he would have to work hard if he were to bring it to the forefront of his memory. "Did she want an abortion?"

Archer had been sitting back in his wicker chair with his drink, picking invisible lint from his tan slacks and pinching the crease as though to test its permanence. Now he shot forward. "You know, I'm not sure. It seems to me she may have been against it at first and he had to talk her into it. That wasn't too hard to do, I suppose, given her mental condition.—Well, you remember what she was like."

Indeed, Chandler had been trying to remember what she had been like ever since his talk with Magnuson. "But what was the professional opinion of her illness?" he asked.

"Something mental, Solomon." He interrupted the protests Chandler was beginning to make. "I don't know what exactly. I suppose I did at one time. I left that to the fellows at the sanitarium. Personally, I think her biggest problem was that she was a rich malingerer. The old world was just too sordid and complicated for her to stomach, and so she put on this little act that she was mentally ill, and the doctors we had back then said, 'We know very well that this is all a masquerade, but listen here, my dear, the very fact that you have to make this little masquerade is proof in itself that you are ill.' "

"What was the prognosis?"

"I think we all thought it was pretty good at the time, and that she would be home soon, or at the very least that it would be some sort of on and off arrangement. Of course that kind of diagnosis I was just telling you about probably went a long way in convincing her that what she had known perfectly well as a sham was really an illness. That couldn't have helped her any. The game wasn't a game after all. And I've no doubt it was a game she liked. She wanted a special kindness. If she's a real lunatic today it's because of all the years she spent in those places."

"You think you were justified in committing her?"

"My God, Solomon, she was discharged half a dozen times, and always had to go back in. Then there was that business of those pregnancies. There wasn't just one, you know, there were two."

"Then why should Frazer all of a sudden accuse us—and from his deathbed too—of being accomplices in a piece of history that happened thirty years ago?"

"If you want my opinion he feels guilty about the business himself. I don't know that he should, but he does. He just wants to spread the guilt around before he goes. It's not nice, it isn't true, but it doesn't hurt anyone, and probably lets him ease his conscience. You can tell he's uncertain about all of this himself. That's why his accusations are so goddamned cloudy and cagey and anonymous." Here he leaned forward and his voice developed the air of a gossip. "It isn't Frazer's fault, and yet, goddamn it, it is his fault too. I always thought Hope wasn't unbalanced so much as just plain retarded. In the beginning, anyway. She was just born with a low I.Q. Oh, she could get by in most situations. But she was just too . . . passive . . . and simple-minded . . . and socially embarrassing. She was like that when Frazer married her, and if Frazer didn't know the lay of the land, why then he should have known. It's my opinion that not only did he know but that was precisely why he married her. He wanted a beautiful, messed-up vegetable. He was always a bit strange with women, and secretive too. It wouldn't surprise me if he didn't get his kicks out of having them trample on him. Then after he made his bed with her he discovered he couldn't handle her, or trust her, especially with other men."

In parting he advised that as a kindness to Farquarson in his final days they ought not to let on that they knew he was the author of those letters. Chandler for his part decided to say nothing of Magnuson's news that Farquarson was dead.

Alone, Chandler went into the bedroom to take his digitalis. Poor Hope. He had never felt right about the advice and service he had given Farquarson concerning her. Archer had articulated what he could not bring himself to say: she had not been insane. Retarded perhaps. Or merely in need of counsel or therapy. Maybe all she had needed was rest. Perhaps the best remedy would have been nothing more complicated than a divorce. If she were now insane it was likely the result of what had befallen her inside all those sanitariums. She had been imprisoned on and off for nearly thirty years, was still imprisoned now. Without trial or right of appeal. Without ever being dangerous to that society she was cloistered from or guilty of any crime against it. He remembered her as a young and beautiful woman. Now she was old, almost as old as his own wife, and her children were almost as old as his youngest. He dared not imagine what she looked like now. God help him, but to have helped Farquarson in such a business he must have abused the knowledge and advantage his profession gave him and whatever sentiments of tolerance and understanding he had had back then. Had he confused illness with depravity, treatment with punishment, and interpreted what was admittedly an embarrassment and nagging problem for Farquarson as an intolerable situation best remedied by shutting up the poor man's wife? It was an injustice he could never forgive. Meanwhile the years had demonstrated that if anyone in this dirty business was mad it was Farquarson, her husband. Or that insensitive Archer. Or even the deluded and conveniently forgetful Chandler himself.

He went out onto the screen porch in the shade of all those evergreens. The handyman had just come down his ladder, where he had been cleaning the needles out of the rain gutters, and was poking with his finger into a box of nails and whistling. Chandler watched him for a while, then went back inside, poured himself a drink, and lost himself in thoughts of Farquarson. How he wanted Farquarson's reasons for shutting up his wife to run deeper than selfishness and retribution. Far better that they reside in that insufferable and inexpressible shame and guilt he wanted Farquarson to have felt about the failure of his wife and marriage; wanted to believe that he had planned to bring her home until the illegitimate children persuaded him—mistakenly, no doubt—that he had no alternative but to leave her there; that he had not divorced her even when he believed there was no hope for her recovery because of that bond of pity he was bound to feel and that duty he was determined to perform; that he had agreed to (and probably not instigated) the abortion not because he suspected he was not the father of the child who, if it were born, would legally be a Farquarson and an heir to the Farquarson fortune, but because he did not want a mentally retarded child or any child brought up by an unbalanced mother, weak as these reasons were.

He could forgive Farquarson far easier than he could himself. He had helped to arrange the abortion as he had later helped to arrange the placement of Cavan into Farquarson's house and that of the mulatto girl in a public orphanage. He had been more than just an agent in all of this. He had been counselor and judge. What was he to this poor woman that he had taken upon himself the right to have a hand in determining the fate of all her children? And what was she to him?

She had returned to haunt Frazer in his final hours and Frazer had managed to pass her ghost along to him. Archer seemed absolved. To him the mystery had been no mystery at all. He had read the first page or two of his anonymous letter and had set it down, saying to himself, Oh, it's Frazer about that business with his wife that happened a good many years ago. He could be perceptive precisely because in his own mind he had done nothing unconscionable that he had had to sublimate these many years. For him there were no moral implications, no memories to haunt him.

Chandler was resolved to go in person to Farquarson's. Accordingly, he telephoned the man he used now in those rare times he required a chauffeur, Max McBrown, formerly a full-time chauffeur for Farquarson, who now chauffeured in his own car and on a part-time basis several retired North Shore businessmen. He drove up from Evanston, and they went together to Lake Forest, Chandler sitting in the back of the unpretentious car.

Young mothers and nurses were out with buggies and toddlers on the sidewalks and paths along the road, and it seemed that everywhere Chandler looked there were pregnant women. Children were riding bicycles in the street and slowing down the new convertibles with their tops down, jammed with teenagers. Groups of older people were out upon the lawns of the large houses, and one hostess wearing a green plastic visor was showing the guests her spring bulbs in her border. In the villages, with their train stations and shopping centers built in the 1920's and 1930's in the old English style of whitewash-and-timber, or stucco, and pitched roofs with gables, there were more bicycles and convertibles, and station wagons and several classic cars and Model-T Fords; the restaurants and ice-cream parlors were crowded, and the people were walking along the sidewalk beneath the awnings, eating ice cream. To Chandler it almost seemed as it had been thirty years ago. He could even make himself believe that despite the high taxes, housing developments, and sewage systems that polluted the lake, these suburban villages with their magnificent houses and landscapes and wooded settings would somehow manage not only to survive, but survive unchanged. He dozed off and dreamed of orchards and pastures and fields of grain and kitchen gardens that stretched across the continent with no roads or fences or cities or towns larger than the buildings at a crossroads and only small stands of forest and isolated white clapboard farmhouses and great red barns set out against the skyscapes of clouds and random meandering footpaths and wagon ruts of sand and grass and rivers that had to be forded. Everything was sunlit and quiltlike and open and rolling and the orchards were in fruit or flower and in the gardens bushel baskets stood beside the vines and the grass in the pastures was always ankle-high and green.

Then the car slowed down for a crowd of some thirty boys ranging in age from seven to twelve that emerged from a thicket of sumac and grapevines growing in a lot between two large houses and started in a body across the road. They reminded Chandler of his own boyhood, when he had played in such thickets with other boys, squatting in that secret, breezeless world on the dappled, hard-packed clay, the sun glinting through the intertwine of leaves. "Look out, little soldiers," Max said quietly to himself, touching the horn softly only once. As the car passed slowly between them, the boys on both sides of the road pretended to open fire with the cap guns, plastic machine guns, and beebee guns they were carrying, catching the car in an imaginary crossfire. At first Chandler was surprised and frightened, as though for a moment he thought the guns were real. Almost immediately, however, he was enraged not only at the boys for their show of violence but at himself for having felt fright at something as innocent as this, and he was almost for sticking his head out the window and shouting back at them. But was it all so innocent? Why was he feeling fear and revulsion, for he was certain that at other times he would have looked on this game of soldiers not only with tolerance and nostalgia but with approval? It was more than merely his resentment at being made their victim, albeit mock, but as though he saw in his own mock fate the possibility of the real fate of a million others. He was not lacking twinges of culpability. After all, why hadn't he been repelled before?

He saw some consolation, however, in all of this. Although the boys depressed him, he could himself be thankful that he had felt that depression.—And Hope Farquarson, it suddenly occurred to him, it was possible that she was mentally disturbed after all, even hopelessly insane, and had been from the beginning, and everyone all along the line—Farquarson, Magnuson, Archer, himself—had done the right thing, or at the very least only what, given the circumstances, they could have done. What was sane in this unhappy business was the compassion and responsibility and regret, no matter how eccentric, that Farquarson even at this late hour could feel for her. As was the guilt and contrition that he, Chandler, felt too. And the beauty was that although the grounds for the existence of these feelings were slight, or nonexistent, they existed anyway!—That they existed at all! That they were abroad in the world among living men. In men of good will who, quite apart from any nonsense of martyrdom, were unsatisfied in the end and could say of themselves, This was not my best . . . I might have been wrong . . . This is not the way the world should work . . . I am at fault . . . Unfortunate humanity . . .

But by the time they arrived at Farquarson's, Chandler was once more given over to apprehension and doubt. Something he could not locate was amiss in what he saw, as though the grass needed mowing, the flower beds weeding. A breeze that would have liked to tear into sheets and sails was blowing. The garage doors were wide open, and there was Max calling for Chandler to come and look at this, his voice sharing for the first time in Chandler's apprehension. The tires of all the cars were flat. A pair of second-story casements in Farquarson's bedroom was open, and a ladder set up against the half-timbered wall leading directly to them. The front door was wide open, too. Instinctively, both men stood on the lawn and called to the house through the megaphones of their hands, reluctant to enter and as anxious to have anyone who did not belong there leave by the back way as they were for someone who did belong there to come out and bid them enter through the front. Only the wind in the woods and the rushing of the lake below. They could be in the northern woods for all the silence and isolation. Then they saw the dead man lying on the bark mulch scattered beneath the rhododendrons. Dead for some time, too, was Max's observation. A heart attack, Chandler wondered? Neither man had seen the dead man before.

They went into the house to call the police, but the phone which Chandler held in his handkerchief was dead, the wires cut. A sense within the house of empty rooms, of sheets draped across the furniture, the shut-in smells of a hospital one would expect to find not in a large house but in a small, overheated room. The dust in the sunlight slanting through the many windows swirled up like smoke. Side by side they wandered through the house, the two old men, the lawyer wearing a kind of large slouch hat that made him resemble some magician or heavyhanded thespian and that was best worn in the company of a cape, the other with his large, black, bald, and furrowed head and neck beneath the chauffeur's cap. It was as though they had blundered onstage behind the curtain that had just fallen on the final scene of the last act of an Elizabethan tragedy. The housekeeper was in her bathrobe in her bedroom, on the floor beside the bed, bludgeoned to death with an ax. The nurse was upstairs in her room, naked on her bed, likewise bludgeoned, likewise dead. "I know those women," Max said, as if this should have rightfully prevented the fact of their deaths. His uniform of cap and jacket and that formal and military manner, as though his body could bend only at one place, and that only slightly at the waist, in contrast to the awful messiness of the corpses. While Chandler trembled in the doorways he went at least partway into the rooms, imposing his own darkness between the windows and the beds. "A maniac," Max said. The door to Farquarson's room was locked and they decided not to break it down but to go instead for the police. But outside they recalled the ladder and open windows and, after taking counsel, Max climbed the ladder, handkerchiefs in either hand, disappearing between the curtains into the shadows of the room. Several times his face appeared in passing before the window, or stationary there, only to be pulled back into the darkness. What seemed a dangerous period of time elapsed before his face came there to stay. He shook his head, leaning out.

"Dead too?" Chandler shouted, surprised at the callousness of the question on his own voice.

Max nodding his head in reply before shaking it again in disbelief.

My God, thought Chandler, as he watched Max back down the ladder, where is Magnuson? And later as they drove for the police, And what has Magnuson to do with all of this? Two questions that were to plague a good number of people for days—months—even years to come.

BOOK FOUR

DISCOVERIES

CHAPTER THIRTY-THREE

THE MAYOR
SPEAKS

In the days that followed no less than ten corpses were discovered at four different murder sites. In response to such awful news, numerous rumors unnerved the amazed and terrified citizens of the city and its suburbs, and were in many instances given credence in the editorials of the press. It was a communist plot to get rid of patriots; a right-wing plot to get rid of Communists; an FBI plot to get rid of Communists; a communist plot to get rid of other Communists; a black plot in revenge for the lynching of a local black youth who had been visiting his grandmother in Mississippi ("Ten whites for every black man slain"); a simple gangland massacre; the work of a secret society of sexual degenerates, steel rods having been found inserted up the rectums of all the victims, a rumor that gained so great a vogue that the police were finally forced to deny it, which only increased the gullibility of those who had believed it in the first place. These rumors, and many others, were the subject of conversations between total strangers in restaurants, taverns, buses, elevated trains, even along the streets themselves. The Letters to the Editor sections of the newspapers and the radio talk shows, on which people were free to telephone in their views, were turned over almost exclusively to the amateur speculations of the citizenry. Indeed, some of the newspapers and radio stations not only offered rewards for information leading to the solution of the crimes but prizes for the most ingenious and imaginative explanations. Hundreds of letters suggested that because of the slaughter of the farm animals in Wenzel's barn the police should search for a man who had once worked in the Stockyards; other letters suggested they look for a mad doctor or veterinarian. A caller into a radio station theorized that the killer was a mathematician; or had at the very least a strong sense of numerical order, the bodies having been found in lots of a 4:3:2:1 ratio (four at Farquarson's, three at Wenzel's farm, two at Bang's Lake, one at Rotterdam's apartment), which explained why there had been no more crimes, the series having been completed. Another letter suggested an interest in geometry on the part of the killer, and had drawn a series of four triangles of decreasing size neatly overlapping one another on a map of Chicagoland, the top point of each a murder site. One caller even proclaimed that the killer was no less than Death himself, that this was a signal that retribution for the republic as a whole was close at hand, and that all would soon see Death ride his white horse across this continent; he could find verses in the Bible to verify this. Almost hourly new rumors circulated that a man had just called a radio show or written a suppressed letter to the newspapers giving information that stamped him irrefutably as the murderer.

With the death of Tanker the people had felt themselves purified and secure in that notion that justice follows crime as surely as death follows life, and that the best punishment for such a crime as murder is always death. If they had missed the excitement of that search they no less enjoyed the righteousness and peace they felt within themselves and among their neighbors when it had reached its satisfactory end. If it was pleasant to suspect everyone it was equally pleasant to suspect no one. But now they had learned they were no longer merely witnesses to a confrontation between the police and a single criminal but were the victims of perhaps the greatest and cleverest mass murderer in the history of their city, a man—or men—who might strike them down at any moment in any place by any means, and who they were all equally suspected of being as well. Although the killings of this madman were unusual in that he had not struck once a week for sixteen weeks but had concentrated his slaughter in a single night, at most two nights, and then had killed no more, there was the fear that if he did strike again the deaths would again be widespread, multiple, and indiscriminate. Because of this fear men and women appeared at their jobs bleary-eyed, having sat up all night watching one of the several all-night round-table discussion programs on television on which, more than likely, the host of the show had tried frantically to keep a suspicious caller on the line while the police traced the call; or having sat up in a chair while the family slept in the bedrooms, with a shotgun or deer rifle across their laps. Sales of guns and ammunition, locks, and large, aggressive, and even dangerous dogs increased until locksmiths and dog trainers could no longer keep up with the demand, and the gun racks at sporting goods stores were emptied.

The police meanwhile were slow to sort out and define the crimes, never mind solving them. At first the murders at each of the different sites had been reported as separate crimes, unrelated to each other. Later they were correlated, but only after what had seemed insurmountable confusion in the co-ordination and communication between the various police agencies involved. As far as anyone could tell there was no rational pattern to the crimes, although a few officers argued for something more organized and diabolical than indiscriminate slaughter. But if they suspected the presence of a pattern they also despaired that it would reveal itself to their detection. They were confused by the diversity in the social scale of the victims, the failure of anyone to detect the killer at the murder scenes, or discover his victims, and the variety of murder weapons he had employed. Good police officers broke down before maps and charts of distances between the four murder sites and the times of death, trying to establish a sequence in time only from one crime to another, ignoring opportunity and motive. To compound the confusion and further drain their already overextended manpower, all departments received crank calls and letters and confessions of a magnitude dwarfing those of any previous crime, all of which had to be investigated. A man had called Nancy Rhinelander's mother in Denmark, Wisconsin, and claimed to be the murderer because he could describe, accurately apparently, the location of a mole on her daughter's body, convincing Mrs. Rhinelander that he was who he said he was. A letter was received by the police of Grand Rapids,

Michigan, containing an alleged lock of Bonny Wenzel's hair. Other items such as nail clippings and dried blood were also received, including in one bizarre instance a freshly severed human big toe, accompanied by a note explaining that the writer, who was the murderer, had cut it from the foot of Mrs. Owens. The police knew very well that Mrs. Owens had all her toes.

From the very beginning Skipper Moony and several of his friends, all of whom were missing, were considered prime suspects in the crimes. He and two of his friends were discovered sleeping in an orange grove near Orlando, Florida, and rumors claimed he had been hustled in violation of his civil rights in a private car back to Chicago, handcuffed and with a raincoat over his head, a revolver always against his ribs. Stories emerged from the County Jail of brutal beatings and the flagrant violation of the most elementary rights. His friends, who were soon released, told of coerced confessions and mistreatment, and in the newspapers there were photographs of them posing with their T-shirts rolled up, pointing out their bruises for the inspection of their lawyers. Neither police, press, or public, however, seemed satisfied that Skipper was responsible for the crimes. There was a prevailing sentiment that he was a scapegoat, and that his incarceration and investigation were a cover-up for police inefficiency and the possible involvement of important public persons in the crimes.

In the meantime, despite the conviction of many law officers that all the murders could not be attributed to one man and that a gang or conspiracy of some sort had to be responsible, the police were conducting a search for two men whose fingerprints, unknown to the public at large, had been discovered at all four murder sites. In fact it was this discovery more than any other that linked the four sites and the ten victims as the work of a single party, and dropped others from the list. Two more unlikely suspects working in consort could not be imagined. A call went out for Joseph Helenowski, a recent escapee from a mental institution, and suspected murderer of a destitute Indian, Alvin Raincloud, in Washington Square on the night before the first of the murders. To the surprise of many, a muted call went out also for Arnold Magnuson, prominent Chicago businessman and founder and president of the Magnuson Men, who worked out of the agency that bore his name. The official word was that Magnuson had been a visitor at the Farquarson house at the time of the murders, and that he was missing and presumed kidnapped and murdered. Unofficially a rumor circulated that had Magnuson somehow involved in the commission of the crimes. But at a time rife with rumors and speculations, most of them far-fetched, this seemed the most improbable of all. Magnuson, of the Magnuson Agency, involved in murder? Most citizens dismissed this hypothesis with a laugh and a wave of the hand, even if the informant's brother-in-law was a policeman who knew another policeman assigned directly to the case.

Meanwhile the missing Helenowski had been sighted by a troop of Boy Scouts in the woods near Eau Claire, Wisconsin, by tourists on a houseboat in the Seine, by an elderly couple hitchhiking in the middle of Montana, and by a man with a telescope at the wheel of a cabin cruiser heading across Lake Michigan. The missing Magnuson had been observed escorting a bevy of chocolate-colored girls in São Paulo, wandering in a daze across a cornfield in Iowa, inquiring about the Soviet Union at a travel agency in Newark, and emerging from a raspberry patch and offering to purchase a sandwich for five dollars from a lady in an isolated farmhouse in Alberta, Canada. Neither man, however, had been apprehended.

As the first part of a program to put an end to these reports and rumors, the mayor of Chicago, the Honorable Thomas Conley, ordered an executive session of certain city officials in City Hall. He wanted to acquaint them with the particulars of the case and to explain official city policy in the matter of handling it. Those summoned were Luther Lindl, recently named by the mayor to head a newly formed crime commission; Police Superintendent Maurice Comiskey; Chief of Detectives James Doyle; City Legal Counselor James McDonough; City Health Superintendent Jacob Hernstein; and the mayor's personal publicity director, Mark Horn.

The mayor, a Democrat and Chicago-born, had risen through the ranks of ward politics and did not resemble the Irish politicians and mayors of eastern cities so much as he did some Yugoslav commissar. He was squat, robust but roly-poly, wore plain gray business suits with blue ties, or blue suits with gray ties, and spoke with an accent that was that of any Chicagoan of Polish descent. He was drab, usually unemotional, and extraordinarily powerful. He used this power in doling out that patronage that was instrumental in maintaining him in office, and in naked and stubborn displays that often bordered on illegality and corruption. He was admired by the people of the city for his wise understanding of the sorry ways of this world, for the power he possessed, and for his use of it to his and sometimes their advantage. He was admired in much the same way as the leaders of certain Slavic countries are admired for being, somehow, the embodiment of their national character, and for being strong. He arranged frequent parades of city employees, usually down Michigan Avenue, and could be certain of a good turnout of both marchers and crowds. These parades were less reminiscent of the good old American Fourth of July and Memorial Day parades than they were of May Day parades in a Slavic country ruled by a totalitarian leader. They were often used to unveil new city equipment—sanitation trucks, fire trucks, squad cars—in much the same way that new military equipment was unveiled in those of the Slavic countries. The name of Thomas Conley, a "Good Mayor" or "Our Beloved Mayor" or "The People's Mayor," or more popularly lately, "The Mayor of All Our People," draped around the bodies of immense, brand-new yellow garbage trucks that crept down the avenue in the slow deliberate formation of Soviet tanks in Red Square, the sanitation workers sitting on them like tank corpsmen. Foot soldiers, burly men in crew cuts, marched by in formation of their profession— "Schoolteachers for Mayor Conley," "Policemen for Mayor Conley," "Sanitation Workers for Mayor Conley," those ranks pushing their brooms before them down the street as they marched beside street-cleaning machines with great whirling brushes. There was no embarrassment for the mayor in any of this, for the pretense was always that this was arranged not by the mayor himself ("King Tom," as he was called by his enemies) but in gratitude and affection by the mayor's many friends.

In a city of over a million Poles, far more Poles than any other nationality (including Irish, of whom there were comparatively few), the mayor was in almost everything but name a Pole. It was high testimony to his political skill that all the highest elective offices in the city were held by Irish, and at Conley's insistence the party only ran Irish candidates on the ticket.

The mayor was himself a man of modest means, and fewer interests, and still lived with his family in a Chicago bungalow in his old neighborhood on the street on which he had been born and had never left. He had two passions in his life: the city of Chicago, its reconstruction, welfare, and good reputation; and the helping in one way or another of those friends and supporters who had in some way helped or befriended him and whom he judged it was his duty to promote and protect. Coincidentally, these two passions were in his judgment the greatest virtues a man of public service could possess. Usually the two were easily reconciled. But the recent police scandal in the city had presented him with a severe conflict between the welfare and reputation of the city—which was his city, and which, given his long tenure of office and the passive trust the people had put in him, was himself, and he felt this modestly—and his helping his supporters and good friends. This scandal involved not only the old news of payoffs to police by criminal elements, but even police burglaries, and the relationship between organized crime and the police—as was recently evidenced by Lazzaretto, a retired and peculiarly wealthy police captain (his wife, he maintained, "had been an heiress"), traveling in the company of Allegro, the alleged leader of Chicago crime who, as it turned out, had been Lazzaretto's lifelong friend. In this conflict the city had emerged victorious, and in appointing Luther Lindl to head the crime commission he was merely preparing for that day, which could be any day now, when he would appoint him superintendent of police. The mayor hoped that as an outsider without previous political or even practical police experience and who was therefore innocent, Lindl would improve the integrity, caliber, and eventually the morale of the demoralized force, and pacify the local and even national outrage at the recent misconduct of the force, which reflected on the mayor's own administration. But more than anything else the mayor hoped that Lindl would modernize the force, for he wanted to make it the best police force in the world, just as he wanted to make the city the best city in the world. This had been a painful decision, and in order to implement it he would not only have to fire the present superintendent, Comiskey, but pass over the list of captains who had come up through the ranks.

The problem of Arnold Magnuson presented him with a different conflict. The reputation of the city, and the people's faith in it, was here pitted against something far more intangible, such as truth, or justice, or rule by law (he was not sure which), and so beyond a certain lip service to the loser, in this case rule by law, it was not a difficult choice to make. The city had been rocked by the death of Farquarson, a name associated with the famous downtown department stores and banks, the meat-packing industry, the steel mills, the city athletic teams. And if this were not enough, the most famous man in the city, by name anyway, and the man most associated with law and order in the city, Magnuson of the Magnuson Men, was himself implicated in Farquarson's death, along with the murder of nine others. Something had to be done.

"I asked you to come here today, gentlemen," the mayor said

to the men around the conference table, "to discuss this problem of Mr. Magnuson, one of our famous citizens, who is missing, and see if we can't work something out together." He spoke always in a soft monotone, with a suggestion of humility and even apology in his voice. He was almost stubbornly inarticulate, as though he knew, as did his listeners, that actions speak louder than words, and made no attempt to disguise the fact that for him public speaking was an onerous and probably unnecessary chore. His speeches were usually little more than brief statements. He called immediately on Chief of Detectives Doyle to give his report on the case.

Doyle was a small muscular man who gave the impression he could be observed most often standing behind a desk in shirtsleeves with his shoulder holster showing and talking tough on the phone. He read from numerous stapled sheets, speaking from the corner of his mouth. It was true, he said, that Magnuson's fingerprints had been found at each of the four murder sites, as had those of the escaped madman Helenowski. Besides, witnesses had been able to place him at every site at one time or another on the first night of the murders, with the exception of Wenzel's barn (where incidentally his fingerprints had been found on Wenzel's truck parked inside the barn and on the weapon that had been used to kill Wenzel), although one of the Moony boy's friends thought he had seen Magnuson's Duesenberg parked in the Moonys' yard, and customers in Al and Bonny Wenzel's Bang's Lake Inn had overheard him ask Bonny Wenzel for directions to her husband's barn. They had finally been able to draw up a chart of Magnuson's movements on the first night of the killings, ending with his being driven home to his apartment on the Gold Coast. The next day they could account for him continuously, beginning with his interrogation by police officers in his own apartment in the morning. But that night, with the exception of a visit to the home of a former black police officer, Marcus Washington, on the South Side, he had vanished completely. Early the next morning a police officer had talked to him on the telephone in his LaSalle Street office, and he had been seen briefly by a complement of his own Magnuson Men at a Polish picnic on Milwaukee Avenue soon afterward. After that he had vanished and had not been seen or heard from since. The rumor was true that on the first night of the crimes Magnuson had appeared at the house of Mrs. Rotterdam impersonating a police officer, and had learned from her the location of her husband. It did not seem that he could be an accomplice of the madman Helenowski, since he was always seen alone. For the same reason it could not be easily argued that he had been abducted by the madman and forced to serve as an unwilling hostage when one considered that Magnuson was roaming about the city freely for the next two days. If he was himself in pursuit of Helenowski, why hadn't he informed the police of the crimes? He had talked with police officers at numerous times on those days. And although he had been hired to investigate the death of Farquarson by Solomon Chandler, the latter believed that most of the murders had been committed prior to the time that he was hired. Indeed, the only reasonable explanation for Magnuson's behavior was that he was insane, and that it was unlikely that rational men could make any sense of his irrational actions.

The mayor spoke. "Gentlemen, I pray to God we find this fine man, dead or alive, if only so his family can stop all this worrying about him and get some sleep. When we find him, gentlemen—if he isn't murdered and I pray to heaven he's still alive—I would be the first man to be certain he could explain this business by saying he was a prisoner of this ruthless killer or that he was chasing him and trying to stop him from killing these people. But if he can't explain this business, gentlemen, then I pray to heaven that our doctors can tell us he's insane so that we can all feel sorry for his fine family and put him away quietly so we can forget this business and he can get the help he needs. But let's face the facts, gentlemen. If he's involved in this business it would be best for him and for his family and for everybody else if he had been killed in the line of duty while trying to protect those people. Because if he's found dead, gentlemen, nothing can ever be known for certain, and these writers can speculate all they want, and nobody has the right to stop them, but they can't prove nothing against this fine man either." The mayor was in the process of working himself up emotionally, which was revealed not in his voice, which remained a soft-spoken monotone, but in the pink splotches on his otherwise gray face and in gesticulations, both fists shaking before his shoulders as though they held castanets or were pounding on some imaginary prison door. He now called upon Dr. Hernstein, the city health officer, to speak.

Dr. Hernstein was very old, with a bald and freckled head and horn-rimmed glasses, and spoke with an East European accent. It was his opinion that Magnuson's extraordinary behavior could be medically explained—and he wanted to emphasize the "could be"—by the presence of a psychosis with cerebral arteriosclerosis. In such an affliction the physical damage to the brain, caused by an inadequate supply of food and blood to the brain cells because of the hardening of the walls of blood vessels, would occur first, with the symptoms of the psychosis following. Each afflicted man would imprint his personality upon the standard symptoms of the disease and make it his very own. This was important to bear in mind when examining the behavior of Magnuson. The early symptoms were often physical and mental letdown; they knew that Magnuson had remained cooped up in his Gold Coast apartment for months before the first night of the murders, and those people who had seen him during this time reported that he was depressed. In most cases the onset of the acute psychosis would be sudden, as it must have been in Magnuson's case, since there was no report of extravagant behavior beforehand. In a man of Magnuson's age, who was retired, widowed, and without a future to speak of, one would have thought the psychosis would have brought about confusion and depression to the point where the man was no longer capable of any integrated action. Instead, it would seem he had responded like a younger man who was still vigorous and ambitious, by entertaining delusions of persecution and grandeur and placing himself in situations where he acted with glory, and without so much as a hint of a shortcoming in his performance. It was possible that he might well act incompetently but view himself as acting competently. Might act immorally but view himself as acting morally. In a sense he would become his opposite, although he would not be aware of the transformation. There were such cases on record. The law-enforcement officer becomes the criminal. Or interferes in the course of justice under the misguided notion that he is helping justice. The surgeon, the healer of people with his knife, becomes the destroyer of people, killing them on the operating table. While in his own mind all the incisions he makes are in the proper place, at the proper depth; the arteries severed are the arteries that should be severed, the organ removed the organ that is diseased. And if anyone corrects him he calls them fools and knaves, just as any normal man would if someone were to tell him he was doing something contrary to the evidence of his own senses. This would be tragic in a man like Magnuson, who in his lifetime had been so very competent, successful, high-minded, civic-minded, moral. It was the worst possible affliction for men like him. And not readily detectable at first in such a man either, since he was accustomed to authority and deference and was not likely to admit to any error of judgment or consult with others for advice, nor was he a man others would quickly criticize. There was an outside possibility that the brain damage was due not to cerebral arteriosclerosis but to general paresis, caused by syphilis, since the damage and mental disorder in both instances were fairly similar. An early symptom for general paresis, interestingly enough, was a weakening of moral fiber. In either case the affliction was fatal, and although madness might be for a time arrested, the case could never be cured. Needless to say, Magnuson was a seriously ill man and not responsible for his actions. A great tragedy. For the man, the city, his family. He, like the mayor, hoped for everyone's sake that Magnuson was found murdered by the madman Helenowski. If so, he was certain an autopsy would reveal severe focal lesions of the brain. But if he were found alive he was certain they would find him suffering from one of the two diseases. In fact, it might be wise to make such information available to the public at this time. It would tend to quiet the most outrageous of the rumors and prepare the way for the diagnosis just in case Magnuson did turn up alive. In tomorrow's newspaper a prominent local psychiatrist, whom the city had supplied with certain information, would begin a series—under commission from the newspaper—in which he would present much the same medical hypothesis for Magnuson's behavior that he, Hernstein, had presented here.

Luther Lindl appeared confused. He raised his hand, waving the pencil he held. "Am I to understand," he said, "that the city is in league with this psychiatrist in putting this medical view of Magnuson before the public?" A cautious man by nature, he could see from the embarrassed faces around the table that he had spoken out of turn. He knew he was soon to be appointed superintendent of police and he was indignant that the mayor would invite him to a meeting where the truth was to be doctored and the news managed. Especially when, if you believed the press reports and City Hall's own publicity releases, he had been appointed to head the new crime commission and clean up the corruption of the city like a marshal in an untamed western town. He knew he had been appointed to the crime commission to appease a handful of reformers and the national leaders of the Democratic Party, in whose good standing the mayor wished to remain. But he knew that he would soon be appointed to the superintendency so as to create and administer an efficient, modern police force trained to meet the urban problems of these times. He had no interest whatsoever in affairs like this mass murder involving Magnuson and the escaped madman Helenowski. If he had an interest in combating crime it was organized crime, and men like Allegro, Fiore, and the late Scarponi, and in easing out and transferring to positions of little power the incompetent and corrupt captains, lieutenants, and sergeants on the force. A professor of sociology and then also a dean at Southern Illinois University in Carbondale, he had no previous experience in a police department anywhere, other than in the role of consultant. He was a manager, technician, and theorist who had begun his career with a strong interest in the relationship between an urban community and its police force but had lately become preoccupied with the theory of administering a large police department and in automating and motorizing the department in its war against traffic and crime. Like the mayor he was obsessed with creating the most efficient police force in the world. He was only in his late thirties and with his short flat-top crew cut and bow tie he resembled less a professor or superintendent of police than a cornbelt farmer.

While the mayor pretended he had not heard Lindl's question, or if he had, that it did not matter, McDonough, the city's legal counselor, had taken over from Hernstein in an attempt to answer it. Without looking at Lindl he spoke defensively, with some anger.

"Well, I only wanted a clarification," Lindl said, as though to tell them they were misreading him if they thought the matter of Magnuson was important to him. "That's all."

At this, Superintendent Comiskey, who had been watching Lindl with amusement, almost laughed aloud. He knew they had been summoned here not to make a decision, or even so much as advise the mayor in the making of his decision, but only to be informed of a decision already made—by McDonough and Horn, more than likely. Comiskey's eyes looked distorted behind his glasses, and his face, which frowned perpetually and was twisted up to the left, seemed to inform anyone who spoke to him, You're a liar, and I'll remember you. Although he did suffer from day-long migraine headaches, he would have been a bitter man in any case. A dedicated law officer and an honest man, he had known too many years of disappointments and loneliness to be otherwise. His sense of humor, which at one time had been formidable if sarcastic, he now indulged in only to himself, so that he often appeared to be talking to himself. This was the first time he had met Lindl, the man he had learned would replace him in the weeks ahead. So this is the outsider, he said to himself. Not only not a member of the police force but not even a Chicagoan, so that the insult to the department and the city was twofold. Superintendent Comiskey had worn a uniform, whereas

Superintendent Lindl would wear a business suit. The "new man," he said to himself, for His Highness King Tom's "new city." He felt that more than anyone else the mayor had sacrificed him personally. To his wife he had threatened to retire from the force after only twenty years, and then after thirty years, and then every year since. For years he had sent away for bulletins and magazines on cheap retirement places, like Mexico and Aruba, and lately Yugoslavia and Spain, and discussed them with his wife (they were childless, and since he had been superintendent she was the only person he ever talked with informally) around the kitchen table in the evening. He was worn out by being a tough guy, a character it was always barely in his power to play.

He and the red-faced unhappy Doyle, who had also been observing Lindl, caught each other's eye, and past secrets and present condemnations passed between them. They both had known Magnuson as far back as when he was a cop. Comiskey had always said of him that "he was a tough nut to crack," while Doyle liked to refer to him, oddly, as "that Roman at the bridge." Comiskey had seen him as that breed of officer who placed his own integrity above the welfare of his fellow officers, correlating the law with his own integrity, but who placed justice above the law. Now Magnuson, who must have fallen on bad days, was to be a madman, while the old guard, so-called, was being purged. Doyle, passed up for the superintendent's job, which in ordinary times would have been his, would be forced into retirement by Lindl within the year. They were all going down with that old trooper Magnuson, and His Honor Mr. Conley, who should have gone with them, knew which way the wind was blowing.

Lindl was one sort of young Turk, McDonough and Mark Horn were others. Comiskey despised them all; "slicksters," he called them. McDonough, in his mid-thirties, loud-mouthed and tough-talking, and acting always as though he alone had His Excellency's best interests at heart, looked more like a German than an Irishman. He lied shamelessly in public as His Royal Highness's trusted spokesman, defying anyone to disbelieve him. With newsmen he could be simultaneously belligerent and evasive, as though he could sidestep you and knock your brains out as you stumbled past, whereas Comiskey, when asked a question he could not answer truthfully, would remain silent and glare at the reporter with disgust, staring him down. To Comiskey there was something brutal about the man; he would have been better suited as a sadistic guard at a marine corps stockade than as the legal counselor for the city. And wasn't he also rumored to be His Worship's closest adviser?

And Horn? Where the hell did they get that guy? Only in his mid-twenties, he drove an olive-colored Cadillac and dressed like a jewelry salesman or Dago gangster. He had been hired by His Lordship to "dramatize" his roles as a political, reform-minded leader. He was self-confident and brash, and trumpeted his influence and friendship with His Royal Majesty about the cocktail bars of the city. His hands reminded Comiskey of melting candles. He looked like the kind of man whose footsteps you could slip on like banana peels. Something cold about all three of them. They were like machines. McDonough was the steel, Horn the oil, Lindl the engineer. Comiskey could be thankful he would not have to deal with them. His Royal Highness could have that bunch, and he was welcome to them.

The mayor, normally taciturn, now decided this was an occasion to defend and unburden himself. He was convinced the city had been attacked unfairly, which was another way of saying that its mayor had been attacked unfairly, and he had rankled with these attacks. He saw his city as something akin to a Greek *polis* and the worst sin a citizen could commit was to work against "our city." He was worried that not only would the mass murders not be solved but the gangland slayings were about to begin anew. The Republican governor of the state had referred to the recent wave of murders as the "Chicago problem," while the national and international and even the local press referred to it as a "Chicago crime." The mayor began calmly enough by pointing out that nine of the ten murders were committed outside Chicago. But then in a quick change of subject he was close to shouting. "Chicagoans are proud to be Chicagoans. They love their houses and apartments and lawns. They love their city and their city officials. Whether they voted for them or not . . . A Chicagoan knows who he is, gentlemen. The whole world knows who he is. Somebody from Los Angeles—they don't know who he is. Somebody from Detroit—they haven't got any idea. They don't even know who a New Yorker is. The world knows we're not savages. The world knows we're civilized. But according to these writers, some from our very own city, we're all crooks and animals. The people's police force and the city government is corrupt and consorting with criminals. Why can't they tell the truth about our city? We're not criminals. We're not bad men. We don't want to hurt no one. We want everybody to be happy. We want peace and quiet. We want justice. We want the criminals to be caught. We want to protect our people." His fist struck his open palm for emphasis at the end of each of these brief sentences. "We're just like other people. Why can't they write about the good things in our city and about us, gentlemen? Nobody's perfect, gentlemen. Not the mayor, not the city, not the country. I've made mistakes." He paused, then repeated himself as though persuaded that his audience would not believe him, "I've made mistakes . . .

"Why don't they write about our new city with our new housing units and wonderful lakefront? Why don't they write about our dedicated schoolteachers and the fine job they're doing in our schools? Or about the fathers working overtime to keep their families together? Or the welfare workers helping out our senior citizens? Why do they write just about murder and this poor man's sickness? Because that's just sensationalism, gentlemen, writing about him only when he's sick. There's more to life than this, gentlemen. Where were these writers when he was an upstanding citizen? Why didn't they tell the story of the Magnuson we used to know, the fine citizen, the good father, the hardworking businessman, the patriotic American?"

These were opinions he felt personally and deeply, and had kept smoldering within himself for some days. It was as though only here in private among these men could he unburden and reveal himself. "I love this city," he said. "I love all its people. It's our city. There aren't any black or yellow or white or Irish or Polish Chicagoans, gentlemen. There are just Chicagoans . . . They can't frighten us. The city and its mayor isn't afraid of anyone . . . This is a great city. This is a great country . . . " He broke down, his eyes wet and red, and patted his brow with his handkerchief. "I have nothing more to say, gentlemen."

So this is how it came about that if Magnuson could not be absolved of any wrongdoing in the recent wave of murders, it was to be hypothesized until believed that, by reason of insanity of a sort, he could not be held responsible for his crimes.

CHAPTER THIRTY-FOUR

SKID ROW

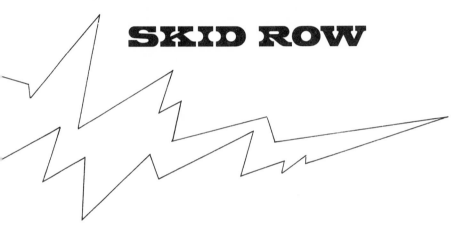

Throughout the time the police departments of the United States, Mexico, and Canada searched for Magnuson, Magnuson was in Chicago, across the Chicago River and the newly constructed highway, in view of the very skyscrapers of the Loop that had been his home, on the smoky, glittering sidewalks of Skid Row. His wardrobe had changed and, because he scavenged the streets, continued to change almost from day to day. He wore a cloth cap with earflaps, a dirty flannel shirt and a gray T-shirt, an old double-breasted suit jacket half a dozen sizes too large for him, and tennis shoes so small that his feet were swollen. The seams of these shoes were torn, the laces crisscrossed taut across the instep, the tongue exposed. He had replaced his own broken eyeglasses with a used pair with steel rims that had been made for a head far smaller than his own. In order to reach his ears the curves of the bows were bent almost straight, and the small round lenses were pulled flush against his brows, cutting his flesh. They distorted his vision and hurt his eyes. Usually he carried them folded up in his hand and held them up to his eyes like a lorgnette whenever there was something he wanted to read. The many small cuts on the soft skin around his eyes, made when the lenses of his own glasses had been smashed against his face, had not entirely healed and still smarted when he cried. One eye was still half-closed. He had been bitten on one ear, and the lobe was scabbed and on some days bandaged, and in his other ear he was almost deaf. His broken nose was still swollen and misshapen, with an impaction in the nostrils so that he breathed laboriously through his mouth, which he held open, looking as though he were always confronted by a sight that astonished him. He thought that his arm could have been broken and that it was healing crookedly. The scabs on his body became smaller each day, while his bruises passed through a range of colors. As he limped down the streets he would often stoop over and reach back with both his hands to grab the small of his back. He had not had a haircut and his sideburns were heavy with white hairs, and his hair was long and ragged above his collar, and he had a beard that although short was soft and almost yellow. Even if he did physically resemble the man he once had been, who, of those who knew him in the past, could have predicted he could descend so low that they could connect him with such a man as this?

Here on these wide and littered streets that stretched west, where the dawn was always either too hot or too cold, he was among derelict, transient, and impoverished men. They looked drugged or sleepy and slouched with their heads lowered and their hands in their pockets as though always underdressed for weather that was always cold. They had been rained on, snowed on, sunburned, frostbitten, wind-chapped, and their faces had that gray pallor and wrinkled texture of men exposed to the weather, smoke, and dust of a northern city. They were men who had failed in life, or who never had a chance to do otherwise: the feeble-minded, the crippled, the maimed. They were southerners, and westerners, and midwesterners from the nearby small towns and farms, and migratory workers, and merchant seamen, and pensioners without families who could live only here on their incomes, and Chicagoans with steady jobs and families who disappeared here for weekends or even months to lead their secret and shameful lives, drawn to the capital city of their own collapsing empire. It was a city without children, and with few women, and few Indians and Mexicans, and even fewer black men.

Here the small shiftless groups were like prisoners milling about in the yard of a concentration camp, and any man alone seemed to stagger stupefied, as though walking away from the clouds of some explosion at his back.

Here Magnuson could be anonymous, invisible, worthless, a citizen of this sanctioned city of the outcast and damned and already dead. Here he could be happy, if only by reason of the justice in his punishment and the equilibrium he detected in his fate. Here the people and the place and his own condition were all equal not merely to the depression that he felt but to that failure his life had been. He was one with his punishment, which was to say himself. With no family or friends, no money or possessions—for he had put most of his money in a locker in Union Station—no past, and no future that differed from the present, except to finish the job of living out his life, he went about the cruel asceticism of his day-to-day existence. Oftentimes his companions seemed less criminals and paupers to him than monks and desert fathers, while he himself had experiences of the senses that were almost religious. Strange visions were given to him, whether from the shock and injuries of the awful beating he had taken about the head or from the alcohol he now drank to excess, and the lack of wholesome food, or even food at all, or because he had by his recent experiences and present mode of living purified himself, and thereby prepared himself for such experiences and visitations, he could not say.

He seemed to be in the underworld, in a city sprawling on a plain where the dead were constantly arriving on foot from the land across the river. He thought he could see on the pavements groups of sickly men in argument with groups of corpses and skeletons, the living men pestered and persuaded to fulfill some bargain by the dead. Sometimes these dead men appeared before him, rising out of the pavement as though upon an elevator, with their palms open, whether to beg or only to indicate that they were empty-handed, they did not say. Or they were encountered grouped around some reading matter, a map perhaps. Sometimes he heard them moan around a black man playing a harmonica on a street corner. Sometimes he saw them pounding up and down the pavements in dusty armies, the long-dead and living dead of this republic. The dead pioneers and frontiersmen of this old New World. These sons of a continent that was to have been plowed into a garden. The victims of an optimistic spirit in marriage with a pessimistic soul.

Sometimes he caught sight of a man he took for Helenowski,

looking as though he had just come from months of wandering and fasting on the desert, where his eyes had been blinded by the burning sun. Usually he would see him only when he himself was drunk or hungry, and only then at night or dawn, as though the man were taking shape amid the morning fog and the smoke of the fires the newsdealers burned in barrels. Once when he thought he saw him in a tavern at the end of the bar pointing his finger at him, he motioned him outside. But when he went into the alley and waited alone in the reflections of the flickering neon sign for what he thought might well be his death, no one came. Another time he was convinced the man was following him, and he turned to confront him, waving his arms and shouting for him to go away. But the man only looked at him as though he were shouting in a foreign language, and continued his pursuit as soon as Magnuson turned again and walked away. There were days and nights when Magnuson believed the man was everywhere, that he saw his features in each of the thousand faces he encountered on the streets, as though the man had multiplied himself and was everywhere and everyone at once. Once when he turned the corner of the sidewalk he found himself face to face with the man. He was dressed in the very clothes from hat to tie to shoes that he himself had worn on that long night of violence and had left in Farquarson's bedroom, clothes that had then been wet and muddy and were now threadbare, dusty, torn. It could have been himself he faced. Once he saw him just after sunrise on a street corner with a dirty army blanket around his shoulders and a seagull feather in his hatband, trying to convince a group of drunken drowsy Indians in their Levi's, cowboy boots and hats, broad leather belts, and with their fleshy or eagle noses and bow legs, whose sole aim seemed to be to keep their eyes open and their bodies from toppling into one another as they swayed and knocking each other down like dominoes, that he was an Indian chief. He had his wallet out from beneath his blanket and was holding identity cards up for inspection. Usually Magnuson would cross the street or turn back to avoid him, or tramp for miles to lose him if he were following him.

Later he began to suspect from the composite of his own recollections and the information contained in the many pieces on the murders in the newspapers that Farquarson had not been murdered after all, but had died a natural death from the cancer, or its complications, that he had suffered from, and that Helenowski, who believed in his delusion that he was Death, had believed, upon finding Farquarson already dead, that he had struck him down no less than if he had stabbed him in the breast. This meant that when he found Farquarson's note beside the bed, in which Farquarson claimed that in a letter to Wenzel he had named his killer, he believed not only that he was named but rightly so. If this were true there had been no reason for the other murders, since it was the murder of Farquarson that provided the motive for all of those that followed. This suspicion troubled Magnuson enough that he went in search of Helenowski in order to confront him with it and learn, if possible, the ironic truth, the verification of which would be even further evidence of his humiliation. Half drunk, he wandered into a tavern he had heard was frequented by Indians and sat at the bar, pouring a shot into his beer. But Helenowski was not among the crowd, which was silent and glaring at him and which, he recalled now, had been speaking Spanish when he entered. They were not Indians but Mexicans. No one would speak or move or look elsewhere as long as he, the *americano*, was in their bar. Then a large Mexican took the stool beside him and, cooing at him in Spanish, inserted a dirty index finger into his ear which he proceeded to turn, boring deeper. Magnuson fled.

Ironically he himself became known on Skid Row as "Chief." If he had to give a name he said his name was Reed, his mother's maiden name. But when he became a familiar sight upon the streets he was given a name by someone at some time that caught on with the men he drank with and slept with and talked with, and that name was Chief. Did he resemble an Indian, he wondered? Or did they believe that he could have been the chief of something? Or was it one of those names given in jest because it was so much the opposite of the man himself, like a large man who is called Tiny? One day a young policeman greeted him on the street. He said, "How is it going, Chief?"

At the Salvation Army mission where he often came and helped to pass out the hymn books at the service and the soup at the suppers, he was called by the soldiers "Mr. Reed" but became known to his fellow vagrants as "Soupy." He liked doing small favors for other people, especially the selfish and complaining men often found along these streets, and he often asked his fellow residents of the flophouses, including men younger and healthier than himself, if he could get them anything. He spoke only rarely, and often not at all, and those men who knew him only casually must have thought he was a mute. When he attempted speech he was often strangely inarticulate, as though out of practice. Whenever he had something important to offer the conversation he would raise his hand to signal he would interrupt, but usually his lips would only tremble, and his companions, having learned he would maintain this pose without speaking, and suffering for him, would pass on to other speakers and other subjects. Sometimes a man would pat his shoulder. "That's all right, Soupy," he would say. He liked the Salvation Army the best of all the missions because to him they seemed the most compassionate. At the mission he liked the sound of male voices singing the hymns and those songs of popular sentiments that were old when he was a boy. He mumbled through all the songs self-consciously, his head lowered. The singing far more than the sermons touched his soul.

The sermons, or the "man-to-mans" as the major who gave them called them, were politely attended by Magnuson, although he was sometimes embarrassed by what was said. The major spoke as though theirs was a world without fathers, brothers, daughters, or even other men, peopled only with mothers and sisters and the sons he sometimes called boys. He emphasized the love of Christ for them and the salvation that awaited the end of their travail, but most of all he commiserated with the daily condition of their lives upon the streets, oftentimes as though to prove he understood and shared their miseries. One night a small man with wavy hair and steel-rimmed glasses, and no uniform, addressed them instead, introduced by the major as a distinguished visitor. In the heavy burr of a Scottish accent he orated with tearful eyes of that time when he had been a chaplain in the British army in the First World War and had looked down upon a large common grave heaped with dead American soldiers. He had been overwhelmed by the youthful beauty in their dead faces, and the glory of their sacrifices, and had resolved there and then that he loved the American soldier boys and that someday he would come to America in person to tell them of his gratitude and love. In closing he asked if there were any veterans in the audience, and blessed each man who raised his hand. Most of them had listened with dazed faces, as though still confronting whatever tragedy it was that sent them here years ago, while Magnuson saw with horror in his own mind piles of rotting bodies heaped on top of each other in a common foreign grave. During the prayer sessions that followed the sermons some men wept unashamedly, and others dropped to their knees before folding chairs and clasped their hands before them, an action Magnuson admired but could not bring himself to imitate.

He liked best the sidewalk bands and the brave, vibrating baritones, sopranos, and tenors of the soldiers. He would often remain among the small crowd until the last hymn was played, and he often followed the band back to the mission. There was something martial and sentimental in the music, and it struck deep chords within him that fired his numb and dying spirit, touching strings of self-righteousness and self-pity while consoling him that the world worked right in its course of misery, and he felt like singing and weeping and getting into step and marching off to do the work of the Lord. Whenever he heard the brass, drum, and tambourine, he came out into the street as though they summoned him. He was surprised at the many men who paused to listen to the music and the sermons, workingmen on errands with packages or envelopes beneath their arms and men in business suits standing side by side with the worst of derelicts, mesmerized as though hearing in the Renaissance harmonies of the brass and the medieval pounding of the drum and rattle of the tambourine above the pot some compelling ritual or rhythm missing from their lives that seemed to promise them that, if they listened closely and let themselves go forward, it would tell each man who he was.

Magnuson was often moved to pity the Salvation Army soldiers, especially the women and girls. In their old-fashioned bonnets, dark stockings, skirts, and shoes, with faces that were too thin or too fat and too pink or too white, they were either too attractive for the uniform and the life they led or else too homely and plain to be comfortable at anything else. His eyes ached with the tears he refused to show when they sang and preached and played their trumpets, French horns, and tubas. Perhaps they were as much at home here, and destined to belong here, as were the fallen and ungrateful men they spent their lives upon, and the ridiculous uniforms they wore were the sackcloth of their own deliberate humiliation. Sometimes when the band had finished a hymn, and he had been moved to weep, he removed his hat and went up to each of the soldiers in turn and in the power of his passion wrung the hand of each man and kissed each woman on the cheek, managing to call them, as they called each other, brother and sister.

Most of his days he spent in long tramps up and down the streets, rarely venturing more than a block or two out of the area designated as Skid Row. Often he would be dull and even depressed on these tramps and find himself at the Chicago River, which separated the Loop from Skid Row. He would pause on any of several wind-swept bridges and watch the green water swirl inland from Lake Michigan, curving around the concrete and stone foundations of warehouses, railroad stations, and the Opera House that walled it in. The water looked wintry, cold, deep, and he sometimes longed to be carried inland with it, across the prairies of Illinois and down the Mississippi to the Gulf, the length of the nation. He could even see himself floundering in the man-made current, his head above the water, an arm raised in a gesture of help or farewell, carried under one bridge and then another. Other times he felt euphoric on these tramps, as though to keep moving was proof that he had survived and had somewhere to go. He feared nothing from the future. The worst had happened. Only now did he realize that what he had feared most in his life had been the public degradation of a physical beating or of an act of cowardice before the threat of force, and he suspected that this fear had helped to shape the man he had become. He had had an invincible image of himself in which it was to have been his manly tragedy not to be beaten but, if he was forced to, to beat others, even if that beating was against his will and nature. Now he had taken his beating. An awful beating. It was as though he had conquered death. Or life. In the purity of his painful wounds he seemed to have reached a self that he could not remember was his own, a self that had remained buried but unsullied by the overlay of all those years, as though beneath the wrinkled skin and brittle bones there was a day-old child.

Once he walked past a panhandler without giving him a coin, lost in the foolishness of his own reverie that had him grinning and talking to himself, and received a cuff on the back of the head that sent him sprawling to the sidewalk. Another time he ignored out of fear a pair of ragged black men panhandling in the middle of the block and after passing them received without comment a kick in the pants. In neither case did they attempt to rob him, although the streets in the first instance were deserted, and in the second crowded with uninterested people.

The flophouses and fifty-cent- and dollar-a-night hotels he slept in nightly, for he feared the street and the possibility that the police would pick him up for vagrancy (although he had spent several nights inside a large collapsed cardboard carton he had dragged into a hole at an excavation site), depressed him as the bars, missions, and streets did not, and he tried never to stay in the same place for two nights running. Here his loneliness would overwhelm him in the night. The dirt, vermin, and timeless stinks of man, of sweat and vomit and urine and infected wounds and ineffectual disinfectant, would spark his latent sentimentality, and he would weaken to the point where he questioned the reasonableness of the justice in his fate and the value of this species, man. Here lies, false sentiments, inconsideration of one's fellows, stoicism or self-pity, and the self-justification of a man's own luckless and degraded condition were the usual fare of conversation. In the windowless cubicles in which he slept fully clothed on a cot with only an army blanket to cover him, incredibly crude drawings decorated the filthy plaster or wallboard walls. Anatomically inaccurate sketches of faceless women with their legs spread, of penises discharging semen, and of oversized male genitals, half of the penis hidden in the mouth of a man or woman, and splotches of real semen, hard, impervious, shiny as shellac. Someone had written HEL in his own semen, and Magnuson wondered if his supply had been exhausted before he could complete the word and whether he had intended to write HELL or HELP.

The conversation here, when it took place at all, was often of army experiences and war. One night a drunken man who said he came from Missouri began to bawl and recall his service in Hawaii in the army during the Japanese attack on Pearl Harbor. He had been in town and was returning to the base during the bombing. From his battered grainy suitcase he pulled a large brownish photograph pasted on gray cardboard. It was of himself naked except for a hula skirt, formally posed in a photographic studio in Honolulu. A handsome boy in his late teens who appeared as though he had been told that it was fashionable to pose for such a photograph, but as the camera snapped, began to have his doubts. The picture caused much laughter among the particular group it was shown to, and was passed about the men. Its owner, after a while, stumbled drunkenly among them, surprised at their reaction to the picture and their laughter at him, and tried to get it back. They held it away from him, passed it on to the next man, sat on it, and held it behind their backs. He claimed he had been a heavy drinker ever since the bombing of Pearl Harbor.

Another man from Kentucky claimed there was a passage in the Bible he had shown to his sister—a religious and inviolate woman who chastised him for drinking—that if properly interpreted explained and justified the turning of certain weak-willed men to drink. He had shown this passage to his sister, and she had almost been convinced. He asked now for a Bible. One was located and he searched frantically for the passage, but failed to find it.

Magnuson himself kept a photograph he treasured for a reason that was unclear to him, and which in the eyes of other people might have made him look ridiculous. It had been taken on Skid Row against his will. A bartender at a tavern Magnuson frequented had come to work with a new camera he wanted to try out, and the two B-girls and whores, Tiny and Belle, each of whom weighed over three hundred pounds and looked fifty although they were not half so old, had insisted on having their picture taken with the soft-spoken and retiring Chief. Magnuson had been given one of the prints. Gray and glossy, with the quality of a pornographic photograph, it had in its center the drawn, bewhiskered face of Magnuson squeezed out of shape by the pair of fat, pasty, overly made-up faces, the round babydoll eyes beneath the curly false eyelashes staring inward with mock lascivious interest at the uncomfortable and frightened Magnuson. It was the only personal item he kept on his person.

Although he saw, or thought he saw, Helenowski often on these streets, his was not the only familiar face from his past that he encountered. One morning he came face to face with Fritzi Schneider as he strode briskly from an area west of Skid Row back toward the Loop. He was dressed like a gym teacher who thought himself a playboy and was wearing, as always, those dark glasses. Involuntarily Magnuson stopped and opened up his mouth in fear that the man would recognize him and take pleasure in having him arrested. But Schneider did not recognize him, and, interpreting his stopping and open mouth as the prelude to asking him for money, said toughly as he passed, "Will you get out of here?" He saw Tip O'Neil down here too. In a tavern, at the bar among a group of his cronies. A retired Chicago police captain in filthy clothes and drunk on Skid Row. He was telling everyone how he was up here in Chicago only for a visit to his daughter and was going back to Florida in a day or two, and, inevitably, about all the influential people of the city who asked for his advice and called him "Tip" while he called them something like "you old bastard." Before Magnuson could realize his danger, he came so close to O'Neil in his wish to greet him that O'Neil had the opportunity to stare at close range into his face. But nothing registered in those weak blue eyes. There was no memory there, no residue of intelligence, only the washed-out sparkle of some sentimental Celtic dream. "Here, buy yourself a beer, buddy," he said, and pressed a quarter in Magnuson's palm. What pleasure it gave Magnuson that he could recognize these men but that they could not recognize him in turn. He had changed, and they had not. Nor would they change. But he was born anew. He was someone he had not been before.

Once around the streets of Union Station he encountered a big black man begging, a rare sight in this area. He sat on a dolly with crutches beside him. Missing one leg and wearing dark glasses, he proffered a cup of the pencils he sold for no specified amount. Hanging by a string from around his neck was a sign that read: Two-fisted Jefferson, Blind Ex-Heavyweight Contender. To Magnuson there was a striking resemblance between this man and Two-Gun Washington. It was stronger than merely the similarity of the names and the loss of the same leg. But Magnuson could not reconcile the humiliation of this act of deceit and public begging with Two-Gun Washington, who had seemed so regal, disdainful, aloof. At the risk of discovery he hung about the man, his whiskered jaw gaping. Finally the ex-boxer, from behind the mask of his dark glasses, spoke as though to the air before him, "Get out of here, old man. You bad for business," while saying, "Thank you, thank you," from the corner of his mouth whenever he heard a coin drop in the cup. Once he called to Magnuson, "I call the police, old man, if you don't get away from here." This frightened Magnuson, and he retreated half a block. When he summoned the courage to return, the beggar rolled away on his dolly with his crutches under his arms to a new location down the block. But Magnuson followed at a respectful distance. Finally the beggar began to rise threateningly from his chair on his one leg, forcing Magnuson back until Magnuson ended up staring at him dumbly from half a block away. Do all of them have two identities, he wondered? Is everyone someone else?

Later, the beggar attempted bribery. "What do you want, old man? You want one of my pencils? Here, you can have one if you go away." Other times he resorted to threats. "See this pencil, old man? I going to throw it at you if you don't go away. See that sharp point it got? It going to stick in you if I got to throw it at you." Sometimes he added menacingly, "I mean business too." Finally defeated, and complaining to himself, he rolled away for good.

The one man Magnuson met on Skid Row who appeared to recognize him was Thorsen. He never called Magnuson by name, nor did he ever refer to the business of the murders for which Magnuson was wanted, but appeared to treat Magnuson, whom he saw often and in whose company he sometimes preferred to be, as an old acquaintance he could be immediately familiar with. As though he knew him of old and there was no reason to call up the past between them, a past that might have been painful to each. And yet Magnuson could not be certain that he was recognized, although he did not believe he was in any danger even if he were. In the newspapers there had been the report that Thorsen, who had disappeared during the night of the murders, had been sought by the police, picked up, investigated, and released.

To Thorsen Skid Row was a spa he visited on his vacations and holidays from work and during any interim of indecision as to where he would go and what do next in his life. Here he enjoyed cheap meals and lodgings, which appealed to the parsimony of his nature, living among lonely, isolated, and nameless workingmen like himself. Although he frequented taverns, he would never drink whiskey, and never more than two small glasses of beer. With his cardboard suitcase, bound up with two rotting leather straps, that never left his hand and that he used as a pillow in the hotels at night, and with what seemed to be his best clothes always on his back, straw hat, large polka-dot bow tie, he gave the impression that he had either just arrived or else was on the verge of leaving.

He preferred the company of men as loquacious and obstinate as himself. His own conversation was always of himself, where he had been and what he had done. "I been there," he would say in his intense, high-pitched, accented voice. "I been everywhere. I done all kind of things. Sure!" Once he had scolded a well-dressed man with a woman in furs on his arm, who had asked him the way to the Opera House, which was just across the river, by informing him that if he had been to all the places he, Thorsen, had been, and done the things he had done, and seen the things he had seen, he wouldn't be interested in seeing any opera.

Apart from talk about himself he liked to engage men in conversation about the West. He had worked out there in the old days, he would state bluntly, breaking in wildly on a conversation in progress with the boldness and desperation of a man asking other men for help. He had been a farmer, a cowboy, a miner, a member of a threshing gang, had built a railroad, had by Jesus done all kinds of things. The West, he claimed, consulting some image in his head, was either wilderness or garden—whichever varied from day to day. Migratory workers, railroadmen, and even some cowhands from the West argued with him that such was not the case, that the West was fast becoming neither one nor the other. There were rich farms to be sure, irrigated farms especially, but they were big businesses, big factories, often owned by big corporations. And there wasn't that much rangeland left, and no real wilderness either. Even the National Parks were full of tourists. Outraged, Thorsen would argue with them, call them liars, tell them they did not know what in hell they were talking about, again citing the first-hand experience he had had out West in his youth. "I should hope to kiss a pig there's cows and cowboys there!" he said.

He also talked of Europe, the Old Country, as he called it; but here, unlike the West, he admitted to some ignorance, for he had left Norway at the age of twelve and over the years had only occasionally touched at European ports. He was informed by former servicemen and merchant sailors that it was awful over there, there was poor sanitation, bad food, and no American food either, impotable water, much ignorance, most people living like peasants, which they were, and that most of the people would be glad to be over here if they could. This he did not contradict but listened to reflectively in his own hardheaded way.

He once justified his passionate interest in the West by relating the melancholy story of the favorite uncle he had known only as a small boy in Norway. He had immigrated to America and settled in Chicago with a part of the family several years before Thorsen himself had immigrated. The uncle, a young and handsome man with a blond mustache, had told his family one day that he was weary of Chicago and was going out West to try his luck and make his fortune there. He spoke no English. The family had seen him aboard the train, and with one bag in hand and in his best suit of clothes, he had gone West. No one in the family had ever heard from him again. Not even a postcard. They had searched for him, as much as they could, but had never heard a word about him. He had stepped aboard that train and simply disappeared. The family had planned and discussed search missions for years, but nothing had ever come of them. This still troubled him, Thorsen admitted, and he thought he might go West in search of his uncle, although according to Magnuson's slow figuring the uncle would now be close to a hundred years old.

The story also troubled Magnuson; he became obsessed with the possibilities of the man's disappearance, and several times asked Thorsen specific questions. The family had feared he had been murdered by bandits or killed by Indians. A man swallowed up by the continent, lost in the vastness of America. Disappeared. Confronting a continent alone in a foreign language. Who knew, Magnuson thought, maybe some small town in South Dakota or Oregon had been named after him. Maybe he had become a farmer, a banker, and his descendants were now the aristocracy of some small town. Maybe he was convicted, rightly or wrongly, of some crime, and was sent to prison, where he died, or when released was so ashamed that he could not bring himself to notify his family. Maybe he had been hanged. Maybe he had ended a drunkard on the Skid Row of some western city. There were thousands of towns out there, millions of farms. How many people had gone West that way and just disappeared?

One morning Thorsen approached Magnuson on the street and asked him to investigate his uncle's disappearance in the West. In his shaky European hand he wrote down his uncle's name and description on a piece of paper, along with the name of the town in Norway where he, Thorsen, could be reached, and handed it to Magnuson with twenty dollars, promising to pay him more, all he felt he had honestly earned, when he discovered his uncle, or his grave, or at the very least had information on his fate. It was the only time Thorsen acknowledged that he was aware of Magnuson's identity. He had heard the call of the open road and had resolved that conflict in his heart as to which way, east or west, he was to go. That evening he stepped aboard a bus that went to Michigan, heading for the Farquarson summer house on Walloon Lake where, in addition to the twenty thousand dollars he had saved over the years and buried in a box among the rhododendrons on the Farquarson estate in Lake Forest and now carried stuffed inside a red flannel shirt inside the cardboard suitcase he hugged against his chest, another twenty-five thousand was buried in a coffee can behind the boathouse. He had mined this money out of the earth of this New World, and at this late age he was to take his fortune and head for home. He was seventy-eight and believed with the conviction of a stubborn Christian who had received the word from God Himself that he would live without illness to the age of one hundred and five. It was a figure he had arrived at years ago.

Thorsen had had a lifelong desire to buy a small sailboat and sail it alone across the Atlantic and up the fjord to the town where he was born. In dreams and daydreams he had seen himself in sou'wester and oilskins, his hand gripped around the tiller and his pipe gripped in his mouth, with no other sail or stack in sight, himself and the small boat pitted against the epic swells of the green and white seas. Instead, he now decided that he would purchase a strong and seaworthy lifeboat and row that alone across the Atlantic.

He wanted to feel his hands around the oars, wanted to propel the boat across the ocean with those hands. He studied them and knew they would not fail him, like wind or sails. In those palms, knuckles, nails, ten digits, he placed a confidence that another man might place only in God. He did not question but that his voyage would be successful. He had the rest of spring, the whole summer, and the early part of fall in which to make it. He would buy a good supply of canned goods, favoring sardines and lima beans, and boxes of mason jars in which to put his drinking water. He would travel by bus to some island off the eastern coast, Nantucket or Long Island, or even Nova Scotia, buy a boat there, and begin his voyage. Maybe he would even start from Detroit, and row across those inland Great Lakes, and up the St. Lawrence to the sea.

The bus Thorsen boarded was crowded, and was now speeding through the darkened city down broad residential boulevards, long and multiple blocks of brownstone houses, and so many black faces on the streets that he was reminded of his service as a cabin boy and ports of call with names like Takoradi, Douala, Accra, Lagos. Then out of the window gray, milky canals, slips and lakes, and out on the marshes, with Lake Michigan beyond, the towers of fire from the steel mills of Gary, Whiting, Michigan City set out like windmills. Like some vast city in the sulphurous, mephitic marshes of Hell. Or that doomsday vision of a holocaust or hell to come. The red flames roaring against the black sky and landscape of the night. Industry everywhere, smelting the bowels out of the continent, employing, who knew how many, thousands, millions. Beautiful fires! Powerful fires! Satanic fires! Thrilling to behold! The new beauty of this New World! The fires of work, of creation. But a feeling that if those fires were even stronger, or somehow broadcast about the marshy landscape like flaming beams, they would reveal not only slagheaps and junkheaps but corpses and skeletons, and instruments of war, and blocks of marching men, and fleeing citizens, scattering like insects around the flame.

Then they were in the country and speeding through Michigan. Many in the bus were already asleep. Thorsen closed his eyes and settled back against the seat. It was evening, moments after sundown. His mother in the Old Country—or was it only Mrs. Owens? She was standing in the flower garden, motionless, clippers in hand before a clump of peonies, with a clump of hollyhocks behind her. In an old dress, a sweater across her shoulders, gloves, and an old hat. A cloud of gnats swirled above her head; swallows swooped in and out of the barn with the silence of bats. She seemed lost in meditation, stupefied by the onrush of evening exploding silently from the last moments of the fiery sunset, until she resembled the statue of a goddess in a garden. It seemed to him that all his life was encapsulated in this single image, and he fell asleep with it fixed in his mind, his calloused hands pressed against his face, transported by the heavy bus down the rural roads of Michigan to his treasure in the North and the first leg of that odyssey that would take him home.

While in Chicago on Skid Row Magnuson sat on a curb beneath a street light with his legs crossed and a knee clasped in both his hands. He was swinging his leg and moving his lips and gazing with his mouth open at the smoky traffic in the street, suffering the hours until he would once more drag himself down the sidewalks among the crowds of tramping hungry men in search of a tavern in which to spend the evening and, later, of a lodging in which to spend the night.

CHAPTER THIRTY-FIVE

THE DEATH
OF FIORE

Fiore was confounded that contrary to his countermanding of his original order to murder Scarponi, Scarponi had been murdered anyway. If that was not trouble enough, the Tanker in killing Scarponi had killed a cop. He suspected a double cross more than malice or incompetence on the part of Romanski, who had introduced him to Tanker, and was already plotting his death. He would be safe with Romanski dead since, other than Fiore himself, Romanski did not have powerful friends. He had hoped to appease all his enemies, including the police, and to redeem and protect himself by locating and killing the offending Tanker, and had already engaged two men from New Orleans to do just that when the news came in that Tanker had fallen beneath a police barrage. He had set the two men to studying Romanski instead. The affair was complex and dangerous but the fact that he had always worked with amateurs and outsiders was

528

cause for him to congratulate himself and to feel that he was reasonably safe. He did not really suspect that the hand of Allegro would be brought against him, although Allegro figured mightily in those intimations that sometimes flooded all his senses and whispered to him that this time his time had come. He was also a strong believer in his fate, as it was revealed to him by dreams and signs, and lately whenever he chanced to listen to the radio, either in his apartment or in the car, he seemed always to tune in on Scarponi's "Opera Hour," and, as though the dead man were haunting him through the music his program played, always to hear in his morbid and jumpy mood arias sung by tenors, basses, baritones, and sopranos, most of whom were dying, and the power of their passion combined with the imminence of their doom moved him to the verge of tears. Manon exhausted on the desert plain outside New Orleans and terrified of the darkness (*"Sola, perduta, abbandonata"*); Mario in *Tosca* in his cell before going to face the firing squad (*"E lucevan le stelle"*); the duet between Rigoletto and his daughter, Gilda, inside the sack he has himself caused to be stabbed (*"Lassù, in cielo"*); Alvaro in *La Forza del Destino*, railing against the injustice of his having to remain alive after having killed Carlo who, as he was dying, stabbed his sister Leonora, who, as she was dying, is commanded by Padre Guardiano to humble herself before God (*"Non imprecare"*); the duet of Aïda and Radames in their tomb (*"O terra, addio"*) while above them in the temple Amneris prays to Isis (*"Pace, t'imploro"*); Otello having stabbed himself with a dagger after choking Desdemona (*"Niun mi tema"*); Edgardo in *Lucia di Lammermoor*, hearing the bell announce that Lucia is dead, declaring to her spirit, *"Tu che a Dio spiegasti l'ali,"* before stabbing himself; Turiddu in *Cavalleria Rusticana*, sensing his doom in the impending duel, bidding his mother farewell (*"Mamma, quel vino è generoso"*); Canio in *I Pagliacci*, having stabbed his wife and her lover in the middle of the play, remarking to the horrified audience, *"La commedia è finita."* To him such coincidences could be explained only by a sinister foretelling of his destiny.

Whenever he ventured out he tried to do so in company, often with the policeman who served him as a bodyguard when he was off duty and available, but this was difficult, since by nature he liked to be alone. His apartment provided him with adequate protection, for he owned the building, and only a few apartments were rented to tenants who were not relatives of his. All were dependent on him and owed him favors, and he could count upon them to serve him as soldiers and spies. A benevolent man, he liked to do favors for his relatives, liked them living all around him and together in the same building. It made him feel like a prince inside his fortress.

A creature of habit, Fiore rose late every morning and called his girlfriend Francine first thing, talking to her from his bed while he petted the Pomeranian, which always slept with him, nestled up beneath the blankets like a mole. This morning Francine was in good humor although she sounded sleepy and somewhat drunk. She was in her bed and smoking a cigarette and telling him about this George, this young college kid she had met in a bar late last night and taken a liking to. He had followed her home and she had invited him in and ordered him to sleep on the couch in her living room, bringing out a blanket and pillow, but he had moved in the night and was now sound asleep with his pillow and blanket on the floor at the threshold of her bedroom, so that she could not open her door without pushing him aside and waking him. She thought he was persistent, cute, funny, frustrated. "And he's married too," she said. "Running around at his age. He must have had a fight with his wife."

"Oh well, kid," Fiore said, for he always called her "kid," "send him home where he belongs, to his little lady. Don't she give him nothing?" He was flattered that a married college kid would be interested in Francine, a divorcee in her late thirties, and she had known that he would be flattered. Large-breasted, with a good figure, although her calves were muscular and her legs were bowed, in a tight dress with her long peroxided hair displayed above her tan, Latin-looking face, she could be dazzling. He knew she could handle herself, that she would not put up with any nonsense if she had no mind to and that she was telling the truth about the separate beds last night. Since he tolerated an occasional one-night affair as long as the man wasn't anyone he knew, there was no reason for her to lie. He was not a jealous man. He did not take women seriously and because he did not, he could not take sex seriously. He did not have strong sexual desires, but he liked to have a steady woman at his beck and call who was known around as his girl, and liked her company a night or two a week for companionship and display far more than sex. He liked to take her to prestigious and expensive bars and nightclubs and ply her with many drinks. He liked to give her money and buy her clothes, at any time of the year, but with extravagance on her birthday and at Christmas. In the selection of stockings, negligees, and underclothes he believed he exercised impeccable taste, preferring them sheer, lacy, and costly, and in color either tangerine or black. He liked his privacy and his own selfish habits too much to ever think of marriage.

The apartment was high-ceilinged and kept dark, the shades drawn behind the drapes, so that there was a timelessness about any daylight hour and the place was reminiscent of a Sicilian house shuttered against the heat and sun. He made himself a cup of instant coffee and drank it in the chilly shadows of the dining room, on the plaster walls of which he had commissioned an artist famous for his work in second-rate Italian restaurants and pizzerias to paint a mural in pastel colors of Italian landscapes and peasant scenes. There, as though seen in a cellar, were Mount Vesuvius and the Bay of Naples, no less in the foreground than the two-dimensional olive trees and the singing, grape-laden peasant boys and girls. He turned on the radio to an aria sung by a tenor threatening to implore and thunder with his tragedy and, trembling, he quickly shut it off, convinced that this was yet another sign of vengeance from beyond the grave.

The Pomeranian, meanwhile, had exchanged the covers of the bed for an easy chair in the living room, on which Fiore had scattered last night's dirty linen (the wife of one of his cousins who lived across the hall did the house cleaning), burrowing deep beneath the sheets and pillow case where it recommenced its sleep. Unfortunately, it was this chair that the drowsy Fiore, as he heaved himself about the rooms, chose to throw himself down upon in a sudden fit of melancholy. As he lifted the corner of a shade and peeked out between two adjacent buildings at a distant patch of bright blue sky, coffee cup in hand, he heard at most from the chair a muted sigh or squeak, felt at most a slight rearrangement of the bedclothes beneath one buttock, and took it to be no more than what he was long accustomed to: the rupture of a distant distressed spring.

Later he opened a can of dog food into a bowl and lumbered through the apartment tapping a spoon against the rim and whistling and calling out, "Here, Princess, here." No small bark and rapid patter of small feet. For a moment he stopped all this tapping and whistling and calling out and it sounded for all the silence as though he were dead or deaf. He searched what he could of the furniture, searched every nook and cranny that his girth permitted him to reach. He threw the remaining bedclothes from the bed piece by piece upon the floor. A bare mattress. Nothing else. He began to panic. The apartment door was locked, none of the windows was open. "Come on now," he called out, "don't play no games." In the living room he tossed the six cushions from the monstrous couch, then went to the armchair and disentangled from the heap of linens, as though it were already wrapped up in its shroud, the crushed and smothered corpse. For some time he was at a loss as to what to do.

"So it is dead," he said to himself. And then to appease his own responsibility in the death, "It must have been a heart attack or something." The dog which had been so much a part of his life was now garbage. Even so he could not simply place it in the pail in the kitchen, and just where in this concrete world was he to bury it? Finally he was able to pick it up without touching it by manipulating two pieces of cardboard and to drop it into a heavy paper sack which he then carried down to the basement and the titanic incinerator. There had not been a fire in it today (his brother-in-law was the superintendent of the building), and he threw the sack in on top of a mound of rubbish, clanging the door shut in terror when out of a cardboard box he displaced slid a large stiff, dead gray cat with dried blood around its open mouth.

Since today was payday for the employees of his burlesque house up in Niles, he spent the early afternoon in the apartment making out the payroll. He would often pause in the act of writing down a figure or sliding a bill into an envelope. He thought he had caught the patter of feet, the clatter of the dog dish as it was nuzzled about the floor, a soft bark, a scratching on the door. Now and then he would startle and look up, convinced the Pomeranian was sitting on the threshold of the bedroom watching him. Or from the sofa behind his back. He had lost a good habit and a piece of luck. The paperwork wearied him, and a taste of futility, like blood and copper pennies, filled his mouth. It felt like a tiny hole had been opened somewhere in his mountain of flesh, somewhere he could neither see nor touch, and the sap of his life was spilling out and leaving him weak, like the loss of blood. Even the meal his cousin's wife brought him, having prepared it in her own apartment across the hall, did not bring back his strength. A grilled T-bone steak topped with mushroom caps and a plate of pasta shells in butter which he ate with a pile of buttered toast cut into triangles and a sunny-side egg. He caught himself with a bite of steak in his hand feeling beneath the table for the wet nuzzle of the little dog against his open palm.

He got his payroll sheets, ledgers, and small strongbox together and dressed himself from the long rack of plastic-covered clothing in his darkly varnished closet. He was an admirer and collector of clothes, and had a special fondness for vests, which he never wore, along with hats and shoes of which, unlike the rest of his wardrobe, he had a large selection to choose from when shopping, since his head and feet alone of his body were relatively normal in size. He was conscious only after he had turned the ignition of his Cadillac and the engine had started that he was still alive.

He drove northwest of Milwaukee Avenue, passing that new nightclub owned and managed by the Doctor, Allegro's uncle—an obvious tax dodge if there ever was one. A large stuccoed building out of some 1930's California movie set, it contained inside a high diving board and a pool in which girls performed water ballet beneath a flood of multicolored lights. It had been built not in the Loop nor on Rush Street nor just off the expressway nor out in the country nor near the airport nor on the lakefront but in the middle of an endless middle-class neighborhood of Chicago bungalows that might still be called the sticks, and on an avenue that was famous mainly for its bus line taking people to and from their shopping and their work. Prairie was on either side of the club and a hot-dog stand stood in the middle of an even larger prairie across the street. Farther up he passed a Scarponi Liquor Store, one of the first the firm had built. Once again he felt the sapping of his spirit, in company with that suspicion that he had been delivered into the hands of fate. Could the neon sign that flashed SCARPONI in its red, white, and green letters affect him so? He missed the dog beside him on the seat.

His own nightclub, called the Lido, was in an unincorporated area just over the Chicago line. Next door was another nightclub called the Round-Up, which he also owned. The Lido had a tipping cocktail glass for its neon sign while the Round-Up had a comet with a tail of shooting stars. At present the Round-Up was closed, and had been for months, for only one of the clubs was ever open at a time. Whenever the public clamor to stamp out vice became too vocal to ignore, the public officials would revoke the entertainment license of whichever club was then open. The next night, however, the other club would open in its place, the bartenders and entertainers moving over from next door. This arrangement had been going on for years and was satisfactory for all concerned. Fiore never lost a day's take, his employees never lost a day's wages, his customers never missed a night of striptease if they wanted it, the decent citizens were satisfied with the power of their moral zeal as witnessed in the action of their public officials, and the public officials themselves appeared to crusade against crime by closing down the club while at the same time they received a payoff for licensing the club to open up next door.

Inside the Lido he was surprised as always at how shabby and tacky the place appeared in daylight, as though it were built of plywood and cardboard and put up with thumbtacks. At night it was flawless, exotic, enclosing that purple darkness that was like the midnight itself, stretching infinitely and erasing any sense of walls. He passed through the maze of partitions where the bouncers checked identification cards and onto the nightclub floor. He plumped down at the twenty-six table, set his pile of pay envelopes, ledger, and cashbox on the green felt, and smoked a long cigarette with his fat, ringheavy hand before his face while the bartender brought him a Scotch and water packed with ice. The bar had yet to open, but because today was payday and the day the dancers and musicians held such rehearsals as they had, the employees were already drifting in.

He had the habit of paying out his payroll in cash and in person. He managed to do this despite the diversification and magnitude of his business interests, for in mentality he was not far removed from the owner of a small restaurant or grocery store. He liked the idea of being a boss, a patron, a businessman, and had always wanted to be the chief of a business, large or small. He was at once flattered and embarrassed when his employees went out of their way to ingratiate themselves self-consciously by calling him "boss." It was common knowledge that it pleased him.

One of the bouncers asked where the little dog was today, reminding Fiore of his loss and his own danger and proximity to death. "She died this morning," he said. Adding, "A heart attack or something." He studied the eyes of the bouncers for any sign that they suspected his predicament, or had any advance knowledge of his fate. But their eyes were ambiguous, no more evasive than usual. Their names were Jimmy and Jerry, and they were dark-complexioned men who looked as though Inca blood were in their veins. At night they checked identification cards, escorted parties by flashlight to their tables, and directed the strippers to those customers from whom they thought the girls could best cadge drinks. They were patient and polite and wore wary and apologetic looks about their faces, as though they dreaded that at any moment a customer would force them to punish him with force. They sadly justified their occasional beating of a customer as due to the customer's own bad taste and stupidity, in which judgment they were always right. They were men of Fiore's own selection and in his absence they managed the club. To Fiore they were men like himself, a group apart from the other employees whom the three of them had at times to treat like small, unpredictable, but manageable animals, keeping them in line.

Today as those employees in their street or rehearsal clothes congregated loosely around the twenty-six table where, resembling an inert, froglike khan, he had enthroned himself upon the stool, he imagined in a moment of sentimental resignation that he was presenting each not merely with their pay but with farewell gifts. He was saying good-bye to the lot of them, this circus of assorted sorry human specimens, a ringmaster bidding farewell to his freaks and clowns and boes.

Ted and Gene, the bartenders, the one a hunting guide in Wisconsin during deer season, the other a former high-school football star. Both had big families and second jobs. What was it guys like that wanted out of life? They liked to work, to put in long hours. They liked to make large paychecks. They couldn't think beyond those paychecks, the overtime, the hourly wage. They were large men, full of their own tough talk and masculinity, but it was the far smaller, soft-spoken, and almost prissy bouncers who roughed up and in some cases battered with bats and blackjacks rowdy and abusive men.

Lila the twenty-six girl. Three times divorced. In the dark from a distance she looked like a Hungarian baroness, up close in the light like a lady wrestler. She sat by herself in this dark corner, drinking tall Bourbons, her face looming out of the darkness in the pallor of the fluorescent lamp that shone down upon her green table, and when she worked, which wasn't often, what did she do but write down the scores of the dice? She was merely sullen at best these days, and fast reaching that day when she could no longer pretend to be pleasant to men, much less seductive. The poor dumb dame, Fiore thought, what the guys must have put to her in her lifetime.

The three black musicians, Duncan the piano player and the husband-and-wife team of Wallace the bass player and Sylvia the drummer, all of whom, Fiore supposed, were middle-aged. They came to work in old cars or else on who knew how many buses traveling who knew how many miles from some warren on the South Side, waiting in the early morning hours after the club closed for the rare late-hour buses. When they performed the men wore tuxedoes, Sylvia an evening dress. During intermissions Wallace and Sylvia, who switched to the guitar, performed on stage, playing popular songs for a dollar tip and no applause. There were rumors that a number of years ago all three musicians were famous jazz recording artists for a "race" label. There were also rumors that they smoked marijuana and even took heroin, and that the men slept with the white burlesque dancers. Fiore, along with his bouncers, did not take this seriously, for he considered the blacks by reason of their color, and the girls by reason of their profession, ignorance, and sex as unimportant if not inhuman. As far as he was concerned, the girls could have been fucked by large dogs.

The dancers had already overly made-up their faces, which was incongruous with the slacks, scarves, and turbans they were wearing. As they gathered around his table, they brought the dizzying aromas of their perfumes and powders, reminiscent of the lineup in a brothel. Ginny the rangy fleshy blonde rumored to have a special fondness for "dark meat," as the bartenders called it, and of whom Sylvia was jealous. When she danced she kept her eyes on Duncan in his dark corner, smirking at him as she removed each piece of clothing as though they shared a common joke, while he called out lewd and provocative remarks that sometimes made her lose a beat or even break down entirely and laugh. Elsa, a new girl from Austria, where she claimed to have been trained as a ballet dancer. Almost stubby with small breasts and muscular thighs, she was too shy or proud to be good at cadging drinks from customers. And Carlotta, a young girl with a pair of illegitimate children who sprayed gray streaks into her hair. She was unpredictable and wild, could actually become aroused by dancing crazily before men she had herself aroused and could be incited by their shouts to open up her G-string. Sunny, with her sleepy eyes and sleepy smile, who had lately become lackadaisical, complaining about the strain of dancing. She did not have her old enthusiasm, and she had recently discussed with Fiore the possibility of her entering a brothel down in Kankakee she thought he might have connections with. She thought that life there would be secure, comfortable, lazy. And raven-haired Donna, an old-timer at the club who was almost glamorous except that her stomach was flabby and scarred. Years ago she had worked as a call girl, and her favorite anecdote and apparently the highlight of her life was the time a famous pop singer and movie star in town for a heavyweight fight had fucked her in his hotel room for several hours without coming. Fiore was amazed at the ignorance of these women. Their lives lay outside the small powers of his empathy. He expected they liked doing what they did. Although they all danced poorly they thought of themselves as part of the entertainment world and spoke of famous strippers with the awe of young poets for their dead masters. For the most part they abused men, but in some instances they were themselves abused. They seemed to have no other relationship with men than this.

Bunny Bunkowski the comedian, dressed in knee-length pants that were low on his hips and supported by long suspenders, saddle shoes, and a beanie with a propeller on top, large buttons pinned all over his clothes that said such things as "A nice pair" and "Soft shoulders" and "Bottoms up" and "All-day sucker." Even by the standards of the small-house burlesque comedian he was a terrible comic. He was on stage only to give the girls a respite and an opportunity to flatter the customers into buying them drinks, and to introduce the acts. Not only did he receive neither applause nor laughter for his labors but he was greeted with suggestions and even belligerent commands to leave the stage as often as with silence. A substitute biology teacher in the high schools by day and a family man, he seemed embarrassed by his after-hours costume and profession, even though he claimed to have had a lifelong ambition to be a clown. How in the name of good Christ could a man so humiliate himself, Fiore pondered. How could he show up for work, never mind getting up there and doing it?

As his employees stepped up before him to receive their pay he found himself saying under his breath, "You poor pathetic clown" and "You sick sadsack" and "You sorry specimen of a loser." It seemed to him that they could not be just his employees either but all of mankind in all its meanness and hopelessness and vulnerability in an endless line that must have wound through the club and out into the street and down the block, disappearing around the corner. They were stepping up to his table to present themselves with their hands out to receive their dues and calling him their boss, as though acknowledging that a contract existed between them and that he was the ringmaster of those pitiful performances they called their lives. Unconsciously he threw up his heavy, ring-laden hands and let them fall lifelessly upon the table. "Anything wrong, boss?" someone said. Wearily he sighed, shaking his head.

To dispel this unusual and unwelcome melancholy he turned to thoughts of the wedding reception he was to attend tonight with Francine. The bride was Francine's cousin and they would probably sit at the bride's table with the wedding cake and he would slip a hundred dollars in an envelope and slip the envelope to the bride when he kissed her cheek. He could picture the crowd in the large rented hall, the bustle, the dance music. He could imagine the menu of melons and big squares of lasagne and hard rolls he would break in his hands and broiled halves of chicken he would slice the bones from with his knife and broccoli and maybe even eggplant, and he could picture them talking around the table with their mouths full of food and with glasses of champagne and red wine in their hands while the flashbulbs popped as the photographer took his pictures. He could smell basil and oregano and garlic (he was in a mood tonight for herbs and spices) and see through the windows the heavy-set women who had volunteered their services sweating as they cooked and served the wedding supper in the adjoining kitchen.

As he did every payday at this hour, Jimmy the bouncer returned from the truck stop across the street with a pair of fried minute steaks, french fries, and chef's salad. Today though it was as if he had read the hunger in his boss's mind. Fiore moved to the table that had been set up for him on the floor and there sliced and salted and chewed in the semi-dark, his broad back to his employees and contemplating the small stage as though he expected that at any moment the curtains would open and a show begin just for him.

When he left he had Jimmy go out and start the car. As he drove through the city the urban sky became gray and then rosy with the twilight, and headlights and neon signs and street lights were coming on along the streets. The people on the sidewalks seemed strange to him, as though they had just stepped out of their stores to watch the outskirts of the sunset in the sky above the buildings. They seemed to be talking to each other, to be waving good-bye or shaking hands. Waves of melancholia lay upon the city like the smoke of leaves burning in the gutters, suffocating the streets.

He drove deep in the city near Taylor Street, to a garage he owned. There he was to exchange this Cadillac for the larger of the two he owned and to meet Fogarty, the Cicero policeman who sometimes chauffeured him and acted as his bodyguard, and who was to drive them to the wedding tonight. The garage had no gas pumps outside and looked abandoned. Although it was closed for the day all the lights inside were burning. Neither Fogarty nor any of the mechanics appeared to be around. No one shouted up from the pits beneath the cars to answer his hello. He was no sooner in the small office with its greasy walls, calendars of naked women, catalogues of automobile parts piled on the desks, and advertisements for spark plugs, and its only window barred, soaped, and painted shut than the garage lights went out behind him, leaving the light on the desk in the office the only light on in the garage. A man with a pistol stepped out of the washroom just as a second man with a pistol appeared in the doorway of the office, having stepped out of the darkness of the garage. He recognized them as Van Heusen and Passeau, the two men he had brought up from New Orleans to locate and murder Tanker, and with the death of Tanker, had transferred to studying and preparing a plan to kill Romanski instead. Both men were dark-complexioned with high cheekbones and foreheads as smooth as scar tissue and black eyes and with bodies that looked emaciated. They looked partly Negroid, or like Sicilians in whom there was Arab blood, and they spoke with accents that did not sound southern so much as faintly European, as though all races and nationalities had been mixed up in their blood and all languages were twisted on their tongues. Fiore's first thought was that they had lost all the money he had paid them in advance in gambling, and since he was probably the only man they knew of in Chicago who had money, they were robbing him, biting the hand that fed them. What stupidity! Didn't they know the kind of trouble they would be in for doing this? So much trouble, it occurred to him, that if they had any brains at all they would kill him as they robbed him, a plan he was convinced it was their intention to pursue. That it was inevitable that they would be in trouble for doing this would be small consolation to him dead.—The fools! A songlike passion full of rage swelled up in all his four hundred pounds. To die for no reason! For sheer stupidity! For men who must want to kill themselves and take him with them! To think that Fiore would die at the hands of such fools when there was so much life to be lived out there! Why, he would club them left and right and send them sprawling, would wade through them as though through a crowd of little children, would step on their faces, ribcages, groins, shattering their bones like panes of glass, rupturing their organs like paper bags filled up with air. "Come on you guys," he said, not moving and with no trace of anger in his voice, "I got to go to a wedding." He was cold and sweating and staying exactly where he was. He could now interpret the breathless but icy atmosphere about their haunted eyes and wasted faces. They did not want to rob him, only to kill him. All the time he had been paying them to stalk Romanski they had been using his own money to study him. Who was behind them? Allegro, obviously. He had found out about the plans to kill Scarponi from Romanski, and with the Tanker's stupid killing of Scarponi and his even more stupid killing of the policeman, he had strengthened his hand with the other businessmen against Fiore. He would even ingratiate himself with the police, for as they had killed the Tanker for killing one of their own, he would punish one of his own who seemed beyond the vengeance of the law. But what did it matter? He no less than his confederates and competitors had lived his life as though always in an army in a country always at war, and had abided by the severe and often selfless rules that governed such a conflict. There was a sense of forces working on a man, and making demands of him, forces always more powerful than the man himself. He lost his passion and grew docile, exhausted, resigned to fate, like a huge tenor who had just spent himself on a taxing aria.

"Get on your knees," Van Heusen said, pronouncing it, "Git on yo kneesss."

"Fiore is not going to beg you guys," Fiore said with dignity. "Fiore is not going to die on his knees."

"You know the old saying," Van Heusen said in that almost foreign accent, speaking as though he were not used to speaking this language, or even any language at all, and while he was doing something to his teeth with his tongue. "About the bigger they are—." He was not trying to be clever but was afraid that someone on the sidewalk or in the building next door might hear this giant as he crashed upon the floor.

"You got to get down," Passeau added.

Fiore tried to go down to his knees but fell forward instead on all fours, looking down at the floor. "Francine," he said, surprising even himself that he had thought of her now and with the suddenness of snapping his fingers. Spoke it as if the utterance of her name and the emotion that welled up behind it were magic, an amulet that should and could and even would prevent him from flying from this world with the speed of bullets. And had no sooner spoke it than he was being escorted out to the bump-and-grind beat of the black musicians by the pair of bouncers with their flashlights cutting through the dark of outer space while Lila's face loomed out like a death mask floating in the dark above the lighted green felt table on which the dice were tumbling from the leather cup and Bunny with his beanie and propeller and short pants followed him across the floor and laughed, hooking his thumbs in his suspenders and imitating his waddle. Then the curtains opened on the lighted but empty stage, fanning out through the dark below, the overpowering scent of cheap perfume . . .

When Fiore lay dead, Passeau, who had done none of the shooting, pointed out the inadequacy of Van Heusen's plan. "You made him get on his knees," he said. "Now we got to lift him up. Why didn't you make him crawl into the trunk and shoot him there? All we'd have had to do is climb in the car and take off."

Van Heusen, who had hold of Fiore by the armpits and was unable to do more than struggle to hold up that small portion of Fiore he had managed to lift, said nothing, although he had to acknowledge the logic in his partner's complaint. Later, when they had managed to drag the body out of the office and had backed their car up to it and had the chain of the block and tackle used for removing car engines wrapped around it and had it swinging in the air, guiding it toward the yawning trunk as Passeau continued to curse that they were wasting time and endangering themselves unnecessarily, Van Heusen said, wishing he had thought of it earlier, "I don't like to do no shooting around the inside of a car. How do I know a bullet won't hit the gas tank or something and explode? No, we done the right thing my way."

When Fiore was shut up in the trunk Passeau yelled with boyish wonder that he could not see the rear hubcaps of the car, waving Van Heusen to come and see. On the road Van Heusen complained of the way the car handled and worried that to pedestrians they would look suspicious with the fins on the rear fenders weaving down the streets as though the driver were intoxicated and the rear end so low it was bouncing on the frame.

On Canal Street they entered the meat-cutting and sausage company of Santiago and Sons, one of many similar small and rundown meat businesses along the street. Santiago's, however, was part of the famous Farquarson Meat Packing Concern, and many of the meats it processed and packaged bore the familiar and trustworthy Farquarson brand name although no U.S. Agriculture seal of inspection. Since Santiago's sold its products only in the state of Illinois its meats were only state-inspected, which meant a great saving to the company since the state inspectors were not as rigid as the federal and the company could use inferior meats. Although the company was closed for the night, Van Heusen and Passeau had been provided with the necessary keys.

At first glance the interior of the plant was more reminiscent of a garage than an abattoir. The walls were greasy and blood-splattered, the blood more a black color than a red, the cutting tables were bloody and fly-covered, the sawdust on the concrete floor was bloody and full of muddy footprints, and here and there the hearts and livers of animals were hanging in no apparent order on hooks from the ceiling. Van Heusen and Passeau donned pants and jackets they discovered wadded up in a corner that were so soiled it seemed they never could have been white. Then they stripped Fiore of his clothes, which Passeau burned in the furnace of the building while Van Heusen, who had worked in a slaughterhouse as a boy, took a knife and bared the tendons in the corpse's ankles, inserted hooks inside the tendons, and by means of a block and chain suspended him naked by his heels above the floor. He stuck his throat but was disappointed with the flow of blood. "He didn't bleed properly," he said when Passeau returned. "It spoils the meat." Then he told Passeau to shave the corpse, while he himself used a butcher knife to slice through the many deep layers of fat on its abdomen, sweating and swearing with the task, until the abdomen gave out with a mighty sigh of escaping air and Passeau jumped back in fear, causing Van Heusen to laugh. Next Van Heusen disemboweled the corpse, feeding the streaming entrails out in his hands and onto the floor. He told Passeau to break up the offal and shovel it onto the nearby dolly. He himself picked out the liver and heart. Then he took a meat-cutting saw and beginning at the crotch sawed Fiore down the middle until the two identical halves of him, severed down the spine, swung free upon their hooks. Van Heusen stood back to examine his own handiwork and as though with an eye to judging the hanging sides for points. Think of the bacon and salt pork in all of that, he said to himself. And to Passeau who had no previous experience with butchering and was gagging from the stench of the offal he was shoveling, "Now you know what they mean when they say a man's full of it."

"Dressed out does a man look like a hog?" Passeau said, his arm crooked around his nose.

"This man does."

Together they took a side of him on their shoulders one at a time, and slid it along the rope and pulley over to a cutting table. There with knives and cleavers and saws Van Heusen dismembered the carcass and sliced the flesh from the broken bones, chopping it into even smaller pieces and linking Fiore up with all those prehistoric kings who were slain and dismembered by their people, to no less than Romulus, the first king of Rome, cut to pieces by the senators, who buried pieces of him in the ground to ensure the good fortune of the earth. Van Heusen threw the broken bones onto the dolly with the offal, and while Passeau emptied it into the existing drums of offal that were to be picked up by the rendering plant that serviced the Santiago business, he threw the pieces of flesh along with the heart and liver into a large vat that already contained the trimmings and organs of pork and beef and that tomorrow would be chopped and ground and emulsified in water and colored and adulterated with cereals and corn syrup and seasoned with spices and squeezed into skins in equal links and thereafter refrigerated, cooked, and smoked.

The ghosts of how many hogs and calves and steers and lambs did Fiore join in this savage ritual of this famous midwestern city? He was separated and reduced and dispersed and encased in the skins of frankfurters of a quality in which a bad flavor and no small amount of fat and gristle were not unknown. Behold Fiore, a hot dog, a red hot, a frankfurter, a wiener. He was sold cold in cellophane packages that bore the Farquarson label at the supermarkets and cooked at the hot-dog restaurants and pushcarts along the streets and hawked from the metal boxes of the vendors at the baseball games ("Hey, red hots! Get your red hots!"). In this form he was fried and grilled and steamed and boiled and eaten with a slice of rye bread or on a bun, garnished with tomatoes and peppers and dill pickles and spread with mustard and piccalilli and sprinkled with chopped onion and celery salt, or served on top of a heap of sauerkraut, or beside a plate of baked beans. He was bitten off, chomped on, chewed, bolted down, wolfed down, swallowed. He was the son of the city and he knew no boundaries or prejudices, and he went everywhere, and everyone partook of him. All over the city, young and old, rich and poor, black and white, took him into their mouths and ate his flesh.

This then was how the four hundred pounds of Fiore disappeared. Disappeared as the perplexed police and papers would have it later, "as though into thin air."

CHAPTER THIRTY-SIX

FISHERMEN

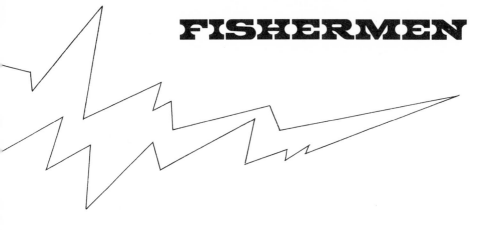

Around midnight of a warm breezy evening three teen-age boys got off the Montrose Avenue bus at the end of the line. They were laden down with rope, trot-line anchors, bamboo poles in bundles held together by rubber bands, minnow bucket, tackle box, and lantern. When they came out of the all-night bait shop where they bought their minnows and rented the boards for setting up their trot lines, they were approached by a man they would later describe as between forty-five and fifty years of age, with high wavy hair streaked with gray and wearing an "old-fashioned" suit. One of the boys observed a pin of a snake wound around a staff in the lapel of his jacket. Another boy remembered seeing him eating a tamale at a hot-dog push-cart on the sidewalk as they entered the bait shop. "Hello, fellows," he said. "Where are you going?"

"Fishing," they said.

He went with them. He said he was a stranger to the city and wanted to know it better. The boys were polite but suspicious. He made them uncomfortable.

From the beginning he talked of sex. He was, he told them, a doctor, a brain surgeon actually, and likewise a psychiatrist, since those two professions were closely allied, and often one could be substituted for the other. His name was Dr. Raincloud. They could call him Al. The stories he could tell them about these young nurses. They would just about proposition a fellow. He had even heard of cases where they climbed right in bed with patients, especially young, good-looking, healthy boys who were always getting hard-ons beneath the sheets. "Sometimes," he said suddenly, "it pays to get sick. Like it's good to break a bone now and then because where the calcium grows back it makes the bone stronger." One of the best places to do it with a woman, he claimed, was beneath an overturned canoe. "I've seen places where there would be hundreds of canoes overturned up and down the beach with you-know-what going on underneath them." The boys were amazed at this piece of information, although on the whole they found his discourse evasive, misinformed, even chaste.

By now they had left the streets, passed the water-pumping station, where they could see through the open windows the great pieces of machinery pumping the water in from the cribs offshore, and were walking through the urine-smelling underpass beneath the Outer Drive. Here he said that although he was a stranger to the city he had a number of good friends here, some of whom had been on hand to greet him when he arrived; others he planned to look up soon on his own. Thereupon he named the mayor of Chicago, the governor of Illinois, the superintendent of police, the alleged head of the crime syndicate, the managers of the White Sox and Cubs, the owner of the Bears, the owner of the largest department store in the Loop, and the owner of the largest meat-packing company in the Stockyards. He expressed surprise that the boys knew who these people were, that they were so well known in the city. By now the boys had decided he was "strange" and possibly a "bullshitter" but that he was a good guy and harmless and probably not, as they had feared at first, "a homo."

Now they were walking through the park, on dimly lit lanes that took them through the lawns and trees. The boys had their equipment on their backs and hanging from their shoulders and they moved cumbersomely, clanging as they walked. On a concrete promenade along the darkened harbor, where the water sloshed in the darkness just below them, a man appeared to be going into a woman on a bench beneath a blanket. For a moment the boys stopped with their mouths open, listening to the sounds. "They drain you," the man said, nodding toward the blanket, walking along. "I'm a doctor, I ought to know. The brains flow right out of the hole with the fluid. And you can catch the syph or clap too, and that stuff turns your brains to jelly."

One of the boys wondered if it was safe if you used a rubber, he had heard they prevented disease.

"That's all right then," the man said. "Because then you can keep your fluid inside you and your brains aren't washed out with it. It can't get out and into her and be destroyed by the machine inside her." He kept looking over his shoulder as he spoke. He added, "You've got to keep them from taking it away from you and killing it and turning you into a mental midget. You've got to use your heads. After all, we're not a bunch of Polacks."

To the boys the few lights in the cabins of the pleasure boats in the harbor, blinking with the gentle rocking of the boats, were signals that told of forbidden ecstasies being had below the decks by those aboard. In the park they cut across they seemed surrounded by the shadows of people sitting in pairs upon the grass and the fishing gear they carried on their backs clanged above the drone and bumble of nocturnal voices that sounded on the verge of dropping off to sleep. At night the city was for them an adult world of sex and privilege where all those fantasies in which they saw themselves as becoming either the troubadours of aloof co-eds or the rape victims of erotic housewives seemed always on the sensational verge of coming true. All three were walking with erections they were fearful the strange doctor would discover, remark upon, and ridicule.

Then they crossed the beach and scrambled onto the long concrete pier at the end of which a red light blinked on a tower above a cluster of lights. There the pier curved to make what was called "the horseshoe," although the pier as a whole was shaped like a cane. On the inside of the horseshoe men fished for herring with long cane poles and lanterns that hung over the side and streaked the calm water in which their red bobbers floated with green and yellow beams that angled down into the translucent depths. On the outside of the horseshoe they fished for perch with trot lines that slanted out without benefit of lanterns into the dark, rough, open water of the lake.

Like many of the fishermen the boys planned to set trot lines on the outside while they fished the inside with poles. But they could not throw out the anchors for the trot lines far enough to suit them, and they kept flinging them out and reeling them in, and the man asked if he could throw out one of them instead. He threw it far out into the darkness where it splashed like a stone, and the boys congratulated him and shook his hand. He asked them if he could tend the line, bait its hooks with minnows, slide the line down into the water, and listen for the ringing of the little bell that signaled a perch was caught. He whispered to one of the boys, "I threw it far out. Farther than anyone." So while all the other fishermen sat on cushions on the inside of the horseshoe and in the warm light of their lanterns, snug behind the thick sweaters and jackets that kept out the wind, their legs dangling over the side, he stood in his suit in the darkness on the outside of the horseshoe, stooped over, with his hands on his kneecaps, like a back in football waiting for the snap, listening for the bells.

The bamboo poles dipped up and down with lake herring, the water teemed with herring, and the fishermen would take the flipping silvery bodies in their hands and smack their heads bloody on the concrete. Although the men on either side of the boys were catching herring, the boys were catching only smelts, and as a joke upon themselves they would take the smelts in their hands and smack their heads upon the concrete. Herrings and smelts were wrapped up in wet newspapers, but perch were kept on a stringer. When a large perch was caught on a trot line the fisherman would shout "Jumbo!" and other fishermen would run to look. The boys shouted "Jumbo!" each time they caught a smelt. A mongrel dog was choking, fishing leader dangling from its open mouth. Its owner accused the boys of leaving rusty hooks about for dogs to eat. The boys ignored him. The man fished and his dog gagged. A man shouted, "Coffee . . . hot dogs . . . sweet rolls!" He wheeled a wagon onto the horseshoe and had a wind-chapped face and wore a white apron over his jacket. Steam rose whenever he drew a coffee from the urn or lifted the cover from the tray that contained the hot dogs.

"Here," one of the boys said to the man watching their trot line. It was a cup of coffee from the boys' Thermos, and he drank it greedily, protecting it in both his hands, as though he not only needed it but was afraid the boys would try to take it back.

Along the shore the random squares of light in the skyscrapers and high-rise apartments winked like candles in a draft glimpsed through fog. The city was as hushed as the lapping of the water against the pier. It was as though the city were floating on a gigantic ice floe, or was a giant iceberg itself, coming closer to the pier with each washing of a wave and retreating on the next. The bells of the trot lines tinkled lightly in the wind. The minnows were still on the four hooks of the trot line, barbed through the back, stiff with death.

He stared out at the lake, his eyes watering with the wind. How black it was at that horizon that led to Michigan! How black it must be on the bottom of the deepest hole! And all the fish swimming through those dark waters and hovering over the sandy, stony bottom with their gills pulsing, their tails curving. There must be millions, billions, trillions of them, full of small sharp bones that could catch in a man's throat. And dead people too, drowned in the storms, washed overboard from the decks or spilled out of the broken boats. The thrill of being carried out into that wilderness of water. The thrashing of arms, the cry of help, the mouth filling up with water . . .

There was a commotion on the outside of the horseshoe. A man was shouting for others to come and see. He had brought a lantern over and was pointing down into the water where the mongrel dog was dog-paddling to stay afloat, its head held above the choppy water that swept it against the pier.

The dog's owner came over holding a wriggling herring in his hand. He slapped his forehead and swore. "Shoo," he said, motioning with the herring. "You dumb mutt, don't keep swimming against the pier. Swim around that way. That way! Shoo!"

"That's a long way," someone said. "He'd never make it."

"He'd only get tangled up in all the lines."

The dog kept coming, paddling desperately to stay afloat with its head bobbing left and right and seeming to rise higher and higher as though it thought it could unscrew itself from the treacherous water and up into the safety of the air.

A man tied a rope around his waist while others laid plans as to how he was to go down and get the dog and bring it up.

One of the boys hauled in the line of the trot line the man had been watching. There was no perch on the line. "I knew it was only the wind ringing that bell," the man said. "You said I could watch it. I threw out the anchor, farther than the other anchors. You're real *amigos*, aren't you? Where is the helping hand you promised to give a newcomer?"

He hurried down the pier with his shoulders hunched and his hands in his pockets as the first traces of dawn began to show upon the lake. Crowds of new fishermen were walking out onto the pier, carrying chairs and gear, and he picked his way among them. A man came up and tried to sell him his catch of fish, swinging a stringer of perch before his face. He could see the ring of bone in their bloody red gills, and could read in the color of those gills the hour when each fish had met its death. On the beach he looked back and saw the long line of fishermen in silhouette against a sky that lightened with the fading of the stars.

He walked down the concrete ledges they call the rocks. A group of teen-age black boys were huddled together in army blankets, shivering and half-asleep, while their fishing rods lay on the rocks, lines in the water. No one else was near. The gray rocks, the gray lake, the gray sky, the faces above the blankets that looked like ashes, the lips purple with cold. Niggers, he said to himself, glaring. He watched them increase before his eyes from half a dozen to a hundred, and from a hundred to a thousand, until they became an enclosing crowd. This multiplying and outnumbering and enclosing, it was what they did best all over the city. All over the country too. But they were only dead men—that was why their skin was black. If you unwrapped the shrouds they had been wrapped in you would find their bodies naked. If they walked about, it didn't mean anything, it was just a matter of appearances.

The sun rose out of the lake, looking at first flat and razor-thin and then like a bloody organ taken from a body, a lane like red tinfoil streaking the suddenly blue water from shore to sun. He was on a beach of white sands where there was a long white bathhouse shaped like a boat. Here and there ancient skinny men lay on their backs with their eyes closed. Their skin was like charcoal and hung in loose folds upon their bones, their hair was long and white and their genitals large and loose in their swimming briefs. They were corpses of men who had worshipped the sun, whose bodies had been stripped and their skin blackened with death.

He watched the waves churn up the pebbles and sand and boil along the shore in their attempts to catch their slower halves. Without removing his shoes or rolling up his pantlegs he waded into the water, swinging his arms and hips, and a wave rushed upon him so quickly he did not have time to turn around and let it hit him backside. It splashed against his chest, lifted him off his feet. He was surprised at the noise and power of the wave and the coldness of the water and turned and high-stepped in his suddenly heavy trousers for the shore.

At his back was the city with its ornate and complicated shapes and planes and depths and angles and heights and widths all jumbled together in brick and stone. The rush-hour traffic was beginning on the Outer Drive and eight lanes of cars whirred and slapped around the curves, and from the city came the sound of a million small engines working. But before him was the lake, and only that, with no shore to be seen on the other side. If he faced east he could be the only man in the world for all it mattered.

He came to a pleasure harbor and a crowded quay. Two men in a dinghy were rowing out to a sailboat. On a moored cabin cruiser a man lowered a six pack of beer in a fish net over the side. On shore, people were still-fishing with casting rods over the chains that made a fence around the harbor, their red bobbers floating in the green water among the flotsam of paper cups, pieces of rotten wood, and white bellies and pink fins of dead perch. Their minnows were in small white cardboard cartons. Away from the water old men sat three and four to a bench, hunched forward with rolled-up newspapers in their hands, watching the boats and the men fishing and the families and children and babies in carriages promenading up and down the wide walk. There was a gentle breeze and sunlight and the slosh of water and the smell of fish. Everyone was happy and lazy, and he recalled an hour of his own childhood, with his family on a picnic in woods along the lake. He sat back on the grass beneath a tree and shut his eyes. The world behind his eyes was full of skeletons with bows and arrows. Arrows sailed back and forth across his mind, sticking into the fishermen, the strollers, the old men on the benches. He opened his eyes and saw that everyone was dead. They had all perished. Everyone in the city. In the nation. Mankind—finished!—extinct! What he saw was just appearances.

He began his journey on foot toward the downtown of the city, walking among the dead and dying, the dead fish, the washed-up drowned, the ghosts who gave the appearance of life. He was on his way to the underworld. He was Death, he had slain everyone, and this was the land of death. The lake of death was on one side of him, the city of death on the other. He passed between them through parks, over rocks and beaches. Riders on horses came down the cinder paths, bouncing in their saddles. At a gun club the firing of pistols and shotguns echoed out over the water. Along the breakwaters crowds stood looking out to the lake with spyglasses and binoculars. A sailboat race was in progress and numerous sails were bunched together, dipping and turning. Cabin cruisers overcrowded with modish passengers in sunglasses and with their feet up on the gunwales streaked along flying American flags from the fantail. On the rocks a policeman on a three-wheel motorcycle lectured an indignant girl in a bikini. At an air force installation, radar apparatus enclosed by a high chainlink fence and barbed wire, soldiers in helmets and toting rifles eyed him as he passed. A chess pavilion on the rocks where men played chess at tables under a half-circular roof, or checkers on boards painted on the concrete ledge. Many men, some dressed like wealthy businessmen, others like beggars, watched the games. He watched them with his arms folded, stroking his chin, looking from one player to the other. They did not appear to move often, and sometimes not at all. All appearances. All dead. He started to walk away but could not restrain his anger and indignation and stopped to shake his fists at the chess players and shout, "You're just a motley bunch of dead men! Don't give me any of your interfering shit! Your nerves are dead. Your souls have been murdered. You were all troops drowned in the war!" A little later he removed his shoes and threw them into the lake, then rolled up his pantlegs in large folds up to his knees. He was drawing closer to the underworld. He was on the shore of death. He was master here and by God he would show these corpses who was on top.

The skyscrapers of downtown rose immediately before him in the haze. He was on a crowded beach. Workers eating lunch. Homosexuals. A man with curly blue hair was burying another man with curly green hair in the sand. Young single girls with airline bags. Young wealthy mothers with their children, playing in the sand. Lovely women, these rich women. He wanted to tell them he was rich and virile and a born leader. That he had the power of death over everyone and everything and that by God he was not afraid to use it either. He sat down in the sand near a woman wrestling with her small children. He hugged his knees and refused to look at her. His teeth were chattering and he could hear himself babbling about his son.

He was larger than the people on the beach. They were like beetles in comparison. He was growing larger too. He could feel his chest and stomach puff up beneath his fingers. He experienced the sensation of rising in an open elevator, the ground rapidly becoming distant beneath him, as though he were rising skyward in a balloon. He was swelling up with death. He would displace tons of water if he waded into the lake. Beneath him the city was like a scale model of itself made from blocks, the tallest of the skyscrapers reaching only partway up his calves.

He was smitten with an unappeasable need for violence. It sent him raving on his back in the sand. His chief enemy was dead, the conspirators against him were dead, all Americans and all mankind were dead. They were at his feet. Even so there was still this dissatisfaction and fear and compulsion to destroy. Unexpendable energy! Unconquerable rage! Unremediable injustices! Blessed violence! In the absence of victims he could tear himself apart with his own hands, rip off his ears, bite through his lips, pull out his hair by the fistfuls, poke out his eyes, break off his fingers, bite into his flesh, wrench off his penis and testicles and throw them at the women corpses, twist off his legs and throw them into the lake, claw open his stomach and pull out his bowels.

Around dusk, when the Oak Street Beach had lost its crowds and the wind was up and the sand blowing, and the few bathers remaining were lying on the ground beneath blankets dusted with sand or standing up wrapped in blankets, and the buildings of the city were in a cool blue shadow in the dusty air that was again laden with the noise of traffic and now of distant horns, and the color of the lake had turned to gray again, a man in a blue suit was seen to walk into the water. The people on the shore began to shout and jump to their feet, waving. The man, up to his waist in waves, and dancing, turned around and waved as though in greeting or farewell. The people shouted louder, waved harder. The man turned around and came out of the water and stomped up and down the shore impatiently, hugging his elbows and shivering, smiling. Boys and girls peeked out from beneath their blankets. They nodded toward him, laughing. Farther down the beach a dog was swimming, retrieving driftwood.

A little later the man walked back into the water. This time the bathers watched with a nervous concern, as though saying to each other, I wish he wouldn't do that, but they did not shout or wave him back. The lights were coming on in the city behind them, and the residents of the Gold Coast were coming onto the beach to walk their dogs. Someone came with a kite.

This time the man did not come out of the water. When he was up to his armpits and dancing in those gray waves, white-capped farther out, and while he was in the trough of what appeared to be more swell than wave, he threw himself face first into the water, was carried out, was carried down, was pulled ashore by his hair. To the stunned witnesses on the beach who gathered around the futile attempts to revive him, it did not seem that he could have been underwater long enough to lie before them, as he did now, drowned.

It was on the same day of Helenowski's suicide that Magnuson's sojourn on Skid Row came to its close. Perhaps that hanging judge inside him had grown satisfied with the degree and nature of his punishment and penance and would now agree to let him go, as though these grim streets had been for him both monastery and prison. Perhaps it was only because his wounds had healed and he was cognizant that the search for him was no longer so widespread and intense. Or perhaps, like Thorsen before him, he knew only that, like some migratory bird, it was time for him to rise and go. He showered at a bathhouse and got a haircut at a barber college, then went to Union Station, where he removed from a pay locker the shopping bag that contained the money and clean clothes he had stored there before he went to live on Skid Row. The station lavatory where he changed was like a Roman mausoleum with its gray marbles and white tiles and porcelain urinals as large as sarcophagi, so grand a place it seemed that men did not come here to clean and relieve themselves but to debate the business of the state. He took a place among a long row of men in sleeveless T-shirts shaving before a gallery of mirrors above the sinks, and looked at his own face as he washed it in his hands. Had his face changed? It no longer looked white and pink but gray, as though it had been stained and soiled and the dirt that had worked into the creases and pores could not be removed. It was a degraded face. But more than this, it was less the face of an embittered and embattled judge than of an idiot who had suffered much indignity and was at peace with himself for knowing who he was. For a moment he almost cried with shame. For a voice deep within him was whispering, You were a real man, Magnuson. You amounted to something in this world. You had a conscience, a grand sense of responsibility. You did your duty as a husband and a father and as an American and as a man. You fought the good battle. You lived your life the only way you could have lived it and did only what you could have done, and you would do it all over again, just the same way, if you could. But another voice was whispering too. It said, Magnuson, regret everything. You would not live that life again. Not the way you lived it. Where was the tolerance and kindness and humility and love, all of which in some degree you had? You were nothing, Magnuson. The noble self, the rugged individual, the divine "I," one man against the gods—no better than a bug. Worse even, for you went against your nature.

Then he crossed the bridge over the river, once more one among the wind-battered crowd, once more hurrying in step with all the others, and went into the Loop to the bus station. He was thinking of northern pine forests and freshwater lakes. He was finished with the city. He wanted to go fishing.

The bus station was cramped with shops and short-order counters with indoor neon lights, which gave the impression that it was an arcade of pinball machines and shooting galleries. Everything seemed littered, broken, soiled. The lobby was overcrowded with travelers, most of whom seemed to be those people in this society who could not afford to own a car. Seedy salesmen selling unimaginable products; men in old-fashioned suits and carrying packages wrapped up in string; Negroes; a few students with guitars; soldiers with duffel bags; drunks. The crowd and bustle confused him. It was as though he had returned to the city after spending years in a mountain monastery.

He had a premonition of the end. He felt pressure—physical pressure—as though he was out of his element and the atmosphere would crush his chest. It was his age, those injuries, the lack of fight. He decided to make out his will. He took a napkin from the hot-dog counter, unfolded it, and scribbled on it with a pencil stub. If he had become famous in his life—and finally infamous—even though he was a failure, was nothing, was no better than a mote, then at least let him be an honest man in death and leave a will with instructions befitting such a man as he had really been. An inconsequential burial, done in his own way, among his own kind. If he acted against the wishes of his son and daughter, his partners and the agency, the powers of the city, so be it. Although he thought that if the truth were known, they would all prefer to have him buried his way. It would relieve them of their responsibilities, it would not embarrass them. He woke up a pair of unshaven men sleeping like bookends on the benches, and gave them each a dollar to sign their names as witnesses.

Then he was on the upper level of the speeding bus with the city in the smoke behind him, looking out the window at the rolling Wisconsin countryside quilted with shadows and a sunlight so golden it suggested fertility, fairy tales, health. Big red barns with Dutch roofs, clumps of silos, and farmhouses, some with Scandinavian gingerbread, grouped together on high ground, as though each farm was a small Bavarian or Bohemian castle. Sinkholes in pastures, herds of dairy cows, a small cheese factory, a schoolbus the color of an ear of corn pausing in the middle of a puddle on a gravel side road, and ahead the wooded ridge of a long moraine.

Then it was night and the passengers were reading paperbacks and the newspapers of small towns he had never heard of in the cold and private cones of the night lights that revealed only the page and the pair of hands, or were slouching in an uneasy and public sleep or whispering to their neighbor in the dark, droning like the voice in the confessional. The group of Germans in leather coats and hats, looking like the kind of men who would loiter about a *Bahnhof* at a dark hour, who had been drinking wine and wondering in German about the town where they were going to live and work, were now asleep and snoring. Two soldiers in uniform with shaved heads were comparing the rigors of basic training; an old widower was telling the teenage girl next to him about the deathbed promise he had made to his late wife that he would never remarry; a woman with a southern accent was telling the black woman she sat beside of the trials and tribulations of being married to "a drinking man." It seemed to Magnuson that the bus was full of frightened and unhappy and lonely people. Women who were weak and ill, the wives of men who had died or were imprisoned or had deserted them. Men who, when they reached the small towns that were their destinations, would not stay in the homes of friends or family but in old hotels or boarding houses. They sat in the dark, these men, with their night lights out and their foreheads pressed against the cool glass of the window, staring at the unseen passing countryside with nostalgia, loneliness, even terror. As though for them the sanctuary of family and home could never be a certainty, and although it was what they wanted most, it was also what they wanted most to leave.

The rare car they encountered on the roads seemed to be driven by locals on their way home from a just-closed tavern, drunken, reckless men but familiar with the roads. Magnuson couldn't remember the last town they had passed through, and the countryside had been dark for miles. They must be in the forest, then. The cool air. The smell of pine. Lakes everywhere, like puddles, out there on either side in the dark. Fish, big fish. Indians. He was journeying into his dream.

They were on the Menominee Indian Reservation, he and his wife, at the same log cabin trading post where they always bought their provisions and the bottles of cloudy beer that had a picture of Chief Oshkosh on the label, waited on by the same silver-haired man in that same red flannel shirt, or one exactly like it, he had worn every time they had seen him in the past twenty years. It was shady here and a flag flew from a pole in the mossy yard, and although summer the air was so cool they could see their breath; from behind the trading post came the roar of a waterfall.

Then the pine-smelling cabin on the lake at the edge of the

forest. The ritual of splitting pine logs for firewood and of fiddling with the damper on the stove, and the meals of fried eggs and baked beans with ketchup and fried panfish and beer and coffee, the menu for breakfast no less than supper, and in the evening as he lay in his bunk beneath the army blanket the whippoorwills, and in the middle of the night the loons, and at dawn the whippoorwills again, and all night long he could hear the plying of muffled oars and the wash of things ashore and the splash of fish from as far away as across the lake. One day he went on a back road to fish another lake and he came across a tavern on the porch of a cottage where the beer was kept in an old white kitchen refrigerator and there the Finnish tavernkeeper sold him a sack of frozen mushrooms he had gathered himself in the spring, and Magnuson marveled that a man could find his own food in the forest, and be able to tell one mushroom from another, and he fried them in butter in his black skillet, and they turned black, and when he cut them with his knife he noticed that fish scales were on the back of his hand. At night he would drive for miles to taverns the size of halls and lodges where stuffed fish and deer heads hung on the shellacked knotty-pine walls, and there he would eat the fish fry and drink dime draughts of beer while the red-faced Swedes and Poles and his own son and daughter danced to polkas and hillbilly music on the dance floor next door and the bartender told the laughing bar above the Milwaukee Braves baseball game on the television in the background the tall tale of how he facilitated the cleaning of the smelts he had brought home by the barrel from the smelt runs in the spring by running them through his wife's wringer washing machine. And his wife sitting on the stool beside him said, "Arnie . . . we ought to pick up some chubs and try trolling deep water in the morning." Something like that. But the cold water and the fresh air and the early rising and the good beer were taking their toll and he was falling asleep on the stool. He managed to raise his glass, noticing that his hand still smelled of the fish he had slit that morning and noticing the old Indian in the dirty battered slouch hat sitting against the wall and staring at him with his one eye which may or may not have been blind. And his wife said, "Arnie . . . honey . . . " Something like that.

Then in the bait shop he was looking down at the minnows and suckers in the tanks into which water was running; on the dock he was looking down at the big pike in the traps that seemed to turn the very water they hovered in dark and dangerous; in the boat he was standing and looking down into the water as he leaned against the weathered piling, looking as though he were weeping, still fishing for the walleyes that lurked about the bottom of the pilings; and in the boat and looking down into a shallow bay and seeing everywhere that the boat passed fat pollywogs boil up out of the mud, millions of them, and swim off, half-frog, half-fish, half-completed creatures in a world of their own. He kept leaning over and looking down.

The lake was like glass and the rowboat drifted with a gentle current as he stood in the stern, casting toward the shore and speaking with his wife as she stood upon the dock. He could not hear exactly what it was she said but he answered her as best he could, and she did not seem surprised by what he said. So he kept casting out and reeling in and looking down and answering what it was he thought she said. Then it became apparent that she thought it was time for him to come in. "No, no," he said. "I'm in good shape!" And, "I'm hale and hearty." Things like that. He did feel healthy and all of a piece. For the first time in his life he felt the press of tranquility upon his spirit, and believed that it would not have been so bad if his life had been different and he had been a simpleton or saint. All the birds in the woods surrounding him, he had wished he had learned their names and how to recognize them and to distinguish, one from another, their songs and calls. And what did he know about the fish he angled for?—Nothing at all! And the plants and the trees in the forest he was drawn to as though by magic? He couldn't tell one leaf from another. And the plant life in the water beneath his feet, a whole forest of it down there in this little lake alone, and he could not recognize or name a single plant. He had loved the forest and wanted to make it his home, but he knew the city and had always called it home. While his wife spoke with him there had come the noise of hammering from across the water, for on the opposite shore men were roofing. Now where there had been men hammering, there were men laughing, and he could make out through the trees a peak of the roof, but not the men upon it.

Then he drifted out until he disappeared behind a wooded island across the lake.

CHAPTER THIRTY-SEVEN

THE MADHOUSE

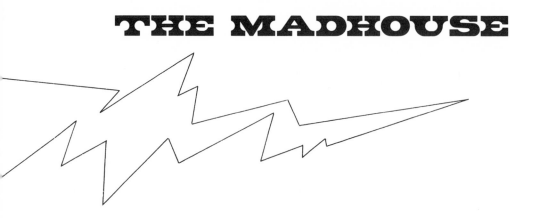

John Cavan, the detective of his own past, is on the last leg of that investigation that will take him home. He no longer cares to make the trip alone, and has persuaded Kay Wanda to accompany him. In scarf and sunglasses, a picnic basket on her lap, she sits beside him in the open MG as they drive southwest of the city through miles of flat cornfields and pastures of grazing cattle and alongside canals with barges until, as though it is in the middle of midwestern America, they come upon a Victorian imitation of a Tudor manor house or castle. Considering the farmland that surrounds it and its own landscaping of giant shade trees and expansive lawns, it seems it could be best explained as a golf course and country club for farmers. But the grounds are fenced with those institutional iron pickets, and in the grass of a small knoll tilted toward the road field-stones have been painted white and laid out beneath the flagpole to spell the institutional if holiday name of Villa Moderne. Once the country estate of a Chicago robber baron, set among the several thousand acres of his private hunting preserve, it is now a private mental hospital whose room and board and therapies are more easily afforded by citizens of wealth. Here the Farquarsons and the Westermanns and the Bradford McCarthys and the Cavans commit their cracked or fragile personalities for rest and pampering and the uplift of being analyzed, dredging up their histories of nervous breakdowns, depressions, suicide attempts, alcoholism, barbiturate and amphetamine addictions, abortions, disastrous marriages and love affairs, until those personalities are sufficiently salved and patched together to take again into the rough-and-ready slapstick of the world. Here Hope Farquarson, the mother of John Cavan, is in residence as a patient. Here John Cavan, having learned from Farquarson's lawyer that she is his mother, has come to see her for the first time since he was born.

Inside the main building the people milling about the corridors and reception rooms and libraries could pass for the guests at a fashionable resort or summer spa. "Unless they're in bathrobes or whites," Kay whispers, "I can't tell the patients from the staff from the visitors."

Cavan returns the nod of a man in handlebar mustache, scarf, and shooting jacket who looks as though he is about to take a brisk turn about his grounds with half a dozen Afghans on a leash. "I even have the feeling," he whispers, "that the other visitors—if there are other visitors—think we're patients."

"Are you sure the woman you talked to was a receptionist?"

Cavan is not sure at all. She did wear her glasses on a chain around her neck, fingering them where they rested on her ample bosom, which made her look official. On the other hand, when he informed her whom he wished to see she had said something like, "Isn't that sweet of you to take the time and trouble?" and walked away.

Here comes a barrel-chested, beer-bellied man with a seersucker jacket over a sweatshirt, and an unkempt beard almost as wide as his chest and small glasses with wire frames. Is he a patient? Psychiatrist? Visitor? He pins Cavan up against the wall. "How's your own work going?" he says.

Cavan, convinced he is mistaken for someone else, admits he guesses his work is going fine.

The man turns Cavan around so that both men stand side by side and face the wall, as though in a *pissoir*. "Do you mind if I read you a poem?" he says, taking a piece of paper from his pocket and breathing a bitter breath that reeks of whiskey into Cavan's face. Without waiting for Cavan to answer he reads in a timid voice a verse about a poet standing in the middle of the prairie in mid-continent—the Dakotas perhaps—on top of what was an ancient Indian burial ground before it was leveled by bulldozers. The spot is directly beneath a string of transcontinental telephone wires from which comes the hum and jangle of a thousand garbled voices speaking from coast to coast, and on which a family of cedar wax-wings perches, passing berries back and forth from beak to beak. Suddenly Cavan recognizes that the man beside him is no mad would-be poet, nor even ordinary poet, but a famous poet whose work he himself read and studied in his college textbooks and anthologies. He thought he recognized the face! His name is Wheat-stack. And the body of his work is something of a Whitmanesque celebration in free verse of the American spirit, a vision of America as a democracy of poet-princes, a new Athens of sprawling, robust cities and magnanimous universities of healthy boys and girls. He is also called the poet of wildfowl, which he catalogues in great chunks, and is famous for his genius at seeing the wilderness in harmony with the works of man: the beauty of helicopters over marshes, Canadian geese over Manhattan, a motorcycle racing through the redwoods, the rainbow colors of gasoline upon the waters of a brook. What on earth was a poet of his reputation and stature doing here?

His astonishment does not go unnoticed by Wheatstack, who thinks it has been caused by the poem. "Maybe you're right," he says shyly. "It's too raw. Unfiltered. Too much like van Gogh and his crows and cornfield." He mumbles something about how he will have to show this poem to his doctor, confessing that he writes a poem daily for her critical analysis, as he maneuvers Kay away from Cavan, having determined perhaps that she is the more interesting and sympathetic of the two. Upon learning that she is a kindergarten teacher, he engages her in a discussion of the techniques for inspiring young school children to compose their own verse. From Kay's look of astonishment it is apparent that she too recognizes the man. It's crazy, Cavan tells himself. Why would a man like Wheatstack hu-miliate himself and degrade his art by writing for his analyst? Was she his critic? His patron? His Beatrice?

He wanders down the corridor and looks in upon a large recep-tion room where a few patients or visitors are watching television, a western with all the attendant shouts and horse hooves and gunfire, as though their minds are busy elsewhere, one woman with her finger in her mouth and poking out her cheek and a man with his hands up beside his eyes like "see-no-evil" blinkers. As he leans against the jamb he realizes that he might have been born here, actually born here—or in a place like this. In one of these rooms, in one of the beds behind one of these doors. And was conceived here too, in some janitor's closet, or out on the grounds behind a tree. Delivered among barred windows and straitjackets and electric shock apparatus, a baby spirited out through a crowd of lunatics.

He becomes uncertain as to what exactly he is watching with the others on the television. Images of past westerns are compounded in his mind and superimpose themselves upon the battle being waged upon the screen: bannisters broken beneath the weight of bodies that pass on to flatten tables on the floor below, bottles broken on the backs of their heads, chairs on shoulders; men beating each other with fists and knees until the victor pulls the vanquished by his neckerchief up from the puddle in the muddy road and smashes a fist once more in his unconscious face, sending him once more into the mud; Indians shot off their horses by the hundreds.

Thank goodness he is rescued by the matronly woman with the glasses on a chain, who informs him that his "aunt" is in her favorite spot by the Goldfish Pond and to get there he has only to follow the signs. He in turn rescues Kay from Wheatstack, whose conversation has passed from little children reciting poetry in kindergarten to treating lunatics by means of "poetry-making therapy" to grown women laboring beneath a heavy bearded man in bed.

On the grounds of Villa Moderne they follow a network of paths marked by little rustic signs stuck in the ground that point the way to such places as the Farm, the Vegetable Garden, the Chapel, the Tennis Courts, the Croquet Lawn, the Goldfish Pond. They are greeted by any number of strollers who smile and say "Nice day." They could pass for groups of alumni, and parents in the company of their sons and daughters, milling about the campus of a small private college before graduation exercises or the homecoming football game.

The Goldfish Pond is walled by shrubbery, and there on a wrought-iron garden bench Hope Farquarson sits alone. Yellow nasturtiums run in a tangle in the border at her back and red geraniums are in imitation Italian Renaissance vases at her feet. She sits in sunlight with her hands folded in her lap, smiling as she stares into the shallow concrete pool shaded by a kind of pagoda roof, where several large black and gold carp hover above a bottom of copper pennies and nickels that have turned green. Her clothes are an expensive if incongruous mix, and several years behind the fashion. Her face beneath the wide straw hat, almost more sombrero than beach hat, is handsome and textured with the wrinkles of someone who hikes and skis or sits as often as she can in sun. This then the moment that Cavan, entering the garden around the pond, has anticipated. Before him sits his mother! Before him in the flesh! The flesh of his own flesh that made him within her flesh and gave him birth! But she has been looking his way for several minutes now and it is obvious that she does not recognize him. How then is he to begin? Does he introduce himself? Funny that in his daydreams of this scene he always picked up the action after the initial moment of their meeting, which was a tearful and passionate embrace of recognition. But this woman before him is a stranger. Just another old woman in the park. Just part of the human scenery on any given day.

Self-consciously Kay and Cavan take a place in the grass close by her bench. After nodding and smiling back and forth they engage her in remarks upon the weather, of which she says, "The day is just one of God's big smiles." And passes on to suggest that they make the equation that the sun equals love equals God. Kay mentions that they have met the famous poet Wheatstack here, to which Mrs. Farquarson replies that she is herself a poetess and would they like her to recite her favorite poem? They would indeed. Nothing they would like better.

But neither Kay nor Cavan can follow the poem, much less make heads or tails of it. Full of abstract nouns, each of which if written down would be capitalized, interspersed with O's and thee's and thou's, it seems to pile allegory onto allegory. It is all about Love and Light and Birth and Rebirth and Kindness and Song and Mercy and Purity and Calm, rewards bestowed upon those who are Worthless and Humble and Humiliated and Undeserving and Happy and Philosophical, as though, thinks Cavan, whatever real experiences she has had in life must be disguised by this featherbed and marshmallow of allegory and abstraction. If this does not make listening difficult enough, she delivers her verse in an apologetic whisper that is often overwhelmed by the singing and rustle of the birds fighting for the berries in the bushes. In the end Cavan is left with the impression that she has suggested that man has been put upon the earth to stuff his head with thoughts of God, and that she has ad-

monished them that to forgive is to understand and that to understand is to be at peace. The only line he remembers is, "Revenge is
for the flowers." The poem is entitled, she tells them, "Peacefulness,"
although originally she called it "Love." But the poem always gave
her such a "peaceful feeling" . . .

"I could see how you might waver back and forth," says Kay.
"Because it is about both, isn't it?"

After which they all lapse into silence, Kay and Cavan leaning
back on their elbows and turning their faces to the sun. When they
try to engage Mrs. Farquarson a second time they find they talk
only between themselves, while Mrs. Farquarson smiles as though
in her sleep. When they persist she shushes them and indicates her
head, as though to tell them not to interfere with the voices and
activities busy there.

To try to talk to her is, to Cavan, like waving a hand before
the face of a blind man. On his feet he approaches her almost as he
would a blinding light. "Do you know who I am?" he says.

It is as though he has not surprised her so much as embarrassed
her, as though he has committed an act of incredibly bad taste, and
she can only smile and shake her head, pretending to listen to the
civil war between the birds in the bushes and the songs and calls
proclaiming mates and territories and to watch the three goldfinches
battle with their wings in the water of the birdbath across the pool.
"You are a wonderful idea," she says, looking at him with that happiness and innocence that seem to say to him, Don't you understand?

"You're my mother," he says, coming closer, only to pause as
though awaiting her invitation before approaching further. "I'm
your son . . ." But the words "son" and "mother" are only words,
and ring false in his ears. He feels foolish, as though he has called
a woman he encountered on the sidewalk mother, declaring that
he was her long-lost son.

A painful drama in which Kay can play no part. She looks out
above the bushes at the tops of silos and the roof of the many-gabled
barn, the buildings of Villa Moderne's own working farm with its
beef cattle and herds of milk cows and poultry house and orchard
and raspberry patch and acres of truck crops, all of which, in accordance with the late robber baron's will, are to be used by the
sanitarium, making it self-sustaining. Crows caw from the fields
around the barn, and honeybees bumble in the nasturtiums, several
to the flower. Just beyond the bushes a tractor plows the plots for

the patients' own vegetable gardens. A man in khaki shirt and trousers, stained with sweat, enters the garden and scratches the grass around the Goldfish Pond with a bamboo rake.

Mrs. Farquarson is shaking her head as though she cannot puzzle it out but knows in any case that there must be some mistake. "Perhaps you were an idea I had once," she says. Adding as she breaks into laughter and slaps her palms pathetically upon her thighs, "If you were, it's certainly funny to see you turn up like this! I'm sorry if it—made you real." But later she says, "No, you must have it all mixed up in your head. Your Mother's dead." (It is mother with a capital M.) She goes on to explain, "You see, these ideas keep getting born in our head." Only to interrupt herself, "What did you say you came for?"

"To find . . . love," he says, mumbling the word, embarrassed by it, surprised that he could even get it out. Adding to protect himself, ". . . in some form . . ."

"Then you shouldn't be here," she says. "It's not here. It's not in anything you can see or touch. It's up there—in the air. It's an idea—up there!—No, no, no use looking up, you can't see it. You have to be a wise philosopher to even think about it. Women can make wonderful philosophers. They can—really."

"Do you know where you are?" Kay says, hoping to ease Cavan's injury by demonstrating that his mother is indeed insane.

"In the Garden." Giving it that capital G.

"And where is the garden?"

"In the Village."

"And beyond the fence?"

"A Wilderness."

"And you want to be in here?"

"Don't you?"

"No," Kay says. "I don't."

"But they don't hurt you here, and quite often they're even very kind to you." Smiling, she rocks back and forth while her lips formulate in silence the babble of what must be a magic prayer, her eyes, half-closed, resembling those of someone blind. What is going on inside that head, Kay wonders? The images of Happiness and Peacefulness no doubt. A crowd of people wearing smocks and carrying hoes and rakes upon their shoulders and tramping down the road, planting and weeding and tending gardens. A great army of gardeners and farmers and butterfly catchers and mowers and orchardmen and beekeepers and swimmers and bird watchers and schoolgirls and simpletons and dwarfs and pilgrims and saints and bicyclists and fishermen and goosegirls and nurses and milkmaids, upon each of whom shines a spectacular sunlight that is the manifestation of the Love of the Great Idea, the One God, the Universal One. And if there is any vestige of any concrete notion of human love left inside her it must be something like a misty vision of a college or high-school baccalaureate processional of young women in the ankle-length white linen summer dresses of years ago, crowns of daisies in their Gibson-girl hair, and a train of daisies undulating from one end of the procession to the other, carried on their shoulders, while their young swains with impish faces, bow ties, and shiny shoes, a bunch of violets in their fists and a book of verse or a Bible marked at a particular page under their arms, grin from behind the huge roots of the ancient oaks beside the way.

Even later in the day, after the trip back to Chicago, as Kay lies in bed with Cavan in his unlighted Gold Coast apartment, when that gray city light of early evening slants through the open slats on the venetian blinds and stripes the sheet they lie beneath, a bottle of Moselle propped upright by their hips, she cannot get rid of Hope Farquarson. The woman abstracted experience, found goodness only in abstraction, had managed to make love itself into an abstraction. An out-of-the-body existence, made all the more ironic because the woman, obviously beautiful when young, was beautiful still, and sensual just in the way she smiled and moved and wore her clothes. Had men driven her to the protection of this extreme, a father, lover, husband, who had burned the nerve ends of whatever raw affections she had been able to muster? Or was she simply not very bright to begin with, a poor dumb, beautiful, rich girl who men wanted to shield from the brutal world and love with their bodies and display like a trophy when she wanted only to become a philosopher and search for love in the cumulus of her own cerebellum? Kay remembers girls like this in college, the beautiful girls especially, demoralized because they thought their men loved their bodies and ignored or ridiculed their minds, although in compensation it seemed the men were willing to concede that the girls were their superiors, morally. Kay herself is not unfamiliar with the injury of this inequality. She wonders if Hope Farquarson is the unhappy consequence of this prejudice in the extreme.

Poor Cavan, lying there with his arm across his eyes. He must have entertained a daydream in which his mother not only recognized him but embraced him, called him son, her own, tears in her eyes. Must have believed that his very presence and the bond of blood between them would be potent enough to shock her from her madness and make her well. Must have believed that blood could be as strong as love.

"I've seen it all, Kay," he says. "That was the last stop. I can't learn anything from going back. I'm only finding out who I'm not, finding out where I don't belong."

She agrees. "It's all ahead of you now."

"The foolish errands are in the future. Forgive me if I'm feeling a bit low right now, if I'm feeling a little blue."

Even the ringing of the downstairs buzzer inside his room does not rouse him from his doldrums. "Don't answer it," he sighs. It rings and rings. And rings some more. When it stops the windows rattle. Someone is throwing handfuls of pebbles or pennies up from the street!

Voices on the sidewalk:

"Open up, Cavan. We know you're up there."

"Don't turn your back on your old pals just because you've become a billionaire."

Softer counsel: "Think he's got a girl up there?"

"Who? That bitch Myrna? That slut Sonja?"

"No, no. A call girl. He can afford to pay for it now."

The voices of Burkhardt, Motluck, Vollmer.

In the apartment above Cavan's the jazz pianist and heroin addict and sometime taxicab driver and massage parlor pimp throws up his sash, complaining down into the twilight that their pebbles have hit his window and that their shouting is giving him a headache and that they are a bunch of goddamn fools for not buzzing off since it is apparent the guy is not at home. Somehow, though, they persuade him to go downstairs and knock on Cavan's door. "It isn't locked," whispers Cavan, as he and Kay, in each other's arms, await the opening of the door. But it remains closed and the man is upstairs again at his window shouting down that of course he isn't home. But dear God, the fool, he is now persuaded to go downstairs and let them into the building so they can see for themselves! They are trooping like arresting policemen up the stairs. On instinct alone Kay is out of bed and racing for the door with her hand outstretched to slide the bolt, only to determine that she will lose the race and to step instead into the wardrobe along the way, where she crouches behind a rack of sports coats just as Vollmer, Motluck, and Burkhardt, as she predicted, bound into the apartment without first knocking on the door.

"Well, well," says Vollmer. "If it isn't Little Lord Lazybones."

"I . . . just woke up," says Cavan, yawning.

"If I had a son," says Motluck, "I'd lead him up to the bed-side and say, 'Son, take a good look. That man's a millionaire. If you'll just be quiet and listen to the man, he'll tell you a secret that will make you rich.'"

"Your sons are going to have everything you never had, Mot-luck," says Burkhardt. "Responsibilities . . . a job . . ."

"So the vice squad made a mistake," says Vollmer. "Throw some clothes on and we'll let you take us to the Pump Room and pop for drinks." He slides open the door to the wardrobe and reaches in, banging hangers, only to jump back, whistling. Only to approach again, parting the clothes as though they are tall grass. "You prob-ably don't know this, Cavan," he says, "but there's a naked girl in your closet."

Burkhardt, bug-eyed and trembling, makes for the closet like an alcoholic for a tumbler of whiskey. "Let's have a look," he says.

"Well, there's not that much to see," says Vollmer. "She's sort of crouched down and twisted around with her hands over her head. What I would call a posture of concealment and guilt."

"Come out of there, young lady," says Motluck, pointing at the floor beside the bed. "You've got some explaining to do to Mr. Cavan."

"More than likely she was waiting for Mr. Cavan to fall asleep," theorizes Vollmer, "so she could tiptoe out and steal his wallet."

"Then how come she's naked?" asks Burkhardt.

"Why, you silly goose," says Vollmer, "so just in case he woke up and saw her he wouldn't be able to describe her clothes."

"Cavan, Cavan," says Motluck. "If only you weren't so predict-able. It's not as if we didn't call the shot from the street."

Behold the naked Kay Wanda emerging from the wardrobe without benefit of any of the many jackets and coats at her disposal. Behold the three grown men transformed into shy and frightened boys and giving ground, averting their eyes and coughing into their fists. She, however, stares at each in turn, picks up her slacks, which she slings over her shoulder, and walks, long-legged, round-shoul-dered, small-breasted, slim, through their ranks.

"Now I know why *Playboy* is published in Chicago," says Mot-luck under his breath, receiving a swat across his behind with the slacks.

She glances over her shoulder at each man in turn before she enters the bathroom and slams the door. Or, as Vollmer would claim later, "Deliberately thumbing her nose at us with her ass."

While Cavan dresses, Vollmer and Motluck belabor him with

their latest hare-brained scheme. Which calls for Cavan to turn the Farquarson estate in Lake Forest, which they have heard he will soon inherit, into a giant country club–apartment house affair. Cavan is to donate the grounds and buildings as his share of the venture while Motluck and Vollmer are to be in charge of operations and Burkhardt is to be their financial adviser, each drawing a salary and a certain percentage of the concessions, rents, and dues. Cavan doesn't have to worry about a thing. He can retire to Puerto Rico if he wants, sit in the sun and sock away his dividends. The amount of money they will make is astronomical. Burkhardt is called on for his financial report since, as a responsible if junior employee in an advertising firm, he, unlike pilot Vollmer and in-between-things Motluck, is reputed to have a knack for business. "Give him the long-range slant in one big package, Burkhardt."

But Burkhardt is still flabbergasted at the sight of the woman he now hears showering behind the bathroom door, and does nothing other than complain that he really doesn't want to and they really ought to go. He does manage to get out, "You can't keep up these big mansions today . . ." The beginning of a memorized argument submitted to him earlier by Vollmer.

Motluck, however, helps out: "Look at those dukes in England opening up their big houses to the public to picnic in for a shilling or sixpence or something a head."

"Picture this," says Vollmer. "A massive beach party behind the house, hundreds of bachelors and bachelorettes bobbing on big rubber seahorses in the waves. Touch football and softball games all over the lawns. Helicopters landing in the driveway, bringing house guests in from the airport—."

"A fortune to be made from the liquor and contraception concessions alone—."

"You have to consider the philosophy behind the venture," Vollmer says. "Not to mention the public need. It's a known fact that guys go out to pick up dames in taverns and that dames go out to get picked up by guys. They go through a period when they devote their lives to this. Now our operation brings them together under the same roof day and night. We're the taverns they go to, the motels they end up in, and the apartments they live in all in one."

"And think of the prestige of the address; and not just for one old man but for several hundred horny boys and horsy girls."

"When you come down to it, Cavan, it's downright American—."

"Un-American to think otherwise—."

With the help of Kay, now dressed and ridiculing Motluck and Vollmer's scheme, and of the turncoat Burkhardt, who cannot bring himself to look at Kay, Cavan manages to beat the pair of schemers to the door. "Let me think about it," he says, bundling them out. He knows they have only dreamed up the scheme while drinking this evening and will forget all about it in the morning. "I'll let you know when we get back—."

"You're going away?" says Vollmer, suspiciously.

"If we get as far as Los Angeles we'll stop and look you up," says Cavan.

"To see California is to see America," says Vollmer. "Chicago is just Chicago. It's not the real phoney America."

"I thought you said California was death." Kay says.

"You learn to live with it," says Vollmer.

"See America first!" says Motluck, pumping his fist like a cheer-leader.

"See America and die!" says Vollmer. "At least that's what the travel posters in Europe say."

"Big posters," says Motluck. "In technicolor. The Manhattan skyline at sunset. The Grand Canyon—"

"The Everglades—"

"Disneyland—"

"State Street—"

"And in big red, white, and blue block letters beneath the color picture this caption—"

"SEE IT AND DIE!"

But despite the clowning it is an awkward parting at the door. As though all acknowledge that they are not saying "Good evening" but "Farewell," and Vollmer especially does not want to go. To Cavan it seems that an irresponsible and even happy portion of his life may well be over, and that regardless of where he goes the likes of Motluck and Vollmer are not likely to be there. "Wooden planes and iron men," Vollmer says, giving him a mock embrace. But for the first time the saying is out of context. It doesn't mean anything; it isn't funny any more.

The next morning who does Cavan encounter but Sonja Maki. He is on the sidewalk, looking at an art poster in the window of a Gold Coast restaurant, she is in the booth beside that window, eating English muffins with her coffee. He glances up from the poster to see her face, she from the medical book she has been studying to see his, with only the plate glass between them. The sun is in her eyes, she has to shade her eyes and squint; he can barely see her through the brilliant reflection upon the glass. An unlikely time and place for a renewal of the old romance; even so he is overcome with gypsy violins, candlelight in Balkan restaurants. "Hello," her lips say silently. "Hello," say his.

Inside, he nods, she nods. He sits, she squirms. She seems embarrassed by his presence. He feels mute, spineless, jointless. They sit in silence, communicating with their eyes that infatuation that does not go deeper than their skins.

At last she says, "You let me down."

"How so, Sonja?"

"You jump out of windows."

"What was the alternative for such a coward like myself?" He is surprised that he is trembling.

"Fancy," she says, "here on the Gold Coast all along. I thought you must have gone to Africa."

"I've been here—working at a printing plant—for the past few weeks—the night shift—bundling pocket books and magazines. The kind that have women with raised skirts or torn dresses on their covers. I just quit the other day. A man has to move up in this world—has to move on." Although it is the truth, he can see she does not believe him. "Look at the paper cuts on my hands," he says. He wonders that he could bring himself to tell her the truth about his job; in her eyes it must demean him. It occurs to him that she doesn't associate him with the recent scandal of his father. She probably doesn't even remember his last name, probably doesn't have the time to read the papers. He discovers he could never bring himself to tell her who he is.

"I want to see you again," she says suddenly, looking into his eyes, spreading grape jam upon her muffin.

"What about your friend?"

"Carlos?"

"Yes."

She shrugs, looks at a bus passing in the street.

"I suppose I'm a character in his books now?"

"You're barely mentioned."

"I suppose I'm shown—?"

"Jumping out of a window, yes."

"Slapstick—."

"Yes."

"Well, that's how it was, Sonja. I deserve that kind of comedy."

"I needed you," she says with sudden intensity.

"I need you, too," he says, surprised at his own shift in tense. Surprised, too, that he could say it, knowing that she would only draw him into her own past in the mistaken notion that he might be strong enough to change it. Why, he would lose himself before he found himself, in her—in them! Surely she knows by now his power isn't much.

"I want to see you again," she repeats.

This time he says, "I want to see you, too."

And means it too. Even though he knows that he will never reach her, will never know her point of view. Nor will she know his, nor will she ever try to know it. Nor will he ever have the courage to reveal it to her. There is no romance in revelation; there is no mystery in knowledge.

"So long, Sonja," he says, rising, certain that if she were to call him he would come.

The night finds him in the company of Kay again, strolling along the breezy lakefront on the concrete ledges they call the rocks. Once more his despondency will not give way. "So you didn't go East after all," he says, for the thought and its implication has only just occurred to him, and he has asked the question less in anticipation of good news than of another telling blow. "When will you go now?"

"Soon," she says, looking at him, almost giving it a question mark.

He listens to the water lapping below his feet and ponders what it must be like to drown. Thinks of Bonny Wenzel thrown into the lake behind her tavern, and her son, drowned in those same waters years before, the child trapped beneath the raft. Thinks of his father, who was drowned not far from where they are standing now, killing himself as the psychiatrists in the newspapers had predicted. And Nancy Rhinelander, whose lighted window in the Farquarson house he can see inside his mind, along with himself quivering on the lawn below, waiting for her to walk before the sash. He supposes that what passed between them was, in its own complicated and self-protective way, a kind of love. He resurrects the other victims of his father, the Wenzels and Mrs. Owens and the Moonys, all of whom he knew, and Alvin Raincloud, whose dead face he looked upon, and Rotterdam the beer salesman and Meyer the Magnuson Man, whose pictures he remembers from the papers, and they tramp back and forth across his brain like ghosts. He can understand how men could look upon this lake as giving up the gift of grace and consolation in exchange for breath and bones. The seeds of the same sins and sickness of his father are in himself, that much he acknowledges as the nature of his curse. If he believed in eugenics the simplest condition of his punishment is celibacy or vasectomy, biological suicide. The most difficult, to learn to live and suffer with his father's crime. And to do so alone, besides. Who would not be repelled by the enormity of his origins? Who would not look upon him as a leper or pariah? Whom could he ask to share his secrets, as he has this girl upon his arm? From the dark an unseen ship's horn; an unearthly call, like a ram's horn signaling him to make ready to atone.

On the horizon the running lights of a large ship. He imagines an ore boat on its run to Duluth, and that he is aboard her as a deck hand, a coalpasser, even a steward. He is out there in that darkness surrounded by water, hanging over the rail outside the galley, wearing a white apron and a cook's hat, or a black turtleneck sweater and black shiny-visored cap, his face blackened with coal dust, smoking a pipe, lulled by the steady shudder of the screw and the rush of the wake below. To sail up and down those inland lakes, passing through canals, gliding in and out of slips. He will disappear upon the water, create a new past, surfacing in the years to come in the waterfront of a new city—Erie, Cleveland, Buffalo, Duluth—a new man with a new future and a new name. He is tormented with wanderlust, the longing for anonymity, escape, the roles of immigrant, orphan, sailor. "I wonder where I'll go when you go East."

"Maybe you'll follow me."

"Maybe I won't be so far behind as all that."

Ahead in the lights of lanterns along the rocks a company of small Japanese men, wearing sneakers and baseball caps, pleasure-fish for smelts with nets and cranes. They look like engineers and architects, move like gym teachers, speak in Japanese. A net is hauled up, dripping water, containing for the amusement of the laughing fishermen the glitter of half a dozen flipping smelts.

"Fish always make me think of childhood," she says. "And church too."

"And fishermen?"

"The same—when I was a teenager I wanted to be a missionary."

"Then you've been baptized?"

"I've been christened—I've been confirmed."

"As far as I know I've never even been christened."

"Then I christen you," she says, scooping up some water from the net poised above the barrel in which the smelt are dumped and flicking it at him playfully, "John Fisher."

"I saw a Negro baptism once. In Lake Michigan, on a beach on the South Side. Come to think of it, my picture was taken by a photographer and was in the *Sun-Times* the next day. There I was, the only white person in it, standing in shallow water and watching with my arms folded across my chest. I even cut it out and saved it. It was the first time I had my picture in the papers."

When they return a fire engine is in the street before Cavan's apartment, a long hook-and-ladder with a city fireman in uniform behind the wheel, rented by the middle-aged playboy who lives in the townhouse next door and parties nightly, flying a flag with a cock-tail glass on it from a flagpole above his door. The guests costumed as pirates, peasant maidens, beachcombers, and matadors climb aboard and crowd the polished sides, hanging on. The playboy, in Black Watch slacks and a fireman's hat and seated at the wheel that steers the engine's rear end as it swings around the corners, waves to Cavan, whom he recognizes, and invites him to bring his girl aboard. But Cavan declines, rushing Kay up the steps and inside the door.

Only to rush her out the door and down those steps once the fire engine has clanged its bells and gone on its way. Determined to satisfy that wanderlust he felt upon the rocks, suspecting that in the act of moving on there will begin the remedy for his depression, he takes her for a drive along the north shore of the lake, his favorite drive, calling at Lake Forest. There, at the Farquarson estate, they peek through the locked iron gate at that Tudor-style mansion with its gables, overhangs, half-timbering, leaded casements, now only a dark mass against the night sky, resembling a burnt-out, haunted castle. "Think you could live there, Kay?"

Of course Kay could live there. Murders or no murders. Could live there like a princess. Could even share it with the ghosts. "Could you afford to keep me there?"

He couldn't. He would have to sell the place even if he did get it. His only share in the estate, it has been challenged by a host of Farquarson's distant relatives, all warring among themselves, on the grounds that Farquarson, when he made the will, had been insane. But this isn't the half of it. Legal battles over the estate can be expected for years to come. Mainly because the coroners and medical experts have given as the times of death for Farquarson, Bonny Wenzel, and Al Wenzel a range of hours that overlap each other, making it possible, in theory anyway, that any one of them could have died before the other. Which means that if Farquarson were still alive at the time of Bonny Wenzel's death, those same distant Farquarson relatives who are challenging Cavan's share of the estate will inherit Bonny Wenzel's portion, the largest of the estate. But if Farquarson died before her, then her heirs will inherit her share. But if she died before her husband, his heirs will inherit her share. Therefore the battle taking place is not only between the Farquarson relatives, but between the Farquarson relatives and Bonny Wenzel's heirs, and between Bonny Wenzel's heirs and Al Wenzel's heirs, with Cavan left on the sidelines, watching the fray. Can Kay imagine the Farquarson empire that spans the continent with its skyscrapers, oil fields, wheat fields, meat-packing plants, and banks in the hands of Bonny Wenzel's heirs, her numerous second-generation Polish or Bohemian nieces and nephews, factory workers, or the wives of workers with large families of their own? Or in the hands of Al Wenzel's heirs, his retired German-born parents, who were in their eighties, and several Catholic orders and numerous Catholic charities, one set of heirs or the other becoming overnight magnates, czars, tycoons, matching-vest types with big cigars, powers to be reckoned with in the world of finance and, who knew, even in the conduct of the state? For the first time today, indeed in several days, Cavan bursts out laughing. "Isn't that what America is all about?" he asks Kay. Immigrants and the sons of immigrants making their fortune. Yes, you could bank on it. One way or another the famous Farquarson estate was to enter the mainstream of the democracy.

"But if we did get the house," he says, "maybe we could turn it into an orphanage. Or a school or hospital for children. With your experience as a teacher I'd let you run it."

"And what would you do?"

"I'd like to begin my new life in service of some sort. Maybe an orderly in an asylum."

"You could always be a teacher."

"Not a professor though."

"Grammar school is more in your line."

"But a grade higher than kindergarten. I don't have your motherly patience. Of course I could always be a policeman."

"You're afraid of guns."

In the car again he says, gripping the steering wheel in his hands as though trying to bend it, "Come with me to Texas!"

"Texas?" she says, thinking, Texas?

He wants to go to Texas. He is driven to go to Texas. He wants to leave tonight. He has recently learned from Farquarson's lawyer that he has a younger sister who is half black and half white and down and out in her luck and was last seen living there. He wants to pick up the trail, meet her, right, if he can, all wrongs.

"What about your promise?" she says. "No more quests. No more going back."

Yes, but it is the terrible injustice in her case that drives him crazy. After all, whatever he has gotten out of life, and is yet to get, is just as much her birthright as his. After all, her father may have been black but he hadn't killed a dozen men. And she may well be the only blood relative left for him to meet—and the only one he will ever meet that is sane.

She sees how the thought of this new detective work has raised his spirits, and she is careful not to bring them down. "You'll have to be careful that you don't hurt her," she cautions, "that you don't falsely raise her hopes. She's gone her own way and she may be someone you won't have much in common with, someone you might want to change. It's right, of course, that you would want to help her—." She does not dare to say yet what she really means, that of course he cannot find her because as far as she is concerned she is not lost. Rather it is Cavan who is lost and who would find himself by finding her. Go not as a missionary or mentor, John, she wants to tell him. Go as a brother. As a half-brother. Or else stay home.

To her surprise and satisfaction he agrees to postpone the trip and think about its implications more. In the meantime will she drive with him around the lake, Wisconsin, the Upper Peninsula, over the Mackinac Bridge, and down through Michigan? "What do you say, Kay?" he says, already heading north, already speeding.

She says, "It's white slavery.—And I want to buy a toothbrush along the way."

On the way they debate the future—a purely hypothetical future, you understand. She argues for a retreat into the country to an abandoned rundown farm in Wisconsin or Michigan or even to a patch of land they have to clear themselves with a grub hoe. She wants dirt roads, the middle of the woods, a return to the soil. Jeffersonian democracy, forty acres, a mule for every family. Wants to relive the experiences of the frontier mothers and fathers. To do without cars and television and telephones and all those other gadgets. Wants to grow and can her own vegetables and milk her milk goat and do her own sewing and teach her own children and lend a hand in the building of the barn and cabin. She quotes Thoreau and paints a picture of quilts and calico. He argues for an assault upon the city by living and working in the worst slums of Chicago among the ill and impoverished and dispossessed, the victims of injustice and ignorance and prejudice, sharing the squalor of their lives as they help them get upon their feet. She doesn't want any part of saving souls. He, however, is willing to take the risk. She persuades him to her point of view only when he persuades her to his. They will do both and will decide later which of the two ways of life will come first, on this much anyway they are agreed.

"And I've decided to take your name," he says. "My own surname is a phoney and you'll agree there's a good reason for me not to take my father's."

She protests his joke and asserts she will have something to say about who takes her name. Besides, she is quite willing to take a man's name if she marries again.

He explains that even if she marries someone named Lovesong that won't affect the rightness of his having assumed her name. He has a choice in the matter, and she doesn't, and the court will grant him any name he chooses. But where is the meaning in picking a name out of the blue? Shouldn't he take a name of someone who means something to him? She is to look at it this way, she has the name and he doesn't, so why shouldn't he take hers? And if by chance she married him someday, why then she wouldn't have to change her name at all. "John Wanda," he says. "That's me."

But she thinks he is merely carried away with the enthusiasm of his own generosity and courtliness and gratitude for her company. She promises to say nothing if he feels differently in the morning.

They are well up into Wisconsin now. It is her turn behind the wheel. "Tell me a story," he says, dozing off. "Tell me about your family. Tell me about the greenhouses."

He reminds her of a small boy in a children's book. "I've told you about them. Why don't I tell you a story about how we all went fishing instead?"

"Tell me that one," he says. "A fishing story. I like those kind."

See Father and Mother and Kay and Older Sister through the early morning fog on the channels of Grass Lake, fishing with their long cane poles for croppies among the roots of the willow shrubs that crowd the banks, growing out into the water. See the small red and white bobbers start to circle; see the croppies circle with the line and come out of the water, a spinning slice of silver. Take a good look at the Wanda family in the rowboat rowing, looking for a better spot. Father like a rawboned crew cut midwestern deacon with his dirty greenhouse fingernails and his ten-gallon straw hat that embarrasses his daughters, and Mother in that gray sun helmet of an archeologist or African explorer that equally embarrasses them. And handsome Sister in an army fatigue jacket much too large for her with the sergeant stripes still on the sleeves and a headband of edelweiss holding back her hair, dreaming over her casting rod of ski slopes and a husky husband and a gang of little boys, all on skis. And Kay herself in the high-school sweater with the football letter, fingering the gold football she wears on a chain around her neck, watching the dark water of the channel glitter with the skimming of the breeze. It is a world of channels, marshes, willows, reeds. A cold wind, cold water. Redwing blackbirds in the marshes, reeds bending in the wind. Mother has a pickerel. Father takes it off the hook. Other boats glide by as though upon a pleasure pond. Mother holds up her pickerel. A grassy bank among a clump of softwood where a party has moored its boat and is drinking coffee, their lines and bobbers in the channel. Once more Mother holds up her pickerel. Sunlight now, and ahead the open water of the lake. Father is identifying water lilies, pointing with his pipe, giving the Latin names—

She has long since ceased to speak to Cavan. Someone else is in the boat now, seated between her father and mother. Another member of the family. Timothy, spoiled and pampered Timothy, her own small son born out of wedlock when she was only in her teens and raised by her parents as their own. Even Peter Pfister never knew the boy was hers, never even so much as guessed, nor does Timothy, who calls her sister. Nor is it easy for her to think of him as being other than her brother, her little brother. And yet he is her son. Lanky, auburn-haired, pea-soup eyed, baseball-crazy Timothy, whom Mother and father call their "All-American boy." Has the time finally come to reveal herself and take the name of Mother? Does she dare? She doesn't think she feels like she is his mother. Perhaps it is too late, and she can only love him as a sister, and he can only love her as her brother. But to have him is to have herself. Is to be herself at last. Her real self. His mother. She is certain that a man like Cavan—if a woman were to share a life with him—would accept a boy like Timothy as his own. Whether because he is weak or strong she doesn't know; she hopes she never cares. She wants, perhaps against her nature, for a man, perhaps against his nature, only to be good and kind. After all—and she smiles—if he does take the name of Wanda, Timothy's name is already Wanda, as is her own . . .

John Cavan, sedated by the story of the Wanda family fishing, thinks back upon that mass black baptism he remembered earlier. He is with friends, students from Illinois Tech, on the Thirty-first Street Beach, lazing on his towel in the glitter of the lake and sand, watching the congregation of the Baptist church file across the beach. Women in their Sunday dresses, carrying pocketbooks and umbrellas, the few men bow-legged or limping in dark suits, the pair of preachers in clerical robes over mechanic's overalls, the young women in white sheets and caps that make them resemble nurses or Coptic nuns. They fan out along the shore, the women begin to moan a hymn. The preachers wade out into the water above their waists. Other men roll up their pantlegs and their white shirtsleeves, then wade out to form a line to pass the candidates along. They go out one after the other, the young women in the white sheets, a fear or blankness on their faces. The taller preacher holds the Bible while the smaller one invokes the name of Father, Son, and Holy Ghost above their heads, then dips them back into a wave from which they emerge dripping, choking, holding their noses. On the shore the women chant and clap, some even jump up and down or do a rhythmic dance in place, more like a tribe in Africa than any Christian congregation. The waves, meanwhile, grow bigger, grander, greener. They gather water and momentum. The preachers dance and float; their heads bob; they cast apprehensive glances over their shoulders. Spontaneous conversions are being made. Women in skirts and nylon stockings kick off their shoes and wade forward in a daze; so does an occasional man stripped down to his white shirt and pants, plowing through the water as though about to dive and swim across the lake. On shore a black man playing bongo drums says to his friends, "No wonder people think we're just out of the trees." A ten-year-old blond girl talks about her swimming lessons with the black guard on his perch. A pair of muscular black men wrestle on a blanket before a gallery of girls. Cavan's friends are playing bridge upon a blanket. Cavan is in the water watching. Watching the women emerge from the baptism wearing only underwear beneath the soaking, cloying sheets, and the girls along the shore who wade out into the water in their ecstasy, holding their skirts above their hips. Watching the small preacher, caught unawares at last, momentarily disappear into the crescent of a wave.

And suddenly his recollection takes a different turn, so unexpected that it shoots him forward in his seat. The men in the line out in the water are taking his own arms into their hands and passing him along from man to man. He is going out into the water. Now the little preacher lays his hands upon him, recites above his head, dips him back into a mighty wave. Submerged totally and rising with his hair plastered, his flesh dripping, his eyes closed, and his mouth open to catch his breath and speak his name . . .

CHAPTER THIRTY-EIGHT

THE FUNERAL

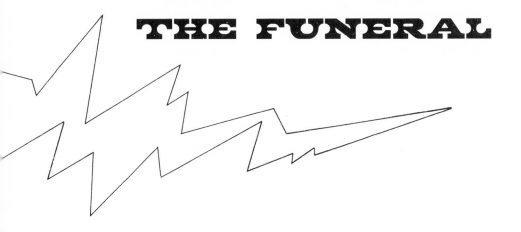

When Shannon returned to Chicago from his business trip on the West Coast he was met at the airport by his wife, who said, after kissing him, "He's been found."

"Alive?"

"Drowned." He had been fishing on some lake up in Wisconsin. Had fallen overboard. The empty boat discovered beached along the shore. The lake dragged. The body recovered yesterday. Identified as Magnuson.

Thank God, he thought, that they hadn't had to shoot him down. He said, "Do they know how it happened?" He was thinking of suicide, murder.

"Apparently an accident," she said. There had been an autopsy. The lungs full of water. But a massive coronary had pitched him overboard.

"Do they have any idea how long he was dead?" He hoped at least a month.

"Only a few days," she said.

As she drove him in their station wagon to their house in nearby Park Ridge he kept saying to himself, So Magnuson is dead. Drowned. In a lake. What on earth was he doing up there anyway? Hiding out? That's what they would say, anyway. So Magnuson has turned up at last. Who would have thought he would have come to such an end?

Even in Los Angeles, where he had gone to promote a southern California branch of the Magnuson Agency and to negotiate the services of the Magnuson Men at the Los Angeles Dodgers baseball games, along with laying the groundwork for their use at the Democratic and Republican political conventions, should one or the other or both parties choose Los Angeles as its next convention site, while managing also to visit an electronics laboratory to investigate and purchase new devices for communication and detection, the mystery and scandal of Magnuson, the president and founder of the agency he represented, had followed him. Political and business figures alike had embarrassed and challenged him repeatedly by their references to Magnuson's involvement in so bizarre and baffling an affair. He had feared that even out there the scandal had hurt the image of the agency and its Magnuson Men and, what was worse, had hurt the image of Shannon himself.

Fortunately, Shannon had missed the worst of the rumors and scandals of the past month by being absent from Chicago. They had fallen instead upon the shoulders of his partner in the agency, Kenneth O'Bannon, the manager and administrator of the business. O'Bannon was not a public person, was not well known in the city, and had nothing to lose by a certain amount of adverse public focus on himself. Shannon, however, was very much a public man, the promoter and publicizer of the agency. He had an image to preserve, his own as much as the agency's. Better to have caught the fire in Los Angeles than here in Chicago. Better for himself and for the agency.

At home in his large Cape Cod house he made himself several drinks and took a swim in the back yard swimming pool. His wife joined him in a sky blue rubbery bathing suit and they swam several lengths together, side by side. She was an athletic, freckled, heavyset strawberry blonde and he liked to call her fondly to her face "a real man's woman." In her presence he felt the world was solid gold and that the course of his life had been exactly right. It was as though without her heavy but comfortable hold of him he would float away and disappear as just so much air. His wife left the pool only to reappear in her terrycloth robe and call him to the television set. The local news was on, the mayor of Chicago, Thomas Conley himself, in response to the discovery and identification of Magnuson's body, was reading a brief statement from a podium above the city seal. His glasses slid to the edge of his nose as he stumbled over the words on the paper he held before him. In his heavy Chicago accent and monotone he referred to the Magnuson Agency as "that famous agency of our great city." To the Magnuson Men themselves as "those fine men that do their duty for all our citizens." When he finished his statement reporters attempted to question him, but he said, "I have no comment, gentlemen," and, removing his glasses, walked away from the rostrum. Shannon knew that that would help. To the mayor, Magnuson and the Magnuson Agency were in good measure the city—his city. To suspect Magnuson was to suspect the city. To condemn Magnuson was to condemn the city. To condemn the city was to condemn its mayor.

So, he said to himself again, Magnuson is dead. Like it or not the old man had been a father figure, and he felt a sudden elation that at last the man was dead. At long last he would have the freedom to do what he wished within the agency and publicly around the city. Once the worst of the scandal was past he would abandon his low-profile image and make the name of Shannon as important and as well known around the city as had been the name of Magnuson. With Magnuson dead and O'Bannon interested only in the privacy of management, Shannon could now assume the political, social, and charitable role within the city, which had been Magnuson's to make, but which Magnuson had ignored.

His three oldest children, a boy and two girls, all teenagers, were sitting in their bathing suits with some of their friends around the pool, and he decided to stay inside and have another drink. His children were all beetle-browed with heavy blond eyebrows that always looked as though they had gotten sand in them, like his, and who wore their blond hair Pan-like. They reminded him sometimes of goats. Some distant and secret look about their eyes. Unlike other teen-age siblings they seemed to genuinely like each other and enjoy each other's company. Unlike most of the other children in the suburb they were not reticent or sullen in front of their father but entirely candid with him, even if they did manage a politeness that bordered on formality. They did almost everything he advised them to, and everything he ordered them to do, and yet he was certain they were fiercely determined to do only what they wished to do, and that somehow they did it, too. He suspected that, more than the other children, they led secret lives of which he knew nothing. They wore a salesman's mask in his presence and, unlike other siblings, were able to wear it in collusion, one looking out for the other. Although it made him uneasy to suspect the mask not only hid their selfishness and hedonism but their true opinion of him, which was not far removed from contempt, he was willing to accept the mask, and was resolved never to let them know he knew that what they showed him was neither true nor real. He was as willing to admit that somehow he had managed or even contrived to fail them as he was to give them up to the world and let them go where they would. He did not doubt their durability. They would get what they wanted. They had had it easy. Their great-grandfather had been a hod carrier, their grandfather a policeman. They would not have to hone themselves like knives to move up as Shannon and his father had. They were already there, waxing fat. The agency and all its success and wealth were open to them. As open as America itself. In a way he even admired the skill of their duplicity and their independence from their parents and the clannishness among themselves. If he suffered a little it was the price he had to pay if he wanted his son to be a man, his own man, and his daughters independent women.

His baby son caught his eye, waving his arms and smiling from the small reclining crib. The beginning of a second and late family. The mistake, the menopause child. Born with both legs broken, he seemed to be trying to kick those legs inside their casts. The boy was talking baby talk, and Shannon knelt beside him to listen. He was overcome with affection. He would know this boy. This boy would know him. He would not make whatever mistakes he had made with the other children. "I'll take you on an airplane ride with me to California someday," he whispered. "Just you and me. Or to Ireland, eh? What do you say, Kevin, sweetheart? What do you say?" To his surprise he caught himself whispering to the boy in the next breath, "Magnuson is dead."

He had always harbored a dream that when it came time for the chief to die his funeral would be arranged and choreographed by no other than himself. It was to have been a masterpiece of pomp, publicity, and public relations, a funeral fit for a general of the army. The mayor would have ordered the flags of the city to be flown at half-mast, city employees would be let off work. All the city and county politicians and police officials and the top businessmen of the city and their wives, along with many of the players and owners of the White Sox, Cubs, Black Hawks, and Bears would be on hand to pay their respects, not to mention the multitude of citizens, many of them men who had once worked or still worked as Magnuson Men. For Magnuson had managed to touch both the city and suburban camps of Democrats and Republicans, and the well-to-do and poor alike, and his death could have brought the city together in a mass display of respect and grief as the deaths of few other men could. Even though he was not a Catholic he would have lain in state in a large downtown cathedral and, in this ecumenical age, would have been eulogized by the cardinal. He would have been dressed in the white braid-laden uniform of a commander of the Magnuson Men (something Shannon himself had thought to design). There would have been some flinty quality of dignity about Magnuson in his stately repose, and something anachronistic too. He would have looked like a commodore from World War One. On either side of his coffin an honor guard of Magnuson Men, the tallest and handsomest fellows they had on their rosters, in the sky blue and gold uniform, the visored hat, the white gloves. And for pallbearers another escort of Magnuson Men, or a selection of city officials, or the stars of the city's professional athletic teams, or maybe the sons of police officers killed in the line of duty. They would carry the coffin out of the cathedral and into the streets. The funeral would be scheduled for the noon hour when the offices would have emptied for the lunch hour, and the blocks around the church would be jammed with people. A chain of policemen would link arms to hold back the throng. Police on horseback would wade into them, clearing an exit for the hearse. It might have been raining, too, and the coffin placed into the hearse among a sea of black umbrellas. At the cemetery an honor guard of the Magnuson Men Industrial Patrol in their navy blue uniforms would fire their rifles in salute above the flag-draped coffin. A police bugler would close it out by playing taps.

But that dream now seemed impossible. The reputation of Magnuson was in serious question, if not disgrace. Even though the agency still bore his name, perhaps it was best to dissociate him from the Magnuson Men as much as possible. Already Shannon had begun to leak stories to the press that Magnuson had had almost nothing to do with the agency, and nothing at all to do with the administration of the Men.

He called the mayor's office in City Hall to learn what the plans were for Magnuson, and was put through to James McDonough, the city's legal counsel, who told him they were about to get in touch with him. Mark Horn, the mayor's personal publicity man, joined them on the line. To Shannon's surprise, they were determined to give Magnuson a large, public funeral, and were contemptuous of Shannon for believing they would do otherwise.

"You can't cover up someone as big as your boss," McDonough said. "You throw him in the troublemakers' faces. You dare them to come out and say it isn't so. There's no problem with the other people. They believe what the mayor tells them."

"The key word," Mark Horn kept repeating, "is 'tragedy.' It was a 'tragedy.' For Magnuson. For the city. For everybody. The adjective for that word was 'tragic.'" "Tragedy"—they were to remember it. They were to use it.

"Here's what we figure happened," McDonough said. "Magnuson stumbled on this killer, see, and tried to stop him but he was made a prisoner by the killer instead, and then the killer tried to kill Magnuson, only he just gave him a bad bump on the head. After that it was a case of amnesia."

Horn pointed out the promotional problem they would all have to face during the funeral. Unfortunately, the threat of scandal still lingered over Magnuson, and although the mayor and his people wanted to dignify Magnuson by lending their presence to his funeral, no one who had known him, or who now possessed a high office or rank, wanted to be made out to be his champion or intimate.

"I want it to look like the mayor is very busy with city business," McDonough said, "and that he took out just enough time to come and pay his respects."

Horn said he would try to create that impression. He felt Magnuson's own family should be in the forefront of the funeral. To play up "the human element," as he called it, because it was "a human tragedy." The State Department had located Magnuson's daughter in Africa and she was flying home tomorrow with her fiancé or boyfriend or someone, although it hadn't been able to locate the son in Europe yet. The daughter was in the U.S.I.S.; the son, he thought, had several college degrees. They wanted to have the press focus on them. He thought they ought to make a sympathetic impression.

McDonough said he had found out that the son was in his late twenties but wasn't married, and he expressed the fear that he might turn out to be queer.

Shannon was asked if Magnuson had any other relatives that he knew of, and recalled from the recent investigation something about his having cousins in Minnesota.

"Let's get them," McDonough said. "What are we waiting for? Put them right up front with the casket."

"We want a crowd of policemen filling that church," Horn said. "And marching outside behind the coffin. Everywhere photographers and cameramen take pictures, we want them to see uniforms. It ought to be just like the funeral we had for that young cop Carbone when he was killed. The same atmosphere, the same stern stuff and dignity. Like Magnuson really was an officer shot down in the street."

"We ought to bring in some police representatives from other towns in the state," McDonough offered. "And from big cities all over the country."

Shannon suggested they might want some Magnuson Men in the procession. But McDonough was disdainful. "The police have got more dignity than a bunch of ushers," he said. Horn agreed.

It was taken for granted that all the police captains and elected city officials would be in attendance. But maybe they could persuade the governor to be there too, or at least the lieutenant-governor as his representative. After all, Magnuson had been a Republican. McDonough would get one of the local state senators—who was a Republican but one of the mayor's men—to make an appeal to the governor.

"We want representatives from all three faiths at the service, too," Horn said, and promised to secure a rabbi.

"He was a Lutheran," McDonough said, pronouncing it "Lut'ran." "We got to get one of those guys. The mayor will call the cardinal."

"I don't think we want our people to say anything at the service," Horn said. "Just have the Lutheran minister recite a prayer and say a little something about Magnuson—the usual stuff. Maybe we could get the daughter to say something—read a poem maybe—and leave it at that."

"If she could just break down while she was reading it," McDonough seconded, "it would be too good to be true."

Finally they discussed at length the problem of the pallbearers, and decided that a contingent of young police cadets was best.

Shannon was elated with such good news. He immediately called his partner, O'Bannon, who was at the office, and acquainted him with the funeral plans that City Hall had in mind for Magnuson. Which was fine with O'Bannon. It wasn't his concern.

But an hour later O'Bannon received a letter in the mail that was to make it very much his concern. It was from Magnuson, and contained his will, written in pencil on a paper napkin. It gave explicit instructions not only for the disposal of his estate, but for his funeral and interment. The envelope bore an Eagle River, Wisconsin, postmark, close to where Magnuson had been drowned. It bothered him that he could not reason out why Magnuson had sent it to him. Had he expected him to keep quiet about his whereabouts? Had he planned to be far away from that postmark by the time O'Bannon had received it? Or had he somehow foreseen or even—God forbid— known for certain that he would die?

He was surprised that Magnuson had not only made him responsible for the funeral arrangements but had also appointed him the executor of his estate. He had always expected that at most he would share that office with Shannon, for he had believed that Magnuson had favored Shannon more than himself, especially with his rare confidences. This had always secretly disturbed him, for he was certain his own affection and concern for Magnuson were stronger than Shannon's. Now it would seem that Magnuson in his last hours had acknowledged that this was so. He felt Magnuson must have chosen him for good reason. In turn he believed he owed the old man much.

He wanted to carry out the funeral instructions, eccentric though they were, if he could do so. He judged that the will could easily be contested—and probably would be—and might even be invalid, although it did appear to bear the signatures of two witnesses. Certainly no one would blame O'Bannon for not acting on its instructions first thing. He believed that if he consulted City Hall on Magnuson's last wishes, the people there would want them countermanded. He was not a rebellious man, far from it, but he was accustomed to working in private and making his own decisions for the good of the agency as a whole (whereas he sometimes suspected Shannon worked in public only for the good of Shannon). Even so, he probably would have consulted Shannon and the mayor's office had he not seen a way around his dilemma. He would call Shannon immediately after the funeral tonight, tell him what he had done, and persuade him to keep quiet about the earlier call he had made to O'Bannon setting forth the city's plans. Shannon would be angry, but would have no choice but to acquiesce. After all, who could blame O'Bannon? He was the executor of the estate, and given the instructions in the will, and his ignorance of the city's plans, what else, legally, could he have done?

Magnuson had wanted his funeral to be swift, private—secret. He had wanted to be in the ground as soon as possible, and O'Bannon arranged to have him buried tonight. He called the cemetery in the western suburbs where Magnuson had a plot beside his wife and told them to prepare the grave. He then called a funeral parlor and arranged to have a hearse meet the Wisconsin train at the Northwestern Station and to take the coffin immediately to the cemetery where the funeral party would be waiting. This was all in accordance with the instructions in the will. Magnuson had asked to be buried in "a plain wooden box," but O'Bannon decided to have him buried in whatever they had shipped him in from Wisconsin.

The next instruction promised to be more difficult to satisfy. At first O'Bannon had no idea how he could solve the problem on such short notice. Finally he called the Mighty-Men Incorporated, a hiring agency located just west of the Loop on Skid Row that hired out laborers by the day. Usually these men were transients and derelicts who wanted no more than the stake of a day's pay. He asked for twelve male laborers to be sent around to the offices of the Magnuson Agency as soon as possible.

"One other thing," he added. "Some of these guys—a couple of them, anyway—have to be black."

There was a pause and what O'Bannon interpreted as a disgusted sigh on the other end. Then the manager, whose name was Sugarman, said he could get into trouble acquiescing to such wishes, and in fact the company had a policy against any hiring by a person's color, and he for one thought it was a good thing, too. If he could not honor a request for white men, he could not very well honor one for black. And besides, he added, proving that he was one of those Chicagoans who delight in sarcasm, which he possessed in place of a sense of humor, unleashing torrents of it through the smallest openings, did not the Magnuson Agency hire only white men as ushers, or so he had heard, and no colored boy had ever shown him to his seat in Comiskey Park. O'Bannon countered that this was special work, outside the routine of the agency, and was more in the nature of manual labor. Thereupon Sugarman commented that maybe when the Magnuson Agency had dirty work to be done they wanted some black men to do it—or did they want the colored boys to serve supper to the whites? O'Bannon countered that this was not what was intended, that the work would be the same for everyone, and would be in the nature of lifting and carrying, and very little of that, and would not take long either, if all went on schedule, the men being free in a matter of hours. He wanted some black men, he said, because he wanted to be fair, that was all. Besides, he lied, the work was in a black neighborhood after dark, and he thought it safer if at least some of the men were not out of place. He went on to name the figure of the wage he would pay, which was high, along with the gift he personally promised the manager. At this Sugarman agreed to do his best.

Far sooner than O'Bannon had been led to expect, the receptionist entered his office to report in a whisper of disbelief that a bunch of shabbily dressed men, many of whom were Negroes, were reporting to the reception desk and asking for Mr. O'Bannon. They had even argued with her that they were expected. Her look said that she was certain he would contradict them.

He nodded. "How many men are here?" He was amused that she would transform a few Negroes into "many."

"Twelve," she said.

O'Bannon apologized for not forewarning her, assured her that they were indeed expected, and instructed her to escort them into the office adjoining his own.

He then went to the doorway of his own office to watch them enter. As they filed through the large outer office, weaving between the many desks and drawing looks of hostile wonder from those clerks still at their desks, his mouth opened in astonishment. Sugarman! The son-of-a-bitch! O'Bannon had expected two, maybe three, Negroes in the twelve, for Magnuson had specified only that some of the men were to be black. Now he counted eight. Was it purely chance that eight of the first twelve men Sugarman had hired were black?

The Negroes seemed to be older men, and wore anything from baggy overalls to mismatching suit coats and pants. All had mustaches of some sort, all wore caps with great duckbills, or fedoras that seemed all crown. They were a range of colors, heights, physiques, although to O'Bannon they all looked pretty much alike. Most of them looked as though they were ready for an honest night's work. This could not be said of the four whites. They were young men, southerners, in cheap, dirty sports coats and loafers, still hung over from last night's, or even this morning's, drunk. They hung back from the blacks, apparently intimidated by their number.

When they were all safely in the office, O'Bannon returned to his desk and called a liquor store on Wells Street and ordered two bottles of Scotch delivered to Sugarman. Next he pondered Magnuson's instruction that his coffin be draped in an American flag. As far as he knew, Magnuson had not been militaristic, or even patriotic, nor had he served in the armed forces. He did recall, though, that during the late 1930's and World War Two Magnuson had served in the Illinois national guard and had been elected by his fellow guardsmen to the rank of captain. He had learned of this once when Magnuson had reminisced about a plan the national guard had in case of a race riot on the South Side of the city like that which had erupted in Detroit during the war. It appeared that Magnuson had had a hand in devising the plan, and was responsible, should the emergency arise, for executing it. All the Negroes in the area were to be driven down certain designated streets, all exits save one blockaded by national guardsmen with rifles and machine guns, that exit leading to the bridge that went over to the two islands in the Jackson Park Lagoon. There they were to be interned until the trouble subsided. O'Bannon had a picture of the black people being driven like cattle, refugees in their own city, with what possessions they could gather up on a moment's notice wrapped up in blankets and tablecloths, a mob of fat women, bent old men, nappy-headed children, and teenagers with their hats marching, or even being made to double-time, for many blocks and perhaps miles in a cloud of hot summer dust. He wondered if they were to have been impounded to keep them from murdering whites or to keep whites from murdering them? The plan sounded so outrageous and alien to the workings of this city and this republic as he knew them that had anyone but Magnuson told him of it, he would have doubted that it could exist. And it was odd too, that during that world war with the fierce fighting on the two fronts of Europe and the Pacific and the war effort at home it should have been Magnuson's duty to be in charge of such a plan. Suddenly he recalled seeing a photograph in Magnuson's apartment, on his wife's desk, of Magnuson in his army captain's uniform, the Sam Browne belt, his hair dark and short and parted in the middle. He had planned to send a man out to buy a flag, but it now occurred to him that Magnuson might be eligible for a flag from the government, and since he was a parsimonious man by nature and always anxious to save a dollar where he could for the company, he called the Veterans Administration and upon learning that Magnuson was indeed eligible, sent the man there instead.

He then entered the large office often used as a conference room where the twelve men were waiting. They sat in the low Danish chairs around the low teak tables, hunched over like men whittling, bringing to the room the air of barbershops and park benches. He interrupted a small black man, in clothes much too large for him and a cigarette dangling from his lower lip, in what appeared to be the act of selling clothes. He had pulled a pair of white socks and undershirts from a shopping bag and was displaying them against his chest, a dollar bill held crap-style folded between his fingers.

After exchanging greetings with the men, O'Bannon told them that they would be leaving soon to do their job and that he, personally, would accompany them. The work would not take more than minutes. Then he mentioned the wages he expected to pay for the evening's work, promising a generous bonus in the bargain, which made the men both interested and suspicious. Then he consulted his watch and said, "Are you hungry?" When several said they were, he fetched a clerk, gave him thirty dollars from his wallet, and instructed him to take the men to a nearby cafeteria for supper. He told the men, "Get anything you want to eat. It's on the company." But before they left he took the clerk aside and warned him not to lose sight of any of them and above all else, not to let them have anything to drink.

In his office again he called a taxi company and ordered five cabs. The dispatcher promised they would be in front of the building at the designated time. Then he ordered a corned beef sandwich and a cup of coffee. He wanted a moment alone. Most of the employees in the office had left by now, and only random lights were left burning above desks and in offices, and the few people encountered in the corridors were wearing coats. He wondered if he could get through the night.

Lately he found he liked his isolation from other men, liked to be alone with words and figures. He attempted to check some cost-accounting figures only to move on to correcting the style and grammar of several business letters he had written personally that afternoon only to discover that his mind had drifted away to that man who had been Magnuson. To think that a man like Magnuson could come to such an awful end. He had been an honest man, hardworking and self-made, mentally tough if not exactly shrewd, morally uncompromising, self-assured to the point of a self-righteousness that at times could be exasperating and offensive. But beneath that surface of gruff impatience and intolerance he could be kind and generous to the fault of sentimentality. His mind, however, had been unable to range outside a certain self-imposed circumscription, as though he was always under some compulsion to rein himself in, hold himself back, keep himself down, even though as events had proven—if wealth and fame and power count for anything in this world—it was his destiny to expand and rise. He seemed to have had the gift of luck, to have been the captain of his life, making of it what he wanted and what other men admired, and yet he had lost his sanity and reputation for integrity and honor, and wound up in the end with nothing but disgrace and death.—He imagined he could see and hear the train that was bearing Magnuson's body across the dark Wisconsin countryside, past lakes and forests and farmlands, a milk-train calling at every darkened town. And for a second that chilled him to the bone he knew the anonymity and loneliness of that darkness, that journey, that coffin in the baggage car.—May the good God save Magnuson's immortal soul!

The messenger returned from the Veterans Administration with the American flag folded in a triangle. Then the men returned from supper, and O'Bannon now sent word that it was time to go.

Down in the street the fleet of yellow checkered taxis was waiting. Four cabs took three men each of the twelve, while O'Bannon rode alone in the lead cab with the folded flag upon his lap. As the caravan drove westward across the monotonous checkerboard of the now dark city O'Bannon stared out the rear window and counted the number of following cabs, feeling like some desperado anxious not to be rid of his pursuers but to make certain that he was still pursued. The cemetery was in the western suburbs on a plain landscaped with occasional trees. At the main gate the gatekeeper came out of his stone and crypt-like guard house and gave them a small map of the cemetery and directions where to go, informing them that the rest of their party had already arrived. They followed the narrow paved lanes that wound between this world of grass and tombstones, the five pairs of headlights, the five yellow checkered taxicabs. Obelisks, winged victories, shepherds, Virgin Marys, Greek goddesses, crosses, and just plain stones loomed up out of the darkness on either side, the monuments of a landscape that seemed infinite. Have this many people lived, O'Bannon wondered? Have this many people actually died? After several wrong turns and debates at crossroads, with the five cabs, unable to turn around, backing up by the light of their tail-lights, they found the right lane and eventually the black hearse that awaited them.

O'Bannon presented himself to the chauffeur of the hearse, signed the necessary papers, and the driver opened the hearse doors. Inside was a plain wooden coffin on top of which the chauffeur now lashed the flag. Reluctantly the twelve hired men were getting out of the cabs.

O'Bannon herded the men together and at last informed them

of the nature of their jobs. Six men were to serve as the pallbearers of the coffin, the remaining six were to serve as honorary pallbearers and follow behind. This was according to the instructions Magnuson had set down in his will. O'Bannon arbitrarily appointed the six men closest to him as the bearers of the coffin. But the men voiced their suspicion and apprehension, searching among the gravestones as though expecting that at any moment the Devil himself might appear, and there was a general murmuring against the place, the hour, the job. The more rebellious men O'Bannon took aside, patiently persuading them to do their job, saying it would be a shame to have come so far and not to finish now. He was successful to the extent that the coffin was slid out of the hearse and carried off by the handles, three men to a side, while the other six men began a ragged march behind. But they could not have gone more than a few yards when the murmuring began anew, and could not have gone more than a few steps after the murmuring began when the coffin was set down and arguments ensued. "I don't know this dead man," one man was crying above the hubbub. "I'm not taking no dead man I don't know anywhere. I got no business here. This the business of his friends."

"If the man had any friends," someone else said, "we wouldn't be here, doing their work."

"Somebody got to do it," an old man said, as though referring to the occupation of garbageman. "He ain't going to get there by himself."

The headlights of the taxis were still on, as were the motors, as though the preparations for a quick retreat were wise in such a place at such an hour, while the cab drivers and the chauffeur huddled beside the hearse, watching in befuddled silence as once more the procession managed to move off between the tombstones.

The sky was overcast and there was neither starlight nor moonlight, and a strong wind was blowing, balmy with suggestions of the South. At the horizon the weak but widespread aura of the lights of the city and its suburbs resembled a false twilight or dawn or the raging of a distant battle. Then the coffin was on the ground again, this time on a mound, and the men arguing above it among themselves, one faction complaining about this kind of work, the other that the complainers were holding up the completion of the job. When the argument became a quarrel O'Bannon stepped in, reasoning with the opposing sides. The more rebellious of the pallbearers he attempted to replace with honorary pallbearers, but two of the men, even though they argued against picking up the coffin again, would not give up their posts. In the end his intercession only inflamed the argument and he felt like the white hunter in some second-rate jungle adventure film in which the native porters upon reaching the frontier of a remote kingdom they have heard condemns to death all strangers grumble in the ranks and set down the packs they carried on their heads and on litters, refusing to move on. He wished that, like the white hunter in the movie, he had a whip or rifle butt with which to drive them on, or a native foreman to do it for him.

To his disgust, he suspected they had managed to get hold of liquor and had been drinking in the cabs. The wind reeked of Bourbon. He suspected they were halting only so that they might take a drink and pass the bottle, for when they stopped some of them turned away from him as though to cough and reached inside their coats as though to scratch their ribs, and he distinctly heard the sloshing of liquid in a bottle.

Until now the four whites had hung back from the Negroes, speaking only when spoken to, and then responding with a timid smile. Now all joined in the good-natured arguments and teasing of the blacks, shared their sense of humor, spoke their language even, so that in the dark, with all those southern accents, it was nearly impossible for O'Bannon to distingish white from black.

According to the directions, the gravesite could not be far from the road, but somehow in the darkness, with all the starts and halts and false starts of the coffin, the procession seemed to have become lost among this city of statuary and gravestones, and arguments broke out among the men along the coffin as to which way the party was to go, while those who were supposed to walk behind the coffin got ahead of it and squabbled with each other in their attempts to point the way. O'Bannon had the map, which he consulted often by the fire of one of the men's cigarette lighter, while the men looked over his shoulder and made their own suggestions as to where they were and where they ought to go. By now the coffin had grown heavy, and the pallbearers switched off with the honorary members of their party, largely, O'Bannon felt, because a stint behind the coffin gave them an opportunity to take a drink. At first they added two men to the coffin, one to the front and another to the back, making eight in all; and then, deciding it was too heavy to continue carrying by the handles, they lifted it upon their shoulders and carried it crookedly because of the difference in height between the men. Some of them became familiar with the corpse and talked to him, referring to him as "dead man."

"You a heavy old dead man."

"Dead man, don't give us no trouble."

"Hang on, dead man, we going to get you there."

They raged with graveyard humor, summoned up in their jokes and challenges and blasphemies a world of ghosts and spirits and resurrected corpses that terrified O'Bannon to the roots of his hair. And as they trudged along, stumbling over the mounds and bumping into the stones, he wondered if he couldn't hear in the wind the Negroes humming the traces of dirges out of slave ships and Africa. The wind got beneath the flag and billowed it up, and the pallbearers had to use their hands to hold it down, along with holding their hats on their heads, while the cigarettes they were smoking as they carried the coffin on their shoulders flared up like fire. A corner of the flag blew free and draped the men on one side, and they cried out in alarm and struggled to get out from underneath, almost dropping their side of the load, and as O'Bannon ran to help he had a vision of Magnuson's corpse spilling out and the pallbearers wrestling with it beneath the flag.

They seemed to have tramped for hours across this alien countryside, to have gone in circles, to have gone back and forth, passing the same gravestones, the same names, the same dates, when finally in the gloom ahead they saw the small tent and lantern and the pair of gravediggers, young men with sideburns and tattoos and in work clothes, sitting before the tent and around the lantern on the mounds of sod, looking in the night like soldiers before their campfire. Now these gravediggers rose in surprise at the sight approaching, for they had heard the party wandering about the cemetery, swearing and laughing, but had been too awestruck and fearful to call out their location in the dark, and too amazed that any real procession of so many people could not see their tent and light, when half a dozen times it had come close enough for them to glimpse it winding through the tombstones, with no light, in the dark.

The coffin was no sooner delivered than the hired mourners departed and even O'Bannon, who had planned to spend some time over the open grave and coffin, pondering and praying and resurrecting Magnuson within his mind, was too on edge to do more than cross himself in a hurry and move away, leaving the remainder of Magnuson's ceremony of bereavement and atonement to the pair of gravediggers drinking coffee from their Thermos as they leaned upon their spades.

One of the gravediggers had removed the flag from the coffin and, folding it into a triangle, returned it to O'Bannon. As they made their way back to the taxis it occurred to O'Bannon that he did not want the flag and that there were no instructions in the will as to how to dispose of it. He was fairly certain that neither of Magnuson's children would want it, and as he was somewhat embarrassed at carrying it himself, impulsively he asked the company if anyone would like the flag. His offer was greeted with silence, with the exception of one man who said, "No, I don't want no flag. What would I do with a flag?" Saying this, or something like it, over and over again all the way back to the cabs. There one of the men approached him—he thought it might be the same man who had been selling second-hand clothing in the office—and said if he really wanted to get rid of that flag he guessed he could take it off his hands. With this O'Bannon presented it to him, and the man carried it back to the office on his lap in the cab.

At the agency he told the men that if they would wait a minute he would soon have ready for them that bonus he had promised them over and above the pay they could pick up in the morning at the Mighty-Men office. He then returned to his office and removed the cashbox from the safe, and began filling small yellow pay envelopes with cash.

As he worked he pondered the strange and even unfair provisions of the will that he was charged with administering. Magnuson had been more than generous with Shannon and himself, giving them every opportunity to purchase the Magnuson share of the agency on terms that were more than reasonable. The Salvation Army and a few other charities, including one for the families of slain policemen, also benefited. But to his own son and daughter he deliberately left very little, cutting them off by the wording of the will from any significant inheritance of the estate. What on earth had been his reasoning for this? Had they disappointed him that much? Was he doing it out of spite or somehow did he think he was doing it for their own good? Did blood and family and tradition count for so little with some men? As if the experience of his children was to be bereft of his own, as if he had worked for nothing, saved for nothing, been lucky and successful for no other purpose than to return it all to the general coffers. As though Magnuson's children, after the immigration and poverty and labor of their grandfather and the labor and success of their father, were to become first-generation immigrants all over again. As though once having made the fortune, the line of the old inheritance was to come to an end. The photographs of O'Bannon's three daughters stood before him on the desk, and he wondered if he could ever cut them off, send them out into the world upon their own, penniless and fatherless, even if he thought it for the best.

By now the men had changed into their street clothes and had collected with a grim patience outside his door. Thereupon he called each man by name into the office, one man at a time. There he thanked him for the outstanding job that he had done and shook his hand, using both of his own. Then, in accordance with the dictates of the will, he presented him with a pay envelope containing fifty dollars, five brand-new ten-dollar bills.

Now there was nothing left for O'Bannon to do tonight except call Shannon. In the morning he would write a letter as the will instructed, canceling the gravestone Magnuson had ordered for his wife. It was to replaced by a single stone to serve for both husband and wife, barely high enough to trip over and only wide enough to bear the inscription which, O'Bannon judged, would be covered by any unmown grass and obliterated entirely when the stone settled. It was to say only:

MAGNUSONS

A NOTE ON THE TYPE

This book was set in Caledonia, a Linotype face designed by W. A. Dwiggins. It belongs to the family of printing types called "modern face" by printers—a term used to mark the change in style of type letters that occurred about 1800. Caledonia borders on the general design of Scotch Modern, but is more freely drawn than that letter.

The book was composed, printed, and bound by The Book Press, Brattleboro, Vermont. Typography and binding design by The Etheredges.